BOOK ONE

FOREVER FAITHFUL

Waiting *for* Morning

KAREN KINGSBURY

Multnomah® Publishers *Sisters, Oregon*

This is a work of fiction. The characters, incidents, and dialogues are products of the author's imagination and are not to be construed as real. Any resemblance to actual events or persons, living or dead, is entirely coincidental.

WAITING FOR MORNING
published by Multnomah Publishers, Inc.

Published in association with the literary agency of Arthur Pine Associates, Inc.

International Standard Book Number: 1-59052-020-3
Cover images by Getty Images
Cover design by The DesignWorks Group

Printed in the United States of America

For information:
MULTNOMAH PUBLISHERS, INC.
P.O. Box 1720
Sisters, Oregon 97759

Library of Congress Cataloging-in-Publication Data
Kingsbury, Karen.
Waiting for morning/by Karen Kingsbury.
p.cm. ISBN 1-57673-415-3 (alk. paper)
ISBN 1-59052-020-3
I. Title.
PS3561.I483L66 1999 98-45973
813'.54–dc21 CIP

04 05 06 07 08 — 15 14 13 12 11 10

Dedicated to
my best friend, Donald,
If life's a dance…
then I pray the music keeps playing forever.
Being married to you is the
sweetest song of all.

To Kelsey,
my softhearted little Norm,
I can see in you the beautiful
young woman you are becoming…
especially your eyes,
which so closely resemble your dad's
and your Father's.

To Ty,
my precious son…
whose flowers have given me
the most beautiful bouquet of memories.
I cherish watching you grow
in the image of the daddy you
so clearly emulate.

To Austin,
my greatest miracle…
watching you throw the ball
and make layups
is daily proof of God's unending love
and faithfulness,
even in the darkest days.

And to God Almighty,
Who has—for now—blessed me with these.

NOVELS BY KAREN KINGSBURY

Where Yesterday Lives
When Joy Came to Stay
On Every Side
A Time to Dance
A Time to Embrace (sequel to *A Time to Dance*)
One Tuesday Morning
Oceans Apart

THE FOREVER FAITHFUL SERIES
Waitng for Morning
A Moment of Weakness
Halfway to Forever

THE REDEMPTION SERIES
(Co-written with Gary Smalley)
Redemption
Remember
Return
Rejoice
Reunion

THE RED GLOVES CHRISTMAS SERIES
Gideon's Gift
Maggie's Miracle
Sarah's Song

www.karenkingsbury.com

Acknowledgments

Writing a novel about the devastating effects of drunk driving was a difficult, emotional journey and one that could not have been taken without borrowing from the pain of others. Searching for that dark place of despair and devastation, I read countless stories of tragic, senseless loss. I pored over the Mothers Against Drunk Drivers Memorial web site and often conducted research through eyes blurred with tears.

For that reason, I wish to thank Mothers Against Drunk Drivers and every person who has ever helped change or tighten a drunk driving law. You may never know this side of heaven all the lives you have saved in the process. I pray you keep on.

Thanks also to the amazing staff at Multnomah Publishers. From sales to marketing to cover design to publicity...please know that God is working through you in ways that will continue to produce books that change lives, especially books like this. Thanks so much for all your help.

Of course, as with my last book, my writing would be nothing without the God-given talents of my editor, Karen Ball. You are a friend and a mentor, and I hope to keep learning from you as long as the Lord allows. Thanks a million times over.

Also thanks to my husband and family for their support and encouragement during what is always an emotional process—the writing of a novel. I am nothing without your collective smiles, cheers, hugs, and endless love throughout the days.

As with other projects, my parents and extended family were again an encouragement that I value deeply. Thanks to you and to the friends in my women's Bible study and other close sisters in Christ who hold me in prayer, asking the Lord to use my writing for his glory.

And finally, a special thanks to my dear friend, Julie Kremer.

One day nearly a decade ago, Julie's husband got a phone call from their teenage daughter. Her friend's car had broken down on the side of the road. Julie's husband did not hesitate but left immediately to help.

While he was out, he was hit and killed by a drunk driver, leaving Julie and two teenage children alone.

I never knew Julie's husband, but I will forever be touched by the way Julie forgave. She brought a Bible to the man who killed her husband, and after that, continued to keep her eyes on the Lord.

Thank you, Julie, for teaching me what it is to forgive…and for giving me a reason to write *Waiting for Morning*.

One

I am in torment within, and in my heart I am disturbed.

LAMENTATIONS 1:20A

Sunday Evening

They were late and that bothered her.

She had been through a list of likely explanations, any one of which was possible. They'd stopped for ice cream; they'd forgotten something back at the campsite; they'd gotten a later start than usual.

Still Hannah Ryan was uneasy. Horrific images, tragic possibilities threatened to take up residence in her mind, and she struggled fiercely to keep them out.

The afternoon was cooling, so she flipped off the air conditioning and opened windows at either end of the house. A hint of jasmine wafted inside and mingled pleasantly with the pungent scent of Pine-Sol and the warm smell of freshly baked chocolate chip cookies.

Minutes passed. Hannah folded two loads of whites, straightened the teal, plaid quilts on both girls' beds again, and wiped down the Formica kitchen countertop for the third time. Determined to fight the fear welling within her, she wrung the worn, pink sponge and angled it against the tiled wall. More air that way, less mildew. She rearranged the cookies on a pretty crystal platter, straightened a stack of floral napkins nearby, and rehearsed once more the plans for dinner.

The house was too quiet.

Praise music. That's what she needed. She sorted through a stack of compact discs until she found one by David Jeremiah.

Good. David Jeremiah would be nice. Calming. Upbeat. Soothing songs that would consume the time, make the waiting more bearable.

She hated it when they were late. Always had. Her family had been gone three days and she missed them, even missed the noise and commotion and constant mess they made.

That was all this was...just a terrible case of missing them.

David Jeremiah's voice filled the house, singing about when the Lord comes and wanting to be there to see it. She drifted back across the living room to the kitchen. *Come on, guys. Get home.*

She stared out the window and willed them back, willed the navy blue Ford Explorer around the corner, where it would move slowly into the driveway, leaking laughter and worn-out teenage girls. Willed her family home where they belonged.

But there was no Explorer, no movement at all save the subtle sway of branches in the aging elm trees that lined the cul-de-sac.

Hannah Ryan sighed, and for just a moment she considered the possibilities. Like all mothers, she was no stranger to the tragedies of others. She had two teenage daughters, after all, and more than once she had read a newspaper article that hit close to home. Once it was a teenager who had, in a moment of silliness, stood in the back of a pickup truck as the driver took off. That unfortunate teen had been catapulted to the roadway, his head shattered, death instant. Another time it was the report of an obsessive boy who stalked some promising young girl and gunned her down in the doorway of her home.

When Hannah's girls were little, other tragedies had jumped off the newspaper pages. The baby in San Diego who found his mother's button and choked to death while she chatted on the phone with her sister. The toddler who wandered out the back gate and was found hours later at the bottom of a neighbor's murky pool.

It was always the same. Hannah would absorb the story,

reading each word intently, and then, for a moment, she would imagine such a thing happening to her family. Better, she thought, to think it through. Play it out so that if she were ever the devastated mother in the sea of heartache that spilled from the morning news, she would be ready. There would be an initial shock, of course, but Hannah usually skimmed past that detail. How could one ever imagine a way to handle such news? But then there would be the reality of a funeral, comforting friends, and ultimately, life would go on. To be absent from the body is to be present with the Lord; wasn't that what they said? She knew this because of her faith.

No, she would not be without hope, no matter the tragedy.

Of course, these thoughts of Hannah's usually happened in less time than it took her to fold the newspaper and toss it in the recycling bin. They were morbid thoughts, she knew. But she was a mother, and there was no getting around the fact that somewhere in the world other mothers were being forced to deal with tragedy.

Other mothers.

That was the key. Eventually, even as she turned from the worn bin of yesterday's news and faced her day, Hannah relished the truth that those tragedies always happened to other mothers. They did not happen to people she knew—and certainly they would not happen to her.

She prayed then, as she did at the end of every such session, thanking God for a devoted, handsome husband with whom she was still very much in love, and for two beautiful daughters strong in their beliefs and on the brink of sweet-sixteen parties and winter dances, graduation and college. She was sorry for those to whom tragedy struck, but at the same time, she was thankful that such things had never happened to her.

Just to be sure, she usually concluded the entire process with a quick and sincere plea, asking God to never let happen to her and hers what had happened to them and theirs.

In that way, Hannah Ryan had been able to live a fairly worry-free life. Tragedy simply did not happen to her. Would not. She had already prayed about it. Scripture taught that the Lord never gave more than one could bear. So Hannah believed God had protected her from tragedy or loss of any kind because he knew she couldn't possibly bear it.

Still, despite all this assurance, tragic thoughts haunted her now as they never had before.

David Jeremiah sang on about holding ground, standing, even when everything in life was falling apart. Hannah listened to the words, and a sudden wave of anxiety caused her heart to skip a beat. She didn't want to stand. She wanted to run into the streets and find them.

She remembered a story her grandmother once told about a day in the early seventies when she was strangely worried about her only son, Hannah's uncle. All day her grandmother had paced and fretted and prayed....

Late that evening she got the call. She knew immediately, of course. Her son had been shot that morning, killed by a Viet Cong bullet. A sixth sense, she called it later. Something only a mother could understand.

Hannah felt that way now, and she hated herself for it. As if by letting herself be anxious she would, in some way, be responsible if something happened to her family.

She reminded herself to breathe. Motionless, hands braced on the edge of the kitchen sink, shoulders tense, she stared out the window. Time slipped away, and David Jeremiah sang out the last of his ten songs. Lyrics floated around her, speaking of the Lord's loving arms and begging him not to let go, not to allow a fall.

Hannah swallowed and noticed her throat was thick and dry. Two minutes passed. The song ended and there was silence. Deafening silence.

The sunlight was changing now, and shadows formed as evening drew near. In all ways that would matter to two teenage girls coming home from a mountain camping trip with their father, it couldn't have been a nicer day in the suburbs of Los Angeles. Bright and warm, a sweet, gentle breeze sifted through the still full trees. Puffy clouds hung suspended in a clear blue sky, ripe with memories of lazy days and starry nights.

It was the last day of a golden summer break.

What could possibly go wrong on a day like this?

Two

How deserted lies the city, once so full of people!

LAMENTATIONS 1:1A

Sunday before Dawn

Long before the sun came up, Dr. Tom Ryan stirred from his rumpled sleeping bag and nudged the lumpy forms on either side of him.

"Pssst. Wake up. One hour 'til sunrise."

The sleeping figures buried themselves deeper in the down-filled bags, and one of them groaned.

"Ahhh, Dad. Let's sleep in."

Tom was already on his feet, folding his sleeping bag in a tight, Boy-Scout roll and wrapping it with a nylon cord. He poked his toe first at one form, then the other, tickling them and evoking a giggle from the chief complainer.

"Daaad. Stop!"

"Up and at 'em. We have fish to catch."

Alicia Ryan poked her head out of her bag. "We have enough fish."

Tom was indignant. "Enough fish? Did I hear a Ryan daughter say we have enough fish? *Never* enough fish. That's our creed. Now come on, get up."

More groans, and finally Jenny Ryan's mass of blond curls appeared near the top of her sleeping bag. "Give it up, Alicia. You know how Dad is on the last day."

"That's right." Tom was already pulling a sweater on. "The last day of the Ryan camping trip is famous for being the best day to catch fish."

Alicia sighed and struggled to sit up. She reached for a rubber band and shook her thick brown hair, gathering it into a ponytail. At that hour, Cachuma Lake was cold and damp, and Alicia shivered as she pulled her sleeping bag around her shoulders once more. "What time is it anyway?"

"Not important." Tom unzipped the tent and ducked through the opening. "Time is for the civilized world. Today, there is only us and the fish."

Alicia and Jenny glanced at each other, rolled their eyes, and snickered. "We're coming," Alicia shouted after him. They stretched and climbed into their jeans and sweatshirts.

The annual camping trip was held at Cachuma Lake mostly because it was famous for its fishing. Nestled in the mountains northeast of Santa Barbara off San Marcos pass, the lake was a crystal blue oasis in a canyon that typically experienced temperatures twenty degrees higher than those on the nearby coast. Swimming was not allowed in Cachuma Lake, which supplied all the drinking water to Santa Barbara. For that reason it attracted puritan fishermen, those to whom fishing was a serious venture.

Each year Tom Ryan and his girls spent three days at the lake. Days were devoted to fishing—and occasionally drifting near enough to a secluded cove to watch deer graze unaware. Sometimes they fished in comfortable silence, but many hours were spent with Tom and his teenage girls talking about boys or the importance of a college education or what it meant to live a life that pleased the Lord. There were lighter moments on the water as well, particularly when they recalled embarrassing escapades or memories of other camping trips. Once in a while they laughed so hard they rocked the boat and scared away the fish.

There were afternoon hikes along the narrow shoreline trails, and sometimes they would drive ten minutes to nearby Zaca Lake for a swim or a nap on the beach. Back at the campsite they built a bonfire each evening, cleaned fish, and fried them for dinner. Then in the hours before they turned in, the girls would play cards while their father played his worn acoustic guitar and sang favorite hymns and church choruses.

Campsites were not far from the shore, hidden among gnarled oak trees and without the benefit of running water or modern bathroom facilities. The Ryans brought water in ten-gallon jugs, food in an oversized Coleman cooler, and an old canvas tent that had been in the family for fifteen years. Camping at Cachuma Lake was *roughing it* at its best, and Tom Ryan wouldn't have taken his girls anywhere else.

Jenny stuffed her sleeping bag into its sack and poked her sister in the ribs. "Hey, since it's the last day and all, I just might have to catch more fish than you." She was the youngest, and a friendly competition had always existed between the two.

"Oh, okay." Alicia pretended to be concerned. "I'll try to be worried about it."

Tom kept their aluminum fishing boat docked lakeside while they camped, so there was little to carry as he and the girls waved their flashlights at the trail and made their way to the water.

"It's freezing!" Jenny's loud whisper seemed to echo in the early morning silence. The path was damp and still, awaiting the crest of new-day sunshine to warm it and stir life into the wooded shoreline.

"Remember that feeling this afternoon when we're packing the gear and it's a hundred degrees." Tom grinned.

"I can't believe it's been three days already." Alicia moved close to Jenny so that the girls walked shoulder to shoulder.

"Time flies when you're fishing, that's what I always say." Tom inhaled the air, filled with energy, loving the early hour of the day.

They climbed into the boat and took their seats, adjusting their flashlights so each could see. Tom watched the girls with pride. Like experienced fishermen, they maneuvered about the tackle box and baited their hooks.

"We're off." He flipped the switch on the battery-powered motor, and a deep puttering sound broke the reverie. The sun was climbing quickly, and the girls set aside their flashlights as the boat slipped away from shore.

Four hours later they were back. Jenny was the winner with three catfish, two bass, and a beautiful twelve-inch rainbow trout.

"You guys aren't much competition." She held up her string and sized up her catch. "You were right, Dad, nothing like an early morning run on the lake."

"Oh, be quiet." Tom laughed and shoved his youngest daughter playfully. He and Alicia had caught just five fish between them. "Let's get back to camp. We have a lot to do if we're going to be on the road by two."

Alicia stepped out of the boat and led the way up the trail toward camp. Suddenly Jenny stiffened and pointed at the trail in front of her sister.

"Alicia!" Jenny's scream was shrill and piercing. Tom and Alicia froze, and Tom followed Jenny's pointing finger….There, coiled two feet from Alicia's muddy hiking boots, was a hissing diamondback rattlesnake.

Tom's heart jumped wildly. "Alicia—" he kept his voice calm, "don't move, honey." He pulled Jenny away and motioned for her to move farther behind him. He had treated snakebites before, but he'd never encountered a snake. This one was already angry and easily within striking distance.

"What should I do, Daddy?" Alicia sounded like a scared little girl.

God, please, protect my girl. And give me wisdom…

"Okay, honey—" he spoke quietly and with more confidence than he felt—"don't let your feet drag in the dirt. Lift them one at a time…very slowly…and walk backward, away from the snake."

Alicia whimpered. "He's staring at me, Daddy. What if he bites me?"

"You'll be all right, sweetheart. That won't happen if you back up slowly." *Please, God, let me be right.* "He doesn't want to bite you."

Alicia nodded. She was an energetic girl, ambitious and rarely given to moments of stillness. But now she moved painstakingly slow, and Tom was proud of her. Right foot, left; right foot, left. Three feet, then four separated her and the hissing snake. Right foot, left...right foot, left.

Tom grabbed her hand and pulled her toward him. Together they backed up even farther to where Jenny waited for them. Alicia crumpled in her father's arms and started to cry.

"Oh, Daddy, I was so scared," she mumbled into his grubby T-shirt.

Tom could feel his pulse returning to normal, and he stroked her hair silently. He could treat snakebites when he was in an emergency room with a vial of antivenin. But here, an hour from urgent care, Alicia might not have made it. "Thank you, God." Then to Alicia, "You did it just right, honey."

Jenny moved in then, wrapping her arms around her father and sister. "I thought you were going to step on him."

Alicia looked at her. "I would've if you hadn't screamed."

Both girls shuddered, and there was a pause while they clung to their father. Fifteen feet away, the snake stopped hissing, uncoiled, and slithered off the path into the shrubbery.

Tom broke the silence. "You know what it was, don't you?"

Alicia sniffled loudly and pulled away from him, running her palms over her jeans. "What?"

"He wanted to see Jenny's catch. Rumors spread quickly along the shoreline in these parts. He had to see for himself."

Alicia and Jenny grinned and wordlessly cued each other so that they ganged up on him and rubbed their knuckles against his head.

"Okay, okay, come on, you monkeys." He took their hands and led them once more toward the campsite. "Let's get the site cleaned up and the car loaded. Mom's waiting for us."

Brian Wesley's body lay contorted, twisted underneath the rear axle of a '93 Honda Civic, while heat from the sweltering Los Angeles pavement radiated through his flesh. He drew breaths in quick, raspy gulps. In the cramped, dark place where he lay, the stench of grease and gasoline was suffocating. His pulse banged loud and fast, the sound of it nearly drowning out the roar of nearby traffic. He had to get air, had to calm the wild beating of his heart, the violent trembling of his hands, and the anxiety that engulfed him.

It had been three weeks since he'd had a drink.

Brian wiped the sweat and grime from his hands onto his worn Levi's and used the last of his remaining strength to steady his fingers. With fierce determination he gripped the torque wrench and made one final turn. There. He tried to breathe more slowly. One Civic rear axle, good as new. Three repairs to go.

If only he could take a few moments to settle his nerves, sip some cool water, maybe chew a piece of mint gum or eat a candy bar. Something, *anything*, before he lost his mind. Every part of him was screaming for a drink. He closed his eyes, and he could feel the fiery liquid sliding over his lips, satisfying the craving that coursed through his veins.

From somewhere near the shop's office, he heard footsteps. They were loud and threatening, making their way toward him.

"Wesley!" The voice barked out over the sound of humming machinery and noisy afternoon traffic.

From underneath the Honda, Brian studied his boss's shoes and struggled to compose himself. He had seen this coming for days. He straightened his legs and used the heels of his worn work boots to push himself out from underneath the car.

"Yeah?" He blinked twice and felt his lip twitch wildly.

Steve Avery, shop manager and owner of Avery Automotive, sized him up like a sack of rotting leftovers. Brian stood and noticed his hands were shaking badly. He forced them into his pockets with a nervous jerk. Avery muttered something about laziness and then turned abruptly.

"Follow me."

I'm finished. Brian swallowed painfully. *Too many guys, not enough work.*

They made their way past several cars in various states of repair and then through a door down a long corridor. Once inside, the roar of the garage died instantly. Avery led the way and made no effort at small talk as they entered a boxy, air-conditioned office.

"Sit down, Wesley." The boss remained standing, sifting through heaps of clutter that covered his imitation oak desk. He did not look at Brian. "I'm laying you off, effective today."

Brian gulped and his heart rate doubled. "Me?"

Avery looked over the rim of his glasses and glowered making Brian feel like a fearful failure of a man. "Yes." Avery spat the word. "Know why?"

Brian shook his head. He couldn't breathe, so talking was out of the question.

"Complaints, Wesley. That Honda was supposed to be done two days ago. These past three weeks you've had more customer complaints than in all your six months combined."

"Well—" Brian tried to steady his voice—"I know business is slow and, uh, with less guys we each have a lot more work and all. So, uh, if you wanna cut my hours some maybe we could, you know, work something out."

Avery stared at him, one eyebrow slightly elevated. "This has nothing to do with slow business. It's you, Wesley. You're the one who's slow. You're lazy and you're making stupid mistakes. There's no discussion here. You're finished."

For an instant Brian thought his anger might actually overcome his anxiety. "Now wait a minute—!" He rose to his feet.

"Sit down!"

Brian's knees buckled as he collapsed back onto the metal folding chair.

"You're not pulling your weight, Wesley. Get your things and leave."

Brian hung his head and rose slowly to his feet. Before the door closed behind him, he felt the distinct blow of one more verbal dagger.

"Too bad you gave up the bottle.... You work better drunk."

Brian stormed around the garage while the others worked quietly, keeping to themselves. He snatched his extra work shirt from the office closet, grabbed his power drill off a dusty shelf, and painstakingly picked up dozens of bits and ratchets, organizing them into his tool chest. Finally, he rolled the ten-drawer red steel container toward his pickup and, with the help of a buddy, heaved it into the bed of his beat-up, white Chevy pickup.

He climbed into the truck, grabbed the wheel with both hands, and dropped his head in defeat.

Brian knew Avery's dig was a lie. He wasn't a better mechanic when he was drinking. Fast maybe, but too sloppy. It was why he'd lost every job he'd ever gotten in the past five years. Customers smelled alcohol on his breath and reported him to the boss, or he'd drink through lunch hour and forget to report back until the next morning.

The drinking had been killing him, destroying him and Carla and everything he'd ever dreamed or desired.

He had tried to quit once three years before. He'd lasted two days. Two lousy days before he woke up in the front seat of his parked car, outside a shady liquor store, at four o'clock in the morning, an empty bottle of Jack Daniels lying on the floor next to him.

After that he'd been a binge drinker for two years. There were five DUIs, two license suspensions, numerous alcohol education classes, and two separate car accidents—once when he rear-ended a neighbor's car and wound up in a head-on collision with a maple tree a block from home, and again when he pulled onto the freeway headed the wrong way. Someone had flashed headlights at him, and he'd turned into a guardrail, narrowly averting a tragedy. No one was really hurt in either accident, and he continued to drink—often waking up with a raging headache and no idea how he'd gotten home.

Carla cried and begged and threatened to leave, but she wasn't serious. Life would always go on as it had—his addiction far more powerful than he.

But all that changed six months earlier when Carla gave birth to their first child, a son, Brian Jr. The boy was a precious reminder of everything Brian had forgotten about life, a tiny living incentive that kindled within him a strong desire to change.

After Brian Jr.'s birth, Brian got the job at Avery Automotive and cut back on his drinking. Finally, three weeks ago, he quit for good. It hadn't been easy. He'd been forced to break ties with Big Al, his drinking partner, and he'd avoided driving by his favorite bars. His hands trembled nonstop, and he had frequent anxiety attacks.

But for the first time in his twenty-eight years, he believed he was a different man. He pictured himself putting in another two years at Avery Automotive and then taking a job with one of the dealers. A high-paying job with medical benefits and a dental plan. He'd buy a new truck and maybe some better tools. Eventually, he and Carla and Brian Jr. could move out of the noisy apartment and rent a small house in a safe neighborhood.

These were big dreams for Brian Wesley, and they had kept

him sober when he didn't think he could last another moment. Now, though, his dreams were good as dead.

He drove out of the shop's parking lot and considered his options. Left turn or right? Left and a mile west on Ventura Boulevard was The Office—a dimly lit sports bar where Brian had drunk away numerous paychecks in the past decade. Right and two miles east was the apartment complex where Carla and Brian Jr. would be spending the afternoon blissfully unaware of Brian's job status.

Right. Turn right. His hands trembled more violently and a thin line of perspiration formed on his upper lip. Panic simmered in his belly, and he gripped the steering wheel harder.

Just one drink, another voice argued. *One drink with the guys, enough to find the courage to face Carla.* He could feel the cool glass, smell the heady scent of forbidden liquor. *One drink. Just one drink.*

He turned his head and stared east. *Carla and Brian Jr.*

Carla would be so disappointed. Especially after he'd struggled to stay clean these past weeks. His arms were shaking now, his knees starting to knock. The drink was calling him, insisting. *One drink...one small drink.*

Three weeks of sobriety had to be worth something, some kind of reward. Besides, if he went home now, he and Carla would have it out, and he'd only wind up out after dark looking for any bottle he could get his hands on. *Do it now*, the voice said. *Just one drink. One drink. Calm your nerves and then go home. She'll never know the difference.*

"I can't...can't let 'em down," he hissed through clenched teeth. He could go home now, tell her the truth, and by tomorrow have a job somewhere else. There were dozens of garage jobs out there. "Just go home." He could feel the anxiety choking his voice, making each breath a struggle. "Come on. You can do it."

He inhaled. It was hard to get enough air. He set his jaw and forced the wheel to the right, toward Carla and Brian Jr.

Then, at the last possible moment, he wrenched the wheel in the other direction, and his pickup swung to the left.

In three minutes he was at The Office. And as he walked inside he could almost feel that first drink sliding smoothly down his throat, washing away his fears and anxiety—and all that remained of his dying dreams.

Nick Crabb was tending bar at The Office that afternoon, straightening bottles and wiping down the counter when a wide-eyed man walked in and stared at him.

"Where's Rod?" The man's feet seemed planted in the entryway.

Rod Jennings was manager at The Office. He worked five days a week and from everything Nick knew about him, he hadn't missed a shift in two years. Rod had a special thing with the regulars, and the guy standing before him had the unmistakable look of someone who had done a great deal of drinking.

Nick dried his hands on a damp towel. "Sick. Food poisoning."

The man blinked and then his shoulders slumped and he sighed. "Figures." He moved toward the bar slowly, hesitating with every step. His hands were shaking, and he glanced over his shoulder nervously.

"Get you a drink?"

The man continued forward in jerky motions until he worked himself onto a stool. "Whiskey on the rocks, straight up." He drummed his fingers anxiously on the bar, his eyes darting from bottle to bottle.

Nick hesitated for a moment. There was something strange about the guy…still he was a customer. Nick grabbed a tumbler, filled it with ice and whiskey, and set it on the bar. "You know Rod?"

"Yeah…old friends, Rod and me." The man's hands trembled

so badly that when he raised his glass he lost a few drops. Then he put the glass to his mouth and the drink disappeared. He set the glass down hard and with more confidence nodded toward the bottle. "Another."

In the other room the opening theme to *Rocky II* began playing. Nick poured a second drink. And a third. And another and another and another.

By the time the sad-looking man at the bar was on his twelfth or thirteenth drink in less than two hours, Nick was beginning to get worried. If only Rod were there. He would know whether the man had passed his limit. As it was, Nick had no idea. He was new at The Office—working to pay tuition at California State University Northridge. He watched the man nervously. He'd never had to cut anyone off before. Besides, the guy was Rod's friend. The last thing he wanted to do was offend the boss's buddy.

Nick wandered into the lounge where *Rocky II* was down to the final fight scene. Over the past two hours, an occasional customer had wandered in for a quick drink, but for the most part it was just the lone customer at the bar. From across the room Nick heard the man tap his glass impatiently.

"Another. Get in here and give me another."

His speech wasn't slurred. But he was getting loud and overbearing. Nick sighed and returned to the bar. "You sure?"

The man narrowed his eyes. "Don't get smart with me."

Nick shrugged and reached for the bottle. "You might want to give it a rest, that's all." He nodded toward the television. "Catch the last part of *Rocky* or something." He splashed house whiskey into a fresh glass of ice, and the man took it roughly. He downed it in three gulps and tossed several ten-dollar bills in Nick's direction. He stood then, somewhat slowly, and reached into his pocket, fumbling for something. Nick was about to offer to help when the man stopped and stared at him, his expression suddenly vulnerable.

"You know—" his voice was low and Nick strained to hear

him— "Rod should have been here."

Nick counted the money and placed it in the cash register. "I told you, he's sick."

The man nodded and began fumbling in his pockets again. This time he found his keys, gripped them tightly in his fingers, and looked up. "Rod would have called her."

Nick cocked his head back and studied the stranger. It almost looked like there were tears in his eyes. "Called who?"

"Carla...and then none of this ever would have happened."

Nick leaned against the bar and crossed his arms. "Who's Carla?"

The man's expression hardened again. "Ah, forget it. You know, there ain't nothing wrong with this world can't be fixed with a drink or two."

Nick studied his customer. "Whatever you say."

The man stared at him through narrow eyes. "What would you know about it? You work back there, looking down at guys like me, guys who drink too much."

"Hey, you okay, man?" Maybe, just maybe, this guy shouldn't be driving. Even if he didn't seem drunk.

The man clutched his keys tightly and shook his head. "Never mind me...get back to work." He turned around and headed for the door.

"Hey, wait a minute. Answer me." Nick came after him. "You okay? To drive, I mean?"

The man stopped and turned around. "Mind your own business."

Suddenly Nick was sure. The man shouldn't be driving. "Hey, buddy, why don't you sit down for a minute. I'll call you a cab. It'll be on me."

"You tryin' to say I can't drive myself home?"

"I'm saying I'll hire you a cab, man. Either that or wait a while before you leave."

A string of expletives split the air. "I'll do whatever I want. And right now I'm going home."

Nick wasn't convinced, but the situation seemed out of his hands. His boss had laid out the definition of a drunk on the first day: if someone could talk fine and walk fine and you were still worried about them, ask. Yeah, well, Nick had asked. There was nothing more he could do.

The man reached for the barroom door handle and missed, grabbing a fistful of air and nearly falling onto the floor in the process. Then with a jolt he threw his body against the door and disappeared into the parking lot.

Nick cringed. Several minutes later he heard the roar of a truck and then the sound of squealing tires as someone pulled out of the parking lot onto Ventura Boulevard.

Tom glanced at the clock and grimaced. They'd gotten on the road later than he'd wanted, but they'd still be home before dinner. He glanced at his daughters and grinned.

They had been driving for nearly two hours, and still the girls had not run out of things to talk about. School was about to start and with the annual camping trip behind them, Jenny and Alicia clearly couldn't wait to see their friends, get their class schedules, catch up on the latest teenage gossip. Tom glanced at them in the rearview mirror of the family's Ford Explorer. Sweet, silly, precious girls.

He sighed and tried to memorize their giggling faces. They were fifteen and thirteen that year, and Tom knew his summers with them were numbered. His little girls were growing up.

Years ago when he and Hannah married, he had assumed they'd have sons. When instead they had Alicia and Jenny, Tom made the most of the situation. The girls went fishing with him every summer from the time they were able to walk. They tossed a football with him and played Little League ball as good as any boys in the neighborhood.

But they also climbed onto his lap at night, melting his heart with their silky lashes and wide-eyed adoration. He was their hero, and they were each his princess. For now he was still the only man in their hearts. He knew that would change soon. Precious little time remained before they would be gone with families of their own, so he treasured this trip even more than the others.

He had never known times like this with his father. His parents divorced when he was ten, and though his father promised to stay close, there was never enough time, and the roadway of his adolescence had been paved with unfulfilled intentions and missed opportunities. One boyhood memory stood clear in his mind. He was in Scouts, twelve years old, and it was the morning of the father-son Pinewood Derby. His father was dating a new woman that month and barely had time for Tom. Still, he promised he would meet him that day.

Tom could still see himself, a skinny, freckle-faced kid watching and waiting expectantly for his father that afternoon. One hour, then two. Other fathers offered to include him but Tom said no. His father would come, he was sure. He waited and waited until finally his friends and their fathers began to leave. As he climbed back onto his ten-speed and headed for home, angry tears trickled down his hot cheeks, and he made a promise to himself. He would never be an absent father. When he had children, he would be there for them.

Tom Ryan smiled softly at the noisy girls in the backseat. He had kept his promise.

He leaned back against the headrest and tuned them out, studying the heavy flow of L.A. traffic on Highway 101 through dark amber Ray Bans. He sighed. He already missed the serenity of the lake.

His mind drifted to Hannah. He'd missed her even more… her smile and her laughter, the way she felt in his arms. Amazing, really. After seventeen years of marriage they were still very much in love. He and Hannah were a rare breed anymore, even among their Christian friends. And to think he had almost married someone else. The idea seemed comical now.

He imagined Hannah's reaction when he told her about Alicia and the rattlesnake. She'd probably go on about how the girl could have been bitten and how they were too far into the wilderness to find help and how maybe the camping trip was too dangerous after all.

He grinned. Hannah wasn't one for camping or threading—*impaling,* she called it—worms on fishhooks or getting her fingernails dirty. She was especially afraid of snakes. But Alicia hadn't really been in that much danger. Besides, he was a doctor, a pediatrician. The snake had only added to their adventure. As their annual camping trip went, this was one he and the girls would remember forever.

He maneuvered the Explorer into the right lane and took the Fallbrook exit. A quick stop at the bottom of the off-ramp, and he turned the vehicle left, under the freeway. Typically there would be a wait at the intersection of Fallbrook and Ventura Boulevard, but this time the light was green.

Good. Tom smiled. *Home in ten minutes.* He pulled into the intersection long before the light turned yellow.

Only Jenny saw it coming. There was no time to scream, no time to warn the others like she had earlier along the path at Cachuma Lake. One moment she was looking at Alicia, asking her about Mrs. Watson's English class, and the next, in a mere fraction of an instant, she saw a white locomotive coming straight at them, inches from Alicia's face.

There was a horrific jolt and the deafening sound of twisting, sparking metal and shattering glass. Jenny screamed, but it was too late. The Explorer took to the air like a child's toy spinning wildly and coming to rest wrapped around a telephone pole a hundred feet away.

Then there was nothing but dark, deadly silence.

Four

How like a widow is she, who once was great among the nations!

LAMENTATIONS 1:1B

Sal's Diner had been in business at the corner of Ventura Boulevard and Fallbrook for twenty-five years, and Rae McDermott had worked the counter faithfully for the last fifteen. That summer afternoon she was thankful the lunch crowd had been light. Another half hour and she could leave early. She needed to get some milk at the market before picking up the baby at the sitter's house. She made a mental shopping list as she ran a worn, bleach-soaked dishrag over the counter.

With a sigh, she stretched, then balled up her fists and pressed them into the small of her back. As she did so she glanced outside at the traffic on Ventura…and frowned. A white pickup truck, headed for the intersection, was speeding. Rae felt a rush of dread. The light was red, but the driver showed no signs of stopping.

She moved across the diner, drawn to the scene, desperately hoping the truck would stop. Suddenly, from south of the boulevard, an Explorer came into view on Fallbrook.

"Dear God…"

The scene seemed to unfold in slow motion, and there was nothing Rae could do to stop it. The two vehicles careened toward the intersection, then collided. The impact was so explosive it was surreal, like something from a violent action movie. The Explorer spun off the ground in a cloud of dust and glass and shredded metal, and Rae watched it sail across the street and wrap around a utility pole a hundred feet away.

"Dear God," she whispered again, and dashed across the diner, grabbed the telephone, and dialed 9-1-1.

Sergeant John Miller of the Los Angeles Police Department was a veteran in handling traffic accidents. He had worked traffic for twenty-three years and had seen hundreds of dead bodies. Most of the victims had never seen the crash coming. They were getting off work or heading home from the market with no idea they were living their final moments. Too often Sgt. Miller had lifted a dead child from the backseat of a car or pulled a dead mother out of a mangled vehicle while her baby cried, unaware of its loss. More times than he could remember, he had watched paramedics perform CPR while someone's father or grandfather or sister or niece bled to death on a grease-covered, trash-strewn piece of roadway.

The temptation was to become callous. Survival, his peers called it. Form a tough veneer, a carefully maintained wall between his emotions and the reality of working traffic in a city like Los Angeles. That's how most of the officers he knew coped with their own vulnerability.

But Miller was different. He was a Christian, a born-again believer who had come to understand mangled vehicles and mutilated bodies as part of a fallen world. Often he reassured himself with Scripture..."I know the number of your days, says the Lord...." "What is your life? You are but a mist that appears for a little while..."

No, he hadn't grown callous, but neither did he fear the dangers that lurked on L.A.'s busy streets. Nothing happened outside God's control, and that was all that mattered.

In fact, he believed his presence at various accidents was often divinely appointed. Sometimes, very quietly, he would pray for—or even with—the victim. Once he had held the hand of a man who was bleeding to death as rescue workers used the jaws-of-life to extricate him from his car.

He'd talked to the man through a hole in the shattered windshield. "Do you believe in Jesus?" He volunteered to keep the victim alert throughout the rescue. He wanted to be sure the man would spend eternity with God.

"I know of him."

Father, give me the words... "He is the Son of God, God in the flesh. He died to give you life, and he wants you to have that salvation now. It's yours for the asking."

The other rescue workers continued their noisy efforts, unaware of the dialogue between him and the dying man. The victim had struggled then, choking on his blood. But his words had been vividly clear. "I want that. Yes, please pray for me."

Sgt. Miller did as the man asked. Rescue efforts had been futile, and the man was listed as DOA at the hospital. But the sergeant knew better. The man was very much alive, and he looked forward to seeing him again in heaven.

The very idea of sharing the grace of Jesus Christ with people in their dying moments made him thankful for his position with the LAPD. He likened it to the parable Jesus told of the workers who worked only a short while yet received an entire day's wage. The sergeant saw himself as the man who introduced Jesus to those who only believed a short while yet shared the same salvation as those who had known Christ all their lives. Physical death was a part of life. Because of his work, Sgt. Miller understood that better than most. All the more reason to cling to Jesus, he figured. Death would not have the final say.

Sgt. Miller received the call at 4:25 that afternoon: Accident with multiple injuries at Ventura and Fallbrook. Two fire engines, three ambulances, and four paramedics were on the way, as were two LAPD squad cars. He grabbed his keys and an accident notebook and moved swiftly through the office, out the back door toward his unmarked car. It was his job to orchestrate the roles of each emergency worker, gather witness information, and make sure protocol was followed perfectly in case an arrest was in order.

As always, he asked God to use him mightily in the next few hours and to comfort the victims and their family members.

"It doesn't matter what task you have for me out there, Lord," he whispered as he flipped on his siren. "Just use me."

Brian Wesley opened his eyes. Was he dreaming?

His head hurt....He looked around and saw that his windshield was shattered. Shards of glass covered his legs and the seat next to him, and he realized he must have been in some kind of accident. He ran his fingers tentatively over his arms and legs....Nothing seemed to be broken. He rubbed his eyes and shook his head, trying to clear his vision. It was then that he noticed the front end of his truck was missing.

He gazed across the intersection and saw another vehicle wrapped around a utility pole. People were all around it, working to get inside.

Brian's blood ran cold. This was no dream.

He had gotten drunk and now he'd hit somebody.

"Oh, man, please be okay." His arms and legs shook, racked with the beginning of a raw fear more potent than any he had known before. He tried to get out, but his truck door was jammed. He turned around, kicking it open with his heavy work boots. Eyes wide, heart and head pounding, Brian walked across the intersection.

Today is the first day of the rest of your life...

The cliché floated through his mind—and chilled him to the bone.

Two motorists had stopped and were working alongside a woman in an apron. All were trying to free the people inside the vehicle. As Brian drew closer, he saw them lean inside, then together they lifted the limp, bloodied body of a teenage girl from the backseat and lay her gently on the grassy curbside. The woman with the apron covered the girl's legs with a blanket.

"Oh, no..." It took Brian a second to realize the whining voice was his.

In the distance, sirens grew louder with each passing moment.

Brian tried to swallow, but his throat was so dry it almost choked him. "Hey, man, is she...is she all r-r-r-right?" He was consumed with dread, and he felt his knees start to shake again. The woman in the apron looked up at him, studied him for a moment, and then turned back to the girl. The two men were trying to find her pulse, and one of them began giving her mouth-to-mouth resuscitation.

The sirens were very close now, and Brian could see several emergency vehicles speeding into view. Relief swept him. *Hurry! Hurry! She needs you!* He couldn't take his eyes from the girl lying on the curb. The others continued working on her without acknowledging him. Brian saw the woman in the apron begin to cry and the men sit back on their heels. They were giving up.

"W-w-w-wait...she n-n-n-needs help, man!" He moved toward the girl, but the woman in the apron rose to her feet.

"Get back!" She spat the words at him. "You've done enough!"

One of the men came to put a hand on her arm. "Come on. Let's check the others." They studied Brian for an instant, disgust clear on their faces, then turned to what remained of the Explorer.

Brian saw the girl's face then....It was a pretty face, framed by honey-colored brown hair. But it was a lifeless face. Even he could see that. He sank to his knees ten feet from where the girl lay—ten feet from the body of a girl who would never again hold her mother's hand or kiss her daddy good-night or dance across a living room floor....

A wail erupted from somewhere deep within him. He willed himself dead in her place, willed anything that might breathe life into her once more. Then his wailing became one word, so weighted with regret that he felt it would consume him: *"Noooo!"*

Sgt. Miller arrived at the scene moments after the paramedics and saw both vehicles. The first one, a white pickup truck, had heavy front-end damage. The second vehicle was almost unrecognizable. Miller could see it was a Ford Explorer, one of the safest vehicles on the road, but it might have been made of tinfoil the way it wrapped around the pole. The impact must have been unbelievable, like getting broadsided by a freight train.

Sgt. Miller made his way to where a small crowd gathered near the twisted remains. Immediately an officer filled him in on the situation.

"We have a deceased female, maybe fourteen, fifteen years old; and two additional victims, a male, late thirties, head wounds, massive bleeding."

Miller felt his shoulders slump imperceptibly. A young girl with her whole life ahead of her. He made several notations on the accident report and wondered if she had known the Lord. "Third victim?"

"Female, twelve, maybe thirteen years old, head injury and a broken arm. She has the best chance of making it."

"Identification?"

"We have a home address for the male victim, some pictures. Guy's a doctor. Tom Ryan. Female victims look to be his daughters."

"Next of kin?"

"Nothing yet. Figured we'd do a drive-by when the ambulances leave."

Sgt. Miller nodded. They didn't always do drive-by notification. Quite often family members were notified by a hospital representative. But in accidents this serious, with multiple injuries—perhaps even multiple fatalities—the officers thought it was best to notify the family in person.

"Driver of the pickup?"
"Minor injuries. He's in the squad car, cuffed."
"Drunk?"
"Can't you smell him?"
For a moment, Miller felt defeated. Another family destroyed by a drunk driver. Somehow with all their efforts, they weren't doing enough to stop the problem. He pursed his lips. "You do the test?"
"Preliminary. Failed the straight line. I thought I'd wait for you to get the blood test."
"Witnesses?"
"A lady, Rae McDermott, works in the diner across the street. And a couple of motorists. They're still here."
Sgt. Miller strained to see which of the victims was now laying on a stretcher and receiving attention from two paramedics. It was the young female. "Where's the male victim?"
"They're using the jaws-of-life. He's bleeding pretty bad, trapped in the front seat. I don't think he's going to make it."
The sergeant sighed and closed his notebook. He dismissed the officer and approached the mangled vehicle. Fire department rescue workers were busy on one side of the vehicle, so he walked to the other. Sleeping bags and camping gear had spilled onto the road. An ice chest had opened and dead fish littered the roadway as well. What a way to end a camping trip.
He saw a small passage where the window had been and gingerly stuck his head and upper body inside. The victim's entire left side was pinned beneath layers of metal and draped with fireproof tarps. One paramedic was stationed under the tarp, just outside the driver's door, waiting for the instant he could remove the man and begin treatment. Beyond him, another firefighter used a blowtorch to separate the wreckage while the jaws hummed and screeched, working to peel away the layers of metal.
Miller focused on the victim. There was a gash across the man's forehead, and despite the noise, Miller could hear the

man struggling to breathe. Still, he seemed semiconscious. Reaching out, Miller took the man's hand in his own. He raised his voice over the machinery. "Sir, can you hear me?"

The man jerked his head twice and his eyelids began to tremble.

"We're doing everything we can to get you out of here. Can you hear me, sir?"

Suddenly the machines stopped as the separated layers were removed and set aside.

"Let's do it!" It was the paramedic stationed under the tarp. He moved, pressing fingers to the man's neck, feeling for a pulse. Then he shouted to the others. "Come on, *move it!* We're losing him!"

"Can you hear me, sir?" Sgt. Miller asked again. The vehicle was quieter inside now, almost tomblike. This time the man stirred and seemed suddenly frantic, anxious to speak.

Help him, Lord, help him say what he wants to say.

Suddenly the man's lips parted and he worked his mouth silently. Miller strained to hear him.

"The girls..."

This wasn't the time to tell him about the older girl. The man would have to remain calm if the rescue was to have a chance of being successful. He squeezed the man's hand. "Sir, they're already out. We're working on them right now."

The man seemed slightly reassured. A gurgling sound came from his throat, and he sucked in another breath. "Tell Hannah—" the man gulped, clearly fighting unconsciousness—"tell Hannah...the girls...I love them." He opened his eyes, and Miller saw an unmistakable peace there.

"I'll tell them. Now you hang on. We're getting you out of here and you can tell them yourself."

The man gulped again and his eyes rolled back for a moment and then closed. His lids twitched violently and once more his lips moved. Miller squeezed the man's hand another time. "Stay calm now, you're almost out of here."

But the man grew more agitated, his mouth opening and shutting soundlessly. He was slipping away, but he seemed desperate to speak.

Sgt. Miller moved closer. "It's okay, sir.... I'm here. I'm listening."

The gurgling grew louder and the man coughed. Miller held back a grimace. The man was choking on his own blood. He was gasping for each breath, and his words were slurred, but finally they were audible.

Miller strained to understand.

"Tell Hannah...tell her...please, forgive...forgive...."

He said something after that but Sgt. Miller couldn't make it out. "You want Hannah to forgive someone, is that it?"

The man's entire body relaxed, and Sgt. Miller thought he saw him nod.

"We're losing pressure!" The paramedic's voice was angry. "Come on, let's *open* this thing." The machines whirred once more, and finally the man was free. Two paramedics lifted him immediately onto a backboard.

"He's not breathing! Prepare to intubate."

In a blur of commotion the paramedics worked on the man, doing everything they could to stabilize him.

Passersby had gathered, and now a crowd of stricken onlookers gaped at the bloodied man, watching the paramedics work frantically to save him. In less than a minute he was loaded into an ambulance while the EMTs used an oxygen pump and manually compressed the man's chest.

As the ambulance drove off, Miller looked around and knew his work at the scene was finished. He'd talked to the witnesses, each of whom had agreed that the driver of the pickup had sped through a red light and hit the Explorer without ever slowing.

Miller looked at his notes. The other driver was Brian Wesley, age twenty-eight...five prior DUIs. He'd been arrested and taken to the West Valley Division, where he would be booked. He had been given a blood alcohol test—the results of which would not be available from the crime lab for several weeks.

If the results were positive, Wesley would be formally charged with whatever crimes the district attorney's office thought they could prove—anything from driving under the influence to vehicular manslaughter. A plea bargain might be struck, but because of the man's prior record and the severity of the accident, most likely the case would be ordered to trial.

Then months or maybe even a year later, after delays and continuances, when the memory of the accident had faded in the minds of witnesses, a trial date would be set. The trial would drag on for a month or more, and finally Brian Wesley might be convicted. At that point, barring some sort of judicial miracle, Wesley would most likely serve less than a year behind bars for destroying the Ryan family.

Sgt. Miller removed his sunglasses and rubbed his temples. Tow trucks had arrived at the scene and were busy removing the wreckage of the two vehicles. It was late, nearly 5:30, and his worst task lay ahead.

He remembered how the injured man had struggled to speak, how desperately he'd wanted to relay what might be his final message to his family. What was it the man had said? Something about getting mad…or about not getting mad. The sergeant wasn't sure anymore; the past hour had been so chaotic, so tense. Besides, the accident hadn't been Mr. Ryan's fault. No one could be angry at him. Miller shrugged. Best to forget it, whatever it was. For all he knew, the man had mumbled the words out of shock or delirium.

Either way, Miller remembered the most important part of Ryan's message: Tell Hannah and the girls he loved them.

Sgt. Miller sighed. It was time to tell Hannah.

Five

Bitterly she weeps at night, tears are upon her cheeks....
There is none to comfort her.

LAMENTATIONS 1:2A

They drove in silence, Sgt. Miller at the wheel and Officer Rolando Santiago making notations, checking the accident report. Miller noticed that the streets were quiet here, lined with mature shade trees and upper-end homes with large, fenced yards. People who lived in this part of the San Fernando Valley generally safeguarded themselves against the perils of city living by driving sturdy vehicles and protecting their homes with custom alarms.

Pity none of those alarms could have protected the Ryan family against this....

Three turns later the squad car pulled up out front of a well-manicured home on a pretty cul-de-sac.

Sgt. Miller noticed a wooden sign near the front door that read "The Ryans." Under their name was the symbol of a Christian fish.

"Believers."

Santiago looked at him. "What's that?"

He nodded toward the symbol. "The Christian fish. The family must be believers."

Officer Santiago shrugged. "You never know after today."

Miller didn't reply but climbed out of the car and headed somberly up the walkway. Santiago walked in step beside him and glanced at his watch. "Let's get this thing over with. I've got dinner plans."

Sgt. Miller studied his partner a moment, but all he could see was the protective wall. He drew a deep breath. "Let me do the talking."

For two hours Hannah Ryan had fought off an exhausting list of possibilities while staring out her kitchen window, but still there was no sign of her family. She wanted to pray, and even tried a time or two, but she held back. It only made the fear worse.

Dread had begun to consume her, and as the minutes became hours, she stopped looking for ways to keep busy. Instead she was continually drawn to the kitchen window, as if she could somehow make them appear by keeping watch. They should have called by now, and anger joined the emotions warring within her.

When the squad car pulled up, she was no longer fiddling with the pink sponge, wiping and rewiping the sink, but rather she was frozen in place, barely breathing, staring at the dusky cul-de-sac.

A pit formed in her stomach and in that instant, she knew.

She closed her eyes. *Lock the door. Close the blinds. Get the car keys and leave.* Anything but greet the officers who were walking deliberately up the sidewalk. Hannah drew a shaky breath and forced her feet to carry her toward the front door. *Calm, calm. Be calm.* She wiped her trembling palms on her jeans and turned the knob.

"Yes?" She did not attempt a smile and neither did the officers.

"Hannah Ryan?"

"Yes, can I help you?"

The older officer hesitated. "Ma'am, I'm Sgt. John Miller with the Los Angeles Police Department. May we come in for a minute?"

No. Go away. I hate that you're here. Hannah opened the

door and the men stepped into the foyer. She did not invite them to go any further.

"Ma'am, maybe if we moved inside and sat down."

"Listen, what's this all about?" Hannah began shivering. She rubbed her arms, trying to ward off the sudden chill. She did not want to sit down, and she was not in the mood for a slow explanation.

"Is your husband Dr. Tom Ryan?"

O God...please..."Yes, what is it? Has he been hurt?"

Sgt. Miller cleared his throat. "I'm afraid there was a car accident, ma'am. He's suffered serious injuries, and he's been taken to the hospital."

Hannah steadied herself. "What about the girls?"

"Mrs. Ryan, why don't you come with us? We'll take you to the hospital so you can be with them."

"No!" Hannah knew she sounded frantic, but she couldn't stop herself. "I want to know about the girls. Are they okay?"

Sgt. Miller moved closer and placed a hand under Hannah's elbow. "Your oldest daughter suffered serious head injuries. The younger girl has a broken arm and a concussion, but her condition is much less serious."

"No!" She ripped her elbow from Sgt. Miller's hand and leveled menacing eyes at him. "That *can't* be! You're lying to me."

"You need to get to the hospital, Mrs. Ryan. May I help you get your things together?"

Hannah spun toward the desk in the kitchen and froze in place. Black spots danced before her eyes, and she grasped the wall to steady herself.

"Ma'am, you all right?" Sgt. Miller's voice was kind, but Hannah didn't want to hear him. She kept her back to the officers and hung her head.

"Listen," she said firmly. "You've made some kind of mistake."

No, God...no. It wasn't true, it couldn't be. They had the wrong Ryan family, or if there was an accident, then Tom and the girls were probably just bruised and a little cut up. After all, they were driving the Explorer. The officers must have mixed up the information. It wasn't their fault. Anyone could get the facts wrong. Hannah forced herself to relax, and the spots went away. She moved across the kitchen and grabbed her purse from the work desk.

"You can leave now." She turned around to face them, the picture of control. "There's obviously been some sort of mistake. My family has a sports utility truck—it's very safe." She pulled her keys from the purse and glanced at the Lexus outside in the driveway. "I better go, now."

"Ma'am, it's not—"

Hannah cut him off. "What hospital?"

Sgt. Miller sighed. "Humana West Hills. Emergency trauma center. Mrs. Ryan, why don't you let us drive you over there?"

"No, I'm fine. Besides, they'll need a ride home if the Explorer's been damaged."

"Do you have a friend or a pastor, someone we could call who could meet you there?"

Hannah stared at him. "A pastor? I don't need a pastor. I told you, they were in a big vehicle. There must be some kind of mistake."

The sergeant studied her, and Hannah hated the look of pity in his eyes. "All right, we'll follow you."

"That's not necessary." Hannah felt mechanical and oddly void of emotion. She walked past the officers, ushered them outside, then locked the front door behind her. "I appreciate your dropping by. They were camping, you know. Monday's the first day of school."

Hannah knew she was not acting rationally, but as she pulled the Lexus onto Roscoe Boulevard, she refused to believe what the officer had said.

She glanced in her rearview mirror and pressed her lips

together. Why on earth had they insisted on driving behind her? Every time she glanced in the mirror, they were there, a constant reminder of their ridiculous story. Their presence was unnerving. Certainly they must have more important tasks than following her to the hospital.

Then, for just an instant, her mind began running ahead. What if they really had been hit? What if they were hurt…or worse? And suddenly she felt a wave of dread and fear and loss and devastation so great, it was like a monster lurking in the recesses of her mind, threatening to break free. If it did, Hannah knew it would destroy her.

She held the darkness at bay and concentrated instead on the simple facts at hand and not the unknown. At least she knew where Tom and the girls were and why they were late. People were in car accidents all the time. That didn't mean anything really bad had happened. She could picture Tom joking with the doctors, and Alicia and Jenny teasing each other about the story they'd tell at school Monday.

Hannah relaxed a bit. She would get there, make sure the hospital had their health insurance information, and take her family home. Eating at The Red Onion was out of the question, but they could pick up some pizzas. Hannah looked at her watch and saw it was nearly seven o'clock. They were probably starving by now.

Sgt. Miller followed Hannah Ryan with care. He had radioed dispatch and asked them to notify the emergency room that the Ryans' next of kin was on the way, and could they please have the staff minister on hand.

Miller thought again of the symbol of faith on the outside of the Ryans' house. How close was this woman with the Lord? She was striking, probably in her midthirties with a figure she obviously worked to maintain. She had blond hair, clear blue eyes, and her clothing and jewelry were casually elegant.

Certainly she seemed strong, self-assured, and in control.

Still…

If her relationship with God wasn't built on the deepest roots, Sgt. Miller doubted she would ever be the same after today.

At last Hannah arrived at the hospital. She said nothing as she entered the trauma center flanked by the two uniformed officers. She introduced herself, and immediately a nurse ushered her into the patient area. There she was directed to sit in a quiet alcove apart from the hustle of activity.

The monster in her mind moved closer, and Hannah smiled in a vain attempt to keep it at bay. "This isn't necessary." She looked at the nurse. "Really, if you could just show me which room my family is in."

The nurse motioned toward one of the doctors, and he immediately picked up his clipboard and approached her. With him was a man who looked like a minister.

One of the officers—Sgt. Miller, was it?—met him halfway and relayed something in hushed tones. The doctor nodded and made a notation on his clipboard. Sgt. Miller turned back to Hannah and pulled something out of his shirt pocket: his business card.

"Call me if you need anything, if you have any questions at all." His tone was filled with compassion. "I'll be praying for you, Mrs. Ryan."

"Thank you." Hannah took the card, glanced at it, and slipped it into her purse.

Sgt. Miller disappeared down the corridor with the other officer at his side. The man with the doctor seemed to take a cue from that because he pulled up two chairs. He sat beside Hannah while the doctor sat directly in front of her, their knees nearly touching. The doctor cleared his throat and looked into Hannah's eyes.

“Mrs. Ryan, I’m Dr. Cleary and this is Scott O’Haver, our hospital chaplain.”

Hannah looked from one man to the other and shook her head, her heart pounding. “This isn’t necessary. There’s been some kind of mistake. My family was in a big vehicle.…It was safe. I just need you to take me to them so I can—”

“Ma’am—” Dr. Cleary interrupted her—“please…let me continue.” He looked like a kind man. Something about him exuded authority and confidence. Reluctantly Hannah settled back in her chair.

“My husband’s a doctor, too.” Hannah watched Dr. Cleary’s reaction carefully.

“Yes, I know. I’ve checked his medical records. I don’t think he and I ever worked together.” Dr. Cleary seemed to struggle for a moment. *Oh, no. He’s afraid to tell me. No, God…please, no.* “How are you doing, Mrs. Ryan?”

“I’m fine. If you could just take me to them.…”

Dr. Cleary checked his notes and drew a single breath. He moved closer and set his hand on Hannah’s knee.

No. Don’t touch me…don’t comfort me. Hannah remained silent as she squirmed and slid her hands underneath her legs.

“Mrs. Ryan, I’ve been working on your husband and the girls for an hour now,” he said. “They were in a serious accident, Mrs. Ryan, hit by a speeding pickup truck. The impact was most severe.” He paused and his gaze dropped to the floor for an instant before connecting once again with Hannah’s. She looked desperately for some sense of reassurance. There was none. “Jenny sustained a broken arm and a concussion. We are checking her for internal injuries, but her vital signs are strong. She’s medicated and very sleepy, but I expect her to show significant improvement by tomorrow.”

Hannah sat frozen in place, waiting for the doctor to continue.

“I’m very sorry to have to tell you this, but Alicia didn’t fare as well.”

Hannah began to rock. *No. No. Not Alicia.…Not Alicia.*

He hesitated. "I'm afraid Alicia received more of the impact and suffered massive head injuries." His words were deliberate and measured. "Paramedics arrived on the scene in minutes, but she was already gone. I'm sorry, Mrs. Ryan. She died quickly and without any pain or fear."

"No." Hannah stood up, shaking—and then she screamed. She tried to push past Dr. Cleary, but he held her gently in place until she eased back into the chair, rocking fiercely and wailing. "No! Not Alicia, no!"

The chaplain circled an arm around her shoulders and leaned toward her. Hannah felt herself losing consciousness, and she crumpled slightly in his embrace.

"Please…" She implored him with every fiber, begging him to be wrong. "She can't be dead, Doctor. I want to see her."

Dr. Cleary drew another breath. "I'm sorry, there's more. About your husband, Mrs. Ryan…"

No…not Tom. It's too much, God. Her heart was racing, banging about in her chest.

"Upon impact your husband hit the steering wheel and suffered blunt trauma to his chest. This caused him to bleed from the aorta, the main artery out of the heart. He was conscious at first while rescue workers tried to help him out of the vehicle. Paramedics were able to intubate him to keep his lungs open, but he was bleeding too badly. He died enroute to the hospital. I'm so sorry, Mrs. Ryan.…They did everything they could."

The only thing that kept Hannah from falling on the floor was Rev. O'Haver. She sagged in his grip, struggling to breathe, to think, to move. But all she could do was say the same thing over and over.…

"No. No! Not my Tom.…Not my baby, Alicia. Please, God, *no!*"

The world was spinning out of control, and her heart pounded hard and erratically. She closed her eyes, fighting against the vortex of emotions that threatened to consume her.

She knew she was screaming, could hear it, but it was almost as though it were someone else...someone whose very soul had been ripped from her chest. With a shuddering sigh, she straightened, leaning back against her chair. She clenched her teeth to hold back the screams still clawing at her throat, and noted numbly that her eyes were dry. The greatest shock of her entire life and she hadn't cried.

"I want to see them."

Dr. Cleary nodded. "That's fine. Perhaps you'd like to see Jenny first? I think she'd recognize your voice, and it might help her come around."

Hannah nodded, mute. Rev. O'Haver helped her up, and she followed Dr. Cleary to a room sectioned off by curtains. There lay Jenny, oxygen tubes in her nose, an IV dripping into her left arm. Her right arm was in a cast from the shoulder to her hand.

Hannah ached inside as she studied her little girl. She longed to cradle her close and tell her everything was going to be okay.

But it won't, will it? It will never be okay again.

She moved closer to Jenny and smoothed a wisp of blond bangs off her forehead. There were bruises on the right side of her face, and Hannah had to choke back a sob as she ran her fingers over them. Jenny stirred, moaned twice, and moved her head from side to side.

"Jenny, honey..." Hannah leaned closer to her. "It's me, Mom."

Jenny opened her eyes, and Hannah could see what effort it took for her daughter to focus. "Mom? What happened? Where's Dad and Alicia?"

Dr. Cleary stepped forward and Hannah glanced up at him. He shook his head quickly and mouthed the word, "Later."

Hannah nodded and took Jenny's hand. "Honey, you need your rest now. Why don't you try to sleep and I'll be right here."

Jenny had already closed her eyes, and when Hannah was sure she was asleep, she turned to Dr. Cleary.

"I want to see Tom and Alicia." Her own voice sounded foreign to her, and she wondered again why she still hadn't cried. Was this the denial people talked about after receiving terrible news? She closed her eyes briefly. Maybe…maybe something deep within her knew this was all some kind of terrible joke, that Tom and Alicia were fine, that there was nothing to cry over—

With an impatient shake of her head, she opened her eyes to find Dr. Cleary watching her carefully. "Please, Tom and Alicia…"

He sighed sadly. "This way." He led her down a hallway into another room. And there she saw them, Tom and Alicia, side by side on stretchers. Hannah wouldn't learn until later how Dr. Cleary had directed the nurses to prepare their bodies so they would appear less traumatized. The nurses had wrapped a towel around Alicia's bloodied head and tilted her face so that Hannah would not have to see her battered left side. They had done the same for Tom, removed his blood-covered T-shirt, and wiped his face clean. They covered his head wounds and placed blankets over him so that only his face and arms could be seen. Later, Hannah would forget everything she'd heard after receiving news of the accident.

But she would remember forever the way Tom and Alicia looked as they laid lifeless on those stretchers.

"Dear God…" She clasped her hands, bringing them to her chin. The tears came then, torrents of them.

"It happened very quickly, Mrs. Ryan. They didn't suffer."

The doctor's words rang in her head, but still she couldn't believe what she was seeing. She moved into the narrow space between the two gurneys and stood there, facing Tom and Alicia. Sobs catching in her throat, she stooped and circled an arm around each of them. Loud, wracking sobs seized her, and she was sure this was how it felt to die.

Hannah felt disconnected from her body, as if she were playing a role or watching some other woman deal with the fact that her life had been destroyed. But this was no stage drama, and she was the only woman in the room. There was no mistake.

Her life had been perfect…too perfect. Something had gone terribly wrong, and now Tom and Alicia were dead.

She knew she should pray, but for the first time in her life she couldn't. Didn't even want to. God had let this happen to Tom and Alicia. Why pray to him now? Why ask him to comfort her when he had allowed her very existence to be shattered? She looked from her husband to her child, studying them through her tears, willing them to move or speak or smile at her. When they didn't, she bowed her head and wailed. In one violent instant her family had been destroyed—and there was nothing she could do to bring them back.

When she finally regained her composure, she straightened slowly. Drawing a fortifying breath, she looked at Dr. Cleary and saw him extend his hand. For a moment, standing there in his white coat, he looked just like Tom. Hannah took his hand and let him support her as she struggled to keep from passing out. But she stayed there between Tom and Alicia, unwilling to move from their sides.

"I'm so sorry, Mrs. Ryan." Dr. Cleary seemed to wait until he had her attention before continuing. "There's something I need to tell you. Sgt. Miller was with your husband at the accident scene before he died. He wanted me to give you a message from Tom."

Hannah felt her shoulders drop, and she reached for Tom's hand as naturally as she had for the past twenty years. But now his touch was cool and unresponsive. She shuddered.

Dr. Cleary's voice grew softer. "Before he died…Tom said to tell you and the girls that he loved you."

A single sob caught in Hannah's throat, and she looked down at her husband through a blur of tears. She struggled to speak, and the silence hung awkwardly in the air.

"I want some time with them," she said finally.

"Take as long as you like."

Forever. A lifetime. A chance to celebrate our twentieth anniversary, and our thirtieth and fortieth. Time to grow old together and watch our daughters become young women. Time to see Tom walk Alicia and Jenny down the aisle, time to share grandchildren and retirement and vacations on warm, sunny beaches—

Dr. Cleary interrupted her thoughts. "I need to get back to work, but Rev. O'Haver will be outside in the hallway if you need him."

The men left, and Hannah was finally alone. She studied Tom and sobbed softly. She hadn't had time to say good-bye. If only she had gone on the camping trip this year. Maybe she would have seen the truck...she could have warned Tom. It was all her fault. If she'd been with them, they would have come home earlier, and this never would have happened.

Tom still looked so alive, as if he were sleeping. She still held his hand, but now she turned to Alicia. Beautiful, self-assured Alicia. Her firstborn.

She took the girl's lifeless hand in her free one. "Mommy's here, Alicia." She thought of proms and graduation, college, the wedding her daughter would never have...and she began to weep once more. Alicia's hair stuck out in matted tufts from underneath the bandages. Hannah let go of Tom's still hand and reached over to smooth the silky locks, making her daughter more presentable. Alicia looked so lost on the stretcher, almost as if she were a small child again. Where had the time gone? Hannah remembered being at this very hospital fifteen years earlier for Alicia Marie's birth, celebrating life and the promises it held for their tiny daughter. She was such a sweet baby, such a happy little girl....

Alicia's hand was cold, and Hannah ran her thumb over it, trying to warm it as she'd done when her daughter was a toddler. Alicia always had cold hands. Hannah wanted so badly to pick her up and rock her, to take away the hurt as she'd always been able to do in the past. She sniffled loudly. "Alicia, Mommy loves you, honey." She sobbed twice. "I'm here, baby. I'll always be here. Wherever I am I'll take you with me, sweetheart."

She remembered a week earlier when Alicia had stayed up late talking to her about boys and how she'd know when she met the right one. Now there would be no boys—no future. Alicia was gone, and it grieved Hannah beyond anything she'd ever known.

She turned back to Tom. "Why didn't you come home earlier, you big oaf? You never were on time." She tried to laugh, but it became one more sob, and fresh tears filled her eyes. "If only you hadn't been so late...."

She let the thought hang in the still air, and she squeezed her eyes shut. When she opened them, she struggled to speak. "I guess...if Alicia had to go, it's better you go with her." She gulped loudly, and when she spoke her voice was barely a whisper. "Stay with her, Tom. She's so afraid of being alone."

She stooped and kissed him tenderly on the cheek, his final message echoing in her mind, breaking her heart. "I love you, too, Tom. I've loved you since we were kids. I always have." She sobbed hard. "I always will."

She carefully arranged Tom's hands on his chest, then did the same for Alicia. But she couldn't bear to leave. She bent over and wrapped her arms around them, holding them close and giving in again to the wrenching sobs....

This couldn't be happening....

Finally, when it seemed as if days had passed, she rose and kissed Alicia on the cheek. She smoothed her hair, knowing it was the last time she'd ever do so. "Good-bye..." She turned to Tom and traced his lips with her finger. Then she kissed him tenderly and studied his face one last time.

Finally she turned and, against every instinct in her body, she left.

Rev. O'Haver waited in the hallway outside and cleared his throat as she approached. "Mrs. Ryan, may I speak with you a moment?"

Hannah stopped and waited. She was struggling to find the strength to move, even to breathe, and all she wanted was to be with Jenny. She didn't need some stranger offering pat answers.

"Mrs. Ryan...I understand you and your family are Christians?"

A single huff escaped Hannah's throat, and she wiped her eyes with the tips of her fingers. "Yes, we are." She paused, trying to make sense of her feelings. "A lot of good it did us."

The reverend hesitated. "I can't imagine what you're going through, Mrs. Ryan, but please know it's normal to be angry at God." He paused again. "I'd like to pray with you, if I can."

Hannah nodded reluctantly and sat down beside the man. He took her hands in his and prayed quietly.

Hannah thanked him when he finished. She hadn't paid attention to the prayer, but it was over and she wanted to be polite. She allowed herself to be hugged, and then she stood without saying another word and headed for Jenny's room. Hannah didn't want to be angry with God, but she didn't want to talk to him, either. There were more pressing things to think about. She had to contact family members, make plans for a funeral, and tend to Jenny....

Jenny was all she had left now, a small fragment of a family that only hours earlier had been perfect...complete.

But though Hannah knew she should be thinking about her surviving daughter and the consolation she would need in the days to come, that wasn't what consumed her as she walked down the hall. Rather she found herself focusing on the other driver...the one who ran the red light and killed her family. And as she thought of him, one emotion reigned supreme.

Hatred.

Six

After affliction...she finds no resting place.
All who pursue her have overtaken her in the midst of her distress.

LAMENTATIONS 1:3

There was solace in keeping busy.

In her new role as victim, widow, and grieving mother, Hannah learned to keep her grief at bay by burying herself in busyness. And there was a mountain of details to handle.

First she made dozens of phone calls in which she told key people about the accident and asked them to contact others. She notified the girls' schools, Tom's partner, and the insurance company. And she organized the funeral.

There was precious little time to weep, to even think about her loss. And that was fine with Hannah. As long as she was busy, she could avoid thinking about a lifetime without Tom and Alicia.

Now Hannah sat in an oversized vinyl chair next to Jenny's hospital bed and glanced at the clock. Eleven in the morning. Nearly twenty-four hours after the collision. In that time Jenny had only awakened once or twice for a few minutes. They'd moved her to the critical care unit, and at the moment she was sleeping again.

Dr. Cleary had been right—Jenny was no longer in danger. Her blood tests and CAT scan were almost normal, but she was sleepy, coming out of the semiconscious haze caused by the injury. The doctor expected her to wake up soon, and then Hannah would need to tell her the truth.

She studied her notes and tugged absently at a lock of hair.

She had notified Tom's parents, his sister in Ohio…her parents in Washington state. She had no siblings, so there were few people to contact. She had called her pastor, Joel Conner, and he had started a prayer chain at New Hope Christian Church in Agoura Hills, where they had been members for as long as she could remember. Several of the women from her Bible study had come by last night to pray with her and offer assistance. Two had brought meals for Hannah to take home.

Hannah refused them all. She'd considered those women friends once, but that was before the collision…back when she had something in common with them. Now she was in a category all by herself, someone to be pitied. The idea of them sitting around talking about her tragedy in quiet voices made her skin crawl. She neither wanted—nor needed—their charity.

But they wouldn't go away. So rather than appear ungrateful, Hannah allowed one of the women to make plans for a brief reception after the funeral, which was scheduled for Wednesday.

Hannah glanced at Jenny's sleeping form—and was struck suddenly by the thought that it was the first day of school. Hannah's church friends would all be at breakfast—an annual tradition on this day—talking about how quickly children grow up, the merits of their various teachers, and how much time they would all have now that the fall routine was back in place.

Hannah's heart grew heavy and tears filled her eyes. She had cried more since the collision than all the other times in her life combined. She leaned her head back and closed her eyes…but images drifted across her mind of her friends' children greeting classmates, working out the kinks in their schedules, and making plans for weekend get-togethers.

She had called the principal of West Hills High and told him about the accident. He would have told the others, so by now Alicia's friends and fellow cheerleaders would probably be convening in the lunch area, consoling each other and crying over the loss of their friend. Certainly many of them would be at the funeral.

But in time they would get over her absence—life would get in the way, and they would be drawn to the thrill of Friday night football games and weekend dances. They would talk about Alicia on occasion, but she would eventually fade into the recesses of their memories.

Hannah sighed and fiddled with her pencil. She felt as if she had aged ten years overnight—she knew she looked haggard. Her clothing was rumpled from sleeping in the chair by Jenny's bed, and her hair was pulled back into an unruly ponytail. Only her crimson, manicured fingernails gave any indication of her former appearance. She had checked the bathroom mirror earlier that morning, and the person staring back at her with empty red eyes and cheeks ravaged by tears did not look even remotely familiar.

Focus. Concentrate on the matters at hand. That was all that kept her from falling into a bottomless pit of despair—something she could not do because she knew if she ever gave in, there would be no return.

She studied her notes again and pressed her lips together. It was time to contact Sgt. Miller. She wanted to know exactly what happened. The other driver had run a red light. She knew that much. But had he been drinking? Was he on drugs? Hannah had a horrible suspicion that there was something more to the accident story, but until she knew for sure, she tried not to think about it. The hatred she already felt toward the other driver was frightening enough without dwelling on it.

Suddenly Jenny stirred and rolled slowly from one side to the other. Hannah moved next to the bed and took her daughter's hand. A torrent of anxiety and dread consumed her, and she willed herself to stay calm. How would she tell this child, this precious daughter, that her father and sister were dead? She had no idea.

*God...*she started, but then cut the prayer short. No, she

would not ask. She didn't want to think about God until she had time to examine her feelings. Besides, she didn't know what power her prayers would have. They hadn't kept her family safe.

Jenny moaned and turned toward Hannah. Her eyes opened and she squinted against the sunshine streaming through the hospital window.

"Mom?"

Hannah figured her daughter could make out her face, but Jenny didn't sound sure of herself.

She leaned over the girl's prone body, hugged her, then pulled away slightly and caressed Jenny's forehead with a single finger. There was nothing she could do about the heavy sadness in her voice. "Hi, sweetheart, how do you feel?"

Jenny glanced around the room. "Where…am I?"

Hannah continued to run her fingers gently over Jenny's hair. "You're at the hospital. There was an accident, honey."

Jenny moved her left hand over the cast on her arm. She thought a moment and her eyes grew wide. "The white truck—"

Hannah said nothing.

Jenny seemed to struggle with her memory, then she jolted into a semi-sitting position. Suddenly she looked wide-awake and frightened. "Mom, he was coming right at us…right where Dad and Alicia were sitting!"

Tears filled Hannah's eyes and she pulled Jenny close once more. "I'm so sorry, baby, so sorry you had to see that."

"I wanted to scream, Mom. There wasn't time…I can't… can't remember anything else."

Hannah started to cry and the sound broke the silence. Jenny looked at her, alarm sweeping her young face.

"Mom, what is it? Where are Dad and Alicia?"

Hannah drew back just enough to see her daughter's face. She held her shoulders firmly and looked deep into her eyes. "Honey, the accident was very serious. Alicia and Daddy…they didn't make it, honey. They're gone."

Jenny's eyes filled with horror, and she searched her mother's face. "They're *dead?* Both of them?" She sounded on the verge of hysterics. "Mom? Are you serious?"

Hannah nodded and pulled Jenny close one more time. *"No!"* Jenny moaned softly, burying her face in her mother's shoulder. "No, not both of them."

She did not scream and carry on the way Hannah had done. Rather she sobbed convulsively, clinging to her mother the way a drowning swimmer clings to a life preserver. Hannah could feel her daughter's pain, and she was heartbroken, knowing there was nothing she could do to take it away.

Finally, when Jenny's weeping slowed, she pulled back and studied her mother. Hannah wondered if the girl was going to faint. "Mom," she whispered, her voice stricken. "It's all my fault."

Hannah frowned. "No, dear, of course not. The driver of the other truck ran a red light. Daddy never saw him coming."

Jenny shook her head, her cheeks red and tear stained. "No, not that part. Earlier. We were getting out of the fishing boat, heading back for camp...Alicia nearly stepped on a rattlesnake. She didn't see it but I did. I yelled at her and she stopped....One more step, Mom, and she would have been bitten."

Hannah hesitated. "Sweetheart, I don't understand. You helped your sister by saying something about the snake. That doesn't make the accident your fault."

Jenny drew a deep, shuddering breath. "You don't understand, Mom. If I hadn't said something, Alicia would have been bitten. Dad could have helped her; she would have been okay eventually. But we would have gotten a later start. Maybe an hour later....And we wouldn't have been going through the intersection when that other driver was running the red light. Don't you see, Mom? It's all my fault."

Hannah began to cry softly. "Oh, honey, it's not your fault.

You have to believe that. The only one at fault is the other driver." Even as she said the words, she thought for an instant about the Lord. He could have saved them, but he didn't. Wasn't he at fault? Just a little?

Jenny began weeping harder. "What are we going to do, Mom?" She looked so vulnerable it tore at Hannah's heart, and her hatred toward the other driver grew until she thought it would choke her. "We're going to go home and get you better. Then we're going to make sure the man who did this is punished."

"They're in heaven, right, Mom?" Fresh tears trickled down Jenny's cheeks.

"Yes, honey, they're in heaven. Together."

Jenny nodded and swiped slowly at her tears. She was sobbing so hard it was difficult to understand her. "I want Daddy..."

Hannah held her for twenty minutes, allowing her to cry and grieve the way she, herself, had not yet done. Finally Jenny grew quiet, and after several minutes she leaned her head back and studied Hannah's eyes.

"I'm...I'm glad Alicia isn't alone."

"Oh, Jenny..."

The girl lay back down and buried her head in her pillow. She stayed like that, sobbing quietly, while her mother rubbed her back until she finally drifted off to sleep.

Leaning back in the chair and pulling the bedside telephone over, Hannah clenched her teeth. She glanced at the business card in her hand, then dialed Sgt. John Miller and introduced herself.

"There's something I need to know about the accident." She kept her voice quiet; the last thing she wanted to do was disturb Jenny.

"I have the report right here," Sgt. Miller said. "Go ahead."

"The man who killed my family, was he drunk?"

There was a pause, then, "We think so. He was arrested on

suspicion of drunk driving. The lab tests aren't back yet, but he did fail a field sobriety test."

Hannah felt like she'd been punched in the stomach. With one careless decision that man had ruined her life. She steadied herself and sucked in a steadying breath.

"Where is he now?" She knew the question was angry, but she didn't care.

"He had only minor injuries. He was booked at the station that evening and released on a bail bond. When the results of the sobriety test are in, he'll be formally charged, and then he'll have to enter a plea—guilty or not guilty."

She had one more question. "Was it his first time? Drunk driving I mean?"

"No, ma'am." Sgt. Miller sighed. "His sixth."

The room was suddenly spinning, and Hannah gripped the arm of her chair for support. She reached for the only solid thing she could grab onto—her anger.

"That man had been arrested *five* other times for drunk driving, and he was still on the road? Still drinking and driving? That's *insane!*"

"I know, Mrs. Ryan. I'm sorry…I agree. Maybe this time they'll put him away."

"You mean there's a chance they won't? Listen, Sergeant. I know none of this is your fault, but I will not sit back and watch the courts let this *killer* back on the streets. I'll fight him and the laws and the entire legal system if it costs every cent I have. Even if it kills me."

There was a pause. "The process will be long and drawn out." Sgt. Miller sounded frustrated. "But there are a few things you can do. You've heard of Mothers Against Drunk Drivers?"

"Yes." Hannah was trembling with rage. How could this be happening to her? She didn't want to think about Mothers Against Drunk Drivers. She was supposed to be having breakfast with her church friends, making plans for the school year.

She was supposed to have two, beautiful, healthy daughters

and a husband who loved her.

Sgt. Miller continued. "There's a woman at the West Valley office, Carol Cummins; she's a victim advocate. Why don't you give her a call and see how you can help? Might make a difference when it comes to a possible trial down the road."

"Who is he?

"What?"

"The killer. What's his name?"

"Brian Wesley. He's twenty-eight, married, has a son."

Hannah was furious. "Good for him! Before Saturday afternoon *I* was married with a *daughter.* But he killed them, and I'll do whatever it takes to get him behind bars. When I'm finished with him, he'll wish he'd killed me, too."

"Ma'am..." Sgt. Miller hesitated. "I saw the Christian fish on your door the other day—"

"What of it?"

Another pause. "I'm a believer, too; that's all. I've been praying for you."

"Don't bother." It was all she could do not to spit the words at him. "I have all the prayers I can handle right now."

"Mrs. Ryan, I'm not trying to interfere. It's just that in these situations it's so easy to lose perspective and turn away..."

When she answered, she didn't even try to temper the coldness in her tone. "I'm sure you mean well, Sgt. Miller, but you're just like every other Christian right now. 'It must be God's will.' 'They're home in heaven now.' 'God still loves you.' 'The Lord has a plan—'"

A wave of emotion choked off her words, and she had to swallow hard before she could continue. "I don't want to hear it. Do you understand? Brian Wesley, age twenty-eight, married with one son, just *destroyed* my life! He took *everything* from me and left me with nothing, not even hope. He murdered my husband and daughter, and so help me God, I'll never forgive him as long as I live. Am I being clear? I don't want to hear a list of platitudes or Bible verses right now. I don't want sympathy or textbook answers. I want my family back....And since I can't have that, I just want Brian Wesley to pay for what he's done."

Jenny lay still, her eyes closed. Her head felt heavy and it was difficult to form thoughts. She knew that the woman she could hear ranting and shouting hateful things was her mother, but when Jenny heard her say those things about not wanting prayers or platitudes, she began to think perhaps the woman was an imposter.

Jenny opened her eyes slowly, waiting for the room to stop spinning. She squinted at the figure by her bed. "Mom?"

Her mother glanced at her. Jenny saw she was on the phone. "Hold on—" she covered the receiver and whispered impatiently—"What is it, Jenny? I'm on a business call."

Jenny stared at her, her mind a blank. Why was Mom angry with her? Dread swept over her as she realized the truth: the accident had been her fault and her mother knew it. "Forget it."

Her mother frowned, her hand still covering the phone. "Don't be like that, Jenny. I'm sorry, okay? This is an important call. I'm talking to the police officer." She sighed impatiently. "Did you need something? A drink? What?"

Jenny felt like a piece of her heart had been sliced off. She squeezed her eyes so her mother wouldn't see her cry. "I said forget it." She rolled over, turning her back to her mother.

Please, please, talk to me...help me...I'm so scared...

But her mother didn't notice. Instead, she resumed her phone conversation. "Okay, I'm back. What I'm trying to say is..."

Tears streamed down Jenny's face as her mother continued to rant at the police officer. What had happened? Why wasn't her mother worried about her, sorry for her? How could a phone call be more important than what she was feeling?

It's because it was Alicia and not me who died. Mom had always loved Alicia more. Jenny wished with all her heart that she could trade places with Alicia. That she could take Alicia's spot in heaven with Daddy and give Alicia back to Mom.

Jenny drew her knees into a fetal position. Then, while her mother continued to yell at the officer, she wept into her pillow, whispering the only words she could think of. "Why, God? Why?...If she doesn't love me, why did you leave me here with her?"

Hannah hung up, her rage so potent it was almost a physical presence. But there was nothing there to vent it on. It seeped through her veins, more powerful than any drug, infusing her heart and soul. She clenched her fists. It was outrageous! How could the courts allow a convicted drunk driver back on the roads to kill Tom and Alicia? She gritted her teeth. She would change the laws—the entire system—if that's what it took.

She ripped a sheet of paper from her pad and began making notations. Her mind raced with plans....She would contact Mothers Against Drunk Drivers....She would attend any court hearing involving Brian Wesley....If she had to, she'd single-handedly change the drunk driving laws in the state of California. The thought of Brian Wesley fueled her rage, but as her notes began taking form, she found herself strangely comforted.

She had a reason to go on.

Brian Wesley—and his punishment.

The next two days flew by. Consumed with her decision to exact revenge on Brian Wesley, Hannah scarcely took in all that happened. In a blur of events, Jenny was released from the hospital, and she and Hannah attended the double funeral service. Family and friends surrounded Hannah, consoling her.

But every time Hannah looked for Jenny, the girl was alone. She sat in the first pew, her head hung low, her casted arm in a sling.

Hannah felt a quick pang of guilt. She was ignoring Jenny, her only surviving daughter. But on the heels of the feeling came her new resolve. Jenny was young and resilient. Her injuries would heal and she would be fine. They would have time together later. Alicia and Tom, they were the real victims.

And, of course, Hannah. This disaster had happened to her, most of all. She would never recover…never find another man like Tom…never know another daughter so sweet and talented and precious as Alicia…

She had lost the most, and she had no energy for consoling Jenny. She was too desperately in need of consolation herself.

Besides, it hurt too much to talk about the loss, to face the present and the emptiness it held every day. No, it was much safer to spend her time living in one of two places: the angry, uncertain future or the bittersweet past. Her thoughts of the future were directed to one end only: seeing Brian Wesley locked up, knowing he would pay for what he did.

The rest of the time she spent in the past, where Tom and Alicia still lived.

Seven

The roads to Zion mourn, for no one comes to her....
All her gateways are desolate.

LAMENTATIONS 1:4A

It had been two weeks since the accident, and Jenny lay sprawled out on her flannel quilt, her fingers fanned against the cool wall beside her bed...the wall that separated her room from Alicia's. Jenny studied her arms and legs and saw that the bruises were fading. But there were other scars—ones she knew would never disappear.

She studied the wall and drifted back to what seemed like another lifetime, the day they were packing for the camping trip. In her mind she heard three soft thuds coming from the other room: the signal she and Alicia had used for years. One thud meant *Urgent! Come quick! Get in here right away!* Two thuds meant *good night*. And three thuds were a simple three-word message: *I love you.*

Alicia's bed was up against the other side of the wall, and each night whichever of them got in bed first would thud twice. *Good night.* When the other sister responded with two thuds of her own, the first would thud three times. *I love you.* And the other would respond similarly.

The day before the trip, Jenny and Alicia had been in their separate rooms, packing their bags; Amy Grant's "Hearts in Motion" had been blaring from Alicia's tape player. A single thud sounded in Jenny's room. She had dropped her thermal underwear and skittered out the door, around the corner into Alicia's room, where she flopped onto her sister's bed.

"What?" Jenny nosed around inside Alicia's duffel bag, checking the things her sister had packed.

"You bringing your tape player?" Alicia held a fistful of cassette tapes. Amy Grant, Steven Curtis Chapman, Michael W. Smith, Jars of Clay.

"My batteries are dead."

"Mine, too. Can you ask Dad if we can stop and get some on the way out of town?"

Jenny had bounced up. "Sure. Be right back." She bounded down the stairs and in a minute returned and threw herself again on Alicia's bed. "Done."

Amy Grant's voice filled the room, and Jenny watched Alicia dance around, snagging a shirt from her closet and jeans from her dresser drawer. Jenny had wondered if one day she might be as pretty and popular as Alicia. Her older sister's cheerleading uniform lay on the floor near her bed, and Jenny bent down to pick it up.

Alicia was involved in everything. Cheerleading, student council, drama. She had so many friends, and she was good at whatever she tried.

"My room's such a mess." Alicia used her foot to move a pile of clothes against her bed. "I never have enough time."

Jenny considered the floor. "Pretty bad."

"Uuugh. It's a total mess." She stopped for a moment and raised an eyebrow. "Don't tell me *you're* already packed?"

"Yep. Wasn't much. I mean, what can you take on the old, annual camping trip? You know Dad. We'll spend half the time on the lake catching fish."

Alicia froze and glanced back at her duffel bag. "True—" She turned abruptly and began digging in her drawer again. "But I have to have the right shorts…and then if it gets cold, I need my woolly sweatshirt…and at night, you know, around the campfire I like my old jeans…" Her voice drifted as she rummaged through a series of drawers. "If I could just find them."

Jenny stood and stretched. She picked up a shirt from Alicia's floor, turned it right-side out, folded it in half, and set it on her sister's bed. "I hate it when that happens."

She made no mention of the fact that she was cleaning Alicia's mess as she bent down and picked up a rumpled pair of shorts. When the pile of clothes was neatly folded on her sister's bed, Jenny headed for the door. "I just remembered something. My Christy Miller book. I have to bring it."

Alicia straightened and looked around her room. "Jenny! Hey, thanks. You're so nice. You didn't have to clean my room."

Jenny shrugged. "No big deal. That way you'll be done faster. Maybe we can play horse out in the driveway with Dad after dinner."

"You're the best sister in the world." Alicia left the tangled web of clothing spilling from her bottom drawer and came to hug Jenny. Then she grinned. "But I'll still beat you at horse."

Jenny had laughed and returned to her room. A moment passed while she searched for the book, and then she'd heard it. Three soft thuds on the bedroom wall.

Was that just a few weeks ago? It seems like years...like it had happened to someone else.

Jenny's lips trembled and she closed her eyes against the tears. At the sound of footsteps on the stairs she wiped her eyes quickly, then turned to watch her mother enter the room. Mom looked angry again, disappointed. *Is it because I'm the one who lived?* Anxiety threatened to strangle Jenny, as it did every time she asked herself these questions. *Would Mom be so angry all the time if Alicia were still here instead of me?* Alicia had had so much going for her. *If one of us was going to live, it should have been Alicia.* Jenny swallowed and blinked twice as her mother crossed the room and sat on the edge of her bed.

"I've been looking all over for you." Her mother sounded tired, robotic. Jenny tried to remember the last time she'd looked or sounded tender.

She couldn't remember one time since the accident.

She turned away and stared at the wall. "I've been here."

Her mother sighed. "You're always here. Can't you come downstairs and spend some time with—"

"With *whom?*" Jenny turned back toward her mother. "The family? We don't *have* a family anymore, Mom, remember? You keep telling everyone how that drunk driver killed your *family*. So who cares if I stay up here? I'm not your family."

Her mother shrank back, a pinched look around her eyes.

Jenny sat up and forced her face closer to her mother's. "I guess you're right, Mom. Our family is dead. Now there's just you and me, and that's not enough, is it? We'll never be a family by ourselves."

She threw herself back down on the bed and rolled onto her side. She couldn't stand looking at her mother for another second.

"Jenny..."

She flinched at her mother's tentative touch on her shoulder. There was a pause, and when her mom went on, her voice was cold.

"I'm sorry I said what I did about my family being killed. Of course we're a family. But there's a lot to do now, and I can't spend my time sitting up here rubbing your back and helping you get over this. That man, that *drunk driver,* is about to be charged for what he did to your dad and Alicia. When he is, I want to be there. I want to make sure he's locked up for a long, long time. I'm sorry, honey...but I'll probably be very busy these next few months."

Jenny remained silent, unmoving, studying her fingers as they moved slightly, back and forth, across the wall near her bed.

"Honey, what I'm trying to say is I'd like your help in this. We owe it to Daddy and Alicia to make sure that man doesn't ever kill anyone again. It won't help for us to hide away in bed and miss them. Not now, anyway. There's too much to do."

Jenny felt tears burn her eyes and couldn't keep her shoulders from trembling. What was her mother talking about? *I'm just a kid!* she wanted to scream. *How can I possibly do anything that would help send that drunk driver to prison?*

For that matter, what difference could her mother really make? None at all. Besides, who cared, anyway? Alicia and Daddy were gone. Nothing could bring them back now.

"Jenny." Her mother's voice was flat. "Are you listening?"

Jenny rolled over and faced her mother. "If you're asking me to get up, put a smile on, and help you make some kind of plan to lock up drunk drivers, I won't do it."

Her mother's face grew a shade paler. "Why are you lashing out at me?"

Because I hate you. Because you hate me for being alive. "Because. You think you have to get back at that guy. Seek revenge or something."

"Well, Jenny, what do *you* want to do?" Her mother sounded exasperated. "Ask the judge to let him go?"

"I don't *know!*" Jenny's whole body shook, and she couldn't make it stop. "The Bible says to forgive, and you always taught us we should live our lives by what the Bible says, right?" She watched her mother closely. *Please, please, be my mom again. You believed in God…in the Bible.…You used to smile and hold me and tell me he would always protect us.…*

But there was no smile on her mother's face. She stiffened, and she wouldn't meet Jenny's eyes. "That's different. The man who did this needs to be punished. Don't you think so?"

"I think we should *forget* about him!" Jenny clenched her fists. "Going to court and fighting him won't bring back Daddy and Alicia. I think we should stay home and remember the happy times."

Her mother stood up abruptly, and Jenny suddenly felt so cold she thought she'd shatter into a million pieces. "That won't bring them back either." Her mother's words were like pieces of ice. "Forget I said anything, Jenny. Stay up here as long as you like. And when you're ready to deal with what happened, I'll be downstairs trying to get on with life."

Her mother walked out of the room, and Jenny turned once more toward the wall. Hot tears filled her eyes, and she sobbed softly into her pillow. "Alicia, where are you? I need you so badly."

Through her tears she remembered how they had dressed alike as little girls, walking hand-in-hand to their Sunday school class each week.

"Yes, Jesus loves me," they would sing as they skipped along. "The Bible tells me so."

Oh, Jesus, please help me. I don't want to live without Alicia and Daddy. Mom doesn't understand. She doesn't care about me.

A scene from the funeral flashed in Jenny's mind. A great aunt had come up to her and squeezed her hard, suffocating her in a fog of strong perfume. "Now listen, dear," the fleshy woman had said. "Be a good girl and don't make things harder for your mother than they have to be."

Jenny remembered looking up at the woman, confused.

The great aunt continued. "You must understand she's suffered a great loss here. Now it's up to you to be strong for her."

Jenny had nodded uncertainly. "I'll try."

"You try hard, now, you hear. Your mother needs you."

The woman's words had haunted Jenny several times since then. She squeezed her eyes shut, and another wave of sadness washed over her. *It's my loss, too. Who'll be strong for me?*

"Alicia, come home," she cried softly. "Pleeease, Alicia. I miss you."

Then she raised her hand toward the wall and thudded softly. Three times. And three more.

Over and over and over again.

In the days of her affliction and wandering
Jerusalem remembers all the treasures that were hers in days of old.

LAMENTATIONS 1:7A

In the haze of grief and anger and bitter rage that consumed her, Hannah realized she was neglecting Jenny. But she felt helpless to do anything about it. She simply did not have the strength to do more than provide for the girl's most basic necessities.

It took all her energy to remember her life as it had been...to remember Tom. She always started back as far as she could remember. That was how it was with Tom. Her catalogue of memories simply did not contain a single day without him.

There had been very few rainy days in Hannah's childhood. An only child, she'd been doted on by both parents. Her grade school years were spent at Cornerstone Christian School where she generally excelled, and each week there was church and Sunday school and dozens of playmates and an entire church family who knew and loved her. What Hannah wanted, she got—and usually with little effort.

She'd grown up surrounded by children from similarly privileged families, where parents stayed together, went to church together, and seldom faced anything more serious than a bad case of tonsillitis or a flat tire on the family van.

Back then it only made sense, though. Hannah was a good girl, and in return, the Lord gave her a life free of speed bumps or bends in the road.

Hannah had many playmates, but her best friend in the

whole world was a boy one year older than she, who lived across the street, three houses down. His parents attended the same church as Hannah's, and the two grew up swinging side by side on the church playground.

His name was Tom Ryan.

On a warm summer day sometime after Hannah's eighth birthday, she rode her bike past Tom's house and skidded on loose gravel. She tumbled over the handlebars and came to a stop on her knees and elbows. Tom, almost ten at the time, dropped his basketball and came running.

"Hannah, are you hurt?" Tom had stooped down and lifted her gently to her feet. He dusted the gravel off her arms and legs and dashed into the house for a wet rag, which he gently swiped over her road burns. "Are you okay?"

"Yeah...thanks." A strange sensation was making its way across Hannah's suddenly flushing cheeks.

Tom found a bandage and carefully applied it to the worst of her cuts. "There, that should do it."

Hannah watched him wide-eyed and knew from that moment on she would marry Tom Ryan one day. She didn't talk about it with Tom, or anyone else for that matter. It was something she took for granted, like the passing of the seasons.

They became even better friends, shooting baskets in his driveway and talking about plans for the future. He wanted to be a doctor; she wanted to have a big family to make up for the siblings she never had. During the school year they did homework together, and in summer they walked to the neighborhood pool and lazed away the afternoons holding diving competitions from the pool's high dive or racing underwater to see who could hold their breath the longest. Hannah hated to lose.

In fact, the only flaw in Hannah's life was her temper. One summer when Hannah was ten, she and Tom were playing basketball when they were joined by a boy who lived two streets down.

After the game, the boy looked at Hannah disdainfully. "You

shoot baskets like a wimpy girl."

Furious, she worked on her shot for weeks after that and refused to speak to the boy again. In her freshman year, Hannah shared a class with the boy and ignored him mercilessly.

"What's with you?" the boy asked her one day.

Hannah sneered at him. "I shoot baskets like a wimpy girl, remember?"

The boy clearly had no idea what she was talking about, but even after he'd apologized, she made a point to avoid him.

"Sure hope you never get mad at *me*, Hannah," Tom had told her once that year. "When you get mad, you don't stop. Ever."

"I think that's why God's so good to me." Hannah had smiled pleasantly. "He knows I'm not good at forgiving."

Through childhood and many of her early teenage years, Hannah was a flat-chested pixie with delicate, cornflower blue eyes, unremarkable features, and gangly arms and skinny legs. The only thing striking about her was her thick, wheat-colored blond hair, which got in the way when she played sports. Hannah thought it was more of an inconvenience than anything.

Tom, however, was a strapping boy with a muscular physique long before he hit his teen years. He had a ruddy complexion, short dark hair, brilliant teasing blue eyes, and a knack for making Hannah laugh out loud. In many ways, Tom was the brother Hannah had always wanted.

They never talked about themselves in any romantic sense, even as they grew older. But Hannah was in no hurry. They had always been together, and they always would be. She wasn't sure how Tom felt, but each night she prayed that when the time was right, Tom would ask her to be his wife. She could not remember a time when God hadn't answered her prayers exactly as she had prayed them, so she had little concern regarding her future with Tom.

When Tom turned sixteen and began dating the majorette from the high school drill team, fourteen-year-old Hannah was not terribly concerned. She was still in middle school, still dressing and acting and looking like one of the boys. She figured her relationship with Tom was bound to change when she turned sixteen and was granted permission to date. That was when she and Tom would fall in love.

Instead, when Hannah turned sixteen, Tom made a decision to attend college at Oregon State University in Corvallis. His father had graduated from OSU, and the family had relatives nearby. Tom would need to leave immediately after graduation because Oregon State had given him a full baseball scholarship, and the team trained all summer.

When she heard the news, Hannah felt as if the bottom had dropped out of her heart. How did this fit into the plans she'd made? She expected Tom to attend college, but she never believed he would leave California and move all the way to Oregon.

She prayed with renewed vigor.

Before he left, his family had a going-away party for him. Hannah was in the early goings of summer league softball that month, but she missed practice the day of Tom's party and went to the mall. There she picked out a sleeveless, rayon dress that danced in the breeze and fell softly on the budding curves of her developing body. She applied a layer of mascara to her fair eyelashes and curled and brushed her hair until it shone and lay in gentle waves around her shoulders. Finally she slipped her tanned feet into a pair of white-heeled sandals that accented her shapely colt-like legs. Before she left, she checked the mirror. Even she was amazed at the transformation—overnight she had become a young woman.

When she arrived at Tom's house, his mother answered the door.

"Why, Hannah...you look so pretty, all grown up." She smiled warmly at Hannah and ushered her inside. "Tom's in the other room. I'm sure he'll be glad to see you."

Hannah held her head high and went into the den. Tom was surrounded by a handful of boys, all seniors at West Hills High, all members of the varsity baseball team.

As she entered the room, each of them stared at her in a way that was just short of rude, but Hannah relished their attention. If Tom were going to leave the state for four years, he would have to remember her as more than the buddy down the block in jeans and a baseball cap.

"Hey, Hannah." Tom looked uncomfortable, and Hannah knew he was registering the change in her appearance. There was a moment of awkward silence before he cleared his throat and said softly, "Nice dress."

Tom stayed by her side the rest of the evening, teasing and making her laugh the way he'd done all their lives. When his teammates tried to have their share of time with Hannah, he found some excuse to take her away or involve her in another conversation.

When she left that evening, he walked her home. They stopped just out of view of her house. Tom leaned casually against the bark of an old shade tree and studied her in the moonlight.

"Kinda feels like the end of childhood, doesn't it?"

Hannah fiddled with a loose curl and nodded. "Yeah. I can't believe you're going to be gone four years."

Tom nodded and angled his head, studying her. "You sure look pretty tonight, Hannah. The guys were going crazy over you."

She shrugged delicately and giggled. "They're just used to seeing me in a uniform with my hair pulled up."

Tom caught her gaze. "Yeah. Me too."

The silence between them grew awkward then, and Hannah made circles in the grass with the toe of her sandal. There was a faint scent of honeysuckle in the early summer air, and she knew she would remember this night as long as she lived.

She smiled. "We had so much fun growing up together... shooting baskets all day and catching crickets at night. Remember that time we had a contest to see who could eat the most watermelon?"

"I won."

"You won and then you got sick all over the front lawn, remember?"

Tom gripped his stomach and grimaced. "I still have a hard time eating watermelon."

"But later, after you felt better, we talked about what we wanted to be when we grew up, remember?'

Tom laughed.

"You always said you wanted to be a doctor."

He nodded. "That much hasn't changed. You always said you wanted to have a big family, lots of kids."

Hannah glanced down, thankful he couldn't see her blushing in the haze of shadows under the shade tree. "I guess I still have some time for that one."

"Hey, Hannah, do me a favor, huh?"

"Sure."

"Pray for me. It's gonna be hard starting over in a place where I don't know anyone and being so far away from home."

She met his gaze head on and smiled. "I always pray for you, Tom. I won't stop now."

He drew a deep breath, and Hannah could tell he was wrestling with his feelings. "Well, I guess I better go. I still have to finish packing."

She was suddenly anxious to keep the conversation going as long as possible. "Will you be back? At break I mean?"

"Yeah. Christmas and summers. Whenever the team isn't conditioning."

"I wish I could see you play."

Tom's eyes lit up. "Hey! You can!...We play at USC and UCLA. You could ride over with my parents. That'd be great!"

"Yeah!"

"And I'll write and tell you all about college life."

"Mmmhhm."

"And you can catch me up on life at school and everything that's happening in the old neighborhood."

"Sure..."

They both fell silent, and Tom glanced back toward his house. "Well, Hannah, come here and give me a hug."

She stepped forward, and they embraced like favorite cousins at a family reunion. When they pulled back, Tom ran his thumb lightly underneath Hannah's neatly curled bangs. "Don't change, Hannah."

She could feel tears welling up, and she smiled uncertainly. "Have a good trip."

"Yeah. See you later."

And with that, life as Hannah had known it changed dramatically. The summer passed uneventfully with only one letter from Tom. She saw him briefly during Christmas break and sat with him and his family at Christmas Eve service. Then she didn't see him until April, when she and his parents went to UCLA to watch his baseball game.

They spotted him before the game and waved, and Hannah felt her face flush at the sight of him. Tom was an outfielder, recruited for his strong arm and high batting average. Though a freshman, he was a starter, and that afternoon he hit a game-winning double. Hannah could barely contain her pride.

But when the game ended, a pretty brunette with a breathtaking figure ran up and threw her arms around Tom's neck. He kissed her lightly on the cheek, and then took her hand in his.

Hannah felt as if she'd been punched in the stomach. She wanted to run back to the car and spare herself this awful moment, but Tom and the girl were approaching fast, and there was nowhere to hide.

"Hey, thanks for coming." Tom was breathless and sweaty, and Hannah thought he looked even more handsome than he had a year ago.

Tom glanced at the girl beside him. "This is Amy." He looked at the others. "She does stats for the team." He and Amy shared a smile. "These are my parents, and this is Hannah, my buddy from the old neighborhood."

"Nice to meet you." Amy wore heavy makeup; Hannah felt utterly plain beside her. Amy smiled warmly at Tom's parents and barely paid heed to Hannah.

Hannah gritted her teeth. Plain or not, she would not be outdone. Tom belonged to her not this, this...

"Are you an actress?" Sarcasm dripped from Hannah's every word, and Tom cast a curious glance her way.

Amy laughed uneasily. "No, do I look like someone famous?"

Hannah volleyed a similar laugh back at Amy. "No, I just thought with all that thick, gray, pancake makeup, maybe you were practicing for a play or something."

Amy's face went blank, and there was an awkward silence. Tom looked as if he could have strangled Hannah, but instead he cleared his throat and said, "I met Amy at the beginning of the season."

"Yes," Amy purred, squeezing Tom's hand. Hannah was forgotten as Amy smiled sweetly at Tom's parents. "Your son is quite an athlete."

They all chuckled and agreed how wonderful Tom was. And before five minutes had passed, he was pulling Amy by the hand and bidding good-bye to Hannah and his parents. For Hannah, the entire scene seemed to take place in slow-motion, as though it were a horrible dream.

On the ride back to the Valley, Tom's parents said very little. They seemed to understand that Hannah was hurt. When they pulled up in front of Hannah's house, Tom's mother squeezed Hannah's shoulder. "She won't be around long. She isn't Tom's type."

Hannah prayed that Tom's mother was right, but Amy did not go away. She and Tom dated through his sophomore and junior year, while Hannah graduated from West Hills High and began attending California State University Northridge, three miles from home. Tom and Amy were together constantly, even during breaks.

Church was the only place Hannah knew she could see Tom alone. Amy was not a Christian and had no intention of ever becoming one, according to Tom's mother.

"She's a nice girl, but she's all wrong for Tom," his mother would say on occasion when Hannah visited. "He still has medical school ahead, and she's not the waiting type. Besides, Tom needs a nice Christian girl. Someone like you, Hannah."

"Tom doesn't see me like that, Mrs. Ryan."

"One day. Give him time."

But a few weeks before the start of his senior year, Tom and Amy came home with an announcement. They were going to be married in June, right after he graduated.

Hannah was shocked and angry. She had dated occasionally, but her heart resided where it always had—to Tom, even if he didn't know it. She and Tom belonged together. Everyone at home felt the same way, her parents and his, and the kids they'd grown up with.

Everyone but Tom.

The summer passed, and Tom and Amy returned to Corvallis to make plans for their senior year while Hannah was left to ponder her suddenly uncertain future.

That fall Tom wrote Hannah a letter. In it was no admission of love or longing, but rather a rambling of memories of their childhood and the happy times they'd shared. Hannah read the letter five times before tucking it carefully into her top drawer. Why, she wondered, was Tom thinking about her and their past when he should be busy making plans for his future with Amy?

Christmas break came, and Hannah learned that Amy had returned to Walnut Creek in Northern California, where she and her mother had plans to shop for a wedding gown. Tom came home and spent hours hanging out in front of his house, bouncing his old basketball in the mild winter afternoons, his face pensive and troubled. More than a few times, Hannah glanced out her window and saw him gazing toward her house.

Three days before Christmas there was a social at church. Hannah arrived late, and while she was talking with the pastor's wife, she heard a familiar voice.

"Hey, Hannah, what you been up to?" Tom was taller than before, his shoulders broad and full like his father's. Hannah blushed furiously, and then thought of Amy, shopping the boutiques of San Francisco for a wedding gown.

"Oh, hi." Her voice lacked any enthusiasm. "I thought you were back."

Tom studied her, and she knew there was little about her that resembled the rough-and-tumble girl he once shot baskets with.

"Can't believe I'm almost finished up at OSU."

Hannah smiled, her defenses firmly in place. "Then there's the big wedding."

Tom's expression changed and his eyes clouded. "Yeah...the big wedding."

Cheerful chatter filled the hall, and Tom looked around, slightly bothered. "Let's go outside and talk. It's been a long time."

She wondered what the point was, but she nodded. "Okay. I'll follow you."

Outside they found a bench nestled against the church wall facing the parking lot. They sat down, shoulder to shoulder, much as they'd done hundreds of times before. They were silent as they took in the Christmas lights and listened to the hum of conversation in the distance.

"You ever feel like you were about to make a big mistake?" Tom leaned against the side of the bench and faced Hannah.

She pulled her knees up to her chin and wrapped her arms

around her legs. Something about the cool night air and the intimacy of the moment caused her defenses to drop.

"Sometimes."

Tom gazed heavenward. "Amy's not a Christian.... She's not..." He looked at Hannah. "She's not a lot of things."

She thought about that for a moment. "You asked her to marry you." Their eyes met, and for the first time since she'd known Tom, it felt as though there was something more between them than just the bond of childhood, something Hannah couldn't quite grasp.

"Yes, I did..."

Hannah felt bold in the darkness. "Why'd you do it, Tom?"

He shrugged. "I don't know. Seemed like the right thing at the time. She sort of orders everything around her, and...I guess her parents were expecting me to propose. I mean, she was talking about our honeymoon and where we'd live when I'm in med school months before I ever asked her."

"Sounds lovely."

Tom stifled a grin. "You don't like her, do you?"

Hannah was silent.

"'Are you an actress?'" Tom mimicked. "Come on, Hannah. You were pretty obvious that day."

She lifted her chin. "I don't have anything against her."

"Oh, okay. If you say so."

"I don't."

"Now, Hannah. You weren't just a little jealous?"

"Of her? *Please*, Tom. Give me some credit."

There was silence again.

Tom sighed. "You know I kinda wish you were jealous."

Hannah ignored that. "What really matters isn't what I think of Amy, it's what you think of her." She waited. "You must love her."

Tom exhaled slowly through pursed lips. "I don't know. I did love her, sometimes I think I still do. But every time I imagine spending my life with her, I end up thinking about..." His voice trailed off and he caught Hannah's gaze. "Did you get my letter last month?"

"Yeah. I didn't know what to write back. It seemed like you were remembering how things used to be."

"Kind of."

She studied him. "Want the truth?"

"Okay."

"After I got that letter, I wondered if you were really happy."

Tom sighed again. "When did you grow up and get so smart, Hannah?" She grinned, and his eyes grew softer. "And so beautiful."

For once, she didn't know what to say.

"Mom tells me every time you have a date. She says you haven't found the right guy yet."

Hannah blushed and glanced down at her trembling hands.

"I don't know, everything seems all mixed up. I'm engaged to a girl who isn't even interested in the Lord, when you're right here, my bestest buddy, all grown up and totally devoted to God. Don't you ever wonder how come you and I didn't get together?"

Hannah's eyes narrowed and a million memories came to mind. "Sometimes."

"How did everything get so twisted?"

She shivered, partly from the night air and partly from the direction their conversation was taking.

"Cold?" Tom looked concerned.

"A little."

He held out his arm. "Come here."

She moved closer and leaned against him. The chill was gone immediately.

He rested his chin on the top of her head. "You know something? These last three years at college I've really missed you."

"Maybe you just miss being a kid."

"We had fun, didn't we?"

She could feel him looking at her, and she knew he was

going to kiss her. Finally, when she could no longer stand it, she looked up into his eyes.

"Hannah," he whispered. Then the moment she'd dreamed of all her life happened. As though it had been destined since before they were born, they came together in a single kiss—one that was slow and filled with every good feeling Hannah had ever known.

When they pulled away, Tom looked startled. "I'm sorry." He was breathless, and she could feel his heart beating wildly against her chest. "I'm so confused right now."

"I'm not a little kid anymore, Tom."

He shook his head, and she thought she saw tears in his eyes. "I know. That's the problem. Ever since you walked into my house that day in that silky dress...you know, at my graduation party." He studied her for a moment. "Ever since then I've wondered about whether we'd..."

"Mhmm." She smiled sadly.

"You, too?"

"Yeah. I've wondered."

"But then I met Amy and..."

"And what?"

"I guess we'll never know."

"*What?*" Hannah jerked away. Of *course* he knew. He'd kissed her, after all!

"Well—" Tom drew back a bit and looked nervous—"I mean...I *am* getting married..."

"I don't see a ring on your finger yet."

"Yeah, but Hannah...everything's all set. I don't know..."

"That's a cop-out, Tom."

"A cop-out?"

"Yes! You're not married yet. Break it off."

He chuckled softly. "You don't know Amy."

She put her hands on Tom's shoulders and shook him. "Listen to you! You don't marry someone because you're afraid of what'll happen if you break up."

He gazed at Hannah thoughtfully and sighed. "I know. There's more to it than that."

She waited a beat and dropped her hands. "So, you do love her." It wasn't a question.

Tom shrugged. "I have a lot to work out, I guess. Come on, let's get back in."

Tears formed in her eyes. "Don't do it, Tom. Don't marry her."

"Hannah..."

She was unashamed of her tears as they spilled onto her cheeks. "Don't marry her."

"Hannah, please." He pulled her close and cradled her head against his chest. "Don't make this harder than it has to be."

He paused, and she knew he could feel her body jerking quietly as she cried.

"Come on, Hannah. What happened to my bestest buddy?"

Hannah pulled away, anger sweeping over her, and met his gaze straight on. "She grew up." With that she wiped her eyes, sniffed once, and stormed back into the church. She didn't talk to Tom again. A month later she heard he was going ahead with the wedding.

Stricken with pain so severe she could hardly breathe when she thought about it, Hannah turned to her best protection—anger. She harbored a grudge against Tom the size of a mountain. How could he make such a horrible decision? Especially after that night at church? She had kissed him, bared her heart to him, and still he had chosen Amy.

As the day of the wedding drew near, Hannah vowed to stay home and avoid Tom whatever the cost. The event was scheduled to take place the first week in June at Knollwood Country Club in Granada Hills, just five miles from the West Valley neighborhood where Tom and Hannah grew up.

In the weeks before the wedding, an invitation arrived at Hannah's house. Her mother responded, stating that all but Hannah would attend. At about the same time, Hannah graduated from Cal State Northridge, and Tom was one of more than a hundred people who attended her graduation party. Hannah felt him watching her from a distance that night, but she ignored him. When he approached to congratulate her, she turned abruptly and began a conversation with someone else.

She had a right to her anger. He had broken her heart, and she would never forgive him.

The day before Tom's wedding, Hannah's parents were at work and she was staging a cleaning frenzy, doing her best not to think about Tom and Amy, when the doorbell rang. She set down the window cleaner and headed for the door.

"Coming!" She stretched and ran her fingers absently through her hair. It was unusually hot and sticky for June, and as she made her way through the house, Hannah thought about driving to the beach that evening. Maybe there she could sort out her feelings.

She opened the door and caught her breath. It was Tom, dressed in worn jeans and a white T-shirt, looking desperately troubled.

Hannah felt her expression go cold, and before he could speak, she slammed the door shut.

He stopped the door with his hand and pushed it open again. "Wait!"

Hannah's hand flew to her hip and she glared at him. "Go away, Tom. I have nothing to say to you."

He sighed. "Hannah, will you stop trying to hate me for one minute. I came here to tell you something."

"Say it. I have things to do."

Tom drew a deep breath and rubbed his palms on his jeans. "May I come in?"

She exhaled dramatically. "I guess." She stepped aside, and he followed her into the foyer.

They stood face to face, studying each other. Finally Tom broke the silence.

"It's off." His voice was breathless, and he looked like he hadn't slept in days.

Hannah frowned. "What?"

"The wedding…I called it off this morning."

Her eyes grew wide. "The day before—?"

He held up a hand. "I know, it's crazy. But it would've been crazier to marry her."

"What did your parents say?" Hannah was so shocked she forgot her anger.

"They were glad I realized it today and not tomorrow."

"What about the…"

"My parents are contacting the guests. Amy and her folks are flying back to San Francisco tonight."

Hannah softened. "She must be furious."

"Yeah, you could say that. She thinks I ruined her life."

"Ooooh boy. I'd never forgive you."

Tom grinned. "Yeah, I know. You haven't talked to me since that night.…Of course, I should have remembered that from when we were kids."

Hannah was afraid to break the silence that followed, but she had to know. "Why'd you change your mind?"

Tom moved closer to Hannah. He raised his hands and framed her face with his fingertips. "I couldn't marry her, Hannah." He hesitated, and she knew if he didn't say something soon her heart would beat out of her chest.

He looked at her intently. "I couldn't. Not when the only girl I've ever really loved—" he moved closer still—"is you. I didn't know it until today, when I realized what would happen after tomorrow. I'd lose you forever.…I couldn't marry Amy after that." His eyes searched hers, looking for her reaction. "Hannah, I love you."

In that instant, she knew her prayers had not been uttered in vain. Indeed, God had seen to it that everything had turned out exactly as she had planned. In his timing, not hers.

Tom stroked her face. "I'm sorry, Hannah. I should have broken it off months ago. Then you wouldn't be so mad at me." He tenderly took her hand in his. "Still hate me?"

Hannah felt tears spring to her eyes. A single laugh escaped, and she pushed at him in mock frustration. "I should hate you forever, you big brat."

"Forever?" Tom grinned.

"Yeah—" Hannah heard the laughter leave her voice—"for waiting to the last minute to realize what I've known all my life."

He caught her around the waist and pulled her close. "I know. But now...can you forgive me, Hannah?"

She paused. "It depends..."

Slowly, he moved his face closer to hers and kissed her as he had so many months ago at the church. A minute passed before he spoke again. "On what?"

She kissed him this time, and when she caught her breath she knew the grudge was gone. "On what you have in mind." She grinned.

He pulled away, and Hannah had never seen him look more serious. "Marriage. Children. Forever." He kissed her again. "I want to spend my life with you."

They were married that summer, and by Christmas, Hannah was pregnant with Alicia. Jenny came along two years later, and Hannah nearly bled to death in childbirth. There was considerable risk that she would not survive another pregnancy, so she and Tom agreed that their family was complete. God had blessed them mightily. They could get on with raising their girls, and then one day they would share a long and happy retirement together.

At least, that was how it was supposed to be.

In the days after Tom's death, when weariness wore her defenses down, Hannah searched for reasons why God had taken Tom and Alicia. What had she ever done to deserve such punishment? Why her? Why, when God had brought her and Tom together in the first place, would he take her husband and leave her so desperately alone?

It was easier to ignore such questions—easier to ignore God, for that matter. She had prayed to him, served him, and loved him all her life. She thought she knew God, but apparently not. He had given her a past filled with sunshine and left her with a future full of darkness. Because of that, Hannah wasn't sure she wanted to know the Lord anymore. She had nothing to say to him. Anything she might ask him for was already gone forever.

In her other life, the one she lived before the collision, Hannah often fell asleep praying. These days she did not find comfort in prayer. How could she? While she passed the time in a blur of tears and rage and vivid memories, Brian Wesley remained free on bail. Three weeks passed from the time of the accident while detectives gathered evidence and criminalists studied the man's blood sample, finally determining that he had been driving with a blood alcohol level of .24—three times the legal limit.

Since Hannah was not praying, she filled her mind the only way she knew how. She remembered. Nights were the worst. She missed Tom so much it threatened to kill her.

She physically ached to touch him once more, to hold him and kiss him and tuck her feet under his legs as she had always done before falling asleep. She would toss and turn in the empty queen-size bed, finding solace only by drifting back to the beginning. Tom at nine years old, shooting baskets in his driveway; she and Tom racing their bikes down the street, the wind in their hair on some endless, golden summer day; Tom alive and young and handsome at his graduation party, seeing her in a dress for the first time; Tom making her heart beat funny every time he was near....

It was the same every night, one memory after another, as if by remembering, she could somehow bring him home to her. Back where he belonged.

Where he had always belonged.

Nine

Her people fell into enemy hands, there was no one to help her.

LAMENTATIONS 1:7B

Drunk driving laws in the state of California were clear. If a person had a blood alcohol level of .08 or higher, he would be charged with drunk driving. What wasn't clear was the punishment exacted for the offense. A drunk driver could face anything from a one hundred dollar fine to several years in prison, depending on a list of variables. That list included whether the person had prior convictions, and especially whether the drunk driver was involved in an accident that resulted in the death or serious injuries of others.

Los Angeles Deputy District Attorney Matthew J. Bronzan was assigned the case against Brian Wesley more than four weeks after the accident that killed Tom and Alicia Ryan. Drunk driving was his specialty, and he had requested this case. Now, on this October morning as he mulled over a stack of documents and crime scene photos, he was beset by a range of conflicting emotions. He grieved for the family who had been shattered by this man's selfish actions. Brian Wesley was a convicted drunk driver, a man with a history of getting behind the wheel and driving intoxicated. This angered the prosecutor greatly. Dealing with the senselessness of drunk driving deaths always did.

But as he sat at his government-issued desk, in his cramped office at the Criminal Courts Building, Matt Bronzan also felt a deep-rooted surge of excitement. This was the case he'd been waiting for. *The People v Brian Wesley* would change California drunk driving laws forever.

There was a knock at the door, and Sgt. John Miller poked his head inside. "Busy?"

"Hmmm. Come on in."

Sgt. Miller pulled up a chair and sat opposite the prosecutor, leaning back so that the chair's front two legs came up off the ground. "Heard you got the Wesley case."

Matt lifted the stack of paperwork on his desk and let it fall down again. "Right here. Got it this morning."

"First time you heard about it?"

"No. Read about it in the papers. I asked for it."

Sgt. Miller crossed his arms and drew a deep breath. "Then there won't be a plea?"

Matt sat back in his chair and leveled his gaze at the sergeant. "Not a chance."

There was silence a moment, then Sgt. Miller stood and paced toward the window. He stood staring through the dirty glass.

"I was there, you know. Saw the dead girl. Watched her sister lifted onto a stretcher and placed in an ambulance. Stayed with their father until they took him to the hospital." Miller remained motionless, his back to Matt. "Mr. Ryan knew he wasn't going to make it, Matt. Made me promise to tell his wife and girls he loved them."

With a sigh, Miller spun around. "I don't want to see Wesley walk."

Matt glanced down and sorted through the photos on his desk. He found one of Alicia taken at the accident scene, her face bloodied, eyes closed. He thought then of the mother who had lost both her husband and oldest daughter in a single instant. "He's not going to walk. I can promise you that."

Sgt. Miller nodded. "I know you're a believer, Matt. And I know it isn't politically correct to talk about such things on the job. But the man's wife, Hannah Ryan, she's a Christian. The other girl, Jenny, is home now, and social services tells me things aren't good. Hannah's turning away help from her church; she's bitter and angry and barely notices Jenny. It's a mess."

Matt sighed and set the picture down. "It always is. Sometimes the anger kills you."

Sgt. Miller looked uncomfortable. "I know you're busy, Matt, but maybe you could give her a call, Hannah Ryan, I mean. Set her up with someone at MADD, give her some direction."

"Sure. I could do that. Her number's here somewhere."

"Good. Well, I gotta run. Let me know if you get a trial on this thing. I'll testify whenever you need me."

Matt thanked him and watched him leave. Then he picked up the photo of the girl and studied her face once more. It was there all right. Something about the nose or the cheek bones, maybe the shape of her face. Victoria Stevens all over again. Beautiful, intelligent Victoria—

Matt stopped the train of thought. He refused to dwell on Victoria. Instead he studied Alicia's picture again and sighed. What would it be like to have a daughter like this? And to lose her? He was forty-one and married to his job, so he'd had no time for relationships. And that sure wouldn't change now. He needed to stay focused.

Because Brian Wesley was about to help him make history.

In the past, prosecutors had taken cases such as the one against Brian Wesley and been fortunate to win a vehicular manslaughter verdict. But recently, other states had upped the ante. In Louisiana and Tennessee, prosecutors had finally convinced juries that this type of drunk driving was not vehicular manslaughter. It wasn't even second-degree murder. If a repeat offender deliberately chose to drink and drive, and in doing so caused a victim to die, it was nothing less than first-degree murder.

Matt nodded. There were only a couple cases he knew of where that charge had stuck, but it *had* been done before. The problem was it had never been done in California.

Until now.

Matt looked at the picture once more and wondered about Hannah Ryan. Who was she? And how was she dealing with the death of her family? How did anyone deal with this type of thing? Matt clenched his jaw. He knew how powerful anger could be...how it could kill.

He set the pictures down carefully, then he bowed his head and prayed. *Lord, if you are willing, let this be the case. Let the standard change, and let the people of this state understand that there will be no more tolerance for drunk driving. And Lord, help Hannah Ryan, wherever she is. Help her forgive, help her go on. Don't let anger win again. Like it did with Victoria.*

He looked up and sifted through his rolodex until he found the number for Mothers Against Drunk Drivers. There was one person who could help Hannah survive.

He picked up the telephone and began to dial.

Ten

Is any suffering like my suffering that was inflicted on me, that the LORD brought on me in the day of his fierce anger?

LAMENTATIONS 1:12B

Hannah was sitting at the kitchen table, reading over a small stack of newspaper articles about the accident and events surrounding the arrest of Brian Wesley.

"Drunk Driving Suspected in Crash that Killed Local Father, Daughter," read the headline of an article that had appeared in the *Los Angeles Times* the day after the accident. A picture of paramedics working around Tom's mangled Explorer accompanied the article.

The story began, "A West Hills man and his daughter were killed Saturday when the vehicle they were riding in was broadsided by a pickup truck driven by a man suspected of drunk driving. Tom Ryan, 41, and his daughter, Alicia Ryan, 15, were killed in the accident. A second daughter, Jenny Ryan, 13, was taken to Humana West Hills Hospital where she was in stable condition."

Hannah's eyes drifted to another article, this one from a few weeks later. "Tests Show Driver in Deadly Accident was Drunk."

She studied the small black-and-white photograph of Brian Wesley. Her enemy. A predator who had taken aim at her family and destroyed it. *I hate you.* She stared hard at the picture. *Whatever it takes to get you locked up, I'll do it.*

A Bible verse slipped through her mind as if she were reading it off the newspaper before her. It was Colossians 3:13:

"Forgive, as the Lord forgave you." Hannah shuddered. *Forgive? Forgive Brian Wesley?* The idea left a rancid taste in her mouth. *Not this time, Lord. No way.*

She blinked away the verse and read the newspaper article. "The driver who rammed his pickup truck into the side of a sports utility vehicle three weeks ago, killing two people and injuring another, was legally drunk at the time of the accident, according to a report released today from the Los Angeles Police Department. The department's crime lab has determined that Brian Wesley, 28, of Woodland Hills, had a blood alcohol level of .24, three times the legal limit, at the time of the crash, which killed Tom Ryan, 41, his daughter Alicia Ryan, 15, and injured a second daughter, Jenny Ryan, 13."

Jenny. She'd grown so silent, so angry these last few weeks....

Hannah shook her head. She couldn't think about Jenny now. She had to get ready for trial. There would be time for Jenny later. She kept reading. "'There will be no plea bargain in this case. We're looking to prosecute this case to the fullest extent of the law,' Deputy District Attorney Matthew J. Bronzan said. 'Maybe even beyond the fullest extent. This might be the case that changes drunk driving laws in the state of California.'"

Hannah considered the prosecutor's words. *"This might be the case that changes drunk driving laws."* She set her jaw. This *would* be the case. She read the prosecutor's name once more: Matthew J. Bronzan. Amidst the horror and shock and grief, she had an ally, a friend. Someone on her side.

She glanced at a sheet of notebook paper beneath the stack of newspaper articles. She'd written Matthew Bronzan's office number and a list of questions she needed to ask him. What did he mean he was looking to prosecute this case beyond the fullest extent of the law? What was she within her rights to do? How could she help? Was there any chance a plea bargain would be struck? The list went on.

She reached for the phone just as it began to ring. Hannah

stared at it, confused for a moment. The phone used to ring constantly. Now, nearly five weeks after the accident, no one called.

Hannah realized she was partly to blame. She had refused help from her church friends, and finally they had stopped calling. The hospital certainly had no reason to call now with Tom gone, and Jenny's friends didn't know what to say so they didn't call. Hannah couldn't remember the last time the phone rang.

"Hello." She no longer recognized her own voice.

"Hannah Ryan?" The woman at the other end sounded pleasant.

"Yes."

"This is Carol Cummins. I work with Mothers Against Drunk Drivers. Matt Bronzan gave me your number."

Matt Bronzan. How did he *get my number?* "Oh...hello."

"Mr. Bronzan tells me there's a hearing tomorrow. Brian Wesley will be officially charged, and they'll have to decide whether the case will be settled by plea bargain or whether it will be held over for trial."

Hannah picked up the article she had just been reading. "The paper said there wasn't going to be a plea bargain."

"They still have to go through the motions, hear the arguments from Mr. Wesley's attorney, and present arguments of their own."

"But who makes the final decision?" She could hear the panic in her voice.

"Matt Bronzan has the last word. It comes down to what he thinks he can prove in court." Carol paused. "If he sets the charges high, and Mr. Wesley refuses to plead guilty, there will be a trial."

"Good. I'd like to see it go to trial."

The woman paused again. "Sometimes. Sometimes not. It depends on the jury. If they think the charges are unreasonable, there's a chance Mr. Wesley could walk with no punishment at all."

Hannah's rage bubbled closer to the surface. "That could happen?"

"Yes. That's why these cases end in plea bargains so many times. At least that way the drunk driver gets some kind of punishment."

"I can't *believe* that." Hannah's hands trembled with rage.

Carol Cummins sighed. "Unfortunately, that's the way things are in the legal arena of drunk driving cases. Three out of ten jurors identify with the defendant. They listen to the evidence and hear about the violent accidents and needless deaths, and they think, 'There but for the grace of God go I.'"

"Three out of ten?" This was all new to Hannah, and it made her head spin.

"Surveys are done all the time asking people if they've ever driven drunk. Generally thirty percent of Americans have." She paused. "They look at the guy on trial and see themselves. Usually they decide the guilt is punishment enough, and they convict him on a lesser charge or let him go."

Hannah stood up and paced across her dining room floor, the cordless phone cradled against her shoulder as she studied the previous day's article. She focused on the tiny photograph. How could anyone identify with Brian Wesley? Who in their right mind wouldn't want to see a repeat drunk driver locked up? She exhaled loudly. "What do you mean, *lesser charge?*"

"Sometimes a prosecutor will attempt to prove two or three charges at once. If the jury doesn't feel strongly enough to convict on the more serious charge, they can find a defendant guilty of a lesser charge."

Hannah stopped pacing. "But if what you said before is true, that three out of ten will identify with him, the jury's always going to go for the lesser one."

"Exactly."

Hannah closed her eyes, struggling against the wave of rage that pushed at her. She couldn't believe what she was hearing. "What's Mr. Bronzan going to do?"

"I'm not sure. I only talked to him for a few minutes, but he feels very strongly about this one."

"Meaning?"

"There's a chance he'll charge the driver with something very serious and leave it at that."

Hannah considered the possibilities. "But then there's a chance Brian Wesley will get off. Go free. Is that right?"

Carol's voice was quiet. "That's right."

Hannah resumed pacing. "Why hasn't something been done about this?"

"Drunk driving, you mean? We're trying, Mrs. Ryan. That's what Mothers Against Drunk Drivers is all about."

"I want to help." Hannah's heart was fluttering about in her chest. *Whatever it takes.* "Tell me what to do." Hannah paced toward the dining room table and set the articles down.

Carol drew a deep breath. "Well, most of our efforts focus on public awareness. If we can make people more aware of the consequences, we can accomplish several things."

"I'm listening."

"We can reduce drunk driving, for one thing. You've heard of our campaigns. 'Friends don't let friends drive drunk.' 'Be a Designated Driver.' 'Tie one on,' which is our red ribbon program."

"I've seen those. Tied around car antennas, you mean?"

"Right. We pass them out at our office and at various storefronts. People tie them on to show a united force in the war against drunk driving."

"I had no idea…it's so…"

"Organized? Yes, it has to be."

"And the key is public awareness?"

"Right. It stops a percentage of drunk drivers, but it also educates the public."

"The public?"

"Yes. Jurors are chosen from the public."

The words sank in, and Hannah nodded. Of course. She

scribbled the word juror and underlined it several times. "I get it. The more people who understand, the less likely a jury is to let a drunk driving defendant go free."

"Exactly."

Hannah tapped her pen on the notepad. "You say public awareness, and I picture television ads and billboards. I guess I don't see how I can help."

"We have something called a victim impact panel, Mrs. Ryan. Three or four people who've been directly affected by drunk driving travel to schools and local government meetings and make presentations."

Hannah felt tears forming in her eyes, and suddenly her voice was too choked to speak. After a moment of silence, Carol gently continued. "We encourage panel members to bring pictures, their loved one's favorite clothing, anything that will make what has happened more real."

Tears slid down Hannah's cheeks and she sniffed softly. "I could do that, Mrs. Cummins." She paused. "I will do that. When can we meet?"

"Call me Carol. And we can meet soon." The woman's voice was filled with compassion, and Hannah knew she had another ally. "I think we should attend the hearing tomorrow. Are you free?"

Hannah felt an ache in her gut—and a hole in her heart. Tom was gone. Alicia, too. Jenny was back in school, and the two of them barely spoke. Was she free? She shook her head. Her calendar would be open the rest of her life. The only thing that mattered was getting Brian Wesley behind bars. Now… now there was a way to make that happen.

She could tell people what had happened to Tom and Alicia. And maybe, if she worked hard enough, she would do more than put Brian Wesley away. Maybe she would change drunk driving laws forever.

She exhaled sadly. "Yes. I'm open. And please…call me Hannah."

"Okay, Hannah. The hearing is at ten. Judge Rudy Horowitz is presiding. Let's meet outside the courtroom at quarter 'til."

"I'll be there."

"I'll introduce you to Mr. Bronzan. You need to talk to him, see what he wants you to do before you get involved in a victim impact panel."

"All right."

"Oh...and if you could, bring a small photograph of Tom and Alicia. I have a pin with the Mothers Against Drunk Drivers' logo. We'll put their picture inside, and you can wear it anytime there's a hearing."

Hannah was silent, but she couldn't stop the single sob from slipping out.

Carol's voice was compassionate. "I'm sorry, Hannah. I know it's hard. But every bit helps. Sometimes in all the legal maneuvering, the victims are forgotten."

Hannah nodded and gulped back what felt like a torrent of tears. "I'll bring the pictures."

Carol paused. "No one knows your personal pain, Hannah, but that dark place you're in? I've been there."

Hannah's shoulders slumped. She hadn't thought about it before, but it made sense. Carol must have lost someone in a drunk driving accident, too. She closed her eyes tightly, her heart heavier than before. "Thanks, Carol. I'll see you tomorrow."

The conversation ended, and Hannah replaced the phone on its base.

Pictures of Tom and Alicia.

Hannah drew a steadying breath and remained motionless, bracing herself against the kitchen counter as she stared distantly through the living room window into the backyard. They had lived in this house for fifteen years, ever since Tom had finished his residency. The swing set stood where it had since Tom and she assembled it one Christmas back when the girls were four and six.

She studied the swings, and she could see Alicia, her long, honey-colored hair flowing down her back in a single ponytail. As a child, Alicia had spent hours on that swing set. Hannah could remember working in the kitchen, making dinner and passing the time watching her little girl swing back and forth, smiling and singing. She was such a happy little girl.

The image faded, and Hannah padded slowly across the living room to the bookcase and her collection of photo albums. She examined the dates on the side of each until she found the most recent. She took it from the shelf and ran her hand over its cover. Just as she was about to open it, her eyes fell on another album, one from more than a decade ago.

Hannah smiled sadly. She had never been one to toss photographs in a drawer and forget about them. Her album collection was complete, intricately organized.

She removed the older album and opened it, turning the pages reverently. As she did, her breath caught in her throat. On the third page was a picture of Alicia, two years old, sitting in a wagon. The little girl was wearing only a diaper, a lopsided grin, and a white plastic cowboy hat. Alicia's hair had gotten darker as she grew older, but back then her wispy blond locks stuck out from beneath the hat at all angles. Hannah closed her eyes and remembered the moment. She could feel the sun on her shoulders as she snapped the picture…hear Alicia's voice chirping happily, "I'm a little cowpope! Happy little cowpope!"

Hannah laughed out loud, despite her tears. Alicia had been five before she could say *cowpoke* correctly.

Another image came to mind then, and Hannah felt her smile disappear. Alicia, two years old, lying on a hospital bed, deathly white and hooked to IV lines. It had happened a month before Jenny was born. Alicia was taking a nap and Hannah, exhausted from the final days of her pregnancy, decided to slip into her own bedroom and lie down.

She woke to the sound of Alicia choking, gasping for breath. She'd raced to the kitchen to find Alicia curled in a ball, lying on the floor, an open bottle of kitchen cleaner nearby. Hannah had forgotten to put it away.

Dear God, help me! Prayer had been a natural response then.

In the end, as he had always done back then, God came through. Doctors observed Alicia through the night and then sent her home the next morning, singing a merry song about flowers and sunshine as she skipped to the family car.

Hannah shut the photo album, set it aside, and covered her face with her hands. She wept then as she hadn't since the day of the collision. "Why?" she shouted. "*Why,* God?"

She cried out again and again, releasing the anger and frustration and gut-wrenching grief that grew deep within her. Why would God watch over Alicia when she was two, only to walk away from her when she was fifteen? As hard as she tried, Hannah couldn't understand why God had stopped listening to her...why he had turned his back.

"What did—I ever do—to deserve this?" Hannah was sobbing too hard to catch her breath.

Eventually, her sobbing grew quieter, and she stared at the picture of Alicia as her mind drifted. Her favorite hymn came to mind, and Hannah found herself humming along. "*Great is thy faithfulness, great is thy faithfulness, morning by morning new mercies I see. All I have needed thy hand–*"

Hannah jerked, realizing what she was doing, what she was saying. *Stop!* She angrily forced the song from her mind. It was a horrible song, full of lies. The Lord was not faithful; the mornings were without mercy, without any hope or reason for moving beyond the edge of the bed. And everything she had ever needed from God he had taken from her the day Tom and Alicia died.

Hannah's eyes stung with fresh tears. The words of that hymn used to describe the perfect life she and Tom shared. The organist had played it at their wedding. The choir had sung it when Alicia—and then Jenny—was dedicated. If ever there was a hymn Hannah had been able to sing from her heart it was "Great Is Thy Faithfulness." Now the song was nothing more than a painful reminder of how God had let her down. *Great* was *thy faithfulness*.

No matter what else might happen, she would never, ever sing that song again.

She was still sniffling softly, still holding the photo albums, trying to find the strength to search for a picture of Tom and Alicia that she could take to tomorrow's hearing, when she heard the front door open.

"Mom?" It was Jenny.

"In here." Hannah wiped at her tears. She heard her daughter traipse through the house and set her books on the kitchen counter. Then she watched as the girl poked her head into the living room. Poor Jenny. She looked as though she had aged a decade since the accident—and Hannah saw something unspeakably sad in her eyes.

Before Hannah could say anything, Jenny looked intently at her face...then at the photo albums on her lap. Rolling her eyes, Jenny sighed softly. "Never mind." She turned and headed for the stairs.

"Jenny, wait." Hannah stood, too weak from grief to move.

The only reply was the sound of footsteps making their way up the stairs, toward the bedrooms.

"Jenny! I want to talk to you!" New tears filled Hannah's eyes, and she collapsed back onto the floor, her legs curled under her.

You're losing her, too. Hannah closed her eyes against the small voice. *Go. Talk to her before it's too late.*

She shook her head. She wouldn't chase Jenny. The girl was being selfish and insensitive; if she didn't want to talk, then so be it. She grabbed a tissue from the nearby end table and blew her nose. Then she put the older photo album away and pulled the newer one onto her lap.

"Sometimes the victims are forgotten." Hannah clenched her teeth and searched the collection of photos. Tom and Alicia would not be forgotten. Not as long as she had anything to do with the court proceedings.

She drew a deep breath and scanned the photographs until she found a shot of Tom and Alicia. They were grinning into the camera as they worked over the gas grill during a family barbecue at the beginning of summer. It was a close-up and probably the best recent picture of the two of them.

She ran a finger over their faces. Tom had said he didn't know how he'd get through either of his daughter's weddings. Especially after Bob Carlisle's song "Butterfly Kisses" became popular. Any time he heard the piece, Tom would beat his chest once, just above his heart. "Ughh. Kill me with that song. When my girls get married, they're gonna have to pour me out of the church in a bucket. Better buy stock in Kleenex while there's still time."

There was no need now, no weddings to dread, no oldest daughter to walk down the aisle. *Poor Jenny, baby. One day you'll have to make that walk alone.* Hannah worked her fingers under the plastic sleeve and removed the photograph, setting it on the table next to the tissues.

She flipped forward a few pages until her eyes fell on another photo, this one of her and Tom taken that past June. They were atop a pair of rented horses, about to ride through the Santa Monica Mountains. Hannah closed her eyes, and she could feel the cool ocean fog against her skin; her senses were filled with the salty summer air and the sweet smell of horse sweat as it drifted up from beneath the saddle. They had ridden for several hours before returning and driving to Malibu Park, where they had sat side by side on a bench overlooking the deep green canyon and shared peanut butter sandwiches.

Hannah kept her eyes closed. Everything about that moment seemed so real...

Was she still there, sitting beside Tom, waiting for him to tell her it was time to go home? Maybe every devastating thing that had happened since then had only been part of a terrible nightmare....

She waited—and heaviness settled over her. No. She was

not at Malibu Park. And Tom would never sit beside her again.

In this life…

She shut the reassurance out. There was no comfort in dwelling on thoughts of eternity. If there *was* an eternity. Today was all that mattered.

And today, Tom and Alicia were gone.

She sighed and opened her eyes, allowing her gaze to fall on the picture once again. Tom looked so young and alive, so handsome. He had pulled his horse up to hers and casually draped an arm around her shoulders. Then she'd handed her camera to a stable boy.

"Memories for another day," she'd said and Tom had groaned. He had always teased her about her excessive photo taking.

"Here we go. Dan Rather, capturing the moment for posterity." He raised an eyebrow and met the grinning gaze of the stable boy. "Don't laugh. Your turn will come, boy." Then he grinned at Hannah. "One day I'll have to build us a separate wing just to hold our photo albums. That's how many memories we have for another day."

She looked at the photo, and she could still see the laughter in his eyes. Tears slid down her face again….Would they ever stop? She shook her head, feeling as though she were falling down a deep, dark well. Would she ever snap another photograph? She couldn't fathom it. Not when the only memories that mattered were those that were already made. She lifted the photo album, clutching it against her chest.

"Oh, Tom…where are you? How can you be gone?" She sniffed and rocked back and forth, cradling the album close. "I'm so alone, Tom."

She squeezed her eyes shut, staying that way a long while, hugging the cold, plastic-covered page against her heart—and with it, all that remained of the man she'd loved since she was a child.

He has handed me over to those I cannot withstand.

LAMENTATIONS 1:14B

The meeting took place in a windowless room located on the first floor of the Los Angeles Superior Court Criminal Courts Building. Only two parties were present: Harold Finch, defense attorney for Brian Wesley, and deputy district attorney Matthew Bronzan.

Matt knew his opponent well. Finch was a hard-nosed defender whose primary source of income came from defending drunk drivers. The man's business card sported the image of a martini glass and announced, "Caught having too much fun? Drunk driving arrest got you down? We can help." Matt kept the card tucked into the frame around his desk calendar. A reminder to keep fighting the war, keep battling the cases until the words *fun* and *drunk driving* would never appear in the same paragraph.

Finch referred to himself as "the drunk driver's best friend," and one day Matt did some research to see what made his opponent tick. He was surprised at what he found.

Rumor was that fifteen years earlier, Edward Finch—Harold's older brother—had developed a promising future in law. Common knowledge had it that the two brothers had attended law school together and planned to go into practice one day. Back then, they were hardworking, clean-cut young men; lawyers who dreamed big and planned to change the world by righting wrongs, one case at a time.

Edward never got the chance.

The summer after he graduated law school, he attended a wedding where the air-conditioning broke down during the reception. Hundred-degree temperatures had people sweltering in the ballroom, and Edward spent much of his time camped out at the punch bowl. From everything Matt had heard, Edward Finch had never been a drinker, and he didn't know until the third glass that the punch was spiked. Of course, after that it didn't matter. With all the dancing and mingling, there was only one way to cool down...so Edward drank crystal goblets of punch until he lost count.

Apparently Edward's young wife tried to talk him into calling a cab or getting a room at the hotel, but Edward wouldn't hear of it. So they got in the car. Halfway home there was a police officer pulled off the road, writing someone up for speeding. Drawn by the flashing lights, Edward let his car drift off the road—until he rear-ended the police car, narrowly missing the officer. No one was injured, but the officer took the accident personally. According to court records, the officer later testified that Edward had acted in a "belligerent manner," that he'd been clearly intoxicated and said, "Next time I drive drunk, I'll take better aim."

Edward swore up and down he'd never said anything of the sort, but his trial took place three weeks after a well-publicized incident in which a young mother had been killed by a drunk driver while walking her daughter to school. The jury made an example of Edward Finch, and he received a one-year sentence in county jail.

Midway through the term, his wife left him. When he got out of prison, he was a broken man, a convict with no apartment, no money, no license to practice law, and no chance at his much dreamed-about career. From everything Matt heard, Harold did what he could to help his brother, suggesting odd jobs and encouraging Edward to appeal for reinstatement with the California Bar Association. But depression set in, and Edward began drinking in earnest.

Last anyone had heard, the man roamed the streets in urine-drenched rags, slept under park benches, and was hopelessly addicted to alcohol. A victim of unjust circumstances—at least, that's how Harold saw it.

Matt understood Harold Finch better after finding out all of this, and in some very small way he pitied the man. The knowledge of Finch's past made him human.

Wrong, but human.

In the wake of what had happened to his brother, Harold Finch changed gears and apparently decided that the best wrong he could possibly right was the wrong done to his brother. He would help drunk drivers if it took a lifetime to establish their rights. Early on, so it was said, Finch had been utterly sincere.

"You know the old saying—" Finch was famous for telling jurors as he cocked his head and linked his fingers over his extended belly—"'There but for the grace of God go I.'"

But somewhere along the road of defending DUI offenders—many of whom were responsible for tragic deaths and mayhem—Finch had changed. Gone was the lawyerly attitude and appearance. In their place was the look and demeanor of a pimp, complete with pinstriped suits and vests with shiny gold buttons that strained against the man's sizable gut. Finch also began calling himself Deuce Dog, a play on the slang for DUIs: deuces.

High profile drunk driving cases always seemed to wind up in Finch's hands, and between appointments he strutted through the courthouse, chest puffed out, brimming with confidence and pride.

Matt figured Finch was a case of someone who'd grown callused, hardened to the devastation he defended so well. Bad company had finally corrupted what were, at the beginning, good intentions. The way Matt saw it, Harold's brash and cocky attitude was probably a cover-up for the pain he felt for his brother. Nevertheless, Matt did not want to lose to him.

Not this time.

Matt had gone toe-to-toe with Finch on many cases, and most resulted in plea bargains. Matt hated plea bargains. He'd agreed to dozens of them over the years, but only because he knew the system as well as his opponent did. Sometimes it was better to plea-bargain and send a defendant away with community service obligations, a fine, and a mark on his record. Especially when the alternative was to waste valuable court time prosecuting a case that could very well result in a not-guilty verdict.

Only twice had Matt and Finch battled it out before a jury. Both times Matt had won convictions. The first involved an elderly woman who suffered major head injuries after a drunk driver had run her down while she was carrying a gallon of milk home from the market. Finch's client was convicted of reckless driving and received two hundred hours of community service along with a fifteen hundred dollar fine. Hardly satisfying, considering that the last time Matt had checked, the elderly woman remained in a vegetative state, strapped to a hospital bed at a sour-smelling nursing home.

The second case involved a nineteen-year-old boy who drove his fifteen-year-old cousin home from a party. The nineteen-year-old misjudged the lane boundaries and hit a hundred-year-old maple tree at fifty miles per hour. His cousin had died on impact. Both boys had been legally drunk.

Finch's client was convicted of reckless endangerment, and because it was the boy's first offense, prison time was waived. He, too, received community service and a fine.

Although Matt had won convictions in both cases, clearly Finch had been the victor. His clients were not confined to a nursing home or a graveyard. Their lives went on as they had before, without even a single night in prison to remind them of the consequences of their choice to drink and drive.

Matt gritted his teeth. He'd spent years prosecuting drunk drivers, but still jurors had never connected driving under the influence with intent to kill.

Until now.

Matt's jaw tensed. God willing, he—and the case against Brian Wesley—were about to change that fact.

A blast of cheap cologne filled the room, and he glanced up to find Finch standing there, the ever-present cocky smile on his face.

"Well, well—" Finch tossed his martini business card across the table—"guess we got ourselves another plea to work out, eh, Bronzan?"

Matt met the man's gaze steadily. "Not this time."

Finch's expression changed. "A bit jumpy today, aren't we?" He let loose a tinny chuckle and pulled a document from the stack before him, eyebrows raising a fraction as he studied Matt. "Read it, counselor."

Matt leaned back against the hard wood chair and crossed his arms. "Your client is a repeat drunk driver who caused two previous collisions despite alcohol education. And now he's killed two people. His blood alcohol level was three times the legal limit." He fixed Finch with a hard stare. "There will be no plea...*counselor.*"

Finch paused, and a knowing look danced in his eyes. "Perhaps, *Mr.* Bronzan, you should read the plea before summarily dismissing it."

Matt glanced at his watch and pulled the document closer. "Unless Mr. Wesley plans to admit to murder, we don't have much to talk about."

Finch was silent while Matt scanned the document. He sucked in a deep breath. The plea was brilliant, of course. Matt had expected nothing less from Finch. Dime-store cologne and gold vest buttons aside, the man knew his stuff. Had the plea been for reckless driving or any such minor charge, Matt could have rejected it easily. But Finch had upped the ante. His client was willing to plead guilty to vehicular manslaughter. Even more, he was willing to serve thirty days in jail for the offense.

In all Matt's years of prosecuting, he'd never seen such a

serious crime admitted by way of plea bargain.

There was only one reason his opponent would present such an offer. Matt studied Finch's beady eyes, and what he saw there confirmed his suspicions.

Harold Finch was scared.

Glancing at the document once more, Matt thought of the heartache a trial would cause Hannah Ryan and her surviving daughter. He thought of the many times a jury had refused to convict a drunk driver of even second-degree murder, let alone first-degree. The Ryans would suffer indescribable pain if the jury let Brian Wesley leave the courtroom a free man....

Then he thought of Tom and Alicia...of the family broken apart, destroyed by Brian Wesley's choices. He remembered others like the Ryans who had been dragged through the criminal justice system only to be let down when penalties were inadequate. No, there would be no plea bargain this time. This was the case he'd been waiting for.

Finch looked pleased with himself as he cleared his throat and motioned toward the plea bargain. "Well, Bronzan, do we have a plea?"

Matt slid the document across the table and watched it settle in front of Finch.

"No. We want a trial."

Finch chuckled and looked down the bridge of his fleshy nose at Matt. "Now, I've worked with you for many years, Bronzan. And even though we've been on opposite sides of the courtroom, I've always taken you for a smart lawyer. Clear on the ways of justice. But if I'm not mistaken, I do believe you're losing your edge."

Matt ignored the comment. "Tomorrow this office will officially charge your client with first-degree murder. At that time he can choose to plead guilty or not guilty."

Finch's laughter died abruptly and his gaze hardened. "I don't need a lesson on law, counselor. Look, we're offering prison time here."

"When I'm finished with your client, we won't be talking thirty days jail time, we'll be talking five years in the penitentiary. Maybe more." Matt considered his opponent and how he'd changed over the years. "There won't be a plea, Finch. You can't change my mind."

Finch waited, but when Matt remained silent his eyes narrowed angrily. "Most generous plea I've ever made." He sighed dramatically as he collected the document and stuffed it into his briefcase. "Next time we offer less. Much less."

"There won't be a next time. Not on this case."

Finch arched an eyebrow. "That right? You'll see, counselor. You'll get in court and start talking first-degree murder, start making the vehicle out to be a weapon and Mr. Wesley out to be a killer. Then you'll see the faces on those jurors and you'll panic. A third of the folks in this great nation drink and drive, my friend. And that includes jurors." He studied Matt. "They won't give you first-degree murder. It's drunk driving, after all. Guy goes out, drinks a few beers, has a little fun with the boys, and drives home. The accident was just that. *Any* jail time is out of line as far as I'm concerned." Finch slammed his briefcase shut. "But in this case my client and I have tried to show compassion for the victims. We offered thirty days in good faith."

Matt remained seated, his arms casually crossed. "Thirty days? In exchange for a husband and father, a daughter on the brink of adulthood? Thirty days for two lives?"

"Thirty days is better than nothing, Bronzan. The victims' family would have been happy with that." Finch shrugged. "Now you're going to drag them through a messy court battle. A battle you're going to lose, counselor. And they're going to lose, too."

Matt stood and stretched, and suddenly a mountain of anxiety rose within him. *How can I turn down voluntary jail time? What if Brian Wesley walks?* He released his breath slowly and waited as Finch continued relentlessly.

"Turn down a manslaughter plea and you have nothing left." He shook his head. "First-degree murder? Huh! My client will walk, Bronzan, mark my words."

"The only walking he'll be doing is from his cell to the yard and back."

"You could take the plea and still come out the winner, here, Bronzan. It's not too late."

Matt straightened. "Are you finished?"

Finch shook his head sadly. "You really have lost it, counselor. No way a jury's going to make drunk driving a murder-one issue. Not in the great state of California."

Matt waited, silent, as Finch headed for the door.

"I'll be asking for a delay."

Matt cocked his head. "Just one?"

Finch's eyes grew cold. "One per month until we run out of reasons. By the time this thing takes the floor, the world will have forgotten all about Tom and Alicia Ryan."

Matt thought of the pictures, photos taken at the accident scene. Broken glass and blood and camping gear spilled onto the road. He thought of the young girl laid out on a stretcher, her body stilled forever…so reminiscent of another whose life had been wasted…

He leveled a look at Finch. "Not me. I'll never forget."

The defense attorney studied him as if he were a curious oddity. "You've forgotten the first rule of law, counselor, don't get emotionally involved. First-degree murder?" He scratched his head, his face contorted in disbelief. "You're out of your mind."

Finch left the room and shut the door behind him. Matt stood there, staring after him, his hands in his pockets. *Finch is worried. He's afraid I'm right.* He closed his eyes and sighed deeply. *Please, Lord, let me be right.*

After tomorrow there would be no turning back.

Twelve

This is why I weep and my eyes overflow with tears.
No one is near to comfort me.

LAMENTATIONS 1:16A

Hannah smoothed a hand over her black rayon slacks and straightened her short-sleeved blouse. The hearing was in two hours, and she planned to be early. She walked briskly down the hallway toward the bedroom.

"Jenny? Are you up?"

Silence.

Hannah sighed. Since their disagreement the day before, Jenny had hidden away in her room, even refusing dinner. Hannah strode up to her daughter's bedroom door and knocked twice. No response.

"Jenny, open the door right now!" Hannah shifted her weight and began tapping a steady rhythm with the toe of her shoe. She could hear Jenny moving on the other side of the door and finally it swung open.

"What?" Jenny's eyes were tear stained; her voice sounded thick, as though she were fighting a cold. She was dressed in rumpled pajamas and fuzzy, Dalmatian slippers.

At the sight of her disheveled, clearly miserable little girl, Hannah was pierced with guilt and heartache. She stopped tapping and sighed, her voice sadder than before. "Honey, you haven't said two words to me since yesterday. I need to know your plans. I'm getting ready to leave for the hearing this morning."

Jenny crossed her arms. "What do you want to know?"

"Well, for starters—" Hannah forced herself to sound understanding, even patient—"are you going to school or coming with me?"

Jenny was silent, her eyes glazed with unresolved anger and grief.

Hannah sighed. "Jenny, I think you should come with me today. Carol Cummins called yesterday. She's the woman from Mothers Against Drunk Drivers." Hannah hesitated. "She said sometimes the victims get forgotten in these court proceedings."

Jenny huffed. "No kidding."

Hannah frowned. What on earth did that mean? "I'll ignore that comment. What I'm trying to say is, we need to be there to represent your dad and Alicia. We're the only ones who can do that."

"Dad and Alicia are dead." Jenny turned, plodded across the room, and fell onto her unmade bed. "I'm staying home today."

Hannah's heartbeat quickened and she felt her face grow hot. "That isn't an option. You need to get dressed and make your bed. Then you need to either get yourself to the bus stop or come with me to the hearing."

"I don't feel good."

Hannah's heart sank. Jenny had always been the picture of health. Before the accident, she was routinely recognized for perfect attendance in school. Now she'd missed twelve days since returning to school, and she rarely woke up enthusiastic about anything. "Honey, you've missed too much school already."

Jenny began crying again. "I thought you *wanted* me to miss school! So you can haul me off to court and show me off, so everyone can stare at me like...like I'm some kind of *freak* or something!"

Hannah clenched her fists. *Why can't you understand? Jenny, what's happening to us?* "Never mind. Don't come to the hearing. I just thought you might feel better if you did something constructive."

Jenny sat up, her shoulders hunched wearily. "What's constructive about sitting in a courtroom while people walk around feeling sorry for you?"

"Someone has to represent your dad and Alicia." Hannah heard her voice getting louder, and she struggled to regain control.

"This isn't about Daddy and Alicia. It's about that guy who hit us. You want him locked up and...and you want to use me as some kind of...I don't know, some kind of puppet to make everyone feel sorry for us."

Hannah felt as if she'd been slapped. She reeled, taking a step backward. "That's not fair, Jenny! That man *destroyed* our family. Yes, I want him locked up. So he won't do this to anyone else. If our being there could possibly help get him off the streets, then your dad and Alicia's deaths will not be in vain."

"That's a lousy reason to die, Mom. I need them here. I want them *here*. Besides, I don't care what happens to that guy. I'm not going to court...not today or any other day! It won't bring Dad and Alicia back, and that's the only thing that matters."

Hannah felt the sting of tears. She wanted to go to Jenny, comfort her, and hold her. Take away the hurt. But Hannah's own pain seemed to create an invisible wall between them too high to scale. "Fine. Don't go. But I'll expect you to get dressed and be at the bus on time." Hannah glanced at her watch. "You have forty-five minutes."

"I said I don't feel good."

Hannah's sympathy evaporated. "Listen, Jenny, unless you want to repeat this year, you need to go to school. I don't feel good, either. It's part of life these days."

Jenny was silent again, and Hannah turned to leave. How had this happened? How had she and Jenny grown so distant? If only Tom were here. He would know what to say, how to reach her....

She collected the photograph of Tom and Alicia and placed

it carefully in her day-planner. She had lost so much, and somehow it seemed like the losing had only begun. In the end, when the court proceedings were behind her…would she have lost Jenny, too? Hannah wiped at a single tear, grabbed her car keys, and forced herself to think of the events that lay ahead.

For an instant she considered praying, considered asking God to help Jenny understand. Maybe if she begged him to repair their damaged relationship, he would help them, restore them, so that at least they would have each other. But the thought of praying made Hannah's skin crawl. It was the same creepy feeling she used to get when she and Tom would see a television commercial for the Psychic Hotline.

That was when the idea came to her. She ignored it for a moment, but it wouldn't go away. And for the first time in her life, Hannah considered an unthinkable possibility: Perhaps everything she'd ever learned and believed about God was just fable and fairy tale. Perhaps God didn't really exist at all. At least you could see the Psychic Hotline people, but God…what proof was there?

No God. It was a plausible explanation, and as Hannah tested it in her heart and mind, she felt herself becoming convinced.

Yes, that had to be it. There was no God. No father in heaven who had deserted her, no Lord who had allowed her family to be destroyed. Perhaps all of life was only a random crapshoot.

The idea was strangely comforting, and by the time Hannah climbed into her car and headed for the Criminal Courts Building, she had accepted it as truth.

Brian Wesley sat on a cold wooden chair in a holding room adjacent to Courtroom 201, home of the formidable Judge Rudy Horowitz. He fidgeted with a paper clip, twisting it back and forth until it broke into tiny metal strips. Across the table from him sat his lawyer, Harold Finch.

"You understand the order of events today?" Finch's chest heaved as he tried to catch his breath. The hearing was in fifteen minutes, and Finch had just arrived to court. Late, as usual.

Brian turned in his chair and studied his trembling fingers. "They charge me with murder. I tell 'em I'm not guilty."

"Right." Finch studied him. "Try to sound sure of yourself."

Brian nodded, his eyes downcast.

"You remember what I've told you about Judge Horowitz?"

"No nonsense. Doesn't like drunk drivers."

"Good." Finch breathed easier. "You been off the bottle?"

"Sometimes. I drink a little now and then, but no driving, man. Don't worry."

Finch's face grew red and he frowned. "It's going to take more than that, Mr. Wesley! You need to stop drinking. This case will go to trial, and if the prosecutor can prove you're still drinking, there's a chance you'll be convicted of first-degree murder."

Brian gulped and his palms began to sweat. When he could speak again, his voice was pinched. "You said that wouldn't happen."

"It's never happened in the history of California." Finch set his elbows on the table and leaned closer to Brian. "But jurors are changing. They're only sympathetic to a point. If they think you're going to drink and drive again, maybe hurt *their* families or friends, they just might put you away."

Brian picked up a broken piece of the paper clip and ran his finger over its smooth length. "I'm trying to stop, man."

"How about AA? You connected with a group yet?"

"I went once. Some guy led the thing...kept talking about higher power this, and God that. I couldn't relate, you know?"

Finch waved a hand in dismissal. "The God stuff is part of the deal. No one says you have to believe it, but if you're not in with an AA group, you'll lose the jury's sympathy for sure."

Brian looked down again, and his eyes fell on another paper clip. He reached out and pulled it closer. "So...what? Pretend I'm some kind of Jesus freak?"

"God, Jesus, Buddah, higher power...whatever. Just go along with it. This has nothing to do with your personal belief system. It has to do with keeping your pickled behind out of prison. Understand?"

Brian nodded and bent the paper clip until it was unrecognizable.

Finch summed up Brian, and his face became a mask of doubt. "I plan to win this case, Mr. Wesley. But I am going to need your cooperation."

"Got it."

"All right, that's better. Listen, I have to talk to someone down the hall. I'll be back in ten minutes, and we'll get set up in the courtroom."

Brian did not look up as his attorney left the room. A ripple of terror ran through him like a current of electricity. *How did I get here?* His heart skipped a beat in response. *Wasn't I doing my best work ever, sober for three weeks? How did everything get so messed up?* He closed his eyes and he could see Carla, the devastated look on her face when she picked him up at the county jail the night of the accident.

She had said nothing until they were in her car. Then her voice had been barely more than a whisper. "How could you, Brian?"

He hadn't answered her. He had still been drunk, after all, and there was no point defending himself to Carla. But she'd been relentless, horrified at what had happened. "Brian, do you understand? You *killed* two people!"

He tried to explain that it was an accident...of course he hadn't meant to hurt anyone. But Carla was furious and unforgiving. For days after the accident she stayed away from him, almost as if she were afraid of him. When they spoke, she talked of nothing but the accident, the impending court proceedings—and the biggest issue of all—when Brian was finally going to quit drinking.

A week after the accident Brian could take no more. He moved out and took up residence on the sofa bed at a friend's nearby apartment. Jackson Lamer was a party buddy from Brian's high school days, faithful and true, always ready with a cold one when the chips were down.

"Dude, whatever you need," Jackson had told him after hearing about the accident. He popped the top of an aluminum beer can and handed it to Brian. "Rides to court, AA meetings. Whatever, dude. You're in righteous, big-time trouble, and that's what buds are for, man. Just let me know."

Jackson was a keeper, the kind of friend Brian wished he had more of.

Police had impounded Brian's car, and the few times he had needed a ride in the weeks since, Jackson had come through. Days were difficult, wondering if he should look for a job or wait until the courts were through with him. But evenings were better, he and Jackson would pass the hours sharing a twelve-pack, talking about old times.

Since the accident, only Jackson had been faithful. Everyone else had forsaken him: Avery Automotive, Carla, even the beer. Back in the old days, the drink always made things okay, but ever since the accident, there was no peace—not in drinking or sleeping...and definitely not in thinking. Day or night, whenever he closed his eyes, he was haunted by them. The girl lying lifeless on the side of the road; her father trapped in their family car, his life slowly draining away. A mother and sister left alone, brokenhearted.

He hated himself for what he'd done to them.

He tried to block out their faces, but they pushed their way into his mind anyway. And with them came images of demons, laughing, taunting him, offering him another drink. Brian swallowed hard around the lump in his throat.

The legal proceedings were pointless. Whatever happened in court, he was already trapped in the worst kind of prison.

He looked around, searching for another paper clip, but found none.

The AA meeting had offered no relief. Finch had called with

the information, explaining that there was a meeting one mile from Jackson's apartment. Brian remembered the evening well. He had stayed clean for the occasion, and that evening Jackson had dropped him off.

"Give it a try, man." He'd shrugged. "Who knows, maybe I'll join you one day."

Brian walked through the double glass doors nervously, signed in, and found a seat. The room was filled with twenty or so men and women ranging in age from early twenties to late fifties. Most of them looked comfortable, like they'd been meeting together for years.

"We have someone new in our group tonight." The leader looked right at him as he spoke. "Mr. Wesley, will you stand and tell us a little about yourself and why you're here?"

Brian wished he could disappear, but he stood, his knees knocking within his worn jeans. "Brian Wesley. I, uh...I was in an accident last week. Uh...my attorney told me about this."

A knowing look came over the leader's face. "Brian—may I call you Brian?"

Brian nodded.

"Brian, was that the accident at Ventura and Fallbrook?"

He looked around the room, suddenly embarrassed. "Yeah."

The leader seemed to wait for him to elaborate. When he stood silent, the man went on. "You were driving under the influence, is that right?"

Brian nodded again and shoved his hands deep inside his pockets.

"Can you tell us about it?"

"Uh...well...no."

The leader nodded. "Okay." He paused. "I'm sure a few of us read about that accident." He looked at the others and his voice filled with compassion. "A father and daughter were killed when Brian, here, drove his truck through a red light at Ventura and Fallbrook. Is that right, Brian?"

Brian's temper flared. "I said I didn't want to talk about it!"

"I understand, but we don't keep secrets in this group. We're here to help you."

Brian wanted to run from the room. "I don't need help. I'm here because of my attorney."

"You're not alone, Brian. A few of those sitting around the room here have been involved in serious accidents. Accidents they caused by driving drunk. But they've found forgiveness in Christ and have accepted his gift of new life."

Brian shook his head. The guy sounded like some kind of religious freak. Who was Christ anyway, and what did new life have to do with drunk driving? What sort of God would want anything to do with him after what he'd done to that family?

His response had been quick. "I don't believe in God, man."

The leader smiled kindly. "That's all right. He believes in you. He wants to meet you right where you are, Brian."

Brian had listened to the man's religious drivel for ten minutes before leaving the meeting early. If there was a God—and he seriously doubted the idea—Brian knew he would have died in that accident. The pretty blond girl and her father would have lived. It was simple as that.

He hadn't gone back to the AA meetings.

Brian looked at the clock. The hearing would take place soon. He pushed the pieces of broken paper clips with his forefinger until they formed a small letter *s*. He hadn't talked to Carla in three weeks, and he suddenly wondered about Brian Jr. What would the boy think when he realized what his father had done?

He thought of his own father. Red Wesley was a boozer from way back. He floated from job to job, and when Brian was four, he deserted the family and took up with a barmaid across town. Brian's mother got married again, this time to a wealthy, tea-drinking investor. He didn't exactly love Brian, but he bought him whatever he needed, and in his father's absence, material goods weren't all that bad. After a year or so they lost track of Red Wesley. Ten years later his mother was notified that Red had died. Alcohol poisoning.

All his life Brian had been determined to be a better father than Red.

I'm just like him. Brian dug his elbows into his thighs and dropped his head into his hands. *I don't care what they do to me. Lock me up for twenty years. Thirty, even. Then Carla can meet someone, and little Brian can have a different daddy. He deserves better.*

He squeezed his eyes shut and the images returned again. The girl, her blond hair matted with blood...her father moaning from inside the car. The demons, black faces dripping with blood, sneered at him, taunting him.

"Okay, God," his hands shook and his pulse quickened. The dryness in his throat seemed to reach down into his gut. "If you're real then I give up. Take me now. I don't want to live another minute."

Brian waited. Nothing. "I thought so."

He pushed the paper clip pieces around until they formed the shape of a glass. He glanced at the clock once more and wrung his hands together, trying to still their incessant trembling. *Let's get this thing over with so I can go home and have a drink.*

Jenny lay on her bed staring at the ceiling. She still wore the same rumpled pajamas and had barely moved in the two hours since her mother left. It was nearly ten, and the school bus had long since come and gone. Jenny clutched her stomach and rolled onto her side. She hadn't lied to her mother, she really did feel terrible. Her heart pounded and her chest ached...getting air was hard because she couldn't relax long enough to draw a deep breath. Her sinuses throbbed from hours of crying. She had felt this way since the previous afternoon and had passed the night restlessly, desperately trying to sleep.

"Oh, I don't care, Lord!" She rolled onto her side. "Take me. I don't wanna live anyway."

She grabbed her pillow and shoved it over her face so she couldn't breathe. Seconds passed, and she willed herself to hold firm, keep the pillow in place. Just a few minutes and she would be with Daddy and Alicia. *Take me, Lord. Please.*

Suddenly, when it seemed her lungs would burst, she threw the pillow onto the floor, gasping in great gulps of air.

I can't even do that right. Please take me, Lord.

If only she weren't so weak. She should have held the pillow longer. There had to be another way. Carbon monoxide. Sleeping pills. A razor blade. Something.

Mom doesn't want me. My friends won't talk to me. Please Lord, I want to be with you and Daddy and Alicia.

She tossed and turned, rolling from side to side, gulping in quick, jerky breaths. What was wrong with the air in this room? It was stale, warm. No matter how many times she sucked in, her body screamed for more oxygen. She wove her fingers into her hair, grabbed two fistfuls and pulled as hard as she could. *I hate this, Lord. I want to die. Carbon monoxide. Sleeping pills. A razor.* She ran through the options again and again and again. Until finally she couldn't keep her eyes open a moment longer, and she drifted off to sleep.

Thirteen

The Lord has rejected all the warriors in my midst;
he has summoned an army against me.

LAMENTATIONS 1:15A

Hannah was pacing a short, nervous pattern in front of Judge Horowitz's courtroom when a woman appeared with two large photo buttons pinned to the lapel of her cream-colored jacket. The first held the insignia of Mothers Against Drunk Drivers; the second bore the picture of a kind-looking man in his thirties. The woman was forty-five, maybe forty-eight. Her hair was pulled back, and her eyes held a gentle glow, as though she had found a peace that was rare in a world of suffering.

The woman approached and held out her hand. "Hello. I'm Carol Cummins."

Hannah wondered if Carol could see her heart pounding in her throat. "Hannah Ryan."

"I thought it was you. We're usually the first to arrive and the last to leave." She smiled and motioned toward the courtroom. "Matt Bronzan is probably already setting up inside. Let's go in. I'll introduce you."

Hannah felt her pulse quicken. What would Matt Bronzan think of her? Did she look like a victim? Would she evoke enough sympathy from the people who had the power to put Brian Wesley behind bars? She thought a moment and tried to take on the look of a victim. As she did, she glanced at the photograph in her hand and remembered the truth.

Tom and Alicia were gone. There was no need to pretend.

"I brought the photo."

Carol took it and studied it a moment. "They look very happy." She raised her eyes, and Hannah saw distant pain there.

Hannah looked at the picture once more. "Yes. We all were."

"Well..." Carol drew a deep breath. She took the photo and snapped it carefully into a photo pin, then handed it back to Hannah. "I'd like to hear more about your family some day, Hannah. But right now we had better get inside. The hearing's in just a few minutes."

Hannah pinned the photo of Tom and Alicia to her rayon blouse and nodded. She was ready to meet Matt Bronzan.

Inside the courtroom, Matt straightened a pile of notes and set them down in front of his chair. Adjusting his tie, he glanced at the clock on the back wall. The others would be here any moment. He swallowed hard and rubbed his damp palms together. His decision was made. He was about to go through with it.

He prayed for wisdom and success. It was time. The system had gone along for too many years without recognizing how serious drunk driving and its consequences were. He prayed that this case would change that.

The back door opened, and he turned to see two women walk in. He recognized Carol Cummins from MADD, and he studied the other woman with her. She was striking, despite her swollen eyes and loose clothing. Hannah Ryan. He was sure of it.

"Matt." Carol stopped at the railing separating the spectator section from the rest of the courtroom.

"Good morning, Carol."

She slipped an arm around the other woman's shoulders. "This is Hannah Ryan. The defendant killed her husband and—"

“I know who she is,” Matt cut in kindly. His gaze held Hannah’s for a moment, then he reached out and took her hand in his. He hesitated. There was so much he wanted to say, but nothing that could help. “I’m…I’m so sorry, Mrs. Ryan.”

Hannah nodded, and Matt saw her eyes fill with tears. She seemed unable to speak so Matt continued. “I’m glad you’re here today. It does make a difference.” He paused. “If you don’t mind, I’d like to explain a little bit about what I’m going to do today, what’s going to take place.”

Carol turned to Matt. “I told Hannah about the first-degree murder possibility.”

“Right.” Matt still held the woman’s hand, and he looked intently at her. “Yesterday I met with the defendant’s attorney. They offered a plea bargain.”

Anger flare in Hannah’s eyes. “A plea bargain?”

“The defendant was willing to plead guilty to incidental vehicular manslaughter. According to their agreement, he would have served thirty days in jail and paid a fine, a thousand dollars I think it was.”

Hannah dropped his hand. “You settled?”

“No. I told them we weren’t interested.”

The woman’s face flooded with relief. “So what’s the charge?”

Matt paused. “We’ll charge him with driving under the influence and causing bodily injury while under the influence for the injuries your daughter Jenny sustained. Those charges don’t carry prison time, though.”

“What about the rest?”

Matt hesitated. “First-degree murder. All or nothing.” He studied Hannah and looked to Carol. “Have you explained any of this to her?”

“Yes. She understands.” Carol tightened her grip on Hannah’s shoulders. “If the jury doesn’t agree with the charges, Mr. Wesley walks away a free man.”

Matt drew a deep breath and returned his attention to

Hannah. "My office has been waiting for a case like this, and we believe it's time. The defendant, Brian Wesley, has prior convictions and prior drunk driving accidents. He's had his driver's license suspended, and last year it was revoked. He has participated in alcohol education courses and signed agreements as part of his parole conditions promising never to drink and drive again. At the time of the accident, he had no valid license, and tests showed he had consumed a significant amount of alcohol before driving home." Matt softened his voice. "All of which makes this a very serious situation."

Hannah swallowed hard and stood a bit taller. She hesitated a moment. "Do you think we have a chance?"

Matt smiled. "I think so. First-degree means Mr. Wesley used his vehicle as a weapon and set out deliberately to murder. Premeditated murder, really. It's a tough charge, but there are a few landmark precedents in other states. The question is culpability. To what degree was Mr. Wesley culpable in the deaths of Tom and Alicia."

Hannah's brow wrinkled in a frown of concentration. Matt figured she was trying to makes sense of all he'd told her. "No one's ever been convicted of first-degree murder for driving drunk and killing someone?"

"Not in California, no."

Carol crossed her arms. "We've tried a time or two—" she nodded to Matt—"at least Matt here has. But in the end the jurors simply haven't been ready."

Matt shifted his weight. "We're hoping this case, and the timing, will change that. Thanks to the education from MADD and other organizations, people want drunk drivers off the road. I think they may be ready to do something more drastic than ever before." He met Hannah's watchful look. "I really believe we can get a conviction in this case."

"If you do—" Hannah hesitated. "*When* you do, how many years will Brian Wesley get?"

"The penalty for this charge is twenty-five years to life. It'll depend on the jury's recommendation and the judge."

Carol met Hannah's eyes. "That's one thing we have going for us this time. Judge Horowitz is fairly conservative. He doesn't have much sympathy for people who choose to drink and drive and then kill someone in the process."

"Of course Wesley would never serve twenty-five years." Hannah's eyes narrowed at this, and Matt went on. She needed to know the facts. "He could be out in five, even three years with parole."

"Three years! If he gets sentenced to—"

She broke off when a door opened and Judge Horowitz appeared, his black robe flowing behind him. He climbed effortlessly into his elevated chair and began sifting through documents on his desk.

Another door opened, and Matt watched Harold Finch enter the room. Behind him came the man Matt presumed was Finch's defendant. Trailing the procession was a bailiff. The trio walked past Matt and the two women and found seats at the defense table. Finch whispered something to his client.

Matt turned and found Hannah staring at the men. "That's Harold Finch there on the right," he whispered. "He represents the defendant and typically—"

"Which one is Brian Wesley?"

Matt caught his breath at the anger in Hannah's voice. "I'm not positive, but I assume he's the younger guy on Finch's left."

Hannah was still staring at the man when Matt excused himself.

The hearing was about to begin.

Hannah barely noticed Matt leave or the judge bang his gavel and ask the court to come to order. Her attention was fixed on the man sitting next to Harold Finch.

Somehow she had expected him to be dark and sinister, with the cold eyes of a killer. Instead he was clean-cut with a trim build. He looked like the youth minister at their church. Hannah studied him and felt a wave of nausea wash over her. She clenched her teeth. It didn't matter how he looked. She hated him. *How could you?* She glared at him, boring her eyes in the back of his skull. *How could you kill my family?*

The judge's voice interrupted her thoughts. "In the matter of *The People v Brian Wesley,* I believe the state has a formal charge to file. Is Mr. Wesley present?"

The young man next to Finch nodded. "Yes, sir."

Hannah's gaze remained locked on Wesley as she absently fingered the photo button on her blouse. The nausea intensified. Suddenly the room was spinning, and she had to fight off a wave of lightheadedness. *Don't faint, don't faint, don't faint.* She drew a steadying gulp of hot, courtroom air.

You can do it. She nodded. Yes, she could. This wasn't about how she felt. This was about what she'd lost. And it was about making Brian Wesley pay for his sins. She closed her eyes for a moment and willed herself to be strong. *I'm doing my best, Tom, really I am.*

The judge continued. "Is counsel present for the defendant?"

The man Matt Bronzan had identified as Harold Finch stood. "Yes, your honor."

Judge Horowitz peered down and acknowledged Finch over his oval reading glasses. "Mr. Finch. I assume you will be counsel for the defendant throughout this matter?"

"I will, your honor."

The judge peered at Matt. "Mr. Bronzan."

"Your honor." Matt rose briefly.

"You'll be representing the state in this matter, is that right?"

"Yes, your honor."

"All right then." He glanced at the docket on his desk. "Mr. Bronzan, please would you inform this court as to the official charge against the defendant, Brian Wesley."

"Yes, your honor." Matt stood and stepped back from his

chair. Hannah liked the way he held Judge Horowitz's gaze. "The people of the state of California do hereby officially charge Mr. Brian Wesley with first-degree murder in the drunk driving deaths of Tom Ryan and Alicia Ryan. In addition, we charge Mr. Wesley with driving under the influence and causing bodily harm while driving under the influence for the injuries suffered by Jenny Ryan."

The judge nodded and wrote something on the form in front of him. He looked up. "Are there other charges?"

"No, your honor."

The judge allowed his glasses to slide further down the bridge of his nose so that his squinty eyes could be seen clearly over them. "This is a drunk driving case, is that right?"

"It is, your honor." Matt caught his hands behind his back, and his sleek, dark Italian suit opened enough to expose a crisp, white, button-down, tailored dress shirt and a conservative silk tie. Hannah studied him. He moved with an athletic grace, confident and self-assured. Though she'd only just met him, she trusted him completely. If anyone could put Brian Wesley away for a decade it was Matt Bronzan.

The judge continued. "And you understand, Mr. Bronzan, that by charging the defendant with first-degree murder, you can not later charge him with a lesser crime?"

"Yes, your honor." Matt didn't falter.

"All right then, the charge has been entered." Judge Horowitz turned toward Brian Wesley and his attorney. "Mr. Wesley, the state has charged you with first-degree murder in the deaths of Tom Ryan and Alicia Ryan. The state has also charged you with driving under the influence and causing bodily harm while driving under the influence. Do you understand the charges?"

Hannah's attention flew to Brian. She could only see his back and the side of his face, but his trembling was visible across the courtroom. Good. Hannah didn't feel sorry for him. He was a monster.

Brian rose slowly to his feet and cleared his throat. "Yes, sir. I understand the charges."

"How do you plead?"

Brian glanced down at Finch, and Hannah saw uncertainty on the young man's face. *He deserves this. I hope he's terrified.*

The attorney nodded slightly. "Uh..." Brian faced the judge once more. "I, uh...not guilty, sir. On all counts."

"Very well, then." The judge scribbled something again. "This matter will be handed over to trial. We'll have a preliminary hearing next month and then, presuming there's enough evidence, I imagine it will take several months to get the case scheduled on the docket."

Matt cleared his throat. "Your honor, I'd like to make a request."

The judge nodded. "Go ahead."

"The defendant has been convicted of drunk driving several times. He has caused two other accidents while driving drunk, and he was driving with a suspended license at the time of the accident. We are seriously concerned that he will drink and drive again, and that other innocent people will be put in danger as a result." Matt paced casually back toward his spot at the table. He picked up a piece of paper. "The state would like to file a motion to have Mr. Wesley detained until such time as a trial can be arranged."

Finch immediately leaned over and whispered something to Brian, then rose quickly, tugging his tight vest firmly over his stomach. "Your honor, we strongly disagree with the state's request in this matter. Mr. Wesley is in the process of finding a job. He has a wife and young son who need his income and support. In addition, he is attending Alcoholics Anonymous meetings. His vehicle has been impounded by the state; therefore, we do not feel he represents even the remotest risk to society."

The judge was silent for a moment, and Hannah willed him to side with Matt. *Lock him up! I can't see Tom or Alicia. Why should he get to see his family?*

Finally the judge looked at Matt. "As you know, Mr. Bronzan, it would be highly unusual to jail a drunk driving defendant until the time of trial. As Mr. Finch pointed out, the state has apprehended the defendant's vehicle. I don't believe he will be a danger so long as he stays off the road. I'm afraid I'll have to dismiss your motion."

"Very well, your honor." Matt nodded and returned to his seat. Hannah leaned forward, ready to shout out if she had to. Why had Matt given up so easily?

Harold Finch took the cue and snatched a document from the table. "One more thing, your honor. Mr. Wesley has some medical problems relating to the accident. He's in physical therapy at the present time and will be for several months to come. Should this court find enough evidence at the preliminary to hold Mr. Wesley over for trial, I will be filing a motion for continuance until such time as Mr. Wesley is physically able to aid in his defense."

Hannah was on her feet, about to protest, but Carol gently pulled her back down. "Not now, Hannah. This is part of the game. It doesn't mean anything."

Doesn't mean anything? Hannah glared at Finch. How *dare* he ask for a delay so Brian Wesley could receive physical therapy? Tom and Alicia were *dead,* and now the animal that killed them needed time for healing before he could face his punishment? Hannah could hardly believe it. She narrowed her eyes, fighting the rage that welled up within her and threatened to strangle her.

Judge Horowitz raised a wary eyebrow. "Mr. Finch, I am aware of your reputation and your knack for delaying the inevitable. It is my intent to see that this trial makes it into my courtroom as soon as possible."

"Yes, your honor, but—"

"I am not finished, Mr. Finch." Hannah almost jumped up and applauded at Judge Horowitz's firm tone. She clasped her hands together, listening intently as the judge went on. "I understand that in this case the defendant was involved in a serious car accident and because of that, I will grant your motion. This time. You will need to present this court with documentation within one week stating exactly how much 'physical therapy' Mr. Wesley will need. We will go ahead with a preliminary next month. Then, if the case is handed over for trial, I will review Mr. Wesley's medical records before scheduling a trial date."

"Thank you, your honor." Hannah wanted to slap the smug look off of Finch's face as he sat down.

"Nevertheless—" Hannah's attention jerked back to Judge Horowitz. "You will *not* use the judicial system to file motion upon motion in an effort to delay this trial. I understand how delays might benefit your client, but I simply will not have that game played out in my courtroom. Is that understood?"

Finch smiled agreeably. "Absolutely, your honor."

The judge turned to Matt. "I'll notify you about the preliminary."

Matt nodded, and Hannah marveled at how he maintained his composure. He looked unaffected by Finch's victory. The judge dismissed them, and in a matter of seconds Finch and Brian Wesley disappeared.

Matt met Hannah and Carol at the railing. "No surprises here."

Hannah crossed her arms. *No surprises?* "Then why'd you ask the judge to hold Brian in jail until trial?"

The corners of Matt's mouth raised slightly. "It didn't hurt to ask." He thought a moment. "And maybe it set a tone for the seriousness of this case."

Carol stretched. "I liked it. Definitely took the defense by surprise."

Hannah's head was swimming. She had no idea there were so many innuendoes and subtle nuances involved in prosecuting someone who was so obviously guilty. "What about the delay?" She studied Matt's face and found strength from the confidence she saw there.

"It won't be the last."

Her mouth dropped open. "But the judge said he wasn't playing that game."

"The judge wants Finch to think that. Truth is, if Finch can come up with a good reason for a delay, Judge Horowitz won't really have a choice."

Hannah wanted to scream. "Why?"

Carol put a hand on her arm, and Hannah found the touch comforting. "If the judge refuses a continuance, he gives the defense grounds for appeal."

"In other words if we earn a conviction," Matt added, "Finch can come back later and say his client didn't have a fair trial. He was too rushed to defend his client fairly."

Suddenly Hannah understood and her temper flared again. "That isn't fair."

"We're trying to change that, but we have to play by the rules."

Hannah nodded.

"Listen—" Carol turned toward her—"You're probably drained. Let's go grab some lunch." She looked at Matt. "Join us?"

He shook his head. "I'm afraid I have a full afternoon. But please—" he directed his attention to Hannah once more—"call me anytime if you have questions or concerns."

Hannah would have done anything to help this man win the case against Brian Wesley. "I want him locked up, Mr. Bronzan."

Matt nodded. "We all do." He looked from Hannah to Carol, then back again. "I'll contact you when I have a preliminary date. And certainly if I have any information about the trial."

"Thank you." Hannah fiddled with the photo button once more, and Matt leaned closer.

"Your husband and daughter?"

Carol stood by respectfully as Hannah nodded. "Tom and

Alicia…at a family barbecue last summer."

Matt's expression filled with a mixture of compassion and frustration, and Hannah warmed to him even more. He seemed to understand all she'd lost…

He looked up at her and sighed. "A man like Brian Wesley should never have had the chance to get behind the wheel."

Hannah suddenly had to fight the urge to break down and give way to the tears she'd held off all day. Matt Bronzan was indeed her ally, her friend. He would see this case through and win a conviction. She was sure about it. "I know you'll do everything you can."

He moved to gather his documents. "You have my word."

Hannah watched him leave through the same door she'd seen Finch and Brian exit earlier. Then she turned her attention toward Carol. "Lunch sounds great. I want to get involved as soon as possible." She hesitated, and when she spoke again it was with fierce determination. "I need to get involved."

She and Carol left the courtroom, and Hannah felt herself finding purpose as they talked about the basic structure of the MADD organization, how victim impact panels worked, and what would be the best uses of Hannah's time.

Much later that afternoon Hannah finally drove home and pulled into the driveway.

She turned off the ignition, leaned back in the seat, and gazed at the house. Would she ever be able to do this, come home and walk through the door without being haunted by all she'd lost.

All Jenny had lost.

She felt the heat of shame filling her face. Jenny. Hannah blinked back sudden tears as she realized this was the first time since early that morning she'd even remembered her youngest daughter.

Fourteen

This is why I weep and my eyes overflow with tears.

LAMENTATIONS 1:16A

Carol Cummins had been a member of MADD for nearly ten years. Like others in the organization, her involvement wasn't something she had planned. Rather, she wound up an activist after her husband, Ken, was killed at the hands of a drunk driver.

The man who hit her husband had faced no trial. Instead there was a plea bargain, a backstreet handshake of a deal that resulted in the defendant serving three days in jail and paying a nominal fine. Ken had carried no life insurance, except what was provided by his work, so Carol was left with two fatherless babies and piles of unpaid bills.

Carol and Ken were believers, and the church they attended came through on the bills. Still, there remained a sense of injustice and an anger that no brother or sister in Christ could ease. Frustrated and stricken with grief, Carol turned to Mothers Against Drunk Drivers.

At first, she'd had a vague understanding of the group's purpose. Started by a mother whose daughter had been killed by a drunk driver, MADD's goal was threefold: Educate the public about the dangers of drunk driving, reduce the number of drunk driving accidents that occurred each year, and increase the penalties for those convicted of the crime.

Carol immersed herself in the workings of the organization, passing out literature at schools, organizing press conferences, attending trials of numerous drunk drivers, and gathering signatures to help get tougher laws in California. Her mother lived nearby, so she watched Carol's young children, allowing her to devote her efforts to MADD. She worked tirelessly for more than a year.

Then the breakdown occurred.

She had been speaking at a high school, relating the details of Ken's death and informing the students how just one drink could impair a person's ability to drive.

"Whatever you do," she concluded that morning, "never, ever get into a car with someone who's been drinking."

From the back of the auditorium, a boy stood up and pointed proudly at himself. "That counts me out!" He grinned and looked around for approval. A handful of teens sitting near him giggled, and there was a moment of uncomfortable whispering among the crowd.

"You—" Carol spoke clearly into the microphone, looking at the boy through eyes filled with fury—"You are no better... than the animal who killed my husband."

The giggling stopped abruptly, and the boy slithered lower among his group of friends. Then, aware she had somehow crossed a line, Carol excused herself, gathered her notes and posters and photographs, and left the auditorium.

She drove aimlessly, crying and pounding her fist on the steering wheel. She had made peace with Ken's absence. She had found comfort in her relationship with the Lord. So why was she falling apart? Slowly the truth had dawned...

She had never forgiven the man who killed Ken.

On the heels of that first realization came a second, equally devastating awareness: She did not intend to forgive. Not now, not ever.

She had steered her car toward Malibu Canyon that afternoon and found a quiet spot on the beach where she wrestled with God until sundown. Scripture after Scripture came to mind...*Forgive as you have been forgiven....Unless you forgive, you will not be forgiven.* For every verse that the Lord presented, Carol fought and argued: Too much time had passed since the accident....There was no way to find the man....He didn't deserve to be forgiven.

But in that quiet space of beach, between the pounding of waves on the shore, Carol heard God speak. Forgiveness was not a feeling, it was a choice. And before she returned to her mother's house to collect her children that evening, she surrendered to the One who loved her, and she made that choice. She forgave the man completely.

It was as though she was set free in every area, especially in her efforts for MADD. Everything she did from that point on paid off tremendously. Three years after Ken's death, California tightened its drunk driving laws so that a person with a blood alcohol level of .08 or higher—instead of the former .10—was considered legally intoxicated. Still, as rewarding as that was, it was nothing compared with how it had felt to imagine the face of a drunk driver and forgive him.

It was in this that Carol found meaning in life without her beloved husband.

So when she and Hannah Ryan had gone for lunch a week ago, right after the hearing, Carol had admitted to her new friend that she'd gotten involved with MADD because her husband had been killed by a drunk driver. But because she knew the angry place Hannah was in, she refrained from sharing the rest of her story.

Especially the part about forgiveness.

Now she set a scrapbook of news clippings on her desk and checked her watch. Hannah would be there soon, anxious to exact vengeance on Brian Wesley and anyone else who dared drink and drive.

Carol sighed and looked about her office. Most of the volunteers with MADD shared a workstation or made phone calls from small cubicles. Not Carol. She was full-time and had her own office—small, but private. She glanced at a bumper sticker on the back of her office door: "God is bigger than any problem I have."

She knew it was true, but this time she wondered at the position in which God had placed her. Throughout the court proceedings Carol would stick by Hannah's side, representing MADD and providing a very real reminder of the victims. She would accompany Hannah to trial and comfort her when she fell apart.

And yet…there would be more than that. Carol felt it deep inside. *You brought us together for a reason, Lord.*

She wasn't sure about Hannah. It seemed the woman was blaming the Lord for what had happened to her family, and Carol ached for the loneliness Hannah must be feeling. It was one thing to lose your husband and daughter—Carol could relate to that type of pain. But to lose your sweet fellowship with the Lord, too…

Carol closed her eyes and squeezed back tears. *Help me, Lord. Show me what to say to bring her peace and comfort, maybe even forgiveness.*

She reached into her top drawer and retrieved her worn Bible. Many victims who came to seek or offer help at MADD had no faith. There had been dozens of times when the most Carol could offer was to pray for them. But something about Hannah Ryan was different. Carol had a feeling there were deep roots of faith buried beneath the woman's pain and misery.

There was a knock at her door.

Carol set her Bible back in the drawer. "Come in."

Hannah stepped inside and quickly took the only available chair. She looked painfully thin and frazzled. "I spoke with Mr. Bronzan." Hannah folded her hands over the top of her purse and crossed her legs nervously. "The preliminary hearing is scheduled for next month."

Carol studied Hannah. "How does that set with you?"

"Mr. Bronzan doesn't seem bothered by it. He says it'll give him more time to prepare."

There was a pause, and Carol turned the scrapbook so it

faced Hannah. "Well, I'm glad you could come. These are news clippings we've collected over the years. If you look through them, you'll get an idea of what keeps us busy."

Hannah turned a few pages and looked disinterestedly at the articles. After a few seconds, she stopped abruptly. "Look, Carol...I didn't come here to read clippings. I want to get involved." She hesitated. "Could you tell me about the victim impact panels?"

"We generally wait until after the one-year anniversary of an accident before assigning victims to an impact panel."

"Why?"

"Well, usually victims want to wait." Carol hoped Hannah could see compassion in her eyes. "It's very difficult to get up in front of a crowd and talk about the death of someone you loved."

Hannah shifted impatiently. "It's been almost two months. I'm ready to talk about it now."

The room was silent except for the hum of fluorescent lighting above. Finally Carol drew a deep breath. "Hannah, sometimes it seems we're ready when really we need more time. A lot more time."

"I'm not worried about what *I* need."

Carol waited. Hannah obviously needed to talk.

"What I'm saying is, if I can talk to high school kids or PTA mothers or the rotary club, if I can talk to anyone and tell them what happened to Tom and Alicia, maybe I'll actually reach someone. And maybe that one person will decide not to drink and drive and then—" Hannah's voice caught. "Maybe I can spare someone else the heartache of...of what happened to me."

Carol nodded. "Hannah, I want to talk to you about something off the subject." She fidgeted with a pencil. "At lunch after the hearing you told me you'd known Tom all your life, grew up with him and went to church with him. I began wondering about your faith."

Hannah's expression was suddenly guarded. "My faith is a personal matter."

O Lord, help me...help me reach her. "I know, I'm sorry. It's just...well, I'm a believer, too. I wondered if there was any certain way you'd like me to pray for you?"

"No." Hannah sighed. "I don't see any point, really."

Carol was silent, encouraging Hannah to continue.

"After the accident—" Hannah seemed to steady herself—"I was very mad at God for letting Tom and Alicia die. Now..." She paused. "Now I think I've changed my mind."

"You're not mad at God?" Carol was confused.

"No." Hannah shook her head decidedly. "I don't believe in God."

Carol felt as if she'd been punched in the stomach. *Help me, Lord. What can I say now*? The answer seemed almost audible: *Lamentations. Give her Lamentations.* Carol considered the grief-filled message of that book of the Bible. *No, Lord. Not Lamentations. She needs something more hopeful.*

She cleared her throat. "I think that's normal—to doubt God—after what you've gone through." Carol folded her hands neatly on her organized desk. *Not Lamentations, Lord.* "Maybe if you read the Bible—"

She broke off at the flash of anger on Hannah's face. Hannah's next words chilled the small room.

"I don't need God anymore. And I certainly don't need the Bible. If God does exist, he let me down when I needed him most." Her voice was like industrial steel. "It's easier now just to let go of the whole idea."

Give me something for her, Lord. Please. Again the answer came: *Lamentations. Give her Lamentations.*

"I was thinking maybe Philippians," Carol said. *Certainly not Lamentations.* "Philippians 4, the whole chapter. Maybe that would help you find the Lord's peace and...I don't know, maybe help you remember what's true and good."

Hannah's eyes became even icier. "I appreciate your efforts,

Carol. But I'm not interested. My belief in God died the same day Tom and Alicia did. If I can't have them, I don't want him either."

Carol nodded. She'd said enough. Probably too much. Hannah had clearly reached her limit.

Give her Lamentations.

Carol ignored the urging. "I tell you what, let's go to the video room." She stood and Hannah did the same. "You can watch a tape of one of our recent victim impact panels and get a feel for how it works. Then if you still think you're ready, maybe we could get you started."

Hannah seemed relieved, and Carol wondered if it was because she'd been given the green light for appearing on a victim impact panel or because Carol had stopped talking about the Lord.

The video was powerful—one moving testimony after another poured out of people who had lost loved ones to drunk drivers. Hannah took a tissue from a box at the center of the room. Carol could hear her sniffling softly and saw her dabbing at her eyes every few minutes.

When the film ended, Hannah blew her nose and leveled her gaze at Carol. She hesitated for only a moment. "I'm ready. When can I begin?"

Carol located a folder filled with informational material regarding the impact panels and a questionnaire designed to help victims organize their thoughts before presenting them in a public setting.

"Read through these and give me a call if you're still interested. If you really think you're ready, we could get you on a panel sometime in the next four weeks." Carol paused. "Your goal will be very specific, Hannah. With Matt Bronzan going for a first-degree murder conviction, we need to saturate the public with the idea. Maybe if the notion isn't so foreign, a jury will be more likely to convict."

"I understand." Hannah thanked Carol, gathered her things,

and headed for the front door with Carol close behind. Suddenly Hannah stopped and turned back to her. For the first time that morning, Carol saw vulnerability in the other woman's eyes.

"The preliminary hearing?" Hannah spoke softly.

Carol nodded. "I'll be there." Impulsively she closed the distance between them, hugging Hannah close.

Carol was ten years older than Hannah and decades wiser, but in that instant she felt closer to this broken woman than to anyone she knew. "I'm here for you, Hannah. Call me...if you need anything."

Hannah left and Carol sat down at her desk again. She had lost interest in the day's work, too burdened by Hannah's choice to abandon God. Once more she reached into her top drawer and pulled out her Bible. *Lamentations? What hope was there in that?* She flipped through the pages of the Old Testament until she found the book, then scanned the pages. Her eyes fell on a verse in the second chapter: *"My eyes fail from weeping, I am in torment within, my heart is poured out on the ground because my people are destroyed."*

A chill passed over her. The verse described Hannah perfectly. *But it doesn't offer any hope, Lord. None at all.* She read on.

"He has besieged me and surrounded me with bitterness and hardship. He has made me dwell in darkness like those long dead. He has walled me in so I cannot escape; he has weighed me down with chains."

Carol shook her head helplessly. *I don't understand, Lord. Such a dark word from you. And for what? Why?* She looked down and saw there was more.

"Even when I call out or cry for help, he shuts out my prayer....Like a bear lying in wait, like a lion hiding, he dragged me from the path and mangled me and left me without help....He pierced my heart with arrows from his quiver."

Terrible stuff. How could anyone say such things about God? Carol wanted to flip a few hundred pages to the right and read something comforting in Psalms, but she felt compelled to continue.

"I have been deprived of peace; I have forgotten what prosperity is. So I say, 'My splendor is gone and all that I had hoped from the L*ORD....'"*

This was going nowhere. Carol blew out a breath of frustration and tried to remember what she had learned about Lamentations. Maybe there was some kind of introduction at the beginning of the book. She flipped back a few pages. Yes, there it was.

"The prophet Jeremiah wept over the awful devastation of Jerusalem and the terrible slaughter of human life that he saw around him." Carol pondered this for a moment. *But how can such a story help Hannah regain her belief in you, Father?*

She read on: *"No book is more intense in expressing grief than this one."*

The introduction continued, outlining the practical significance of Jeremiah's laments—and then what Carol saw made her breath catch in her throat: *"Even though we may begin with lamenting, we must always end with repentance—as Jeremiah does in the book of Lamentations."*

Tears filled her eyes. It was her very own life...word for word.

Carol felt her throat constrict, and gradually she gave way to a torrent of sobs. Suddenly the memory of Ken was so real she could almost touch him. No wonder God had given her Lamentations. She ran the words over again in her mind. *"No book is more intense in expressing grief than this one."*

She had suffered greatly when Ken died; she had lamented in much the same way Jeremiah had over the city of Jerusalem. At first her grieving caused her to have a bitter, hard heart. Anger consumed her, and there had been no peace until she, like Jeremiah, reached a place of repentance, a heart of forgiveness.

Now it made sense! That was why the Lord had wanted her

to share this particular book with Hannah. Carol had passed the way of Jerusalem.

Now it was Hannah's turn.

Fifteen

The Lord is like an enemy…

LAMENTATIONS 2:5A

The MADD questionnaire was harder than Hannah expected.

"Describe loved ones who were killed by a drunk driver." Hannah pictured her husband and daughter, let memories run through her mind, and then began to write. *Tom Ryan, husband, father, memory-maker. Alicia Ryan, daughter, sister, friend to all.*

Hannah squirmed in her seat and reached for a tissue. Her sinuses were clear for a change, and she didn't feel like crying. But tears came anyway, trickling down the side of her face like some kind of permanent leak. She read the next question. "Where were your loved ones going when the accident occurred." Hannah moved the pen across the page. *Home.*

The next section was more difficult. "Describe what you would like people to remember about your loved ones." Hannah sighed and wiped her eyes. Maybe Carol was right. Maybe she wasn't ready for this.

She looked up and saw that the morning had grown cloudy. A gloomy shadow filled the house, bringing a chill over the place where she sat at the dining room table. She picked up the steaming mug beside her and breathed in the smell of apple-cinnamon tea. Carefully she lifted it to her lips and sipped slowly, allowing the hot liquid to soothe her raspy throat.

In the past she might have been listening to David Jeremiah or some other Christian artist as she worked. But she had packed those CDs away a week ago. No point in singing about God if she didn't believe in him.

She reached behind her and flicked on the chandelier lights above the table. Soon the days would grow shorter, and then the holidays would be upon them. The first Thanksgiving without Tom and Alicia. The first Christmas. Hannah tried not to think about it as she studied the questionnaire once more.

When the phone rang, Hannah sighed and set down her pen. Reaching across the table she picked up the cordless phone and pushed the blinking button. "Hello?" Again she was struck by how foreign her voice sounded—dead, toneless, emotionless...like someone who had lost the ability to feel.

"Mrs. Ryan? This is Mary Stelpstra, principal at West Hills Junior High."

Hannah felt her heart sink. Something was wrong with Jenny. "Yes?"

The woman hesitated. "Mrs. Ryan, I think we need to set up a meeting to discuss Jenny."

Not now. "What about her?"

"Well, it isn't something I wish to discuss over the phone. Are you available this morning? Say around eleven?"

Hannah stared at the unfinished questionnaire. Eleven gave her an hour to complete it. "Yes. I can be there."

"Fine. I'll meet you in my office."

Hannah hung up and sighed. When would the nightmare ever end? She returned to the form and saw that it gave her just five lines to write everything she hoped people would remember about Tom and Alicia. *Five lines?*

She moved on to the next question. "What do you think about people who drink and drive." This one was easy. Hannah picked up her pen and scribbled furiously. *Drunk drivers are selfish animals, killers with no regard for human life. They are the worst sort of people on earth.*

She reread her answer and thought of Brian Wesley, sitting nervously beside Harold Finch and hoping for a delay so his injuries could heal before he might have to face a jury.

She clenched her teeth and threw the pen across the room.

The questionnaire wasn't making things better! Even if she *could* reach someone, save someone from drinking and driving, it would never bring back Tom and Alicia. She began to moan and it became a cry that filled the empty rooms of their home. "*Tom!* I can't do it. I can't do this without you!"

She laid her head down on her folded arms, and the tears came hard. She missed Tom and Alicia so badly she thought she might suffocate.

Wiping at her eyes, she glanced at the clock. 10:45. With a start she stood up, blew her nose, and grabbed her car keys. It was time to meet with Mary Stelpstra.

West Hills Junior High sat adjacent to the high school, and neither building was like other stark, stucco-covered Los Angeles schools. Instead these two structures were bright, cream-colored with blue trim, and anchored in a sea of grass. Behind the school were rolling hills and trees and a picturesque football stadium. It looked more like a private university than a public junior high school.

This was where Alicia had earned the right to be head cheerleader and captain of the drama team. Here at West Hills Junior High, Jenny had run track, showing signs of being a promising sprinter. Of course, that was before the accident. As were the times when, after school hours, the Ryans had used the school's expansive green fields for informal Frisbee contests and softball games. It was a beautiful school—and it was filled with too many memories to count.

Hannah ignored all of it.

She strode stiffly toward the principal's office and signed in. In less than a minute, Mary Stelpstra swept into the waiting area and ushered her into her office. She shut the door behind them. "Please, Mrs. Ryan, sit down."

Hannah sat. Ever since the accident it seemed people were forever telling her to sit down. As if whatever news was about to be shared was simply too difficult to hear while standing. Hannah knew she must look terrible, her eyes tear-stained, her makeup smeared...but she was tired, and she didn't care what people thought of her. Right now she cared only for her youngest daughter. "You said there was something you wanted to discuss about Jenny?"

"First let me say on behalf of West Hills Junior High, we are so sorry about your loss, Mrs. Ryan." The principal had the polished sound of a school administrator. She continued. "Our staff, our students, we all loved Alicia very much. We feel her absence sorely."

Tears again. Hannah reached for a tissue and dabbed at the corners of her eyes. She waited for the principal to continue.

"Lately, though, we've spent more time worrying about Jenny. She's missed a lot of school, Mrs. Ryan."

Hannah relaxed slightly. *Was that all? Jenny's attendance?* "She hasn't felt good. I don't think it's anything physical, really..."

Mrs. Stelpstra nodded. "I understand. Actually, her teachers are working with her, helping her with missed assignments. Her absences are to be expected after what she's gone through."

Hannah was relieved, but curious. If they were willing to work with Jenny on her absences, then why the meeting? "I guess I'm not quite following you, Mrs. Stelpstra."

The principal sighed and pulled a folded piece of notebook paper from her desk drawer. "I didn't ask you in because of Jenny's absences." She paused and unfolded the paper, glancing at it and then handing it to Hannah. "I asked you in because of this."

"What is it?"

"Something Jenny wrote in English class yesterday. It's quite alarming, really, Mrs. Ryan. And I wanted to be sure you knew about it."

Hannah felt her stomach turn and noticed her heart had skidded into an unrecognizable beat. She was suddenly terrified as she reached for the paper, her hands trembling. She recognized Jenny's handwriting and read the title scrawled across the top of the page: *"The Best Place to Live."*

Hannah looked at Mrs. Stelpstra curiously. "Was this an assignment?"

"Yes. Jenny's composition teacher asked the class to write an essay on any place in the world where they'd like to live."

Hannah returned her gaze to Jenny's paper and began to read.

"I can really only think of one place where I want to live, and it's not here. Last summer my dad and sister died in a car accident. A bunch of people tried to save them, but they died anyway. Now it's just me and my mom.

"Mom's busy most of the time with court stuff. She wants to make sure the man who hit our car will go to jail for what he did to my dad and sister. I don't know. I don't really care about him. My mom does, though. She doesn't care about anything else. Not even me."

Hannah closed her eyes. *Of course I care about you, Jenny.* She forced herself to keep reading.

"I spend a lot of time in my room now, and I think maybe I'm having anxiety attacks. I read about them once in a book. I get sweaty, and it feels like I can't breathe, like maybe I'm going to die. Sometimes this makes me scared but most of the time it doesn't. I sort of wish it would happen.

"I feel like I'm in some kind of holding place. Kinda like life ended when the accident happened, and now there's just this waiting time. I still believe in God, but my mom doesn't. I heard her telling someone from church the other day that she stopped believing in God when Dad and Alicia died. I don't blame her. I even thought about it. About letting go of my faith. But I can't. I believe Dad and Alicia are in heaven, and I want more than anything in the world to be with them."

Hannah stopped and clutched the paper tightly, closing her eyes against the tears that were coming faster now. *I'm right about there being no God, I know I am.* But she was shocked to learn that Jenny had found out. It was something she should have shared with the girl herself. *This can't be happening. It keeps getting worse, Tom. I can't do this by myself.*

Mrs. Stelpstra handed her another tissue and waited patiently. Hannah wiped her eyes, steadied herself, and continued reading.

"Sometimes that's all I think about. Dying and stuff. How I can get from here to there so we can be together again. Mom wouldn't care. It would be easier for her if I was gone. Then she'd have more time for all her stuff with MADD, and she wouldn't have to wonder why I don't feel good and how come I'm not going to school. I don't know. I've thought about it a lot. The different ways and stuff. But nothing seems easy, and I just roll around in bed at night wondering about it. I can't sleep, that's for sure. I miss Dad and Alicia so much. If there was an easy way to do it, I would. I would in a heartbeat.

"Because of all the places I would like to live, the only one I can think of right now is heaven."

Hannah set the paper down on the principal's desk as if it were contaminated. "I...I don't know what to say. It's like a nightmare that never ends."

The principal nodded. "I understand."

"It keeps getting worse, you know?"

Mrs. Stelpstra's voice was filled with kindness. "We see this kind of thing when one of our students has suffered a severe trauma." She paused. "Have you noticed anything unusual about Jenny's behavior? Anything that would lead you to believe she might...actually consider acting on this?"

Hannah blinked. Surely Mrs. Stelpstra didn't mean..."You mean killing herself?" Hannah couldn't believe she was having this conversation.

"That is what Jenny seems to be alluding to, Mrs. Ryan, don't you think?"

Hannah glanced back at the paper lying on the desk before her. "Yes. I guess so. But Jenny would never really do such a thing, Mrs. Stelpstra. I know my daughter."

"You must remember, Mrs. Ryan, things are completely different now than they were before the accident. Obviously Jenny never would have considered suicide before. She was a very happy, very carefree girl, secure in herself and her place in your family. Now...well, it seems she feels somewhat forgotten."

Hannah's defenses reared. "Wait a minute! I haven't done anything to make Jenny feel this way. We're both suffering... and doing the best we can to get through this...this...."

"I'm not trying to accuse—"

"Then don't!" Hannah drew a slow breath and tried to regain control. "Jenny's right. I've been busy with MADD. I don't want Tom's and Alicia's deaths to be for nothing."

"And Jenny?"

"I spend as much time with her as possible. When she wants to be alone, I let her."

Mrs. Stelpstra paused and retrieved Jenny's paper once more. She glanced over it again in silence. "Some of the letters are smeared...I think maybe she was crying when she wrote it."

Hannah sighed. "We've both been doing a lot of crying. That doesn't mean she's suicidal."

The principal hesitated. "I'm worried about her, Mrs. Ryan."

"I'm worried about her, too, about *both* of us." Hannah leaned forward. Why didn't this woman understand what she was going through? "I'm worried about us finding a way through this pain so we can have a relationship again. I'm worried about whether the drunk driver who did this to us will be locked up or whether he'll walk free." She paused and leveled her gaze at the woman across from her. "But I am *not* worried about Jenny killing herself."

"This paper—"

"That paper is Jenny's way of trying to get attention." Hannah was angry and no longer trying to hide it. "She would never, ever, not in a million years think of killing herself. She knows better than that."

Mrs. Stelpstra set the paper down and leaned back in her

chair. She considered Hannah thoughtfully. "Well, I suppose you know her better than we do."

"Of course I do." Hannah stood, and almost as an afterthought she grabbed Jenny's paper from the desk and folded it, placing it roughly inside her purse. She turned her attention again toward the principal. "Thank you for looking out for my daughter, Mrs. Stelpstra. I even thank you for taking the time to call me in today and share your concerns. But please, don't contact social services or start worrying about needing a suicide counselor." Hannah searched for the right words. "We've suffered the worst ordeal of our lives, and it's nowhere near over. I think we can expect Jenny to be a little upset."

Mrs. Stelpstra nodded and seemed resigned to let the issue go. "I didn't mean to make things worse, Mrs. Ryan. I just thought you should know."

Hannah reached out and shook the woman's hand. "Thank you. Let me know if you have any other reason for concern. But for now I think this needs to be between me and Jenny. I'll talk with her, but again, don't worry about her paper. She doesn't mean anything by it."

Hannah walked from the office, keeping an iron control on the trembling that wanted to overtake her. As she made her way back to the car she faltered. Jenny? Suicidal? Could there possibly be merit to Mary Stelpstra's warning? What if Jenny really didn't want to live? What if she had actually thought about taking her own life?

Impossible. She shook her head firmly and forced herself to keep walking. *Ridiculous.* She knew Jenny too well. They had been through a lot these past months, but Jenny was too stable to consider suicide.

She would talk to Jenny about the paper. But she would not worry about it.

By the time she got home, she had nearly erased the meeting with the principal from her mind. She was focusing again on the questionnaire Carol Cummins had given her. She would finish it this afternoon and get it over to the MADD office. That way she would still have time to read through the other information before dinner. It didn't matter how difficult the material was. She would need every available day to educate the public about the truth....Drunk driving really was murder. If they got the message out now, she was certain Matt Bronzan would win a conviction.

She climbed out of the car and headed for the house. One day she'd have to talk to Jenny about the letter. But not now. Not when there were so many more pressing issues at hand. Jenny's problems would simply have to wait.

Sixteen

The L*ORD determined to tear down the wall around the Daughter of Zion.*

LAMENTATIONS 2:8A

On a sunny November morning, an hour before the preliminary hearing in the case of *The People v Brian Wesley*, Jenny arrived at school and headed for the library. She walked inside and peered over a bookshelf. Good. The library was empty except for the librarian, and she was immersed in a magazine. Jenny had only ten minutes before her first class, so she would have to work quickly. She padded quietly toward the computer section.

She had tried to work things out on her own. She had prayed, and in the last few weeks she had even tried talking to her mother. It wasn't her mom's fault. She was just too busy to notice how Jenny was feeling, and Jenny didn't blame her.

She sat down at a row of computer screens and logged on. At least her mother had made some sort of effort recently, asking her questions about how she was doing and whether she was coping. Jenny waited for the welcome screen to appear. Her mother's questions had made her wonder if maybe she had seen the essay, but it didn't really matter. Mom was too busy working for MADD to be worried. Between Carol Cummins, Matt Bronzan, and Brian Wesley, Jenny knew she was the last person on her mother's mind.

The Internet screen popped up, and Jenny clicked the search button. Next she typed three words, "Suicide AND methods AND quick." Glancing nervously over her shoulder, she saw that no one was watching. Then she clicked *OK*.

A list of web pages appeared, and Jenny's eyes grew wide. More than sixteen hundred sites! She scanned the first few and saw that many of them offered advice to troubled people and listed the ways a person could determine if their loved one truly was suicidal. Jenny scrolled past those sites. Her eyes fell on one. "Suicide and Assisted Suicide—It's Nobody's Business if You Do." She clicked it, and a colorful page appeared bearing the same headline. The opening paragraph doubled Jenny's confidence.

"There can be nothing more fundamental concerning individual freedom than this: Our bodies and our lives belong to nobody but ourselves. Our bodies do not belong to our friends, our families, and especially not to the state."

Jenny read on as the web page detailed the ineffectiveness of laws against suicide and then commented on a book that detailed the most successful methods of suicide.

The library was still quiet, but Jenny knew the bell would ring soon, and students would file in. She read quickly.

"With every suicide attempt, there is a chance the effort will fail and the person will wind up a vegetable. For that reason it is better to use fail-safe methods. The problem then, however, is that these methods either hurt—as in hanging or slitting wrists—or they're messy—bullets, jumping off buildings. Sleeping pills are very uncertain because they often cause vomiting before enough of the drug is absorbed into the blood. Therefore, the best technique involves taking the perfect combination of certain pills or inhaling carbon monoxide. When done right, this will lead to a quiet, painless death."

Jenny felt a pit form in her stomach. She hadn't expected the web page to be so graphic. She glanced around quickly and swallowed twice. Her eyes returned to the computer screen and fell on a quotation set apart from the rest of the text. It was a Bible verse. Proverbs 31:6: *"Give strong drink unto him that is ready to perish."*

Jenny sat back in her chair and considered the verse. According to the web page, this proved that God found value in suicide. The idea didn't really match up with what Jenny had been raised to believe...but if God didn't have a problem with suicide, then maybe it really was the best idea.

She felt her confidence grow as she closed the page and scanned the list once more. She found the title of the suicide book from the site and clicked it, but to gain access she had to register for a death service. With a shiver, Jenny closed it and looked for another. Two minutes before the bell rang.

She scrolled past several generic sites until she found one marked, "Untitled." She opened it, and a page appeared with an index of suicide-related topics that people had posted over the past week. She opened one marked, "The Correct Methods." It was written by a paramedic. Jenny began reading:

"I have been a paramedic for seven years, so I have personally responded to many suicides. If you are going to commit suicide, you need to take some things into consideration. First, if you care about your family or whoever you live with, you will do it outside or somewhere easy to clean. Second, if you really want to die, DO NOT call 911. Third, leave a note so they have some idea what made you want to die. (it will help the survivors with the grieving process)."

The paramedic went on to discuss specific drug overdoses and other methods and why they would not work. He detailed drugs and drug combinations that would counteract each other, nullifying the intended fatal effect. He also described ways a paramedic could help an unconscious person after a drug overdose so that they would not die. Jenny was spellbound.

"Hanging is a mistake. Every hanging I have been to, the person dropped less than two feet; therefore instead of breaking your neck at the C1-C2 level (cervical vertebrae referred to as a "hangman's fracture"), you strangulate instead. Effective but lots of misery...I know many effective ways, but I am in the job of saving lives so I can't help ya there."

Jenny sighed. She'd thought for sure the article would tell her how she could do it right. Well, at least she knew what not to do. The bell rang, and Jenny clicked the print button. Three pages rolled out of the printer, and Jenny grabbed them, closed down the web page, and signed off the Internet. Some of the information had been good. Jenny ran over it again as she headed for class. *Don't leave a mess, don't call 911, and don't forget to leave a note.*

She felt a rush of relief and for the first time since the accident was filled with something that felt like hope. The Internet was wonderful. Sixteen hundred web pages on suicide. She could get more information tomorrow and the day after that. Pretty soon she would know enough to make a plan, and then maybe next month or the month after that, she would carry it out...finish what should have taken place in the accident.

Before entering her geometry class, Jenny stuffed the printed pages into her notebook. For an instant she remembered how it had felt to be Jenny Ryan before the accident. That Jenny would never have considered killing herself and she shuddered. In some ways the whole notion of suicide scared her. It was crazy. She would have to consider her options carefully.

If only things had gone like they should have...if only she'd died in the accident. Her mother probably wished she had. With all the appointments and lawyers and court dates to deal with, Jenny was only in the way. She replayed the moments before the accident and frowned. How had she survived? Oh, sure, everyone said it was a miracle. Jenny thought it was a curse. She had seen the pictures. She should be dead.

Well, soon she would be, thanks to all that information on the Internet.

And then she and Daddy and Alicia could be together forever. She closed her eyes and pictured it. A never-ending camping trip in the sky.

Brian Wesley rubbed his sweaty palms together and glanced nervously at the courtroom clock. He was early. The preliminary hearing didn't start for thirty minutes.

A bailiff walked up. "You here for *State v Martinez?*"

Brian shook his head and swatted at a stray lock of hair as it fell over his eyes. "No. *State v Wesley.*" The bailiff nodded and walked away.

Life had become a sea of legal maneuverings, and Brian wondered if he'd ever find a way out. If the judge thought they had enough evidence—and Brian's attorney, Harold Finch, thought they did—Brian knew he might serve most of his life in prison. Sweat broke out across his brow. He'd heard about prison once. One of the older guys at the shop did time when he was in his twenties. He'd entertain the technicians with war stories and nuggets of wisdom. Brian remembered some of them. *You don't want to go there, man, but if you do, look out for the soap. If three or more guys come at you, man, just take off running. Oh, and lift something for the belt. Fork, rock, something. Don't go unarmed. Guys die that way all the time. Especially in the shower.*

Brian felt sick to his stomach. How had everything gone so wrong?

The back door opened and Brian turned. A woman entered. She was in her forties, maybe, with a file under one arm and a book in the other. *Too many lawyers in the world.* Brian watched as she scanned the courtroom, locked eyes with his, and then walked toward him.

"I'm not with the Martinez case." Brian fidgeted with his ear lobe. What was she staring at?

"Me neither." She sat down, looking like she had no intention of going anywhere.

"Look, lady, I already have an attorney."

"I'm not an attorney." She turned her body slightly so that she faced him.

Brian sank lower in his seat and fixed his gaze straight ahead. "I gave at the office."

The woman seemed unaffected by his sarcasm. She cleared her throat. "I'm not looking for donations, Mr. Wesley."

He turned to her. "How do you know my name?"

"I know all about you. I know about the accident, about the man and his daughter who were killed. I know about the surviving daughter, and how even though her wounds are healed, a part of her will always be broken because of what you did. I know about the dead man's wife, too."

Brian stared ahead and said nothing.

"You've caused a lot of pain, Mr. Wesley. And whatever is decided here will certainly be what you deserve."

"I don't need to listen to this—" Brian started to stand.

"Wait, Mr. Wesley." The woman reached out and gently took his wrist. He caught her look and paused in surprise. There was nothing condemning in the gaze fixed on him.

Slowly he sat down. "What do you want?"

The woman sighed. "I know your type. You are an alcoholic, so you have driven drunk all of your life. You should have been more responsible, and you deserve punishment."

Brian waited impatiently. "I don't get—"

"Let me finish, Mr. Wesley." She paused a moment. "You have done an awful, devastating thing, but in your heart of hearts I know you did not set out that afternoon to murder two people. You did not intend to destroy that woman's family."

Brian blinked. No. No, he'd never intended that.

"You see, Mr. Wesley, whatever they decide to do with you in this courtroom, you will never truly be free the way you are."

"What's that supposed to mean?"

The woman looked back at the door as though she were waiting for someone to appear. She seemed to be in a hurry when she continued. "Do you know Jesus?"

"Jesus Christ? You mean, like, am I religious or something?"

The woman nodded.

Here we go. "I don't do the church thing, lady."

She smiled again, and he was struck by what he saw in her eyes...calm...*peace.* More peace than Brian had ever seen. Something inside him ached at the sight of it. Why couldn't he feel that? What did it take to look that way...feel that way?

She went on. "I'm not talking about a church thing. I'm talking about a relationship with Jesus Christ. Whether you're in prison or out, you need a savior, Mr. Wesley. And even though you don't do the church thing, Jesus loves you. He loves you, and he's waiting to forgive you."

"I didn't do anything to him." Brian heard the hard edge in his voice.

"Yes, you did." Again, no condemnation. She spoke it like it was a simple fact. "You nailed him to a cross with your sins. He went there to pay the price for what you did that afternoon by choosing to drink and drive, destroy that family."

Brian couldn't think of a comeback.

"Here—" the woman handed Brian a hardcover book—"It's a Bible. Read the gospel of John, and see what you can learn about Jesus."

Brian stared at it. *New International Version Study Bible* was written across the front cover. "Uh...no thanks, lady." He glanced at the courtroom clock. "I need my attorney. Not a Bible."

"Take it. It's yours." She checked the back door once more. "God's given me this job, Mr. Wesley. Jesus loves you. The Bible says so. Read it and see for yourself."

Brian reached for the Bible and felt its heaviness in his hands. "I'm not going to read it."

She smiled sadly. "I'll be praying that you change your mind. Believe me, it won't matter what your punishment is, you'll never be free until you learn the secret of that book."

Brian watched her stand, but before she turned to leave she stopped. "Oh, I'll be checking in on you now and then, Mr. Wesley. Take care."

She moved down the row and disappeared out the back door of the courtroom. Brian glanced down at the Bible in his hand and considered tossing it in the trash can at the back of the courtroom. Instead he opened the front cover and saw writing and a phone number.

"Mr. Wesley...remember, the keys to your prison cell lay between the covers of this book. Call me if you have any questions."

Hannah found a seat in the courtroom ten minutes before the preliminary hearing and noticed Carol Cummins heading toward her.

"Did I miss anything?" Carol gave Hannah's hand a quick squeeze.

"No. Mr. Bronzan is not even here yet." Hannah kept her voice to a whisper.

"Is Jenny coming?"

Hannah scowled. "She had to be at school early for a project or something."

Carol hesitated. "How's she doing?"

"It's hard to tell. She spends a lot of time in her room. Whenever I try to talk to her she gets hard, almost angry at me."

"Have you thought about sending her to a counselor?"

Hannah blinked at the question. A counselor? Of course not. Jenny wasn't sick, for heaven's sake. "No. We never thought much of counselors."

There was a pause. "That's because you had the Wonderful Counselor."

Hannah felt something like a rock in her stomach. "Yeah, well, on that note maybe we *should* look someone up."

Carol's voice softened. "You still have the Wonderful Counselor, Hannah. You just need to go to him."

Hannah sighed. Why couldn't Carol leave this alone? Hadn't she made her feelings clear? "I told you I'm finished with that. Clearly God, if he even exists, did not want to spend a lifetime walking by my side. He left me, remember? From here on out I'm on my own. And so is Jenny."

Carol reached into her notebook and took out a slip of paper. It was covered with scribbled notes. "I wrote these down for you." Carol handed the paper over. "Just some Bible references. I know it sounds crazy, but they're all from Lamentations. I really related to them. Maybe sometime when you have a moment to yourself..."

Hannah took the paper because to refuse would have been rude. She folded it and tucked it into a pocket in her purse, then cocked her head to one side and looked at Carol. Sadness filled her at the sincerity on her friend's face. "I appreciate what you're trying to do, Carol. Really. But it isn't going to work. When I'm alone and nothing makes the hurt go away, I don't go to the Bible. How could I believe anything it says after what happened?" Carol didn't have an answer for that. But then, Hannah hadn't expected one. "I go to my photo albums. Pictures of me and Tom when we were kids, wedding photos, and...and pictures of my little girl—" Hannah's voice broke and she bit her lip. When would the pain stop?

Carol placed a gentle hand on her shoulder. "I'm sorry. I'm not trying to make things worse."

Hannah swallowed, but it took her a moment to speak. "I know. You mean well. But please, no more talking about God and the Bible and how much my old church friends could help. I have you, after all—" she smiled through teary eyes—"and Mr. Bronzan. That's enough for now."

The preliminary hearing was underway.

Matt had given a thorough rundown of the state's evidence, and in response, Harold Finch had tried to convince the judge that his client may not have been legally drunk at the time of the collision. He delivered a long-winded dissertation explaining how it takes so many minutes per drink for alcohol to permeate the bloodstream and how it was possible Brian Wesley's senses had not yet been impaired when the crash occurred.

At first Hannah had been alarmed but from where she and Carol were sitting, she could see the calm in Matt's face, and her concern eased. When Finch finished, the judge ordered a five-minute break, and Hannah watched Matt rise and turn his attention toward her. He smiled and made his way through a small gate in the railing to where she and Carol sat. There was something tender in his eyes, and Hannah had the oddest feeling that somehow this man could relate to her pain.

Carol motioned toward the lobby. "I have to make a few phone calls. I'll be back." She stood up and left as Matt approached and leaned against the back of one of the seats. He nodded a greeting to Hannah. "Glad you could make it."

"I told you, Mr. Bronzan, I'll be here every time there's a hearing." Hannah stared at the back of Brian Wesley's head for a moment and felt her anger rising. "I want him locked up as much as you do."

"Call me Matt."

She met his gaze and smiled a smile that never reached her eyes. "Okay, Matt. Call me Hannah. By the way, you did great up there."

"This is only the beginning. It'll get a lot more heated once we get to trial."

Hannah hesitated. "Then...you're not worried about the... the..."

Matt shook his head. "The argument about Wesley's blood alcohol level? No. I had a feeling we'd get that from Harold Finch. It's a new defense in these cases."

Hannah nodded uncertainly. There was so much involved. She didn't know what she'd do if it weren't for Matt.

The judge returned to his chair, and Matt put a hand on her shoulder. "Carol tells me you're ready to do victim impact panels."

Hannah nodded and closed her eyes. For an instant she saw Tom and Alicia, lifeless, as they'd looked lying on stretchers that day in the hospital. She opened her eyes and the image disappeared. "Yes, we're planning to do one next month. Sometime before Thanksgiving."

"Let's get together before then so we can compare notes. You know, come at this thing from the same angle. It's crucial that everyone who hears you or reads what you say understands about the first-degree murder charge. If we're going to break ground here, we'll need the public's support." He checked his watch. "I've got an appointment right after this hearing, but maybe next week?"

"Absolutely. Whenever you're ready."

"Okay, we'll talk soon." He turned and made his way back to the table.

The judge rapped his gavel once more. "I see that all parties are again present." He gazed about the courtroom. "I've had time to review the preliminary evidence on both sides, and I have determined there is ample evidence to hold the defendant, Brian Wesley, over for trial in each of the charges he faces."

Hannah felt a surge of relief. Matt had been right.

The judge continued. "I've checked the docket and—"

Harold Finch was on his feet. "Your honor, I would like the court to remember that Mr. Wesley is currently undergoing therapy for injuries he received in the accident. We would like—"

"Sit down, Mr. Finch," the judge interrupted. Finch looked surprised as he obeyed the judge's order. The judge glared at him. "You have already informed the court of Mr. Wesley's injuries and his need for therapy. Now, if you'll let me continue—" he faced Matt—"The holidays are fast approaching, and since we must allow time for...Mr. Wesley's *healing* process, I have set a trial date of May 14."

Six months. Hannah hung her head and looked to Matt for his reaction, but as always, he appeared calm and confident. He kept one hand in his pocket, and Hannah was struck by how professional he looked. The jurors were going to love him. "That works fine for the state, your honor."

She glanced at Harold Finch. He was trying to contain a

smile and failing badly. "That should work for my client, as well, your honor. We'll certainly file a motion if Mr. Wesley is still in therapy at that time and needs a continuance."

The judge raised a single eyebrow. "Mr. Finch, let me say something again, in case you have forgotten. This court is well aware of your reputation to delay trials, presumably for the benefit of your clients and to the detriment of the memories of many witnesses. You will not be permitted to play that game in this courtroom. See to it that your client is either healed or transferable by wheel chair. The trial date is May14."

Finch looked as if he might object but changed his mind. "Yes, your honor."

"If that's all, then I'd like to call attention to the next matter on the docket..."

Matt gathered his things, and Hannah watched as Finch and Brian Wesley stood and left the courtroom.

She stared, frowning. What was that tucked into the crook of Brian's arm? Her eyes widened, and fury washed over her as she nudged Carol. "Look at that." She nodded toward the defendant. "It looks like he's carrying a Bible."

Carol looked in the same direction as she stood and swung her purse over her shoulder. "Hard to tell from here. Could be."

Hannah kept her gaze locked on the book in Brian's hands. "I can't believe it! I think it really is." Hannah clenched her teeth, fighting off the powerful urge to throw something at the man. "He probably got it from one of those prison ministry people. Bunch of do-gooders. I wish they'd just leave well enough alone. There's no point witnessing to a man like that. There's no way God—if there *is* a God—would let a worm like Brian Wesley hang around heaven."

Seventeen

Together they wasted away.

LAMENTATIONS 2:8B

Brian got back to Jackson's apartment that afternoon and hid the Bible under his pillow. Wouldn't want Jackson to see it and think he'd freaked out and gone religious or something. The afternoon passed, and that night Jackson brought home a case of Miller, which they shared while talking about the trial.

"Dude, I don't know. I smell trouble this time." Jackson's forehead creased with genuine concern as he crushed an empty aluminum can in his hand and popped open another cold one.

"Tell me about it." Brian turned his can bottom-side-up and guzzled the last bit of beer before grabbing another. "Man, I'm looking at a lot of years behind bars."

Jackson belched loudly. "You've got that expensive dude, what's his name?

Brian laughed, but it sounded hollow even to him. "Finch. Harold Finch."

"That's right. Hey, man, who's paying for that dude?"

"My old man. Called him up in Virginia, and he wired me the bucks. He's loaded."

"Cool." Jackson took several long swigs and set his can down hard. "I thought your old man died."

"Yeah. . . ." Images of Red Wesley, sprawled out drunk on the sofa flashed in his mind. Brian swished a mouthful of the cool, amber liquid around in his mouth and swallowed hard. "Died a long time ago. The money comes from my stepdad, man. He figures I'll stay away if he sends me money. Especially when I'm in trouble."

Jackson thought about that a moment. "That's cool. How loaded is he?"

"Not that loaded. I definitely have to hold a job, man, if that's what you're thinking."

Jackson nodded. "Well, hey, dude, at least you got old Finchman. You might get off yet." He motioned toward the half empty Miller carton. "Hey, man, toss me another, will you? The night's young!"

When Brian opened his eyes the next morning, he had no memory of how or when he finally went to bed. He knew he and Jackson had drunk into the night, but exactly how long, he couldn't say.

He shifted, groaning, and felt something hard beneath him. He tossed and turned and tried to get back to sleep, but there seemed to be a pile of bricks directly under his head.

When he could no longer tolerate the discomfort, he finally reached around near his pillow. His hand found something hard and heavy, and he pulled it out. His eyes widened.

"Oh, man…" The Bible. He'd put it there the day before.

He stared at it and sat up in bed, wincing at the wave of nausea that washed over him. He leaned against the headboard and drew a deep breath. What did he want with a Bible, anyway? He opened the front cover again.

The lady's words were haunting. *"The keys to your prison cell lay between the covers of this book."*

Man. No one talked like that in the bars. Even Carla didn't talk like that. She griped and complained about his drinking. She ragged on him as often as she could. But she never talked about the keys to his prison cell.

Now, through the haze of an incredible hangover, Brian understood the lady's words. She wasn't talking about a cage made of bars and brick. She was talking about drinking. The prison of alcoholism.

As he studied what she'd written, he noticed something else. A few letters and some numbers written underneath her message. It looked strange, like a foreign code of some kind: *Phil. 4:13.* Brian studied it for a moment and then a realization hit. Maybe it was a Bible story or something. Words from the Bible. Yeah, that must be it.

He'd never held a Bible in his hands, let alone read one. But as he lay tangled between the sweat-soaked sheets that morning, his head pounding, he turned the pages gently until he reached the index. He scanned the list of chapters and found dozens of names he'd never heard of.

Then he saw it: *Philippians.* Hey, it was the closest thing to what she'd written. He checked the reference beside it and turned to the corresponding page. Now, what the heck was 4:13? He scanned the text and realized that occasionally there were large numbers that seemed to divide the writing into sections. He found section 4, and noticed that every sentence or two there were other, smaller numbers. His eyes darted past 11 and 12, and finally settled on 13. He read the words slowly: *"I can do everything through him who gives me strength."*

Brian read the words over and over again until his head began to clear and tears filled his eyes. *"I can do everything through him who gives me strength."*

The keys.

Tears spilled onto the delicate pages, and he carefully closed the Bible.

Now if only he could learn how to use them.

The young women of Jerusalem have bowed their heads to the ground.

LAMENTATIONS 2:10B

The call came three weeks later, early one morning, while she was studying the book of Romans. By that time, although she still prayed for Brian Wesley every day, she had decided he was not going to call. He had probably tossed the Bible first chance he had and never gave it another thought. That did not discourage her; she had seen the same rejection from a number of drunk drivers, and she knew she could not change their behavior. God did not ask her to be successful, just faithful. She would continue to pray for change in drunk drivers' hearts as long as she had life.

Her phone rang and she answered on the second ring. "Hello?"

Silence.

"Hello? Is someone there?"

Dimly, she heard the shaky sound of someone either crying or breathing heavy in the background. "Uh…it's…it's me. Brian Wesley. You know from, uh, court the other day."

She closed her eyes. Thank you, Lord. "Yes, Brian, I remember. Have you been reading the Bible?" She hoped her voice sounded compassionate. She could tell this was difficult for him.

"No. Well, I mean, I looked at it or whatever, but…no. I haven't read it. No."

She waited, but he didn't go on. "Is there something I can do for you, Brian. Would you like to pray?"

"No! Nothing like that. Just, well...maybe if you had time...could you, like, you know, meet me somewhere? Just to talk."

The woman considered her schedule. She had planned to meet her daughter for lunch, but she could postpone it. For a moment she considered suggesting a nearby park, but then she caught herself. She didn't know the man, and although she cared deeply for his soul, she did not want to put herself in any danger. "Tell you what, I'm pretty booked today, but why don't you meet me at Church on the Way tomorrow morning?"

"Church where?"

"Church on the Way." She gave him directions. "I'll be sitting in the front row. We can talk in my office."

She listened while Brian drew a deep, shaky breath, then released it slowly. "I guess."

He hung up abruptly, and she replayed the conversation in her mind. There had been so many who had not called after her initial contact....

Then she hung her head and prayed.

The days were growing colder and Jenny sorted through her sweaters. They were too small. This happened every year, and when it did, she and Alicia would rummage through Alicia's closet. Whatever was too small would be passed on to Jenny.

A chill passed over Jenny, and she rubbed her bare arms. She knew exactly which one of Alicia's sweaters she wanted, and she padded softly into her sister's room.

It had been a week since Jenny had stepped into Alicia's room. It was still exactly as her older sister had left it before the camping trip. Her bed was made and because of Jenny's efforts that day when they'd been packing, the floor was neat. An invitation to a birthday party still stood erect on Alicia's nightstand. A list of scribbled dates and phone numbers lay on a scrap piece of paper beside her phone. Her walls still held poster pictures, one of Amy Grant and another with two cuddly puppies peering over the top of a fallen log. "God help me over the troubles of today," the poster read. Jenny allowed her eyes to linger on the message before turning to Alicia's closet.

A hint of White Shoulders perfume lingered on her sister's clothes, and Jenny closed her eyes. She ached inside for the sound of her sister's voice, for the touch of her hands as they wove her hair into a French braid. All Jenny's life she'd been part of a pair of sisters...without Alicia she felt lost beyond anything she could have imagined. She remembered a time two years ago when Alicia had gone to summer camp with their church. She'd been gone five days, and the afternoon she returned Jenny had waited outside for her to pull up in the church van.

"Jenny!" Alicia had squealed as she jumped from the van, her sleeping bag flying behind her.

Jenny remembered how they'd hugged in the front yard until they were laughing so hard they had fallen in a heap on the grass. "I missed you," Alicia had said when she caught her breath. "Next time you come, too."

Jenny opened her eyes. The sweaters looked much better on Alicia than they did on the hangers. She sorted through the rack twice, but the sweater she wanted was missing. It was a navy pullover with two white horizontal stripes that circled it just above the waist. It had been Alicia's favorite. Mom would know where it was.

"Mom!" Her mother had an appointment at MADD that morning, or maybe with the prosecutor or someone else at the court building. Something. She was always busy these days.

She heard her mother approaching and watched as she peeked into the room.

"What are you doing?" Hannah's hands flew to her hips.

Jenny felt tears sting at her eyes at her mother's mean tone. "I'm looking for a sweater, if that's all right with you."

"In Alicia's closet?" Her mother came a few steps closer and seemed to survey Alicia's clothes, to make sure nothing was missing.

Jenny rolled her eyes. "Yes, mother. In case you forgot, Alicia and I always shared clothes. When she outgrew her stuff, she gave it to me."

Her mother sighed. "I know. I'm sorry. I just thought we should leave things the way they are in here." She tried to pull Jenny into a hug.

Tears spilled onto Jenny's cheeks as she jerked away. "Don't touch me."

"Jenny—"

"No! You don't love me at all, do you?"

"Now, Jenny, that isn't fair. I just don't want—"

"Stop! I know what you want. You want this room to be a shrine. You and I can tiptoe around the house pretending to be alive, but really we're just existing in some kind of…I don't know, some kind of tomb or something."

"It's not like that, Jenny, I—"

"Forget it!" Jenny cut her off, but a whisper of fear ran over her. Was that shrill and trembling voice really hers? "All I wanted was to wear one of Alicia's sweaters. The blue one with the white stripes. I'm cold, okay? Alicia would have wanted me to wear it. But it's…it's missing!" Jenny's tears gave way to sobs, and she felt rooted in place, unable to move as the sobs washed over her.

Hannah slumped back against the poster of the two puppies, stared at the ceiling, and began to cry. "I'm so sorry, Jenny. I do love you. I don't…want you to think just because Alicia's gone…"

"Spare me, Mother, please!" Jenny shook her head. "I don't want to hear it."

Her mother's shoulders shook as she hunched against the wall, her eyes tightly closed. When she opened them, her words were barely a whisper. "The sweater's at Kerry's. Next door."

Jenny hesitated for a moment, wondering if she should thank her mother, or hug her, or say something to mend the distance that continued to grow between them. In the end, she just walked away, wiping her tears as she pushed past her mother.

Kerry and Kim Basil had been friends with Alicia and Jenny most of their lives. Kerry and Alicia were the same age, as were Kim and Jenny. Until the accident, Kim had been one of Jenny's best friends, but now, like so many girls Jenny knew, Kim seemed to be avoiding her.

Jenny knocked on the Basils' front door and waited until the girls' mother answered. She was a heavyset woman who always seemed to have something home-baked in the oven. "Jenny!" The woman wiped her hands on her apron and pulled her into a warm hug. "We've missed seeing you around here."

Jenny savored the feel of a mother's arms around her, but she didn't feel like making small talk, so she pulled away, thankful the woman hadn't noticed her tear-stained face. "Mrs. Basil, Kerry borrowed one of Alicia's sweaters last spring, the blue one with the white stripes. Would you care if I go up and get it?"

"No, dear, go right ahead. The girls are already gone. They take the bus, you know."

Jenny nodded. She used to take the bus, too. Before the accident. Now her mother drove her to school, usually in an uncomfortable silence. Jenny started for the stairs. "Thanks, Mrs. Basil."

"Try the closet shelf," the woman called after her.

"Okay."

Kerry and Kim shared a room, and Jenny had almost never seen it clean. Today was no exception. Jenny glanced around, then headed toward the closet. When they were younger, the four girls had played dress-up and Barbies and a dozen board games in this room. Jenny narrowed her eyes and studied the stacks of sweaters on the closet top shelf. She spotted Alicia's sweater almost immediately and took it gently from where it lay near the bottom of a stack.

She held it up, and she could see Alicia, grinning and challenging her to a foot race at Winter Camp last year. Jenny looked back to see if Mrs. Basil had followed her up. Then she took the arms of the sweater and pulled them around her neck. She held the sweater that way, desperately wishing that Alicia still lived inside it. Her fingers brushed over the soft blue cotton, and she felt the tears again. She folded the sweater gently and tucked it under her arm.

As she turned to leave, Jenny's eyes fell on a folded piece of paper atop Kim's dresser. Kim's name was scrawled across the front, and Jenny recognized the writing. Stacy Carson. Before the accident, the three of them had been inseparable. Jenny, Kim, and Stacy—they'd been a threesome that rarely quarreled, unlike so many other girls who hung out in trios.

Jenny moved closer to the dresser, checking the doorway once more for Mrs. Basil. She studied the paper and saw it was lined. A note. From Stacy to Kim. Curiosity got the better of her, and she lifted it gently from the dresser. She knew what she was doing was wrong, but she couldn't stop herself. The paper unfolded in her hands and she began to read:

"*Hey Kimmie, it's me. Can you believe it? I finished the math test early!!! You should be so lucky. It's not as hard as I thought. Anyway, I talked to Leezer yesterday, and she says she wants me and you over for the sleepover this weekend. Yowwsa! I can't wait. Oh, yeah. She said something about Jenny, but I told her what we talked about. You know, that we feel bad for her and everything—everyone misses Alicia. But Jenny's different now. She's not the same, and the rest of us have to accept it. I told her what we decided. You know, that Jenny really wasn't our friend anymore. She was fine about it. She said she thought Jenny was acting weird, too. She said that happens sometimes. Anyway, Mr. Glintz is staring at me so I better stop. Can't wait for Leezer's party. Love ya! Stace.*"

Jenny felt her blood run cold. These were her best friends.

Writing about a party at Lisa Hanson's house, and she wasn't invited. Was she really that different? She folded the note and set it back on the dresser, then made her way downstairs, outside, and back up to her own bedroom.

She threw herself on the bed and gave way to the flood of tears drowning her heart. Staring at the wall that separated her room from Alicia's, she sobbed loudly, unconcerned about her mother's reaction or the need to be strong for the sake of appearance. Alicia's blue-and-white sweater remained clutched tightly in her arms while the minutes passed. Eventually her weeping stopped.

"Jenny?" It was her mother. Jenny heard the door open.

"What?" She rolled over to face her mother and reached for a tissue.

"It's time to go. I can't be late, honey. I have an appointment at the—"

"I don't care where your appointment is." Jenny thought about staying home, about telling her mother she simply wasn't up to another day at school...another six hours of watching people who once laughed and talked with her now whisper and stare at her in pity...six hours around Kim and Stacy, who were only pretending to be her friends.

No one cared about her anymore. Not her mother, not her friends. No one from youth group had called in weeks. Even God didn't care, at least it didn't seem like it. She sighed and stared at the ceiling.

"Jenny, I won't have one of your temper tantrums today. You need to get out of bed and get ready. We have to leave in five minutes."

Jenny closed her eyes and remembered the Internet. Hope stirred within her at the thought. She needed Daddy and Alicia so badly, and today she had a break after lunch. Maybe she could find out more online information. She stood up slowly, blew her nose and stretched. "You don't need to watch me, Mother. I'll be down in a few minutes."

She moved quickly, suddenly motivated, her mind tracing the electronic paths she would take later that day when she resumed the most important task of her life.

Finding a way to join Daddy and Alicia.

Nineteen

City bus No. 2315 rattled and rumbled east on Vanowen Street, part of a steady flow of morning traffic past Shoup and Topanga Canyon and on into Van Nuys. The bus would take Brian part of the way, and he planned to walk the rest. The brakes screeched as the bus pulled over and Brian got out.

He still couldn't believe he was doing this.

He walked three blocks until he saw it: Church on the Way. *Strange name.* He stood there staring at the building, doubting himself. What was the point in making the journey in the first place?

Brian thought about the man at the AA meeting who'd talked about Christ this and Jesus that. Man! What was he doing here, anyway? He wasn't some religious freak. He didn't need anyone's help. This was *his* problem, *his* mess to figure out. He glanced about and saw a graffiti-covered bench nearby.

What am I doing here?

He turned away from the church, sat down on the bench, and dropped his head into his hands, massaging his temples. Why had she given him the stupid Bible anyway?

The words he'd read came back to him: *"I can do everything through him who gives me strength."* There was something so appealing about the thought. Brian blinked and stared blankly at the traffic whizzing past. He had never been very strong. Not even in high school. His friends could always benchpress more than he.

Somehow he knew the Bible words weren't talking about physical strength, anyway. The more he said the words over in his mind, the more he knew what they meant. Inner strength. The strength to say no when Jackson brought home a sixer of brews. Brian sighed. He'd never had that kind of strength.

The traffic continued, and Brian thought the flow of cars was a lot like his life. The drunken nights and hungover mornings would continue in a never-ending series unless he found the guts to stand up, walk into that church, and stop it. The keys to his prison cell. He gazed over his shoulder, then slowly stood.

With a steadying breath he made his way to the front door and stepped inside. For the first time in his life, in a way that he could not explain and did not feel responsible for, he felt an overwhelming surge of hope.

Hannah climbed out of her car and wandered past a hot dog vendor, down a winding sidewalk shaded by elm trees, and into the back entrance of the Superior Court Building. By now, she moved with confidence. She knew where to go, and she quickly made her way to Matt Bronzan's office. He was expecting her.

His door was open and she peered inside. A subtle hint of men's cologne hung in the air, and Hannah felt herself relax. There was something reassuring about the man, something that went beyond his role as prosecutor.

Matt saw her and returned his sleek, black pen to its upright holder. "Come in." He rose and motioned for her to sit down. "I was just doing busywork."

Hannah settled into the chair and gazed out his window. There was silence for a moment. "It's a beautiful day."

Santa Ana winds had kicked up, and a warm breeze had lifted the veil of smog from the valley. The Santa Monica Mountains were crystal clear, as if all Hannah had to do was reach out the window and she could run her finger over their sharp edges.

Matt followed her gaze. "A last burst of summer."

Hannah nodded and turned her attention back to him.

"Seems funny, with Thanksgiving a week away."

They studied each other and Matt spoke first. "Do you have plans?"

Images of the fight she'd had with Jenny earlier that morning flashed in her mind. "No. Not really."

"It's early, still."

"Yes." Hannah's eyes narrowed and she studied her golden wedding band.

"But you think you're ready for victim impact panels?" Matt spoke slowly and he seemed at ease in her presence.

Hannah nodded. "It'll matter more now than later. Yes…I'm ready."

"Carol's told you about them, how they work?"

"She'll put me with two other victims and assign us to public speaking events. High schools, civic meetings, that sort of thing."

"Right…and you'll have to tell the story, the details about what happened."

Hannah gazed down at her hands again. "I can do that."

"People want to hear about the accident, the loss you've suffered. But then it's up to you to close the discussion with a sales pitch."

Hannah cocked her head. "Sales pitch?"

"Yes. People are drawn by tragedy. They want to know how it happened and why, how they can avoid that sort of thing in their own lives."

Hannah remembered a time when she'd been drawn to such tragedies, too. Back when they only happened to other people.

Matt inhaled deeply. "That's when you talk about first-degree murder."

"Should I say that's what you're seeking in this case?"

Matt nodded. "People will want to know what's happening to the defendant, what penalty he's facing. Tell them he's going to be tried for first-degree murder. Then tell them a little bit about first-degree murder and how it relates to drunk driving."

Matt slid a sheet of paper across the desk to Hannah. "I wrote out some notes for you. Just a description of the charge—murder with the intent to kill—and the reasons some drunk drivers fit the bill."

Hannah glanced over the sheet, noting key phrases: several priors, previous accidents, alcohol training, driving without a license. "These are the same things you said at the preliminary hearing last month."

"Right. It's important that we keep the message short and consistent."

"Because of the audience?"

"Partly. See, the media covers these victim impact panels. Same theory. People are drawn by tragedy, so the papers and news stations send reporters and take your story to the public."

"So we're really reaching more than just the people in the audience?" Hannah thought she was beginning to understand. "We're reaching the people at home, too. Right?"

"We're reaching jurors, Hannah. It's that simple." Matt leaned back and crossed his legs. "You sell the audience on murder-one, you sell the jurors. At least that's the plan."

Hannah sighed and stared out the window again. "Sometimes I can't believe I'm here." She turned to Matt again. "You know, making plans for victim impact panels and discussing murder-one with a prosecutor."

Matt smiled sadly. "Hey, come on, now. We prosecutors aren't all that bad."

Their eyes connected. "I'll never think of you as bad, Matt. You're the good guy...my only hope right now."

Matt shifted in his chair uneasily. "Hannah, don't take this wrong, but aren't you a Christian?"

Oh no, not again. She was growing so weary of this conversation. She folded her arms tightly in front of her. "I was once. A long time ago."

"I thought so." He turned his attention to a small photograph tucked into the frame of his desk calendar. She couldn't quite make out the faces, but she felt her heart constrict when he ran a finger over the image. It must be someone he loved. A girlfriend?

"I'm a believer. Did you know that?"

She shrugged. "I think Carol mentioned something about it." She was no longer enjoying their conversation, and she glanced at her watch. It was time to go.

Matt watched the emotions washing over Hannah's face. This wasn't easy for her. "You don't want to talk about it, do you?"

"No." Hannah fidgeted with her wedding ring. "Ever since the accident…I've had a hard time believing God really exists." She paused. "We went to church, we tithed, gave to the poor, obeyed his word."

"And look where it got you." Matt understood perfectly. Far better than he'd ever wanted to.

"Right." Hannah looked away. "I wouldn't want to serve that kind of God, even if he were real."

Matt nodded. "I remember feeling that way."

Hannah looked up, surprised.

"It was a long time ago."

It was time. Time to tell Hannah why this all meant so much to him. He glanced down at the photo, at the laughing couple smiling up at him…

He removed the photo from the frame on his desk calendar and held it out to her. "This was my best friend Shawn. And his girlfriend Victoria."

Hannah leaned closer and studied the photo. Matt swallowed hard. It hurt to remember his friends when they were young and full of life. Hannah lifted her gaze curiously and waited for him to explain.

Help me, Lord. Help me tell this so she'll understand. He wasn't quite sure why it mattered so much.

He only knew it did.

"Shawn was my best friend growing up. We played ball together and went off to college together. Victoria came into the picture a couple years after that."

Matt gazed at the picture, and then, as though a flood-gate had been removed, Victoria was there before him. And Shawn. He could see the three of them making their way across the campus at Loyola Marymount University, carefree and brimming with enthusiasm, planning study sessions and beach trips, Saturday pizza parties and whatever basketball game was coming up.

Shawn Bottmeiller had been Matt's best friend since high school. They'd both been forwards on the Westlake basketball team. Off the court, Shawn was a slow-moving, handsome dreamer with little drive or ambition, who imagined himself with a career in the NBA. He was lanky with a pretty shot and as much natural basketball talent as anyone who'd ever graced the court at Westlake High.

Matt had been everything Shawn was not. He was a blur of motion, filling out college applications and scholarship forms two years before high school graduation. Matt did not have Shawn's striking looks, but he was fiercely athletic, and hours in the weight room had given him a chiseled body. What he lacked in talent and natural skills, he made up for with hard work and dedication. Matt was a realist, and from the time he could spell his name he'd known he would be a lawyer one day.

"A crummy old lawyer?" Shawn would ask sometimes when they were breathless and sweaty after a game. "Why would ya wanna go and do some fool thing like that. This is the life, man. Hoops, hoops, and more hoops. And girls, of course."

"Someone has to take care of the bad guys," Matt would tell him.

"Oh, I see. You'll be one of those poor, struggling lawyers

who wastes his life getting criminals locked up just to watch 'em get out on some early release program. That oughta be real satisfying, man."

"Okay, how 'bout you, Shawn? Gonna live at home all your life?"

"I—" Shawn paused for effect—"will be playing hoop in the NBA, stopping by your dreary little law office when I'm feeling charitable and giving you free tickets to watch me play."

"Oh, okay. Is there a plan B?"

Shawn looked insulted. "Plan B? Matt, you've lost faith in me, man. I'm still growing, you know. Gonna be six-foot-eight, and then they'll be banging down my door asking me to play for them."

"Do the words 'hard work' mean anything to you? 'Cause that's what it's going to take to get that kind of attention. I for one plan to work my tail off to make state."

"Hoop and work." Shawn looked as if he'd gotten a sudden taste of lemon. "The words don't go together in my book. Hoops are too much fun, man."

Before their junior year, Matt drew up a workout schedule he believed would give them the edge when basketball season came. "Three hundred jump shots a day, two hundred free throws—" Matt was excited as he explained the routine to Shawn—"lifting for an hour, then sprints. And dribbling. We take the ball with us wherever we go. By the time school starts, we'll be better than any forwards in the league. State championship, man. All the way!"

Shawn looked at him, arched one eyebrow, and dropped himself into a beanbag chair. "During summer vacation? You must be missing a screw, my man. Summer is for catching rays and watching babes."

Matt shrugged. "Suit yourself. But don't whine when I make all-state. Then the recruiters will be knocking down *my* door, and you'll find yourself scrambling for a junior college team who'll let you walk on."

"Moi, me, the great one." Shawn laughed. "They'll beg me to play for them, man."

"We'll see."

Matt made time for the beach that summer, but only after he had completed his daily basketball regime. When state playoffs came, Matt led the way averaging thirty-two points per game and eight rebounds. Shawn skated by averaging nine points and three boards, but Matt's prediction had been accurate. He was selected first team all-state, while Shawn received only an honorable mention.

The next year Matt, who had sprouted to six-foot-four, accepted a scholarship to play basketball at Loyola Marymount University. Shawn was forced to attend a junior college. Two years later he transferred to Loyola Marymount, where the closest he got to a basketball court was his seat in the student section. Still, he rarely missed one of Matt's games.

Midway through their junior year, Matt and Shawn took an advanced English comp class and there, sitting in the first row of the large auditorium, was Victoria Stevens.

Being friends for so much of their lives, Matt and Shawn had reached an agreement regarding girls: No girl came between them. Period. They might both find a girl attractive, but if one of them had the opportunity to date her, the other celebrated the victory. There was no room for jealousy in their friendship.

Victoria Stevens was the first girl who threatened that. Everyone on campus knew about her. She was more beautiful than any girl they'd ever seen and utterly unattainable. For the first month, they filed into class early to get a better look at her, but neither of them could figure out a way to meet her.

Then one day they were leaving class after the bell when providence placed Victoria right in front of them. Drawing on his once considerable defensive basketball skills, Shawn slipped his finger under her elbow and dislodged her books. Matt watched the whole thing and saw Victoria's befuddled expression as her books mysteriously tumbled to the ground. Shawn was there at her side as she stopped to pick them up.

"Oh, hey, let me get those for you." He flashed her his famous grin and she met his gaze. Then just as quickly she looked beyond him to Matt, and her eyes lit up.

"Hey, aren't you on the basketball team?"

"Yeah." Matt smiled uncomfortably. Shawn had made the first move. He needed to back off.

Shawn cleared his throat. "Yes, and I taught him everything he knows." He dribbled an imaginary ball, pulled up near Victoria, and shot an invisible three-pointer. He remained motionless for a moment, then raised both hands signifying that the basket was good. "Nothing but net."

Victoria cast a questioning glance at him, but she couldn't hold back her laugh. Shawn and Victoria began dating, and soon they were seeing each other exclusively. On occasion Matt would catch her looking at him longer than she needed, but there was never any reason for him to doubt her affection for Shawn.

One afternoon the three of them were studying when Shawn had to leave for an appointment with his counselor.

"You don't say much, Matt," Victoria said when they were alone.

He shrugged. "We're supposed to be studying."

She tilted her head pensively. "But you work so hard. School, basketball. Don't you ever just want to have fun?"

Matt considered her thoughtfully. "I have fun being the best."

"You and Shawn are so different. He's so, oh, I don't know...goofy, I guess. I wonder what he'll do in life, you know?"

"I think he's going to law school with me." Matt grinned.

Victoria looked surprised. "Really. I didn't know he wanted to be a lawyer."

"I don't know that, either, but he seems to follow me

around." Matt stifled a laugh. He didn't want to get too friendly with Victoria while Shawn was gone.

"Sometimes I wonder what would have happened if *you'd* knocked my books down and not him." She was no longer smiling.

"So you knew about that, huh? He used to do that on the court all the time. Come up behind some poor guy, nudge the ball, and take off without ever looking back." Matt looked down at the textbook and doodled with a single finger.

Victoria lowered her head and caught his eyes again. "Don't you wonder, Matt?"

He drew a breath and released it slowly. "Look, Victoria, you're a beautiful girl, and I'd be lying if I told you I wasn't attracted to you. But you're dating Shawn, and that's about as far as my wondering usually goes."

Victoria nodded once. "Okay. Shawn's a lot of fun and I enjoy dating him. But still..."

Matt looked up once more.

She met his look. "One day...who knows?"

Matt held her gaze a moment longer, then exhaled dramatically, leaned over, and tapped the textbook opened up in front of her.

"So, what is it you're studying anyway?"

Shawn and Victoria continued dating, and her presence in his life seemed to change him. He became more responsible, more aware of the future and its looming reality. While Matt dated occasionally, for the most part he was too busy studying and playing basketball. He spent his free time with Shawn and Victoria, and the threesome became as integral a part of his college life as the school's hardwood gymnasium floor and stuffy locker room.

Before graduation Shawn followed Matt's lead and applied for admission to Pepperdine Law School. His father worked in the movie industry, and money would not be a problem. Funds weren't as easily abundant for Matt's family, but his grades, student involvement, and application essays were such that he received a full scholarship.

Shawn burst into Matt's dormitory when he received the news. "I'm in, man! You and me. Law school. Conquering the bad guys."

Matt stood up and slapped his friend on the back and the two embraced. "Don't worry. It'll be even better than the NBA."

Shawn grinned. "Now, I doubt that, man. Seriously. But hey, this calls for some kind of celebration."

"Yeah, let's plan something. The three of us."

Shawn pulled a small velvet box from his pocket. "I'm seeing Victoria tonight."

Matt glanced from the box to his friend. "What's this?"

Shawn opened it, and there inside lay a glimmering diamond solitaire engagement ring. "Tonight's the night, man."

Matt's momentary disappointment turned quickly to elation for his best friend. "Hey, that's great. She have any idea?"

"Oh, you know the female gender." Shawn flashed his famous grin. "Probably been expecting it for months."

"You sure you're ready?"

Shawn grew suddenly serious. "I've never loved anyone like I love her, man. She's my life."

That night, Shawn and Victoria went to dinner at Gladstones on the beach. They ate steak and lobster and later walked on the sandy strip beneath the restaurant where Shawn got down on one knee and proposed. Matt got the whole story later, all the details—including how Victoria grew teary-eyed and accepted.

The two were walking hand-in-hand along Pacific Coast Highway looking for a less crowded stretch of beach when a Volkswagon careened out of control and struck them from behind. Shawn was knocked onto the shoulder of the roadway, scraped but not seriously hurt; Victoria took the full force of the hit. She flew twenty feet in the air before landing on the pavement, motionless. Shawn scrambled to her side and cradled her broken body, begging her to hang on. He was still holding her that way, sobbing, when paramedics arrived and told him what he already knew. She was dead.

The driver of the Volkswagon had been drunk.

Matt did his best to help Shawn get over her death. They started law school and tried to keep busy. But they were both devastated.

The drunk driver was given ten days in prison and a five hundred dollar fine. He'd been convicted once before, but he was young, and the judge thought he'd be better off taking alcohol education courses than wasting away in a prison. Shawn hated the man, could have gladly killed him given the chance. But none of it would bring back Victoria, and as the one-year anniversary of her death grew near, Shawn dropped two of his classes and spent hours sitting on the grassy Pepperdine hillside overlooking Malibu Beach.

Matt had tried talking to him, tried to help him work through it. But all to no avail. On the one-year anniversary of Victoria's death, Shawn Bottmeiller took a gun from his parents' closet and wrote two letters—one to his parents expressing his love and sorrow for what he was about to do; the other to the man who killed Victoria. In it he expressed his anger and hatred, his inability to forgive the man for what he'd done.

"When you killed her, you killed my dreams. You killed me. Today I'll finish what you tried to do a year ago."

Then he drove to the beach, walked down to the sandy strip where he had proposed to Victoria a year earlier, and shot himself in the head.

Matt, always the realist, always the achiever, doubled his efforts at law school and determined that Victoria's and Shawn's deaths would not be in vain. He finished law school top of his class and took a job at the district attorney's office in Los Angeles. In the process, he met Sgt. John Miller and saw something different about him. When he learned about the man's faith, Matt began attending a Bible-believing Christian church, and a decade after the deaths of Shawn and Victoria, he gave his life to the Lord.

Then, when he had enough experience, he began specializing in one type of case, the only type that really mattered to him.

Cases against drunk drivers.

That had been eighteen years earlier, but now as he watched Hannah Ryan studying the photo of his two friends, it felt as if it had happened yesterday.

Hannah looked from the photo to Matt, and was surprised at the grief she saw on his face.

"Do your friends live here?"

Matt blinked, as though the question startled him, then shook his head slowly. "No." His gaze drifted to the photo, then back to Hannah. "The day Shawn asked Victoria to marry him, she was killed by a drunk driver."

Shock swept over Hannah, and she had to resist the strong urge to go to Matt, to put her arm around him and comfort him. No wonder she'd always felt such understanding from him.

But he wasn't finished.

"One year later, on the anniversary of Victoria's death—" Matt's voice was ragged with sorrow—"Shawn killed himself."

Hannah sat slowly back in her seat. Like her, Matt had lost so much. Because of men like Brian Wesley...the kind of men Matt had worked so long and so hard to prosecute....

"And so you spend your life prosecuting drunk drivers...."

"As many as I can."

She could think of nothing to say. This was the compassion she felt from Matt, the understanding. He knew her pain, knew it personally.

Matt drew a deep breath. "After that, I doubted God for a while, too." He lifted his eyes from the picture, and Hannah was struck at the peace she saw in his gaze. "But then I found out the truth. God's ways are not our ways. This world is a fallen place, and bad things do happen to good people. They even happen to Christians. Truth is, I couldn't have made it through without his strength."

Tears stung at Hannah's eyes, but she refused to give in to them. What Matt was saying had the strong ring of truth to it, but she couldn't accept it. Couldn't believe God was real...that he'd done nothing but watch as her family was ripped apart...as Matt's dearest friends were destroyed....

Matt tucked the photograph back into the frame. "I know you don't believe it, Hannah. But God loves you. Even now."

She didn't reply to that. Instead, she nodded. "It must help...prosecuting them."

But he slowly shook his head. "Not really. The law is still pretty loose where drunk drivers are concerned. That's why this is such a big deal. We'll be making history if we win this one."

Hannah glanced at Matt's left hand and couldn't hold back the question. "You're not married, are you?"

Matt shook his head. "Never had time. I've spent ten years right here, increasing public awareness, waiting for the day when we could get it into the murder-one category."

Good. This was safe ground. This was the kind of conversation she wanted to focus on. "Now here we are."

Matt smiled, and again she saw understanding in his expression. "Not yet. We still have a lot of work to do."

"And that's where the victim impact panels come in."

"Exactly. If we can fill this room with a dozen jurors who are familiar with the idea that killing someone in a drunk driving accident can be murder one...well, that'll make my job that much easier."

Hannah nodded. Her role was clearly defined and she was thankful. She would do this, working for the memories of Tom and Alicia, alongside Matt Bronzan, who had his own memories to fight for. They would win their murder-one conviction and then, in their own ways, they could get on with life.

"Hannah..." Matt's voice interrupted her thoughts. "Do you mind if I pray for you?"

Her heart constricted. "Now?" She desperately wanted to avoid this, but she didn't want to hurt him.

Matt smiled again. "No, not now. But throughout the trial. I don't know..." He paused. "You've lost so much already. I guess I can't imagine losing all that and God, too."

Hannah glanced out the window and waited. After a long while she finally spoke. "You can pray, Matt." She looked at him and felt tears well up in her eyes. "But everything I want, I've already lost."

"I know. I'm not trying to change your feelings. But Hannah, my door's open. Anytime you want to talk, if you need anything, I'm here. And I will be praying."

She believed him, and it gave her a sense of comfort. And hope. She stood up then. "I'd better get going. I have to meet Carol."

Matt rose and reached for her hand. "Thanks for coming." He looked suddenly self-conscious. "I probably told you more than I should have. But I thought you should know where I'm coming from. What I believe, what drives me."

She nodded. She was grateful he had done so...and she felt a closeness to him that warmed her. With a start she realized she was holding his hand a bit too long, so she let go and crossed her arms. "Thank you, Matt. Maybe after the trial we can put this thing behind us—both of us. Unless there's another delay, of course."

"I'm not worried about it." Matt slipped his hands in his pockets. "More time means more days to convince jurors that Brian Wesley is guilty of murder-one."

Hannah tilted her head. "Some people would think that doesn't sound very Christian."

"My obligation to forgive doesn't erase my obligation to provide punishment. Without rules and penalties, this country would have fallen apart decades ago. I like to think that my job is actually quite Christian. Further questions?" He grinned.

Hannah studied him. "You certainly can argue."

"Only when I believe in the cause." He moved around his desk and opened his office door a bit wider. "Let's stay in touch. I want to know how the first victim-impact panel goes, okay?"

Hannah nodded and thanked him again.

As she walked slowly back to her car, she considered Matt and Carol, their strong beliefs, and the role they played in this, her season of grief. She sighed. The world was filled with non-Christians, atheists even. All her life she had shared classrooms and committees and airplanes with them. She drove behind them on freeways, shocked at the boldness of their Darwinian fish and the mockery they made of the Christian world view. They seemed to rule Hollywood, the media, and the voting polls. They had elected Clinton, after all. Millions of them walked the United States.

Yet in this, her darkest hour, when she herself had finally come to join the ranks of nonbelievers, she found herself relying completely on the strengths and abilities of two very devout Christians.

My eyes fail from weeping, I am in torment within,
my heart is poured out on the ground
because my people are destroyed.

LAMENTATIONS 2:11A

The sun was sinking slowly behind the mountains, and Hannah wondered if theirs was the only house in America that didn't smell of turkey and gravy and home-baked pumpkin pies. She had asked Jenny about celebrating Thanksgiving and got little response. Now it was four o'clock in the afternoon, and Hannah had just about finished making a small platter of tacos.

"Jenny, time to eat," she called from the kitchen. She wiped her hands on a paper towel and set the tacos on the table.

"I'm not hungry!" Jenny shouted from upstairs.

Hannah sighed. She should have skipped cooking altogether. It wasn't as if making tacos instead of turkey could eliminate fifteen years of Thanksgiving memories. The smell of greasy hamburger made her nauseous. She walked to the foot of the stairs and yelled again. "Jenny, we agreed on tacos for today! I've cooked them and they're ready. Please come down here and eat."

Hannah could hear her daughter padding out of her bedroom toward the stairs. "Mother, I told you I'm not hungry."

"Why didn't you tell me that before? I wouldn't have bothered."

Jenny drifted down a few stairs so that Hannah could see her face. "If I wasn't around—" Jenny was almost snarling—

"you wouldn't have to cook at all. That's what you want, isn't it?"

Hannah stared at her for a moment, then her anger started to build. "I want two things, young lady, and maybe you'd better take notes so you don't forget."

Jenny rolled her eyes, something she never would have done before the accident. Now, she did it constantly. Hannah continued. "First, I want us to stop fighting. It's getting old. We're supposed to be helping each other through this, and instead we're like enemies. It's ridiculous."

Hannah waited, but Jenny remained silent, her arms folded defiantly. "Second, I want you to get down here and eat your tacos."

There was silence again. Finally Jenny released a frustrated burst of air. "Fine. Whatever. You wouldn't know anything about losing your appetite because you don't even miss Daddy and Alicia."

"What?" Hannah's temper rose another notch. "How can you even say that?"

"It's true! All you care about is that guy who hit us—Brian whatever his name is. You want him in prison so badly you've forgotten about Daddy and Alicia."

"That's a lie and you know it, Jennifer Ryan! Everything I'm doing is because I miss Daddy and Alicia, I miss—"

"Then how can you even think about eating *tacos*?" Jenny's eyes blazed. "On Thanksgiving Day? I just don't understand you, Mother."

Hannah fumed silently. "Forget it. Go back upstairs and sit alone in your room. I thought we could start something new, enjoy a dinner together, just the two of us. But forget it."

"Fine." Jenny turned and stomped back upstairs, down the hall, and into her room.

Hannah wandered back to the kitchen table and sat down. She took a single taco from the platter and set it on her stark plate. It was cold, and tiny white flecks of hardened lard had appeared on the fried tortillas. Hannah pushed her chair back from the table, dropped her head into her hands, and closed her eyes.

How had so much changed since last Thanksgiving?

Suddenly she was there again. She could smell the turkey, hear the televised football match between the Cowboys and the Redskins....She could almost see Jenny and Alicia, giggling and darting about the house while Tom and a handful of church friends chuckled in the background.

Each year they had filled the house with a ragtag group of stragglers, friends who had no family in the area. She had never been the greatest cook, and last Thanksgiving was proof. In the seconds before dinner was served, the sweet potato casserole caught fire, setting off smoke alarms throughout the house.

"Just like Dad always says," Alicia had teased. "You know it's dinner at the Ryan house when the smoke alarms go off."

Hannah had been frustrated, but Tom had come up behind her and circled her waist with his arms, whispering in her ear. "Don't worry about it, honey. You can't be good at everything."

Hannah remembered turning around and collapsing against his chest. "Yes, but it's Thanksgiving. I should be able to pull off a meal like this after more than a decade of experience. At least once a year."

"But you're good at so many other things."

Hannah pouted. "Like what?"

Tom put a finger under her chin and lifted it gently as he gazed into her eyes. "Like loving me. Loving our children. God gave me the best woman I could ever hope for. You go ahead and burn the sweet potatoes. Burn the whole meal, for all I care. I could never love another woman like I love you, Hannah Ryan."

She blinked, and the memory faded. The wilting tacos looked even less appetizing now. She could still feel Tom's breath on her neck as he'd whispered those lovely things to her. Tears slid from beneath her closed eyelids, and they fell hot on her cheeks. *Tom, I need you. I can't do this alone.*

With the holidays there would be so many yesterdays to wade through. First Thanksgiving. Then, starting tomorrow, the whole world would be making frenzied preparations for Christmas. The entire holiday season seemed overwhelming.

How could Tom and Alicia be gone? Forever? And when would Jenny stop acting so selfish and try to move ahead, as Hannah was doing?

She stood up, took the plate of tacos, and tossed them in the trash. Tuesday would be her first victim impact panel appearance. She had gone over her notes a dozen times, and she was ready. It was time to start making a difference, time to start reaching the jurors.

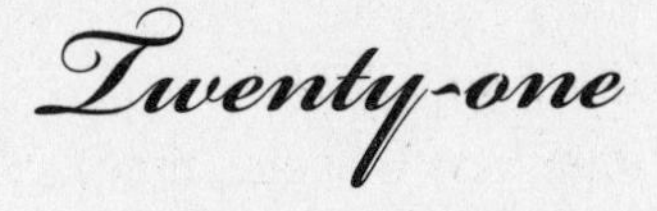

What can I say for you?
With what can I compare you, O Daughter of Jerusalem?
To what can I liken you, that I may comfort you?...
Your wound is as deep as the sea.
Who can heal you?

LAMENTATIONS 2:13

It was days later, and as victim impact panels went, it was an obvious place to start, even if Jenny wasn't excited about the idea.

West Hills High School—where Alicia had been so involved, so popular. If any students would be receptive to a lesson on the evils of drinking and driving, it would be the kids at West Hills. And not just the older students. Hannah would be speaking to the junior high as well, since they, too, had been invited to the assembly.

Hannah slipped into a silk blouse and slim, navy, dress slacks. She had thirty minutes, so makeup would have to be done in a hurry. Leaning forward, she checked herself in the mirror and saw that the dark circles were going away. Sleep was a remarkable cure. Her body had learned to compensate for the nightmare of her waking hours by requiring long stretches of blissful sleep, replete with vivid dreams of happy yesterdays.

Studying her image more closely, Hannah saw it again. There was something different about her eyes, something hard. Before the accident people used to say she had the eyes of a child—eyes that shone with Christ's light. She snorted softly.

Christ's light was nothing of the sort. What people had seen back then was simply a pure, unadulterated joy that came from having her family alive and healthy.

The eyes that stared back at her now looked eighty years old, flat and lifeless. The brightness had been clouded by something Hannah couldn't quite identify, and no matter how she tried, she couldn't will the light back.

Well, not to worry. She knew what it would take—Brian Wesley's conviction. Only then would the cloud lift and the sparkle return.

Jenny entered Hannah's bedroom and stared at her mother with listless eyes. "What time are we leaving?"

Hannah started, studying her daughter for a moment. Why hadn't she seen it before? The light was gone from Jenny's eyes, too. It was all so unfair. She smiled sadly at Jenny. "Let's say in about half an hour."

Jenny exhaled slowly. "Do I have to go, Mom? Couldn't I just hang out in the library and work on my homework?"

Hannah turned to face her daughter. "Jenny, I don't understand you. Do you realize the importance of what's happening today? I get a chance to tell those kids what happens when you drink and drive. I have one hour to explain how wrong that man was who killed your dad and Alicia. Film crews will be there, journalists, reporters. They'll take notes and pictures, and then everyone in Los Angeles will know that Matt Bronzan is seeking a murder-one conviction against Brian Wesley."

Jenny huffed. "I *know,* Mom; you've told me four times since yesterday. But what's that got to do with me?"

Come on, Jenny, you've got to care about this. What's happened to you? "You should be up there beside me, that's what. You're a victim, too, you know. Or am I the only one who's suffering here?"

Jenny looked at her, and Hannah was deeply troubled at how hard the girl's gaze was. Like stone. Or ice. "No, Mom, you're the only one who's *flaunting* it."

At the cold, curt words Hannah opened her mouth, but Jenny cut her off, angry words spewing like molten lava. "You want to take our private misery and lay it out for everyone to see. You cry for the cameras and tell the world how Daddy and Alicia were killed. That way if enough people know, then maybe, if we're *really* lucky, that prosecutor will put Brian Wesley in prison for life."

Jenny paused long enough to take a step toward Hannah. "But, Mom, have you ever asked me what *I* want? No! Because you don't care about me. The only time you want me around is if it works into your agenda."

Hannah swallowed hard. When had her little girl grown so contemptuous of her? "Jenny, please, we've been through this before...."

"I know it and I hate it as much as you do. Why won't you just leave me alone? I don't want to be up there on the panel beside you. I'm not ready to have a question-answer session. I...I don't want to tell someone what it feels like to have your sister killed in the seat beside you." Jenny began weeping then, and Hannah thought the girl looked like she might collapse. "I don't want to do it, Mom. I just don't."

Hannah drew a deep breath and tried to control her temper. She knew she should go to Jenny, hug her and tell her everything was going to be all right one day. But her daughter's temper tantrums had become tiresome, and Hannah sat on the edge of her bed instead. A dozen questions darted through Hannah's mind. *Why don't you care? Why won't you help me? Don't you think I'm hurting, too?*

Hannah released the breath she'd been holding. "Jenny, I can't believe some of the things you say to me anymore. You think I'm only interested in using you, using your pain for publicity? Is that it? Is that what you *really* think?"

Jenny nodded and sniffed.

Hannah wasn't sure how she kept her voice controlled, but she did. "Well, that's a lie, young lady. Nothing could be farther from the truth. I care about you and your future and the way this has changed our lives forever. I love you, Jennifer Ryan, but yes, I am putting my entire life into helping Matt Bronzan convict that killer of first-degree murder. And once he's locked up, once he's punished for what he did to us, we can start fresh, learn to live again. Because this is all we have left. Me and you."

Jenny stared at her mother as if nothing she'd said made any sense. "You think everything's going to be okay just because some guy goes to prison? It doesn't work that way, Mom."

Hannah was tired of fighting. "Finish getting dressed. I'll take you to school. After that it's up to you. Come to the assembly with your class or stay away. Don't sit on the panel with me unless you want to."

Jenny walked away without another word.

The silence continued the entire trip to school. When they pulled up, Hannah reached out and tried to take Jenny's hand, but Jenny opened the car door and quickly stepped out.

Hannah leaned over in the seat, craning her neck to see her daughter. "Jenny, I hope I'll—"

The car door slammed shut.

Hannah entered the auditorium and saw that the media had already arrived and set up. *Oh, good. Thank you—"*

Hannah froze. *Thank who?*

The question stumped her for a moment, but she shook it off. Thank good fortune, thank the media, thank no one in particular.

She made her way across the wood floor, over a maze of heavy black electrical cords lining the back of the auditorium, where two of the three major networks had cameras stationed. Reporters milled about with notepads, interviewing students who wandered past. Hannah notched the minor victory—

Carol had said there was always a chance the media wouldn't show.

She studied the stage. Five desks for the five panel members, each sporting a microphone. Hannah felt her hands growing cold, and she thought about Carol's warning: "Sometimes just before you take the stage, you're nearly overcome with nerves." Carol had several suggestions on how to combat this, but only one that Hannah thought applied to her.

Remember Tom and Alicia.

She reached up and felt the photo pin and knew she would be all right. She wore the pin anytime she went out, anymore. Jurors were everywhere.

Hannah approached the stage, greeted the others, and took her seat between one of the MADD representatives and a highway patrol officer. She glanced over her notes and then at her wristwatch. They were scheduled to begin in five minutes.

The room was filling with giggling teenagers, and Hannah found herself staring anxiously at the entryways. Would Jenny come? Training her eyes on the double doors, Hannah studied the stream of kids still pouring in and spotted her daughter's class. Her heart raced when she spotted Jenny at last. She was the last one in the group to enter the building, and she sat a ways off from the others, alone.

Hannah stared at her, willing her to look up. *Watch me, Jenny*. But the girl kept her eyes downward. *Come on, Jenny, I need you up here. Look at me!* A chill passed over Hannah's arms and she shuddered. Her daughter had become little more than a stranger.

The others had already spoken, and finally it was Hannah's turn. She introduced herself, and a wave of whispers washed over the teenage crowd. Hannah caught some of what they were saying…"That lady up there is Alicia's mom." "Oh, my gosh, this is actually Alicia's mom!" Hannah waited until the whispers died down, taking the opportunity to glance again at Jenny. Her eyes were still on the floor.

Hannah cleared her throat and began. Sparing no details, she explained how Brian Wesley had plowed his car into her family's Explorer, killing both Alicia and her father, Dr. Ryan. The students sat spellbound as Hannah described Alicia's head injuries and Tom's internal bleeding.

"Alicia's sister Jenny was spared, thankfully." Hannah hesitated and for a moment she caught Jenny's gaze across the auditorium. She smiled, hoping Jenny would know it was just for her, but the girl seemed suddenly busy with her shoelaces. Hannah scanned the faces before her. "Even though Jenny lived, she will never, ever be the same again. All because someone made a choice to drink and drive. A choice to kill."

Hannah segued into a list of increasing penalties and tougher prosecution where drunk driving was concerned. Jenny's expression was indifferent as Hannah talked about Matt Bronzan and his quest to reduce the number of drunk driving accidents each year. Hannah explained that if a person chose to drink and drive despite prior convictions and alcohol awareness classes, the stakes were higher than ever before.

"The man who killed my husband and oldest daughter is being charged with first-degree murder." She let that sink in a moment. "First-degree murder. That's usually reserved for people with guns and knives, but now it's been used a few times across the country to convict drunk drivers. The prosecutor believes he can win a murder-one conviction. He believes the time has come to let people know just how serious this is."

Hannah paused then, drawing a breath. This was the hard part. "You know, Alicia should be out there today, sitting with you, joking with you." She looked at Alicia's cheerleader friends. "Cheering with you. She should be here. But she's not, and it's all because someone chose to drink and drive."

She waited, studying the faces in the crowd, some crying, many who had been over to the house to visit Alicia and Jenny in years past. Her eyes narrowed, and she forgot about the television cameras for the moment. "Alicia is gone. Her father is gone. Nothing we say or do here today will bring them back."

She shot a glance at Jenny—the girl's head was bent down nearly to her knees. *If only she would listen.* "We can't bring them back, but we can make a difference. We can make it so that their deaths were not in vain."

There was silence while the students waited. Hannah had the feeling that at this point they would do whatever they could in Alicia's memory.

"If you cared about Alicia, then please, take a stand against drunk driving. Go out from here and say enough, already. No more!" She met the somber gazes directed at her. "Spread the news about what's going to happen to Brian Wesley. Get the truth out: you choose to drink and drive, knowing the risks involved, then you're going down for first-degree murder. Murder one! Please. If you loved Alicia, do this one last thing for her. Thank you."

The students remained motionless, and the muted sound of crying and sniffling filled the room. Hannah glanced at the cameras and saw one directed at Alicia's three cheerleader friends who were crying, clinging to each other.

"Thank you, Mrs. Ryan." Betty Broderick from MADD nodded in Hannah's direction, then turned to the students. "Now, if you have any questions..."

Hannah knew she had reached these kids, and she felt a sense of accomplishment, elation even. She had notched a victory for MADD that day, a victory for Tom and Alicia. The news would broadcast what she'd said, or at least parts of it, and by tomorrow people across Los Angeles would be aware that drunk driving might lead to a first-degree murder conviction.

Hannah felt a ray of hope for the first time in weeks. She couldn't help it. Four months of this and Brian Wesley wouldn't stand a chance.

She could hardly wait to speak to other groups.

She looked out at the students and saw a handful of arms raised. As Betty Broderick started responding to their questions, Hannah sighed. She had gotten through it. Jenny must be so proud of her! She glanced to the spot where her daughter had been sitting—and sudden tears welled up in her eyes.

Jenny was gone.

Twenty-two

The visions of your prophets were false and worthless;
they did not...ward off your captivity.

LAMENTATIONS 2:14A

Christmas was fourteen days away, but Brian Wesley wasn't waiting for December 25. The celebration was now. He'd been forming the plan for days, and he was finally ready to carry it out.

Brian smiled at himself in the mirror. He had a reason to be excited as he got ready that morning. He had been sober again for three weeks.

At first he had credited his sobriety to the strange Bible words, as if somehow that code, that Phil. 4:13 or whatever, had made a difference. As if maybe Christ, if there was such a person, really had given him strength. Or in case that lady had prayed for him like she promised, and his staying clean was some kind of answer.

He knew better now. Staying sober had nothing to do with God or prayer or Bible words. It was merely a matter of deciding not to drink.

He wasn't even sure why he'd called the lady in the first place. Probably because he was fairly freaked out about the trial, worried about spending life—or any time, for that matter—behind bars. Maybe it had something to do with that bit about the keys to his prison cell. The trial would be here before long, and prison was looking more and more likely. Freedom was bound to interest him.

Still, when he thought back to that day at Church on the

Way, how he'd poured his heart out to some strange woman, he decided he must have been losing it. Imagine, going to church and talking with some middle-aged religious freak about the Bible. Crazy. He was embarrassed about it now, to think he had actually considered turning religious or seeking some kind of revelation or conversion.

There was an explanation, of course. The drinking had made him crazy enough to visit her. Finch had told him he didn't stand a chance in court if he couldn't lay off the bottle. The woman and her "prison keys" had merely been in the right place at the right time, when he was feeling particularly vulnerable.

Brian straightened the covers on the bed in the spare room of Jackson's apartment and considered his heritage. He came from a long line of religious scoffers. He chuckled out loud. Imagine him—Red Wesley's son—falling into some Jesus cult or something. Brian shuddered at how close he'd come.

Christianity was for losers. Being sober helped him see that.

Brian made breakfast and tossed an empty egg carton in the trash. The can was full of Jackson's empty beer cans. He and Jackson had finally made a rule: no beer in the common areas. All drinking was to be done in private. That way if Brian wanted to stay clean, he didn't have to watch Jackson get oiled every night. Jackson had stuck with the rule. Good old Jackson.

Brian dressed in a clean pair of Levi's and a knit pullover. Today was the day. He paced about the apartment wondering how best to go about it. He stared at the telephone. His money was almost gone, and he considered calling his old man and asking for more. As stepfathers went, Hank Robbins was good that way. Brian stopped pacing and sat down. He hadn't thought about his stepfather—or his mother, for that matter—for years. *I wonder how they're doing...?* Brian knew now, of course, how his stepfather felt about him. He held none of the illusions he'd had as a young boy, back when a new bicycle or an ATV or a Ford Mustang on his sixteenth birthday felt like love. The man had only put up with him because of his mother.

He remembered when he first learned the truth.

He'd been seventeen and out with friends...and he'd come home early. Unlocking the front door he heard Hank talking. The old man never raised his voice. If he had a difference of opinion with someone, he would walk outside, wait a while, and then work things out when he came back inside. He was a cool one, old Hank.

But that night as Brian entered the house Hank was shouting....

"I don't *care* what you want! It's completely unreasonable. I will not have that boy live here a moment longer than necessary!"

"You wish it were tomorrow, don't you?" His mother sounded like she was crying, and Brian strained to hear. "He's my son, Hank. Doesn't that mean anything to you?"

Hank's voice grew softer. "Yes...but he's also the son of a no-good, alcoholic loser. You know I've done everything in my power to provide for that boy. I promised you that when I married you, and I've kept that promise. At least give me that."

His mother sniffed. "I know. Brian's never wanted for anything. I just wish...I wish you loved him."

"Caring for Brian has nothing to do with love." Brian remained frozen as the words ripped at his heart. Hank's voice became softer, kinder. "It doesn't matter, really, does it, honey? I love you....I've always loved you. But when that boy turns eighteen, he's on his own."

His mother was quiet, as though considering Hank's words. Then she sighed loudly. "I guess you're right. I just hate to think of him out there by himself. He's still so young."

"Sooner he learns the ways of the world, the sooner he'll become a man." Hank hesitated. "Don't worry, dear. I'll help him out a little."

The money. Brian felt a pit form in his stomach.

His mother spoke again. "You always do, Hank. Brian is

lucky he has you." There was silence for a moment. "I just thought maybe he could stay a few more years..."

Hank's voice grew loud again. "No! The subject is closed. Now let's not have anymore nonsense about this. The boy is trouble, darling. Pure trouble. He'll be lucky if he graduates from high school. He's a drinker and a partier. He's just like his father."

"Don't say that!"

"It's true! The writing's on the wall."

"Oh, Hank, I don't want him to grow up like Red. I want the best for him." His mother sounded sad again.

"I can afford to help him. And then we can get on with life and all the..."

Brian couldn't listen to any more. He sneaked out the front door and jogged out to his Mustang. Tears blinded his eyes as he drove off, and eventually he wound up at the beach, sitting on the hood of his car, gazing at the cold, stormy-gray surf long after sunset.

"The boy is trouble, pure trouble.... He'll be lucky if he graduates from high school.... The writing's on the wall.... He's just like his father... just like his father... just like his father."

After that Brian stayed away from home as much as possible. Then, right after he graduated, he told Hank he needed his space, wanted freedom. The old man willingly shelled out a thousand dollars so Brian could set up an apartment. Brian was doing mechanic work at a shop a few miles away, and the payments weren't a problem.

But late at night, when his party buddies had gone home and the silence was deafening, Brian wondered what his life was worth. His father had left him; his mother had chosen Hank; and Hank...well, the old man had been nothing but a phony from the get-go.

It was during those long nights, when daylight seemed forever away, that Brian began drinking in earnest. He had always been able to party, but those awful, lonely nights had nothing to do with celebrating. He needed an escape, and Budweiser became his best friend. Constant, reliable, and always able to put him at ease.

By the time Brian thought twice about his nighttime beer consumption, he was an alcoholic, a willing slave to the demons of drink. That year, with so many hungover mornings, Brian's work ethic began to slip until he was on the verge of losing his job. He knew what he needed to do, but nothing worked. He and the Buds were, well, buds. There was no separating them. Not until one night a year later.

The night he met Carla Kimball.

Carla was a pretty girl with the most beautiful hair Brian had ever seen. Thick and wavy, it shimmered down her back and caught the attention of every man in the place.

She was oblivious. She sat alone at the end of the bar gazing into a glass of straight orange juice. She was barely five feet tall, no more than a hundred pounds including her hair. She looked like a little girl playing grownup—one without a care in the world.

The moment Brian saw her he set his beer down and leaned toward his buddy. "Now there's a catch."

Brian wasn't exactly a lady's man, but he held his own. When he saw a girl he wanted to know better, he generally approached her and introduced himself. But as he watched Carla from across the bar that night, he couldn't get up enough courage even to stand.

Finally, just before closing time, the girl stood up and sauntered toward the juke box. She considered the selections and then seemed to changed her mind.

"Looks like she's getting ready to leave," Brian's buddy said.

Brian swallowed and decided he needed to make his move or lose the chance forever. He walked up to her, and, standing nearly a foot taller, he smiled down at her and told her his name. If he lived a hundred years, he would never forget the way she grinned at him that night.

"Took you long enough." Her eyes danced playfully.

"What?"

"I've been watching you. You've been trying to get the guts up to talk to me all night."

Brian glanced at the stool where she'd been sitting. "Is that right? What? You got eyes in the back of your head?"

She had giggled again, her laughter ringing like wind chimes on a pleasant summer morning. "Maybe."

They sat down, and Brian learned her name and why she was drinking straight orange juice.

"My mother was an alcoholic. She died last year before I could get her help."

Brian digested that information. "Same with my dad." It had sounded strange to hear himself call Red *Dad*. "He left when I was a little kid. Died of alcohol poisoning."

"I guess we're kind of like…kindred orphans, then." The smile disappeared and sadness filled Carla's face. "Nothing good comes from alcohol."

Brian checked their surroundings. "Might be a stupid question, but if you hate the drink, what're you doing in a bar?"

Carla's laughter rang out again. "I like people. And people hang out in bars. Besides, I'm the designated driver. My friend's counting on me."

Brian had been ready to order another Budweiser, but in light of Carla's comments he refrained. Besides, the bar was closing and it was time to make his move.

"Your friend…" He hesitated. "Is it, uh…you know…is he…"

"You mean is it a guy?" She laughed. "No. My friend, Shelly." Carla glanced across the bar at a girl and guy kissing in the corner. "But the way things look, she won't be needing me after all."

"Meaning?"

"Meaning I think she found someone else to go home with."

"I see."

"There's just one problem."

"What's that?" Brian drew closer to her, flirting for all he was worth.

"It's her car. If she goes with him, I'm stuck."

From across the bar, Carla's roommate approached them. "Hey, Carla, give me the keys."

Carla looked at her drunken friend suspiciously. "Who's driving?"

"He is. Now come on, give 'em to me."

"What about me?" Despite her question, Carla did not look terribly bothered. Was this a common routine with these two?

Carla's friend glanced at Brian. "You'll find some way home. You always do."

Well, that answered that.

As her friend walked away, Carla shook her head. "She'll be sorry in the morning and I'll forgive her. Happens all the time."

Brian stretched. "It's getting late..."

"We have time." She shrugged, and again Brian thought she looked like a little girl.

"Hey how old are you, anyway?"

"You first."

"Okay." He sat up proudly. "Nineteen. Of course you'd never know it by looking at my driver's license." He winked.

Carla's face fell. "So you're a big-time drinker? Fake ID. Nights at the bar, the works."

"Now wait a minute, I like meeting people, that's all. Just like you." Brian hoped his breath didn't smell too badly of beer. "Besides, you must have a fake ID. Otherwise you wouldn't be here."

Carla huffed. "I'll have you know I'm twenty-one, a very sophisticated and mature woman by your standards."

The bartender had finished cleaning. "Let's go you two, last ones out."

They stood and strolled toward the door, and Brian grinned down at her. "You may be sophisticated and mature, and I may be little more than a school boy, but you, my dear, are without a ride. And this immature guy with the fake ID would like to give you a lift home."

Carla studied him closely, her face inches from his. "All right." She paused. "But let's get one thing straight before we start something here."

Brian waited anxiously. He was already making plans for Carla to spend the night. If not now, then next week or the week after that. It would happen, he was sure.

Carla's eyes grew serious, the laughter gone. "I don't date drinkers, Brian. You drink, I'm outta here."

He raised a solemn hand and struggled to appear as serious as she did. Whatever it took. This was one girl he didn't want to lose. "You have my word on it, Miss Carla Kimball."

Brian couldn't remember how long he kept his promise. He and Carla went home together that night and never looked back. She had shared an apartment with an aunt and had been looking to get out. A week later, Brian helped her move in with him, and they grew deeply attached, more so than anything Brian had ever experienced. For a while he didn't even miss the beer.

"I love you, Brian," Carla would tell him.

He'd respond with a nuzzle or a kiss, anything to avoid saying the words. Brian didn't want to love anyone, not after what his mother and Hank had done to him. Need was something he could relate to. Love…well, that was something altogether different. Carla had told him if he ever became a drinker, she'd leave him. Brian wasn't sure, but he thought there was a chance that at some point he might drink again. Just one or two beers, nothing serious. But if Carla left because of that, there was no point loving her now.

Two years later Brian did start drinking again. One or two beers quickly became a sixer, and then half a case. He'd come home late and lie about where he'd been. It took Carla a month to learn the truth, and when she did, she stared at him sadly.

"I loved you, Brian." The expression in her little-girl eyes tore at Brian's heart. "But I can't stay with you if you keep drinking."

He apologized and made a handful of lofty promises. Twenty-four hours later he was drinking again, and a month after that, Carla packed her things and said good-bye. She moved in with a friend and refused his phone calls.

That's when Brian knew the truth. He loved Carla more than life itself.

He found her at her friend's apartment a week after she moved out, and he confessed his feelings. "I should have told you sooner." There were tears in his eyes as he spoke. "I love you. I've never loved anyone like you, and I'll never love anyone this way again. Please…work with me. Help me get past this thing."

Despite her strong convictions, Carla had loved Brian too much to stay away. She moved back in and agreed to help him. They got married in a simple civil ceremony, and he stayed sober for nearly a year.

The next time Brian began drinking, Carla didn't threaten to leave. There was no point. She was in for the long haul, and the certainty of her commitment gave him no reason to let up. Not long after, he had his first drunk driving arrest, and then another, and three more after that. There were the accidents and alcohol-training courses. When little Brian Jr. came along, Brian renewed his determination to stop drinking. But that, too, had been short-lived.

Carla stayed, but her laughter stopped sounding like wind chimes on a summer morning. Instead it sounded hollow, as though she were only pretending to be happy. Worst of all, she didn't look like a little girl anymore.

She looked like a woman who'd been through a war.

Brian glanced at the clock on the wall and saw that an hour had passed. He didn't like remembering Carla that way. It was nicer to think of her as she'd been the night they first met, when she sat alone drinking orange juice at the end of the bar. Before she cared whether he drank or not.

He sighed and stood up, tugging his stiff jeans into place. He was through drinking now, through for good. And it was time Carla knew about it.

He sorted through a pile of rumpled one-dollar bills and two folded tens. Thirty-two dollars. All the money he had left at this point. He thought about the gift. Thirty-two dollars should be enough for what he had in mind.

He went downstairs and waited at the bus stop. He was getting used to buses now. They were cheap. On the ride to the mall he wondered how Carla was doing, whether she missed him or not. They hadn't talked since the preliminary hearing. Brian had started drinking pretty much nonstop after that—right up until the day he'd met that lady at church.

He shook his head. He didn't want to think about the lady or the booze. Drinking was in the past now. He got off the bus and strode into the side entrance of the mall. Frenzied shoppers crowded the aisles, searching for the perfect Christmas present.

Brian moved quickly in and out of the crowd until he saw the store he was looking for. Spencer's Gifts. They had the best jewelry, and they didn't charge a month's wages for something simple.

Brian had bought Carla's wedding band here.

He walked in and found the jewelry case. There they were: gold-plated hoop earrings. Brian could picture the look on Carla's face when she opened them. He pointed at the pair, nestled in a cardboard box.

"Can you giftwrap 'em, man?"

The clerk—a teenage boy with blue hair and a tiny hoop that pierced his lower lip—stared at him blankly. "You mean, like, with Christmas paper?"

"Yeah. Giftwrap."

The kid laughed. "Dude, that's for, like, the big-time jewelry stores. But hey, I'll give you the box."

"Right. Okay. How much is it?"

The blue-haired boy rang up the sale. "Eighteen twenty-five."

Brian gulped. He counted out the ten-dollar bill and eight ones. Then he fished in his pocket for a quarter and took the package. He darted across the corridor, found a giftbag for two dollars, then took a piece of scrap paper from the cashier and began writing.

"Carla, I know I've said it before. But this time I'm serious. I'm done drinking for good. I bought you two hoops because I'm twice as sorry, twice as serious. My promise, like these earrings, will go on and on. True as gold. I need you, babe. Help me through this trial. Stay by me. Merry Christmas. I love you. Brian."

He left the mall, boarded the bus, and half an hour later he stood outside the apartment where Carla and Brian Jr. lived without him. He was almost as nervous as he'd been that first night in the bar, but finally, clutching the small gift in his left hand, he made his way to the front door and knocked.

Seconds passed, and Brian wondered where she could be. It was the middle of the day, and Brian Jr. should have been napping. Carla was always home for Brian Jr.'s nap.

He knocked again and waited. Finally he heard the click of the lock and the door opened a few inches. Carla stepped out, closing the door behind her.

"Brian..." She looked nervous and he felt a wave of fear. Carla never looked nervous. Angry, sad, frustrated. But not nervous.

"Carla, honey, I have good news..." He stood straighter and smiled tentatively. "I stopped drinking. For good this time."

With one hand still on the door handle, she sighed. "Really, Brian...you came all the way here to tell me that?"

He felt another wave of fear. "I need you, baby. I brought you something for—"

"No, Brian. I don't want anything from you. We're finished." She glanced back at the door, clearly anxious.

Brian sucked in a deep breath. "Carla, I know I've let you down before. The kid, too. But—"

"Brian, stop! This is crazy. You're...you're on trial for murder. *First-degree* murder. You're going to spend the rest of your life in prison. We're finished, Brian. Now go home."

He tried to move past her but she held her ground. "Come on, Carla, let me in. I have a present I want to give you. Then you can see for yourself that I'm serious this time."

"Brian," Carla hissed. "Go home! I don't want your—"

At that instant, the door behind her opened and a man appeared. He was wearing boxer shorts and a T-shirt. His hair was wet...he looked as though he'd just taken a shower.

"What the—" Brian took a step toward the man, but Carla put her hand on his chest and stopped him.

"Brian...don't. I'm...I'm seeing someone else now."

The stranger put his arm protectively around Carla and glared at Brian. "I believe the lady asked you to leave."

He stared at Carla, and then at the strange man beside her. He felt lightheaded, sick to his stomach. For one horrible moment he thought he would faint there on the doorstep—or possibly die of a heart attack.

Once more he looked at Carla, and he could see the pain in her eyes. She spoke in a voice that was little more than a whisper. "I'm sorry..."

Without saying another word, Brian turned and walked away. At the end of the row of apartments, he passed a smelly dumpster. He stopped and stared at the package in his hand, then tossed it angrily over the side of the bin and kept walking.

He wandered out onto Ventura Boulevard and headed east, away from the intersection where everything in life had changed four months earlier. A block away he saw a liquor store. Before he knew it, he was inside. He found their least expensive bottle of whiskey and handed over what was left of his money.

He gave a sick chuckle. "You gift wrap?"

The old man behind the counter twisted his face. "What's that, boy?"

"Aww, never mind. Private joke." Brian took the bag and twisted it tightly around the neck of the bottle. Then he boarded the bus and went back to Jackson's apartment. Drinking had to be done in private, those were the rules. Brian took his bottle to his room, tore off the cap, and began swallowing fast.

"It's finished, Brian.... It's finished. I'm dating someone else now."

He hadn't even gotten to see Brian Jr. He'd been gone only a few months and already he'd been replaced. Brian was too shocked to be angry. Anger would come later.

He raised the bottle, and the liquid burned his throat as he took three long gulps. The walls were flexing, in and out, back and forth. He looked around and the entire room was in motion. He sank slowly to the floor. Suddenly they were all staring at him, crowding the room so that it was hard to breathe.

There was Red Wesley, laid out flat on a sofa while his mother sobbed at the kitchen table. Hank announced in a loud voice, *"He's just like his father...can't you see it? He's just like his father."* Carla was there, too, and the stranger with his arm around her shoulder. *"It's over, Brian. I'm dating someone new...someone new...someone new."*

He took another long swig from the bottle and closed his eyes. He didn't care anymore. He only wanted to be alone. Forget about Carla and promises and gold hoop earrings.

The bottle was more than half gone, and Brian felt himself losing consciousness. The room was spinning faster, and he closed his eyes. Suddenly a loud noise pulled him from his stupor. This time when he opened his eyes, he saw something that sent a surge of bile into his throat.

Right in front of him was the blond girl and her father, their car wrapped around the utility pole. Only now the girl was crying, and Carla was standing over her, trying to help her breathe. Suddenly they all turned on him, glaring at him, hating him.

"Go away!" Carla shouted and she ripped the gold hoops from her ears. *"You're a murderer and a liar and a loser! I hope you rot in prison."*

As quickly as they'd come, they faded away, and he could see more clearly. There was still something left in the bottle. He raised it to his mouth, missing wildly at first and then finally finding the mark. Nausea welled up, but still he drank, swigging down what was left until the bottle was empty. There was a strange noise, like air leaking from a rubber tire. He tossed the bottle aside and looked up.

Demons filled the room before him.

Dripping blood and spewing venomous taunts and accusations, they crowded in around his face. He swung at them, shouted at them to stay away, but they drew nearer still, hissing and smelling of death and sulfur. They were carrying something, and Brian saw that it was a rusted, black chain. Before he could get up or run away or close his eyes, the demons bound his wrists and wrapped his arms tightly against his body.

He was utterly trapped, and the demons began hissing one word, over and over. Brian's heart beat wildly and he struggled to break free. *What was the word? What were they saying?* The noise grew louder, each word a hate-filled hiss.

Finally Brian understood.

Forever. Forever, forever, forever.

He was trapped. The demons had him and they would hold him forever.

He wanted to break free, to scream for help and chase the demons away before they killed him. But instead he felt his insides heave. Once, twice, and then a third time, until it seemed his stomach was in a state of permanent convulsion.

And then all he wanted was to die.

Brian woke up, face down in a puddle of pasty vomit, his entire body shaking violently from fear and alcohol poisoning.

The room smelled like rotten, undigested food and urine. He noticed his pants were wet, and he realized he must have soiled them. His head throbbed, and he recoiled as he touched his hand to his hair. It was matted with crusted vomit. Suddenly he remembered the hissing creatures. Using only his eyes, he glanced from side to side.

The demons were gone.

But this brought no relief. They would be back. He knew with every fiber in his being that it was so. He struggled to his feet, wiped the vomit from his eyes and nose so he could breathe better, and staggered toward the phone.

It was time to call the Bible lady.

Twenty-three

The hearts of the people cry out to the Lord.
O wall of the Daughter of Zion, let your tears flow like a river
day and night; give yourself no relief, your eyes no rest.

LAMENTATIONS 2:18

In the end, they skipped the tree and presents and agreed to go out to dinner on Christmas Eve. Hannah thought that even that was a stretch since neither she nor Jenny wanted to be reminded that the rest of the world was celebrating Christmas. The "Silent Night"s and "O Come, All Ye Faithful"s were not a reminder to fall and worship at baby Jesus' manger—they were a reminder of his broken promises.

Jenny might still believe, but Hannah knew better.

December 25 would be merely another day to prepare for the trial, another chance to work on victim impact panel information and clip newspaper articles dealing with drunk driving.

The restaurant was packed, and their Christmas Eve dinner was filled with long periods of silence and uncomfortable conversation. When their plates were cleared, Hannah set her napkin down and leaned her forearms on the table.

"Jenny, what do I have to do?"

Jenny stared at her, her eyes listless and empty. "What?"

"To make things right again. Between us."

Jenny doodled a circular design in the Alfredo sauce on her dinner plate and said nothing.

Hannah hung her head for a moment. What would it take to reach the girl? She looked up again. "See? You don't talk to me...you won't even look at me."

"There's nothing to say, Mother."

Jenny sounded so tired that it pierced Hannah's heart. But she pushed the feeling away. If Jenny was tired, it was her own fault. Hannah had tried everything she knew to help her daughter! "That's great, Jenny. We've lost everything that matters to us; our lives have changed forever, and you tell me there's nothing to say? Well, here are some suggestions. Tell me how you're doing, how you're feeling...ask me how we're going to make it. How about that, huh?" Hannah knew she didn't sound sympathetic, but she didn't care. She'd had it with Jenny's self-pity. "Maybe then we'd find something to talk about."

Jenny leveled her gaze at Hannah. "I think it's a little late to be asking."

Late for what? Jenny wasn't making sense. "Meaning...?"

Jenny stared at her plate and resumed doodling. "Meaning maybe you should have asked me those questions when... when...oh, never mind."

A cord of concern rang on the keyboard of Hannah's mind. Jenny was no longer angry, and that was a relief. But now she wasn't speaking or making eye contact, either. She wasn't anything—except completely detached.

Hannah closed her eyes briefly. *All I want is my family back...the way it used to be! Is that so terrible?* When she spoke once more, it was with the weight of more burdens than she thought she could carry. "I love you, Jenny. I'm sorry if I've been busy."

Jenny shrugged. "It's okay."

The conversation stalled again as the waitress cleared their plates. The silence as Hannah paid the check and they walked to the car was oppressive.

Back at home, Jenny immediately excused herself and disappeared to her room. Hannah watched her go and felt like an utter failure. Jenny was free-falling away from her, and Hannah was helpless to do anything about it. *Don't look too deeply at this. It'll all be okay after the trial.* She wandered through the quiet house and sighed, studying the framed photographs.

They had smiled so easily back then. She couldn't remember Jenny smiling even once since they'd lost Tom and Alicia. Maybe this was how it was going to be from now on. No holidays. No smiles. No communication.

Tomorrow there would be a garden of golden memories to be walked through, but Hannah didn't want to go there now, not yet. She didn't want to stroll through yesterday and savor the fragrance of all they had once been. She would rather work on her drunk driving speeches. She didn't want to think about any of it, and she certainly didn't want to think about Jenny, alone in her room, besieged with her own thoughts of Christmases past, probably crying herself to sleep.

The truth was suddenly unbearable.

Hannah turned off the downstairs lights and padded slowly up to bed. The world was a heavy place, especially when it rested squarely on your own shoulders.

That night, somewhere between lying awake and falling asleep, Hannah moved her leg and in the process slid her foot under a section of the covers that was weighted down with a heavy book she'd tossed there earlier. Still, for an instant the weight wasn't a book at all. It was Tom, his leg, comfortably stretched across the sheets just inches from her own. Hannah stirred, and the weight remained. She enjoyed the feeling of Tom's leg on hers, heavy and warm. Suddenly a realization pulled at her. If his leg was here, that meant—

"Tom?" She sat straight up in bed and breathlessly peered through the darkness. Then slowly, as she had at least ten times before, she realized who she was and where she was and what her life had become.

She was a woman alone who had lost everything.

And tomorrow was Christmas.

Since his father died four years earlier, Matt Bronzan usually spent holidays with his mother. She lived two hours north and he enjoyed the drive. But that year his sister had flown their mother to Phoenix so she could be with her grandchildren for Christmas.

Matt didn't mind being alone. He lived in a four-bedroom ranch home in an elite subdivision in Woodland Hills and had come to appreciate the house's solitude when he needed a break from court. In the week leading up to Christmas, his housekeeper had set up a twenty-four-inch decorated tree on an end table and purchased a four-pack of cinnamon buns at the mall.

When Christmas morning dawned, Matt heated the buns and brewed a pot of Starbucks Holiday-blend coffee. He sat down at his glass-topped dining room table, savoring the rich aroma as he ate. When he was finished he did something he did every morning. He opened his burgundy leather Bible and began reading.

He was in Romans 12 that morning and he savored the words, searching for every morsel of truth therein: *"Love must be sincere. Hate what is evil; cling to what is good. Be devoted to one another in brotherly love.... Practice hospitality...."* The words jumped off the page and landed squarely on Matt's conscience.

"Be devoted to one another...brotherly love...practice hospitality."

Images of Hannah Ryan came to mind, and suddenly he saw her not as a woman to be pitied for losing her husband and daughter but a woman to be pitied for turning her back on the Lord. He'd done everything he could to help her with the trial, but what had he done to help her in her faith struggle? According to Carol Cummins, Hannah had refused all contact with her church friends, and she had few, if any, relatives in the area. He pictured Hannah and her daughter sitting at home alone....He remembered how difficult Christmas had been for him after Victoria's and Shawn's deaths. He bowed his head then, overcome with gratitude that God had drawn him out of his own doubt and depression so many years ago. *Give me wisdom, Father. Use me...*

Drawing a deep breath, he reached for the telephone.

Hannah answered on the third ring. "Hello?"

"Hannah...it's Matt Bronzan."

She hesitated, and Matt wondered if he was making a mistake. "Hi, Matt. Don't tell me you're working on Christmas day?"

Matt chuckled. "No. I'm hard on myself, but even workaholics take off December 25."

"Yeah, I guess."

He thought a moment. "You don't sound too good."

She waited too long to answer. She'd been crying. He'd be willing to bet on it. He drew a steadying breath and jumped in with both feet. "Listen, why don't I swing by and get you and Jenny? The three of us can drive out to Santa Monica and walk along the pier."

"You mean...right now?"

"Right now. It's a beautiful day. We can talk about whatever you want. And we'll buy Jenny some cotton candy or something."

Hannah hesitated again. "Why, Matt?"

"Because...I've been there, remember? And I wish someone had kidnapped me for the first three or four holidays after my friends died. Believe me, anything will be better than staying alone in an empty house filled with memories."

He wanted to tell her that God had used Scripture to impress the idea on him, but he knew better. Hannah Ryan didn't need a list of Bible verses. She needed brotherly love and hospitality....

"Okay." Hannah didn't sound sure. "I guess. Be here in an hour."

She gave him directions and the conversation ended. Matt slipped a sweatshirt over his head and felt a sudden prompting to pray for Jenny. The whole time he was getting ready, constant prayers were in his mind, prayers for the sweet girl who had refused to attend any hearings, the girl who Hannah said had become more withdrawn with each passing week. Something was about to happen to Jenny, Matt could feel it, and he prayed for her as if his life depended on it.

Hannah was sitting in a living room chair studying a tree in the front yard when Jenny walked by.

"Honey, we're going to the beach with Mr. Bronzan." Hannah realized she didn't sound very enthusiastic.

Jenny stopped in her tracks and stared at her mother. "Mr. Bronzan?"

Hannah met her gaze. "Yes. The prosecutor, remember?"

"I know who he is. Why are we going to the beach with him? Today? On Christmas?"

Hannah shrugged. "He asked."

"Oh, I get it. That way we can spend the day plotting how to ruin Brian Wesley's life. Is that it?"

For the first time in days Jenny sounded angry, and Hannah almost enjoyed it. Anything was better than the indifference that had come over her lately.

"He said we can walk along the pier and talk."

"About what?" Jenny put a hand on her hip.

"I don't know. Maybe about how lousy it is that drunk drivers get to celebrate Christmas and the ones they kill never will again."

Jenny rolled her eyes. "Like he would know."

Hannah turned to face Jenny. "I will not have you talking that way about Mr. Bronzan. He's the one who can take away the pain we're in. He's on our side. And yes—" she swallowed—"he would know. He had a close friend killed by a drunk driver many years ago. It's not something you forget."

Jenny considered that for a moment, and hope sparked in Hannah's heart. Then her daughter shrugged. "I'm not going."

Hannah wanted to cry, but she felt as though there were no tears left. She sighed and reached her arms out to Jenny. "Come here, Jenny. Please."

Jenny took one step backward. "No. I don't want a hug, Mom. Just leave me alone. I'll be fine."

Hannah struggled to her feet as if every movement was an effort. She closed the gap that separated her from Jenny and reached for her shoulders. "Come with me, Jenny. It'll do us both good."

Jenny pulled away. "No! I won't. I'll be fine..." She turned and headed for the stairs.

"Jenny, please...you're making this so much worse."

Jenny stopped on the fourth stair and spun back around. "Mom, there's nothing *I* could do that would make this worse than it already is."

"You are not an adult, and if I tell you to come, you'll come." Hannah followed her daughter toward the stairs.

"I'm not going, Mother. I don't want to be with Mr. Bronzan. I want to be with Daddy and Alicia. If I can't do that, I want to stay home. I wish I never had to leave this house again!" She turned and ran the rest of the way up the stairs.

Hannah realized she would have to call Matt. She had no right spending Christmas Day with him while her daughter lay alone on her bed. She reached for the telephone and stopped. Maybe Jenny needed to be alone. Maybe that would give her time to sort out her feelings. Besides, she and Matt needed to talk about the trial.

She leaned into the stairwell and spoke loud enough for Jenny to hear. "Since you're not willing to go, you can stay home. Don't leave the house, though, is that understood?"

Silence.

"Jenny?"

"Yes, I understand." The cool indifference was back.

"Jenny, try and use this time to think about your attitude. You've changed so much since the accident."

"Yes, Mother."

"We both lost when that man killed Daddy and Alicia. Maybe you could think about that and stop taking it out on me."

"Yes, Mother."

Hannah sighed. She was rambling, and Jenny wasn't listening to a word. She heard a car pull up, and Hannah glanced out the living room window to see Matt climb out and make his way up the front walk. "Jenny, Mr. Bronzan is here. I'll be home in a couple hours."

"Enjoy your *date*, Mother."

The word was like a sharp slap, and Hannah froze. How could Jenny say such a horrible thing? Hannah felt tears sting at her eyes. *She pushes and pushes...* She shook her head. *Maybe we'll never get beyond this...*

"Enjoy your date." Jenny's words echoed in Hannah's mind, accusing her, pulling her down. Oh, why had she ever agreed to go with Matt in the first place?

He was a business acquaintance, a friend. Nothing more. There couldn't be more because she was still in love with Tom.

She would always be in love with Tom.

As her mother slammed the door shut, Jenny skittered across her bedroom floor and gazed out the window. How *dare* that man take her mother to the beach on Christmas Day. Her dad had only been dead four months. Jenny watched the way he opened the door for her mother and slid into the seat beside her. The high and mighty Matt Bronzan could tell her mother whatever he wanted. Jenny could see the writing on the wall.

She slumped back across the room and locked her bedroom door. Maybe Mr. Bronzan was a blessing in disguise. Maybe he would move into her mother's life and make it whole again. But where did that leave her? Jenny thought about the answer and realized it was a simple one. If her mother was preoccupied with Mr. Bronzan, then maybe the time had come.

She reached under her bed, pulled out a small plastic bag of pills, and dumped them on her bedspread. Her mother would be home in two hours, maybe three. She stared at the heap of pills and ran a finger through them. If she took them now, she would be unconscious in fifteen minutes, but death would take a while longer. Maybe an hour, maybe more.

Jenny knew how long it took her to die depended on the number of pills and how quickly her metabolism worked. Factors she couldn't control. If she did it now, she might even be dead before her mother came home. But if not, she needed to have the door locked so she could buy a little more time. That way, though her mother might find a way to break into the room, she wouldn't have enough time to save Jenny's life.

The pills were multicolored, coated with a gelatin for easy swallowing and digestion. Sleeping pills and some outdated pain medication she'd found in her father's medical bag. The Internet had taught her that there was little mess with pills. That meant her mother wouldn't have a lot of trauma.

Jenny hesitated. She was so close, so desperate to be with Alicia and Daddy. Suddenly she heard the voice. It spoke to her often these days and it always said the same thing: *Take the pills. Take the pills. Do it, Jenny. Take the pills.*

If she did it now they could be together in one hour. She drew a deep breath. *God, give me the strength.*

The pills looked ominous, dozens of them heaped up in the center of her bedspread. Jenny picked up a small handful and rolled them around in her palm. *Don't be mad at me, Lord.... You know I love you.*

Suddenly there was a soft thudding sound. Then another and another. Three thuds, coming from Alicia's room. Jenny dropped the pills and stared at the wall. Three thuds. The signal she and Alicia had used all their lives.

I love you.

Jenny's hands began to tremble and then her arms, until finally her scalp was tingling. There was no one in the next room. The sounds echoed in her mind, and she wondered if she had heard them or only imagined them.

Jenny willed herself back to last Christmas when she and

Alicia were in their rooms, racing to clean them before dinner. But it wasn't Christmas past. It was Christmas present.

"Alicia..." Tears spilled from her eyes and she squeezed them shut. "I love you too."

Jenny wasn't sure how long she sat that way. Eventually she fell asleep, huddled against a mound of pillows, her hand resting on the wall that separated her room and Alicia's.

The beach was empty that afternoon, and Hannah figured it was because most people had better things to do. She and Matt walked along the pier slowly, gazing out to sea. The day was cool and overcast, not quite seventy degrees, and a breeze blew off the Pacific Ocean. Hannah was glad for her bulky sweatshirt.

Matt was so easy to be around. During the drive he'd talked about a few other cases he was working on, and the time had passed quickly. Now, as they studied the succession of waves hitting the shore, a comfortable silence fell between them.

"Your case is coming along." They stopped walking and Matt leaned against the white wood railing. "I wasn't sure if you wanted to talk about it."

Hannah nodded. "Is it looking strong?" She folded her arms and studied him, making sure that several feet separated them.

He gazed back out to sea. "I keep looking for a loophole, a weakness, some way the defense will be able to convince the jury this wasn't murder one."

"And?"

"I don't see one." He turned toward her, and his eyes held a wealth of sincerity. "It's a strong case, Hannah. I really think we can do it."

She gazed through the slats of wood that made up the pier, looking down to the water below. When she was a little girl she'd always been afraid of the slats, afraid she'd fall into the ocean and drown. The slats didn't bother her now. She was in way too far over her head to worry about drowning. She lifted her eyes to Matt's. "I've got four victim impact panels lined up for January and February."

"They're making a difference. I've seen you on TV a couple times now."

Hannah glanced up, eyes wide. She'd been on TV? "You have?"

"Yes. You look determined—and beautiful, in a tragic way. And very angry."

He thinks I'm beautiful. Hannah's gaze fell, and she chided herself for enjoying the thought.

"People watch that kind of thing, they read it in the paper, and pretty soon they start to see drunk driving a little differently. After hearing your story, some of them will be fed up. Once the public takes on that sentiment, murder one is only a matter of time."

An ocean breeze blew Hannah's hair back, and a chill ran down her neck. She gritted her teeth. "Good." She pictured Brian Wesley locked in a solitary, rat-infested cell. "I wish they still did hangings in the public square."

Matt raised his eyebrows and his voice grew soft. "Is that what this is all about?"

"What?" Hannah snapped. "I hate Brian Wesley. Surely you of all people understand that."

"I understand." Matt's gaze fell for a moment and then found her eyes again. "But I don't like what I hear in your voice."

"Oh, please." Hannah didn't have patience for this. "Brian Wesley is the reason we're doing this. You know that."

Matt thought for a moment. "I want to see Brian locked up, but only because that's the punishment he deserves. He's not the reason we're pushing for murder one."

"He's *my* reason."

Matt shook his head. "He's just one drunk driver, Hannah. We want to change the way people look at drunk driving on the whole. Then maybe we can prevent the kind of thing that happened to your family."

Hannah paused. Matt was right, of course. That should be the reason. Still, that wasn't what motivated her to get up before a crowd and bare her heart about the collision.

Picturing Brian Wesley in prison was what motivated her. Nothing more, nothing less.

"Hannah—" Matt interrupted her thoughts. He rubbed his hands together to keep them warm. "Is everything okay with Jenny?"

She shrugged and began walking again. She could feel the hard, angry lines creasing the skin around her eyes, and she pressed her lips together. *I bet I don't look beautiful now.* She shook the thought away. There was no point worrying about how she looked. Smiles came from the heart. Her face was a direct reflection of her feelings.

She thought about Jenny. "At first...after the accident, Jenny was mad at me. Not Brian Wesley. She doesn't hate him like I do. She never has. She hated me, and we fought all the time." Hannah's heart ached as she remembered how quickly her relationship with Jenny deteriorated after Tom and Alicia's deaths. Hannah searched for the words. "But now, I don't know...it's like she's given up. She's thirteen years old and she acts like she's finished living."

Matt's expression changed. "You don't think—"

Hannah caught the look in his eyes and shook her head. "No, nothing like that." Hannah didn't mention the school principal and her concerns that Jenny might be thinking about suicide. "Jenny's a very stable girl. But she and Alicia were so close and now...it doesn't seem like she knows how to go on."

Matt nodded as he walked alongside her. They were approaching the end of the pier. "I had this strange feeling earlier that I was supposed to pray for her."

"Really?" Hannah felt a twinge of anger. She didn't want to talk about prayer this Christmas day. That life was behind her.

But Matt nodded and went on. "I prayed while I was getting ready and the whole time I felt that something bad was about to happen to her."

Hannah rolled her eyes. "Great. Figures that'd be the kind of thought you'd get about Jenny. When God is against you, he doesn't pull any punches does he?"

Matt was quiet and they walked the last few yards to the end of the pier. A seal splashed near the pilings below, and they watched him for a few moments. "God isn't against you, Hannah." Matt's voice was quiet, and she had the distinct impression he was trying not to start an argument.

She braced herself against the white railing and stared up at the cold, gray sky. "It doesn't matter. I don't believe there is a God anymore. Not after what happened."

"It's a fallen world. People get hurt. Injustice happens." Matt rested his back against the railing and faced Hannah. "That's because of mankind, not God."

She wanted to scream at him, to push him away. How dare he tell her it wasn't God's fault? "He could stop it. If he's really a great and mighty God, then he could have caused Tom to be ten seconds slower that afternoon. Or made Brian drive ten seconds faster. Something. But he didn't keep it from happening and that's—that's why I stopped believing."

"Sometimes he has a different plan."

Hannah sighed and moved forward, leaning her body on the railing and gazing down at the churning sea below. "I never *wanted* a different plan. Only Tom and Alicia...all of us—" Her voice caught, and she sank down on a nearby bench. Tears spilled from her eyes and she wiped them dry.

Matt knelt on one knee next to her and ran a hand soothingly over her shoulder. "It's okay. You can cry. The Lord understands..."

She tried to shut out the words. She had heard enough about the Lord. "Please, Matt..."

"I know, I know. You're not ready."

Matt's voice was like an anchor in what seemed to be the greatest storm she'd ever faced. Still she disagreed with what he was saying. "I'll never be ready. God abandoned me, and that's not the kind of God I used to believe in."

"Hannah, the Lord never—"

"No!"

"Give me a chance. The Lord does understand. John 11:35 says—"

"I don't want to hear it!" She buried her face in her hands, shutting out both the sound and sight of Matt Bronzan. "Please, Matt."

There was silence, and when Hannah opened her eyes, Matt was standing again, leaning against the railing, studying her. "Okay. No talk about God. But don't let yourself drift too far away. You might not be able to find your way back."

As though I'd want to...

She wiped the tears off her cheeks. She'd been gone long enough. She wanted to get home, back to Jenny and the miserable existence that was their life these days.

Matt seemed to sense her thoughts. He stuck his hands deep into his pockets and straightened. Hannah pictured Tom and remembered how he had moved so similarly, with the same athletic grace.

He reached out his hand. "Come on, let's get you back home and see how Jenny's doing."

The sound of the front door opening brought Jenny instantly awake. She glanced around the room and felt her arms. She was alive, but she couldn't remember why. Then she saw the pills scattered on her bedspread and her heart sank.

She had fallen asleep.

Now her mother was home and it was too late.

She gathered the capsules and quickly dropped them in the plastic bag. She could hear her mother's footsteps making their way closer to her room. Leaning over her bed she tossed the bag of pills far underneath. She didn't know what had made her fall asleep, but she wasn't going to worry about it. There would be other opportunities.

And when they presented themselves, she would be ready.

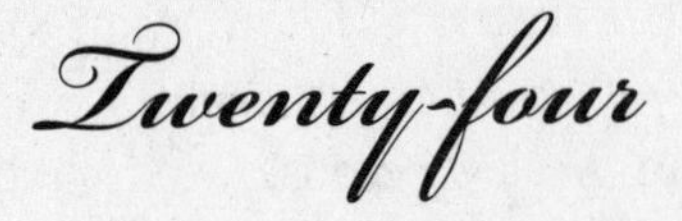

Twenty-four

He has besieged me and surrounded me with bitterness and hardship. He has made me dwell in darkness like those long dead.

LAMENTATIONS 3:5–6

January blended into February and then into March while Hannah kept herself too busy to worry about Jenny or the impending trial or anything but the victim-impact panels. The media ate it up, reveling in the story for all its human interest elements and ground-breaking possibilities. Before the end of March, Hannah appeared on two local television talk shows and *Good Morning America.* They showed pictures of Tom and Alicia and talked in reverent tones about Hannah's strength, her determination to see that justice prevailed.

"A day is coming," Hannah would tell them, "when I will finally be at peace. That will be the day Brian Wesley is convicted of first-degree murder."

Sometimes Hannah wondered about Brian, where he was, what he was doing. Once she asked Carol about it over lunch, but the woman didn't seem the least bit worried.

She shook her head. "It isn't healthy for you to worry about this." Carol hesitated. "Remember back a few months ago…I asked you to read Lamentations? Have you done it?"

Hannah sighed and set down her club sandwich. "No. And I don't plan to. If I remember, Lamentations is in the Bible, and I'm not interested in reading the Bible anymore."

"Hannah—"

"Please, Carol. Between you and Matt, I'm beginning to

think there's a conspiracy. 'Poor Hannah, throwing away her faith when she needs it most.' I don't want to be your project, Carol. If there is a God, then he might as well take the stand right next to Brian Wesley. Because when it comes right down to it, God allowed this. He could have stopped it. So why in the world would I want to read Lamentations, or anything else God has to say?"

Carol seemed flustered. She sipped her apple juice, as though giving herself time to gather her thoughts. "I...well, I've been praying about it. I feel there's a message for you there, Hannah. Every time I ask the Lord...when I don't know what to say to help you...Lamentations comes to mind."

Hannah picked up her sandwich and brought it to her mouth. "Let it stay there, Carol. I'm through with Scripture." She took an angry bite, chomped it, and swallowed. "Now what I really want to know is what's happening with Brian Wesley?"

Carol glanced down at her plate and poked at the remainder of her sandwich. "I don't know."

Hannah continued. "I keep thinking of that day in court when he had a Bible under his arm. If it was a Bible. I mean, it's possible he's going around thinking he's some kind of Christian or something."

Carol looked up and spoke in a quiet voice. "Would that bother you?"

Hannah's face grew hot and her heartbeat quickened. "Yes, it would bother me!"

"I think you spend too much time worrying about Brian Wesley. It isn't healthy. Really. You have enough going on. Leave Brian to our friend Matt."

They changed the subject, but in the weeks that followed, when Hannah was preparing a speech or talking before TV cameras or clipping newspaper articles, she couldn't stop wondering about Brian. The thought of him carrying a Bible repulsed her, and she wasn't sure why. Especially in light of her conviction that God wasn't real anyway.

But if he was, it would be just like God to save the man who killed her family. Forget about Tom and Alicia. But Brian Wesley? *He* would be a man worthy of God's time and attention. That great, merciful God.

Hannah's sarcasm ran deep, and she fed it regularly with bitter thoughts. Just let God try and save Brian Wesley. She hadn't been pouring herself into the victim impact panels for nothing. God couldn't save Brian Wesley from prison. Wesley—and God—were about to go down in flames.

The trial was only weeks away.

But troubling thoughts of Brian Wesley weren't all that distracted Hannah from her mission. Jenny continued to withdraw. The principal contacted Hannah two more times—once in January and again in February—worried that Jenny was slipping through their fingers. Both times Hannah had a conference with the woman.

"I think she needs to see a counselor, someone with experience in grief." The principal eyed Hannah, who politely thanked the woman and left without discussing the matter further. The second time, the principal's warnings got to her.

When she left the school office that afternoon, she went straight to the local bookstore. Moving quickly through the aisles she located the self-help section, picked out a book on teenage depression, and thumbed to the section labeled, "Recognizing the Symptoms."

Hannah read them carefully. "*Change in behavior...change in conversational patterns...change in eating habits...sense of withdrawal...change in appearance...talk of suicide.*" Any of these, the book said, could signal deep depression or even suicidal tendencies.

A chill ran through Hannah, and then she chided herself. *You're overreacting. This is ridiculous. People from families like ours don't suffer from depression. They get upset; they get over it. They become fighters; they change public opinion about drunk driving;*

they fight for a murder-one conviction.

What they didn't do was kill themselves.

She shut the book and returned it to the shelf. When she walked out of the bookstore that day, she promised herself never to consider such an absurd thing again.

Jenny was going through a hard time, that was all. But she would be fine. She was only putting on an act because she was angry at Hannah for being so involved in MADD. When the trial was over, Hannah would lessen her involvement, take some time so she and Jenny could rebuild what they'd lost.

Yes, when the trial was over, life would fall back into place.

April arrived and with it a motion from the defense. Matt called and explained it to her over the telephone. Brian Wesley was still suffering back pain, still needed medical attention and wouldn't be able to assist in his defense until July 14 at the earliest. The motion would go before the judge in a few days.

Hannah had expected the delay, but still she cried for two hours when she heard the news. The idea of Brian running free for another three months nearly suffocated her. Carol attended the hearing with her, and they sat together, watching as Matt went to work, handling himself with his usual poise and professionalism. The judge listened to both sides and called a recess. They had their answer before the lunch break.

"I've decided to grant the delay." Judge Horowitz's voice did nothing to hide his ill feelings toward the defense. "But I'm through playing games with you, Mr. Finch." He scrutinized Finch from his high place in the courtroom. "It is not my idea of 'fair and speedy' when reasons are concocted to delay the inevitable. Your client will face trial, and he will do so July 14. Not a day after." The judge waved his hand in dismissal. "Be gone from my courtroom."

Hannah left court that day convinced that the delay would help the prosecution, that it would buy time for her to continue with the victim impact panels and give Brian Wesley one less reason to appeal the case.

Still, when she arrived home she felt drained and defeated. She sank into the old leather recliner. She would be speaking later that week to a hundred local attorneys, and yet the very idea of it left her cold. It was hard to get excited about changing laws when the process moved so interminably slowly.

She was pondering this when Jenny walked past carrying a glass of milk, heading back upstairs. The girl was still missing a lot of school, and even when she did go, she came home and spent her afternoons upstairs. Hannah was tired of it.

"Hello, Jenny."

She continued toward the stairs.

"Aren't you going to say hi?" Hannah heard the lack of enthusiasm in her own voice. There was no warmth, no love...nothing but emptiness.

Jenny paused and turned, and Hannah fully expected her daughter to ignore her question.

Instead, she gave one simple response. "Hi." The word was monotone, spoken in obligation.

Hannah sighed. "You missed a hearing today."

Jenny stared at her.

Hannah was sick of her daughter's silence. "'Oh, really, Mom, what hearing did I miss?'" Hannah mimicked the response she had hoped to hear from Jenny, and this time she did not give the girl time to respond. "I'll tell you. They delayed the trial. Not April anymore, but July. July 14."

Jenny shrugged. "So?"

"*So?* Jenny, what's *wrong* with you?" Hannah surged to her feet, her voice loud and shrill.

"Nothing." She turned toward the stairs.

"Wait!" Hannah stomped her foot. "Why don't you care about this? Don't you see? The man who killed your father and Alicia is having his way with us!"

Jenny took two angry steps toward Hannah. "I could ask

you the same thing, Mother." The girl was shouting now, and Hannah realized again that she preferred an angry Jenny over an indifferent one.

Her daughter's eyes suddenly filled with tears. "Why don't you care about *me?* Daddy and Alicia are gone, but I'm here, right here in front of you. And all you care about is that man who killed them."

"That's not true and you know it!" Tears slid down Hannah's face as her voice rang through the house. "I do care! It's *you* who doesn't care, Jennifer Ryan. We're both victims here. I want you beside me at these hearings."

"Well, I want a mother who spends her time with me instead of trying to convince a bunch of strangers all over the city why Brian Wesley is such a bad guy."

"You don't understand, do you?" Hannah tried to lower her voice. "The victim impact panels are making a difference. They're changing the way people view drunk driving. And one day they'll be responsible for saving lives."

Jenny screamed at her then. "What about *my* life, Mother? What about saving me?" The words were no sooner out than Jenny stopped, a horrified look on her face. She covered her mouth with a trembling hand, drew back several steps, then turned and ran toward the stairs.

"That's another thing!" Hannah followed her retreating daughter. "I'm tired of all your threats and little ploys for attention. *Everyone's* tired of it. I love you, and I want things to be right between us. The sooner you realize that, the better."

Jenny stopped and turned back toward Hannah once more, her mouth open. "Ploy? Is that what you think?" Hannah caught her breath at the hatred in her daughter's eyes. "You'll see, Mother." Jenny turned and ran up the stairs, shouting once more as she disappeared up the stairwell. "You'll see!"

Hannah shouted louder than before. "Stop threatening me, Jenny! I do love you, but you'll never know it acting like that."

"Shut up, Mother!" Hannah heard a door slam shut.

"Shut up, Mother..." The words hit Hannah like a slap in the face, and she reeled backwards, sinking once more into the recliner. A picture filled her mind of their family walking into church one sunny, Sunday morning. She and Tom had held hands while Alicia and Jenny, maybe twelve and nine years old, skipped along in front of them.

She closed her eyes and savored the memory. As she did, she could almost hear their voices.

"Love you, Daddy. Love you, Mommy." The girls waved as they reached the door of their Sunday school classroom.

Tom crouched down and met them at their level. "Okay, one last time. What's your memory verse?"

"'Blessed are those who hunger and thirst for righteousness, for they will be filled. Matthew 5:6.'" The girls rattled off in sweet, singsong voices.

Hannah held the image, studying them a while longer, remembering them....she was surprised how quickly the girls' memory verse came to mind after all these years.

Maybe that was the problem. Maybe teaching the girls those Bible verses had been a bad thing. Now that God had proven himself to be a fraud—or at least not the good God everyone thought him to be—maybe the Scripture verses were actually harmful.

Hannah thought about the fight she and Jenny had just had. *"Shut up, Mother. Shut up, Mother."* She couldn't get Jenny's words out of her mind. Finally she stood up and grabbed her car keys. She needed to make a visit, needed to be close to someone who loved her.

Jenny heard her mother drive away and sighed in frustration. She glanced about her room. She was angrier than she'd let on about the trial being delayed. She'd had it all worked out and now this meant waiting.

Unnecessary waiting.

Her mother thought getting a first-degree murder verdict was the most important thing in life. Well, Jenny would show her. She had the pills ready, the note written.

The day of the verdict, that was the day she had chosen.

While her mother was waiting for the big decision, she would finally join Daddy and Alicia. Later that day, when the trial was over and the last cameraman had gone home, her mother would truly be free. She would be finished with everything that held her back—the trial, the victim impact panels... and Jenny. After the verdict, her mother would never need to worry about how to make things right between them.

She'd been so close. Now she would have to wait until after July 14. Verdict day would probably come a few weeks after that.

She flopped on her bed and lay on her stomach, her arms wrapped around the pillow. Maybe she should just do it now and get it over with. She could still hear the voice, whispering to her, telling her to go ahead and be done with it.

She rolled onto her side, restless, agitated. She didn't want to attend the trial. She'd told her mother at least a hundred times, but still she pushed. *She never listens to me. No wonder we fight so much. What does she expect?*

In the fog of confusion that filled her mind, Jenny wished she and her mother could be at peace with one another before the big day. Suicide was forever. There would be no turning back, no time for regrets.

For a moment she was assailed with doubts. Maybe there was another way. If only things were like they used to be between her and her mother. Jenny felt tears sting at her eyes again.

Alicia had always been their parents' favorite, but before the accident Jenny had at least felt loved, appreciated. She would give anything to have that feeling again. If she felt her mother truly loved her—instead of just saying she did—then Jenny would attend the trial and maybe even throw away the pills.

Yes, if she could be sure of her mother's love, she might be able to live her life out and then join Daddy and Alicia whenever the time came.

"I have come that they may have life and have it to the full...."

The Scripture filled Jenny's mind and she sat up, hugging her knees to her chest. That had been happening a lot lately. The strange voice would whisper to her, telling her to take the pills...and then she'd hear another voice, one that was clearer, filled with love, speaking Scripture she'd memorized years ago. But the Bible verses made her nervous....They were always about life and living...and that made her wonder. Maybe God didn't believe in suicide, maybe he didn't want her to take her life, after all.

The problem was her mother didn't love her like she used to. And Daddy was busy loving Alicia in heaven.

She leaned over her bed and reached for the shoebox. Setting it on her bedspread, she lifted the lid and examined the contents: a bag with dozens of colorful pills, a water bottle, and an envelope containing a good-bye letter.

Jenny pulled the letter out, opened it gently, and began to read.

"Dear Mom..." She closed her eyes for a moment and tried to imagine what her mother would be feeling when she read the letter for the first time. She opened her eyes and continued. *"First let me say I'm sorry. I never planned to hurt you with this; it was just something I had to do. Ever since the accident, you've been too busy with your speaking things to spend time with me. Too angry to notice me, even when you're home. It's okay. I understand, really. You lost everything that matters to you. Daddy and you have been together a long time, and I know you miss him a lot. Alicia, too. She was your first child, and I know she's always been a little more special.*

"Then there's me. Ever since the accident, you and I haven't been the same. We fight all the time and finally I decided it was time to go. I'm just in the way here anyway. Still there's a few things I want

you to know. I enjoyed being part of this family, at least before the accident. You were always a good mom, so don't think this is because of you. It's not.

"Also, you can do whatever you want with my scrapbooks and things. Give the clothes to someone who needs them. Maybe since it'll be just you now, you can sell this house and get on with your life. If I'd stayed, I would have wanted to sell it. You can only walk around a museum of memories for so long, Mom.

"Anyway, that's all. I just wanted you to know this isn't your fault and that I'm sorry. I wanted to be with Daddy and Alicia and Jesus. You don't want me talking about Jesus anymore, and sometimes I think I miss him as much as I miss Daddy and Alicia. This is the only way I know to make things right. Love forever, Jenny."

Two tears fell from Jenny's eyes and splattered on the sheet of paper. She brushed them off, folded the note once more, and returned it to the shoebox.

She was ready.

Now it was only a matter of waiting.

The cemetery looked like something from a postcard as Hannah pulled up and parked in the visitor lot. The setting sun cast a glow over the rolling green hills and elm trees, causing the leaves to shimmer in the gentle breeze. Rosebushes lined the roadway throughout the grounds, lending a sweet smell to the springtime air.

Hannah drew a deep breath and leveled her gaze eastward, toward the plot where Tom and Alicia lay buried. Then she checked her appearance in the rearview mirror.

She was still beautiful, she supposed, but not in the way Tom had always liked. He had always loved her eyes most of all, and since the accident her eyes had changed. They looked almost as if they belonged to someone else. Each morning she saw them—hollow, hard, hateful eyes with none of the beauty Tom had loved.

It's all Brian Wesley's fault.

The eyes looking back at her grew harder, angrier. Brian had stolen everything from her, even the way her eyes had once made the man she'd loved weak in the knees.

She tried to will the bright-eyed innocence back into her eyes—after all, she was going to visit Tom, and if in some inexplicable way he was able to see her, she didn't want him seeing her eyes like this.

She tried thinking about happier times, about Tom, their childhood, the way he'd shown up on her doorstep the day before marrying someone else. She thought about their wedding and Alicia's birth and Jenny's.

But her eyes remained empty.

Brian isn't the only one; it's God's fault, too.

You don't believe in God anymore, remember? So it can hardly be his fault.

She ignored the thought. Maybe there was a God, and he didn't like her. Maybe this was his way of showing that.

There was nothing she could do about her eyes. Not until she heard a guilty verdict. Then they would light up again.

She climbed out and stretched, gazing at the blue sky. *Tom? Are you there? Are you looking down on me?*

The temperature was cooling, and Hannah didn't want her visit cut short, so she strode across the grassy knoll, weaving her way around various plots and tombstones until she found them—two simple, granite grave markers and a section of earth covered with new grass.

She sat gingerly on the edge of Tom's stone and ran her fingers over his name. *Dr. Thomas J. Ryan.* The insanity of it all struck her. Tom Ryan, the man she'd loved all her life, dead...buried beneath mounds of dirt while she spent her days trying to change public opinion, trying to figure out how to make a life for herself and Jenny.

It wasn't possible.

She traced the *T* in Tom's name and felt the tears. She'd only come to the cemetery three times since the accident. She would have come more often, but she was simply too busy fighting the war against drunk drivers.

Or rather, the war against Brian Wesley.

"They got a delay." Her whispered words sounded strange in the silence. She traced the *H,* and a single tear fell onto the grass. Maybe that was why cemetery grass was so green—it was watered by the tears of the living. She tried to swallow a sob, but it remained lodged in her throat. "No trial until July 14."

Her finger moved slowly around the *O.* "But…Matt says it'll be okay. He's the prosecutor, you know. The one I told you about before." She placed her finger in the groove at the base of the *M* and began tracing.

"I'm still getting the word out, talking to whoever will listen. Matt says it looks good. First-degree murder for a drunk driver, Tom. It'll be the first time in California."

Her finger moved along the upward slant of the *A.* "Things aren't…they aren't too good with Jenny."

A sob escaped then and several tears fell. She wiped her eyes, and for a moment a torrent of sobs convulsed her chest in an attempt to break free. She sighed, struggling to control herself. Slowly, her finger wound lazily down the *S.* "I don't know what to do about her, Tom. She…she hates me."

Hannah squeezed her eyes shut, and more tears ran down her face. Could Tom see her, hear her? She thought for a moment and then opened her eyes. Slowly she traced the *J.* The only way Tom could see her now was if he was in heaven. And if he was in heaven, then God was real after all.

But if God was real, what were Tom and Alicia doing six feet under? What was she doing talking to a gravestone in the middle of a lonely cemetery on a beautiful spring evening? Hannah sighed and her finger found the *R.* "Tom…I miss you, honey. I miss you so much."

People said the ache she felt from not having him to hold—

from not having his hand in hers and his body in bed with her at night—would fade. But it hadn't. It was stronger than ever. She traced the *Y* and moved on to the *A*. "Tom, I can't do this without you. Where are you? Can you hear me?"

She finished tracing the *N* and buried her head in her hands, giving in to her sobs and allowing the grief. There had been so much involved in planning for the trial that she had rarely taken time to cry in the last few months. Now, with the trial moved to July and Jenny refusing to talk to her, there was finally time. Hannah cried until the cool breeze against her arm reminded her of the late hour. It would be dark soon.

Slowly she lifted her head and let her eyes fall on Alicia's stone. Sliding herself over, she perched on the edge of the granite square and gazed at the name written there. *Alicia Marie Ryan.*

She began tracing the *A*. "Oh, Alicia...Alicia, baby, Mommy's here."

A mother's instinct, strong and palpable, swept over Hannah. Alicia was in trouble. Hannah was consumed by a suffocating fear. The girl was trapped down there, underground where it was cold and dark and frightening.

"Alicia! Mommy loves you."

She nuzzled her face against the cool gravestone, her tears mixing with the loose dirt. "Alicia! I'm here, baby!"

For a single moment, Hannah considered clawing away the dirt, tunneling her way to the casket and prying it open so she could hold Alicia close. Just one more time.

Even if all that was left of her were bones.

He has walled me in so I cannot escape;
he has weighed me down with chains.

LAMENTATIONS 3:7

Three months passed and finally the day of the trial arrived. In the warm early morning of July 14, four hours before jury selection, Carol Cummins read the final chapter in the book of Lamentations. *"Restore us to yourself, O LORD, that we may return; renew our days as of old..."* She finished the chapter, closed the leather cover of her Bible, and stared out her dining room window.

She had read Lamentations twice through since suggesting it to Hannah. She'd read about Jeremiah and how he and his people had felt deserted by the Lord. *"The Lord is like an enemy..."* Hannah might as well have written the words herself.

Carol had read Jeremiah's feelings of abandonment and intentional persecution. It had struck her how, like a single light in a dark place, Jeremiah had declared amidst death and destruction that indeed, God's mercies are new every morning, that his faithfulness truly is great.

She remembered the day she'd come to that realization herself, on the first anniversary of her husband's death.

In the end, Jeremiah's lament had turned from dark despair to a powerful desire for restoration with the Lord. If only Hannah could grasp that truth.

Hannah was poring over a scrapbook she'd made of newspaper clippings and of photographs of Tom and Alicia. When it came her turn to speak, she would be ready, complete with visual aids to show the jury the extent of her loss.

It was hard to believe it had all come to this. All the victim impact panels, all the interviews, all the effort at changing public opinion. In the end it came down to what happened over these next few weeks.

Jury selection would take two or three days. Hannah flipped a page and gazed at a photo of Alicia at her kindergarten graduation.

Matt wanted to stay away from singles. They would have the mentality a prosecutor feared most of all: *"There but for the grace of God, go I..."*

She turned another page and caught the image of Tom, grinning widely as he held a string of rainbow trout on one of his summer camping trips with the girls.

Retired people could be trouble, too. Most of them would be old enough to be Brian's parents. They would sympathize with his youth and be hard-pressed to convict him of first-degree murder when he had so much of life ahead.

Hannah sighed and shut the scrapbook, staring absently at the wedding band that still adorned her finger.

Women jurors would be good, much better than men. Matt had explained the law of averages: a man was more likely to drink and drive. Therefore, men would empathize more with Wesley. They would look at him and see themselves, and that was something Matt wanted to avoid.

Hannah knew Matt intended to play the averages. She ran her hand over the leather binding of the scrapbook. "Wish me luck, Tom."

She felt the sting of tears but willed them away. There was no time for grieving now.

It was eight o'clock and jury selection would begin in two hours.

In the end, it took Matt and Finch two days to choose a jury of seven women and five men. One of the women was single, a redhead in her early twenties. One of them was retired, a volunteer librarian quickly approaching seventy. The men included three who were married, two of whom were parents. One man was single and in his thirties; another in his fifties was divorced after two failed marriages. The alternates were a man and woman, both in their forties, both married.

Twelve ordinary people...representatives of society, the combined voice of justice. Hannah watched them carefully. Did they know the power they held now that they'd been chosen?

It was Friday morning. Opening statements were minutes away, and Hannah was the first to arrive in the courtroom. She found a seat in the front row, directly behind the prosecutor's table. At this point, she had worked so hard she almost felt like part of the team, one of Matt's assistants, battling for justice in a system that rarely seemed just.

Matt entered the courtroom through one of the side doors and found her immediately. "Hannah, how're you doing?" He spoke in hushed tones.

"I'm ready. I have a good feeling about this."

"Have you prayed about it?" Matt stared deep into her eyes, and she felt a connection there, something she couldn't define.

Reluctantly she looked away. If only she could say what he wanted to hear. But she couldn't. "You know I haven't."

"Pray, will you, Hannah? For me. I need all the help I can get."

Hannah nodded, but she could tell by his expression that he didn't believe she would do it. She pushed away the guilt tugging at her.

Carol moved in beside her, took her hand, and squeezed it once. "Here we go."

Hannah leaned over and hugged her. She wouldn't have survived the past year if it hadn't been for Carol. The two had spent nearly every day together at MADD's office, and many times Carol had taken Hannah to lunch to talk about her feelings. Sometimes just knowing Carol had made it through this dark valley was enough to keep Hannah going. She searched Carol's face now. "I feel good about it. How 'bout you?"

Carol nodded and whispered. "The way Matt works, I think we're about to make history."

Matt was up first. He stood, and his dark, tailored suit hung gracefully on his lanky frame. He looked youthful as he approached the jury and nodded a greeting, thanking them for serving as jurors. For fifteen minutes he talked about the details of the case. Then he turned his attention to Hannah.

She knew what he was about to do, and she watched him amble slowly toward where she sat. When he was inches away, he greeted her. Then in a voice loud enough for the jury to hear, he asked if he could borrow the photo button she was wearing. Hannah took it off and handed it to him.

Matt studied the photograph as he made his way back to the jury box. Holding it up for them to see. "This is Dr. Tom Ryan and his little girl, Alicia." He moved slowly in front of the panel so that each member could see the photo. Hannah watched them strain to get a closer look, and she knew Matt had been right. They needed to be familiar with Tom and Alicia, not just with the cold facts of the case.

"Tom Ryan was a family man, active in his church, involved in the lives of his daughters. Each summer he and the girls took a camping trip, sort of a summer's end hurrah. They would fish and hike and boat, but those trips weren't about the number of trout they caught. They were about building love and relationships. Something at which Tom Ryan was brilliant."

Matt looked at the photo once more. "Alicia was just fifteen when she died at Brian Wesley's hands. She was on the verge of everything wonderful in life. She was active in student government, a cheerleader whose smile made an impact on everyone around her."

Hannah shifted her gaze to the defense attorney. He was busy making notations on a pad of legal paper. Probably trying to appear disinterested in Matt's statement.

Matt continued. "Dr. Ryan left behind his other daughter, Jenny, a twelve-year-old who has had trouble smiling since the accident. A young girl who will never know the security of having Daddy waiting at home when she goes on a date. A girl whose dad will not be there to walk her down the aisle when she gets married. A very sad, very troubled girl who once was the picture of carefree innocence."

Hannah could see tears sparkling in the eyes of two female jurors. Matt turned his attention back to Hannah as he crossed the courtroom and passed the photo button back to her. He kept his focus on her as he continued. "And of course there is Hannah Ryan. Tom and Hannah were childhood sweethearts." He smiled sadly. "In all her life, there has never been—" Matt looked deeper into Hannah's eyes, and again she felt a connection she couldn't explain—"probably never will be anyone for her but Tom Ryan."

"Hannah lost her husband and her best friend, her confidante, the father of her children. The man around whom she had built her life." Hannah felt a strange tugging at her heart, and she directed her gaze at her wedding ring. Matt was right. There could never be anyone else.

Matt looked at the jurors and strolled toward them again. "I am here to prove to each of you that what happened to the Ryan family was not—absolutely *not*—an accident."

Matt put one hand on the railing in front of the jury, the other in his pants pocket. He leaned forward, facing the jurors squarely. Then his gaze traveled to Brian Wesley, who sat, white-faced, his hands on the table before him. When Matt finally spoke, his voice rang with sincerity. "Don't let Mr. Wesley, or anyone else who chooses to drink and drive, get away with murder." Matt straightened, nodding to the jury. "Set a standard that other prosecutors can follow. A penalty that will save lives."

He nodded toward them politely. "Thank you."

Hannah caught only fragments of Harold Finch's opening statement. Something about being deeply troubled at the thought of drunk driving being a murder-one offense and how anyone might make such a mistake. She wasn't really listening. Her thoughts were still swimming from all that Matt had said.

She realized Finch was winding up and sat up straighter in her seat, determined to pay attention. "Mr. Wesley had suffered through a bad morning. He'd been laid off from his job and didn't know how to tell his wife." Finch hesitated. "What happened? What happens to a lot of people when they get bad news? He wound up at the bar. He had a few drinks, thought about his troubles, and set out for home."

Finch stood up straighter and hiked his suit pants back into place. "What happened between the bar and his front door was not something Mr. Wesley intended. So what was it?" He paused. "It was an accident. An *accident*." Finch's expression was one of great regret. He shook his head sadly. "Yes, Mr. Wesley made poor decisions. And yes, as a result, there was an accident."

Finch scratched his forehead absently, as though momentarily lost in thought. His hand fell back to his side and he stared at the jurors. "If you decide that drunk driving is akin to first-degree murder, you must understand that the next person involved in such an accident might be you, or the guy next to you. It might be the PTA mother out with the girls, or maybe the hardworking father sharing a few drinks with his buddies over an afternoon football game."

Carol shook her head angrily and leaned toward Hannah. "Like that would make it okay?"

Before Hannah could agree, anger filled Finch's voice. "You and I know the truth, don't we? *We* don't need three weeks of evidence. Lumping someone who makes a mistake, someone who drinks and then drives, into the same category as gun-wielding bank robbers and vicious gang members is ludicrous. Utterly ludicrous."

Tears filled Hannah's eyes and she hung her head. She could see Tom and Alicia and Jenny as they'd loaded the Explorer with sleeping bags and coolers and fishing poles. They'd been so happy, laughing and teasing each other about who was the best fisherman. She remembered hugging them, feeling them in her arms before they pulled away, one at a time, and began the journey that would destroy their family forever.

Brian Wesley *was* an intentional killer, and Hannah wanted to tell that to the jurors before they forgot everything Matt had already said.

Unable to bear it, she wept softly, covering her face with her hands. As Harold Finch took his seat, Carol placed an arm around Hannah and rubbed her back gently. Distantly Hannah heard the judge dismiss the court until later that afternoon. Then before she could collect herself, Hannah heard Matt's voice...felt his tender hand on her shoulder.

"Hannah..."

She looked up and accepted a tissue from Carol. "I'm sorry. I didn't mean to break down."

"You have nothing to apologize for." Matt removed his hand and stooped down to her level. "Don't worry, Hannah. Finch didn't say anything I didn't expect." Hannah sighed and adjusted the photo button on her lapel. "Did they get a good look at Tom and Alicia?"

Matt nodded and Hannah saw the sadness in his eyes. "They did." He hesitated. "Come on. Let's get a bite to eat. I need to get back in an hour to meet with the first few witnesses."

As she rose to follow Matt and Carol from the courtroom, Hannah thought about calling Jenny...but there wasn't time.

Her closest friends in this, her new world, were waiting for her; and so, anchored by their support, she walked past the pay phone without a backward glance.

Twenty-six

Even when I call out or cry for help he shuts out my prayer. He has barred my way with blocks of stone; he has made my paths crooked. Like a bear lying in wait, like a lion in hiding, he dragged me from the path and mangled me and left me without help.

LAMENTATIONS 3:8–10

Court resumed at 2 P.M. and Matt called his first witness.

Rae McDermott, the waitress from Sal's Diner, took the stand. She related the events that led up to the accident. She told the court how she was getting ready to leave for the day when she spotted a white truck speeding east along Ventura Boulevard, approaching Fallbrook.

"From where you stood, were you able to see the traffic signal, Ms. McDermott?" Matt spoke from a place midway between the jury box and the witness stand. He looked down, apparently checking his notes.

"Yes, I could see the traffic signal clearly."

He nodded. "What color was it?"

"Red. It was a red light." Rae glanced disdainfully at Wesley. Hannah could have hugged her.

"So…you watched the defendant, Mr. Wesley, drive his white truck through a red light, is that right?"

Finch was on his feet. "Objection, your honor. Prosecutor is leading the witness. She said the light was red when she looked out, not when the defendant passed through the intersection."

Judge Horowitz looked bored by the interruption. Hannah could have hugged him, too. "Overruled. Continue Mr. Bronzan."

"Thank you, your honor." Matt glanced back at the witness. "What color was the light when the defendant drove his truck through the intersection, Ms. McDermott?"

She jutted her chin out and spoke in a clear, condemning tone. "The light was *red.* It was red as he approached, red when he drove through, and red when he barreled into the Explorer. It was red the whole time."

She shot Harold Finch a glare, and Hannah almost burst into applause.

"And after the impact?" Matt asked.

"I hurried toward the Explorer and began working with two other motorists to help the victims." She shook her head, clucking sadly. "That poor little girl—"

"Objection, your honor!" Finch bellowed. "Please ask the witness to confine her answers to the questions asked!"

The judge nodded and looked at Rae kindly. "The witness will please answer the questions and refrain from elaborating."

Rae smiled up at the judge. "Whatever you say, your honor, sir." Then she shot another glare at Finch.

Matt stared down at his notes again, and Hannah thought she caught a glimpse of a smile. But when he looked up, he was all business. "At some point did the defendant exit his white truck and make his way toward you and the two motorists?"

"Yes."

"Did anything about the defendant suggest to you that he'd been drinking?"

Finch jumped up. "Objection! The defendant had just been involved in a severe traffic accident. It would be impossible for a bystander to know whether the defendant had been drinking or whether he was merely injured in the accident."

Judge Horowitz considered that. "Sustained. Rephrase the question, Mr. Bronzan."

Matt moved closer to the woman on the stand. "What do you remember about the defendant when he approached you after the collision that afternoon?"

"He stunk."

Rae's answer brought a few muffled giggles from the jurors. Hannah glanced at the panel. *Good*. They liked Rae McDermott. Matt waited for the court to be silent again. "He...stunk? Can you elaborate for the court, please?"

"Sure." She flipped her hair back. "I work at a diner, serve drinks to half the people all day long. Heck, done so all my life. The defendant—" she cast another contemptuous glance at Brian—"smelled like booze."

"*Booze* as in alcoholic beverages? Wine...? Beer...? That kind of thing?"

She nodded firmly. "He smelled like beer. In fact, if I were a bettin' woman, I'd say he'd had himself a case of beer before getting in that truck."

"*Objection!* Your honor, there's no way this witness can possibly know how much alcohol, if any, the defendant consumed before getting in his truck."

Judge Horowitz looked slightly amused. "Sustained. The jury will disregard the last part of the witness's answer."

Hannah drew a deep breath and felt a wave of exhilaration. The judge's warning was too late. The jury already had the image in their minds—Brian Wesley stumbling out of his car, reeking of alcohol. There was nothing a judge could say to undo the mental picture.

Matt continued. "Ms. McDermott, can you identify the man you saw that day, the man who drove through the red light, crashed into the Explorer, exited his truck, and then made his way toward you and the two motorists. The man who smelled like beer."

"Sure thing." Rae pointed toward Brian Wesley. "He's sitting right over there."

"Thank you, no further questions."

When Finch was through cross-examining, it was four o'clock, and Judge Horowitz dismissed court until Monday. Hannah stood—and suddenly she was surrounded by members of the media, many whom she recognized from her work with victim impact panels. A chorus of voices vied for her attention.

"Hannah, was there anything that surprised you about the opening statements?"

"Do you have any comments on Harold Finch's suggestion that a guilty verdict would set a dangerous precedent?"

"Are you happy with the prosecutor's approach?"

"Do you have any predictions about a verdict?"

She had become a media darling, and she handled their questions like a professional, understanding why they were drawn to her. The media saw her as the beautiful, angry widow with a cause. They liked her, and they played her point of view perfectly in the press. She took time with them gladly and left only when Matt appeared in the distance and motioned for her.

He smiled at her. "Do you have a few minutes?"

She was breathless from speaking before the television cameras, rocked with feelings that ranged from anxious anticipation over the trial, bitter hatred toward Finch and Brian Wesley, and a cavernous sense of loss.

What she should do was go home. Spend time resting... time with Jenny. Still...

Spending time with Matt was extremely appealing. He was safe and kind and on her side. He didn't fault her for her involvement with victim impact panels, and he didn't badger her to read Scripture. He was her friend, and now—in the wake of a flood of emotion—she wanted nothing more than to find a quiet place and talk with him.

She glanced at her watch. "I've got time, why?"

"I thought we could talk, brainstorm about how the trial might go and how things went today." He began walking down the corridor, and she fell into step beside him.

"Okay. Let's go outside though. It's stuffy in here."

Matt nodded. "You're right. We'll spend enough time inside over the next few weeks."

They headed for the stairs, and as she had earlier, for a

moment Hannah considered Jenny, home alone, despondent. A nagging voice reminded her that she should go home and try to make amends in their relationship, but she had no patience for Jenny's self-pity. She was tired of trying and too busy fighting the war for justice. The trial would be over soon enough. There would be time then for mending the bond between them.

"Thinking about Jenny?" Matt gazed down at her as they moved out into the courtyard.

How could a man who barely knew her be so perceptive. *He's a Christian.* The thought came before she could stop it. *He's an attorney*, she silently retorted. "Yeah. She should be here."

"You're angry with her, aren't you?" Matt lowered himself onto a graffiti-smattered cement bench, leaving plenty of space for Hannah. She sat at the other end and turned to face him.

"Sometimes I think I'm mad at everybody." She studied him. "Everyone but you and Carol. I wouldn't have made it this far without you two."

"Jenny's pulling for you, too."

Hannah huffed softly. "She has a fine way of showing it."

"May I say something?"

Hannah sighed. "What?"

"Be careful. Don't let her think this trial...anything...is more important than she is to you."

"It's not that. She has to understand—"

"Hannah." Matt's interruption was gentle. "Long after this trial is over, whether we win a conviction or not, there will be you and Jenny. Don't lose sight of that."

"We *will* win a conviction." Hannah crossed her arms.

"If it isn't God's will, it won't happen."

Hannah sighed and looked skyward. "Please. Don't start talking about God's will. If it was his will to allow Tom and Alicia to die, then certainly it would be his will to allow Brian Wesley to go to prison for the rest of his life."

"Not necessarily."

A pang of doubt hit Hannah. "Matt...is there something you're not telling me?"

He shook his head. "No, nothing like that. I feel confident about winning a conviction." His gentle eyes scanned her face. "I just don't want us to put all our hope in that. The true hope comes from knowing that you and Jenny will be all right, that God has a plan for your life long after this trial is over and forgotten."

She bit her tongue to hold back the bitter retorts she could have said. Matt was her friend and he didn't deserve her anger. Instead, she directed the conversation back to the trial, asking Matt how he thought the day had gone and what they could expect in the weeks to come.

He answered her questions, but she could see in his eyes that he knew what she was doing. And she was grateful to him for letting her get away with it.

The day had gone too well. She simply couldn't bear to have it—or her time with Matt—ruined by talk of a God Hannah could no longer trust.

By the time Hannah got home it was dark, and the lights in the house were out. She tiptoed up to Jenny's room and opened the door. The girl was asleep in bed.

Jenny doesn't need me.

Hannah was hit by a sudden, powerful urge to kiss her little girl, to brush her blond bangs off her forehead and pray over her as she had done all her life before the collision. But everything had changed now. Jenny didn't want to be kissed, didn't like her mother touching her forehead. And Hannah knew better than to pray.

She sighed, shut the door, and made her way to her bedroom. Jenny didn't need anyone. She had survived one of the worst traffic collisions in the history of the San Fernando Valley. Certainly she would survive another few weeks without

Hannah's undivided attention.

Before turning off the light, Hannah spotted Tom's old, leather Bible, still sitting atop his dresser. Nearly a year had gone by, and Hannah had packed away most of Tom's and Alicia's belongings. But Tom's Bible had been so dear to him, his faithful companion each morning in the early hours, long before Hannah or the girls were awake. Other than photographs, Tom's Bible was the only reminder that he once had lived there, once had shared a room and a life with Hannah.

The worn Bible called to her at times like this, times when the echoes of another endless, lonely night ricocheted off her bedroom wall making it nearly impossible to sleep.

Back in the days when she could sing "Great is Thy Faithfulness" and mean every word, back when she and Tom shared and lived their beliefs, she would occasionally pick up his Bible and scan the pages, enjoying the notations he'd written in the margins.

But Scripture held no hope for Hannah now. She turned her back so that the Bible was out of view, and fell asleep dreaming of the way things used to be.

Twenty-seven

`He drew his bow and made me the target for his arrows.

LAMENTATIONS 3:12

After her mother left for court Monday morning, Jenny dressed, pulled her mountain bike from the garage, and set out for the cemetery. It was four miles away, but Jenny knew a shortcut. With school out and the verdict still two weeks away, she knew exactly what she wanted to do. She hopped on her bike and set out.

Twenty minutes later she pulled up to the spot where Dad's and Alicia's tombstones lay on a grassy knoll. Jenny climbed off her bike and dropped down crosslegged next to the stones.

"Hi, Dad. Hi, Lecia." She wrapped her arms around her knees. A warm, summer breeze drifted through the nearby trees, and Jenny wondered if she should have worn sunscreen. She planned to be here all day.

"I can't believe it's been almost a year. Gosh...if you guys only knew how much I miss you."

A pair of swallows sang out from opposite trees, but otherwise there was silence.

"Mom is so freaked out. All she cares about is the guy who hit us and getting him into prison. She spends all her time on it."

Jenny examined the tombstones closely. "I'll be with you guys pretty soon...I'm waiting for the verdict. That way Mom will be finished with everything all at once. The trial, the guy who hit us, and me. I'm only in the way."

With no other visitors around to bother her, Jenny began to

cry. Her chest convulsed, and she sobbed like she hadn't done in weeks. Not for her father and sister because she would see them again soon. She cried for her family, for the way they had been before...the way they would never be again. When her sobs slowed, she stretched out along the ground, closed her eyes, and placed one hand on her father's stone, the other on Alicia's. She fell asleep that way, tears still drying on her cheeks, reaching out to the only people she knew loved her.

Across town at the Criminal Courts Building, Hannah watched Matt speak with a bailiff and then head toward her. He appeared upbeat and full of energy.

"I've reviewed the list of witnesses." He smiled. "Depending on cross-examination, I should be finished by the end of the week. Finch doesn't have much. If everything goes right, he'll be done Wednesday. That could mean a verdict as early as Friday or the following Monday."

A swarm of butterflies invaded Hannah's stomach. "That soon?"

Matt nodded and gently squeezed her hand. "In a case like this, the sooner we make our argument the better. Juries get bored with statistics and redundant testimony. Two weeks is perfect."

She nodded and spoke in a choked whisper. "Go get 'em, Matt."

The first witness of the day was Sgt. John Miller. He testified about the accident scene, how everything had appeared when he arrived, how badly the Explorer was damaged, and how Brian Wesley had failed two field sobriety tests.

The next witness was Dr. Larry Keeting, head of the crime lab and the person responsible for the results of the blood alcohol test.

Matt immediately took the offensive on the issue of timing and how quickly alcohol absorbs into the bloodstream.

Hannah kept her eyes trained on him, trying to see the scene through the eyes of the jurors.

Dr. Keeting was very clear. Although a person's blood alcohol level can continue to rise for an hour or more after the beverages are consumed, in Brian Wesley's case this would not have changed the facts.

"So you're telling us that it is possible that Mr. Wesley's blood alcohol level was lower than .24 at the time of the collision?"

"Perhaps. Based on progressive absorption, it is possible his blood alcohol might have been as low as .18 at the time of impact." Dr. Keeting was dressed in a three-piece suit and spoke with a great deal of authority. Hannah added him to the list of people she would later thank.

Matt turned slightly toward the jury. "So what you're saying is that even if Mr. Wesley's blood alcohol level was lower than what it was while taken at the station, the lowest it could have been was .18, or more than twice the legal limit, is that right?"

"Yes." Dr. Keeting paused. "Of course, there is great possibility that the defendant's blood alcohol was actually higher at the time of impact. Absorption reaches a certain peak sometime within an hour after consumption. After that, the level begins to decline."

Matt looked surprised, and Hannah stifled a smile. "So, if that were the case, what would Mr. Wesley's highest possible blood alcohol level have been, Dr. Keeting?"

The doctor checked a stack of notes in front of him on the witness stand. "According to our projections, the defendant might have had a blood alcohol level as high as .28."

Finch spent nearly an hour cross-examining Dr. Keeting, but it was like trying to poke holes in a brick wall. Later that afternoon when court adjourned, Matt assured Hannah the testimony had been better than he'd hoped.

"The best is yet to come." Matt smiled as he and Hannah strolled alongside Carol Cummins toward the elevator.

Hannah looked at him. "The bartender?"

He nodded. "Found something out yesterday that will help a great deal."

"Good. He's the last witness, isn't he?" Hannah pushed the elevator button as they waited with a handful of people.

"Right. Wait 'til you hear him. He's great." Matt leaned closer to Hannah and Carol, speaking in a whisper. "Answered prayer."

Carol nodded.

Oh, brother. Hannah looked away. "Come on, Matt. Give credit where credit's due."

She waited for a retort but it didn't come.

Matt gained more points the next day. Brian Wesley's coworkers and former bosses testified about Brian's alcohol problem and how well he hid it. Next came three people who ran state-sponsored alcohol awareness classes. Each provided the jury with proof that Brian Wesley was indeed aware of his problem and that he'd been counseled about the dangers of drunk driving.

A representative from the state's parole board brought in documentation signed by Brian stating that he understood that if he drank and drove again someone could very well die. The department of motor vehicles showed proof that Brian was driving without a license at the time of the collision.

The week wore on, and Hannah sometimes found herself tuning the testimony out while she focused on Brian Wesley. What kind of animal was he, anyway? What had he seen in those final moments before driving his truck into her family? She seethed as she stared at him. He was loathsome and worthless, and he deserved life in prison. Now that he was days away from getting it, her hatred toward him was so intense it left her drained, empty, incapable of any other emotion.

Harold Finch, meanwhile, remained relatively quiet. He

objected occasionally, but not nearly as often as he had at first. Hannah figured he probably didn't want to alienate the jury.

Matt's final witness was Nick Crabb, the bartender from The Office. In brief and succinct testimony, the bartender told the jury that he'd been bothered by the defendant's drinking. He had asked him if he'd needed a ride home, but despite the fact that he'd seen Brian drink large quantities of beer and whiskey, it was difficult to determine if the man was dangerously drunk or not.

"Think back, Mr. Crabb." Matt settled his hands in his pants pocket and gazed thoughtfully at the witness. "Do you remember how many drinks the defendant consumed that afternoon?"

Nick squirmed in his seat nervously. "Well, uh, it's been almost a year now, and we have a lot of people sit at the bar."

Matt nodded. "I realize that, Mr. Crabb. I'm asking—to the best of your knowledge—if you can tell this court how many drinks the defendant had?"

Nick nodded. "Okay. Well, after the accident I wrote some notes."

Finch leaped up. "*Objection*, your honor. We have no way of knowing when the witness actually wrote those notes."

Hannah's pulse raced when Judge Horowitz looked intrigued. He turned to the witness. "Did you date your notes, Mr. Crabb?"

"Yes, your honor. I'm a business student at Cal State Northridge…and, well, I guess I write the date on just about everything."

Judge Horowitz smiled. "And you are willing to testify under oath that you wrote those notes immediately after the accident?"

"Yes, your honor."

"Very well. Objection overruled."

Hannah turned briefly toward Carol, and the two shared a quick grin. This was why Matt had been looking forward to the bartender's testimony. The man kept notes!

Matt cleared his throat and continued. "Let me see if I understand this. After the accident, you wrote down the date and some details about the defendant, is that right?"

"Yes, I have it right here." Nick held up a piece of notebook paper.

"I see." Matt moved closer to the witness stand and peered at it. "And what prompted you to write these notes?"

Nick swallowed and glanced nervously at Brian Wesley. "I, uh...I read about the accident in the newspaper, and I knew the guy'd been drinking at The Office. I served him. I figured I might have to talk about it one day in court, so I jotted down some details."

Matt smiled. "Thank you, Mr. Crabb. That was very conscientious of you."

Hannah saw Harold Finch whisper something to Brian Wesley.

Matt continued. "Now, did you note anywhere on that sheet how many drinks Mr. Wesley consumed on the afternoon in question?"

"Yes...it's, uh, right here." Nick studied the piece of paper. "I served Mr. Wesley about six shots of whiskey and eight beers."

A murmur ran through the courtroom, and Hannah shut her eyes. Fourteen drinks. No wonder Tom and Alicia hadn't lived long enough to say good-bye.

Matt waited for the crowd to still. "So fourteen drinks altogether, is that right?"

"I'm estimating, but I think so. It could have been more."

Matt raised an eyebrow, and Hannah saw him glance briefly at the jury. She followed his gaze and saw that they looked stunned. They might drink, they might know someone who drank...but *fourteen* drinks? "Now, Mr. Crabb, did you make any notations about how long Mr. Wesley had been drinking?"

Nick glanced down at his notes again and gulped. "Yes. He came in after lunch sometime, maybe one, one-thirty. And he left after three."

Harold Finch looked restless but he remained in his seat.

Matt nodded. "Is there any way you can be certain about those times, Mr. Crabb?"

Hannah willed the bartender to say the right thing. *Please...please...*

"Well, there was a movie running on the bar TV, *Rocky II*. Mr. Wesley arrived just as I was putting it in, and it was over by the time he left." Nick glanced at his notes once more. "I figured that had to be at least two hours."

"Fine. So he drank for two hours—fourteen drinks, maybe more—is that right?"

"Yes, sir." Hannah watched the young bartender expectantly. She knew what was coming.

Matt stood squarely in front of the witness stand. "At some point Mr. Wesley decided to leave, is that right?"

"Yes."

"Were you concerned that he might be too drunk to drive home?" Matt kept his tone matter-of-fact. This wasn't the time to point fingers at the bartender.

Nick Crabb sighed, and Hannah saw the burden he carried. He'd been the final line of defense, the only one who could have stopped Wesley from getting into the truck and barreling down Ventura Boulevard. He'd had the chance and he'd missed it.

Nick drew a deep breath. "Yes. Just before he left I decided he was too drunk to drive."

Murmurs rose across the courtroom, and Matt waited a moment. He raised his voice slightly, and the jurors strained to hear. "Did you act on that decision?"

Nick nodded. "Yes. I asked him if he was okay to drive."

Hannah felt her heart sink. She followed Matt as he paced slowly toward the jury. "Do you remember what Mr. Wesley told you?"

Nick sighed again. "Yes. He told me to mind my own business."

Across the courtroom Finch leaned over and whispered

something else to Brian. Hannah glared at them and turned her attention back to Matt.

"Then what happened?"

"I...I told him to sit down a minute...told him I'd call a cab so...so he wouldn't have to drive home." Nick hung his head.

"What next, Mr. Crabb?"

"He got mad."

Matt raised an eyebrow. "Could you explain your answer, Mr. Crabb."

The bartender straightened, and for a moment his eyes connected with Hannah's. He was sorry. Hannah could see that, and she wasn't sure how she felt. This man's testimony would help put Brian Wesley away for a very long time. Then again, if only he'd said something different, done something... physically contained Brian, anything...perhaps they wouldn't be here today. Perhaps they would all be home living life the way they were supposed to. Happily ever after.

Nick was silent, and Matt tried again. "Mr. Crabb, please explain to the jury what you meant when you said that the defendant got mad when you offered to call a cab."

"Well, he told me he could drive home if he wanted to. Then he cussed at me a few times. He told me he was leaving, and he turned around and left."

"Do you have some sort of test, some way of determining whether a person who has been drinking should or shouldn't drive?" Matt slipped his hands in his pockets and leaned slightly against the railing.

"Yes. My boss had told me to watch how customers talk, how they walk. Mr. Wesley seemed okay that way, but he'd had a lot of drinks in a short time, and I was worried. So I did what the boss said to do in that situation. I offered him a cab. When he refused, I thought I was out of options. There was nothing more I could do."

"Okay, now let's see if I have this straight. The defendant, Brian Wesley, spent two hours drinking at least fourteen alcoholic beverages, then refused your offer of a cab and left the bar despite your warnings. Is that right, Mr. Crabb?"

The bartender swallowed, struggling to find his voice. "Yes."

"No more quest—"

"There's something else."

Matt looked at Nick in surprise, and the young man met Hannah's eyes once more.

"If I had to do it over again, I'd tackle him to the floor, tie his hands, anything. The only way out would be over my dead body." His voice was barely a whisper, his eyes were still on Hannah's. "I'm sorry."

Tears spilled onto Hannah's cheeks. She nodded and hung her head. It was easy to hate Brian Wesley, easy to hate any attorney who would defend him. But this man, this college student, was not her enemy. They had both lost that day and clearly he, like Hannah, still suffered.

Finch bounded to his feet, his face red. *"Objection!* The witness's statement went beyond the scope of the question, your Honor."

Hannah looked at the judge and saw him nod sternly. "Sustained. The jury will disregard the last statement."

Matt paused a moment, and Hannah knew he was allowing the jurors time to soak in what had just happened. Nick Crabb had apologized to her. Finally Matt looked up from his notes and thanked the witness, turning him over to the defense.

Harold Finch whispered something else to Brian and then stood up. Hannah thought he looked like a snake. A boa constrictor. She wondered if the jury saw him the same way.

"Mr. Crabb, has the defendant ever done anything to personally wrong you?" Finch's voice was sharp, full of accusation.

Nick blinked twice. "No. I don't know what you mean."

Finch shook his head and cast a knowing look at the jury. "Listen, here, Mr. Crabb. Isn't it true that you were hired by the prosecution, instructed to write those notes, and paid to appear here today in order to ruin the defendant's chances at an acquittal?"

Matt was not typically quick to object, but this time he was on his feet and doing so forcefully. "I object, your honor. Mr. Finch is badgering the witness about something that was not brought up in the direct. If it isn't brought up in the direct—"

"Yes." Judge Horowitz peered over the rim of his glasses at Harold Finch. "If it isn't brought up in the direct, it cannot be brought up in the cross. You should know that Mr. Finch. Objection sustained."

Finch continued to question the bartender for more than an hour, always stopping just short of harassment. Finally he tried to cast doubt on whether Nick Crabb had even tended bar the afternoon of the accident. In response, Nick produced another sheet of paper.

"What's that?" Finch's tone was filled with mockery. "More notes?"

"No, sir." Nick held the single sheet of paper higher so that Finch could see it. "It's a copy of my time card from that day. I asked the owner for a copy of it after the accident, when I figured I might need to testify in court at some point."

Hannah wanted to laugh out loud. Finch had been caught at his own game. Had he avoided this line of questioning, the jury would never have seen the meticulous care Nick Crabb took to present accurate details. Now the idea of the defendant consuming fourteen drinks looked like the gospel truth.

Hannah caught Matt's expression, and he winked. This one was theirs.

She could have kissed him!

Matt had another chance with Nick on redirect, and he used the opportunity to establish the specifics of the photocopied time card. Nick had indeed worked that afternoon. He had started at 11:00 A.M. and clocked out at 3:30 P.M. The details were perfectly in keeping with Nick's testimony. When Matt was finished with the bartender, he turned to the judge and nodded. "The state rests, your honor."

"Very well." Judge Horowitz scanned the courtroom. "It's

nearly three o'clock, so we'll adjourn until tomorrow at which time we will hear from the witnesses for the defense. Court dismissed."

Hannah closed her eyes and said a silent thanks to Matt Bronzan. They were halfway there, and because of Matt, Brian Wesley's days of freedom were disappearing fast.

Carol leaned toward her. "I need to get going. See you tomorrow."

As Carol left, Hannah was engulfed by a sea of reporters. When she had answered each of their questions, her eyes searched the front of the courtroom for Matt. Twenty minutes had passed, and Hannah figured he would be gone, but she found him leaning against the prosecution's table, his arms and ankles crossed, staring at her. Their eyes met, and the air seemed charged…alive…between them.

She waited while he gathered his files.

The trial was half over. Hannah could barely contain the sense of joy and victory she felt. When Matt stood and their eyes met again, she didn't hesitate. She went toward him, into his open arms, laying her head against his broad chest, letting her tears of gratitude fall on his shirt.

His arms wrapped around her back and held her close. And for the first time in decades, Hannah found herself being held by a man other than Tom Ryan.

Twenty-eight

He pierced my heart with arrows from his quiver.

LAMENTATIONS 3:13

Brian Wesley showered earlier than usual the next morning and paid particular attention to his appearance. He would be the first witness to take the stand in his defense, and he wanted to be clean and neat. If he really was a changed man—and he believed he was—then he needed to look the part.

Hot water pounded his shoulders, and steam filled the bathroom of Jackson's boxy apartment. *Lord, I'm gonna need your help today. I can't do it alone.*

Brian closed his eyes. The next few days would be the hardest in his life. First he would testify, talk about his past failures and how he'd become a changed man in the process. Then, at some point, Harold Finch would call Carla as a witness. She would testify that Brian never actually intended to kill another person.

Finch had been square with him. He would serve time in prison regardless of the verdict. Worst-case scenario, driving under the influence held a penalty of several years. And if the jury didn't convict him of first-degree murder, they would certainly give him the maximum for driving drunk. Ten years, maybe more.

Brian's heart began beating fast, and he recognized the beginnings of an anxiety attack. Times like this he could still taste the alcohol, still feel his body reaching for the drink that would destroy him.

"Do not be anxious about anything, but in everything, by prayer

and petition, with thanksgiving, present your requests to God. And the peace of God, which transcends all understanding, will guard your hearts and your minds in Christ Jesus. Do not be anxious about anything, but in..."

Over and over he repeated the verse from Philippians 4. It was a weapon, a demon slayer, and he used it every time they came back. Funny thing, too. Because as long as he could remember, relief from anxiety had always been something that came in whiskey bottles and beer cans. But this...this Scripture thing—having God's word memorized, ready to wield like a weapon anytime the beast of anxiety appeared—this was really something.

Better than the bottle ever was.

That Bible lady had explained it best: Scripture words were alive and active. They worked every time. They never lost their power like some dime-store battery. Brian stepped out of the shower. "*Do not be anxious about anything, but in everything...*" One thing was sure. This Bible thing was truth.

And it was his last hope.

He toweled off and dressed in his best new jeans and a button-down flannel shirt. A bit hot for July, but they were the nicest clothes he had.

He thought about Finch's advice: "*Make the jury love you or it's all over. Don't let 'em smell your fear. Let 'em see a sad man, someone ruined by the bottle, but don't let 'em see a killer. Make promises, even if you don't plan to keep them.*"

He planned to make promises. What Finch didn't understand was that he planned to keep them, too.

Brian sighed and pulled a clean, white sock onto his bare foot. He wasn't sure about Finch anymore. The man was a good enough attorney, worth the money. But he didn't play fair, and that bothered Brian. Ever since meeting that woman down at Church on the Way, a lot of things about his old life bothered him.

For a moment he could see the young girl, lying dead on

the shoulder of the road, hear her father several feet away moaning for help, dying, trapped in his car.

Brian swallowed hard. *"Do not be anxious about anything, but in everything, by prayer and petition..."*

The image faded. He finished dressing and then checked his appearance in the Budweiser mirror that hung on Jackson's apartment wall.

He stared at his reflection. "Gonna need your help today, Lord."

For a moment he studied the man in the glass. He didn't look the same. Something different...something in the eyes maybe. He grabbed a fistful of change for the bus and studied himself once more. Yes, that was it. Something gentler in the eyes.

He wondered if Carla would notice.

An air of expectation hung over Judge Horowitz's courtroom that next Tuesday morning. Harold Finch was there early, and Hannah thought he was wearing a new suit for the occasion. It fit a bit more loosely, but its loud pinstripes, satin cuffs, and gold-plated buttons still gave him the look of a mob boss rather than a lawyer.

Matt looked relaxed as he read a stack of documents and jotted down notes.

Hannah's eyes fell on Brian Wesley. He looked freshly bathed, neatly dressed. His hair was shorter than before...and there was something different about his face.

Hannah wanted to shake him. How could he put on a front, act like someone society could live with when he was a cold-blooded killer? He'd deliberately chosen to kill Tom and Alicia. He would do it again if this jury gave him a chance. He might pretend for a while, but nothing, no one—not God himself—could ever change Brian Wesley.

Is anything too hard for God?

Hannah blinked back the Scripture and huffed out loud. Some things apparently were. Like keeping Tom and Alicia alive.

The proceedings began, and Finch was on his feet calling his first witness. Brian Wesley. Parading about the front of the courtroom, Finch established Brian's background as a faithful worker and husband, as a man troubled by a continual drinking problem. He worked his way up to the point of the collision, highlighting the fact that Brian had been sober for three weeks prior to August 28.

"Now, on the afternoon of the accident, what transpired prior to your visit to the bar?"

Brian frowned slightly. "You mean, why did I decide to drink again?"

Finch waved his hand, shaking his head. "Okay, fine, why did you decide to drink again?"

"Well, I got laid off."

"And were you depressed?"

"Yes."

Hannah held her breath, her blood all but boiling. She'd like to give both of them something to be depressed about.

Finch strutted farther from the witness stand so that he was adjacent to the jurors. His stance, his expression, it all gave the jurors the impression he was one of them...the thirteenth juror.

"So you went to the bar and had a few drinks, something to lighten your spirits, is that right?" Finch's tone was hostile and Hannah struggled to understand. Weren't they supposed to be on the same team?

Brian stared at his attorney with a strange expression, almost as if he were angry with the man. "It was a stupid thing to do. I'd been clean for three weeks, and if only I'd just gone home to Carla—"

"Just answer the question, please, Mr. Wesley." Finch didn't look pleased....Sighing and exchanging a long-suffering look with several jurors, Finch continued. "Why did you go to the bar, Mr. Wesley? Did you go there planning to kill someone?"

Brian's face twitched slightly. "No, of course not."

"Did you go intending to hurt someone, perhaps destroy someone's vehicle in a traffic accident?"

Brian shook his head.

"Answer out loud for the court, please," Judge Horowitz said. He looked interested in the testimony for the first time that day.

"No, I didn't intend to hurt anyone."

"Fine, then let's go a little further. You sat at the bar for a certain amount of time. Do you know how long you sat there, Mr. Wesley?"

Brian shrugged. "I didn't take notes or nothing."

"Answer the question to the best of your knowledge."

"I don't know. My memory's a little hazy on it, you know?"

Finch's jaw dropped half an inch, and Hannah caught Matt's suddenly alert look. Certainly this wasn't the line of testimony Finch and Brian Wesley had practiced.

Finch cleared his throat. "I am not asking for a vivid account. I am asking you to tell this court, as best you can remember, how long you sat at the bar on the afternoon of August 28."

"Okay." Brian looked determined to come up with an answer. "I think that guy was probably right, that bartender guy. Two hours maybe."

Finch looked about to swallow his tongue. "Fine. At the end of that time, when you left the bar, did you think you were drunk?"

Hannah expected Finch to ask Brian how many drinks he'd consumed in that time. When he didn't, she figured he was starting to fear Brian's answers. She couldn't blame him. Brian's testimony was strangely unsettling....Of course, it was favorable for the prosecution, but why on earth was he making statements that might harm his case?

Finch was waiting for an answer. "Do you understand the question, Mr. Wesley?"

Brian nodded and then caught himself. "Yes. I understand. I don't know that I really thought about it, to be honest. I drank a lot, and I wanted to get home."

"So you didn't think you were drunk, correct?"

Matt leaned forward slightly, as though he were about to object, but he waited, poised on the edge of his seat.

Brian's face grew red. "Listen, man, don't put words in my mouth."

A hush fell over the courtroom, and Finch stared at Brian, clearly stunned. In a strained voice he requested a moment alone with his client.

The jury was ushered out, and for ten minutes Brian and his attorney talked in hushed but heated tones. Hannah sat stone-still as she watched them reach some kind of apparent agreement.

"Your honor, we're ready for the jury again." Finch wiped a layer of perspiration off his forehead and shot a glare at Brian.

Hannah's head was spinning. What was happening? Why was Brian suddenly fighting with his own attorney? Then it struck her, and she leaned toward Carol. "It's an act!"

Carol considered her. "Maybe."

"Carol, come on! Don't you see it? They make it look like Finch is the bad guy, the slimy defense attorney. Brian's the guy who's trying to come clean, trying to be straight with the jury. The jury sympathizes with him, and we lose the conviction. It's all an act!"

Carol looked from Brian to Finch and back to Hannah. "Let's watch and see what happens."

The jury was back in place, and Finch's friendliness seemed forced as he phrased his next question. "Were you drunk when you left the bar that afternoon, Mr. Wesley?"

Brian leaned back in the witness stand. "I might have been. I didn't think about it."

"Okay." Finch stayed near the stand. His hands twitched at his sides, and Hannah thought he looked like he might strangle Brian if he gave anymore unexpected answers. "Did you plan to leave the bar that afternoon—*maybe* drunk—and drive your car through a red light on Ventura Boulevard?"

"No." The sadness on Brian's face pierced Hannah. It was an image that didn't fit into the category of behaviors she had assigned him. He was an animal. Animals didn't look sad.

"Did you plan to kill Tom and Alicia Ryan on the afternoon of August 28?"

"No..." Brian's voice dropped off, and when he spoke again Hannah watched everyone in the courtroom strain to hear him. "It was an accident."

Finch shot a satisfied look at the jury, dabbed at another layer of perspiration, and then turned to Judge Horowitz. "No further questions, your honor."

Matt rose slowly to his feet and studied Brian for a moment. "Did you know that drinking shots of whiskey and glasses of beer would affect your blood alcohol level, Mr. Wesley?"

"Yes."

Matt nodded and moved slowly toward the jury. He turned back to Brian. "Did you know it was against the law to drive a vehicle with an elevated blood alcohol level?"

"Yes." Brian seemed defeated and Hannah felt smugly glad. *This is just the beginning, buddy.*

"Did you sign a statement promising to never drink and drive and agreeing with the fact that to do so was to risk the lives of innocent motorists?" Matt's voice was calm, matter-of-fact.

"Yeah, I knew it."

Matt nodded again. "And you chose to do it anyway, is that right?"

"Yes. It was a stupid mistake."

"Just stick to the question, Mr. Wesley. Did you choose to do those things regardless of the consequences, yes or no?"

"Yes."

"Mr. Wesley, *Webster's Dictionary* defines *accident* as a tragic event that does not involve fault. Do you understand that definition?"

"I think so...yes."

What in the world was going on? Brian was clearly not fighting his own cause on the stand. Hannah shifted uneasily in her seat.

"Based on that definition—a tragic event that does not involve fault—can you honestly tell us that what happened on the afternoon of August 28 was an accident?"

Brian paused for a moment, and Hannah could see that he was wrestling with his answer. "No."

At the quiet admission, Hannah's mouth went dry, and her heart beat so hard she thought it might explode. Had Brian Wesley just said what she thought he'd said?

He met Matt's gaze without flinching. "Based on that definition, I can't...I can't call it an accident."

Reporters stationed along the back of the courtroom began scribbling furiously as a hum of discussion broke out among those in attendance.

"Order!" Judge Horowitz glared at the gallery. "I will not have you disrupt this court." He looked at Matt. "Continue."

"No further questions, your honor." Matt shot an amazed look at Hannah, and then returned to his spot at the table.

Finch worked the rest of the day trying to undo the damage done by Brian's admission that the crash hadn't been an accident, but it was useless. Hannah didn't know what kind of act they were playing, but whatever it was it had backfired.

If the trial ended now, Hannah felt certain they'd win their conviction.

The week dragged on with a physicist testifying that Brian's blood alcohol may have been lower than the police test showed because of the rate of alcohol absorption into the bloodstream. On cross-examination, the witness admitted that

Brian's blood alcohol may have been higher, as well.

"A waste," Matt told Hannah when court was adjourned for the day. "Nothing that'll hurt the case."

"So things still look good?" Hannah felt stronger in Matt's presence, as if being near him brought her closer to a point of healing.

"Yes." Matt patted her hand and then hesitated. "Hannah... how's Jenny?"

She started and stared at him. Jenny? She hadn't thought of Jenny in days. Weeks...

She shrugged. "I'm not really sure. Still moping, still riding her bike aimlessly around town, pretending she's a loner."

Matt sighed. "Be careful, Hannah. She's still a little girl. She needs you."

I need her, too. She blocked out the thought. "You don't understand. She's different than...than before the...than before. I can't reach her anymore."

"Okay." Matt looked troubled. "I don't mean to meddle. I'm worried, that's all." He was silent a moment. "I'm still praying for her."

Hannah resisted any overt show of doubt. She looked deep into Matt's eyes trying to understand how he could maintain his faith in light of the pain all around him. "Whatever makes you feel better, Matt."

On Thursday morning, Finch called his last witness, Carla Wesley. Hannah studied the young woman through critical eyes. Brian Wesley's wife had a good figure, but was otherwise hard and unattractive, with dark circles under her eyes.

White trash. Hannah glared at Carla as she took the stand and hated her for choosing to love a man like Brian Wesley. *Judge not, lest you be judged....* Hannah pushed the Scripture from her mind. How long would it take before Bible verses no longer flashed at her?

Finch established who the woman was and that she and Brian were no longer living together. Carla testified that she had been aware of Brian's drinking problem. Then Finch moved to the heart of the issue.

"Was Brian a violent man, Mrs. Wesley?" Finch leaned against the jury box.

"No."

"I'm sorry, I couldn't quite hear you. Could you repeat the answer?"

Carla fidgeted in her seat and glanced at Brian, who kept his gaze downward. "No. He was not a violent man."

"Was he an angry man?" Finch appeared confused, as if he were trying to solve a difficult riddle.

"No. He wasn't angry."

Finch nodded, still puzzled. "Then he must have had tendencies toward murder, is that it, Mrs. Wesley?"

Carla shook her head quickly. "No, of course not. Brian was always..." She glanced at her husband, and for an instant Hannah saw their eyes meet. "He was always a gentleman."

Hannah huffed softly. *Gentleman.* Brian and his wife were equally worthless as far as she was concerned.

Finch scratched his head. "The prosecution is trying to convict your husband of intentionally killing two people, Mrs. Wesley. You've known him many, many years. Certainly you would know if he had ever planned to kill someone. Would you say you know Mr. Wesley very well?"

Carla's eyes filled with tears, and a smudge of mascara appeared under her right eye. Her voice was choked when she answered. "Yes. I know Brian very well."

"So you would know if he had homicidal tendencies, the desire or intention to kill someone?"

Matt had been observing the proceedings passively, but now he rose to his feet. "Your honor, I object to the last question. Mrs. Wesley cannot testify as to the intentions of her husband. Mr. Finch knows that. The witness needs to stick with what she personally observed or heard him say."

Judge Horowitz nodded. "Objection sustained. Disregard the last question."

Finch paced for a moment and wound up a bit closer to Carla than before. "Mrs. Wesley, did you ever hear your husband say he intended to kill those people?"

Carla batted at an errant tear making its way down her cheek. She sniffed and shot another look at Brian. "No. Brian had a drinking problem, but he never wanted to kill anyone."

For an instant, Hannah felt a pang of empathy for Carla Wesley. Both women had lost, and neither of their lives had turned out the way they'd planned. Hannah swallowed hard and her compassion dissolved. Still, that woman had chosen to marry a creep like Brian. It was difficult to feel sorry for her.

Finch made his way back to the table. "No further questions, your honor."

Matt rose once more and nodded politely at Carla Wesley. His tone was kind. "Mrs. Wesley, did you ever warn your husband about his drinking problem?"

Carla gulped and stared at her hands for a moment. "Yes. Lots of times." She looked up at Matt again. "But he was an alcoholic. He couldn't stop drinking—" she glanced at Brian—"not even for me."

Matt nodded. "Very well. And did you ever warn your husband that if he didn't stop drinking and driving, he was going to kill someone?"

Hannah held her breath.

Carla paused, clearly unwilling to answer.

"Answer the question, please, Mrs. Wesley." Judge Horowitz sounded impatient, ready to see the testimony finished.

Carla sighed and her shoulders slumped. "Yes. I warned him."

"You warned your husband many times that he had a drinking problem, and you warned him that if he didn't stop drinking and driving he was going to kill someone. Is that right, Mrs. Wesley?"

Carla refused to look at Brian as she nodded. "Yes." Another tear fell onto her cheek. "I warned him."

Hannah shot a look at the jury and saw they were caught up in the implications of Carla's testimony. Matt cleared his throat and continued. "You warned him, but he did it anyway, is that right?"

"Yes, obviously." Carla pursed her lips and sat up straighter in the witness stand. Hannah wondered about Carla Wesley's mother. Where had she gone wrong in raising Carla to marry a man like Brian Wesley. *What about your own daughter?* Hannah was startled by the sudden question that rattled through her mind. *Jenny is fine. We'll have time together after the trial.* The voice vanished as quickly as it had come.

Matt nodded again. "Thank you, Mrs. Wesley. No further questions, your honor."

"Call your next witness." Judge Horowitz waved a hand toward Finch.

Finch rose, pausing momentarily, then, "The defense rests, your honor."

Hannah exhaled slowly. It was over. No more surprises, no more questioning. It was finally over.

"Very well then." Judge Horowitz adjusted his glasses, drew a deep breath, and directed his gaze first at Finch and then at Matt. "We will take a brief break until 2 P.M. At that time we will hear closing arguments." He banged his gavel and left through a door behind his chair.

Hannah watched as Matt sorted through a stack of documents, and Finch and Brian whispered in some sort of consultation.

"Well, this is it." Carol turned to Hannah.

Hannah massaged her temples. "I can't believe it's finally over."

Carol nodded, her eyes distant. "I remember this part." She looked sadly at Hannah. "Be careful."

"What's that supposed to mean?"

"You've convinced yourself that a conviction will bring you peace, it'll release the anger that's tearing you up. It's the answer to all the problems left behind when Tom and Alicia died."

"It's all I want." Hannah felt the beginning of tears.

"I know. That's all I wanted, too. But it took me a long time before I found the secret to having peace in my life again."

What was she talking about? Didn't she know how much Hannah's head was pounding? How confused she was already? Hannah didn't need this. "It's no secret, Carol. When that animal is locked up, Tom's and Alicia's deaths won't be in vain."

"But there won't be peace."

Hannah was silent.

Carol reached out and took Hannah's hand in hers. "And even a conviction won't bring Tom and Alicia back."

"Don't you think I know that?" She had fought the front line of this battle, and now they had almost reached a victory. There would always be sadness, but a guilty verdict would bring Hannah peace no matter what Carol said. Immediate, perfect peace.

Carol's eyes were so sad Hannah wanted to weep. "Okay. But if you still feel empty when it's all over, I'll be here."

"The only way I'll feel empty is if Brian Wesley walks out of this courtroom a free man. And personally, I don't think that's going to happen. Now let's change the subject before you ruin my day."

Twenty-nine

They mock me in song all day long.

LAMENTATIONS 3:14B

Closing arguments were about to begin, and for the first time all week the jury looked wide-eyed and attentive. An air of excitement buzzed through the courtroom as reporters speculated and spectators recounted evidence in the case. If history were going to be made in Judge Horowitz's courtroom, they wanted to remember every detail. Especially the lawyers in attendance. Someday it would make for great storytelling: the case that changed California drunk driving laws forever.

Matt spoke first, reminding the jurors of Brian's history of drinking and driving. He moved quickly to the day of the accident. "No one wants to get news from the boss that he's been laid off." He walked slowly back and forth in front of the jurors, meeting their intent gazes. "Mr. Wesley packed up his things, loaded his truck, and headed for the road. That's when he made his first choice. He could have gone home. Instead he went to the bar."

Matt stopped and leaned against the railing. He walked the jurors through Brian's every movement that afternoon, emphasizing the choices Brian had made: the choice to go to the bar, the choice to drink, the choice to get drunk, the choice to drive home, the choice to ignore warnings from Carla, the state, and finally the bartender.

"Brian Wesley made deadly choice after deadly choice. Regardless of his history." Matt stared at Brian for a moment, and Hannah watched the jurors do the same. Matt faced them again. "Brian Wesley signed a document agreeing that to make those very choices was to risk life. He knew his choices were deadly." Matt paused. "He told you so himself."

He told you so himself. Hannah closed her eyes, and suddenly she was sucked back to a moment, decades earlier...it was Tom's mother saying those words, days after he proposed to her.

Hannah had been fretful that afternoon. "I don't know, Mrs. Ryan, he spent so long loving that other girl..."

Tom's mother had set a plate of warm cookies on the table and motioned for Hannah to sit. "Oh, no, dear. He never loved her like he loves you, not for a moment."

"But how can I know he really loves me?"

"Hannah, dear, you know he loves you. He told you so himself."

Told you so himself...told you so...told you so...

If there had been a way back—a river to swim, a bridge to cross, an ocean to sail—she would have taken it. She would go back to that warm, Southern California afternoon when she and Tom's mother were speculating about the future, and she would start over again. Relive every day, every minute with Tom. And Alicia. And Jenny. The way everything was before. And when it came to that terrible day last August, she would stop time.

If there was a way.

Hannah felt the sting of tears, and she opened her eyes reluctantly. Matt was still speaking, and she chastised herself. She had to pay attention. It was Brian Wesley's final hour. After this she would have peace. Finally.

Matt's voice was deliberate and intense. "I want you to close your eyes for a moment. Go ahead, close them." He waited until the jurors did as he asked. "Okay now. I want you to imagine three people you love dearly are in a vehicle...coming home from a summer camping trip." Matt waited. "Can you see them? See their smiles? Hear their laughter, hear the fish tales and the retelling of campfire stories? Can you see them?"

Matt walked silently across the courtroom and stopped in front of Hannah. He held out his hand wordlessly. She nodded, reaching into a bag she'd brought for this moment. Inside were two photos. One of the Ryan family, taken the Christmas before the collision. The other of Tom and Alicia. She handed them over to Matt and watched him carry them carefully back to the jury.

"Keep your eyes closed, please." He began pacing again, this time staring at the photos of Hannah's family. "Coming the other direction is Brian Wesley. A man with so many drunk driving arrests the system's nearly lost count. A man who by drinking and driving has already caused two traffic collisions. A man who has signed a statement—signed a legal document—agreeing that for him to drink and drive again could very likely result in death. His or someone else's. A man who has been warned, over and over again. A man who knows that the gun he's wielding is loaded."

The courtroom was so quiet Hannah wondered if everyone could hear her beating heart.

Matt continued, his voice softer still. "Can you see him? Guzzling fourteen drinks over a two-hour span, stumbling out of the bar and heading toward his pickup truck? Can you hear Nick Crabb asking him to wait for a cab? Listen, now. Hear him swear at this young, inexperienced bartender. Can you see him storm out of the bar? Hear his tires squealing as he peels out onto Ventura Boulevard?"

Matt stopped and stared at the jurors, who sat with their eyes still closed. "This is a man who has chosen to drink and drive despite the risks, despite the potential for death. Can you see him behind the wheel, eyes barely open?"

Matt's words came faster now, louder, his tone more urgent. "Now picture your loved ones again, getting off the freeway, their car loaded with camping gear, almost home. They head for the intersection—the same intersection Brian Wesley is about to plow through. Your loved ones move through that intersection at the exact same instant—" Matt stopped, and when he spoke again, his voice was heavy with sorrow. "And in that moment, those three people you love so much are obliterated by an impact as severe as a freight train. One of your loved ones is dead before she ever knew what happened. Another is dead minutes later. The third, alive…but forever devastated."

Hannah was barely aware of the tears sliding down her cheeks. She watched as Matt drew close and leaned against the railing so that he was only inches from her. "You can open your eyes."

The jurors did so but instead of looking at Matt, they stared at Hannah.

"You have not met Hannah Ryan. She has nothing to add to the testimony in this case. But if those had been your loved ones killed by Brian Wesley's speeding truck, if that were you sitting there—" he gestured toward her—"where Hannah's sitting, would you think it was an accident? No. You'd think it was intentional murder. First-degree murder."

Finch squirmed in his seat.

Matt held up the pictures and stared at the faces of Hannah's family once more. Then he looked back at the jury. "It's up to you."

The jury strained to see the photos, and Matt moved closer, positioning them so each of the twelve could study the smiling faces, frozen in a moment that was gone forever.

"It's up to you to open the door. Pave the road to a new California, a place where people will think twice before drinking and driving. A place where people like Brian Wesley won't have a chance to load up and shoot because they'll be behind bars.

"You hold the keys, and I ask you—" Matt turned the photos so he could see them once more—"I beseech you on behalf of Tom and Alicia Ryan, on behalf of young Jenny Ryan and her mother, Hannah. I beg you on behalf of your own loved ones who deserve safer streets. Please...return a guilty verdict. What Brian Wesley did to Hannah Ryan's family was not an accident. Let's stop calling it one. Thank you."

Finch wasted no time. He struggled to his feet, coughed, adjusted the buttons on his vest, cleared his throat. Papers rustled in his hands. Hannah realized he was doing everything he could to break the mood Matt had masterfully created.

He smiled at the jurors and gestured toward them as if they were family gathered for a summer reunion.

"Now you folks are a lot smarter than the district attorney might think." He smiled broadly, dabbing quickly at the perspiration on his forehead. "The good D.A. asks you to close your eyes and imagine. I never heard of anything so ridiculous in all my life." Finch shook his head disdainfully and leaned his belly over the railing, propping himself up on both elbows and looking hard at the jurors. "How dare the district attorney ask you to close your eyes in this case? I will ask you to open your eyes. Open them wide. Look at the defendant."

Twelve pairs of eyes shifted toward Brian Wesley. Hannah scowled at him through narrow eyes, hating the way he hung his head. Only a worthless human being would try to look humble now. She gritted her teeth. He was detestable. Certainly the jury could see that much.

Finch smiled at Brian, and when it was obvious there would be no eye contact between attorney and client, Finch turned back to the jury. "He's not a killer." The attorney searched the faces of the jurors. "You needn't fear him in dark alleys like some hardened criminal. Mr. Wesley is an alcoholic. He needs help. Your help."

Finch paused and raised an eyebrow. "You know, what happened to Brian Wesley could have happened to you. Drink a few too many, wind up in a tragic accident." He straightened his arms, rising several feet above the jurors. "But that doesn't make you a killer, anymore than it makes Mr. Wesley one. He made a series of poor choices. But Brian Wesley did not set out on the afternoon of August 28 to kill two people. The prosecution has not proven that in this courtroom. They have not proven that Brian Wesley chose to kill that day. No. He didn't set out to kill. He just wanted to get home."

Finch moved away from the railing and adjusted his vest buttons. "He was a guy down on his luck who drank a few too many, a guy who wanted to get home. It was an accident, folks. We feel for the family, the victims. But that doesn't change the facts. Brian Wesley never intended for anyone to die. And murder one means a person must intend to kill. Please, folks—" Finch gripped the railing with both hands and once more leaned toward the jury, his voice filled with passion—"Vote with your heads and not your hearts this time. You convict Brian Wesley of murder one in this case, and the next person serving a life sentence for drunk driving might be someone you love. It might even be you."

Finch was finished, and it was time for Matt's final rebuttal.

"What we are talking about here is the repeat drunk driver." He stopped and faced the jury, clearly concerned. "You don't have to worry about serving life for drunk driving unless you're a repeat drunk driver, careening headlong toward a fatal collision."

He waited and Hannah held her breath. "But there is something you and your loved ones do need to worry about. And I ask you today, as you begin wading through the details of this case, please, worry about it. Worry about leaving here and getting on the streets in a state that allows a man with a string of drunk driving arrests and revoked licenses and alcohol-related traffic collisions—a state that allows a man like Brian Wesley—to be on the road when he should be behind bars."

Matt moved closer to the jury box. "And something else. Mr. Finch told you Brian Wesley was not a man to fear." Matt glanced at Hannah, and the jury followed the direction of his gaze. "To tell you the truth, men like Brian Wesley scare me more than convicted felons. I can avoid the places a convict might hang out. But Brian Wesley? I might be coming home from a fishing trip, chatting with my family, and boom! The people I love most are dead." Matt raised an eyebrow and shook his head. "Laws being what they are today, I can't avoid a man like Brian Wesley. And *that* scares me."

Matt leaned against the railing and folded his arms. "Mr. Finch wants you to think of Brian Wesley as someone down on his luck, just trying to get home. Well, that's all the Ryan family was trying to do. Three days in the mountains, end of summer, school's about to begin. They were coming home."

He faced the jury squarely and slid his hands into his pockets. His voice was strong, but Hannah thought his eyes looked damp as he continued. "What happened to Hannah Ryan could happen to me—" he met their eyes—"or you. Any day. Anytime. Anywhere. Remember, there are two reasons why Brian Wesley should be convicted of first-degree murder. The first is to punish him. He took a weapon, in this case a pickup truck, and made a choice to use it under the influence of alcohol. That's intentional murder, and it must be punished as such.

"But the second reason is just as valid. The second reason is to protect people like Hannah Ryan. People like you. It's time, friends, please. Find Brian Wesley guilty of first-degree murder, and let's put an end to this madness now. Before it's too late."

The judge finished giving instructions, and the case was handed over to the jury. After just two hours the foreman notified the clerk.

They had reached a decision.

He has broken my teeth with gravel; he has trampled me in the dust.

LAMENTATIONS 3:16

Because of the late afternoon hour, Judge Horowitz determined that the verdict would be read at 10 A.M. the next day. The moment Matt heard the news, he was on the phone to Hannah. A quick verdict wasn't good.

"So fast? What does it mean?" Hannah sounded frantic, and Matt's heart went out to her.

"It could go either way." He wanted to be honest. "But usually...quick verdicts wind up in favor of the defense."

Hannah was silent for several seconds. "*What?* That's impossible!" Matt could see the fury that would be in Hannah's eyes as clearly as if he were standing in front of her. It made him wish he'd told her the news in person so he could take her in his arms and comfort her.

"Remember, Hannah, we had the burden of proof. Brian is innocent until proven guilty, and usually it takes longer to study the evidence and determine guilt. Usually."

"Then we'll have to appeal, find a loophole. Something. He has to pay for this, Matt. He can't just—"

"Hannah, I didn't say he was acquitted. I just wanted to warn you. There's a chance. A good chance. We took a gamble in this case and didn't leave the jury much choice. All or nothing."

Hannah made no response, and Matt could hear her quietly sobbing.

"Hannah? Are you all right? I can be there in five minutes if you need me." Matt almost hoped she'd say yes.

"No." She gave two quick, jerky breaths and steadied her voice. "I'm okay. I have to talk to Jenny. She's…she's been in her room all evening."

Matt felt Hannah's heartache as though it were his own. He had to resist the urge to ask once more if she needed him. He wanted to be there. Wanted to help her. But he didn't ask it. He didn't want her to mistake his intentions. Not now. He changed topics instead. "I'm still worried about her."

"Jenny?" Hannah drew a weary breath. "I think she'll be okay. She's just hiding out until the trial's over. When I have peace, she will, too."

Matt sighed. "Hannah…what if the verdict…" He couldn't bring himself to finish the sentence.

"Don't, Matt. Please. I simply can't imagine the what-ifs. It's late and it's been the longest week of my life. My daughter hates me, and after tomorrow I have to put this behind me and get on with making a life for the two of us. Right now I have no choice but to believe that tomorrow you will win your conviction, and finally—" her voice broke once more, and she sounded beyond tired. "Finally, I can have peace."

Matt tapped a pencil on his dining room table and searched frantically for the right words. She wouldn't have peace. He knew she wouldn't. But there was no point trying to convince her. Not right now. "Get some sleep, Hannah."

She laughed, but there was no hint of humor in her voice. "Are you kidding? With Jenny upstairs pouting and the verdict sitting in some sealed envelope down at the courthouse? *You* sleep, Matt. I'll see you tomorrow."

"Okay, but if you're going to be awake anyway, at least pray, Hannah. Please. Jenny needs your prayers."

"She doesn't need prayers, Matt; she needs her daddy and her big sister." Hannah sighed and the emotion drained from her voice. "And not even your God can give her that."

Matt cringed. *Lord, give me the words. Hannah's your child. Jenny, too. Help them, Lord.*

When he remained silent, Hannah drew another deep breath. "I'm sorry, Matt. I don't mean to take it out on you. You've been wonderful through this whole thing. I could never have climbed into that legal ring and duked it out with Finch like you've done. You were my only weapon in the biggest fight of my life."

"That's why God brought me into the case."

Hannah paused. "God has nothing to do with it. He checked out months ago. August 28, I think it was."

Matt could almost see the bitter root strangling everything beautiful in Hannah Ryan. But there was nothing he could say. "Enough. Good night, Hannah."

"Night, Matt." She hesitated. "See you tomorrow."

He clicked the off button on his cordless telephone and set it on the kitchen counter. Hannah Ryan. He wandered to the cupboard, pulled out a glass and filled it with ice water. What would become of her after tomorrow, when she learned that peace wasn't something one could buy with revenge? Win or lose, tomorrow night Hannah would be as unsettled as today. Maybe more so.

The glass was cool against his hands. He wandered into the living room and settled into a leather recliner. He pressed the drink to his face. Hot, hazy, summer days. Why had the Lord put Hannah in his life, anyway? And what would happen if they lost this case?

He surveyed his empty house. Normally after a day in court the solitude brought him peace. Today, for some reason, it made him feel lonely and old. Television didn't help, so Matt turned in early and pulled out his newest copy of the Bible—a clothbound, men's edition. Matt did not keep a well-worn copy of the Bible in his house. He liked reading the Bible through, marking it up as much as possible, and then starting fresh with another copy.

He fell asleep reading Philippians 4, somewhere between the peace that passes understanding and doing all things through Christ who gives strength. But he didn't dream of Paul and his profound letter.

He dreamed of Hannah Ryan.

Hannah studied her bedroom as she hung up the telephone. It had been nearly a year, and Tom's Bible was now packed away with his other things. Only a picture of them taken on their tenth anniversary remained on the dresser. The clutter Tom had always tossed there had long since been cleared. There were none of the keys and coins and receipts that had collected there each week while they were married.

Tom was gone. The room was proof.

She stood and stretched. Her bones were tired, but she wasn't particularly interested in sleep. Besides, the last few nights she'd woken at all hours with the most frightening nightmares. Hannah shuddered. There was no point dwelling on the dreams now. She had business to take care of.

Tiptoeing upstairs, Hannah tried to work up her courage. Anymore it was an amazing feat to get two words out of Jenny, and nights like this Hannah was almost too worn out to try. She knocked at the door.

"What?"

The girl didn't sound angry. She didn't sound anything. After tomorrow they could start working on their tattered relationship, but how long would it take? Months? Years? "Can I come in?"

Silence.

"Jenny? I want to talk to you." Hannah allowed the wall to hold her up as she closed her eyes. "Open the door, Jenny."

Footsteps, then Hannah heard a click. Jenny opened the door a crack, but by the time Hannah looked inside, she was already back on her bed, staring at the ceiling, eyes hollow.

Hannah pulled up a chair and sat down, facing the girl. For a single moment she remembered their old life, when she would climb into the girls' beds with them, snuggling and giggling and making girl-talk long after bedtime prayers. Now there was only awkwardness between them, forcing Hannah to keep her distance. She settled into the chair and tried not to think about it.

"The trial ended today." Hannah waited and for an instant there was a flicker of something in Jenny's eyes. Concern? Interest? Whatever it was, Hannah knew she had caught the girl's attention.

When Jenny said nothing, Hannah felt her frustration begin to grow. "Did you hear me?"

Jenny didn't roll her eyes or sigh as she had done so often lately. Instead she leveled her gaze at Hannah. "Yes, Mother. I heard you."

There was no point waiting for Jenny to ask questions. She wouldn't. Hannah set her chin. "It went well, I think. Matt did a great job presenting the case. But there's still a chance Brian Wesley will be acquitted. We'll know tomorrow."

Jenny stared at her mother blankly.

"I thought you'd like to come. Tomorrow, I mean. I know you haven't wanted to be there before. But it is the verdict, after all. If we win, I want you to be there."

Jenny's face twisted. "If we *win?* Mother, listen to yourself! No one's going to win tomorrow."

"If Brian Wesley goes to prison, we will win. It's that simple."

Jenny sat up in bed. "No, it's not that simple...." She looked like she was about to say something else, but apparently changed her mind. Shoulders slumped, she began picking at her bedspread. "Never mind."

Hannah leaned forward, trying to get up the courage to touch her daughter, to pull her into a hug. Anything to bridge the distance between them. "Things will be different after tomorrow." Silence. "You have to understand, Jenny. After Daddy and Alicia were killed, I didn't know what else to do. I had to fight. Tomorrow Brian Wesley will be taken into custody.

Where he's belonged since he did this awful thing to us."

Jenny looked up, and Hannah was shocked to see that her little girl had the eyes of an old woman. "You honestly think a guilty verdict will make things different? Between us?"

"I know they will, honey. The battle's almost over." She hesitated. "Just this once, could you come to the trial with me? Please, Jenny."

Jenny shook her head quickly. "No. I won't go. I told you that." Her voice was panicky, and Hannah drew back.

"Okay, forget it. I just thought...after all this time...oh, never mind." Hannah stood up and headed for the door. Her heart felt like a dead weight within her.

"Mom..."

Hannah spun around. In that instant, in that one single word she heard the Jenny she'd lost, the one she hadn't heard since they'd said good-bye in the driveway the day they left for the camping trip. The one that never made it home. Hannah searched her daughter's eyes, but she wasn't there. When Jenny spoke again whatever Hannah had heard was gone. The indifference was back.

"Nothing."

"Tell me, honey."

"It's nothing, Mom."

"Jenny...it's been so long since we've talked. Really talked." Hannah hated the awkwardness between them. She paused, desperately trying to think of the right words. "I'm here. Let me know when you're ready."

Jenny's eyes were blank and she didn't nod. Instead she lay down, turned her back to her mother, and faced the wall.

The rejection was more than Hannah could bear. "Fine. Turn away."

"Get out, Mother. I'm done talking."

If that's the way you want it, Jenny... Hannah stared at her, and in a voice so frigid it was foreign even to her, she spat one final sentence at her daughter: "Thanks a lot, Jenny, and oh, yeah, I love you, too." Hannah stormed out of the room, her heart pounding, her eyes dry.

That night as Hannah fell asleep, she realized she had no one to love, no one who loved her. Somehow she had died without anyone noticing. Her corpse was still breathing, but she was dead. As she tossed and turned, battling relentless, unseen, torturous demons, she wondered how it was, someone could love God most of her life and still wind up in hell.

Sgt. Jon Miller was having trouble falling asleep, but not because of unseen demons. Lately he'd been bothered by the accident...the one from a year ago. He had convinced himself it was the testimony. Acting as a witness for the prosecution had brought up memories he'd almost forgotten. The young teenage girls, one dead when he arrived on the scene...and the man, Dr. Tom Ryan. And especially that scene in the car when the man was trying to speak his final words.

He couldn't for the life of him understand why that particular memory kept making its way into his mind. He had done as the man asked, passed on his final message for his surviving family. Sgt. Miller turned in bed and saw that his wife was sleeping soundly. He sighed. His eyes were open, but all he could see was Dr. Tom Ryan, trying to speak, struggling to form those final words.

Tell Hannah and the girls he loved them. That was it, wasn't it?

Miller rolled over onto his other side and shut his eyes. Maybe he should get up and read his Bible. God's promises always helped him fall asleep. He flipped so that he was flat on his back. He was about to pray when he heard the voice.

Remember the rest.

Miller's eyes flew open and he sat up straight in bed. Had he imagined that or had someone actually spoken? He glanced about the room, but nothing had changed. He released the air from his lungs slowly. Sinking back into the pillows he felt his heart race. Must have been a dream. Maybe he was falling asleep after all. He closed his eyes. *Lord, thank you for letting—*

Remember the rest.

His eyes flew open and he shot up once more. His eyes sought his wife, but she was snoring. He propped his pillows and leaned back, heart racing, searching the room for the source of the message. *Remember the rest?* The image appeared again, Dr. Tom Ryan, bleeding to death, trying to gurgle out the last part of a farewell.

Could that be it? Was there something more to his message?

Suddenly the image cleared, and a realization came over Sgt. Miller so strong that he could feel his nerves calming, his heart rate returning to normal.

Dr. Ryan had said *two* things, not one. Tell Hannah and the girls he loved them and...and something else. Something that hadn't seemed very important at the time.

Now if only he could remember what.

Thirty-one

I have been deprived of peace; I have forgotten what prosperity is.

LAMENTATIONS 3:17

They met in a thicket of trees just outside the courthouse some two hours before the verdict. Neither of them wanted to be seen together. Especially praying together.

Heads bowed, voices soft, they lifted their direst concerns to the Lord. Finally, they thanked him for whatever he was about to do. It was getting late, and there were people moving in and out of the courthouse. They sat on opposite sides of the bench, silent.

"Are you nervous?" She studied him. This might be their last conversation outside prison walls.

He shrugged. "It was a quick verdict. Could mean an acquittal." His eyes stayed down and he picked nervously at the rough skin around his fingernails.

"You don't look happy."

He shot her a quick glance. "I'm not."

She nodded. That was understandable. A person could be spirit-filled and still be unhappy.

"In some ways I wanna serve time." He drew a shaky breath. "If they let me walk...I'll never be able to face her."

"You're not in control here, Brian."

"I know, I know. We've been talking about it, me and the Lord."

"Just do what's right. God will take care of the rest."

He looked at his watch. "I have to meet my lawyer."

She stood and gathered her purse. "I'll be praying."

Jenny's hands trembled as she sat at the breakfast table. It was verdict day—for Brian Wesley and for her. She stared at the soggy cornflakes in front of her, but she could see her mother, darting about the kitchen, grabbing gulps of black coffee. She was reading something, probably newspaper articles about the accident and the victim impact panels. Her life's passion.

"What are you doing today?" Her mother set her coffee cup in the sink and glanced at Jenny.

Mom was obviously still mad about last night, and suddenly Jenny was sorry she'd been rude. It would have been nice to be at peace on their last morning together.

She took another bite of cornflakes. "Nothing."

Her mother waited, impatient to leave. "Fine. I'll tell you how it went when I get home. Not that you care."

Jenny watched her grab the car keys from the counter and head for the garage. No kiss. No good-bye. She listened as her mother drove off, and then she trudged upstairs, shoulders heavy, heart empty.

It was time.

After all the planning, it was finally time. She pulled the box from beneath her bed and examined the contents once more. Pills. Water. Good-bye note.

Not that you care.... Not that you care.... Her mother's words haunted her, but she shook them off. She did care. Not about the trial, but about Daddy and Alicia. It would only be a few hours now until they were together. If only she'd hugged her mother or said good-bye. Two lonely tears slipped from her eyes and landed on her bedspread.

Sniffing loudly, she dried her eyes and sat up straighter. There was no time for regrets now.

She had to get busy.

It was almost time. Hannah felt as if she'd waited her entire life for this moment. The courtroom was filled with people spilling into the hallways, straining to get a view of what was about to happen. Hannah took in the scene as it unfolded. Brian and Finch huddled at one end of the table; Matt and his assistants at the other.

Matt had met her downstairs earlier and assured her that if Brian was acquitted on first-degree murder charges, the state would see that he served the maximum time for drunk driving. It was the least they could do.

"Don't talk like that," Hannah said. They stood against a wall, facing each other in a quiet corridor near his office. Their voices had been hushed and inches separated them.

"Hannah, you have to be realistic. What if they come back with not guilty?"

She didn't hesitate. "I'll kill him myself."

"Hannah..."

"I'm serious."

He had sighed and pulled her into a quick hug. "Let's go. It's time."

That was an hour ago.

Carol Cummins leaned over and whispered to her. "If anyone can pull this off, it's Matt Bronzan."

Hannah nodded. "He's worried."

Carol studied Matt for a moment. "You'd never know it."

A hush fell over the courtroom as Judge Horowitz entered and took his seat. The moment of the verdict had arrived.

The judge glanced around. "I see that there are a great number of people interested in the outcome of this trial. I warn you, matters will be conducted in a quiet manner. I will not allow my courtroom to become a media circus." He banged his gavel. "Court is in session. Will the bailiff please bring in the jury."

The bailiff moved toward a door on the side of the courtroom, disappeared for a moment, then returned with the jurors in single file procession behind him. The jurors took their seats.

The pills were calling her, beckoning her to a better place where she and Alicia and Daddy could spend eternity together. She opened the water and picked up three orange capsules. *Please, God, let this work.* She slipped the pills into her mouth and took a swig of water. For a moment Jenny thought she was going to gag, but then she took another swig and felt the pills go down.

There were dozens of pills on her bedspread. She picked up three more capsules, and this time they went down easier. She reached down and found three more. Swallow. Three red. Swallow. It was easier than she'd thought. Before she knew it, the pile was gone. She had done it.

Now all she had to do was wait.

Matt watched the jury file in and take their places.

The judge looked at them. "Has the jury reached a decision?" Matt glanced at Hannah and saw that her eyes were closed, her hands clenched tightly. His heart constricted. *Father, I'd do anything to give Hannah the peace she so desperately seeks. Help her, please.*

The jury foreman stood up. "Yes, your honor."

"Very well. Please hand the verdict to the bailiff."

The foreman did as he was told, and the bailiff carried it to Judge Horowitz. He read it silently, his expression unchanging. He leaned over and handed it back to the court clerk. The judge looked about the courtroom. "The clerk will now read the verdict."

A petite brunette in her late fifties stood, her mouth near

the microphone. She unfolded the verdict and cleared her throat.

A strange feeling was working its way through Jenny's body. She felt her heart beat erratically. Her hands shook...then her arms...finally every part of her was trembling violently.

Was this it? Was this death?

The room started spinning and all the edges blurred together.

"I have come that they may have life...I have come that they may have life...I have come..."

Scripture filled her mind—bringing doubt with it.

Suicide was murder. Wasn't that one of the Ten Commandments? *"Thou shalt not kill....I have come that they may have life..."*

Jesus didn't want her to take her life. Daddy, either.

She needed to get to the bathroom. Someone online had told her if she took the pills then changed her mind, her only hope was to vomit. *Get up!* But her legs would not obey. She stuck her finger down her throat and gagged, but nothing came up.

Jenny beat her stomach with her fists, willing her body to reject the pills, but they sat like a ball of poison in her belly. It was getting harder to breathe. She had tricked herself into thinking this was the answer when it was really no answer at all.

It was a lie straight from the devil. And now it was too late.

The court clerk was reading and Hannah hung on every word.

"We, the jury, find the defendant, Brian Wesley, guilty of the crime of drunk driving." She paused and prepared to read the second verdict. "We, the jury, find the defendant, Brian Wesley, guilty of the crime of first degree-murder against Tom Ryan and Alicia Ryan."

Tears flooded Hannah's eyes, and her hands flew to her face, providing the only privacy in a room where suddenly all attention was focused on her.

They'd done it! They'd won the verdict. Brian Wesley would spend the rest of his life in prison. Matt had been brilliant. The evidence had been glaringly obvious. That's why the verdict had come so quickly.

We won! We won! Guilty! We won...we won. The words ran through her mind, over and over. Every panel, every hour of research, every meeting with Carol, all of Matt's hard work...it all had paid off. It was the victory she'd waited for all year, and now it was time to celebrate. Brian Wesley was going to prison. Murder one. History-making murder one.

Her hands remained spread across her face, and she heard herself weeping now, louder and louder. She felt Carol's arm come around her shoulders, and she struggled to gain control. Dimly she heard Judge Horowitz banging his gavel, calling for order.

She had pictured this moment a hundred times. She'd imagined she would jump up and congratulate Matt, look at the jurors and silently thank them for making the right choice, then proceed to the cameras for a series of interviews.

Instead, she was consumed by the greatest heartache she had ever known.

It was her grandest moment—the moment of justice and peace—but not one of the people she loved was there to share it with her.

If this is peace, how will I ever tolerate a lifetime of it?

Jenny was dizzy. She lay back on her bed and began to cry, but she only heard the deep, raspy sound of her body gasping for breath.

No! Please, no! Her mind screamed the words, but her mouth no longer worked. Suddenly she remembered something from one of the Internet sites. You know it's working if your fingernail beds begin to turn blue. She held up her hands, steadying them, straining to see them as the images blurred. It was impossible to tell, but she thought she saw the deadly blue there.

She gasped once more, but black spots blocked her vision. Suddenly all she wanted to do was sleep.

Please, God. I want to live. I want...

Her thoughts faded. She could no longer feel herself trying to breathe.

Two seconds later, she was unconscious.

Matt released the air from his lungs slowly. "Thank you, God." He turned to face Hannah.

The entire courtroom had erupted into conversation, but his eyes were fixed on her alone. She was hunched over, head buried in her hands, weeping. She needed him, and in that instant he felt an attraction for her that went far beyond the scope of the trial. He chided himself for the feeling. *Must be the intensity of the moment.* He started to rise from his seat, then remembered the proceedings were not officially finished. He sat back down, his neck craned, his eyes still on her.

Poor Hannah. He had won, but not her. She had lost everything. Not even this verdict could change that.

The judge banged his gavel. "Order! Order in the court."

Gradually the people who filled the room and much of the corridor outside fell silent once more. Judge Horowitz gave each of the jurors the opportunity to affirm their verdict. Then he continued with final instructions.

"The bailiff will take the defendant into custody until such time as his sentencing hearing, which will take place two weeks from today in this courtroom at ten in the morning. At that time—" he looked at Brian Wesley—"the defendant and the victims will have an opportunity to speak. That is all for today. Court dismissed."

He banged his gavel one final time, and Brian Wesley stood to face the bailiff. Cameras captured the moment as handcuffs were snapped onto Brian's wrists, and he was led away.

It was the first time Matt had been able to look into Brian's eyes since his testimony days earlier, and what he saw there was surprisingly familiar. Peace. Brian looked content, ready to take his punishment. Matt stared, stunned, and suddenly he knew Hannah's concerns had been warranted.

Brian Wesley had the eyes of a believer.

Matt turned toward Hannah and saw that she was still sobbing. He watched her hands drop, saw her eyes follow Brian as he was led away. He didn't want her to stay around the courtroom. She needed to be home with Jenny. *Get her home. Now!* The urging impelled him from his seat.

"Matt…" She stood up and hugged him, gripping his neck and burying her head in his shoulder.

"Shhh…it's all right. It's over now." He knew the cameras were on them and he pulled away, studying her face. The hatred was still there. And the bitterness and a dozen other emotions with the exception of one: peace.

A reporter made his way over and stood between them. "What's your reaction to the verdict, Mrs. Ryan?"

She straightened and wiped her cheeks with her fingertips. "I think it's wonderful. The streets will be safer when we can be confident about convicting repeat drunk drivers of first-degree murder."

"And what about Mr. Wesley? Do you think he deserves the full sentence, life in prison?"

Matt watched Hannah's eyes narrow, and he cringed at what was coming.

"Yes. He deserves a life sentence. And then he deserves to rot in hell."

Hannah was barely aware of her surroundings as she drove home. She had expected to feel something...elation, excitement, the thrill of victory. *Something*. But as she turned into her driveway she felt strangely numb. Exactly the way she'd felt before the verdict. She glanced in her rearview mirror and saw Matt pull in behind her. He had talked her into going for lunch, but he thought they should tell Jenny the news first.

Together they walked up to the house.

Matt waited while Hannah turned the key. "She can come with us if she wants."

Hannah huffed as she opened the door. "Good luck. Jenny doesn't do anything that involves me these days." She headed for the stairs. "Jenny?"

No answer.

"She must be sleeping. Wait here, I'll wake her and tell her the news." Hannah trudged up the stairs. She had a throbbing headache and couldn't wait for the day to end. She entered the hallway and headed for her daughter's room.

"Jenny, I'm home." Again, no response. She was wasting her time. Jenny wouldn't care, anyway. She turned the doorknob to the room, but it was locked.

Hannah sighed impatiently. "Jenny, it's me. Wake up."

Nothing. Hannah banged on the door.

"Jenny, come on." She was shouting now, angry because she knew her daughter was ignoring her.

"Jenny...open the door this instant! Do you understand me?"

Silence.

Suddenly Hannah heard voices from the corner of her memory....The principal...*"I don't know, Mrs. Ryan, under normal circumstances a girl like Jenny would never consider suicide...but now..."* Then Matt...*"I'm worried about her...you don't think she'd try anything crazy, do you?"*

Terror seized her and she grabbed the door, rattling it frantically. "Jenny, open up!"

Twisting the knob roughly, she pushed her shoulder into the door, but it held. *God, no. Please...*

"Matt!"

He was at her side in seconds. "What—"

"Jenny's locked in there! She won't answer. Open it, Matt. Whatever it takes, just get it open!"

"Jenny, this is Matt Bronzan! Open the door, okay?"

When there was no response, he gently pushed Hannah aside. Then in a single, quick motion he jammed his shoulder against the door, and it flew open. Hannah followed him into the room, and they saw her. Sprawled out on her bed, her skin gray, pills scattered on the floor beside her. At the foot of the bed lay a box with a note on top of it. Matt picked it up, read two lines and dropped it. Instantly he grabbed Jenny's wrist.

"What's wrong with her?" Hannah screamed. She bent over Jenny, shaking her.

"I can't find a pulse!" Matt grabbed Hannah's shoulders. "My God, Hannah, call an ambulance!"

Thirty-two

So I say, "My splendor is gone and all that I had hoped from the Lord.*" I remember my affliction...the bitterness and the gall. I well remember them, and my soul is downcast within me. Yet this I call to mind and therefore I have hope: Because of the Lord's great love we are not consumed.*

Lamentations 3:18-22

Sometime between watching Matt perform fifteen agonizing minutes of mouth-to-mouth resuscitation on Jenny, and hearing paramedics radio the hospital to inform them a suicide-attempt was coming in; sometime between reading Jenny's suicide note in the ambulance, and authorizing doctors at the emergency room to pump her daughter's stomach, Hannah began doing something she hadn't done in nearly a year.

She prayed.

Not that she'd had some deep realization that God was real or that his promises were true. Rather, she had simply reached the end of herself, of everything she knew about coping.

Her prayers were pure, desperate instinct.

An hour after arriving at the emergency room, Hannah was still uttering the same silent prayer as she sat in the waiting room on a cold, vinyl sofa, Matt at her side. *Please, Lord, please let her live. Don't let her die, God, please.*

Thirty minutes passed before Hannah heard purposeful footsteps.

"Mrs. Ryan? We need to talk about your daughter."

Hannah lifted her head, stared at the doctor, and gasped.

Dr. Cleary. The same doctor who had told her the news about Tom and Alicia.

She screamed then. "*No!* Not again! Get away!" She bolted up from the sofa and pushed the doctor out of her way. "Not Jenny! *No!* No more!"

She was screaming, struggling to make it to the doorway, when she felt two firm hands on her shoulders.

"Let me go!"

"Hannah—"

"*Nooooo!*" People were watching, getting up and moving their small children away, but Hannah didn't care. She would not hear the same news about Jenny that she'd already heard about Tom and Alicia. She needed space, needed air, needed out. Anywhere else. She struggled to break free, but now the arms eased firmly around her waist, holding her fast.

"Go away, Doctor! Let me g—" She spun around, and suddenly the fight was gone.

It was Matt. "Matt..."

"Shhh. It's okay. Calm down."

She sagged against him, gasping for air. No matter how many breaths she drew in, she couldn't get enough oxygen. Her words came in short, choppy spurts. "Tell...the doctor...to go...away!"

"Hannah, blow the air out." Matt pulled a few inches back and spoke to her gently, slowly. "Come on...do it."

Something deep within Hannah knew she needed to obey him. She pursed her lips and blew out a puff of air that wouldn't have flickered a birthday candle.

"Again...several times...come on, Hannah, sweetheart." She sank into him, exhaling three times without taking a breath. *Please God...*

Matt met her gaze. "There...better?"

She nodded, but tears filled her eyes as she looked up at him. "Stay with me?"

He nodded and gently led her back to where Dr. Cleary was

waiting. Matt's arm was wrapped tightly around her shoulders, supporting her.

"Let's go in another room." Dr. Cleary started to turn.

"Wait!" Hannah was frozen in place. For an instant her eyes connected with Dr. Cleary's. She had to know. "She's dead, isn't she?"

Dr. Cleary reached out and touched the side of her arm. "No, Mrs. Ryan, she's not dead." He looked about the waiting room and saw that they were alone. "Tell you what, let's sit down right here."

Matt and Hannah sat back on the sofa, and Dr. Cleary sat across from them. His eyes narrowed with concern. "Mrs. Ryan, Jenny's in a coma. She was very nearly successful in her attempt to take her life, and we know she was without oxygen for some period of time." He hesitated and looked at Matt. "Are you the one who performed CPR on her?"

He nodded.

"It saved her life." His gaze came back to Hannah. "But she's still in critical condition. Things could go either way."

Hannah gulped two quick breaths. "What...what does that mean?"

"Breathe out," Matt whispered, and she obeyed.

"Comas are unpredictable." Dr. Cleary shook his head slightly. "She could come out of it today, or not for twenty years. Also there's a chance she may have suffered some brain damage."

Hannah couldn't breathe. She gulped huge breaths of air, but it didn't matter. Matt was telling her something, but she couldn't hear him. She was growing faint..."No...can't be...Not Jenny...It's all my...all my...all my fault..."

Matt caught her as she fell, then she passed out.

Hannah slowly opened her eyes. She was lying on a narrow cot with bright lights glaring at her. She felt woozy, her eyelids heavy…and she wanted to close them. She glanced around.

Where was she?

Sterile bandages were stacked on a nearby counter, and there was a chart on the wall detailing various views of the human ankle before and after injury.

Then it came back in a rush. She was in the emergency room, and Jenny was somewhere lying in a drug-induced coma. Fear gripped her.

God…please, no! She sat up too quickly and rubbed the back of her neck. This can't be happening. Tom and Alicia, dead. Jenny lying in a coma from a drug overdose. She needed to find Jenny and wake her up. She thought of the girl's suicide note. *You've been too busy….You lost everything that matters….I'm just in the way….You can only walk around a museum of memories for so long….You don't want me talking about Jesus….Sometimes I think I miss him as much as I miss Daddy and Alicia….This is the only way…*

A powerful desire swept Hannah then. She wanted to be on her knees, in a chapel. She didn't understand it, didn't question it. Just felt the sense as it filled her to overflowing. She looked around. She needed a chapel.

Before she could get her feet on the ground, Dr. Cleary appeared. "Hannah, how're you feeling?" He came alongside her and took her pulse.

"I need to go—"

"That's fine. Your vitals are good."

"How's Jenny?" Tears filled her eyes and spilled onto her cheeks.

"The same."

"Matt? Mr. Bronzan…did he go home?"

"No. He's upstairs with Jenny. Sitting by her bed. He told me about the verdict. I've been following it in the papers. I know it must have been very hard for you." Dr. Cleary paused. "We're doing our best to make sure the media doesn't find out about this."

Hannah nodded, tears blurring her vision as she stared down at her leather heels. She was still dressed in the same skirt and blouse she'd worn for court. Had the verdict been only that morning?

Dr. Cleary interrupted her thoughts. "It was the right verdict."

She nodded again, silent.

"Listen, Mrs. Ryan, I've asked the hospital social worker to stop in if you'd like to talk. You've got a lot to deal with..."

Hannah shook her head, but she made sure her tone was kind. "I already have a counselor, Doctor, if you'll give me permission to go talk to him."

"Here, at the hospital?" He looked confused.

"Yes." Hannah's head was clearing quickly. She sat up straighter, determined. "May I go?"

"Is he expecting you?"

Hannah nodded. "Yes. Can you tell me how to get to the chapel?"

With every step she took, Hannah knew with increasing certainty that God was, indeed, expecting her. She knew it because he was speaking to her.

He'd done so before; she knew it. But she'd closed her mind, her heart. Now...now her heart was shattered, decimated on the rocks of her rebellion and anger. Now her defenses were gone, and all that was left was brokenness...contrition...

"I have loved you with an everlasting love..."

Yes. Oh, yes...I know...

Still, a hundred thoughts battled for position in her mind, both accusing the Lord and assaulting him with questions. *Why? Why if you loved me? Why if you loved them? Why us? Why when so much of life lay ahead? Why, Lord?*

The questions came as steadily as the click of her heels on the hard linoleum floor. She was still angry with God, but by the time she reached the chapel, she was absolutely certain that he knew that. God was listening. He had never stopped. He was as real as the nightmare that had become her life.

"Come, let us reason together..."

I'm coming, Father, I'm coming...

She pushed opened the chapel door and crept inside. Twelve empty, cushioned pews filled the room, and gentle lights shone on a single object at the front. Hannah moved slowly down the center aisle, her eyes fixed straight ahead.

It was not an ordinary cross, but a life-size one of two rough-hewn wooden beams roped together in the center. It stood there, a challenge to anyone who doubted the depth and height and breadth of Christ's love.

A challenge to Hannah.

Tears flooded her eyes, and she took two steps closer.

She had forgotten about the cross. Oh, it was there on the gold chains people wore at the grocery store, emblazoned across an occasional bumper sticker or novelty T-shirt. But this cross—this symbol of pain and suffering, this weapon of splintered wood and iron stakes slicing into the Lord's back, ripping through the flesh in his wrists and feet, this reminder of how the Savior gasped for air and asked the Father to forgive his killers—this cross would forever show the world what Hannah had forgotten until now.

Jesus loved her.

She stopped in front of the cross.

"He was...a man of sorrows...familiar with suffering....He... carried our sorrows...the punishment that brought us peace was upon him, and by his wounds we are healed."

She closed her eyes, not even trying to stop the tears. Peace. She'd sought it for so long and so hard, and it had been here all along.

"We all, like sheep, have gone astray, each of us has turned to his own way; and the Lord has laid on him the iniquity of us all..."

Reaching out, Hannah ran her fingertips over the splintery

surface of the cross. Anyone who would die that kind of death for her, had to love her. That truth struck her to the core.

Hannah's knees went weak with the force of the sorrow that washed over her. She had suffered much this past year, but it had been worse because she had exchanged the truth about God for a lie. She had rejected any comfort or solace or hope that the Lord would have offered, choosing instead to fight her battles alone. By doing so, she had built an icy fortress of self-pity around her heart, shutting out God and Jenny and anything but her desire for revenge.

The cross towered above her, the beams as thick around as her waist.

She stared up and imagined the Lord looking down at her, forgiving her for walking away. And finally, in that moment, the sorrow was more than she could take. She wrapped her arms around the cross and wept, loud, inconsolable cries for forgiveness. Slowly, humbled by the weight of her sin against God, her arms slid down the rough, wooden beam until she lay in a heap at the foot of the cross.

Jesus had not stopped loving her when Tom and Alicia were killed. Life took place on the enemy's ground. And the enemy would always allow drunk driving and senseless murder and evildoers like Brian Wesley.

But there was more to the battle, and for a season Hannah had forgotten. Yes, this world was Satan's domain, but God had already won the war. The enemy was no longer a threat to Tom and Alicia, for they were celebrating in the very presence of the living God. Tom and Alicia had only been on loan in a place that was never meant to last forever.

Our citizenship is in heaven.... The words were a physical comfort to Hannah as one after another Scriptures filled her mind. She was only passing through, a foreigner in a strange land. Like all who followed Christ, whether she walked this planet eight years or eighty, it was only a journey. She wouldn't ever really be home until she reached heaven's doorsteps.

She wept then, remembering the times she had rejected Jenny this past year and how she had allowed the girl to stumble through the most difficult time in her life with neither her support nor God's.

"I'm sorry, so sorry, Father. Please, don't punish her for my sin..."

When her weeping finally eased, she prayed—and it was as if she'd never stopped, as though there'd never been a distance between her and God.

She was restored. By God's grace and mercy, she'd been restored.

Lord, I'm sorry. I don't deserve her. But please, if it be your will, please...please let her live. She sniffed loudly and ran her fingers underneath her eyes. *Come, Holy Spirit. Please come to me. And whatever happens, Father...Thy will be done....*

Suddenly she had an overwhelming desire to read Scripture. She let go of the cross and rose to her feet, then made her way into one of the pews and opened a Bible. She fanned past the Old Testament, through Matthew and the gospels and on into Revelation.

What did one read after being away from Scripture for an entire year? *Lamentations*. It was as though Carol Cummins was sitting beside her, whispering in her ear. *Read Lamentations*.

Nodding, she flipped back into the Old Testament until she found the book written by the prophet Jeremiah. All year Hannah had resisted Carol's advice to read this book. Now she devoured the words.

Her eyes filled with tears once more when she reached the second chapter. "*The Lord is like an enemy...my eyes fail from weeping, I am in torment within, my heart poured out on the ground because my people are destroyed...you summoned against me terrors on every side...he has turned his hand against me again and again...he has made my skin and my flesh grow old...*

Hannah thought of how her eyes had changed, how her features had grown hard and sour, how even the guilty verdict had not brought her peace. She bowed her head.

"I can't take anymore, God…Please…let her live."

"Hannah."

The voice came from behind her, and Hannah spun around, wiping at her tears.

"Matt…what is it?" She grabbed the Bible and moved to meet him in the aisle.

He took her hands in his. "It's okay. It's Jenny." His eyes shone with joy, and Hannah's heart leapt. "She's awake, Hannah. She's calling for you."

"Oh, dear God, thank you!" Hannah hung her head and cried. How was it possible for one person to produce so many tears?

Matt pulled her close and stroked her hair. "It's okay, Hannah. Come on…Jenny's waiting."

She nodded, her face against his shirt. Then, the Bible still clutched to her heart, she walked with Matt back to her daughter.

Jenny looked tired but alert, and Hannah rushed to her side, gently setting the Bible down near the girl's feet. "Jenny, honey, are you all right?"

Matt stood on the other side of the bed, his voice kind and concerned. "She hasn't said much. Just 'Mom.' Dr. Cleary said that was normal."

Hannah lowered her face so it was closer to Jenny's. "Oh, Jenny, I'm so sorry, honey. I've been awful…it's all my fault."

Jenny swallowed and cleared her throat. "No."

"Honey, don't try to talk. You need your rest." Hannah stared into her daughter's eyes and smoothed a wisp of bangs back off her forehead. "I love you, Jenny. Things are going to be different. I'm so sorry. I want us—"

"Mom…" Jenny's voice was hoarse. "Not your fault…"

Hannah wanted to tell Jenny to rest, to sleep, but she could see the girl had more to say.

"I wanted…to be with Daddy…and Alicia."

"I know, sweetheart, I know." She rested her head on Jenny's chest, holding the girl close. "I'm so sorry, honey…"

They stayed that way a long time, until finally Hannah straightened and once again stroked Jenny's blond bangs. "I understand, sweetheart, really. We'll get help. For both of us. Things are going to be different."

Jenny nodded and her eyelids lowered. "At the end…I prayed. I wanted to live, Mom. Really. I love you."

Hannah wrapped her arms around the girl and held her close, whispering into her hair. "Thank God…thank God you're alive."

Jenny's eyes opened again, and her gaze was questioning. "God?"

Across the room Matt grinned at Hannah. "God?"

Hannah's eyes glistened with old and new tears. "Thank God Almighty. I told you things were going to be different."

Jenny's eyes filled with light, as if God, himself, had breathed new life in them. "Mr. Bronzan says you won."

Hannah looked deep into her daughter's eyes. "Not really. Not 'til about an hour ago."

Jenny nodded. "I'm glad he's guilty." She glanced at Matt and then back to Hannah. "I'd like to go to the sentencing…if that's okay with you."

Hannah felt her heart soar. Not because Jenny wanted to attend the sentencing, but because the girl was alive. And because after all that had happened, her daughter still loved her.

Two hours later, Matt had gone home and Jenny was sleeping. Dr. Cleary had evaluated Jenny and determined that her recovery had been utterly miraculous. Judging by her vocabulary and clarity of thought, the girl was in the process of making a complete recovery.

It was late, nearly ten o'clock, and the nurses had prepared a reclining chair where Hannah could spend the night. Now, with the lights dim and the hum of machinery confirming the fact that Jenny was alive and well, Hannah returned to Lamentations.

Chapter 3 showed the prophet's change of heart. He was no longer lashing out at God, accusing him. She read, curious—and suddenly her eyes stumbled onto something that made her catch her breath.

"I remember my affliction...and my soul is downcast within me.... Yet this I call to mind and therefore I have hope:...Because of the Lord's great love we are not consumed, for his compassions never fail....They are new every morning; great is your faithfulness."

It was her hymn. She'd known it came from the Bible, but until now she hadn't realized where. No wonder God had placed this book on Carol's heart, knowing that therein lay the words to Hannah's favorite song.

The melody ran through Hannah's mind, and she wept anew. Jenny was here, alive and well. They had their entire future ahead of them, and Brian Wesley was about to spend the rest of his life in prison. Indeed, God's compassion would never fail her, his mercies were new every morning. Especially today.

Hannah found even more hope at the end of the third chapter: *"You have seen, O LORD, the wrong done to me. Uphold my cause!...Pay them back what they deserve, O LORD, for what their hands have done...."*

Hannah closed her eyes. God loved her and forgave her. He was going to help her. Brian Wesley was the enemy, the one who had wronged her. Now God would uphold her cause and see that Brian Wesley paid.

She closed the Bible and stared at the ceiling. She could hardly wait for the sentencing.

Thirty-three

You have seen, O Lord, the wrong done to me.
Uphold my cause!...Pay them back what they deserve,
O Lord....And may your curse be on them!

Lamentations 3:59,64–65

It happened on the twenty-second straight night of dreaming about the accident.

At four-thirty in the morning, hours before the sentencing of Brian Wesley, Sgt. Miller finally remembered.

The moment he did, the sergeant's mind was released from what had seemed to be a holy vice grip. Like a modern-day Jonah, he had a message to relay to Hannah Ryan—and the sooner he did so, the sooner he could get on with his life.

He climbed out of bed, showered, and found his place at the dining room table. He wrote the note quickly, making sure to capture every detail.

Then, for the first time in three weeks, he drank his morning coffee in peace.

The cameras were back in full force for the sentencing.

History had been made in the state of California, as evidenced by the articles and editorials that had filled the newspapers every day since the verdict. The facts were in place. Now it was time to capture the feelings.

Hannah and Jenny sat in the first row beside Carol Cummins. Hannah surveyed the front of the courtroom, watching for Brian Wesley. Fourteen months had passed since he had mowed down her family, taken Tom and Alicia from her—finally she would look in his face and tell him how she felt about his actions that day. Her scrapbook sat in a bag at her feet.

From what she'd read in Lamentations, Hannah was sure God would fight this battle for her. She had a right to her anger. If the prophet Jeremiah could rail against a wrongdoer without showing forgiveness, then so could she.

Jenny slipped her hand into Hannah's and squeezed. "Love you, Mom."

Hannah's eyes locked onto Jenny's, and she pulled her daughter close, gently kissing the side of her head. "Love you, too, sweetheart. Thanks for coming. You didn't have to."

Jenny nodded and shifted uncomfortably. "I know. I wanted to."

Hannah hugged her again and remembered earlier that morning. They had awakened at six o'clock, dressed in shorts and T-shirts, and headed for the middle school track where they walked three miles. It was a routine they'd started when Jenny got home from the hospital, and Hannah treasured every step they took together. That morning, Jenny talked about the collision and finally admitted to Hannah that she felt guilty.

"Alicia had so much going for her, Mom," Jenny said as they powered around the track. "It should have been me who died."

"The truth is...you *both* should have died." Hannah was breathless, but she wanted to make a point. "Jenny...the only reason you lived...is because God has great plans for you. You're a miracle, honey."

They walked in silence for a length, and then Jenny surprised her. "It's good to hear you talking about God again."

Back at home, they shared breakfast and spoke little about the hearing. Hannah could sense Jenny's uneasiness, and several times she assured her daughter that she didn't have to go. Hannah could hardly believe she had berated Jenny so badly for not attending the earlier hearings. It was one of many areas the Lord had shed light on since Jenny's suicide attempt.

Hannah would be grateful as long as she drew breath for this second chance with her daughter.

Judge Horowitz entered the courtroom, drawing Hannah's attention back. She sat up straighter and wondered again why she still didn't feel complete peace. She frowned. She could understand why the verdict hadn't brought her peace...but neither had her restored relationship with the Lord.

She felt a gentle prodding. *Hannah, listen to me...*

She recognized his voice, the same sweet calling she'd relied on all her life before the accident. *What is it, Lord? What else can I do?*

Maybe God wanted her to listen closely to the hearing. Maybe after Brian was sentenced she would finally realize that perfect peace—the peace that passes understanding.

After all, this was her chance to face Brian Wesley before the court. She would tell him about Tom and Alicia. Then, when he was hauled off to prison fully aware of how much he'd taken from her...then she would have peace. Wasn't that the message of Lamentations?

Jenny glanced over and smiled weakly. "It's almost time."

Hannah's eyes locked onto the back of Brian Wesley's head. "It's something I have to do." She turned to Jenny. "You understand, right?"

Jenny hesitated, and Hannah saw how much she'd aged in the past year. She was not the carefree girl she had been when they pulled out of the driveway that summer day so long ago. Brian Wesley had taken that, too.

"Yes, Mom. I understand. I'll be praying for you."

The judge banged his gavel twice. "Come to order." He hesitated a moment, glancing at the docket before him. "We will proceed with the sentencing of Brian Wesley, who has been found guilty of the crime of first-degree murder in the deaths of Tom and Alicia Ryan.

"First, I want to state for the record that I have received a pre-sentence probation report on the defendant. Because of his history of alcoholism and driving under the influence, the probation department is recommending the maximum sentence, to be served concurrently with alcohol rehabilitation. The department advises that at such a time as Mr. Wesley should be deemed cured of his alcoholism—"the judge raised his eyebrows skeptically, then cleared his throat and continued—"At that time the department suggests Mr. Wesley should be released at the soonest, most reasonable opportunity."

Hannah tried to make sense of that and glanced at Matt. His eyes told her it was okay, and that was enough.

"Also, I have a letter from—" the judge sorted through a stack of papers until he found what he was looking for—"the defendant's ex-wife. She asked that I read it for the record and I will do so now."

He held the sheet and read:

"'Dear Judge, My name is Carla, and I was married to Brian Wesley for many years. I am raising his son. I saw Brian drink a lot in our marriage, but he never raised a hand to me or our boy. He was not a bad man, even though he drank. I know what he done is wrong and he should be punished. But I would appreciate it if you would be kind and give him the least many years in prison as you can. Things are over between us. Little Brian won't never know his Daddy.'"

Hannah watched Brian hang his head. She huffed lightly and angry thoughts fought for position. *Good. Grieve. I hope the boy forgets you ever existed. You deserve every moment of heartache.*

She couldn't wait to tell him so.

Hannah, listen to me....

What? I don't understand, Lord. I'm listening as hard as I can.

The judge finished reading and paused. "Under the California Victim's Rights Act, I will now allow any victims who are present to speak."

Matt rose to his feet. "Mrs. Hannah Ryan would like an opportunity, your honor."

"Very well, let the record reflect that Mrs. Ryan, a victim, will be speaking next."

Hannah wanted to ask the Lord for strength, but it felt strange. She frowned at the odd feeling and instead squeezed Jenny's hand and met Carol's eyes. Then she reached for the scrapbook, headed for the witness stand, and took her seat.

She stared at Brian and realized it was the first time she'd seen his face during the proceedings. Her eyes narrowed, and she saw Brian struggle beneath her gaze. A movement caught her eye, and she saw Matt cross his arms and study something on the floor.

Hannah adjusted the microphone and stared at three pages of typed notes. Her anger was so intense it might well have been a visible shield about her.

Careful, Hannah. The warning seemed strangely out of place, and she ignored it.

She drew a thin breath. Her hands trembled, and she steadied the letter before her. "More than a year ago my husband, Tom, and my two daughters, Alicia and Jenny...left home for their annual camping trip. It was something they did every year at the end of summer. They were coming home on that August day when—"

Suddenly a sob lodged in Hannah's throat, and she lifted her eyes to meet Brian's. For a moment all she wanted to do was spit at him or slap him or knock him down. She wanted to hurt him physically the way he'd hurt her. She caught a tear on her fingertip and continued. "They were coming home when you killed them. You didn't care about who they were or where they were going when you killed them. So now I'll tell you who they were. Because I think you need to know.

"Tom was..." This was harder than she'd thought. She gulped and swiped at more tears. "He was the love of my life. We grew up side by side and thought we'd be...together forever."

Hannah glanced up; Brian was staring at his hands.

"*Look* at me!" She leaned forward, clutching the stand. She wanted to cross the distance between them and—and—

Her heart pounded as she recognized the truth. Her anger was about to explode into a fit of rage. She had to gain control, to say these things with dignity. She released a single breath and relaxed back into her seat, regaining composure as quickly as she had lost it. When she spoke again the anger was there, but it was contained once more. "I asked you to look at me, Mr. Wesley. You owe me at least that."

When he met her eyes, she paused, then flipped through her scrapbook and held up a photo of Tom. She spoke, not in a voice of sorrow, but of seething, carefully managed fury. The tears came in streams now, and she gave up fighting them. "Tom was all I ever wanted in a man. He was...he was my best friend."

She turned to another page and held up a portrait of Alicia. "You killed my little girl, too. My precious firstborn." She looked up and met Brian's gaze. "You wouldn't know anything about someone like Alicia—" Hannah glanced toward Jenny—"Or my other daughter...Jenny. Because people like you, selfish alcoholics who think nothing of taking a life...people like you don't have anything in common with people like my girls." She looked down at her notes and then back at Brian. "Alicia was beautiful, inside and out. She would have done anything for anyone and usually she did. You killed her and..."

That was as far as she got. She began sobbing. Unable to hold back the sorrow, she put head down in her hands.

She didn't know how long she sat there, weeping, but when she felt someone at her elbow, she lifted her head and saw Matt with a box of tissues. He placed a supportive hand on her shoulder and squeezed gently. Hannah met his eyes and nodded.

Sitting straighter, she sniffed and blew her nose. There were things she needed to say, and she had to say them now, to Brian Wesley's face, or she would spend the rest of her life angry at missing the opportunity.

Peace. After this I'll have peace. She glanced at the judge. "I'm sorry."

Judge Horowitz nodded, his eyes compassionate. "That's all right, Mrs. Ryan. Please continue."

Hannah nodded and swallowed. Then she caught Brian Wesley's eyes once more and finished. "You killed Alicia, and any children she may have borne. You killed her family... because of—of your selfish choice. You killed her future." She shuffled pages until she was staring at the third page. "I no longer have a husband. I no longer have my oldest daughter. And my youngest daughter, Jenny—" tears coursed down her face but she continued—"Jenny has suffered severely because of this. She will not have her sister to share the future with.... She will not have a father to walk her down the aisle when she gets married."

Hannah looked up and found she still had Brian's attention. "For a long time I hated God because of what you did. Now I know I was wrong about that. This wasn't God's fault, it was yours." She was nearing the end, and she leaned forward again, spewing hatred with every word. "You...you are a despicable human being. Worthless...hopeless...heartless...without any concern for the lives of those around you."

Hannah, Hannah, Hannah...

What was the Lord trying to tell her? Why now? Hannah pushed the thoughts away. Whatever it was, she would have to worry about it later.

When she continued, her voice was slightly more controlled. "Today, before this courtroom, I am asking Judge Horowitz to hand down the stiffest, most severe punishment he can legally assign. You are an animal, a ruthless, cold-blooded killer who will kill again and again until someone locks you up."

She drew a trembling breath, and when she spoke again her voice was a snakelike hiss, each word pronounced with increasing rage. "I hope you rot in hell, Mr. Wesley. Because I will never..."

Hannah!

"—ever...forgive you for what you took from me."

Brian hung his head. Hannah collected her scrapbook and excused herself from the witness stand. *There.* She had done it. But instead of the peace she had hoped to feel, she felt choked by the same emotion that had strangled her since the accident: merciless, bitter hatred.

Thirty-four

Moreover, our eyes failed, looking in vain for help;
from our towers we watched for a nation that could not save us.

LAMENTATIONS 4:17

When Hannah said she wanted Brian Wesley to rot in hell, Matt linked his hands and lowered his head until it was resting on his fingertips. *Lord, this can't be what you want from Hannah. Help her, please. The anger is going to kill her.*

He let go a heavy sigh and leaned back in his chair, knowing there was more to come.

"Are there any other victims who wish to speak?" Judge Horowitz looked to Matt, and then Hannah.

"No, your Honor." Matt rose briefly and then sat back down. Brian Wesley was next, and Matt had a sudden urge to join Hannah, to put an arm around her and steady her. He couldn't explain it, but he was sure she wasn't going to like what Brian Wesley was about to say.

"Very well." The judge turned to Finch. "Would the defendant like to speak on his behalf?"

"Yes, your Honor." Brian Wesley made his way slowly to the witness stand. He hung his head and didn't look up until he'd been sitting for several seconds. He had no notes.

Dressed in jailhouse orange, his hair poorly cut, his body bent and rail thin, Matt thought the man looked the part Hannah had assigned him. A cold-blooded killer. A criminal who didn't care who he hurt. But there was something in Brian Wesley's eyes....

Brian lifted his head and searched the courtroom until he

found Hannah, and Matt held his breath as Brian began to speak.

"Mrs. Ryan, I agree with everything you just said. You're right. It was all my fault, and I deserve my punishment."

Matt glanced once more at Hannah; she looked like a human fortress, arms crossed, body back against her chair, eyebrows lowered suspiciously.

Please, Lord...

Brian continued. "I am worthless, despicable, and untrustworthy on the streets of this city. But there is one thing I'm not. And that's hopeless." His gaze didn't waver. "What I did was terrible and wrong, and before these witnesses today I want you to know I'm sorry. I'm sorry, Mrs. Ryan, really—" his voice broke—"if I could change it, I would. If I could go back..."

As Matt watched and listened, he had the surest sense that Brian Wesley's remorse was genuine. He looked at Hannah... did she see it, too? No, one side of her upper lip lifted, and she laughed without the slightest trace of humor.

Brian went on, undaunted. "I can't go back, Mrs. Ryan. But I am sorry. I'll be sorry every day, the rest of my life. But I do have hope because of someone I met after my arrest...someone who's here today. She told me about Jesus and how his blood had already paid the price for my horrible sins. I gave my life to him, Mrs. Ryan."

Hannah's face lost all its color, and she looked frozen in icy shock.

"That woman told me Jesus loved me even though I killed your husband and daughter. But she told me something else. She told me it was right for me to serve time here, now. In this life. I done the crime, and now I need to do the time. She's been the best friend I could ever have hoped for. You know her. Carol Cummins."

Matt watched helplessly as Hannah was cut by the truth. After today Carol would be on Hannah's hate list as well—and it would take all Hannah's time, all her energy, and what was left of her beauty to tend to the bitter root that was even now spreading through her heart. His eyes shifted and fell on Jenny. She, too, looked stunned as she hung on to her mother's arm.

Brian rattled on about the virtues of Carol and how she had brought him a Bible and led him to the Lord, but Hannah was barely listening. *Carol Cummins?* The woman she had confided in nearly every day since the collision? Carol was...the enemy? Hannah turned in her seat and glared at Carol.

Carol sighed and spoke in a whisper. "I'm sorry, Hannah. I wanted to tell you—"

"Don't talk to me!"

The same sense of shock she'd felt when she first learned of the collision hit her again. Her entire world was suddenly upside down, and she wanted to grab Jenny's hand and run from the courtroom.

Brian Wesley was talking to her again.

"I may be in prison for the rest of my days, Mrs. Ryan, and it serves me right. But believe me, I am a new man because God used Mrs. Cummins to change my life forever." He paused and kept his eyes on Hannah's. "I am sorry, Mrs. Ryan. I'll be sorry for the rest of my life. And I don't blame you if you never forgive me."

Brian finished, and Hannah had a hard time making her mouth work as she whispered to Jenny, "I'll be in the hall." The judge dismissed them for a fifteen-minute break, but Hannah was out of the courtroom before he finished speaking.

Matt watched Hannah go. The moment he was free, he left the courtroom and found her staring out a dusty window, her arms crossed.

"Hannah—"

She spun around. "Were you in on this, too? This...this

betrayal with Brian Wesley?"

Matt wanted to pull her close and soothe away the shock, but not with reporters lurking nearby. He held her gaze and shook his head. "I knew nothing about it."

She wrapped her arms around herself and turned back toward the window. Her voice was a strangled whisper. "How could she?"

He had an answer, but not one Hannah was ready to hear. "Come on, let's get back. It's been almost fifteen minutes."

When they returned, Matt saw that Carol was gone. He wondered if the two women would ever speak again.

They took their seats and waited.

Less than a minute later, Judge Horowitz returned and shuffled through a slight stack of papers. "I have reached a decision—" he looked up and met Brian Wesley's gaze—"young man, you have made some very poor choices in your life, and they resulted in a first-degree murder conviction. It is up to me to decide whether you should serve twenty-five years or longer for your crimes.

"I considered the letters for and against you, listened to arguments in which people asked for the minimum sentence and the maximum. Before I read the sentence, I want you to know that I based my decision primarily on your history of drinking and driving. I believe you cannot be trusted with standard alcohol treatment programs or promises to stay away from the wheel of a car. I believe you are a dangerous and very real risk to this community. Because of that, I hereby sentence you to serve fifty years in the state penitentiary."

There was a rustling throughout the courtroom as the news sank in. Judge Horowitz had made legal history; he'd sentenced Brian Wesley to the longest prison term ever handed down for deaths by driving under the influence.

Matt glanced at Hannah and saw she and Jenny hugging. He could tell by the way Hannah's shoulders shook that she was crying. It was everything she had hoped for. A murder-one verdict and a record-breaking prison sentence. And yet…

Hannah looked more heartbroken than ever. *Please, God, help her…*

"Order…" The judge frowned at the crowd. "Order! Immediately!" He returned his gaze to Brian. "With time off for good behavior, it is possible you will be up for parole in fifteen years, but not sooner. That is all. Court dismissed."

Hannah knew the reporters were waiting. This was her big moment, the chance to tell the world thank you. She had won in every possible way except the one that really mattered.

Tom and Alicia were still gone.

And now there was something new that grieved her nearly as much as the loss of her family. If Brian Wesley was telling the truth, if Carol had indeed betrayed her and led him to the Lord, then no prison could contain him now. If he was a Christian, then he was saved by the blood of Christ, heaven-bound and free indeed. He might live a season behind bars, but he would spend eternity in a mansion. Worst of all, one day when Hannah was reunited with Tom and Alicia…Brian Wesley, the man she'd come to hate with a driving passion, would be there, too.

It was the greatest injustice of all, and more than she could stomach. Carol's betrayal felt like a javelin piercing her midsection. Jenny had to be feeling the same, but she hadn't spoken a word. Maybe she didn't understand the implications of what Brian had said.

The courtroom buzzed with activity, and Jenny leaned against Hannah. "You did good, Mom. He won't hurt anyone else."

Hannah squeezed her daughter's hand and dabbed at her tears. She kept her eyes forward and watched while the bailiff came for Brian and led him away. This was it. The moment of peace.

But it didn't come.

Instead Hannah felt strangled and angry and tired and betrayed.

Brian wasn't in prison. She was.

She led Jenny into the hallway and answered a handful of questions from the media. Then she caught a glimpse of Carol leaving the courtroom. She must have sneaked back in before the sentencing, and now she was trying to get away without speaking to Hannah.

She thanked the reporters and turned to Jenny. "Honey, I need to talk to someone. Why don't you go wait over there with Mr. Bronzan." She pointed to where Matt stood in the doorway of the courtroom, talking with several spectators.

Jenny nodded and moved toward Matt. Ever since learning how he had saved her life, Jenny had opened herself to him. Now, just two weeks later, the two were fast friends.

Once Jenny was safely in a conversation with Matt, Hannah raced down the hallway. Carol was about to board an elevator. "Wait!"

Hannah expected Carol to be embarrassed, ashamed of what she'd done. Instead when Carol turned, her expression held no apologies. She waited while Hannah quickly closed the distance between them.

They stood face to face, and Hannah felt her eyes fill with tears. "Is it true?"

Carol did not blink. She nodded solemnly. "I had to, Hannah."

Hannah had fought so long and so hard she had little energy left for this battle, but somehow she summoned anger from the shards of her broken heart. She did not scream or rant, but there was venom in her voice. "You were *supposed* to be my friend."

"This isn't the time..." Carol started to turn back toward the elevator.

"Wait a minute! Don't tell me this isn't the time. You're the one who broke my trust."

Carol sighed. "I don't expect you to understand, Hannah. Not now, anyway."

Hannah's hands flew to her hips. "I'll *never* understand. I poured my heart out to you. I thought you were on my side."

Carol stared at Hannah, clearly puzzled. "Are you so far gone, Hannah, that you don't remember the very basic truths of the faith?"

She stared at Carol. What on earth was she talking about? "Don't give me a sermon—" she waved her hand toward the window—"there are a million people out there looking for a savior, Carol. And you had to give the good news to Brian Wesley? *Brian Wesley?*"

"I gave it to the person God asked me to give it to." Carol hesitated. "After my husband died, I gave a Bible to the man who killed him. It was the only way I could finally let go and forgive. I've been giving Bibles to drunk drivers ever since."

Hannah was stunned. "From your office at MADD?"

"No. From my office at Church on the Way. I head up the prison ministry there."

Carol might as well have punched her in the stomach. "Well, maybe you should have told me sooner so I could be prepared. Hearing Brian Wesley give you credit for his *conversion*—" Hannah spat the word—"was like getting news that Tom and Alicia had been killed all over again."

Carol sighed. "I'm sorry you feel that way. All I can tell you is my concern for you was, and is, genuine. Usually I don't get involved with victims, but Sgt. Miller thought…oh, never mind. I never meant to do anything that would hurt you."

Hannah was speechless. "How did you think I'd react? Surely you didn't expect me to fall facedown in the courtroom and praise God over one sinner repenting of his way. That man killed Tom and Alicia. He is a worthless human being."

Carol's reply was so soft Hannah barely heard it. "Not to Jesus."

She clenched her teeth. "I have nothing else to say to you.

You...You betrayed me. You're on his side, not mine." She leveled bitter eyes at Carol. "I hope heaven is a big place because I want to live eternity without ever seeing you or Brian Wesley."

Hannah didn't wait for a reply as she left Carol standing there. She found Jenny and bid Matt good-bye.

Matt looked concerned. "You okay? Want me to come with you?" Hannah smiled through her tears. At least he was genuine. He was the only friend she had, he and Jenny.

"That's all right." The reporters were gone, and she leaned toward him, wrapping her arms around his neck and resting her head on his chest. They had been through so much over the past year, she almost felt like she'd known him a decade or more. "Thank you, Matt. I'll never be able to repay you for what you've done."

He pulled away and searched her eyes. "Would it be okay if I took you and Jenny out for dinner? It'd be a shame to stop spending time together now. Besides...I want to talk to you about Carol."

Hannah laughed bitterly. "After the past month I'd say we better make it dinner once a week." She thought of Jenny and her voice grew serious. "I don't know what I would have done without you."

Jenny moved closer and hugged Matt's waist. "Me, too, Mr. Bronzan. After I took the pills I prayed God would save me and he did. He sent you."

When she and her daughter left the courthouse minutes later, Hannah had a strong feeling something was missing. She checked her purse and found her car keys and her sunglasses. Then it hit her. She had expected to feel a sense of relief, to walk out of the courthouse that day a different woman. And in that light something was indeed missing. Hannah felt fresh tears as she realized what it was.

It was peace.

Thirty-five

Restore us to yourself, O LORD, that we may return;
renew our days as of old unless you have utterly rejected us
and are angry with us beyond measure.

LAMENTATIONS 5:21–22

The plain white envelope lay on her front doorstep, tucked neatly under the welcome mat. Jenny had already gone upstairs to change clothes when Hannah spotted it and sighed. She didn't know if she had the energy to pick it up. The day had been long, and she felt strangely defeated. The sense of victory and accomplishment had never come, and the peace she had so desperately sought had turned out to be as elusive as justice was.

She stared at the envelope. *Advertising.*

Yet as she moved into the house, something made her stop and pick it up. She slit it open and gently removed the letter. It was simple, less than a page. Hannah began to read.

"Dear Mrs. Ryan, My name is Sgt. John Miller. I worked the accident scene the day your husband and daughter were killed. I came to your house with the news that day, and later I talked with you at the hospital. You may not remember me, but I remember you. For the past several months I've been thinking about the accident almost as if God wanted me to remember something."

Hannah's heart beat faster. *What was this? Why now?*

"This morning, I remembered what it was. I was with your husband in the minutes before he died, and he wanted me to give you a message. He wanted you to know he loved you and the girls—"

Hannah closed her eyes and remembered Dr. Cleary telling

her Tom's final words. Tears stung her eyes and she read on.

"—but there was something else. And that's what I finally remembered this morning. At the time it didn't make sense, and I figured he must have been hallucinating or suffering the effects of blood loss. But now I am convinced that I need to deliver his message to you in its entirety.

"Tom told me to tell you to forgive, Mrs. Ryan. He wanted you to forgive."

Hannah's eyes locked on the word, hearing it as Tom had spoken it years ago when Hannah was mad at the boy who beat her at basketball...and again years later when Tom reminded her there was no victory in holding a grudge against the girl he nearly married, no gain in hating her....

"Forgive her, Hannah...let it go." She heard it as clearly as if Tom was saying it to her.

Then, like a parade in her mind, Hannah recalled a dozen times Tom had told her that over the years. She closed her eyes, choking back a sob. And now...even after he'd been gone for so many months...he was telling her again.

Her eyes ran over the sentence until it was seared in her heart. *"Tom told me to tell you to forgive, Mrs. Ryan."*

Forgive. Forgive. He wanted you to forgive.

She moved outside and sank into the porch swing along the side of the house. It was a private spot bordered by jasmine. Hannah knew Jenny wouldn't come looking for her yet, and she was grateful. Her entire body was numb from the shock.

Tom had known.

He had laid there in the middle of the twisted wreckage of the Explorer, aware his minutes were numbered, and he had thought of her. The collision hadn't been his fault, and he knew that someday, somehow, Hannah was going to hold his death against someone. He better than anyone knew what would happen then. And so his final words had been for her: *Forgive, Hannah. Please forgive.*

"I can't, Tom, it's not fair. I have a right to this..." Her voice was a tortured whisper as trails of tears made their way down her face. "He did it on purpose."

But Tom's words, his final message, remained.

Forgive, Hannah...forgive.

She wept, imagining her dying husband worrying about the condition of her heart. Did he know her that well? Did he know she would turn her back on God? That her unforgiving heart would force her to forfeit a relationship with the savior?

Hannah's answer came from deep within.

Yes. Tom had known.

And God had placed it on Sgt. Miller's heart until finally he remembered Tom's words and brought them to her now.

She wept and prayed and fought the message. She did not want to forgive Brian Wesley. Indeed she would rather die than do such a vile thing. Eventually she crept back into the house and found Jenny napping on the sofa. Hannah found her Bible on the end table and carried it back outside.

Maybe there was something else in Lamentations, something she'd missed. After all, if Jeremiah had felt it was all right to be angry with his enemies, didn't she have the same right? She had been in Scripture many times since the night in Jenny's hospital room...but she had never finished Lamentations. She opened it now and began chapter 4 again, reaffirming her reasons for asking God to pay back Brian Wesley and curse him.

Then she read chapter 5. At first the lament sounded familiar, similar to the rest of the book. Then her eyes fell on something that caused her heart to skip a beat.

"Joy is gone from our hearts; our dancing has turned to mourning. The crown has fallen from our head. Woe to us, for we have sinned!...Restore us to yourself, O LORD, that we may return; renew our days as of old unless you have utterly rejected us and are angry with us beyond measure."

Hannah stared at the words as the reality hit. *We have sinned...restore us... angry with us.* Jeremiah and his people had suffered great loss. They had been victims in every possible way, yet at the end of the book of Lamentations Jeremiah was confessing sin. Repenting. Apologizing. Asking God to restore him and his people and hoping God would not be too angry with them.

Hannah searched her heart and tried to imagine what she had done wrong, what sin she had committed that could possibly require repentance. She had made things right with Jenny. What else was there?

Again, as though Tom were standing before her, she heard the words: *Forgive, Hannah...forgive.*

Tom's words pierced her heart. She was guilty after all.

With a heart so troubled she thought she might die from the pain, she began to pray, wondering, like Jeremiah, if it was too late, if she had made God too angry.

Scripture memorized years ago came rushing back.

"Forgive and you will be forgiven...If you forgive men when they sin against you, your heavenly Father will also forgive you. But if you do not forgive men their sins, your Father will not forgive your sins...forgive as the Lord forgave you."

Hannah closed her eyes and let the truth wash over her. As it did, she read Sgt. Miller's letter once more, hearing Tom's voice as he spoke his words of love to her. She sighed heavily, folded the letter, and stood on wobbly legs.

She knew what she had to do...and she was fairly certain it would kill her. But it was what Tom wanted. What God wanted. It was just a matter of doing it.

Making her way to the kitchen telephone, Hannah lifted the receiver and took the first step.

A woman answered on the second ring. "Hello?"

Hannah paused. "Carol, it's Hannah. I have something to tell you...."

Thirty-six

Because of the LORD'S *great love we are not consumed,*
for his compassions never fail.
They are new every morning; great is your faithfulness.

LAMENTATIONS 3:22–23

A warm breeze picked up speed across a dirty, vacant field and brushed over Jenny and the tall man sitting beside her. Bits of trash and dirty cigarette butts mixed within the weeds that grew from cracks in the asphalt, and Jenny wondered what it was like inside. She was quiet, hands folded in her lap as she turned once more to watch the visitor entrance.

"How long do you think it'll take?" She looked at Matt Bronzan. He'd had so many of the answers they'd needed over the last year...she was sure he had this one, too.

He turned toward her and leaned over, resting his forearms on his thighs. "Takes a while to get through security."

Jenny nodded. There were dozens of strange characters scattered throughout the outdoor waiting area. Occasionally someone would come from inside with a small bag of belongings and wander off toward a dirty, graffiti-covered bus stop. The freeway was only a hundred yards away, and the grime and pollution of inner-city life filled the air.

None of it mattered, though, with Matt beside her. She moved closer to him and sighed. "Sometimes I miss Daddy and Alicia so much...."

Matt nodded. "There'll always be times."

There was an easy silence between them.

"Matt..." Jenny studied his eyes intently. She'd wanted to

ask this question for the last three months, ever since she saw him hug her mother...well, in *that* way. "Can I ask you a question?"

"Sure." Matt smiled at her.

"Do you love my Mom?"

His expression changed and he sat straighter. His eyes looked suddenly bright, and she saw the hint of a smile on his lips. "Well, young lady, where did that come from?"

Jenny shrugged. "I don't know. You're here, aren't you?"

Matt nodded and stroked his chin with his thumb. "You have a point there."

Jenny giggled. "It's okay. I like you being here."

Matt leaned closer, and a pang went through her. His eyes were so full of wisdom. Just like her dad's eyes had been....

"Let's make it our secret for now, okay?"

She grinned. "So I'm right? You do love her?"

Matt shook a playful finger at her. "Oh, no you don't. I'm the lawyer, remember?"

Jenny laughed again. It felt so good to laugh. "Okay, you win. I won't say anything."

"You're a good girl, Jenny Ryan."

She met his eyes again. "But you *do* love her—"

"Jenny..."

She felt her grin widen at the teasing threat in his tone. This was going to be fun. She hugged herself, then her smile faded. Biting her lip, she glanced up at him. "I know it's too soon to tell the future...but Matt, please don't ever go away."

He stared at her, and she felt the warmth of his love—of Christ's love— surround her.

"I'm not going anywhere, Jenny. You can count on that."

"Promise?" She felt like a little girl, clinging to all she had left in the world.

Matt put an arm around her and pulled her close. She snuggled against him, smiling as his answer washed over her. "Promise."

Hannah had moved through several levels of security and now she was in a holding chamber, waiting for the signal. She thumbed through her Bible and found the letter from Sgt. Miller. She had made the appointment six weeks ago, now she had to follow through. And yet she still felt like she wore shackles on her feet, chains around her wrists....

She wanted to forgive, really. But she was having trouble seeing Brian Wesley as worthy. Even now. Forgiveness was Tom's gift, not hers.

A heavy steel door opened and a uniformed officer stepped into the waiting room. "Mrs. Ryan?"

Hannah stood. "Yes?"

"We're ready for you." He looked at her Bible. "You'll have to leave all your belongings with me."

Hannah nodded and did as she was told.

"Right this way."

She followed, feeling as if she were being led to the executioner's block.

The deputy stopped at a door with barred windows and opened it with a key. He stared at the prisoner shackled to a chair inside then turned to Hannah. "Ten minutes."

Hannah stepped inside, refusing to look at him. Not yet. She stared at the floor and found a seat at the simple, pressed wood table. She could see his feet, just across from her. *Help me, God. I still want to choke him, hit him, make him suffer for what he did.*

Forgive...forgive, Hannah.

She squeezed her eyes shut and felt two tears slither down her cheeks. She swallowed. *Please, God. Give me strength.* It was now or never. She had just ten minutes.

He interrupted her thoughts. "You...you wanted to see me?"

Hannah lifted her head and met his eyes—and gasped softly. In that moment she didn't see the eyes of an alcoholic, of a killer. She saw Tom Ryan's eyes...gentle, spirit-filled eyes.

The unmistakable eyes of a godly man.

In the face of those eyes, Hannah did the only thing she could do: she broke down and wept.

Brian shifted uncomfortably, clearly unsure what to say.

The minutes were getting by, and Hannah knew it was time. She fought for control over her tears and wiped her eyes. "You told me...at the sentencing that you were sorry."

He hung his head, and an errant tear slipped onto the table. "I am sorry, Mrs. Ryan. Every day...every minute."

Hannah nodded. Her stomach was in knots and she swallowed hard. And now she knew why she'd felt shackled. She had been locked in a prison of bitterness and hate, and only Tom's dying words had reminded her of God's truth: "You shall know the truth, and the truth shall set you free..."

Free. She longed to be free. At peace.

She had lived in the dark prison of hate for too long. The way out was right in front of her. She took a deep breath.

"I forgive you, Brian." Fresh tears filled her eyes. "It is what my husband wanted...what God wants. And now, it's what I want, too."

The words were no sooner past her lips than she felt it...a rush of peace so real, so sweet and comforting, that it took her breath away. It coursed through her entire body, and she felt like a wind-up toy whose workings had been fully released....

She settled back into her chair, the tension she'd felt earlier completely gone.

This was what she'd waited months to feel, and she chuckled softly. How ironic that it was here, locked in a boxy room face to face with Brian Wesley, that she felt more peace than at any time since her life had been ravaged by the accident. Her smile broadened. How pleased Tom would be if he could see this. A second wave of peace washed over her.

He could.

Brian's mouth hung open, and he looked from side to side,

as though this might all be some kind of joke. Fumbling with his fingers, he began speaking in quick jerky sentences. "You don't...you don't have to forgive me, Mrs. Ryan. Really...It was my fault. All my fault....You don't need to forgive me. I don't deserve it. I don't—"

Hannah held up a hand, and he fell silent. "None of us deserves it, Brian. This wasn't a decision I made lightly. I understand now that no matter what you did, Carol was right. Jesus loves you, and...he wants me to forgive you. For your sake. And for mine."

Hannah felt God urging her to go one step further, and she did so without hesitation. "I believe you mean what you say, that you're sorry and you never want to hurt anyone else the way you hurt me." She paused, amazed at how easily the next words were coming. "I want to pray with you, Brian."

His eyes grew wide. "Carol told me crazy things would happen if I gave my life to the Lord, but I never...not *this* crazy—"

Hannah smiled, wanting to weep all over again. How much time she'd wasted...."We serve an amazing God. I've had to learn that the hard way." She reached toward him and held out her hands, palms up. Slowly, almost reverently, he placed his shackled hands in hers. She closed her fingers around them, the hands that had slapped money down on a bar fourteen months ago, hands that had raised one drink after another to his lips until he was too drunk even to walk a straight line, hands that turned a key in the ignition and steered a truck through a red light into the side of her family's Explorer.

They were the hands of a killer, but Hannah held them warmly. As she did, she felt only freedom, and her heart soared with hope. She bowed her head.

"Lord, thank you for this meeting, for bringing me to this point in my life." There were tears in her eyes and she swallowed hard. "You know what I've been through...what has led me to this decision. And you know that I am sincere when I say I forgive Brian.

"Please be with him now, Lord. He has a long time to spend in prison and...and I pray you use him to touch the lives of others around him." She paused as a sob caught in her throat. "Help him forgive himself, Lord. In Jesus' name, amen."

There was a knock on the door, and the deputy walked in. "Time's up."

Hannah squeezed Brian's hands, and he looked deep into her eyes. "Thank you, Mrs. Ryan."

She pointed heavenward and nodded as she stood to leave.

Without looking back she followed the deputy down the hallway. Her battle against drunk driving was not over. She had her priorities straight now, but she knew, as long as she drew breath, she would stay involved in the fight for tougher laws and greater awareness.

Ahead sunlight flooded the jail, and Hannah was overcome with the need to be back outside, where her future waited. She peered through the double glass doors, and among the sea of people waiting in the lobby, she saw them looking for her. Matt had a protective arm around Jenny. She ached knowing that Tom would never again be there to protect their daughter. But the fact remained that there would be times when the girl needed protecting. This was one of those times....Matt was here and he was real. As she made her way to them, she thanked God for his presence in their lives.

They both saw her at the same instant, and another sob caught in Hannah's throat once they were all together. There were tears in both Matt's and Jenny's eyes as they looked at her expectantly.

"Well?" Jenny took a step closer and hugged her gently, laying her head on Hannah's chest.

Hannah nodded. "I did it—" Her voice broke, and she hung her head as Matt put his arms around both her and Jenny in an embrace that needed no words.

It felt as though a horrible chapter in her life was finally over. As freeing as it had been to go to Brian, to forgive him, the reality of what had just transpired left her drained.

They held each other for a while, connected in every way that mattered, until finally Hannah stopped crying and caught her breath. "I have a crazy thing I want us to do." She looked from Jenny to Matt.

"What?" Jenny wiped her cheeks with her sweater sleeves and looked confused. "I thought you'd wanna talk about Brian and whatever happened in there."

Matt raised a curious eyebrow, and Hannah caught his gaze and held it. "Later. I promise. But right now I want you to sing with me. Please. Both of you."

"Sing?" Matt still had one arm around Hannah, one around Jenny.

Hannah nodded. "My song. 'Great Is Thy Faithfulness.'"

A look of understanding filled Matt's eyes, and he bowed his head. Then in a voice that was both quiet and strong, he began to sing.

And there, in the midst of bedraggled prisoners struggling with their first moments of freedom and hollow-eyed parents waiting and wondering where they went wrong, the song began to build.

Three voices rang as one, reaching the end of the first verse and launching into the chorus: "Great is thy faithfulness, great is thy faithfulness..."

The defeated and desperate around them lifted their eyes and listened until a worn-out woman in the corner stood on shaky legs and joined in. Hannah smiled at her and watched as a white-haired man farther down the bench rose to his feet and added his voice.

Another and another stood until there were ten people standing amidst fifty. Ten hapless, harried souls who, in that moment, found hope in the message. Finally even the hardest eyes around them grew noticeably softer.

"Morning by morning new mercies I see..." Hannah continued to sing, studying the strangers whose voices joined hers.

She saw pain there, suffering…and something deep within her told her they knew what it was to walk away from a loving God when life didn't turn out like it was supposed to. They knew what it was to struggle with pain and anger, waiting for morning.

If she could, she would take each one and tell them they didn't have to give up, that in Christ there really was hope. It might take months or even years but one day, as sure as every one of God's promises was true, morning would come.

She held tighter to Matt and Jenny, warmth filling her heart. She was going to survive. God's love had filled her future with bright possibilities.

Her voice grew stronger.

This was her song. It would always be her song. And some far-off day she would sing it in the presence of her mighty and loving Lord, with Tom and Alicia at her side.

She closed her eyes and with a full heart lifted her hands toward heaven, singing to an audience of One.

"All I have needed, thy hand hath provided. Great is thy faithfulness, great is thy faithfulness, great is thy faithfulness, Lord unto me."

I hope you have gained much by traveling with Hannah Ryan through the truths of Lamentations. There were times—in the early stages of writing this book—when I thought about scrapping the idea, writing something simpler and easier to produce than a story about a family devastated by a drunk driver. Especially a faith-filled family like the Ryans. But I believe God has allowed me this time and place to produce fiction for a reason. People of faith have struggles, too. They hurt and die and are tempted. The characters in my books will likely always be dealing with more than a jilted love. They will be real people, dealing with real issues. And I hope, because of that, they will help you, the reader, grow in your faith.

I pray that the underlying message in *Waiting for Morning* was clear: bad things do happen to good people. And not all Christians respond to tragedy by falling on their knees and reaching for their Bibles. Sometimes we travel a long, dark night waiting for morning.

It's like Jesus said when he assured his disciples, "I have told you these things so that in me you may have peace. In this world you will have trouble, but take heart! I have overcome the world" (John 16:33).

What assurance! What perfect peace! What a glorious morning awaits those who, like Hannah, learn to take their burdens to the foot of the cross.

If you have ever faced such a journey, it is my prayer that after reading *Waiting for Morning* you know you are not alone. Whatever you are facing today, God sees you, he loves you, and he has already won the battle for those whose faith is in him.

I've heard it said that all of us are either coming out of a trial, heading into a trial, or living through a trial. Drunk driving, car accidents, illness, financial struggles, relational breaks, marital unfaithfulness...these are things that happen to everyone. The difference is how we choose to respond, where we find our strength.

Many of you reading this book already have that sweet fellowship with our Lord. For you I offer encouragement and ask you to pass this book on to someone who feels alone in his or her trial.

But for you who have not made a commitment to Jesus Christ, there is no better time than now. Accept his free gift of grace, buy a Bible, find a Bible-believing church. Otherwise when the trials come, you will have no morning to wait for.

May God bless you and keep you in his care and may his face shine like the dawn even in the darkest of days. Until next time...

The publisher and author would love to hear your comments about this book. *Please contact us at:* www.letstalkfiction.com

Discussion Questions

1. Was there a time in your life when you felt you were "waiting for morning"? Describe that time?

2. What did you do to survive? What would you do differently based on what you know today?

3. In what ways did you see God's hand at work during that time? What good has come from it?

4. Which character in Waiting for Morning could you most identify with? Which character could you least identify with? Why or why not?

5. List as many ways as you can remember where God showed His mercy to Hannah in her darkest days. How has God shown His mercy to you in yours?

6. Read Lamentations 3:22–23. What are the promises these verses deliver? Which one is most precious to you at this point in your life? Describe a time in your life when these promises could have helped or did help you.

7. Jenny thought the answer to her problems was to end her life. What led her to believe that? When has the enemy of your soul whispered wrong solutions to you? What were the consequences?

8. Which character(s) represented for Hannah God's promise that He will never leave nor forsake us? How did those character(s) deal with Hannah's anger toward God? How do you deal with the anger of hurting people?

9. Ultimately the lesson in Waiting for Morning is one of forgiveness. Describe a time when you had trouble forgiving someone. How did you act toward that person, inwardly and outwardly? How did that make you feel? At what point did you, like Hannah, find peace in this situation?

10. Oftentimes God uses outward situations or other people to help us get unstuck from a bad place, whether we need to forgive or obey or draw closer to Him. For Hannah, God used the police officer's delayed message from Tom. What has it been for you? What was/is God trying to tell you about your life? Are you listening?

THE FOREVER FAITHFUL SERIES

WAITING FOR MORNING—*Book One*
A drunk driver...a deadly accident...a dream destroyed. When Hannah Ryan loses her husband and oldest daughter to a drunk driver, she is consumed with hate and revenge. Ultimately, it is a kind prosecutor, a wise widow, and her husband's dying words that bring her the peace that will set her free and let her live again.
ISBN 1-59052-020-3

A MOMENT OF WEAKNESS—*Book Two*
When childhood friends Jade and Tanner reunite as adults, they share their hearts, souls, and dreams of forever—until a fateful decision tears them apart. Now, nearly a decade later, Jade's unfaithful husband wants to destroy her in a custody battle that is about to send shock waves across the United States. Only one man can help Jade in her darkest hour. And only one old woman knows the truth that can set them all free.
ISBN 1-57673-616-4

HALFWAY TO FOREVER—*Book Three*
Matt and Hannah...Jade and Tanner—after already surviving much, these couples now face the greatest struggles of their lives: Parental losses and life-threatening illness threaten to derail their faith and sideline their futures. Can Hannah survive the loss of an adopted daughter? Will Tanner come through decades of loneliness only to face losing Jade one final time?
ISBN 1-57673-899-X

ABOUT THE AUTHOR...
Karen Kingsbury is an award-winning author and former reporter for the *Los Angeles Times* and *Los Angeles Daily News.* She is also a recognized author with the Women of Faith Fiction Club. Kingsbury lives with her husband and six children in Washington.

Excerpt from *A Moment of Weakness*

May 1977

The children rode their bicycles into Tanner's driveway, laid them on the pavement and flopped down on a grassy spot in the center of his neatly manicured front lawn. The discussion had been going on for several minutes.

"I still don't get it. Where'd she go?" Tanner plucked a blade of grass and meticulously tore it into tiny sections.

Jade shrugged and gazed across the street toward the two-story house where she had lived for the past three years. "Daddy says she's gonna meet us in Washington. That's all I know."

Tanner chewed on that for a moment. The whole thing sounded fishy to him. Mamas didn't leave for no reason. And people didn't move without making plans first. "Do you think she's mad at you?"

"Of course she's not mad. She loves me. I know it." Jade tossed her dark head, and her eyes flashed light green. Tanner had never seen eyes like Jade's. Green like the water of Chesapeake Bay.

"Why doesn't she just come back? Then you wouldn't have to move."

"I told you, they already decided. We're moving to Washington. Mama went on ahead of us, and Daddy says she'll meet us there."

"In Washington?"

"Yes, Tanner. I told you she didn't *leave* me. She just needed some time alone."

Tanner plucked another piece of grass and twisted it between his thumb and forefinger. "But she didn't say good-bye, right?"

Jade sighed, and Tanner saw tears form in her eyes. "I *told* you, Tanner. She left early in the morning. Daddy said she probably knew I would be sad so she left before I woke up. 'Cause she loves me."

"Did she leave a note or anything?"

"Daddy said he didn't need a note." Jade swiped at a tear, and her voice was angrier than before. "He knows where she's going, and that's why we have to move. We need to get there so we can be with Mama again. She would never wanna be alone that long."

Tanner still didn't understand, but he saw that his questions were bothering Jade. He sat up and crossed his legs, studying her curiously. The only time he'd ever seen her cry was two years ago when she jumped a curb on her bike and flew over the handlebars. But that was different. Now Tanner wasn't sure what to do. He decided to change the subject. "How far away is Washington?"

"Daddy says"—she leaned back on her elbows and stared at the cloudless sky—"it's about as far away as heaven is from hell."

Tanner thought about that for a moment. "But you're coming back, right?"

Jade nodded. "Of course. We'll meet up with Mama, and then Daddy's gotta do a job there. He said it could take all summer. After that we'll come home."

Tanner relaxed. That sounded all right. Even if the whole thing still seemed kind of weird.

"I gotta go." Jade rose and climbed back on her bike. "Daddy needs help packing."

Tanner stood and pushed his hands deep into the worn pockets of his jeans. "You leavin' tomorrow?"

She nodded and worked her toe in tiny circles on the pavement. For a moment Tanner thought she was going to hug him, then at the last second she pushed him in the arm like she always did when she didn't know what to say.

Tanner pushed her back, but not hard enough to move her. "Hey, I'm still going to marry you."

Jade huffed. "Shut up, Tanner. You're a smelly old boy and I'm not going to marry anyone."

"One day you'll think I'm Prince Charming," Tanner teased.

Jade couldn't keep a straight face, and she began giggling. "Oh, okay. Right. Sure...whatever you say." She shook her head dramatically. "I would never marry you, Tanner. Sometimes I think you're crazy."

"Got you smiling, though, didn't I?"

They grinned at each other for a beat and then Jade's smile faded. "I'll see ya later."

Tanner kicked at a patch of grass and sighed. "You better come back when summer's over."

Jade's eyes got watery again. "I *said* I'll be back." She began pedaling down his driveway. Halfway home she turned once and waved.

Tanner raised one of his palms toward her. He'd heard his parents whispering about Jade and her daddy the other day. Tanner didn't catch all the details, but it was obvious his mother didn't think the Conner family was ever coming back.

It was good to know she was wrong.

As Jade disappeared into her house, Tanner felt a subtle reassurance that somehow, someday soon, the two of them would be together again.

OTHER NOVELS BY KAREN KINGSBURY

WHERE YESTERDAY LIVES
1-57673-285-1
In the wake of her father's sudden death, Ellen Barrett must journey back to the small town where she grew up and spend a week with antagonistic siblings. In the process, she must reckon with a man who once meant everything to her.

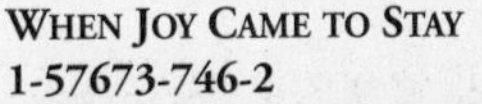

WHEN JOY CAME TO STAY
1-57673-746-2
Maggie Stovall is trapped inside a person she's spent years carefully crafting. Now the truth about who she is—and what she's done—is revealed, sending Maggie into a spiral of despair. Will Maggie walk away from her marriage and her foster child in her desperation to escape the mantle of depression cloaking her? Or will she allow God to take her to a place of ultimate honesty before it's too late?

ON EVERY SIDE
1-57673-850-7
Jordan Riley, an embittered lawyer, sues his hometown to have a public statue of Jesus removed. The conflict causes him to cross paths with a spirited young newscaster named Faith, who opposes Jordan's suit in surprising ways. Perhaps most amazing of all is how Faith begins to disassemble the walls around Jordan's heart. Will love be enough when the battle rages on every side?

KAREN KINGSBURY

AND PRISM COFOUNDER TONI VOGT

THE PRISM WEIGHT LOSS PROGRAM

The PRISM® Weight Loss Program, founded in 1990, has helped more than 60,000 people transform their eating behaviors with a sensible, lifestyle-change approach. Now available in The Prism Weight Loss Program by bestselling author Karen Kingsbury and PRISM cofounder Toni Vogt, the book shows readers how to not just "tame the monster" of food addiction, but destroy it through simple eating strategies and biblical principles. It includes testimonials, descriptions of the authors' personal struggles with food addiction, details of the program, and a fabulous recipe section that will help readers become the fit people God created them to be.

ISBN 1-57673-578-8 HD

What People Are Saying about

KAREN KINGSBURY Fiction...

"Karen Kingsbury has been such a godsend. Her books have brought me to God and have motivated my husband and me to remarry after a bad divorce. After not being able to have kids, we now have an adopted boy and are trying to adopt another. Your books show faith, love, and tenderness, and I love them."

—KATHY, Rancho Santa Margarita, CA

"Karen Kingsbury's fiction has changed my life by reminding me that there is hope amid seemingly hopeless circumstances and that faith in God's redemptive plan is the anchor I can hold on to when life's compasses fail."—AMY, Lawrenceville, GA

"Karen Kingsbury is our book club's favorite author. We often discuss how each of her books not only entertains us, but inspires us to live out our faith in a real, everyday, every-moment way. Thanks for your stories, which challenge us to be better disciples of our precious Lord Jesus."—LYNDA, Covington, WA

"Karen Kingsbury's books have touched my life in many different ways, but *Where Yesterday Lives* really helped me in the death of my father-in-law... Thank you for the great stories."—CHRIS, Zeeland, MI

"I have read every book Karen Kingsbury has written. Each book has brought me to a place of repentance and helped me to forgive myself for things I've confessed to no one but God. Her books have given me hope for the future, the assurance of forgiveness, and the strength to look forward to what the Lord would have me do and that I can accomplish it in His strength! Thank you."—KAREN, Campbell, CA

"The Lord prompted me to find a Christian author I enjoyed, and I found Karen Kingsbury. I have struggled with depression to a certain degree all my life, but when I read her book, I was at the bottom. This was the beginning of a wonderful journey to recovery for me."—DANNELL, Brawley, CA

"A dear friend handed me *A Time to Dance*, and it was the beginning of some much needed deep healing in my marriage. Just knowing that others could walk through muddy waters and make it through to the other side gave me hope and a sense of relief that maybe, just maybe, I too could be okay again. Thank you, Karen Kingsbury!"—JO ANN, Dickinson, ND

"Karen Kingsbury's work always reminds me of God's grace in my own life, especially the times I really didn't deserve it! After each book, my faith is stronger, and I can't wait for the next book to come out!"—NANCY, Salem, IL

"I just love all of Karen Kingsbury's books. Every one has touched me in a very deep way, relating to one or another 'storm' I have gone through and yet giving me hope that God is always there, carrying us when we don't care anymore whether we live or die. I have been to that place, and God did lift me up from the depths of sorrow and pain! Thank you so much!"—HENRIETTA, British Columbia, Canada

"Karen Kingsbury's books never cease to amaze me. When I finish reading one, I not only feel connected to the characters and the events; I feel that I have walked in the presence of Christ and that He has spoken mightily to me. I always cry when I finish one of her books...tears to say good-bye to the friends I've come to know and love and tears of thankfulness to my heavenly Father. I can't wait to read the next one!"—LINDA, Batavia, IL

"My grandmother has been diagnosed with dementia... Right after her diagnosis, she asked me to bring her some books. I took her everything I own by Karen Kingsbury, which is about ten books. She devoured them! They encouraged her and gave her hope."—DONNA I.

"A friend recommended *A Moment of Weakness*. I gave it to my teenage daughter at the time and she read it as well. It opened up a chance to discuss remaining pure until marriage. She is now twenty-two and married a few months ago as a virgin. We had many other discussions, but your book hit home where my lecturing may not have. God has given you a very special talent, and I am sure He is smiling at your use of it. Thank you!"—KATHY, Livonia, NY

"Karen Kingsbury's novels have not just touched my heart but also my soul. When things go topsy-turvy in my daily life (as with four children they sometimes do), I often think of the Scriptures I've read in your books. Your books have not only kept me up at night anxiously waiting for what is going to happen next, but more important, they have helped me in my walk with the Lord."—STEPHANIE H.

"As a biblical counselor, I have used several of Karen Kingsbury's books to reach the hearts of many of my clients. They have been most helpful in this respect, but I also admire Karen's courage in speaking out on tough issues within our Christian culture."—SANDY K.

"The greatest impact Karen Kingsbury's works have had on my life was to help me with forgiveness. Not just to say the words, for that's what's expected of me, but to actually feel it in my heart... I marvel at how God has used you to work in my life and the lives of countless others."—HARRIETTE, Durham, NC

"I've read several of Karen Kingsbury's books, and after finishing them, I was challenged about the depth of my surrender to whatever the Lord allows in my life. Thank you for taking me to another deep place with my Father."—PAULA M.

"From Karen Kingsbury's very first book to her most recent, she has inspired me to be a better person, have a stronger faith in God, and to question how I am raising my family in a world filled with hate and evil."—PATTIE, Oceanside, CA

"When I went off to college, I fell into a dark depression but convinced myself that Christians not only don't suffer depression, but that it is inherently un-Christian to be depressed... I bought *When Joy Came to Stay* and read it in one sitting... I was able to receive treatment for my illness and work on dealing with events and behaviors that led to this depression. The book made it easier for me to see that God can use even dark times to bless us and help us grow."—DEIDRE E.

"Karen Kingsbury's fiction has helped me with my family problems. Karen's books have taught me how to stick together with my family through thick and thin. They have taught me that even when your family may be having a tough time, never give up."—ASHLEIGH, Fairfield, CA

"I can't tell you how much Karen Kingsbury's books have blessed my life. The novels make me think seriously about what commitment means, sticking it out even when all seems gloomy, and understanding the covenant of marriage."

—NATA, Nigeria

"Karen Kingsbury's fiction is so easy to identify with. These books have been a source of refuge in my emotional struggles after going through marital difficulty and divorce. It helps to know that someone understands what people like me go through!"—MELISSA, Bethel Springs, TN

Fiction Readers Unite!

You've just found a new way to feed your fiction addiction. Letstalkfiction.com is a place where fiction readers can come together to learn about new fiction releases from Multnomah. You can read about the latest book releases, catch a behind-the-scenes look at the your favorite authors, sign up to receive the most current book information, and much more. Everything you need to make the most out of your fictional world can be found at www.letstalkfiction.com. Come and join the network!

"Karen Ball has penned a modern classic and given us two unforgettable characters to root for. This is an author to watch!"

—ROBIN LEE HATCHER, bestselling author of *Firstborn* and *Promised to Me*

1-59052-033-5

Gabe and Renee Roman are on the edge—relationally and spiritually. But after years of struggling in their marriage, their greatest test comes in the most unexpected of forms: a blizzard in the Oregon wilderness. Their truck hurtles down the side of a mountain, and suddenly they are forced to fight for survival by relying on each other. But both must surrender their last defenses if they are to come home at last—to God and to each other. Only then will they learn the most important truths of all: God is sufficient, and only through obedience to His call can we find true joy. Can the Romans overcome their greatest obstacle—themselves—in time?

Coming October 2004 from bestselling author
KAREN BALL

Her daughter Faith is the answer to Ann's lifelong prayer to be a mother. But her dream is shattered when the teenager rejects Ann's love and the love of God. After years pass, and God heals their relationship, Ann falls seriously ill. Faith watches her mother weaken, struggling with role reversals and leaning on God as never before. Through all the intricacies of their relationship, all the joys and trials, they are reminded that God is with them. He brings them peace in the darkness, joy in the midst of sorrow, and hope in the face of death.

ISBN 1-59052-265-6

ghout the material. This is because the middle part o
may be regarded as rigid and, furthermore, in a soli
lo not generally exchange places – at least at moderat
ads. The only thing, therefore, which can 'give' is th
c bond. These bonds or springs vary a good deal i
springiness (or, as the layman might put it, in 'strength'
f them are much stiffer than the metal springs to whic
customed in ordinary life. From this it follows, o
at the forces between the atoms are often very larg
e should expect this if we think about the forces whic
eased by chemical explosives and fuels.

gh there is no such thing as a truly rigid solid – that is t
hich does not yield at all when a weight is put on it
ay life the deflections of common objects are often ver
r instance, if I take an ordinary builder's ceramic bric
pright on a firm surface and tread on it, then the bric
ompressed along its length by a total distance of abo
an inch. Any two neighbouring atoms in the brick a
nearer together by about $\frac{1}{500,000}$ Ångström unit (2
., or about one hundredth of a millionth
This is an inconceivably small distance but a perfect
ement for all that. Actually, in large structures the d
are not by any means always tiny. In order to suppo
d, that is to say the roadway and the cars, the suspensi
the Forth road bridge are permanently stretched in te
bout 0·1 per cent, or something like ten feet (three metre
total length of nearly two miles, or three kilometres.
e the atoms of iron which are normally about tv
m units apart when at rest and unloaded are kept abo
gström units further apart than they would be in t
ed state.

atoms really do move further apart when a material
d has been checked experimentally many times and
t methods. The most obvious way is by X-ray diffracti
ched and unstretched specimens. The standard way
ing the distance between the atoms in a crystal is to stu
y in which an X-ray beam is deflected when it pass
h the crystal. This method has been used now for si

gravitation upon the mass of the load and in the case of stopping a moving load (whether a solid, a liquid or a gas) the forces generated are those needed to decelerate the moving mass (Newton's second law of motion). The business of all structures is the conservative one of maintaining the *status quo* and in order to do this they must somehow generate adequate forces to oppose the loads which they have to carry. We can see how a weight presses down on the floor but how does the floor press up on the weight?

The answer to this question is far from obvious and the problem was the more difficult for Galileo and Hooke, in the early days of scientific thought, because the biological analogy is confusing and the tendency is, or was, to begin thinking about a problem in an anthropomorphic way. An animal has really two mechanisms for resisting loads. Its inert parts – bones, teeth and hair – resist by just the same means as any other inert solid but the living animal as a whole behaves in a quite different manner. People and other animals resist mechanical forces by pushing back in an active way: they tense their muscles and push or pull as the situation may require. If I stretch out my hand and you put a weight on it such as a pint of beer, then I have to increase the tensions in certain muscles so as to sustain the load. I am enabled to do this because the tensions in our muscles can be continually adjusted by an elaborate biological mechanism. However, the maintenance of biological tensions requires the continual expenditure of actual work (like driving a car fitted with a fluid flywheel while it is hard up against a wall – the engine is working away and using petrol and the car is pushing against the wall but neither the car nor the wall are moving). For this reason my arm muscles will sooner or later get tired and so I shall have to drink the beer to relieve them. One remains standing, not like a tripod standing inertly on the ground, but by a series of deliberate, though perhaps unconscious, adjustments of the body muscles. One gets tired standing up, and, if the muscular processes are interrupted by fainting or death, there is a dramatic collapse.

In an inanimate solid these living processes are not available. Structural materials are passive and cannot push back deliberately, so that they do not, in the ordinary sense, get tired.

They can only resist outside forces *when they are deflected*; that is, they must give way to the load to a greater or less extent in order to generate any resistance at all. By 'deflection', in this context, we do not mean that the solid moves bodily, as a whole and without changing its shape, but rather that the geometrical form of the solid is to some extent distorted so that some parts of it at least become shorter or longer by stretching or contracting within themselves. There is, and there can be, no such thing as a truly rigid material. Everything 'gives' to some extent and, as we have said, the realization that this is what structural engineering is about is what divides the professional from the amateur engineer.

When I climb a tree the deflections of the boughs under my weight will probably be very large, perhaps a matter of several inches, and are easily seen. However, when I walk across a bridge the deflections may be imperceptibly small. These are only questions of degree: there is always some deflection. Unless the deflections under loads are excessively large for the purpose of the structure they are not a fault but an inborn and unavoidable characteristic of structures with which it is the business of this chapter to come to terms. Most of us have sat in an aeroplane and watched the wing-tips going up and down. This is quite all right; the designer meant them to be like that.

It is probably obvious by this time that these deflections, be they large or small, generate the forces of resistance which make a solid hard and stiff and resistant to external loads. In other words, a solid deflects exactly far enough to build up forces which just counter the external load applied to it. This is the automatic process at the basis of all structures.

How are these forces generated? The atoms in a solid are held together by chemical forces or bonds (see Appendix 1) which may perhaps be thought of as electrical springs since there is nothing 'solid' in any crude sense to make any other kind of spring. It is these forces which bind solids together and also make the rules of chemistry. There is no distinction between the chemical bonds between atoms whose fracture yields the energy of gunpowder or petrol, and the chemical bonds which make steel and rubber strong and elastic.

When a solid is altogethe
strictly speaking, is very sel
are in their neutral or relax

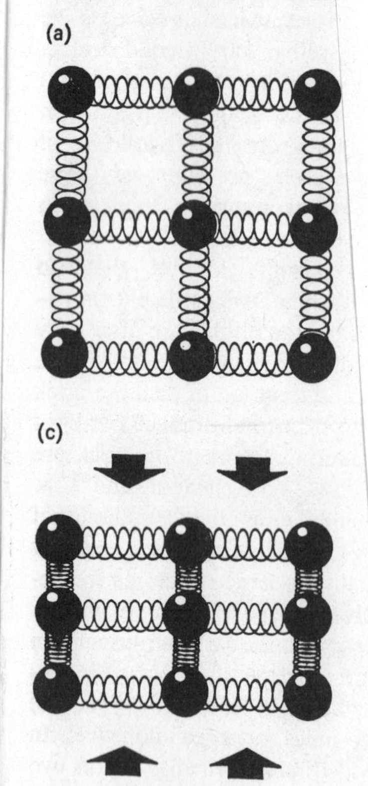

Figure 1. Simplified model of distorti
mechanical strain.
(a) Neutral, relaxed or strain-
(b) Material strained in tensi
gets longer.
(c) Material strained in com
material gets shorter.

to push them closer together (which
stretch them further apart (which
shortening or lengthening the intera

little, throu
the atoms
the atoms
or 'safe' lo
interatomi
stiffness or
but most o
we are a
course, th
indeed. W
can be rel

Althou
say one v
in everyd
small. Fo
stand it u
will be c
$\frac{1}{50,000}$ of
pushed
10^{-14}cm
an inch)
real mov
flections
their loa
cables o
sion by
in their
this cas
Ångströ
$\frac{2}{1,000}$ Ån
unstres

That
stretche
differen
of stre
measu
the wa
throug

years or more and it is nowadays capable of considerable accuracy. It is found that the atoms in a metal, for instance, move apart or together exactly in proportion to the amount by which the metal as a whole is stretched or compressed. Changes in inter-atomic spacing up to about 1·0 per cent have been observed. Some actual measurements up to about 0·3 per cent are shown in Figure 2.

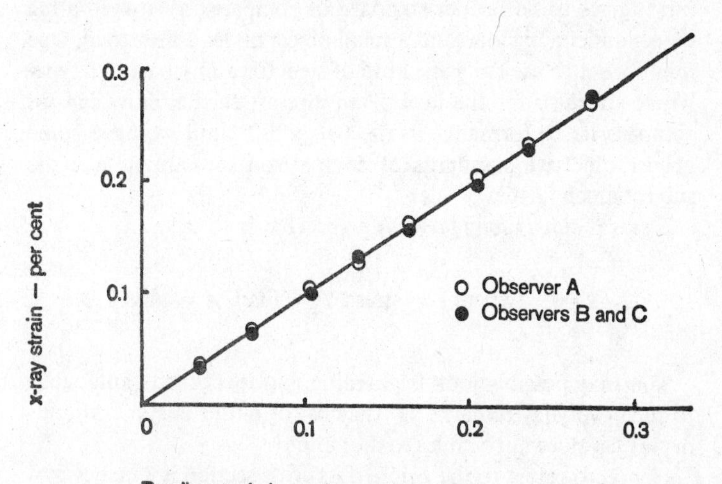

Figure 2. Comparison of strains determined by X-rays (two-exposure method) and strains computed from the curvature of a bent beam. Annealed mild steel.

What are stresses and strains, and why bother?

All this brings us to the question of stresses and strains, words which the layman is apt to regard as alarming, distressing and confusing. This is perhaps partly because the words may conjure up the idea of a wilderness of mathematics but probably more because the words have been borrowed or stolen by non-scientists to describe the mental condition of human beings. In this connotation the words have no very precise meaning and commonly stress and strain are used interchangeably as if they meant the same thing. All this is a pity because in science the two words have quite simple, clear and distinct meanings.

So far we have thought, as much as we have thought about it at all, of the force acting on a material as being the total load upon it. This might be any weight, and we have thought of the deflection under that load as being the total deflection, whatever the dimensions of the object, large or small. This is all very well but it gives us no proper standard of comparison between a big object under a big load and a small object under a little load. One might want to use the same kind of steel for a tiny part in a typewriter and also for the keel of an aircraft carrier: how can we compare its performance in the two jobs? Until we have some proper objective standards of comparison we cannot take the subject much further.

Stress is simply load per unit area. That is to say:

$$s = \frac{P}{A} \text{ (where } s = \text{stress, } P = \text{load, } A = \text{area.)}$$

This may possibly look frightening, but it is exactly analogous to such everyday remarks as 'the cost of butter is 50p a pound' or 'my car does thirty miles to the gallon'.

Hence, to revert to the brick, if its cross section is 3 inches by 4 inches then its end has an area of 12 square inches and, if I tread on it with a weight of 200 pounds, the compressive stress which I cause in the brick is clearly:

$$s = \frac{P}{A} = \frac{200}{12} = 16\tfrac{2}{3} \text{ pounds on each square inch, or pounds per square inch, or lb./in.}^2\text{, or p.s.i.}$$

Similarly if the brickwork pier of a bridge has a cross-section measuring 20 feet by 5 feet and it is crossed by a railway engine weighing 100 tons (224,000 pounds) then the compressive stress in the brickwork will be roughly 16 p.s.i. We can say with confidence therefore that in both cases the stress in the bricks is similar and, if one structure is safe, so most probably will be the other. As far as the bricks are concerned, their molecules are being pushed together with an identical force although the engine is ponderous and I am relatively small. This is obviously the sort of thing that engineers want to know.

In English-speaking countries stresses are traditionally expressed in pounds per square inch or tons per square inch. Continental engineers generally use kilogrammes per square centimetre. With S.I. the use of Newtons per square metre (N/m^2) usually produces embarrassingly large numbers and so we generally use Meganewtons per square metre (MN/m^2); (1 Meganewton = one million Newtons). In this book we shall use p.s.i. and MN/m^2 side by side.* Nevertheless we must be clear that we are applying the concept to the conditions at any cross-section or at a point and not especially to a square inch or to a square metre. Because the price of butter is 50p a pound this price does not apply especially to one pound; it is just as applicable to larger or smaller quantities.

Strain is just as simple: *Strain is the amount of stretch under load per unit length.*

Obviously, different lengths of material stretch different distances under the same load. So:

$$e = \frac{l}{L}$$

where e = strain, l = total amount of stretch, L = original total length.

So, if a rod 100 inches long stretches one inch under load, then it is subject to a strain of 1/100 or 0·01 or 1·0 per cent. So also is a rod 50 inches long which stretches ½ inch, and so on. It does not matter how fat or thin the rod is or what is causing the extension. We are only concerned with how much the component atoms and molecules are stretched apart, and so strain is again, like stress, independent of the size of the specimen. Strain is a *fraction* of the original length and so it remains just a fraction or a ratio (in other words a number) and has no units, British, S.I. or anything else.

*For conversion:

1 MN/m^2 = 10·2 Kg/cm^2 = 146 p.s.i.
1 p.s.i. = 0·00685 MN/m^2 = 0·07 Kg/cm^2
1 kg/cm^2 = 0·098 MN/m^2 = 14·2 p.s.i.

Hooke's law

The first man to grasp what was happening when an inert solid was loaded was Robert Hooke* who, besides being a physicist, was a notable architect and engineer and used to discuss the behaviour of springs and pendulums with the great clockmaker Thomas Tompion† (1639–1713). Hooke, of course, knew nothing about the chemical and electrical forces between atoms, but he realized that a 'spring' as a clockmaker might think of it is only a special case of the behaviour of any elastic solid and that there is no such thing as a truly rigid material, springiness being a property of every structure and of every solid.

Hooke, like Horace, did not suffer unduly from modesty and he staked his claim to priority in a number of fields by publishing in 1676 *A decimate of the centesme of the inventions I intend to publish* among which was 'The true theory of elasticity or springiness'. This heading was followed simply by the anagram 'ceiiinosssttuu'. The scientific public were left to make what they could of this until, in 1679, Hooke published *De potentia restitutiva, or of a spring* where the anagram was revealed as 'Ut tensio‡ sic uis' – 'As the extension, so the force'.

In other words, stress is proportional to strain and vice versa. So, if an elastic body such as a wire is stretched one inch under a load of 100 pounds it will stretch two inches under 200 pounds and so on, *pro rata*. This is known as Hooke's law and is regarded as one of the pillars of engineering.

As a matter of fact Hooke's law is really an approximation which arises from the character of the forces between atoms. There are several kinds of chemical bonds between atoms (see Appendix 1) but they all result in interatomic force curves which are similar in general shape (Figure 3). At very large strains – 5 to 10 per cent or so – stress is anything but proportionate to strain.

* For Hooke in general, see *Robert Hooke* by Margaret 'Espinasse.

† Tompion is the joy of modern sale-rooms where his lovely clocks fetch enormous prices.

‡ Tensio means, generally, not tension but extension in Latin. The truth seems to be that the Romans muddled up the two ideas. Literary writers probably never thought about the matter at all.

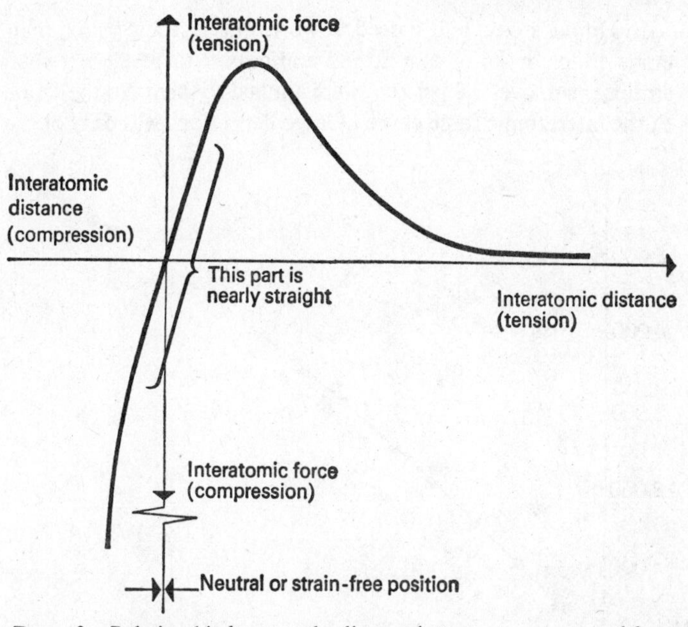

Figure 3. Relationship between the distance between two atoms and force between them.

However, in practical engineering materials, strains nearly always lie in the range $\pm$ 1·0 per cent either side of the neutral or strain-free position and for this range the relation between stress and strain is pretty well a straight line. Furthermore for small strains the whole process of extension and recovery is reversible and can usually be repeated many thousands or millions of times with identical results; the hair-spring of a watch which is coiled and uncoiled 18,000 times each hour is a familiar example. This type of behaviour by solids under loading is called 'elastic' and is widespread. Elastic behaviour, which is shown by the majority of engineering materials, contrasts with 'plastic' behaviour, shown to the extreme by putty and Plasticine, where the material does not obey Hooke's law in the initial loading and does not recover properly when the load is removed. The word 'elastic' is not especially dedicated to indiarubber and sock-suspenders and the science of elasticity is the study of stresses and strains in solids.

In Hooke's day, and indeed down to the last few years, materials either broke or else flowed and ceased to be elastic when strains much over 1·0 per cent were applied to them. So the shape of the interatomic force curve at large deflections was only of the

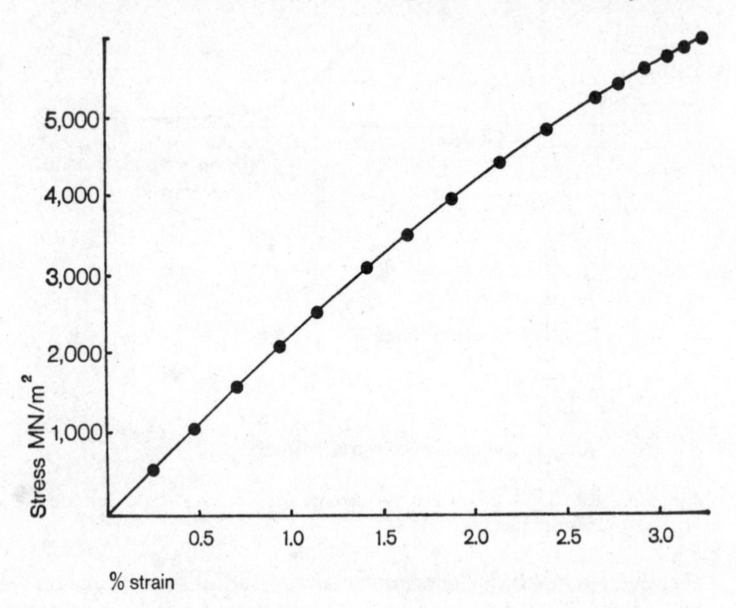

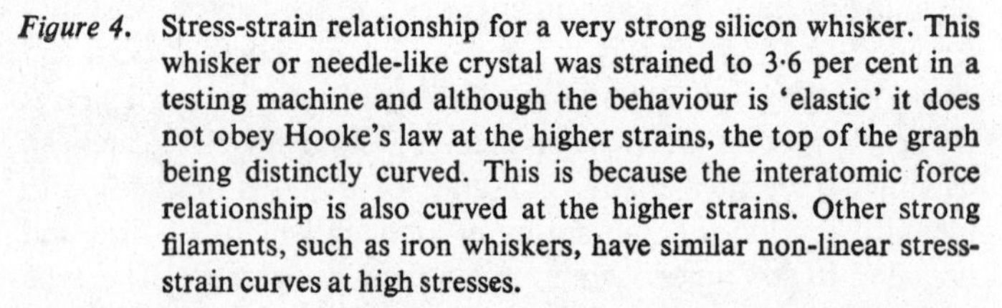
Figure 4. Stress-strain relationship for a very strong silicon whisker. This whisker or needle-like crystal was strained to 3·6 per cent in a testing machine and although the behaviour is 'elastic' it does not obey Hooke's law at the higher strains, the top of the graph being distinctly curved. This is because the interatomic force relationship is also curved at the higher strains. Other strong filaments, such as iron whiskers, have similar non-linear stress-strain curves at high stresses.

most academic interest because such stresses were never reached. Fairly recently, in the writer's laboratory and elsewhere, it has been possible to take very strong 'whisker' crystals up to strains between 3 and 6 per cent and the measurements confirm that Hooke's law is not literally true. The stress-strain curve bends over to follow the interatomic force curve which is derived from considerations, not of engineering, but of theoretical physics.

Figure 4 shows such a curve for a silicon whisker strained to over 3 per cent.

Young's modulus

Hooke stated that the deflections of springs and other elastic bodies were proportionate to the load which is applied to them but, of course, with different structures, the actual deflection under any given load will depend both upon the geometrical size and shape of the structure and also upon the material from which it is made. It is not clear how far Hooke distinguished elasticity as a property of a *material* from elasticity as a function of the *shape and dimensions* of the structure. We can get similar load-extension curves from a straight piece of rubber and from a helical piece of steel which we call a spring – this has always been a fruitful source of confusion. Certainly for something like a century after Hooke's time a state of intellectual muddle seems to have invested the few people who thought about elasticity and no clear distinction seems to have been made between these ideas.

Around 1800 Thomas Young (1773–1829) realized that, if we consider the stresses and strains in the material rather than the gross deflections of the structure, then Hooke's law can be written:

$$\frac{\text{stress}}{\text{strain}} = \frac{s}{e} = \text{constant}$$

Furthermore, Young realized that there was here a constant peculiarly characteristic of each chemical substance which, as he might have said, represents its 'springiness'. We call this constant 'Young's modulus' or E. There is no mystery about the word 'modulus', it just means a figure which describes a property of a material. Thus:

$$E = \frac{s}{e} = \frac{\text{stress}}{\text{strain}}$$

E therefore describes the elastic flexibility of a material as such; the flexibility of any given object will thus depend both upon the Young's modulus of the material from which it is made and also upon its geometrical shape.

It is said of Young that he was 'a man of great learning but unfortunately he never even began to realize the limitations of comprehension of ordinary minds'.* Young published the idea of his modulus in a rather incomprehensible paper in 1807 after he had been dismissed from his lectureship at the Royal Institution for not being sufficiently practical. Thus perhaps the most famous and the most useful of all concepts in engineering, which defines the stiffness or floppiness of a material, was not generally understood or absorbed into engineering practice until after Young's death. Young's modulus is often called 'stiffness' in casual engineering conversation and will sometimes be called stiffness and sometimes E in this book.

E is enormously important in engineering for two reasons. First, we need to know with accuracy the deflections in a structure, as a whole and in its various parts, when it is loaded. A moment's thought about bridges or aeroplanes or crankshafts will show that this is so (Figure 5). Things must still fit together,

Figure 5. Aircraft with strain of 1·6 per cent in wing spar booms.
$$\left(\text{Bend radius of beam} = \frac{\text{thickness}}{2\times\text{strain}}\right)$$

or have the proper clearances, when the load is on.† A knowledge of the E of the material being used is the first thing we need to know in making these calculations. Secondly, although the lay-

*S. B. Hamilton, *History of Technology*, vol. 4, chapter 15.

†I once did a design study of a plastic railway carriage for British Rail. One of the troubles was that, if the doors fitted properly when the carriage was empty, they would neither open nor close when the carriage was full of passengers in the rush hour.

man might suppose, as the early engineers seem to have done, that the stiffness of all common structural materials were very similar ('Well, it's stiff, isn't it, you can't *see* any deflections'), this is in fact very far from being the case and we not only need to know the *E*s of various materials such as wood and steel in order to calculate their deflections, but we must also arrange that the deflections of differing materials in a structure are compatible and that they share the load in the way we want them to.

Since, if we divide stress by a ratio – that is by a number without dimensions* – we must still have a stress, Young's modulus is therefore a stress in pounds per square inch, or what you will. It is that stress which would in theory double the length of a specimen, if it did not break first. One can also regard it as the stress to produce 100 per cent strain. As it will easily be imagined, the actual figure is likely to be a high one, usually at least a hundred times larger than the breaking stress of the material, because, as we have said, materials are apt to fracture in the ordinary way at 1 per cent elastic strain or less. The Young's modulus of steel, for example, is about 30,000,000 pounds per square inch. As we have also said, *E* varies very much according to the kind of chemical substance we are dealing with. A few typical figures are shown on page 42.

Thus the whole range of solids vary in *E* by about 200,000 to 1. Even substances which we normally think of as 'rigid' vary by about 1000 to 1, which is still an enormous range. *E* is very low in rubber because rubber is made of long molecular chains which are flexible and in the resting material they are generally much bent, kinked and convoluted, like a heap of bits of string such as one finds in a drawer in the hall at home. When rubber is stretched, the bent chains are straightened and, as one can easily see, the force needed to do so is very much less than that which is needed to stretch an arrangement of strings which were initially straight. Nothing of this kind happens in a normal crystal where one is pulling directly on the interatomic bonds and the only reason for the large variations in Young's modulus is that the chemical bonds themselves vary a great deal in stiffness. So with crystals, although the general shape of the interatomic force curves is

*i.e. by a strain.

Approximate Young's moduli of various substances

	E Pounds per square inch	E MN/m²
Rubber	0·001 × 10⁶ (i.e. 1,000)	7
Unreinforced plastics	0·2 × 10⁶	1,400
Organic molecular crystal, phthalocyanine, a blue pigment	0·2 × 10⁶	1,400
Wood (about)	2·0 × 10⁶	14,000
Concrete	2·5 × 10⁶	17,000
Bone	3·0 × 10⁶	21,000
Magnesium metal	6·0 × 10⁶	42,000
Ordinary glasses	10·0 × 10⁶	70,000
Aluminium	10·5 × 10⁶	73,000
Steel	30·0 × 10⁶	210,000
Aluminium oxide (sapphire)	60·0 × 10⁶	420,000
Diamond	170·0 × 10⁶	1,200,000

Note. Because the interatomic force curve (Figure 3) passes smoothly through the point of zero stress and strain the true E of a material is always the same in compression as it is in tension at all normal strains. If this were not so then the mathematics of elasticity would be even more complicated than they are. In practice, however, materials such as cast iron and cement, which contain quite gross internal cracks, may sometimes show an E which is lower in tension than it is in compression. This is simply because the cracks gape under tension and 'come up solid' under compression.

similar, the slope of the straight part of the curves varies greatly according to the bond energy and other chemical conditions.

The figure for the E of phthalocyanine tells us at once why a great many solid chemical compounds are not candidates for the status of structural materials. Generally speaking we want a structure to be as rigid as possible: bridges and buildings sway quite enough as it is and there are excellent reasons for making other things rigid as well. Any structure made from a material with a stiffness as low as phthalocyanine would be far too floppy. Steel is about the stiffest reasonably cheap material, which is one of the reasons why it is used so widely. As much as anything it is the relatively low stiffness of plastics, even when 'reinforced', which restricts their use for large objects.

Strength

Next to 'heat-proof' I suppose that 'unbreakable' is one of the most useful words in advertising. Although most of us know that advertising is not an entirely objective profession, somehow or other the message sinks in so that one still meets people who really believe that there are unbreakable objects or, if there aren't, then there ought to be. Since there is always some force which will tear the atoms apart in a solid (since the chemical bonds have a finite energy or, in other words, they are only so strong) nothing is unbreakable. You have only to get hold of the thing firmly and pull hard enough and it will break. The only question is 'how soon?' There is however a very large variation between the strengths of various materials.

Lest there be any possible, probable, shadow of doubt, strength is not, repeat not, the same thing as stiffness. Stiffness, Young's modulus or E, *is concerned with how stiff, flexible, springy or floppy a material is. Strength is the force or stress needed to break a thing. A biscuit is stiff but weak, steel is stiff and strong, nylon is flexible* (*low* E *and strong, raspberry jelly is flexible* (*low* E) *and weak. The two properties together describe a solid about as well as you can reasonably expect two figures to do.*

It is easiest to think about strength in terms of tensile strength. This is the stress needed to pull a material asunder by breaking all the bonds between the atoms along the line of fracture. One can perhaps most conveniently think of it as the stress required to break a bar by pulling it along its axis like a rope. A very strong steel may withstand a tensile stress of 450,000 pounds (200 tons) per square inch (3,000 MN/m^2), while ordinary brick or cement may perhaps withstand 600 or 800 p.s.i. or only 4 or 5 MN/m^2.* The strength of commonly used engineering materials thus varies over a range of about a thousand to one†. The tensile strengths of some common materials are given in the table.

*'Daddy, why can't you make boilers out of cement?'

†For the moment we may be content to say that breaking stress is that stress at which things break. However, let us beware of a trap or incipient muddle. If a bar of 10 square inches cross section breaks under a tensile load of a 100 tons then its breaking load is a 100 tons, but its breaking stress

Some typical tensile strengths in round figures

	p.s.i.	MN/m²
METALS		
Steels		
Steel piano wire (very brittle)	450,000	3,000
High tensile engineering steel	225,000	1,500
Commercial mild steel	60,000	400
Wrought iron		
Traditional	20,000–40,000	140–280
Cast iron		
Traditional	10,000–20,000	70–140
Modern	20,000–40,000	140–280
Other metals		
Aluminium		
cast, pure	10,000	70
alloys	20,000–80,000	140–550
Copper	20,000	140
Brasses	18,000–60,000	120–400
Magnesium alloys	30,000–40,000	200–280
Titanium alloys	100,000–200,000	700–1,400
NON-METALS		
Wood, spruce		
along grain	15,000	100
across grain	500	3
Glass (window or beer-mug)	5,000–25,000	30–170
Good ceramics	5,000–50,000	30–340
Ordinary brick	800	5
Cement and concrete	600	4
Flax	100,000	700
Cotton	50,000	350
Catgut	50,000	350
Silk	50,000	350
Spider's thread	35,000	240
Tendon	15,000	100
Hemp rope	12,000	80
Leather	6,000	40
Bone	20,000	140

is 10 tons per square inch. Engineers refer to the first of these as the strength of the bar and to the second as the strength of the material – fair enough but rather confusing.

When we talk about 'strength' we usually mean tensile strength although materials are more often used in compression than they are in tension. At first sight it is not very easy to see why a material should ever want to break at all in compression. After all, if one is pressing the atoms closer together, why should they come apart? Compressive failure is more complicated than tensile failure, especially as there are several different ways in which a material can run away from a compressive load.

If the material is in the form of a fairly short, squat column, or chock or wedge or something of the sort, then, if the material is at all soft or ductile like mild steel or copper, it will simply squish out sideways, like Plasticine. If the material is brittle, like stone or glass, it will explode sideways (and very dangerous it can be) into dust and splinters. However, if the specimen is long and slender, like a thin rod or panel, then it may fail by 'buckling' such as happens when you lean too hard on a walking stick which bends and ultimately snaps in two. If you put too much weight on a tin can, as by driving a car over it, it will crumple in the same sort of way. This is the kind of failure which is apt to happen to shell structures such as steel ships and metal aeroplanes when they hit things, not to mention the wings of motor cars. For these reasons it is not easy to quote figures in tables for '*the* compressive strength of so and so'. Broadly speaking there isn't one or at least it must be estimated with knowledge and experience. This is one of the reasons why structural engineering isn't particularly easy.

There is no general relationship between the tensile and compressive strengths of various materials and structures, partly because the distinction between a material and a structure is never very clear. For instance, a pile of bricks is strong in compression but has no tensile strength at all. A pile of bricks is undoubtedly a structure and not a material, but then cast iron, cement, plaster and masonry are much stronger in compression than they are in tension and for much the same reason as a pile of bricks: they are full of cracks. Chains and ropes are strong in tension and have no compressive strength because they fold up in compression. They are probably structures not materials. Wood is three or four times as strong in tension as it is in compression because the cell walls fold up in compression, yet wood is thought of as a material not a structure.

Tension and compression structures

For a great many centuries engineers and architects avoided using materials in tension as much as they could. This was not so much because they had no materials strong in tension – wood, for example, is excellent – but rather because of the difficulty of making reliable strong joints to withstand tension. Most of us intuitively feel that a compression structure is safer than a tension one; that a brick tower is safer than an aerial cableway, for instance. In the old days, when tension joints were unavoidable, as they were in ships, they were a perpetual source of trouble. Now that we can make good joints with bolts or rivets, glues or welding, there is no special justification for distrusting a tension structure.

However, in a primitive technology, the problem of a compression joint is very much easier and in the simplest case resolves itself into merely heaping one stone or brick upon another in such a way that the house does not fall down. Dry-walling is a skilled job but not much more so than doing a jigsaw puzzle. As architects became more ambitious and walls higher, it was necessary to arrange firmer, better fitting joints lest the wall slide down with a rumble into a heap of stones. If the stones do not fit each other reasonably well they will roll over each other like a pile of balls and be pushed outward under the superincumbent weight, just as, on a finer scale, Plasticine is pushed outwards. In this way we get magnificently fitted joints between large blocks of stone in ancient buildings. How much of this laborious accuracy was born of engineering necessity and how much of a morbid desire for prestige on the part of men or gods is arguable. Many of these buildings, like a famous car, strike one as being 'a triumph of workmanship over design'.

However high and impressive a wall may be, it remains technologically a very unsophisticated structure because the designer is really only thinking about stresses in one dimension; that is to say vertically. He is always in a difficulty about bridging roofs, doors and other openings. Once he starts thinking imaginatively of stress systems in two and three dimensions, all kinds of possibilities open up, even if he is still restricted to compressive systems. This is why the arch is important. The ordinary simple arch utilizes compression in two directions simultaneously to bridge a gap (Figure 6). This is an apparent

Figure 6. The arch – a two-dimensional compression structure – enables vertical forces to be transmitted laterally around the arch-ring into the abutments. (The wedge-shaped pieces which make up the arch-ring are called 'voussoirs'.)

impossibility which works extremely well. A masonry arch can span 200 feet (60 metres) or so (though 100–200 feet is more common) without much difficulty. This is a very much greater span than any primitive beam or architrave or lintel could bridge. An arch is also durable and there are innumerable Roman arches, such as the aqueducts, in excellent condition today.

The trick of thinking in terms of stresses acting in more than one direction simultaneously is really the key to most advanced architecture and engineering. Once one accepts the two-dimensional concept of the arch or the three-dimensional concept of the dome which is the next logical step, then one can start playing elaborate architectural games. St Sophia, built by Justinian at Constantinople about 530 A.D., is a great dome 107 feet (32 metres) in diameter and made of pumice bricks for lightness, poised upon four great arches which are propped in turn by auxiliary half domes (Figure 7). The result was a nave, completely clear of

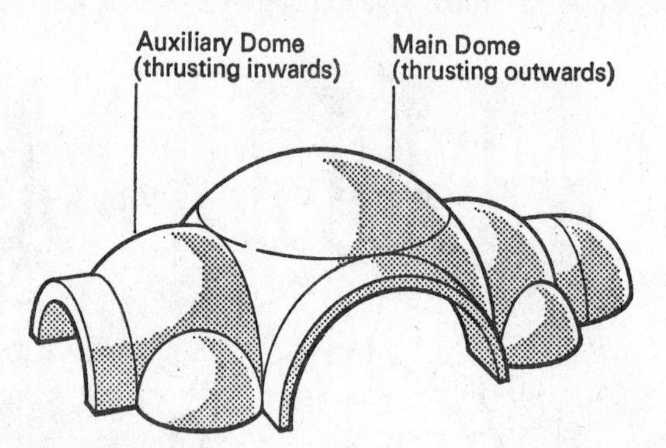

Figure 7. How the outward thrusts of the main dome of St Sophia at Constantinople are supported by means of subsidiary domes and vaults.

pillars, measuring more than 200 feet by 100 feet (60 metres × 30 metres) and about 240 feet (72 metres) high, a clear roofed area greater, probably, than any achieved until the advent of the modern railway station which is roofed with steel trusses. The shapes of Byzantine architecture are usually simple but the Gothic architects ran riot in aisles, fan-vaulting and clerestories. All this, though rather expensive, is great technical and artistic fun as long as you know what you are doing. The essential thing about a masonry structure is that it must be a compression structure everywhere, because masonry is incapable of resisting tensions since the stones will come apart at the joints.

In the three-dimensional labyrinth of a cathedral roof, where thrust chases thrust in Gothic disregard of mathematics, strange things were apt to happen. Tensions crept in, like devils among the gargoyles. In one of the greatest of the Gothic cathedrals, Beauvais (1247), the tower fell once and the roof fell twice. Contemporary architects knew what was wrong in a qualitative sort of way and they propped their structures up with a maze of flying buttresses (Figure 8), just as St Sophia is set about, in a more rational and successful way, with auxiliary domes which thrust inwards and maintain a state of compression in the critical regions. Sometimes the Gothic architects overdid the business of

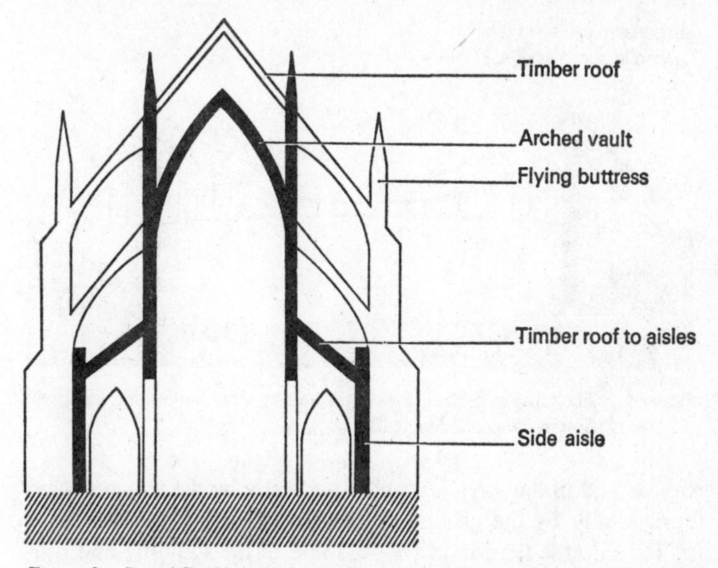

Figure 8. In a 'Gothic' structure the outward thrust of the roof is taken mainly by buttresses.

inward thrusting and had to strut their naves internally to prevent the building collapsing inwards. This strutting was sometimes done by inserting inverted arches, as at Wells Cathedral (Plate I) which, whatever may be thought of it aesthetically, is a mess structurally. It is not surprising that the roofs of churches continued to fall upon the heads of their congregations with fair regularity throughout the ages of faith.

A masonry structure is kept together by gravity; that is, if it is properly designed, the weight of the stones keeps everything safely in compression. If necessary one can pile on pinnacles and towers to get more weight in the right place. Once we start dealing with tension, however, or mixed tension and compression structures, we have to accept that the tensions and compressions must balance out, taking into account the weights of the various parts, of course. In a suspension bridge the cables are maintained in tension by a corresponding horizontal compression in the ground beneath the bridge (Figure 9). In a tent the tension in the

Suspension cables in tension
Towers in compression

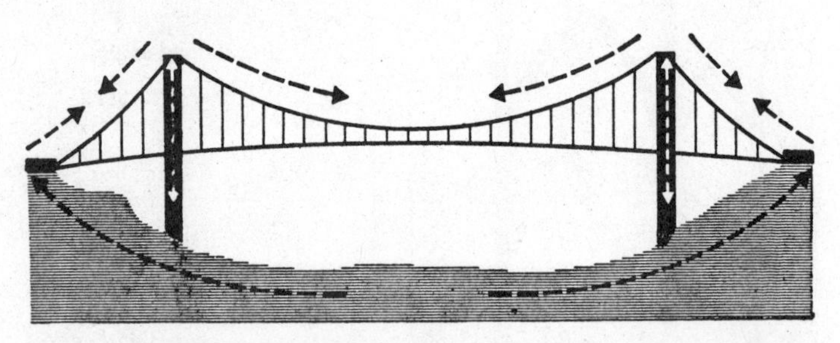

Figure 9. The tension in the cables is reacted by a corresponding compression in the ground beneath.

canvas and in the guys is reacted vertically by the tent pole and horizontally by the ground on which the tent is pitched. In a sailing ship the tension in the sails and in the standing and running rigging is reacted by compressions in the masts and spars. In an animal the bones, and especially the backbone, are chiefly compressive members reacting, not only the weight of the animal, but also the tensions in the muscles and tendons. I raise my arm by shortening a muscle, that is to say by pulling on it, and this puts the bone into compression – which is what bones are usually designed to take. Getting one's leg into bending, which involves tensions, is the easiest way to break it.

It is a great convenience and a great source of safety to be able to pass, as it were, from compression into tension and back again, either deliberately or by accident. In architecture this is one of the arguments for reinforced concrete and for steel-framed buildings, both materials being strong in tension and compression. It is also one of the reasons why iron and steel are such a godsend to engineers, putting a cloak over their ignorances and uncertainties.

Boilers, for instance, are tension structures which may occasionally get into compression (if you let the fire out you can drive an engine under the negative pressure, that is the vacuum in the boiler) without anything very dangerous happening.

The compressive stresses in a submarine can lead to some rather interesting and unexpected effects of strains, which have to be thought about and guarded against. When a submarine is on the surface she floats, like any other ship, because the weight of the submarine is less than the total weight of water which would be displaced if the vessel were totally submerged. If, for any reason, the hull sinks a little in the water, a greater volume is immersed and the extra buoyancy pushes the vessel up again. When a submarine dives, she fills her ballast tanks with water until her total weight just about equals her submerged displacement and so she has no reserve of buoyancy. In this condition she can dive and manoeuvre under water in much the same way as an airship does in the air. However, as the submarine dives deeper, the water pressure increases and the hull is put under more and more compression. Because the air inside the hull is not under pressure the steel in the hull can only resist this compression by contracting. So the volume of the hull, and thus its displacement, is reduced, although the weight of the submarine and her ballast water is, naturally, not changed. There is therefore a tendency for the submarine to sink further, or to become apparently heavier, the deeper she goes – and in certain circumstances this can be dangerous.

At the safe limit of diving depth the compressive strain in the hull plates might be about 0·7 per cent. Since this strain occurs in all three directions the hull may shrink by about 2 per cent in volume. As water is only very slightly compressed, this may represent a loss of about 20 tons or so of buoyancy for a 1,000-ton submarine.* If this weight cannot be counteracted by blowing the ballast tanks or working the hydrofoils, the submarine will sink deeper and deeper until she is crushed by the water pressure

*Or tonnes – near enough. The total weight of ballast water needed in order to enable such a submarine to dive might be around 300 tons. The elastic contraction of the hull may therefore call for quite substantial proportionate adjustments in ballast.

in the depths of the ocean. This is one of the difficulties about making submarines out of reinforced plastics, such as fibre-glass, which are otherwise rather attractive, but which have low Young's moduli. It is nonsense to think, as used sometimes to be said, that sinking submarines and wrecks will float somewhere short of the bottom of the sea. Even if the pressure hulls and compartments which contain air do not actually burst inwards, which must usually happen, they will progressively contract and lose buoyancy and so the wreck sinks faster and faster.

Balloons, pneumatic tyres and the like are a special case of a tension structure where the tension in the skin is reacted by the pressure of the gas or liquid inside. In this way Dracones (large bag-like barges for conveying liquids) and pneumatic boats are usually very light and efficient structures. The air-supported roof – a building held up entirely by internal pressure – reverses architectural tradition in that everything except the air inside is in tension. Since only a very small air pressure is needed, a modest electric blower keeps everything taut and even supports any reasonable snow load for less expense than the capital charges of a conventional building. Plants and animals use the osmotic pressure of their internal fluids in a similar way.

Beams and bending

It is quite easy to see how tension and compression structures work but it is not at all self-evident how the tensions and compressions which we have been discussing really support a load on a beam. This is a pity, since beams of one kind or another (Figure 10) make up a high proportion of everyday structures. The ordinary floor-board is as good an example as any other of a simple beam. As we said earlier it is the function of a floor-board to press upwards on the soles of our feet with a thrust equal to our own weight. Yet it must perform this function even when we are standing in the middle of the floor and the walls which eventually support the plank are remote. Exactly how does this thrust get from the wall to our feet and vice versa?

The answer to this question is known as 'beam theory' to engineers and is more or less the backbone of engineering. Unfortunately it is less of a backbone than a *pons asinorum* to engineering students. Most students merely learn the formulae of beam theory off by heart and regurgitate them at examination times; understanding only comes much later when they have to struggle

Figure 10. Simply supported beam.

with designing something. We shall therefore leave out all that stuff about integrating the shearing force diagram and try to tackle the problem by the light of nature. Once beam theory is understood the world becomes a more lucid and an altogether better place, so take courage.

To understand about beams it is perhaps easiest to return to the idea that there is no very clear distinction between a material and a structure. Large beams are often fabricated, Meccano fashion, from many small tension and compression rods, as anyone can see who looks at a railway bridge. Yet the means by which the load is transmitted in such a lattice beam or girder is not different in kind from the means by which it is transmitted in a solid beam, even so humble a one as a plank or floor-board. In the lattice structure we can generally see the individual members which resist all the pushes and pulls – all of them, since of course no load can get across the empty spaces between the lattice-work. In a solid beam we have to consider the lattice members as diffused throughout the beam, but the stresses are working in the same way.

We might as well start with a cantilever, a beam one end of which is built into a wall or otherwise fixed to a firm base (what engineers call *encastré*) while it is loaded in some way on the

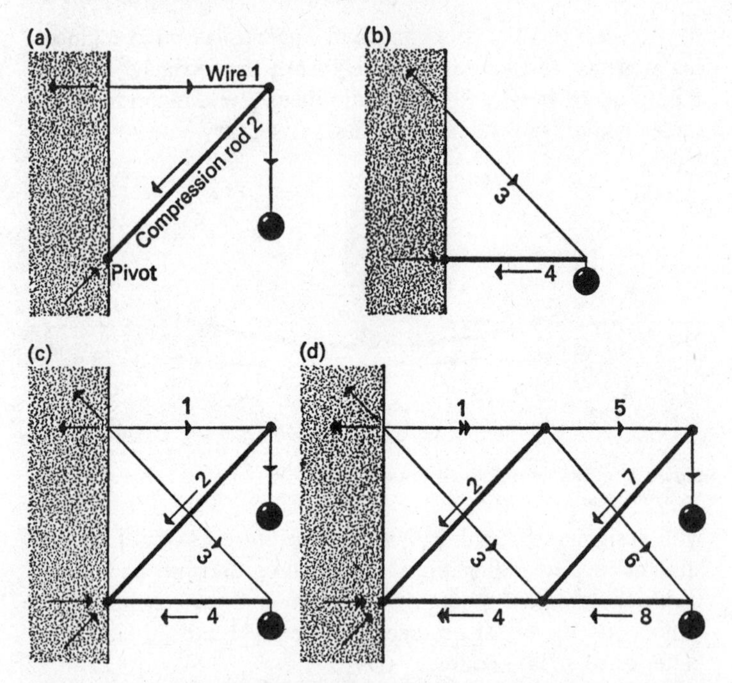

Figure 11. **Beam theory – a beam may be considered as made up from a number of separate panels.**

projecting part. Galileo's picture (Plate 2) of a cantilever will serve as well as any other although Galileo, rather excusably, got his cantilever sums wrong. Let us, however, build up a cantilever entirely by tension in wires and rods.

Consider the simple crane-like structure in Figure 11(*a*). A compression rod (2) is pivoted against a firm wall and is supported by a wire or tension member (1), so that it can carry at its outer end a load, *W*, say. Now it is clear that the push against gravity which is actually supporting the load *W* is generated from the compression in the sloping rod (2). The tension in the wire (1) acts horizontally and only prevents the compression rod (2) from rotating and falling down.

Now we might equally support the weight *W* from another triangular structure such as (*b*) in which the compression rod (4)

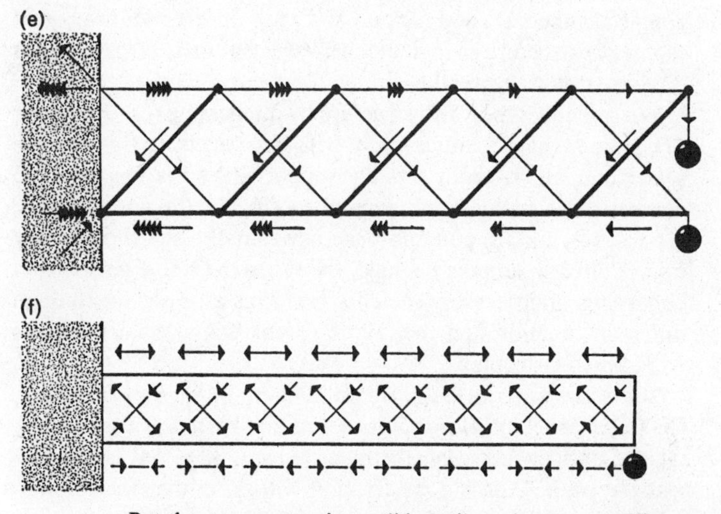

But the stress system in a solid cantilever is not very different from that in a lattice truss.

And, of course, in order to support the weight, the material must be strained and so the cantilever will droop.

was horizontal and was kept from falling down by the diagonal tension wire (3). In this case the upthrust to support the weight W comes from the slanting wire (3) and all the horizontal compression rod does is to prevent the wire from collapsing inwards onto the wall.

These two structures are each as good as the other and we might combine the two to support $2W$, as in (*c*). Clearly the weight $2W$ is directly supported by the two slanting members (2) and (3), one in tension and the other in compression. The horizontal members (1) and (4) pull and push on the wall to prevent the whole structure swinging downwards but their thrusts do not directly sustain the weight.

We can now repeat this structure by duplicating (*c*) so as to get (*d*). Here we have a lattice girder with two panels. In this case the same load $2W$ is again actually supported by the tensions and compressions in the slanting members (2), (3), (6), and (7) while (1), (5), (4), and (8) pull and push horizontally, and though they do not directly support the load, they keep the whole girder from collapsing; indeed every member performs an essential, though different, function and the failure of any of the eight members would be catastrophic.

Notice the way the loads are building up in our simple girder. The outer panel in (*d*) is in all respects similar to the single panel in (*c*). Consider, however, the inner panel in (*d*); that is the one next the wall. A little consideration will show that the tension in the wire (1) is greater that in (5) and in the same way the compression in (4) is greater that in (8). This is because the diagonal or 'shear' members are feeding load in progressively towards the root of the cantilever. In the shear or slanting members, however, the loads are the same in each panel, however long the girder may be.

We can go on and build up a long girder of many panels like (*e*) and here again, if we look at the lattice intelligently, it is obvious that the load in all the diagonal shear members is constant along the length of the girder, however many panels there may be. On the other hand, the tensions and compressions in the top and bottom horizontal members (called the booms or flanges of the girder) are building up and increasing as we move from the loaded tip to the built-in root of the girder, in fact in proportion to its length. For this reason a cantilever will usually break in its most highly stressed members – the horizontal members which are up against the wall – unless we have gone to the trouble of making the thickness of each part proportional to the load which it has to carry. In such a case the lattice may break anywhere, which is an ideal state of affairs and the aim of most stress calculations. When this occurs all the material is equally stressed (like the one-horse shay) and the material is used in the most efficient way. Hence the least quantity of material can be used and the lightest structure will result.

If we now convert our lattice or Meccano girder to a simple continuous beam we shall get a stress system like (*f*). The middle of the beam is mostly occupied with resisting shear, which turns out to be another name for tensions and compressions at forty-five degrees to the axis. These shear stresses are of constant magnitude for the whole length of the beam. The material near the top and bottom surfaces is concerned with resisting the tensions and compressions which the shear stresses have generated. These horizontal stresses near the surfaces build up rapidly and in the worst place are usually far greater than the shears. They are the stresses which are most liable to break structures and kill people. Stressing is not a dry academic exercise of interest only to experts but an affair affecting the safety and pockets of most of us.

If all this stress-chasing seems confusing the best thing to do is to make a model out of Meccano or drinking straws joined with ordinary pins. If one makes a lattice model in this way it is quite easy to understand what it is in a cantilever which actually keeps the load from falling down. Of course, in all this rather complicated pattern of stresses, each stress is only gained at the expense of a proportionate strain and so the cantilever does not stick out rigidly but inevitably droops (*g*) to a greater or less extent.

Cantilevers are common enough in engineering but ordinary beams, particularly those that engineers call 'simply supported', are commoner still (Figure 10). This is the sort of thing you get when you put a plank across any simple gap such as a stream. How is this related to the cantilever? The answer is really quite obvious from Figure 12. The simply supported beam is really two cantilevers turned back to back and upside down. While the biggest stresses in the cantilever are near the root, those in a simply supported beam are in the middle and so such a beam will generally break in the middle.

We can now see that the reason why we don't fall through the floor is that the floor boards and joists produce tensions and compressions at forty-five degrees to the surface of the floor and

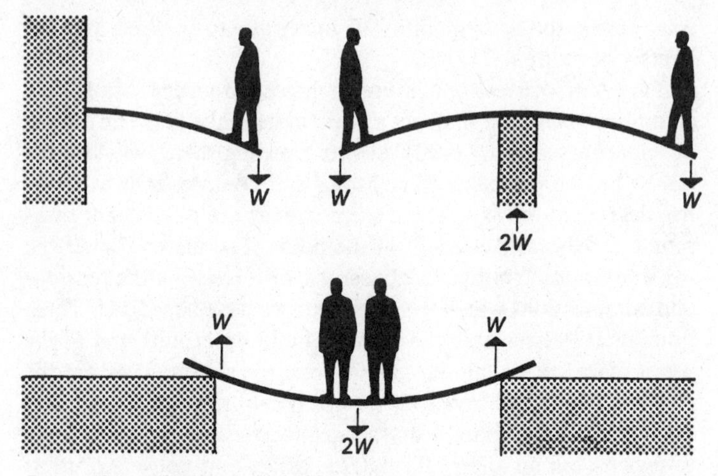

Figure 12. **A simply supported beam may be considered as two cantilevers back to back and upside down.**

these stresses, elaborately zig-zagging all the way from my shoes to the skirting-board, provide the upward sustenance which I need. As well as these shears, and much larger in magnitude, there are tensions and compressions horizontally near the top and bottom faces of the floor boards. If these horizontal stresses become too large, either because I am too heavy or the floor boards are too thin we shall first get alarming deflection in the floor and finally it will break.

The simplest experiment will show that the stresses and deflections induced by bending are, other things being equal, much more severe than those caused by direct tension and compression. If we take a piece of fairly thin wooden plank or rod in our hands, it is quite impossible to break it in tension by pulling on it by hand and the deflections we can cause by hand tension or compression are far too small to see by eye. If we bend the rod, however, we can nearly always produce quite a big and obvious deflection and in many cases it is quite easy to break it. For these sorts of reasons, although beams are extremely convenient, we nearly always have to be careful that they are strong enough and don't produce excessive deflections. The strengths and deflections of a given beam can be calculated by anyone with a knowledge of elementary algebra from the standard formulae which are given in the appendix at the end of this book.

As we have said, all this is not particularly easy to understand but it is really no more difficult than, say, French verbs, and it can be comprehended by quite a moderate intellectual effort. Once this is done, a great deal of engineering becomes much clearer. The truth is that many professional engineers use very little more than elementary beam theory when they design quite ambitious structures. As we shall see this is apt to be dangerous because beam theory in itself, though extremely useful, does not really tell us all we need to know about the strength of a sophisticated structure. However, it is very widely used as a guide to the strength of all kinds of things from crankshafts to ships.

The deliberate and confident use of large beams in engineering is not much more than a century old. Telford (1757–1834) – the 'Colossus of roads', or 'Pontifex Maximus', as Southey called him – probably built more bridges than anyone else in history. He used masonry or cast-iron arches in compression and for the longer spans he pioneered the suspension bridge, using wrought-iron tension chains, notably in the Menai road bridge (1819). Telford hardly ever used large beams. This was partly because a suitable material, such as wrought-iron plates, was not easily available and partly because of the lack of a trustworthy beam theory. An interesting sidelight on the status of strength calculations in Telford's time is that the shape of the chain catenaries for the Menai bridge was determined not by calculation but by setting up a large model across a dry valley.

Working thirty years later, Robert Stephenson (1803–59) had large wrought-iron boiler plates available and he also had the courage of his calculations. He had the brilliant idea* of making a hollow box-like beam of iron plates and running the trains inside it. The idea found its best-known expression in the Menai railway bridge which was opened in 1850, almost alongside Telford's bridge. Stephenson's beams, which weighed 1,500 tons each, were built beside the Straits and were floated into position

*Actually much of the credit must go to Stephenson's designer, William Fairbairn.

between the towers on rafts across a swirling tide. They were raised rather over a hundred feet up the towers by successive lifts with primitive hydraulic jacks. All this was not done without both apprehension and adventure; they were giants on the earth in those days.

At one time, when Stephenson's faith weakened, it was proposed to add suspension chains to help sustain the tubes, but this proved quite unnecessary. Both bridges stand side by side today as elegant demonstrations of tension and bending upon the grand scale. Telford's suspension bridge was lacking in stiffness at first and the bridge swayed alarmingly in the gales which blew down the Straits. There is an account of how one winter night the oscillations were such that the horses of the mail-coach could not keep their feet on the bridge and were thrown down in a dangerous tangle of hooves and harness so that the traces had to be cut by lantern light before the mess could be sorted out. After this the bridge was stiffened and now carries modern traffic.

The general lack of stiffness of suspension bridges made them unsuitable for railways, since the trains might have been rolled off the rails. This was why Stephenson and I. K. Brunel (1806–59) developed beam-like bridges for long spans. Though the Menai tubular bridge is splendidly stiff and has never given any trouble, equivalent modern beam bridges are generally lattice structures because lattices are easier to paint and 'To keep the Menai bridge from rust by boiling it in wine' was impracticable.

A ship is a long tube closed at both ends which happens to be afloat but is not otherwise structurally very different from Stephenson's Menai bridge. The support which the water gives to the hull does not necessarily coincide with the weights of engines, cargo and fuel which are put into the ship and so there is a tendency for the hull to bend. It ought to be impossible to break a ship, floating alongside a quay, by careless and uneven loading of the holds and tanks, but this has happened often enough and will probably happen again. In dry-dock ships are supported with care upon keel-blocks arranged to give even support but there is not much even support at sea where a ship may be picked up by rude waves at each end, leaving her heavy middle unsustained, or else exposing a naked forefoot and propeller at the same moment.

As ships tended to get longer and more lightly built, the Admiralty decided to make some practical experiments on the strength of ships. In 1903 a destroyer, H.M.S. *Wolf*, was specially prepared for the purpose. The ship was put into dry-dock and the water was pumped out while she was supported, in succession, amidships and at the ends. The stresses in various parts of the hull were measured with strain-gauges, which are sensitive means of measuring changes of length, and therefore of strain, in a material. The ship was then taken to sea to look for bad weather. It does not require very much imagination to visualize the observers, struggling with seasickness and with the old-fashioned temperamental strain-gauges, wedged into Plutonic compartments in the bottom of the ship, which was put through a sea which was described in the official report as 'rough and especially steep with much force and vigour'. Her captain seems to have given the *Wolf* as bad a time as he could manage but, whatever they did, no stress greater than about 12,000 p.s.i. or 80 MN/m^2 could be found in the ship's hull.

As the tensile strength of the steel used in ships was about 60,000 p.s.i. or 400 MN/m^2, and no stress anywhere near this figure could be measured, either at sea or during the bending trials in dry-dock, not only the Admiralty Constructors but Naval Architects in general concluded that the methods of calculating the strength of ships by simple beam theory, which had become standardized, were satisfactory and ensured an ample margin of safety. Sometimes nobody is quite as blind as the expert.

Ships continued to break from time to time. A 300-foot (90 metres) ore-carrying steamer, for instance, broke in two and sank in a storm on one of the Great Lakes of America. The maximum calculated stress under the probable conditions was not more than a third of the breaking stress of the ship's material. Even when major disasters did not actually happen, cracks appeared around hatchways and other openings in the hull and decks.* These

*In 1966 the honorary vice-president of the Royal Institution of Naval Architects, Mr J. M. Murray, announced 'Since 1950 only 26 ships have broken in two on the high seas'. Of a considerable number of ships which had come to no harm at sea but which were examined in dock, 20 per cent were found to have cracks in the main hull girder.

openings are of course the key to the problem. Stephenson's tubular bridge was eminently satisfactory because it is a continuous shell with no holes in it except the rivet holes. Ships have hatchways and all sorts of other openings. Naval Architects are not especially stupid and they made due allowance for the material which was cut away at the openings, increasing the calculated stresses around the holes *pro rata.* Professor Inglis, in a famous paper in 1913, showed however that '*pro rata*' was not good enough and he introduced the concept of 'stress-concentration' which, as we shall see (Chapter 4), is of vital importance both in calculating the strength of structures and in understanding materials.

What Inglis was saying was that if we remove, say, a third of the cross-section of a member by cutting a hole in it then the stress at the edge of the hole is not $\frac{3}{2}$ (or 1·5) of the average but it may, locally, be many times as high. The amount by which the stress is raised above the average by the hole – the stress-concentration factor – depends both upon the shape of the hole and upon the material, being worst for sharp re-entrants and for brittle materials. This conclusion, which Inglis arrived at by mathematical analysis, was regarded with the usual lack of respect by that curiously impractical tribe who call themselves 'practical men'. This was largely because mild steel is, of all materials, perhaps the least susceptible to the effects of stress concentrations though it is by no means impervious (Plate 3). It is significant that, in the *Wolf* experiments, none of the strain gauges seems to have been put close to the edge of any important opening in the hull.

Note: problems of walls, arches, beams and so on are dealt with more fully in the author's *Structures*, Penguin Books, 1978.

Chapter 3 Cohesion

or how strong ought materials to be?

*'Again, the things that we see to be hard and dense must needs consist of particles more mutually hooked and must be deeply held compact by branch-like elements. In this class, for example, stands adamantine rock, accustomed to laugh blows to scorn, and stalwart flint, and the hard strength of iron, and the copper bolts that scream as they resist their rooves.'**

Lucretius, *De rerum natura*.†

Before one can start arguing about how strong materials ought to be one should be able to measure how strong they actually are. Although nowadays a certain amount of mechanical testing is done for what might be called academic reasons, by far the most of it is done for strictly practical ends and in fact a thorough knowledge of the actual strength of its materials is, like drains and income tax, one of the things which no advanced civilization can do without.

There are generally two pragmatic reasons for knowing the strength of a material. The first and the most obvious is to have a figure to put into one's calculations on the strength of structures. However since proper scientific strength analysis is a recent affair, much the older and the commoner is that of maintaining the quality of materials. In other words, is this batch as good as the last? A variant of this is, can I use this as a substitute for that?

Of course anything as scientific as a mechanical test has not always found favour with traditional craftsmen or indeed with

*The word is 'claustrum' which means a closing or something closed. Jackson translates it 'staples' which may be correct if Lucretius is talking of door bolts. If however he means structural bolts then the word must mean 'rooves' which are the washers put under the clenched or riveted ends of copper bolts.

†Book II, 444, translated by Thomas Jackson.

business men.* The procedure described in Weston Martyr's (1885–1966) delightful book *The Southseaman*† (which is about wooden shipbuilding in Nova Scotia in the nineteen twenties) was probably much commoner.

> Before any plank was put into place, MacAlpine and Tom and anyone else who happened to be about held a consultation over it. First they examined it very carefully, and then they bent it, tapped it, listened to it, and, as I live by bread, I swear that once, at least, I saw MacAlpine tasting it. At any rate he applied his tongue to the wood, and then went through all the motions of an expert tea-taster – even to that final feat of expectorating through the clenched teeth with precision and gusto.

The first published tensile tests seem to have been done by the French philosopher and musician Marin Mersenne (1588–1648) who was interested in the strength of the wires used in musical instruments. In 1636 Mersenne made a series of tests on wires of different materials but it is doubtful if any use was made of the information.

As far as I know, the first actual record of an objective mechanical test, which had results of practical consequence, occurs in Pepys' diary for 4 June 1662.

> Povey and Sir W. Batten and I by water to Woolwich; and there saw an experiment made of Sir R. Ford's Holland's yarn (about which we have lately made so much stir; and I have much concerned myself of our rope-maker, Mr Hughes who represented it so bad) and we found it to be very bad, and broke sooner than, upon a fair triall, five threads of that against four of Riga yarne; also that some of it had old stuffe that had been tarred, covered over with new hempe, which is such a cheat as has not been heard of.

The Woolwich people may have broken these ropes in direct tension by hanging weights on them, having tied some sort of scale pan to one end and the other end to an overhead beam. On the whole, however, it is more likely that they used a comparative

*According to *The History of the British Iron and Steel Industry* (by J. C. Carr and W. Taplin, Harvard University Press, 1962) the leading British ironmaster of the 1870s used to say 'I know nothing about tests; if they want my brand they can have it; if they don't they can go elsewhere.'

† *The Southseaman*, J. Weston Martyr, Blackwoods, 1928.

test, tying the two competing ropes end to end, in series, and breaking them by means of a capstan. The number of strands in each rope would then be adjusted until there was an equal chance of failure.

Ropes and wires are fairly simple to test since it is easy to grip the ends by winding them round the barrel of a winch or capstan. Rigid solids are much harder to get hold of in tension and so for a long time such testing as was done was confined to compression and bending. Testing machines now exist which have vice-like grips, called 'friction grips', so that one can take an ordinary bar of metal, cut off a short length, and break it in tension. In practice however, this is generally an unsatisfactory arrangement since the grips damage the metal and cause premature failure at the ends so that the result is unreliable. It is usually better to cause an hour-glass or wasp-waisted specimen to be made as this can be arranged to break in the middle where it is thinnest. Even so, the design and making of satisfactory test-pieces calls for a modest degree of skill and experience as the best shape will be different for each kind of material.

With regard to the actual mechanics of testing, it is of course possible to apply the load to each specimen directly, by means of weights. However, since the breaking loads for convenient sized test pieces (say $\frac{1}{4}$ inch thick) are typically between about one and ten tons (a motor car weighs about a ton) and since most testing is done by girls, it is usual to apply the load mechanically or hydraulically and there are a large number of more or less automatic testing machines on the market. All that the operator has to do is to insert the specimen, watch the machine break it, then divide the recorded breaking load by the area of the cross-section at fracture, which is easily measured. The result is the breaking stress.

Of course this figure tells one nothing at all about why the material has the strength which it has and whether it ought to be stronger. On the other hand, in practice, the strength of any one individual engineering material tends to be constant. There therefore grew up a tendency to ignore the whys and wherefores and to regard the tensile and other strengths as innate properties with which the material happened to have been endowed by

Providence in a rather arbitrary way. Metallurgists knew that this or that ingredient or heat treatment would strengthen or weaken an alloy but this knowledge was empirical and the effects were not susceptible to an obvious rational explanation.

Engineers like their materials to be consistent and are not too deeply interested in reasons, so they encouraged the idea that each material has a characteristic strength which could be determined accurately, once for all, if only one did enough tests. Materials laboratories of a generation ago centred upon magnificent collections of large testing machines. We filled a great many notebooks with testing data but learnt very little about the strength of materials.

Indeed it is difficult to exaggerate the impenetrability of the mystery which for centuries hung over the problem of the strength and fracture of solids. Lucretius (95–55 B.C.) set forth at great length the theory of the atomic nature of matter which had been propounded earlier by Democritus (460–370 B.C.). Though the theory was many years ahead of its time it was almost wholly guesswork and rested on no satisfactory contemporary experimental evidence. However Lucretius recognized the problem of cohesion and suggested that the atoms of strong materials were provided with hooks with which to grip each other. In the middle of the nineteenth century Faraday (1791–1867), one of the wisest of men, could do no better than to say that the strength of solids was due to the cohesion between their fine particles and that the subject was a very interesting one. Though both these statements were true they were not a great advance on Lucretius.

Chapter 2 contains a list of the practical strengths of various materials. Like the values for Young's modulus or stiffness, the figures vary a great deal between different substances, but then, so do the strengths of the chemical bonds within them and one might expect the engineering strengths to be proportional to the strengths of the chemical bonds. This is one of the differences between strength and stiffness. One can relate the Young's modulus, E, for a material in bulk to the fine-scale stiffness of its chemical bonds with considerable accuracy. Generally speaking this is not true of strength. The iron to iron bond in steel is not especially strong, it is easily broken chemically when iron rusts.

Rust, iron oxide, is weak mechanically although its chemical bonds are strong. Again, magnesium metal is stronger than magnesium oxide, magnesia, though the energy difference in the bonds is dramatically shown by burning magnesium ribbon in oxygen. Any attempt to relate chemical to mechanical strength works only in a vague and irregular way. About all one can say is that while it is only too easy to make a weak material (or indeed a material of no strength at all) from strong chemical bonds, it is not possible to make very strong materials from weak bonds.

The plastics and polymers which came into use between the wars were, or were claimed to be, the first man-made strong materials to come out of chemical laboratories and they rather went to the heads of the chemists, who supposed, not unnaturally, that these polymers were strong because they had put them together with strong chemical bonds. When the last war broke out, a very able young academic chemist came to work with me. He set to work straight away to make a stronger plastic. He explained to me that it must be stronger because it contained stronger bonds and more of them than any previous material. Since he really was a very competent chemist I expect it did. At any rate it took a long time to synthesize. When it was ready we removed this war-winning product from the mould with excitement. It was about as strong as stale hard cheese.

Griffith and energy

We must now go back to about 1920 when the whole subject could be described as pretty well bogged down. At this time A. A. Griffith (1893–1963) was a young man working at the Royal Aircraft Establishment at Farnborough. He had ideas which cut through the mass of tradition and very dull detail which hung around materials work everywhere but unfortunately nobody took them very seriously. Griffith asked in effect 'Why are there large variations between the strengths of different solids? Why don't all solids have the same strength? Why do they have any strength at all? Why aren't they much stronger? How strong "ought" they to be anyway?' Until fairly recently these questions were regarded as unfathomable or unimportant or just silly.

We now understand in a general way how strong any particular solid ought to be and why it falls short of that strength in practice. Furthermore we know more or less what to do to increase its strength. Much of this success is due directly and indirectly to Griffith. In what follows I have shortened and transposed Griffith's arguments.

To calculate how strong a material ought to be we need to make use of the concept of energy. Energy is officially defined as 'capacity for doing work' and it has the dimensions of force multiplied by distance. Thus if I raise a two-pound weight through a height of five feet I have increased its potential energy by ten foot pounds.* This energy (which comes from my dinner which comes ultimately from the sun and so on) can be transformed into any of the many alternative forms of energy but it cannot be destroyed. Potential energy is one convenient way of parking energy until it is wanted and this energy can be followed through its various subsequent transformations by a sort of accounting procedure which can be very revealing.

The stored or potential energy in a raised weight can be used, for instance, to drive the mechanism of a grandfather clock though in most clocks a spring is usually more convenient, if only because it stores the same amount of energy which ever way up it is.† The strain energy in a stretched material is very like the potential energy which is in a raised weight, except, of course, that the stress is changing as the material is strained whereas the

*The S.I. unit of energy is the Joule which is the work done when 1 Newton acts through 1 metre. 1 Joule (1J) = 10^7 ergs = 0·74 foot–pound = 0·23 calories.

†A clock spring is really a beam – a flat strip of steel wound up into a spiral, like a tape measure, to save space. When the clock is wound, more turns are put into the spiral and, since the total length of the spring remains the same, any given short length is more sharply bent. Being a beam, every small element of the material of the spring is either in tension or compression (Chapter 2).

Incidentally, because a spring produces less energy per turn as it runs down, the early clockmakers had to invent a device called a 'fusee', a sort of conical spool on which was wound a driving chain, to keep the driving force constant. This was why they generally preferred the grandfather clock for time-keeping since an inch of fall of the weight is good for as much energy at the bottom as at the top of the case.

weight of a weight is constant as it is raised to any normal height.

Because of Hooke's law, when a material is strained the stress in it varies from nothing at the beginning of the operation up to a maximum at the final strain. For this reason the strain energy in a material is:

$$\tfrac{1}{2}\ \text{stress} \times \text{strain} \qquad \text{per unit volume}$$

That strain energy is more than a triviality was demonstrated by the bowmen at Agincourt and, incidentally, one is well advised to keep out of the way of a stretched hawser such as is used for checking a ship. The kinetic energy, or energy of motion, of the ship has been exchanged for strain energy in the rope. There is a lot of energy, and, if the rope breaks strain energy is reconverted to energy of motion in the rope and somebody may get killed.

All stressed solids thus contain strain energy and this strain energy can be converted by one means or another into any of the other forms of energy. Most commonly a relaxed stress simply reverts to heat but children have discovered that it is possible to convert the strain energy of catapult elastic into the fracture of, say, glass. Whether or not something of the sort put into Griffith's head the idea of fracture as an energy process, I have no idea.

When a brittle material breaks, two new surfaces are created at the point of fracture which were not there before fracture, and Griffith's very brilliant idea was to relate the surface energy of the fracture surfaces to the strain energy in the material before it broke. Energy has many forms – heat, electrical energy, mechanical energy, strain energy and so on – but it is not immediately clear that the surface of a solid has energy, merely by virtue of its existence as a surface.

From watching raindrops, bubbles and insects walking on ponds it is obvious that water and other liquids have a surface tension. This tension is a perfectly real physical force which is quite easily measured. Consequently, when the surface of a liquid is extended, as by inflating a soap bubble, work is done against this tension and energy is stored in the new surface. In the accountancy of energy, surface energy counts in the balance just as much as any other kind of energy. When an insect alights on water, the surface is dimpled by its legs and thus extended and so the surface energy is increased. The insect sinks until the increase of surface energy just balances the decrease in its potential energy when it sinks no further and is, presumably, happy. Liquids tend, if they can, to minimize their surface energy. For instance a thin stream of liquid, from a tap which is being turned off, will reach a diameter at which it pays it to break up into separate drops simply because these have less aggregate area then the cylindrical stream.

When a liquid freezes, the molecular character of its surface is not too greatly changed and the energy of the surface remains much the same although the surface tension is no longer able to change the shape of small particles by rounding them off into drops. With a number of solids the interatomic forces are stronger and stiffer than they are in common liquids and so the surface energies are higher, often ten or twenty times the values for ordinary liquids.* The reason why we do not notice surface tensions in solids is not that the surface tensions are weak but rather that solids are too rigid to be visibly distorted by them.

Just as we could, perhaps, calculate the weight of the largest insect which could walk on a given liquid, so we can use these concepts to calculate how strong we ought to expect materials to be. As calculations go, this one turns out to be surprisingly simple, once somebody has had the original idea.

What we want to do is to calculate the stress which will just separate two adjacent layers of atoms inside the material. At this stage we need not worry too much whether the material is glassy or crystalline and all we really need to know about the solid is the Young's modulus and the surface energy. The two layers of atoms are initially x metres apart and so the strain energy per square metre for a stress s causing a strain e will be:

$$\tfrac{1}{2}\ \text{stress} \times \text{strain} \times \text{volume} = \tfrac{1}{2}\, s.e.x.$$

*The surface energy of water is about 0·077 Joules per square metre. Structural solids have usually energies around 1·0 J/m². Surface energy of diamond = 5·14 J/m². N.B. The surface *energy* in Joules per square metre is *numerically* equal to the surface *tension* in Newtons per metre.

But Hooke's law says:

$$E = \frac{s}{e} \text{ so } e = \frac{s}{E}$$

So, putting in $\frac{s}{E}$ for e:

$$\text{Strain energy per square metre} = \frac{s^2.x}{2E}$$

If G is the surface energy of the solid per square metre, then the total surface energy of the two new fracture surfaces would be $2G$ per sq. metre.

We now suppose that, at our theoretical strength, the whole of the strain energy between any two layers of atoms is potentially convertible to surface energy, then:

$$\frac{s^2.x}{2E} = 2G$$

so:

$$s = 2\sqrt{\frac{G.E}{x}}$$

Actually, this is a bit optimistic because we have assumed that the material will go on obeying Hooke's law right up to failure. As we saw in the last chapter, Hooke's law is really only true for small strains and at large strains the interatomic force curve bends over so that the strain energy is less than we have calculated, very roughly about half. We can allow for this effect by dropping the two from the strength equation which we have just derived, bearing in mind that we are in no position to quibble about exact values. Thus a reasonable expectation for the strength of a material would be:

$$s = \sqrt{\frac{G.E}{x}}$$

which could hardly be much simpler.

For steel some typical values in S.I. units would be:

Surface energy G = 1J per square metre
Young's modulus $E = 2\times10^{11}$ Newtons per square metre (note *not* Meganewtons)
Distance between atoms x = 2 Ångström units $= 2\times10^{-10}$ metre

Putting in these values gives us a strength of about 3×10^4 MN/m^2 or about five million pounds per square inch. Say ($E/6$). This is rather over 2000 tons per square inch. The strength of ordinary commercial steels is usually about 60,000 p.s.i. or 400 MN/m^2 while very strong wires may reach about 400,000 p.s.i. or 3,000 MN/m^2.

Since the values for E and G vary, of course, for each solid the values we get for the theoretical strengths will vary too. The only thing they have in common is that they are all very much above any strength normally realized in ordinary experiments. In fact steel is exceptional in sometimes reaching strengths as high as a tenth of its calculated strength; the great majority of common solids can show only a hundredth or a thousandth of what theory indicates.

As a matter of fact, thirty or forty years ago, nobody actually and openly disbelieved this calculation. If they had, they would have had to provide an alternative explanation of where the surface energy of a newly broken surface came from, but somehow nobody took it very seriously. There was a discrepancy somewhere and perhaps the less said about it the better.

If we confine our calculation simply to strength as such, we get a different figure for the theoretical strength of each material. However, we can nearly as easily do the sum for the theoretical elastic breaking strain, and if we do this, we are apt to find that the answer we get is very roughly the same for any solid, almost irrespective of its chemical entity. Generally speaking, this strain is something like 10 or 20 per cent.* If this is more or less

*Discerning minds will deduce that the surface energy of a solid must be roughly proportional to its Young's modulus – and so it is. G is more or less equal to $Ex/20$. This arises because it is the same bonds which give rise both to the Young's modulus and to the surface tension.

true, then the strength of any solid should lie between $E/10$ and $E/5$. Hence, although we cannot say that every material ought to have the same strength, we can say that, very approximately, all materials ought to have the same elastic breaking strain. In everyday practice it is palpable that not only do materials not have the same breaking strain but also that the calculated strengths are, without exception, far above any commonly realized practical strength.

Griffith set out to find some physical theory which would bridge this gap between theory and practice. I never knew Griffith himself but Sir Ben Lockspeiser, who acted as Griffith's assistant at this time, told me something about the circumstances under which the work was done. In those days research workers were expected to earn their money by being practical, and in the case of materials they were expected to confine their experiments to proper engineering materials like wood and steel. Griffiths wanted a much simpler experimental material than wood or steel and one which would have an uncomplicated brittle fracture, for these reasons he chose glass as what is now called a 'model' material. In those days models were all very well in the wind tunnel for aerodynamic experiments but, damn it, who ever heard of a model *material*?

These things being so, Griffith and Lockspeiser took care not to bring the details of their experiments too much to the notice of the authorities. The experiments, however, involved drawing fibres and blowing bubbles of molten glass and one day, after the work had been going on for some months, Lockspeiser went home leaving the gas torch used for melting the glass still burning. After the inquiry into the resulting fire, Griffith and Lockspeiser were commanded to cease wasting their time. Griffith was transferred to other work and became a very famous engine designer. The feeling about glass died hard. Many years later, about 1943, I introduced a distinguished Air Marshal to one of the first of the airborne glass-fibre radomes, a biggish thing intended to be

---

Indiarubber has a breaking strain of about 700 per cent, but this depends upon quite a different mechanism which, as far as this calculation is concerned, may be regarded as cheating, see Appendix. The 'plastic' breaking strain in soft metals (say 60 per cent in mild steel) is not elastic, see Chapter 4.

bolted under a Lancaster bomber. 'What's it made of?' 'Glass sir.' 'GLASS! – GLASS! I won't have you putting glass on any of my bloody aeroplanes, blast you!' The turnover of the fibreglass industry passed the £100,000,000 mark about 1959 I believe.

To return to Griffith's experiments, Griffith was not the first man to draw strong glass fibres but he was probably the first man to do it in a systematic way and to provide a plausible explanation oı the results.

Griffith had first to determine, at least approximately, the theoretical strength of the glass he was using. The Young's modulus was easily found by a simple mechanical experiment and two or three Ångström units is a fair guess for the interatomic spacing and cannot be far out.* It remained to measure the surface energy. It was here that one of the advantages of glass as an experimental material lay. Glass, like toffee, has no sharp melting point but changes gradually, as it is heated, from a brittle solid to a viscous liquid and during this process there is no important change of molecular structure. For this reason one might expect there to be no large change in surface energy between liquid and solid glass so that surface tension and therefore surface energy, measured quite easily on molten glass, ought to be approximately applicable to the same glass when hardened. When the end of a glass rod is heated in a flame the glass softens and tends to round off into a blob because surface tension remains active long after permanent mechanical resistance to deformation has disappeared. The force, which is easily measured, needed slowly to extend the rod under these conditions is therefore that which will just overcome the surface tension. From experiments of this type, done with very simple apparatus, Griffith could deduce that the strength of the glass he was using (at room temperature) ought to be nearly 2,000,000 p.s.i. or about 14,000 MN/m^2.

Griffith then took ordinary cold rods of the same glass about a millimetre thick and broke them in tension, finding that they had a tensile strength of about 25,000 p.s.i. or 170 MN/m^2 which is round about the average for laboratory glassware, window panes, beer bottles and most of the other common forms of glass but was

*As a matter of fact Griffith came at this calculation in a rather different way.

something between a fiftieth and a hundredth of what he reckoned it ought to be.

Griffith now heated his rods in the middle and drew them down to thinner and thinner fibres which after cooling he also broke in tension. As the fibres got thinner so they got stronger, slowly at first and then, when they got really thin, very rapidly. Fibres about one ten thousandth of an inch (2·5 mμ) thick showed strengths up to about 900,000 p.s.i. or 6,000 MN/m² when they were newly drawn, falling to about 500,000 p.s.i. or 3,500 MN/m² after a few hours. The curve of size against strength was rising so rapidly (Figure 1) that it was difficult to ascertain a maximum or upper limit to the strength. The increase of strength with thinness was not entirely smooth but showed a certain amount of scatter or

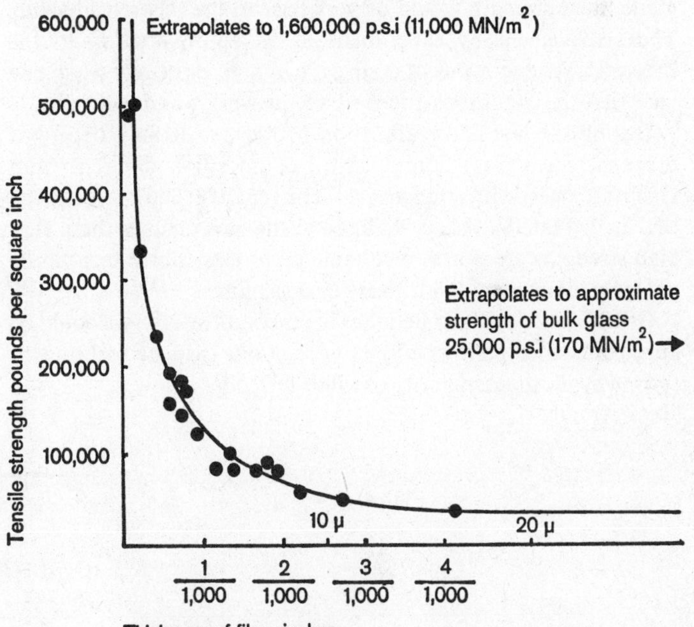

Figure 1. Griffith made and tested thinner and thinner glass fibres. As the fibres got thinner so they got stronger until the strength of the thinnest fibres approached the calculated theoretical strength.

variability. However, there was absolutely no doubt about the general trend.

Griffith could not prepare or test fibres thinner than about a ten thousandth of an inch (2·5 mμ) and, if he had, it would have been difficult at that time to measure the thickness with any sort of accuracy. However, by the simple mathematical device of plotting reciprocals it was possible to extend or extrapolate the size-strength curve fairly reliably so as to ascertain the strength of a fibre of negligible thickness. This turned out to be 1,600,000 p.s.i. or 11,000 MN/m^2. It will be remembered that Griffith had calculated a value a little under 2,000,000 p.s.i. or 14,000 MN/m^2 for the glass he was using. He therefore concluded that he had approached the theoretical strength quite closely enough to satisfy most people, and that if thinner fibres could actually be made, their strength would be very near to the theoretical value. The achievement by experiment of an approximation to the theoretical strength was of course a triumph, especially when one considers the conditions under which the work was done.

During the last few years, John Morley, of Rolls Royce, has prepared silica glass fibres (with a composition different from Griffith's glass) with strengths rather over 2,000,000 p.s.i. (14,000 MN/m^2) (Plate 4). As we shall see in the next chapter these very high strengths are not in fact confined to glass fibres but can be got from almost any solid, glassy or crystalline.

Griffith had demonstrated that the theoretical strength could be approximated experimentally in at least one case, he had now to show why the great majority of solids fell so far below it.

Chapter 4 Cracks and dislocations

or why things are weak

'The fault that leaves six thousand ton a log upon the sea.'

Rudyard Kipling, 'McAndrew's Hymn'.

Griffith wrote a classic Royal Society paper about his experiments which was published in 1920. In this paper he pointed out that the problem was not to explain why his thin fibres were strong, since a single chain of atoms must, inescapably, have either the theoretical strength or none at all, but rather to explain why the thicker fibres were weak.

It was becoming clear, at any rate to Griffith if to nobody else, that in a world where practical materials only reached a small and highly irregular fraction of the strength of their chemical bonds, the weakening mechanism, rather than the bond strength, was what really controlled mechanical strength. It is only quite lately and now that we are able regularly to get strengths which are a large fraction of the theoretical value, that it has become really important and worthwhile to make materials with very strong chemical bonds.

The weakness of glass fibres brings us to the question of Griffith cracks and it also brings us back to Professor Inglis, whom we left in Chapter 2 worrying about why ships broke in two at sea when simple calculation showed them to be amply strong enough. Inglis made calculations about the effect of hatchways and other openings in large structures like ships. Griffith had the wit to apply Inglis's mathematics on a far finer scale, to 'openings' of almost molecular size and too fine to see with an optical microscope.

Stress concentrations

Whatever the scale, the practical importance of stress concentrations is enormous. The idea which Inglis expounded is that *any* hole or sharp re-entrant in a material causes the stress in that material to be increased locally. The increase in local stress, which can be calculated, depends solely upon the *shape* of the hole and has nothing at all to do with its *size*. All engineers know about stress concentrations but a good many don't really in their hearts believe in them since it is clearly contrary to common sense that a tiny hole should weaken a material just as much as a great big one.* The root cause of the Comet aircraft disasters was a rivet hole perhaps an eighth of an inch in diameter. Small holes and notches are particularly good at starting fatigue failures but they also do very well for starting ordinary static fracture. When a glass cutter wants to cut glass, he does not bother to cut right through but makes a shallow scratch on the surface after which the glass breaks easily along the line of the scratch. (By the way, so-called 'cut glass' is ground to shape, not cut.) The weakening effect of the scratch has very little to do with the amount of material removed, a shallow scratch will do nearly as well as a deep one, it is the sharpness of the re-entrant that increases the stress.

It is not difficult to form a physical picture of what is actually happening at a re-entrant such as a crack, especially if we consider the matter upon a molecular scale. Referring to Figure 1 it is obvious that a single chain of atoms in tension must be uniformly stressed and should reach the theoretical strength (1a). The mere multiplication of such chains, side by side, to constitute a crystal, does not prevent each separate chain from still carrying its full theoretical stress (1b). Suppose now that we cut a number of adjacent bonds so as to constitute a crack, then of course we have interrupted the flow of stress in the broken chains and the load in these broken chains has got to go somewhere (1c). In fact it does the most natural thing, which is to go round the end of the opening. Thus the load in the whole of the cut chains may well have to pass through the single bond which closes the tip of

*As we shall see in Chapters 5 and 9, in a ductile metal the anelastic or plastic behaviour of the metal around a small hole may smooth out the local concentration of stress and greatly reduce the weakening effect of things like rivet holes; however, this is not always the case in fatigue, that is under repeated loading.

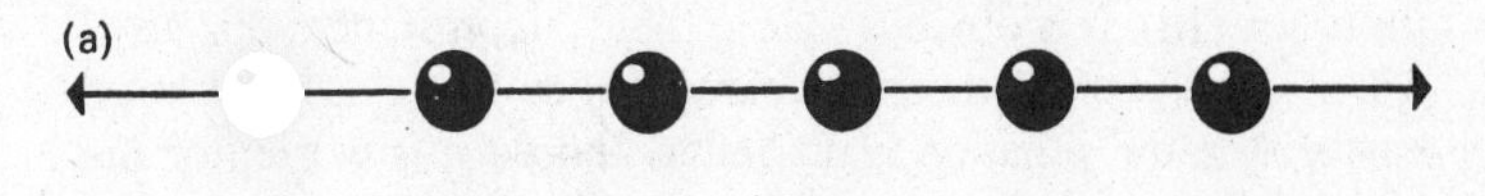

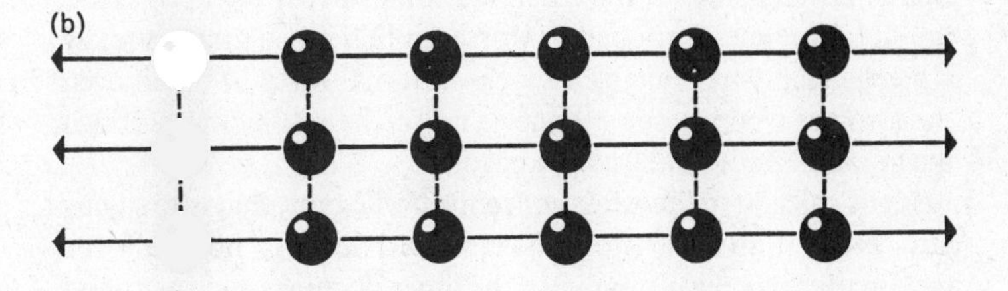

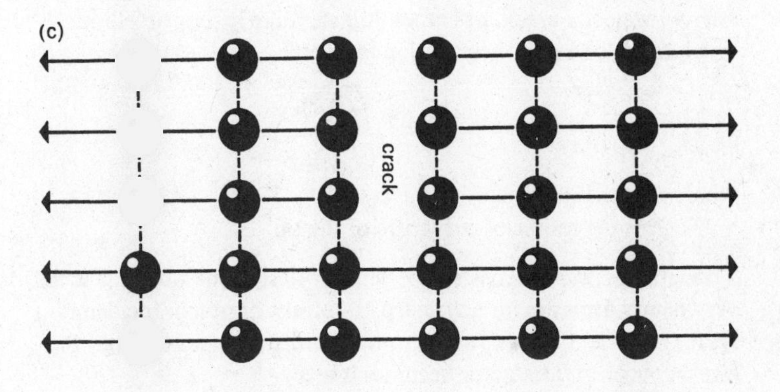

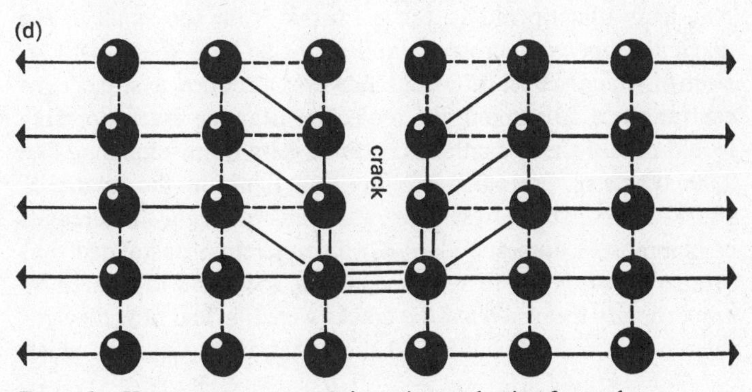

Figure 1. How a stress concentration arises at the tip of a crack.

the crack (1d). It is obvious that in these circumstances this bond will fail long before its companions. When this over-tried bond has broken the situation is no better. Indeed it is worse, for the next bond has to bear, not only the load in all the initially broken chains but also that in the chain which has newly snapped. Thus the situation goes from bad to worse. In this way a crack is really a mechanism which enables a weak external force to break even the strongest bonds one by one. And so the crack runs through the material until total fracture occurs.

Inglis calculated the stress concentration factor, that is to say by how many times the stress is increased locally, not only for rectangular hatchways, but also for other openings such as round and elliptical holes. By making an elliptical hole very long and narrow we get a crack, or something very like it. For an elliptical crack Inglis's stress concentration factor is:

$$\left(1+2\sqrt{\frac{L}{R}}\right)$$

where L is half the length of the crack
R is the radius of curvature of the tip.

Though this was calculated for an ellipse it turns out that it is very nearly accurate for any sharp re-entrant or notch. Incidentally, for a circle, that is to say a round hole, it will be seen that the stress concentration factor becomes three.

Consider now a crack, say, two microns long and of one Ångström unit tip radius. Such a crack is far too small to see under the optical microscope and might be hard to see with an electron microscope. It would however produce a stress concentration of 201 among the molecules near the crack tip. This would reduce the strength of Griffith's glass from something like 2,000,000 p.s.i. or 14,000 MN/m^2 to a figure in the region of 10,000 p.s.i. or about 70 MN/m^2, which is very roughly the strength of common or domestic glass. Griffith therefore postulated that ordinary glass is full of very fine cracks, too small to be seen by any ordinary means. What the cracks were like and how they got there he did not say, but he did show that, if they existed, which was not unreasonable, they would account for the weakness of ordinary glass. He supposed that for some reason they became rarer in thin fibres and almost non-existent in the very thinnest fibres, perhaps because there was simply no room for them.

Griffith cracks

Griffith seems to have supposed that the cracks which he thought existed were scattered throughout the interior of the glass and were perhaps a consequence of a failure of the molecules inside the glass to join up completely when the glass hardened. Looking back, it is curious how long it took us to get rid of this idea of some kind of defect inside the body of the glass.

Griffith's calculations showed that the cracks, whatever they were, must be quite narrow, perhaps a hundredth of the wave-length of ordinary visible light. Since one can never hope to see things which are much smaller than the wave-length of the light which one is using, there was clearly no hope of ever seeing them directly by means of the ordinary optical microscope which reaches its limit with objects about half a micron thick. This is the reason for the invention of the electron microscope which uses electrons with a wave-length of something like a twenty-fifth of an Ångström instead of light with a wave-length of about four thousand Ångströms.

However, before the electron microscope was available, in fact in 1937, Andrade and Tsien decided to look for the cracks by the method of decoration, using of course an optical microscope. This method, which is often very effective, may be thought of like this. Imagine a fine wire which is too far away and too thin to see by any ordinary means. If we can persuade birds to come and perch on it in a row fairly close together we have obviously made it much easier to see the wire. (The Post Office sometimes put corks on the telegraph wires for the same reason.) If we can now persuade more birds to come and perch on top of the first lot we can in principle build up the wire to any thickness we choose. Now it happens that when some substances crystallize they find it easier to do so if some kind of irregularity is present. By choosing the right substance to crystallize on a surface one can often get the new crystals to form almost entirely upon the fine irregularities of the surface and thus show them up.

Andrade treated the surface of glass with sodium vapour and produced linear patterns which seemed to indicate the existence of surface cracks. In this work it is extraordinarily easy to produce ghost images and chimeras, like the canals on Mars, which may or may not be cracks, but even if Andrade's patterns showed genuine surface cracks, which seems likely, this would not prove that there were not also internal cracks.

In the years after the last War it was found that not only were the thinnest fibres strong, but, if they were carefully made, quite thick fibres could also show high strength. Strong fibres were weakened by touching while weak fibres were improved in strength if the surface were removed chemically.

All this was a strong indication that the important weakening defects lay on the surface and around 1957 Margaret Parratt, David Marsh and I spent a lot of time examining the surface of glass. By refining Andrade's sodium technique, Mrs Parratt was able to produce the most beautiful crack patterns on the surface of all kinds of glass and what was more, many, perhaps most of them, did seem to be genuine cracks. Furthermore the frequency of the cracks correlated quite well with the experimental strength of the various specimens of glass. The question was how the cracks got there. In many cases there was no doubt at all: the glass had been in contact with some other solid and the cracks were due to simple scratching or scraping. Plates 5 and 6, Mrs Parratt's photographs, show quite typical scrapes. Very little glass is wholly untouched from the time it is drawn or blown from the melt, and it takes only the lightest contact to create an elaborate crack pattern.

Very probably this simple explanation accounts for the weakness of the majority of common glass.* The high strength of thin fibres may be due in part to the fact that such fibres are very

*The Griffith energy criterion which governs the propagation of cracks is dealt with in Chapter 5. Though internal defects, where they exist, are not different in kind from surface ones, they are generally shorter and thus, as we shall see, may not have an energy incentive to propagate cracks.

easily bent and it is therefore easier to bend them than to scratch them. However, there do remain a number of cases where there are variations in the strength of glass whose surface is genuinely untouched. One reason for this was investigated by Marsh.

When most liquids freeze they crystallize and usually the crystal, being more orderly, is better packed and therefore more dense than the mother liquid. Water is an exception for complicated reasons. Glasses behave as they do because, while they are cooling, they are so viscous that the molecules do not have time to sort themselves out into crystals and so cool glass is a solidified liquid, not a crystalline solid. However the tendency to crystallize is there and given time some glasses will in fact crystallize. This is known as devitrification. Since devitrification involves shrinkages, the glass is often weakened and sometimes falls to pieces in the process. Devitrification is almost universal in ancient glasses which were usually badly made in the first place and have had plenty of time to crystallize; the result, however is, often very beautiful, though these old glasses have become very weak.

Marsh showed that in some glasses there is incipient devitrification even when they are new. He photographed tiny crystallites in the electron microscope and showed that the shrinkage which accompanied their formation was sufficient to initiate a crack which would spread into the main body of the glass (Plate 7).

It must be emphasized that there is nothing very special about thin glass fibres which is specifically due to their thinness as such. If the surface of thick glass can be got smooth and kept smooth it will be just as strong as a thin fibre. In practice, however, this is generally more difficult to do.

If a material like glass does not fail owing to the spread of a crack from some local defect then how does it fail? The answer is that it fails by flowing in shear, just like Plasticine or soft metals. Because the flow stress of glass is very high at room temperature and because glass is very susceptible to fracture by the spread of cracks, glass, and materials like it, nearly always fracture in the familiar brittle manner and we find it difficult to imagine anything different happening. In fact, if glass is prevented from cracking in tension, say by putting it into compression, then it is quite easy to get it to flow like a soft solid; for instance, glass will behave like putty under the blunt point of a diamond indenter but the shear stresses required to cause flow are well above the normally observed fracture stresses – in common glasses at room temperature usually above 500,000 p.s.i. or 3,500 MN/m^2.

Fairly recently Marsh has shown that glass which is quite free from cracks does in fact fail in this manner by flowing, and that when this happens around room temperature, the stresses are usually upwards of 500,000 p.s.i. An interesting point is that the tendency to fracture by the spreading of cracks is relatively little affected by temperature whereas the viscosity or shearing stress is very dependent upon temperature. For this reason, when we heat glass to a temperature well below its melting point the shearing stress is reduced more than the brittle fracture stress and thus we can bend and shape and blow hot (but not necessarily very hot) glass quite easily. Contrariwise, defect-free glass can be strengthened by cooling which raises its viscosity or resistance to flowing. In this way the strength of smooth glass tested at −180°C. is about twice that of the same glass tested at room temperature.

Very generally, there are always two fracture mechanisms competing to break a material – plastic flow and brittle cracking. The material will succumb to whichever mechanism is the weaker; if it yields before it cracks the material is ductile, if it cracks before it yields it is brittle. The potentiality of both forms of failure is always present in all materials.

The strength of brittle crystals and the whisker story

All this accounts fairly satisfactorily for the strength and weakness of glasses, with which are included natural glassy minerals such as flint* and obsidian, but then the vast majority of hard solids, both natural and artificial, are crystalline. There is some kind of popular superstition that crystalline materials are weak. The garage foreman, appearing with your broken crankshaft or back axle, will tell you that it has 'crystallized'. What state it was in

*Strictly speaking flint is micro-crystalline but, mechanically, it behaves very like a glass.

before it crystallized he does not explain; certainly it was not glassy. Needless to say all metals, the great majority of minerals, most ceramics and common solids like salt and sugar are crystalline. From common sense one would not expect the mere possession of a regular, orderly arrangement of atoms or molecules to be a cause of weakness, and of course it isn't.

When we are dealing with hard, brittle crystals, however, the practical strength is generally even lower than that of bulk glass and in their crude state most of the non-metallic crystals deserve the contempt with which they are generally regarded by engineers.

At this stage it is necessary to talk about whiskers. People often mention 'metal whiskers' as if they were the only kind but, as a matter of fact, metal whiskers are less common and less interesting than whiskers of non-metals and it is about these latter that we shall mostly talk. Whiskers have nothing to do with human hair and are in fact long thin needle crystals which can be grown from most substances by accident or by care. They can be grown in a large number of different ways but are typically one or two microns thick though they may be millimetres or even centimetres long.

Whiskers sometimes grow by accident from the surface of metals and if the metal happens to be part of an electrical device then there is likely to be a short circuit which will be annoying, expensive or dangerous according to the circumstances (Plate 9). Metal whiskers of this kind had been known of, in a general sort of way, for a long time but had been regarded as a nuisance or a curiosity. They were not thought particularly interesting, until, in 1952, Herring and Galt chanced to bend some tin whiskers and noticed that they could be bent to a strain of about 2 per cent and still recover elastically. This corresponded to a higher stress than had ever been observed before in tin and perhaps in any other metal. It looked like another case of thin fibres showing anomalously high strength and it naturally attracted a good deal of attention.

Herring and Galt worked with tin. Tin is a metal and somehow everybody expects metals to be strong. What interested me at the time was whether the 'naturally' weak non-metallic crystals could be made strong too. Thinking about this one morning in 1954, I went along to the keeper of the laboratory chemical stores and asked him for something which was water-soluble and formed needle crystals. He gave me a bottle of hydroquinone, a common substance used in photographic developers. The bottle was full of dry crystals about as thick as an ordinary pin and about a centimetre long. Manipulating these crystals by hand with the dissecting tools which biologists use it was quite obvious that their strength was negligible. I then dissolved some of the hydroquinone crystals in water, put a drop of the solution on an ordinary glass microscope slide and allowed the water to evaporate naturally in air so that new, but much smaller, needle crystals were produced as the solution dried under the microscope.

The new crystals tended to be long, smooth, whip-like filaments, initially so thin that they were hardly visible in the optical microscope. By poking about with a dissecting needle it was obvious that these little threads were very strong, exactly how strong it was difficult to say (Plate 12). This was exciting and I was very soon trying crystals of all sorts of substances taken from the shelves of my own and my colleagues' laboratories. With a little skill and low cunning it was possible to get almost any common soluble solid, such as Epsom salts, or even sodium chloride – ordinary table salt – to crystallize in the form of these very thin filaments, whiskers, and in every case these whiskers were obviously strong. It might be supposed that their strength had something to do with the crystals being wet. A man called Joffé observed, about 1928, that some things got stronger when they were wet. (Actually, other things get weaker.) However, drying the whiskers out did not seem to have an important effect upon their strength, as far as I could tell.

One of the difficulties in the early stages of this work was to find any reasonably reliable method of measuring whisker strengths. We used to bend the whiskers under the microscope with a dissecting needle and, having measured the thickness and radius of curvature very approximately we could estimate the breaking strain by simple beam theory. As one might imagine this method was maddeningly inconvenient and very inaccurate.

The whiskers generally began life as exceedingly fine filaments which could be seen to thicken as they got older. I therefore introduced the refinement of bending the infant whisker, by troubling the waters around the moment of its birth, and then simply allowing it to thicken until it broke, this was a little less clumsy but still highly unsatisfactory.

Just at this time (1956) David Marsh came to work with me and one of the first things he said was 'Why don't you build a proper tensile testing machine?' I am afraid that I told him to go away and not be silly. The whiskers were too small to see with the naked eye and nobody could possibly make a testing machine on that scale. Marsh went away and was not silly for he came back with a micro-testing machine which worked, which he had designed and built himself. The Mark III version of the Marsh machine went into commercial production and now no gentleman's laboratory is complete without one. This remarkable machine will, if pressed, test fibres down to one tenth of a square micron cross-section (that is, virtually invisible in the optical microscope) and about a quarter of a millimetre long. It will detect extensions down to less than five Ångström units which is about the resolution of a good electron microscope.*

With this tool in our hands, we were able to get some real results. The first thing we discovered was that we could get high strength from almost anything from Epsom salts to sapphire. Provided it was in the form of a thin whisker, it did not matter what the chemical nature of the stuff was or by what method the whiskers were grown. We must have worked on well over a hundred different substances and there was absolutely no doubt about it.

When we plotted strength against thickness for any given whisker we got a curve which was uncannily like Griffith's size-strength curve for glass fibres (Chapter 3). What was more, when we plotted, not strength but breaking strain, against thickness, we found that it did not matter what the whiskers were made of, for they all plotted on the same curve. Figure 2, for instance, shows the breaking strains of whiskers of two very different substances, silicon and zinc oxide. It is impossible to tell them apart.

*The construction and working of this machine is described in the *Journal of Scientific Instruments* for 1961 (D. M. Marsh, **38**, 229–34.)

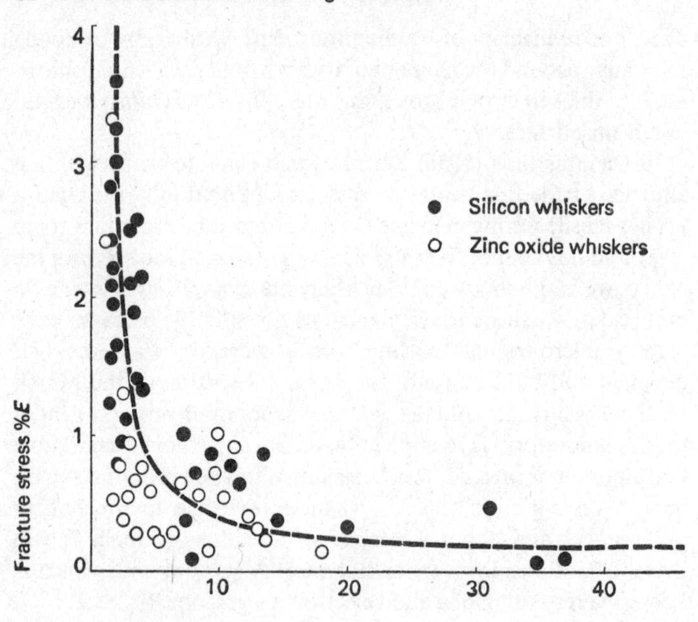

Figure 2. Strength-diameter relation for whiskers. Like glass fibres, they get stronger as they get thinner, but the cause of the increase of strength is different.

The temptation to assume that the strength and weakness of whiskers, and therefore presumably of other crystals, was due, like glass, to surface cracks was of course strong. However, we were unable to find any cracks and there were good reasons, based on the mode of growth, to suppose that they should not exist. When a whisker grows from solution or from vapour there generally first appears a very fine filament or leader which in the electron microscope can be seen to be almost perfectly smooth. This leader then thickens by the spreading down it of new, sleeve-like layers of material. At first these layers may consist of single layers of atoms or molecules, but, naturally, the various successive layers of new material will be fed with molecules from the surroundings at slightly differing rates. Thus the layers which are fed faster will advance faster and may catch up on slower underlying layers which they have no means of passing. The advancing edge or step is now twice the normal height and so would require twice the amount of new material if it were to advance at the same rate as the other layers. In fact, however, it is only likely to be supplied by diffusion at the same rate as the single layers. Thus the double layer moves more slowly than the average and so yet more growth layers pile up behind it and cannot pass. Thus there build up a series of steps with sharp, cliff-like fronts (Plate 10). On the average these steps will be higher the older and therefore the thicker the crystal. When the crystal stops growing, because it is removed from the solution, or for any other reason, these steps will remain on the surface and can often clearly be seen in the microscope.

It is quite easy to see, intuitively, that a crack is a nasty dangerous thing to have about the house but it is by no means so obvious that a step can cause a bad stress concentration. The problem of the step was so little regarded that there was no standard solution in the literature and so I asked David Marsh to get one. Working with a series of transparent resin models in polarized light, Marsh was able to show that a step was just as bad a stress concentrator as the equivalent crack, in fact it might be regarded as half a crack. This experimental solution has since been confirmed by a purely mathematical analysis carried out by H. L. Cox.

Though this work was done to explain the strength of very tiny crystals it is worthy of the attention of engineers who are perhaps somewhat frightened of cracks but take a rather light-hearted view of steps in machinery and structures.

It will be realized that with the step, as with the crack, what governs the stress concentration or weakening effect is not the absolute size of the re-entrant but the ratio of depth to the root radius.

Marsh examined a number of whiskers in the electron microscope and found that, for the substances he was using, the root radii of the growth-steps was roughly constant at about 40 Ångströms. He then compared the heights of the worst steps with the measured strength of the whiskers. The correlation was extraordinarily good and left no room for doubt that this is the true explanation of the size-strength effect in whiskers. Since a large whisker is in no way different from any other crystal except in size it must also be a general explanation of the strength and weakness of all brittle crystals.

That the strength behaviour of whiskers is no different from that of much bigger crystals was confirmed by Dash who took a large (2 cm.) crystal of silicon, which is normally quite a weak material, and polished it very carefully. He then enclosed it in a transparent box which he provided with a mechanism for straining the specimen in bending. He used to take this affair round various conferences and demonstrate to all and sundry that the crystal could be repeatedly bent to a strain of 2 per cent which is equivalent to a stress of about 600,000 p.s.i. or 4,000 MN/m^2, a very respectable figure.

When we come to everyday crystalline materials, however, there is one more link in the argument. It is possible, by taking care, to grow quite large single crystals, as Dash did, but normally each individual crystal in a common material is quite small. Whiskers are small single crystals of rather a special kind but ordinary sizable solids are what is called polycrystalline, that is to say they are made up of a large number of small crystals fitting together in three dimensions like crazy paving or like counties on a map. Although the shape of the individual crystals is irregular the fit at the boundaries is usually very good and in a pure material there is good contact on a molecular scale. In general the surface energy of these boundaries is actually higher than that of fracture planes within the crystals and so, in a reasonably pure material, the 'grain-boundaries' are not usually a source of weakness.

The case is somewhat different however with an impure material. As is well known, when a liquid freezes by crystallizing the crystals tend to expel impurities. For instance ice which is formed on salt water is substantially fresh, to the great convenience of Polar explorers. This effect causes impurities in solids to accumulate at the grain boundaries (and also vacancies, that is, holes) and this may cause the grain boundary to become a line of weakness. This is one of the reasons why the addition of quite small amounts of the wrong impurity can ruin an alloy. A useful application of this weakening effect occurs when we add antifreeze to the water in a car radiator. It is true that the glycol does depress the freezing point of the resulting mixture considerably and so postpones freezing but, when this eventually does happen, the result is a mushy ice without mechanical strength which is unlikely to do much harm to the engine.

For most fairly pure crystalline solids, however, the grain-boundaries are quite strong and, for a hard brittle material, a polycrystalline solid may be regarded as behaving in a manner comparable to whiskers and other single crystals and this, as we have seen, is very like the way glass behaves. In both cases the problem of strength and weakness is almost entirely a matter of surface smoothness. In the case of glass the important defect is usually the surface crack, in the case of brittle crystals it is usually the surface step. The presence of internal defects in a brittle crystal is usually of minor importance.

As we shall see, the problem with a ductile material, such as a soft metal, is quite different.

Dislocations and ductility

So far we have dealt entirely with what are technically known as 'brittle' substances. This does not mean, of course, that they will fall to pieces at a touch and as we have said, some brittle substances are very strong. There is no absolutely sharp division between brittle and ductile substances but generally speaking brittle solids have fairly well defined characteristics. Apart from the small elastic strains which recover when the load is taken off, brittle solids do not distort before failure and fracture is usually by a crack or cracks which run cleanly through the material. Thus the bits will fit together after fracture so that one can often glue a broken vase together quite plausibly. In a ductile material such as mild steel, a good deal of irreversible distortion takes place before actual fracture occurs so that broken parts do not fit even approximately. This is one of the reasons for the high cost of car repairs.

Brittle substances in common use include glass, pottery, bricks, cement and some plastics and these are fairly satisfactory for the purposes for which they are generally used. For the more exacting uses, such as machinery, we generally tend to choose ductile metals. In a brittle solid, fracture occurs by the total separation of two adjacent layers of atoms or molecules under a tensile stress, the rest of the material being undisturbed. A metal behaves rather more like Plasticine. Before actual fracture occurs, in the sense that the specimen separates into two pieces, there is extensive flow, something like a viscous liquid, in the body of the material. This is caused by adjacent layers of atoms, not coming apart, but sliding over each other after the fashion of a pack of cards.

After the adjacent layers of atoms have slipped to a greater or less extent, so that the material is deformed in shear, no serious weakening has necessarily taken place, so that broken bonds have reformed with new partners. In some cases metals are actually strengthened by this process, which is known as cold working. If the process is carried too far the material will however be weakened and eventually broken. The amount of shearing or elongation which a ductile material will withstand varies enormously between different metals and alloys. It nearly always increases when the metal is heated; hence the village blacksmith and his forge. The ability of ductile metals to be permanently distorted and therefore shaped either cold or hot is of course an outstanding advantage of metals. Besides this, it goes a long way to account for their toughness, as we shall see in Chapter 9. However it is also the principal cause of their weaknesses. This is because, as we have said, if a material does not fail in a 'brittle' manner because of a crack at right angles to a tension stress, then it may fail by 'sliding off' (Figure 3) at 45° to it, and if this is the weaker mechanism this is what will happen.

Kelly has shown recently that correct calculations about the shearing strength of solids are rather complicated and that there is a good deal of variation between the theoretical shear strengths of various substances. However we can achieve an approximation to the theoretical shear strength by means of a very simple model and the result is not grossly in error. Consider a model, on paper or in the solid, consisting of sheets of spheres or balls to represent the atoms. There will be certain positions in which such

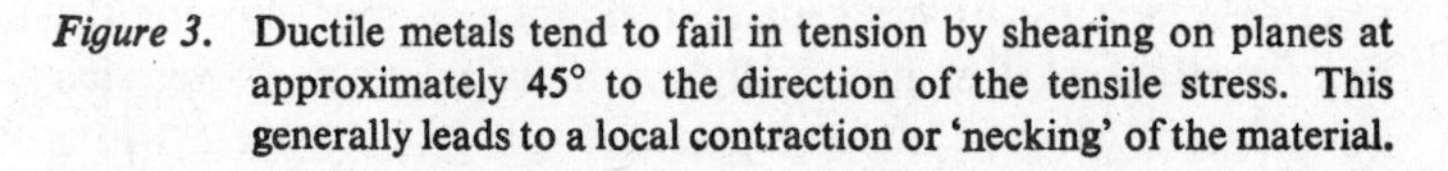

Figure 3. Ductile metals tend to fail in tension by shearing on planes at approximately 45° to the direction of the tensile stress. This generally leads to a local contraction or 'necking' of the material.

sheets of spheres will lie on each other as close together as possible. To disturb the layers from this position involves moving them further apart, which is resisted by tension in the bonds. The rows of atoms, as it were, dislike being dug out of their comfortable trenches of lowest energy.

Figure 4 represents a two-dimensional model such as is afforded by two parallel rows of pennies lying on a table. It is clear that all

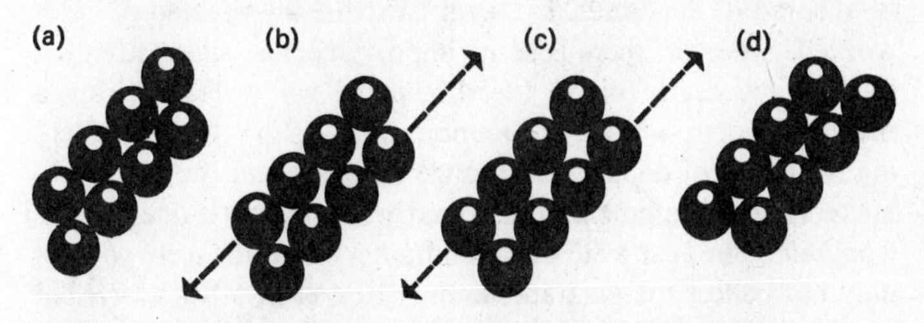

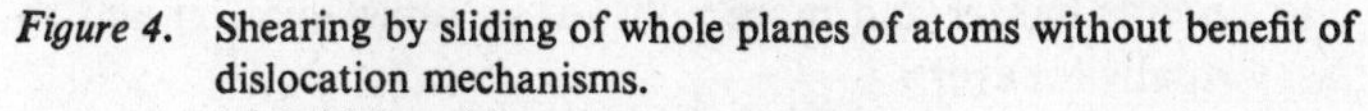

Figure 4. Shearing by sliding of whole planes of atoms without benefit of dislocation mechanisms.
(a) Initial position at rest.
(b) Resistance to slip a maximum, about 15° angular shearing displacement.
(c) All resistance to shearing gone at 30°.
(d) Final position of rest 60° shear.

resistance to shearing has vanished by the time that the atoms are balanced on top of each other, which will occur when the whole material has been distorted in shear through an angle of 30°. Beyond this point the rows of atoms will subside into repose in the next valley and shearing through one atomic spacing will have occurred. The resistance to this shearing will start at nothing, build up to a maximum, and decline again to zero when the atoms get to the top of the hump. Resistance will be a maximum about half-way up the hill, in this case about 15°. The three-dimensional case is slightly more complicated but the peak occurs around 7°. Crystals made from arrangements of atoms of differing sizes may also tend to reduce the angle at which maximum resistance occurs.

Arithmetic of a rather crude sort again gives figures in the general region of 10 per cent of the Young's modulus for the theoretical shear strength. (Kelly's more sophisticated approach gives figures between about 5 per cent and 10 per cent *E*.) In a way it does not matter very much if our figure is not very accurate because it is seldom or never reached when testing real materials in bulk.* The theoretical figure for iron is something like 1,500,000 p.s.i. or 10,000 MN/m² but in practice a crystal of really pure iron shears at about 3,000 p.s.i. or 20 MN/m², commercial steel at about 25,000 p.s.i. and the very strongest steel at 250,000 or so.

Really soft metals like pure gold, silver and base lead can easily be sheared in the hands. If they are extensively sheared or cold-worked, however, there is some improvement in shear strength, though not nearly up to the theoretical value. Hammering a metal to harden it is not uncommon: this was the way of hardening the edges of copper and bronze weapons and the old clock-makers always hammered their brass gear-wheels. (If one refrains from oiling the gear teeth of a grandfather clock, the teeth will not only not collect the dust and so not grind each other away, but also become harder and more polished as times goes on and so last virtually for ever.)

*It will be noticed that, very approximately, the theoretical shearing stresses are generally lower than the theoretical tensile stresses. Thus, near-perfect specimens tend to fail in shear if they can reach very high stresses, as we have seen in the case with glass.

Until about 1934 the Establishment explanation of these phenomena was remarkably unconvincing and seems to have reflected mainly a desire not to be asked embarrassing questions. 'Slip is due to little bits of crystal getting loose and acting as roller bearings between the layers. When too many break away they jam each other and that is the cause of work hardening.' As the Duke of Wellington said, 'If you believe that you will believe anything.'

In 1934 G. I. Taylor, a Cambridge don who invented the ploughshare anchor, a major alleviation of human misery, also invented the dislocation. At least he put up the dislocation as a hypothesis in a scientific paper. The essential idea is extraordinarily simple, so simple that it must be true, and it turns out that it is.

It is most unlikely, said Taylor, that metal crystals are really as perfect as we suppose them to be when we do sums about their strength. Let us suppose that every now and then, perhaps every million atoms or so, slight irregularities occur. What we need is not so much a point irregularity such as a foreign atom, because that could only facilitate movement at one point, but rather a line defect which will allow the army of molecules, as it were, to sweep forward on a broad front.

Crystals, of course, consist of sheets or planes of atoms, which to an electron-sized observer would seem to lie, piled upon one another, in awful and endlessly regular array, virtually for ever, like the pages of some enormous celestial book. What Taylor suggested was that every now and then, but very rarely, a sheet of atoms is not complete. It is as if somebody had slipped an extra sheet of paper between the pages of the book which now, at one point consists of perhaps a million pages, at another of a million and one. The interesting bit occurs of course along the line where the extra layer of atoms comes to an end.

Referring to Figure 5, it will be seen that there must be two places, one on either side of the tip of the extra sheet, where the atoms are distorted to an angle which approximates to the theoretical shearing strength of the crystal. In other words, at these two points the crystal is pretty well broken away.

What is even more important, the dislocation turns out to be

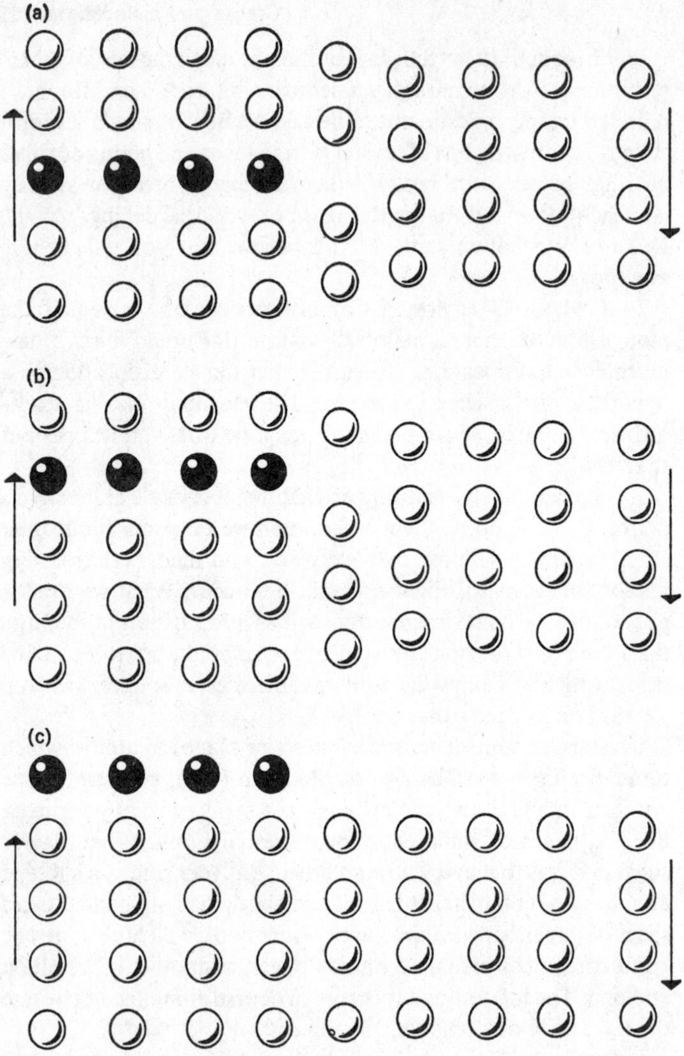

Figure 5. Shearing by means of an edge dislocation. For the reality of this phenomenon see Plate 14.

(a) Edge dislocation (diagrammatic).

(b) Dislocation sheared one lattice spacing.

(c) Dislocation sheared out of crystal altogether.

Note. The shaded atoms are not of course the *same* individual movable. If we put a gentle shearing force upon the crystal as a whole we can easily apply that little extra strain needed to break the whole line of sorely stretched bonds but we find (Figure 5b) that we have merely reformed the whole arrangement one atomic spacing further on. By going on loading the crystal in shear we can repeat the process indefinitely and eventually squeeze the dislocation out of the far side of the crystal (Figure 5c). Furthermore the force needed to do so may be very small.

Engineers and some metallurgists resisted the idea with the whole force of their emotions and even today some of them are still making growling noises in caves in the backwoods. Academic physicists, on the whole, however, fell upon dislocations with glee. For many years nobody saw a dislocation in the flesh, or perhaps ever expected to, but their hypothetical movements (dislocations of like sign repel each other etc.) and breeding habits (when the union of two dislocations is blessed about five hundred new dislocations are suddenly released upon the crystal) could be theoretically predicted and provided a superb intellectual exercise like three dimensional chess.

As a matter of fact nearly all these academic predictions turn out to be true. Taylor supposed originally that slip in ductile crystals was due entirely to those dislocations which were present initially in the crystal due to the accidents of imperfect growth. It turns out that there are generally not enough dislocations originally present in most crystals to account for the very extensive slip which can take place in a ductile material. Large families of new dislocations can however be nucleated either by dislocation interaction (known as a Frank-Read source), or, more frequently, by severe stress concentrations, such as occur at crack tips. These mechanisms enable a stressed metal to be rapidly filled with dislocations (something like 10^{12} per square centimetre) and thus to flow under a steady load or the blow of a hammer quite easily.

---

atoms in each of these diagrams. The shading merely indicates the position of the extra half sheet of atoms. During dislocation movement no individual atom has to move more than a fraction of an Ångström from its original position.

It will be recalled that the dislocation is essentially a line defect which can move about in the crystal fairly freely. When there are many dislocations they do not have to move far before two or more dislocations meet. In rather special circumstances this can result in the creation of new dislocations but the much more usual effect is for them to repel each other. As more and more dislocations are born and move about they impede each other and get tangled up, like so much string. The result is that after a period of free movement the material begins to harden and if one goes on deforming it it will become brittle.

The most familiar example of this is when one wishes to break off a piece of metal such as a wire or the opened lid of a tin can. This can usually be done by bending it backwards and forwards a few times. The metal yields easily at first, hardens somewhat and then breaks off in a brittle fashion. Metal hardened by deformation can be returned to its initial soft condition by 'annealing', that is to say by heating it until total or partial recrystallization occurs, in which case most of the excess dislocations vanish. Thus copper tubes must be annealed after bending to shape or they will be brittle.

Altogether, the dislocation mechanism has been found to explain the mechanical properties of metals very well indeed. Although dislocations do exist in non-metallic crystals they are not usually very mobile and they seldom breed, thus dislocation movement does not play any important part in the way non-metals behave. It is the mobility of dislocations which accounts for the mechanical differences between metals and non-metals. Needless to say, dislocations cannot exist in glasses because glasses are not crystalline.

Part Two

The non-metallic tradition

Chapter 5 Crack-stopping

or how to be tough

'And yet flint is considered to involve comparatively easy work, as there is a kind of earth consisting of a sort of potter's clay mixed with gravel, called "gangardia" which it is almost impossible to overcome. They attack it with wedges and iron hammers; and it is thought to be the hardest thing that exists, except the greed of gold which is the most stubborn of all things.'

Pliny, *Natural History.**

Pliny the Elder (A.D. 23–79) in his highly unreliable *Natural History* gives directions for distinguishing a genuine diamond. It should be put, he says, on a blacksmith's anvil and smitten with a heavy hammer as hard as possible; if it breaks it is not a true diamond. It is likely that a good many valuable stones were destroyed in this way because Pliny was muddling up hardness and toughness. Diamond is the hardest of all substances and the hardness of diamond is useful when one wants to cut or scratch or grind materials and this is its main industrial use. But diamond, like other hard precious stones, is quite brittle so that, even if one could get it cheaply in large pieces it would not be a very useful structural substance.

The worst sin in an engineering material is not lack of strength or lack of stiffness, desirable as these properties are, but lack of toughness, that is to say, lack of resistance to the propagation of cracks. One can allow for lack of strength or stiffness in design but it is much more difficult to allow for cracks which catch the engineer unawares and are dangerous.

Most metals and timbers, and also Nylon, Polythene, fibre-glass, bones, teeth, cloth, rope and jade are tough. Most minerals, glass, pottery, rosin, bakelite, cement, and biscuits are brittle, and so is ordinary table jelly as one can readily prove by propagating a crack in it with a spoon and fork. It is not at all easy to see what it

*Translated by Racham and Jones.

is that makes one thing tough and another brittle because the substances in each of these lists seem to have little enough in common. The distinction is a very real one however. Pottery and commercial tinplate may have roughly the same tensile strength but if a cup is dropped on the floor it will shatter, perhaps almost explosively. If we drop a tin can probably nothing will happen; at the worst we may make a small dent. The actual tensile strength of ordinary glass and ceramics can be quite high; the reason why we do not make motor cars, for instance, from them is not that they are weak but that they are far too brittle. Anybody can tell this from common sense. But why? What is really happening?

First of all brittleness is not primarily a matter of the rate of loading. Psychologically there is a great difference between a statically applied load, that is one which is put on slowly, and a dynamic load, that is one suddenly applied, usually by means of a blow. The distinction does arise and it cannot entirely be neglected but it is much less important than appears at first sight. Generally we use a hammer simply because it is a convenient and cheap way of getting a high local force, which we do by decelerating the heavy head. Usually we should get much the same results by applying the same load slowly. To a certain extent this applies to dropping things on the floor and to car and aeroplane crashes, though as we shall see there are some important reservations. However, in most brittle materials, whether the force which causes fracture is applied quickly or slowly, once failure has begun, the consequent cracks will propagate very quickly indeed, usually at several thousand miles an hour. Thus to the eye fracture appears to be instantaneous.

In a way there is no essential difference between a stressed material and an explosive. When an elastic material is strained, strain energy is stored in the stretched chemical bonds and when the material is fractured this energy is released. At the theoretical breaking strain of the material all the bonds are stretched to their maximum and the strain energy is roughly equal to the chemical energy, as we ought to expect. In practice materials generally only reach a small fraction of their theoretical strength before they break and so the release of strain energy is usually far less than the energy which would be provided by an equivalent weight of explosive. All the same, it may make a very respectable bang. When strong fibres and whiskers are broken, for instance in the Marsh machine, one can realize a high proportion of their theoretical strength. In these cases one is not left after fracture with two or more broken pieces: there is an explosion and the fibre vanishes in fine dust. Only the fact that these strong fibres are generally quite small prevents the operation of breaking them from being a dangerous one.

Impact strength

Before going on to the general question of crack propagation and control, it is worth considering some of the special effects of a dynamically applied load such as a blow. The highest speed at which a stress can be transmitted through any substance is usually the speed of sound in that substance. Indeed, sound is perhaps best thought of as a wave, or series of waves, of stress passing through a substance at its natural speed.

Now the speed of sound in any substance is $\sqrt{E/\rho}$ where ρ is the density or specific gravity of the substance and E is the Young's modulus. Given the common values of E and ρ in structural solids we find that the speed of sound in these substances is very high indeed: for steel, aluminium and glass it is about 11,000 miles an hour or 4,800 metres per second, which is much faster than the speed of sound in air. Such speeds are far faster than any hammer blow and considerably faster than the flight of bullets.

The result is that the hammer or the bullet is pressing against its target for a period, perhaps about a hundredth of a second, which is very long compared with the time which is required to conduct the energy away from the point of impact in the form of waves of sound or stress. As photographers know, a great deal can happen in periods of time as long as a hundredth of a second. What is apt to happen when we strike a solid is that a whole series of stress waves radiate from the point of impact and move off into the body of the material. They reach the further boundaries of the solid in a time which is probably between a ten-thousandth and a hundred-thousandth of a second and are reflected back, as a kind of echo, very little attenuated or diminished in intensity. What happens next depends upon a great many things such as the shape of the solid, exactly where the blow was struck and so on. What *may* happen is that the returning reflected stress waves repeatedly meet the outgoing ones at some critical or unlucky point and thus the stress may pile up at this point until fracture occurs. The stories about singers fracturing panes of glass may well be true.

There are some elegant instances of the sort of things which can happen. The British Ceramic Research Association, for instance, have a routine impact test for ceramic tiles in which a loosely supported square tile is struck a measured blow in the centre of one flat face. In many cases the tile does not break in the middle where it is struck. What happens is that the four corners drop off because the stress waves are reflected and crowded into the corners.

When a shell is fired against armour plate, if the shell does not penetrate, then what is known as a 'scab', a jagged piece of armour, sometimes becomes detached from the inside or back surface. If this happens the scab may bounce about with great speed and energy within the turret and may do as much damage as if the shell had actually penetrated.

In a similar way, when a projectile is fired into a tank of liquid, such as the fuel tank of an aeroplane, it is the exit hole which is much the largest and the most difficult to seal since the shock waves which are readily transmitted through the fluid may burst the back of the tank. Unfortunately the human head is structurally rather like a tank of liquid and the consequences when it is struck by a bullet are well-known. What is less well-known is that rather similar effects may happen with a blow on the forehead which does not penetrate. The important factor in the design of crash-helmets is therefore the cushioning of the shock wave so as to prevent damage at the back of the skull. This is the reason for the internal head-band in helmets which looks as if it was put in in order to provide ventilation.

In engineering it is usual to test materials for toughness by means of a routine impact test of what is called the 'Izod' type. In this test the material is in the form of a bar a quarter or a half an inch square and is often provided with a standard notch to initiate failure. This bar is clamped at one end and the other end is then broken off by means of a heavy hammer in the form of a pendulum. By measuring the difference in the height to which the pendulum swings before and after breaking the specimen the energy of fracture can be estimated. Academically, this test is not very accurate but it does have some value as a rough comparative test between different materials.* It is very popular with engineers.

The Griffith criterion and critical crack length

To return to crack propagation in brittle solids, it does not really matter for our present purposes whether fracture is initiated by a dynamic blow or by a static load. On the whole, if the fracture stress is produced, by whatever means, at a given point, fracture will probably occur there. There are some exceptions to this: a few substances, such as pitch and toffee, are sensitive to the rate of loading. Every child knows that the way to break the most intractable toffee is to hit it with a poker. This will work when slower methods are quite impotent (Chapter 9). However, most normal materials are not much affected by considerations of dynamic and static loading.

Of course it would be ideal to have a material in which it was impossible to initiate cracks at all. Unfortunately in practice this does not seem to be a possibility. As we have seen in the last chapter the surface of even the smoothest glass is infested with tiny invisible cracks and even if it were not, it soon would be when it had brushed against some other solid. What therefore counts most of all is the ease with which the cracks can be made to extend by applying a stress to the material. The basic theory of crack propagation is again due to A. A. Griffith.

Griffith said that two conditions must be fulfilled if a crack was to propagate. First it must be energetically desirable and secondly there must be a molecular mechanism by which the energy transformation can take place. The first condition requires that at every stage in the propagation of the crack the energy stored in the material is being reduced, just as when a car runs

* As we shall see on page 108, it is an approximate measure of the 'work of fracture'.

downhill its potential energy is being reduced. On the other hand, however energetically desirable it may be, the car will not run downhill unless it is provided with wheels and the brake is off. The wheels are the mechanism by which the car runs downhill and implements the transformation of energy.

As we have said, a strained material contains strain energy which would like to be released just as a raised weight contains potential energy and would like to fall. If the material is completely fractured naturally the whole of this energy is in the end released. Consider, however, what happens during the intermediate stages of fracture. When a crack appears in a strained material it will open up a little so that the two faces of the crack are separated. This implies that the material immediately behind the crack is relaxed and the strain energy in that part of the material is released. If we now think about a crack proceeding inwards from the surface of a stressed material (Figure 1) we should expect the area of material in which the strain is relaxed

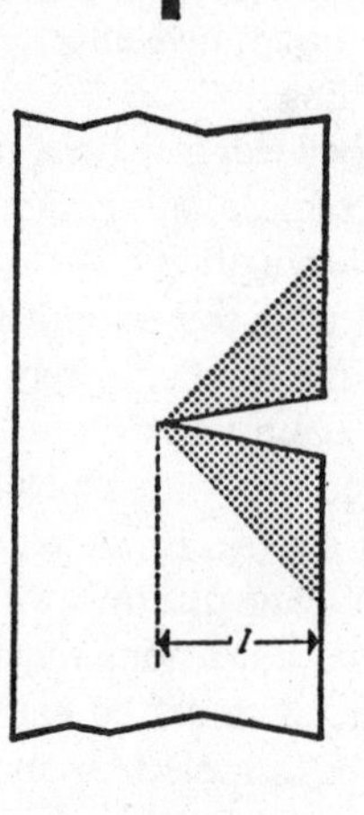

Figure 1. Griffith criterion for crack propagation. As the crack extends the material in the shaded areas is relaxed and releases its strain energy. This released energy then becomes available to propagate the crack still further.

to correspond roughly to the two shaded triangles. Now the area of these triangles is roughly l^2, where l is the length of the crack. The relief of strain energy would thus be expected to be proportional to the square of the crack length, or rather depth, and in fact this rough guess is confirmed by calculation. Thus a crack two microns deep releases four times as much strain energy as one one micron deep and so on.

On the other side of the energy account book is the surface energy, $2G.l$, which is needed to form the new surfaces and clearly this increases only as the first power of the depth of the crack. Thus a crack two microns deep has twice the surface energy of a crack one micron deep but as we have seen it releases four times as much strain energy. The consequences of this are fairly clear. When the crack is very shallow it is consuming more energy as surface energy than it is releasing as relaxed strain energy and therefore the conditions are energetically unfavourable for it to propagate. As the crack gets longer however these conditions are reversed and beyond the 'critical Griffith length' l_g the crack is producing more energy than it is consuming, so it may start to run away in an explosive manner. There is a characteristic critical Griffith crack length for each stress in the material. At the theoretical maximum stress the critical crack length l_g is extremely short and at zero stress it is infinitely long, which is what we should expect.

Algebraically, this can be shown to be equivalent to,

$$l_g = \frac{2GE}{\pi s^2}$$

where l_g is in metres

G is in J/m^2

and E and s are in $Newtons/m^2$ (*not* MN/m^2)

If the energy required to propagate the crack by producing the two new fracture surfaces were really confined to G, the free surface energy (which is seldom much above 1 J/m^2), then simple arithmetic will show that, at any realistic stress level, the critical crack length would be very short indeed, perhaps around a micron.

Fortunately this is seldom actually the case with practical

materials because, in order to produce a new fracture surface, we have generally not only to break all the chemical bonds at the fracture surface (which requires only the free surface energy), we also disturb the molecular structure of the material to a depth which is sometimes very considerable; in doing so we break a great many other bonds as well. In other words, fracture is a brutal process. The total energy which has to be used up in producing a real fracture surface is therefore greater than *G* and is known as the 'work of fracture', *W*, such that,

$$l_g = \frac{2WE}{\pi s^2}$$

– *W* being in J/m^2 again.

Although *W* is always considerably bigger than *G*, its actual magnitude varies very greatly between different materials. With glass, for instance, the molecular structure is only disturbed to a comparatively shallow depth below the fracture surface and *W* is generally around 6 J/m^2 – in other words about six times *G* – and so, although l_g, the critical crack length, is six times as high as it otherwise would be, it is still very short and glass is a brittle material. Most ceramics are not much better than glass in this respect but the ductile metals, such as wrought iron, mild steel, copper and aluminium, have works of fracture which are enormously higher than their free surface energies and range between 10^4 and 10^6 J/m^2. That is to say, *W* is from ten thousand to a million times higher than *G* and so the critical crack length is longer in direct proportion. Thus mild steel structures, for instance, can generally put up with cracks at least a metre long without breaking. This is what makes ductile metals so safe and tough and so popular.

In fact the possession of a high work of fracture – at least a thousand times higher than the free surface energy – is an essential characteristic of all safe and practical structural materials which are used in tension. However the actual molecular mechanism by which so much energy can be absorbed during fracture varies a great deal between the different kinds of solids. With metals it is essentially due to the operation of the dislocation mechanism which was described in the last chapter; we shall discuss how this works in Chapter 9. Timber, again, has a high work of fracture – about 10^4 J/m² – but this is produced by a totally different mechanism which we shall talk about in Chapter 6. The various plastics and composites are different again and we shall come to these presently.

As we saw in Chapter 4 the stress concentration at the tip of a crack is about:

$$K = 2\sqrt{\frac{l}{R}}$$

where l = crack length, R = tip radius.

Note L is the half length of an internal (or elliptical) crack, l is the length of a crack proceeding inwards from a surface. For all practical purposes L may be taken as equivalent to l.

Now in many materials, R, the tip radius of the crack, remains constant whatever the crack length, so that as the crack gets longer, the stress concentration gets worse. In practice R may have a value comparable to atomic dimensions, say about 1 Ångström unit. A crack length of about 1 micron (i.e. 10,000 Ångströms) will therefore produce the theoretical stress at the crack tip when the average stress in the material is quite modest and for longer cracks the stress at the tip will be far higher. However, paradoxically, and as Griffith pointed out, *as long as the crack is shorter than the critical length, nothing will happen – however high the stress at the tip may be.* Thus the chief safeguard against brittle failure lies in a high work of fracture. This is basically why glass (W = 6 J/m²) is brittle and steel (W = about 10^5 J/m²) is tough, although both these materials have roughly the same tensile strengths. With any luck a serious crack in a large steel structure will be spotted by an inspector and remedial action will be taken before anything dangerous happens. As we have seen 20 per cent of ships are found to have serious cracks in their hulls, say a metre or so long. If the ships had been made of a material like glass they would have broken long before a crack became conspicuous. This is basically why engineers are traditionally addicted to 'ductile' materials and really one cannot blame them.

However, in any material, a crack may sooner or later reach its critical length, whether this be a micron or ten metres. Once this has happened, as the crack gets longer, everything gets worse. The stress concentration gets worse and the Griffith energy balance gets more and more favourable to crack propagation. If the load is maintained, the crack therefore accelerates rapidly and soon reaches its theoretical calculated speed which is generally about 38 per cent of the speed of sound in the material. In the case of glass this crack speed is 4,000 miles an hour or 1,700 m/s, a velocity which has been confirmed experimentally. By this time stress waves are probably racing about in the material in all directions at the speed of sound (that is faster than the crack), being reflected off both old and new surfaces, and we are likely to end up with not one crack but with a great many. In other words the material has shattered. This is possible because, at high stresses the total strain energy in the material will 'pay' for a great many new surfaces, indeed at the theoretical strength it will 'pay' for dividing the whole material up into individual sheets of molecules.

A completely brittle material like glass is reasonably safe as long as we are content to operate it at a very low stress level, for instance as a shop window, because the Griffith crack length is then quite long and so the material is safe against minor chips and abrasions. If we want to work at a high level of stress, however, anywhere near the potential strength of glass for instance, we must be prepared to keep the surface free from even the most microscopic cracks for, if even one crack is allowed to exceed the Griffith length, which may be only about a thousand Ångströms, catastrophic failure will occur. This makes homogeneous brittle materials much too dangerous to use in practice when there is any serious stress on them.

The ability to propagate cracks freely under a small stress was not wholly a disadvantage to primitive man who was thus able to shape flint and obsidian, which are more or less natural glasses, into various cutting tools. When the flaking is done skilfully, only light hand pressure with a piece of wood is needed to detach long slivers of material which can themselves be used as knives. Using a non-brittle stone, such as jade, shaping could only be carried out by the infinitely more laborious process of grinding. Most of the tensile stresses in tools are due to bending and by keeping stone tools short and compact stresses could be kept low enough to ensure reasonable durability. A weapon like a stone sword would of course have been quite impracticable.

TOUGHNESS IN NON-METALS

The history of the attempts to prevent cracks spreading or to evade the consequences, is almost the history of engineering. The most obvious way of preventing cracks from spreading in brittle materials is not to use them in tension, in other words to use them in compression. This is what masonry is about and as we have seen in Chapter 2, starting with the simple wall one can go from the arch to the dome and to the most complicated cathedral, keeping everything in compression, or at least trying to do so. Masonry is extraordinarily satisfactory in its way but it is inherently heavy and immobile. There are therefore a number of variants of the same idea. One of these is prestressed concrete in which the brittle component is kept in compression by strong tension wires. Then there is toughened glass, which is homogeneous in the sense that it is all glass, but the outside, which is susceptible to cracks, is put into compression at the expense of a tension in the protected middle.* This has been widely used for car windscreens and, in a much more sophisticated form, is being developed for serious engineering in America. This may turn out to be an important development in new materials. Rather curiously, this line of thought does not seem to occur at all in biological materials which all depend, as do some artificial

*This is usually done by chilling the outside of the hot glass by means of air jets. Glass, like other substances, contracts as it cools and if the outer parts of the glass be cooled and hardened before the inner parts then the outside will, of course, contract more initially than the inside but, since the inside is still soft, it will yield in the early stages of cooling. In the later stages of cooling however both the inside and the outside behave elastically and thus their contractions get out of step. As a result, when the glass has finished cooling the outside is in compression while the inside is in tension.

Strains in glass – as in most other transparent solids – become visible in polarized light and sunlight is partially polarized especially when it is reflected from non-metallic surfaces such as a road or the paintwork of a car. In this way the pattern of the air-jets used for cooling the glass can often be seen in car windscreens. Naturally the effect becomes more pronounced when one wears polarizing glasses.

ones, on reducing the effective stress concentration at the tip of the crack. Again, the methods used by nature are quite widely different from those which the metallurgist employs.

It is rather strange that so little attenion has been given so far to the mechanical properties of biological materials, though perhaps in human terms it is understandable. Many people become biologists and doctors by a reaction against things mechanical and mathematical and contrariwise engineering has been going through a phase of rejecting natural materials. Metals are considered more 'important' than wood, which is hardly considered worthy of serious attention at all.

Cellulose, which is the main constituent of wood, cane, bamboo and all vegetable fibres, is very tough. Cricket bats are made of willow, mallets of elm, polo balls of bamboo roots and loom shuttles of persimmon, a tree which grows in Persia. Aeroplanes used to be made of wood and gliders still are; wooden ships are supposed to be more robust in ice than steel ones. Cellulose cannot be considered as either weak or brittle yet it is chemically a sugar, being made by stringing glucose molecules together. All crystalline sugars are very brittle and so are glassy sugars, that is toffee. Bones and teeth are made from quite simple inorganic compounds which in their normal crystalline and glassy forms are very brittle. Of course it is possible to break a bone or a tooth but this is comparatively rare. Teeth are especially worthy of admiration, being capable, with proper maintenance, of cracking nuts for something like forty years. Even the most modern dental cements are very much weaker and more brittle than tooth substance.

The interface as a crack-stopper

The incentive to investigate the toughness of materials of this kind came, not from the biologists, but from the development of reinforced plastics which present an interesting paradox in the matter of toughness. The commonest, or at any rate the best known, reinforced plastic is fibreglass. This material consists of a very large number of thin glass fibres glued together with a resin. Now the fibres are chemically and physically in no way different from ordinary bulk glass, which, as we have seen, is catastrophically brittle. Furthermore, the resin which is used to bond the fibres is also brittle, perhaps not quite as brittle as the glass, but very nearly so. When the two are put together however, the result is a material which is sold in large quantities primarily on account of its extreme toughness.

A few years ago, John Cook and I set out to examine this effect quantitatively. The difficulty with so many problems in materials science has been that the algebra and arithmetic, though theoretically soluble, are too laborious to be done by traditional methods. This applies to a certain extent to the solution of the detailed stress distribution around a crack and until this was known in some detail it was not possible to predict what a crack would do when it met an inhomogeneity such as the interface between a fibre and a resin.

Nowadays computers are changing all this. The stress concentration at a crack tip was first calculated by Inglis in 1913, as we have said, and his results are classic and correct as far as they go. Since then a number of people a great deal abler than ourselves have worked on the problem but, because of the sheer labour of handling the algebra they were forced either to assume that the crack tip was infinitely sharp, that is had zero radius, or else, with a finite tip radius, to use very approximate methods, or at least to map the stress system only in certain regions. The assumption of an infinitely sharp crack tip leads to infinite stresses at the tip and this is clearly meaningless when one wants to investigate fracture. The other approximation using a finite tip radius did not give sufficient detail close to the actual crack tip where fracture was occurring.

Computer or no computer, I should certainly not have been able to handle the mathematics myself but John Cook likes that sort of thing and using the Mercury computer at Farnborough he was able to map the stresses very close to the tip of a crack which had a finite tip radius.

The rough general picture is of course very much that indicated in Figure 1 of Chapter 4. Generalizing a little, we might plot the stress trajectories, that is the direction in which the stress is handed on from one atomic bond to the next, very much as in

Figure 2 of this chapter. This will perhaps serve to put John Cook's detailed maps of the tip region into perspective. He and I were of course aware that we were making two assumptions which were obviously incorrect. One was that the crack tip was elliptical or rounded, which is clearly not the case in detail in a

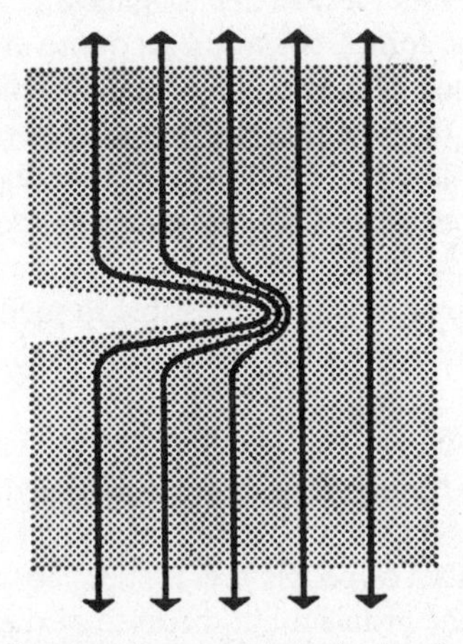

Figure 2. Rough diagram of stress trajectories in a bar uniformly loaded in tension and containing a crack. The stress trajectories become crowded together near the tip of the crack and so the stress in this region is increased.

material made out of atoms. Secondly we assumed that, elastically, the material behaved as a continuum and obeyed Hooke's law. This is also not true in detail either. However, this was the best we could do and we hope that the consequent errors are not too great.

One of the things which John Cook found in his exercises with the computer was that, as far as the stress distribution at the actual crack tip region is concerned, it does not very much matter how the load is applied. Whether the crack is forced open by a wedge, such as a nail or a chisel, or whether it is opened by a remotely applied tensile stress or bending load affects the general stress distribution in the whole body of the material very greatly, but, as far as the region sensitive to fracture is concerned, that is the area a few molecules wide in the region of the tip, the stress pattern is identical. This means that the mechanism of failure is likely to be the same by whatever means the material is broken. This was an important simplification and a step forward.

We may now turn to Figures 3 and 4, which are the actual stress distribution maps which John computed for a crack 2 microns long and 1 Ångström tip radius. The shaded area is empty space at the notional crack tip. The curved lines are not stress trajectories but are contours of stress concentration for stress at right angles and parallel to the plane of the crack. The numbers on each contour represent the stress concentration factor K by which the mean stress remote from the crack is multiplied at each point. As the crack gets longer, the tip radius remaining the same, the stress concentrations get more severe but the pattern and proportions remain similar. The reverse is true, of course, if the crack is shorter.

Figure 3 shows that the stress at right angles to the surfaces of the crack, that is the force tending to open and extend it, is very severe and is concentrated very close indeed to the crack tip. In fact the worst stress is concentrated within an area about equivalent to that covered by a single atomic bond. Its numerical value is the same as that calculated by Inglis for this critical point, though one should not attach too much importance to the exact numerical values in any of this work since all the presuppositions are approximations. However, by the time we have moved forward from the crack tip to roughly the position of the next interatomic bond, the stress has fallen to rather less than half the peak value. Such values are probably roughly true and they show fairly vividly how a great part of the load in a material is concentrated upon a single line of atomic bonds at the tip of a sharp crack, remembering of course that a material is a solid and that a crack tip is a line in a three-dimensional picture. Once the critical bond at the crack tip has broken, the peak stress concentration is transferred to the next bond, and so on, like a ladder in a silk stocking.

Merely using stronger chemical bonds will have a small effect upon the strength of a cracked material by comparison with the stress concentrating effect of the crack and this is why diamond and sapphire are brittle and usually not especially strong, in spite of their hardness and high chemical bond energies. So long as we

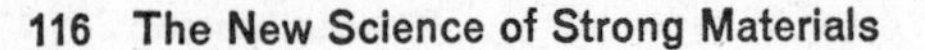

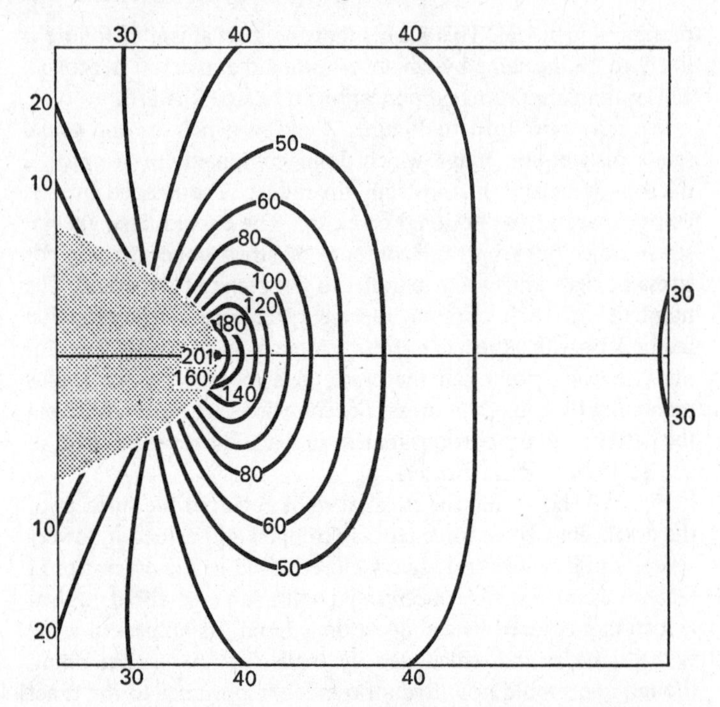

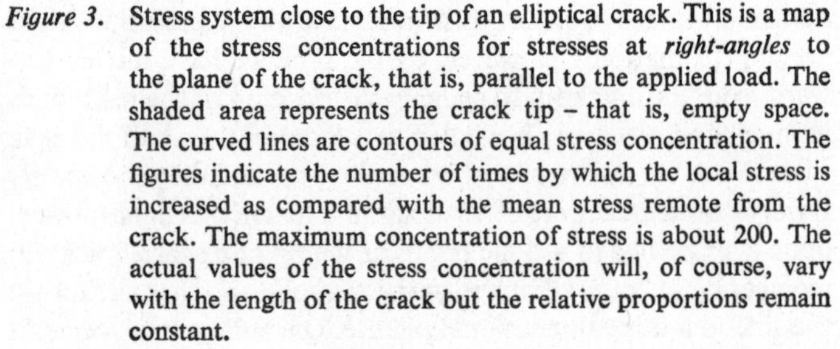
Figure 3. Stress system close to the tip of an elliptical crack. This is a map of the stress concentrations for stresses at *right-angles* to the plane of the crack, that is, parallel to the applied load. The shaded area represents the crack tip – that is, empty space. The curved lines are contours of equal stress concentration. The figures indicate the number of times by which the local stress is increased as compared with the mean stress remote from the crack. The maximum concentration of stress is about 200. The actual values of the stress concentration will, of course, vary with the length of the crack but the relative proportions remain constant.

are dealing with materials which are approximately elastic and approximately homogeneous this is virtually the whole story as far as strength and brittleness are concerned. It does not make any appreciable difference whether the solid is glassy or crystalline or even polymeric, nor does it matter whether it has a high or a low Young's modulus so long as it more or less obeys Hooke's law, virtually up to failure. *Brittleness is not a special condition, it is the normal state of all simple non-metallic solids which cannot generate dislocations and so achieve a high work of fracture.*

Toughness requires some increase in complexity; in a sense it is a property which has to be designed for. In non-metals we can achieve an effective toughness either by devising some kind of work of fracture mechanism without making use of dislocations or else by stopping cracks from running by one means or another. Useful non-metallic materials often work by some combination of the two. (We can sometimes stop a crack by increasing its tip radius – it is fairly common to see holes drilled at the ends of cracks in glass and Perspex in the hope of preventing the crack from spreading any further.) Tough non-metallic materials often contain interfaces or planes of weakness within the materials and many of them are heterogeneous, that is to say they consist of two or more constituents, such as fibre and resin.

We must refer now to Figure 4 which is a map of the stresses *parallel* to the surfaces of the crack. On a first consideration one would not think that there would be appreciable stresses parallel to the crack surface but on reflection it will be seen that this must always be so. As Figure 2 shows, all the stresses have to get round the crack tip and are sharply bent in doing so. These stress trajectories can be thought of, more or less, as strings under tension and they will try to straighten in much the same way. If one passes a string round a post and pulls on both ends there will be a force on the post in the direction of the pull which is reacted by the post pushing in the opposite direction. In other words, there must be a tension in the area just ahead of the crack and in a direction parallel to the crack surfaces. John Cook's computations explored the distribution and magnitude of this tension and the results are mapped in Figure 4.

Unlike the stress at right angles to the crack surfaces which is mapped in Figure 3, this tension starts at zero at the crack tip and increases as we move forward away from it. The maximum is reached at one or two atomic spacings ahead of the crack but the distribution is not very peaky and a fairly high tensile stress level exists over a considerable area ahead of the crack. *Irrespective of the proportions of the crack or the means by which it is loaded the ratio of the maximum value of this stress parallel to the crack surfaces to the peak opening stress at right angles to the crack is constant and has a value of one to five*. This state of affairs seems to be fundamental to all cracks existing in a stretched material.

This is where the internal surfaces in biological materials and reinforced plastics become important. It is significant that these interfaces are generally weaker than the surrounding material. This is not because Nature is too incompetent to glue them together properly but because, properly contrived, the weak interfaces strengthen the material and make it tough.

Consider what happens when a crack approaches an interface of this kind which is roughly at right angles to it. When the area

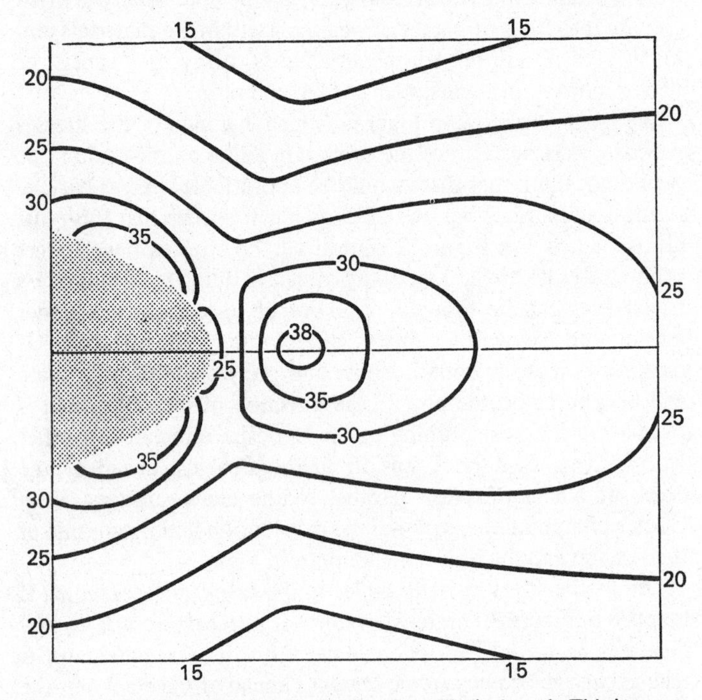

Figure 4. Stress system close to the tip of an elliptical crack. This is a map of the stresses *parallel* to the plane of the crack, that is, at right-angles to the applied loading. For this case the maximum stress concentration is about 40, i.e. one-fifth of that in Figure 3.

of tension stresses ahead of the crack tip reaches the interface, it will try to open it by pulling the two sides apart. If the strength of the interface is greater than about one-fifth of the general cohesion of the material then the interface will not be broken, the crack will cross it and the material will behave as a normal brittle solid. *If however the adhesive strength of the interface is less than about one-fifth of the general cohesive strength of the solid then the interface will be broken before the main crack reaches it and a crack trap or crack stopper has been created.**

This is shown diagramatically in Figure 5 and in the flesh, in a reinforced material in Plate 11. Of course, if the adhesion at the

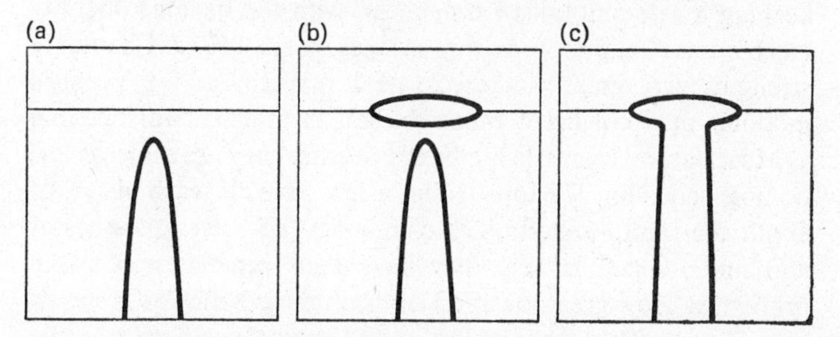

Figure 5. Cook-Gordon mechanism for stopping cracks at a weak interface.
(a) Crack approaches a weak interface.
(b) Interface breaks ahead of main crack.
(c) T-shaped crack-stopper. In practice the crack is usually diverted, as in Plate 11.

interface is too weak then the material as a whole will be weakened so that, when there is no adhesion at all, one has to have some arrangement like cloth or rope or basket-work to hold the material together by friction. For the best results, exact control of the adhesion seems to be critical but when this is achieved, as it seems to be in the best natural and artificial composite materials, very excellent combinations of strength and toughness are created.

*I suppose that one could consider that the crack has been blunted. The tip radius, from being very small, is now very large, practically infinite in fact. It is true that we have now a new crack, at right angles to the original one, but then the tendency to propagate a crack which is *parallel* to the applied stress is usually nil.

Since the condition for effective crack-stopping is that we have to weaken the material by a factor of five, the process does not sound a very promising one. We have, as it were, given up before we have started. As toughening processes go, however, the interfacial weakness method seems to be rather efficient. This is because the true fracture stress at the crack tip is presumably the theoretical strength of the material and this generally lies between 10 and 20 per cent of the Young's modulus, E (Chapter 3). Reducing this to one fifth still leaves a potential strength of between 2 and 4 per cent of E, which is roughly what is achieved in practice in fibre-glass and is a good deal more than one can reach, keeping a safe amount of toughness, with the metallic ductility mechanism (Chapter 9). In any case, as we shall see in Chapter 8, strengths very greatly in excess of 1 per cent of the Young's modulus may not be of much interest in practical engineering.

Most natural minerals are brittle because they are more or less homogeneous but it happens that a few have cleavage planes of about the right strength. The commonest of these are asbestos and mica, which is why they have their peculiar and useful properties. How great the effect of the interfaces may be is shown by a famous experiment of Professor Orowan's with mica. Mica is an ionically bonded mineral in which, because of the arithmetic of the electrical charges in the molecule, every so often there is a layer of metal atoms in the crystal in which each atom has to share a single electron's worth of charge with several near neighbours, so that this layer in the crystal is a weak one. The useful form of mica is called Muscovite (because it originally came from Russia) and in this mica the strength of the bonds on the weak cleavage plane is nominally and very roughly a sixth of the strength of the bonds elsewhere in the crystal.

What Orowan did was to measure the strength of Muscovite mica in tension. In his first experiment he cut from a sheet of mica a normal hour-glass shaped test-piece (Figure 6(b)). This test-piece was flat and quite thin and the planes of weakness lay parallel to the broad flat surfaces. The whole specimen might be regarded, on a molecular scale, as being cut from a number of sheets of paper, weakly glued together. The edges of the specimen, which had been cut mechanically, were, in detail, quite rough. When the specimen was loaded in a testing machine the edges

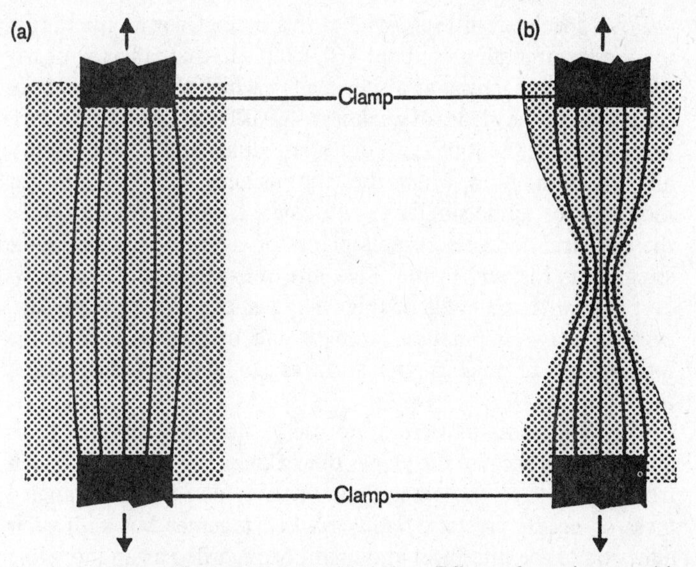

Figure 6. Orowan's experiment with mica. Effect of specimens with stressed and unstressed edges.

(a) Edges unstressed. Tensile strength 460,000 p.s.i. (3,100 MN/m^2).

(b) Edges exposed to average tensile stress. Tensile strength 25,000 p.s.i. (170 MN/m^2).

were stressed as much as the middle and so cracks started at the edges and spread inwards across the material in the usual way. The tensile stress developed in this test was about 25,000 p.s.i. (170 MN/m^2), much the same as ordinary glass and perhaps a little less than commercial steel.

Orowan now tested a differently shaped specimen of the same mica. In this case the sheet of mica, though otherwise similar, was not waisted but was of a rectangular, playing-card shape, somewhat wider than the clamps which gripped it. It was assumed that the stress followed a path similar to that sketched in Figure 6(a). Thus the edges were largely unstressed. The outside surfaces lying on the stress-path between the grips were, of course, fully stressed and no doubt contained all manner of iniquities in the way of scratches and stress concentrations. For these to extend, however, the crack would have had to cross the planes of weakness in the crystal which were in their path.

For a specimen of Muscovite of this shape Orowan found that the tensile strength was about 460,000 p.s.i., that is to say nearly twenty times as strong as a specimen in which the cracks did not have to cross the planes of weakness. 460,000 p.s.i. (3,100 MN/m^2) is about $1\frac{1}{2}$ per cent of the Young's modulus and a very respectable strength. Now Margarite, for instance, which is another kind of mica, quite similar to Muscovite except that it has twice the electrical charge across its planes of cleavage, has negligible strength and is very brittle. This sort of experiment shows however that with materials of this character one cannot really distinguish between practical strength and brittleness so that the introduction of weak internal surfaces can be regarded as raising the strength.

Mica and asbestos were of no use to stone-age men for tools and weapons because the planes of weakness run straight through from one side to the other. Jade however consists of a tangled mass of needle crystals, tightly packed together but with poor adhesion at the interfaces and might be regarded as an inorganic equivalent to a briar pipe or a bamboo root. Jade is therefore very tough and would have been almost ideal for tools and weapons if only it had not been so difficult to work and so scarce.

Since jade cannot be flaked, like flint and obsidian, it could only be shaped by grinding it with sand on a piece of wood for weeks or months. Hence, though very durable, jade implements were very costly and partly for this reason, and partly for the beauty and scarcity of the material itself, they remained symbols of prestige after the introduction of metals.

Jade is scarce because it can only crystallize in that form under geological conditions of heat and pressure which were confined to certain faults in the earth's crust. These occurred in the Far East, in New Zealand and in Central America. Jade axes were being made by the Maoris in New Zealand, almost within living memory. According to Heinrich Harrer axes are being made from a jade-like stone in central New Guinea today. He says that the polishing takes several months.* A curious problem is set by the discovery of a few jade axes in England recently. If these are not the product of a Piltdown-type hoax, then either there must have

*Heinrich Harrer, *I come from the Stone Age*, Hart-Davis, 1964.

been a source of jade somewhere in Europe or else the axes must have been brought an unimaginable distance from the Far East, a journey comparable in its way to that of the monoliths of Stonehenge. However, as Herodotus remarked on finding Scythian artifacts in Delos, they may have 'diffused'.

The instances of effective crack-stoppers in minerals are fortuitous. When one looks at biological materials one is impressed with the enormous care which Nature seems to take over the interfaces when she is being, as it were, teleological. A good example is the construction of teeth, about which a certain amount is known. Teeth consist of a hard, tough surface layer called enamel while the interior is made of a material called dentine. Both constituents however contain elongated inorganic crystals distributed in an organic matrix and the principal difference between enamel and dentine lies in the proportion of inorganic material to organic material.

The hard part of both enamel and dentine consists of elongated crystals of a substance which is nominally hydroxyapatite, $Ca_{10}(PO_4)_6(OH)_2$, although the exact chemical composition varies widely, reflecting the environment in which it was formed, and carbonoapatite, fluorapatite, calcium fluoride, calcium carbonate and so on may be present. These crystals are quite small and in enamel are about 3,000 to 5,000 Å in length and from 500 to 1,200 Å thick. In enamel these crystals are very closely and beautifully packed together so as to constitute 99 per cent by volume of the material. They are separated by a thin layer of a very complex organic material. This separating layer is undoubtedly mainly a protein and was originally thought to be similar to keratin which is the protein in hair. It is now thought that it is a special protein unique to tooth enamel. Incidentally it changes its composition considerably between the foetus and the adult.

Dentine differs from enamel in that the inorganic part constitutes only about 70 per cent by volume. The apatite crystals are also much smaller being 200–300 Å long and 40–70 Å wide. These apatite crystals are embedded in an organic matrix which is mostly collagen.

The adhesion between the hydroxyapatite and the separating

protein layer is of a most complicated chemical nature being partly by hydroxyl bonds and partly by ionic bonds (see Appendix 1). No doubt very precise control is exercised over the interfacial adhesion and thus over the propagation of cracks. The presence of the weak organic layer, however, must enable decay to get a start and, once the enamel is penetrated, the high organic content of the dentine enables the attack to propagate fast. Apparently one cannot have it both ways. If the vulnerable organic layers did not exist teeth would not rot so easily but then they would be brittle and would probably break early in life.*

The use of hydrogen bonds, that is hydroxyl groups (—OH) (see Appendix 1) to control adhesion at an interface is very common in living organisms and it is presumably a convenient method where the environment is continuously wet. When natural materials are used by man in a dry environment difficulties arise. The drying of the hydroxyls, each of which normally has a shell of water molecules around it, leads to the shrinkage of materials like wood. It can also lead to drastic embrittlement, because the interfacial adhesion gets too strong. This can be the case with ivory, which is pretty nearly tooth material. The Parthenon in Athens contained a famous gold and ivory statue of Athene and the Parthenon must have been even hotter when the roof was on than it is today. To preserve the ivory from becoming brittle and cracking, the statue was surrounded by a shallow pool of water which, besides reflecting the light upwards on to the statue, maintained the humidity high in the naos. This pool was kept topped up, and the statue preserved, for about eight hundred years. The remains of the rim of this pool, which was only an inch or two deep, can be seen on the floor of the Parthenon today.

Thermoplastics

So far we have dealt mostly with metals and with natural non-metallic materials of various kinds. The large class of artificial non-metallic solids which we generally call 'plastics' are all based on arrangements of long-chain molecules, usually made preponderantly from carbon atoms. The earliest material of this sort

*I am indebted to Mr J. W. McLean for this account of tooth structure

was 'Bakelite', a polymer made by reacting phenol with formaldehyde; it was patented in 1906. Such materials have the advantage that they can be made permanently hard by heating them to a temperature around 150°C, for which reason polymers with this sort of constitution are called 'thermosetting'. However, because thermosetting plastics consist essentially of an irregular three-dimensional network of molecules, something like glass, they have quite a low work of fracture – seldom more than 100 J/m^2 and usually much less – and so they behave mechanically in much the same way as glass does. As we shall see in Chapter 8, the only way to make thermosetting plastics reasonably tough is to incorporate fibres of one kind or another, in other words to use them in a composite material. Although the addition of fibres is a fairly effective way of making these materials tough it does put up the cost of manufacture and it also restricts the number of applications for which they are suitable.

Many of the objections to plastics of the thermosetting type for household goods and such-like applications have been got over by the development of the 'thermoplastic' resins which came into use on a large scale after 1945. These materials are based on polymeric chains which are not cross-linked, in other words the molecular arrangement is quite different from that of glass. As the name implies they do not harden permanently but will soften repeatedly if one subjects them to some temperature between about 100° and 150°C. Although this characteristic is to some extent a handicap in that they cannot be used, for instance, with boiling water, there are very great manufacturing advantages since the stuff can be squirted out hot in the form of tubes and sections or else into an elaborately shaped mould where it can be hardened almost instantaneously by rapid chilling. These processes are known as 'extrusion' and 'injection moulding' and for many purposes they have proved the cheapest of all manufacturing methods.

Nowadays such materials exist in a great many chemical varieties and their trade names are legion though 'Polythene' and 'Nylon', together with 'P.V.C.' (polyvinyl chloride) are probably still the most popular and the best known, at least in this country. The really phenomenal success of these materials during the last thirty years or so has been due to the combination of cheap and rapid mass-production with adequate toughness – added of course to chemical inertness, lightweight and bright and cheerful, not to say garish, colours.

The text-book example of this sort of thing is polyethylene (Polythene). This consists, basically, of $(CH_2)_n$, in other words it is a linear long-chain molecule much like Figure 7.

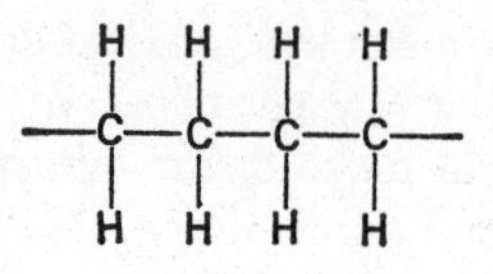

Figure 7.

Other synthetic polymers are chemically rather more complicated but, elastically, apparently not very widely different. But now consider that the E of diamond – which has similar carbon-carbon bonds – is around 170×10^6 p.s.i. (1,200,000 MN/m²). Diamond has a density of about 3·5 grams per c.c., polyethylene about 0·92; when we have made all the necessary corrections however we find that we ought to expect an E of about 10×10^6 p.s.i. (70,000 MN/m²) for polyethylene and similar thermoplastics.

In experimental fact, the E for polyethylene is around $0{\cdot}3 \times 10^6$ p.s.i. or 2,000 MN/m² – about a thirtieth of what theory predicts – and most of the other synthetic polymers are not much stiffer. What is remarkable about the text-books (which describe the chemical structure of the various chains in loving detail) is not so much that they do not explain the discrepancy but that they do not even notice it; nor are they apparently interested in the fact that the work of fracture for a material like Polythene or Nylon is at least a hundred times higher than it is for most of the thermosetting plastics.

Owing to the work of Frank and Keller at Bristol University the probable explanation is now apparent. It has long been known that the chain molecules of many natural and artificial polymers are arranged in a way which is at least partially crystalline. What emerges from Frank and Keller's work is that the nature of the crystals is different in natural and synthetic polymers. As we shall see in the next chapter, in natural materials like wood, the long-chain molecules are arranged roughly parallel to the length of the tree, that is to say, more or less in the direction of the most important stresses. This is why timber develops a good fraction of its theoretical modulus in actual practice.

In materials such as polyethylene, however, Keller finds that the long $(CH_2)_n$ chains are arranged in quite a different sort of way. In fact they are folded on themselves in a zig-zag pattern something like Figure 8, for polyethylene the fold length is usually pretty constant at about 180°Å.

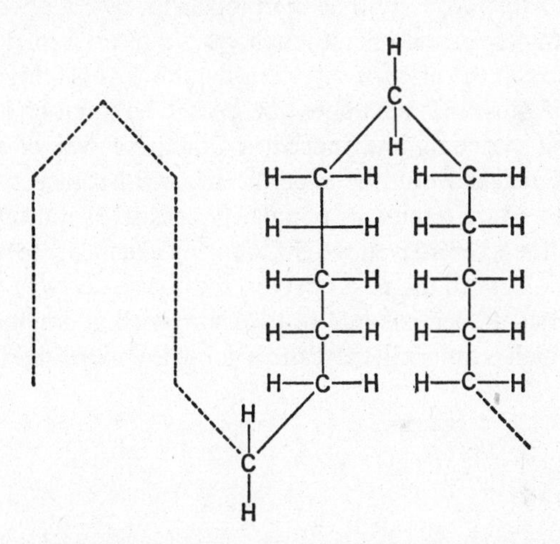

Figure 8. The long flexible chains of polymers like polyethylene frequently crystallize in a folded or zig-zag pattern.

Examining this structure with the eye of an engineer it is at once evident that very little of the stiffness of the carbon – carbon chain will be reflected in the macroscopic modulus of the plastic since the bonds which control the extension are not the covalent primary bonds but the secondary or van der Waal forces which attach the convolutions of the chain to each other.

The experimental values for the *E* of polyethylene do, in fact, fit very well with both the known stiffness of the van der Waal forces and also with that of molecular crystals of the phthalocyanine types. (Chapter 2)

Thus the folded, Keller-type crystallization results in a large reduction in the stiffness of thermoplastics of the polyethylene type. This may, or may not, be a technological handicap, depending upon what the material is meant to do. It does seem, however, that Keller crystallization is wholly beneficial in regard to the work of fracture of these materials. Before the plastic can break, many of the crystals have to unfold, rather like concertinas, and, in doing so, a great deal of energy is expended in unravelling the long molecules (Plate 13).

It is to this property that thermoplastics owe a good deal of their commercial success although, as we have seen, toughness is obtained at the price of very considerable loss of stiffness. Such a molecular arrangement does not seem to be common in natural structural materials and indeed, a Polythene tree of any considerable height would be a public menace because of its low modulus. Wood retains its popularity because it can offer much more stiffness for a given weight than any existing thermoplastic. As we shall see in the next chapter, the consequence of this stiffness is that timber has had to evolve a work of fracture mechanism which is quite different and a good deal more ingenious.

Plate 1

Chapter 1

Wells Cathedral. It has been necessary to insert these elaborate arches so as to prevent the structure from collapsing inwards.

Plate 2

Chapter 1

Cantilever beam loaded at one end. Woodcut from Galileo.
Discorsi e dimostrazioni matematiche (Leyden 1638).

Plate 3

Chapter 1

S.S. Schenectady, designed, more or less, on simple beam theory. A crack has started at the sharp corner of a hatchway on deck and has run down to the keel.

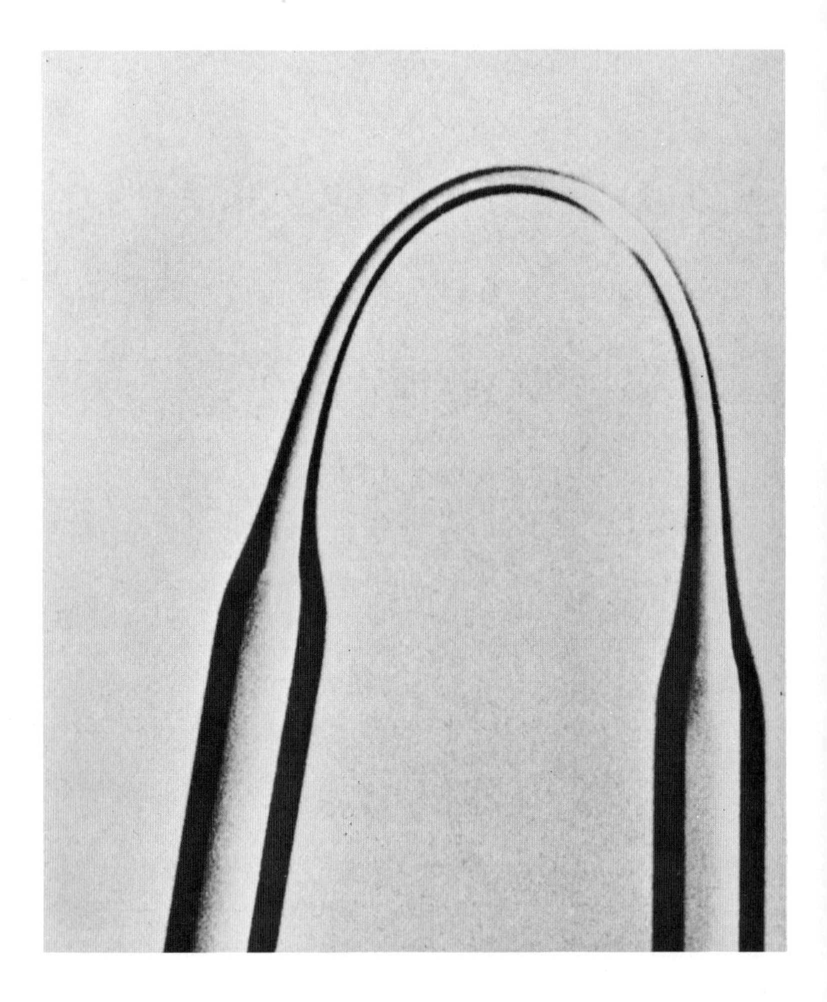

Plate 4

Chapter 3

Glass and other solids when truly free from cracks and defects can exhibit enormous strengths. This silica rod is bent elastically to a strain of $7\frac{1}{2}$ per cent, i.e. a stress of 5000 MN/m^2. (The normal strength of glass is about 100–200 MN/m^2.)

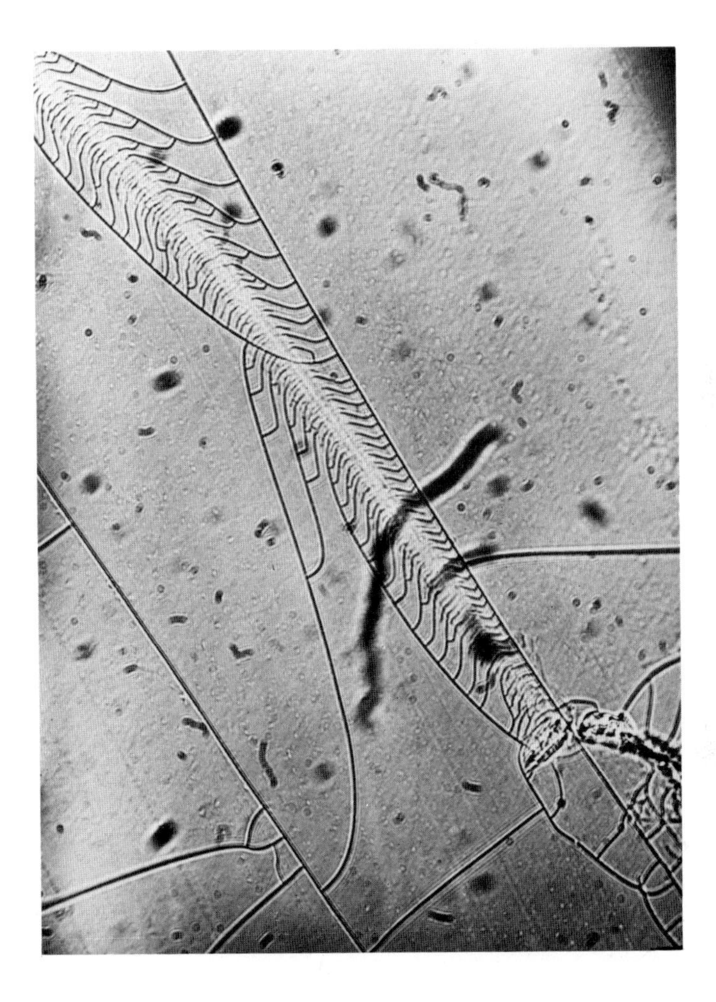

Plate 5

Chapter 4

The strength of brittle solids such as glass is dramatically reduced by surface damage. Even slight contact can cause serious abrasion. This is a photograph of cracks caused by slight accidental contact on the surface of Pyrex glass. Magnification 700×.

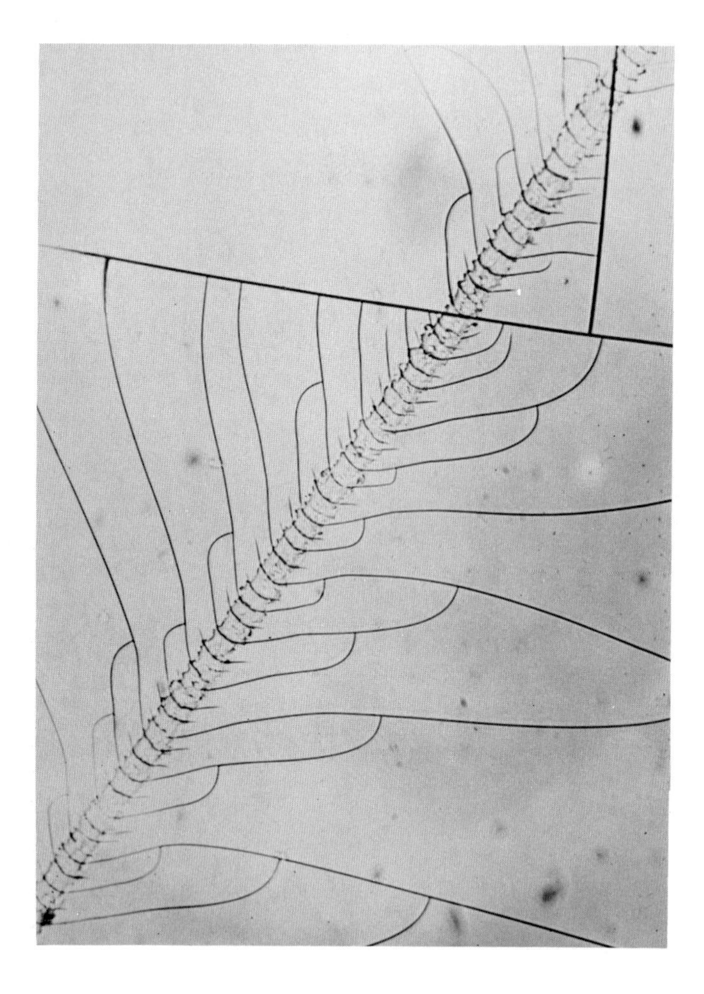

Plate 6

Chapter 4

Cracks resulting from deliberate scrape by a needle-point on the surface of a microscope cover-glass. Magnification 1000×.

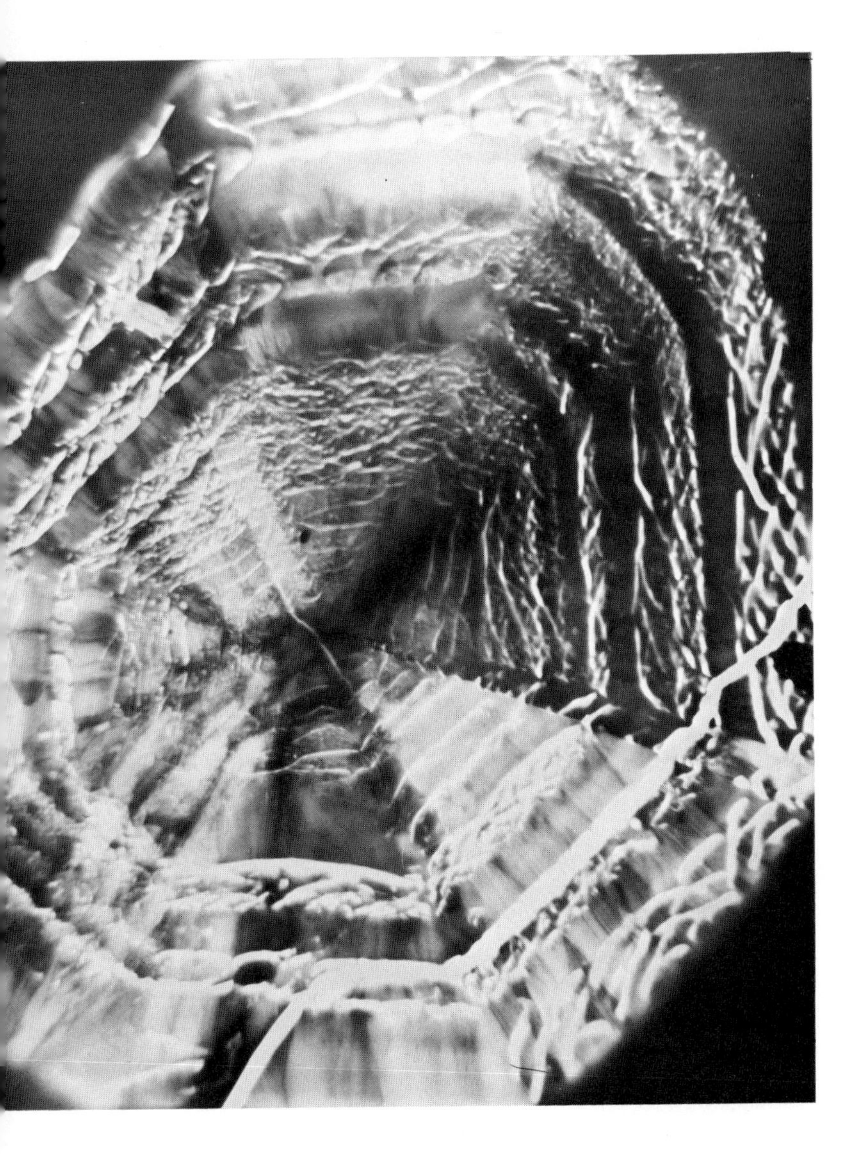

Plate 7

Chapter 4

The strength of glass can also be much reduced by 'de-vitrification', that is to say by the formation of small local crystals. The material contracts during the process of crystallization and frequently cracks in doing so. These cracks often spread from the crystalline into the glassy area. This is a photograph of de-vitrification in silica glass. The central area of the picture is crystalline and much cracked. The black areas in the corners of the picture are glassy material into which the cracks are penetrating.

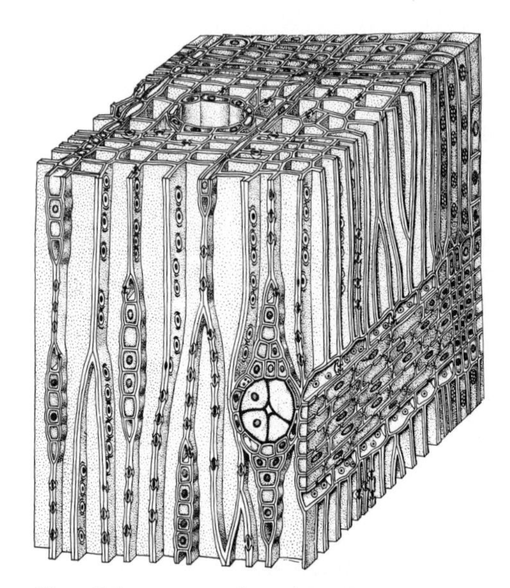

Plate 8

Chapter 6

The cellular structure of wood greatly enlarged. The grain runs vertically. The darker area further from the camera represents 'summer wood', that near to the camera 'spring wood'. A medullary ray can be seen on the right of the picture near the bottom. Magnification 100×. Courtesy of E.S.T. Mondadori.

Plate 9

Chapter 4

Tin whiskers growing spontaneously on the tin-plated surface of a radio component. This is a frequent cause of faults in electronic equipment.

Plate 10

Chapter 4

Whiskers and other crystals frequently grow by the addition of thin growth layers each of which terminates in a sharp 'step'. These growth steps on a large whisker crystal are all moving towards the bottom of the picture.

Plate 11

Chapter 5

Effect of weak interfaces in stopping or hindering cracks. Material on the left contains numerous interfaces, that on the right none. This crack-stopping mechanism is important in artificial composite materials such as fibre-glass and in wood and other biological tissues. These photographs of a copper-tungsten model material were taken by G. Cooper of Cambridge University.

Plate 12

Chapter 6

Whiskers or needle crystals of hydroquinone growing from solution in water. Note the blurred image of a whisker which has broken away from its mechanical restraints and is in the act of straightening itself. Magnification 1000 ×. (The parallel stripes are diffraction fringes and are my fault!)

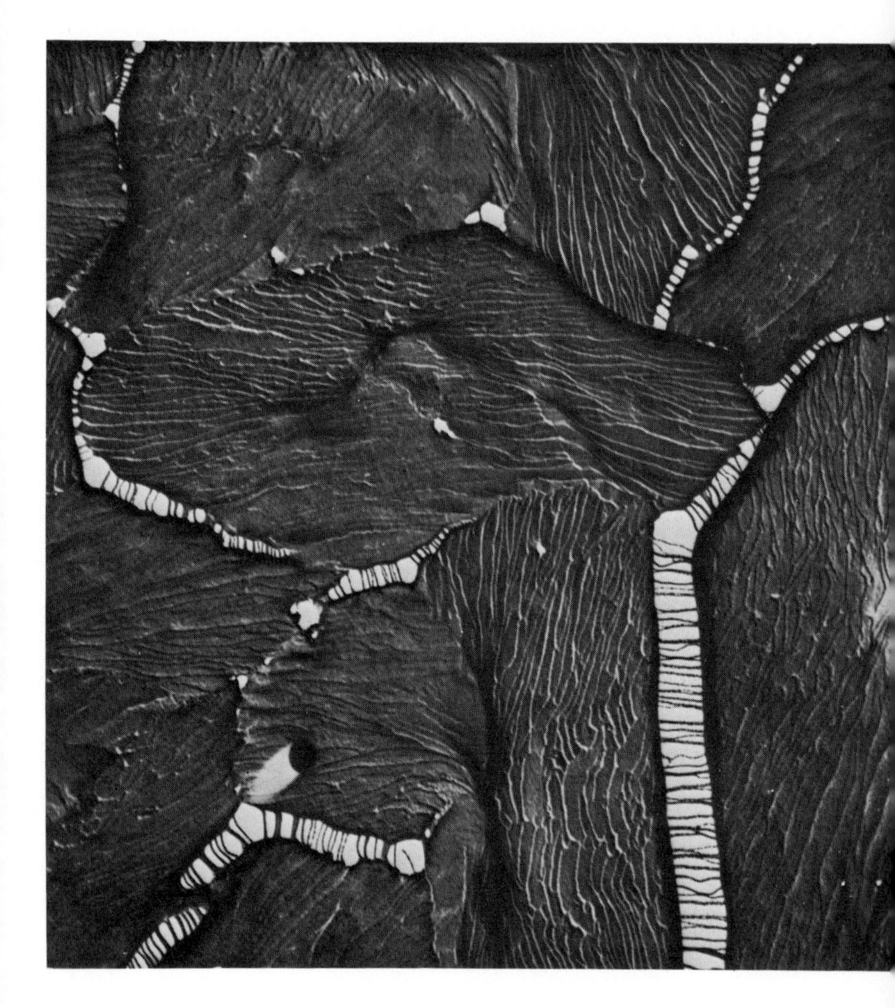

Plate 13

Chapter 6

Fracture in thin polyethylene sheet. The grey plates are crystals of folded polyethylene chains. The new cracks are still bridged by strings of polyethylene molecules which have been pulled out of the crystals. Hence the toughness of polyethylene. Electron micrograph 12,000 ×. Courtesy of Professor Sir Charles Frank.

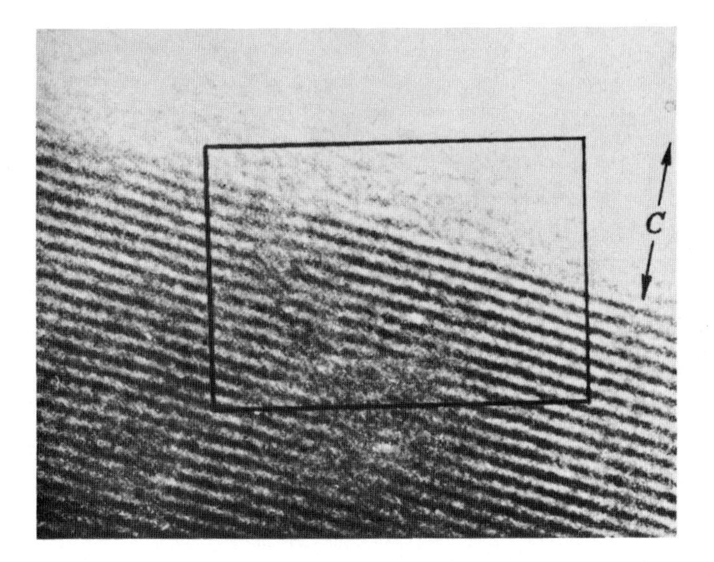

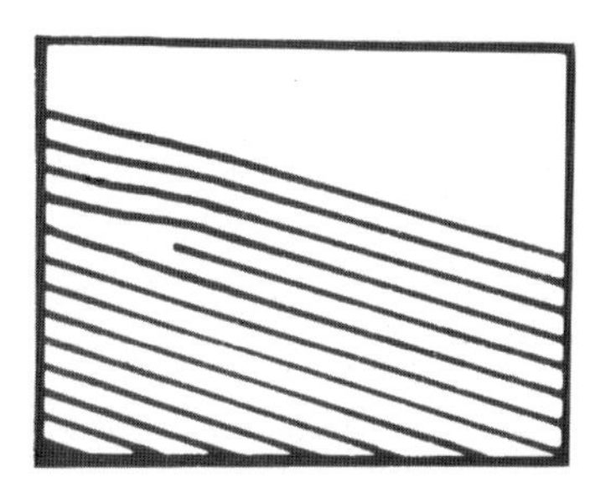

Plate 14

Chapter 9

The dislocation is the most important kind of defect in crystals, especially in metals. This is the first direct photograph of an edge dislocation. The large size of the platinum phthalocanine molecule enabled the lattice spacing of the crystal to be resolved in the electron microscope. Magnification 2,000,000 ×. Courtesy of Sir James Menter.

Plate 15

Chapter 10

Trevithick's 1805 high-pressure locomotive. This was a failure because it broke the cast-iron rails. Note that it is shown here upon wooden rails.

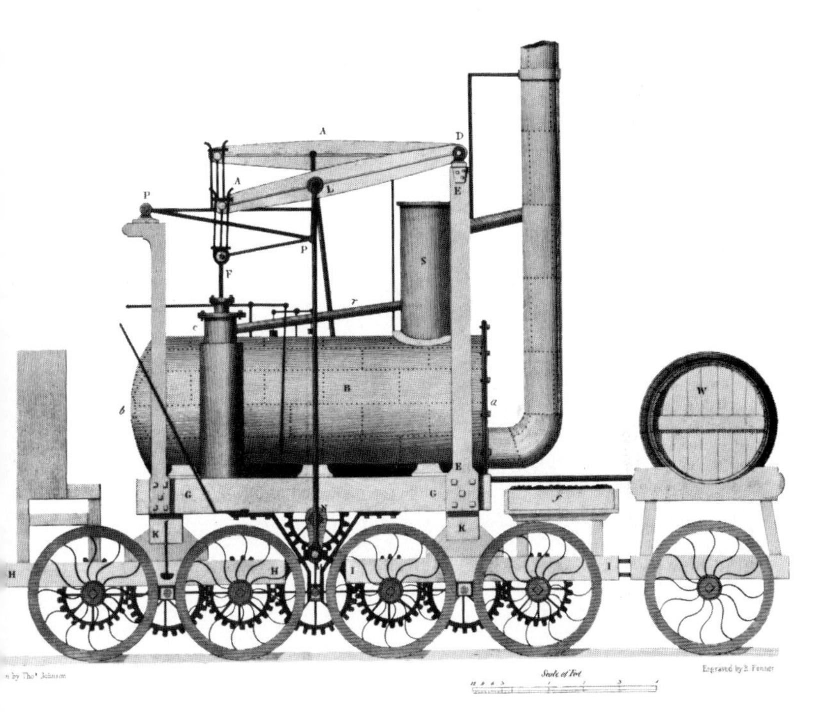

Plate 16

Chapter 10

Attempts to spread the load by using eight coupled wheels. Note that there is no springing except such as is afforded by the flexible spokes. Like other engines this one was converted back to four driven wheels when wrought-iron rails were introduced.

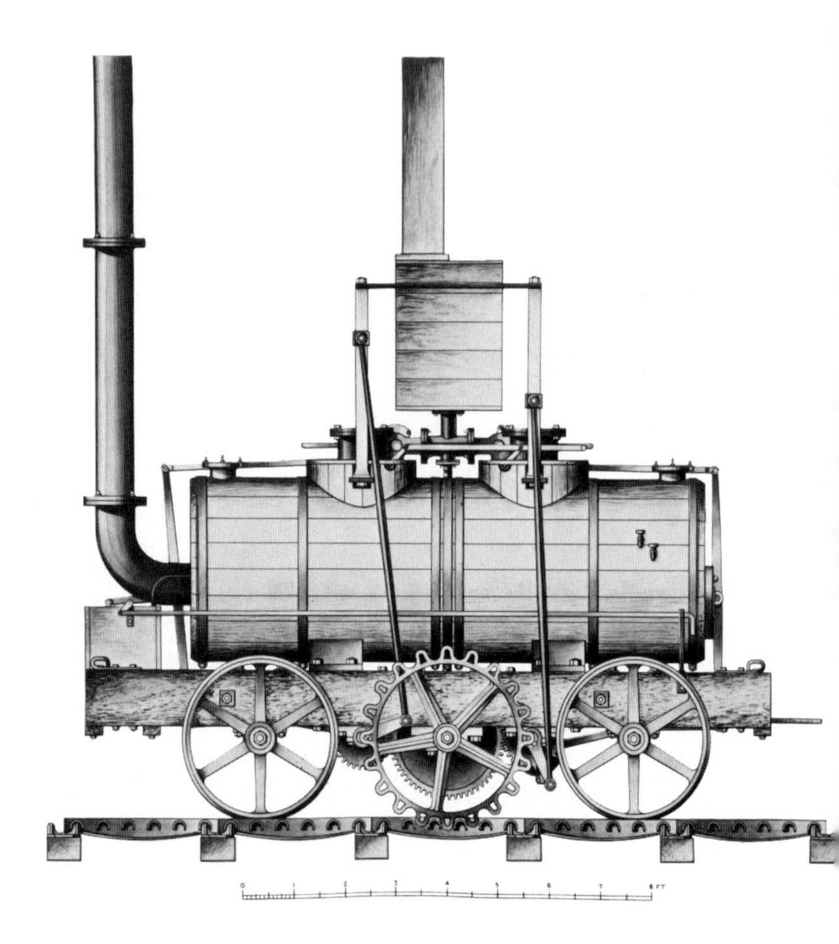

Plate 17

Chapter 10

Rack systems were popular in attempts to solve the problem of getting sufficient adhesion without putting much weight upon the cast-iron rails.

Chapter 6 Timber and cellulose

or Wooden ships and Iron men

'Plastics are made by fools like me
But only God can make a tree.'

During the war, when we were doing research on strong plastics, Professor Charles Gurney used to recite this little ditty to me nearly every day and I found it depressing because wood was in fact a better material for making aeroplanes than the plastics which we could then produce. Even today there are classes of structures such as sailplanes and some kinds of boats for which wood is still the most efficient material available.

Not only are wood and other forms of cellulose technically efficient but they are also fantastically successful, judged by any quantitative criterion. Cellulose is the structural part of all vegetable matter and it is the strength and stiffness of cellulose which displays leaves and greenery to the sunshine so that photosynthesis can take place and become the principal chemical starting point for all forms of life. Cellulose forms on the average about a third of the weight of all vegetation and the world tonnage of plants is almost beyond computation, locking up in cellulose a large fraction of the world's limited supply of carbon. Cellulose seldom occurs in animals but there is one rather dim little class of marine animals, the Tunicates, which are mostly made from cellulose. They look rather like elongated jellyfish and appear to have no structural virtues. However chitin, the structural polymer in insects, is very similar to cellulose.

When we come to the works of man, cellulose is still in the leading place. If we consider the timber which is sufficiently industrialized to get into the official statistics, the annual world consumption (not counting fuel) appears to lie between 800 and 1,000 million tons. The rough timber, fencing, bamboo, reeds, thatch and so on used by farmers and primitive people may possibly amount to nearly as much again, but naturally, no records are available. The world production of iron and steel is somewhere round 450 million tons, that of all other metals is negligible by comparison.* Since, weight for weight, the strengths of commercial steel and timber are comparable, the total of the burdens supported by wood may well be greater than those supported by steel, though no doubt many of the loads which steel carries are the more spectacular.

Since the density of wood averages about one-fourteenth of that of steel it may be that about thirty times the volume of wood is used, taking the world as a whole.

The ratio of the consumption of wood to steel varies considerably between different countries but it is not necessarily an index of the degree of industrialization or of technological advancement. England and Holland both use about 1,100 lb. of steel per head per annum as against about 700 lb. weight of wood. In U.S.A. the consumption of steel per head is about the same, 1,100 lb., but the consumption of timber per head is much more, about 2,400 lb. In Canada it is as high as 3,300 lb. per head per annum. The characteristic of less developed countries is that their consumption of both wood and steel, that is the total tonnage of their artifacts, is less.

Plant growth

Cellulose is an example of standardized production on the part of nature. Although plants vary so greatly in their shape, function and general appearance, the cellulose molecule is the same in all. It may vary slightly in length and in its physical arrangement but these are matters of detail; the chemistry is the same.

All the more advanced plants contain hollow, elongated, spindle-shaped cells (Plate 13) whose walls are made largely of cellulose. (Which is why it is called '*cell*ulose', '-ose' being the chemical termination for sugars, 'fructose' is the sugar found in

*It is rather difficult to get a comparison in money values. The relative prices of timber and steel vary greatly in different countries and also the price of timber itself varies from that of rough timber, which may be much cheaper than steel, up to expensive plywoods which cost far more than steel sheet. Again it depends at what stage of manufacture one makes the comparison. Very, very roughly, however, the cost of 'industrial' timber is about the same as that of commercial mild steel per lb.

fruit, and so on.) These hollow spindles are the fibres which take the loads and provide the strength.

Initially the simple sugar, glucose (Figure 1), is synthesized in

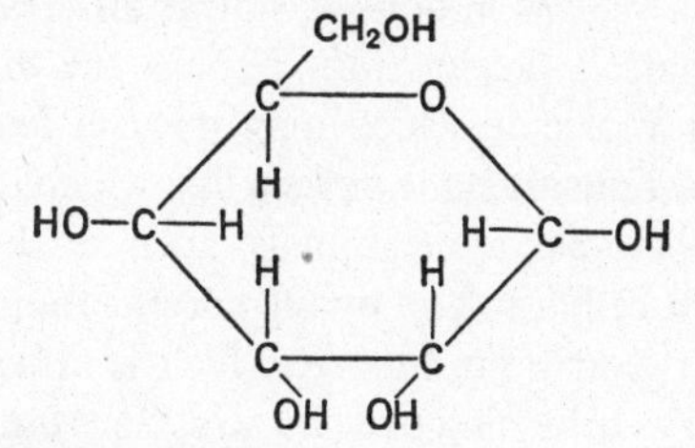

Figure 1. The glucose molecule.

leaves from atmospheric CO_2 and water by the action of sunlight on the green catalyst chlorophyll. Like other simple sugars, glucose is soluble in water (which is why it is easily digestible) because it has five hydroxyl groups (see Appendix 1) which have a strong attraction for water molecules, and also because the glucose molecules are physically small enough to shuffle around fairly freely in a liquid, provided there are not too many of them. Concentrated solutions of glucose approximate to treacle.

Glucose in dilute solution in sap-water thus passes through internal passages in the plant until it reaches a growing cell. In the wall of the growing cell the glucose molecules are joined together

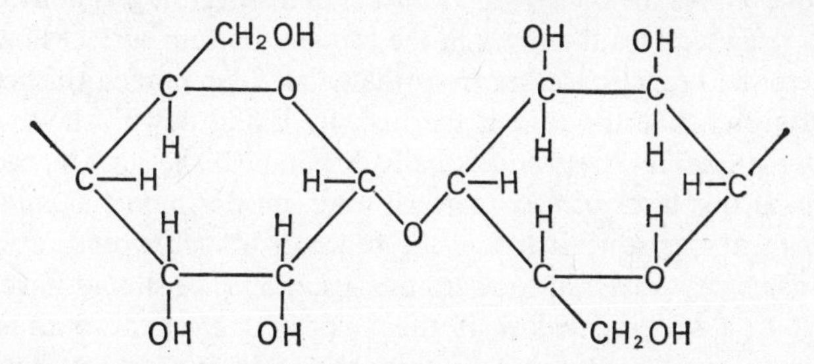

Figure 2. The cellulose chain. It is usually several hundred glucose units long.

endwise (Figure 2) by a chemical reaction known as a 'condensation reaction':

$$-OH + HO- \rightarrow -O- + H_2O$$

The result is an oxygen linkage and a molecule of water which goes off in the sap.

This process is controlled in the plant by substances called 'auxins' though how it is done is not at all clear. The oxygen linkages between the sugar rings remain the vulnerable links in the cellulose molecule which may reach a length of several hundred glucose units. It is the oxygen link which is broken by the enzymes in the stomachs of animals, such as sheep and cows, which can digest cellulose and by the various fungi or rots which attack wood. It is also the linkage which is attacked by simple chemicals, such as bleaching powder, which are used by laundries, and accounts for the gradual weakening of shirts in the wash.

The cellulose chains which are laid down in the cell-wall are long and they have their length more or less parallel to the length of the cell or fibre, that is to say in the direction of the applied stress. The growth of cellulose is altogether a very remarkable business. If we consider an ordinary tree, by the time it is a few years old it has usually acquired a number of little branches, coming out more or less horizontally from the main stem or trunk. Each of these little branches is in effect a cantilever beam stressed in bending by its own weight (Chapter 2). This means, as we have seen, that the upper surface of the branch is stressed in tension and the lower surface in compression, like any other cantilever. As the bough grows thicker and longer, it gets heavier, and this increases the stress in the top and bottom surfaces near where the branch emerges from the trunk. The branch thickens and grows, like the rest of the tree, by laying down a layer of new material all over, under the bark and near the surface, each year. If this layer of new material were put down each summer free from mechanical stresses the beam or branch would droop until the new material took up the strain and we should have a tree like a weeping willow. In the majority of trees this does not happen. The boughs grow out from the trunk at nearly the same angle throughout the life of the tree and the sapling can be regarded as a geometrical model of the fully grown tree. It follows that, in the majority of trees, the new cellulose is laid down in the cell already containing the stresses and strains which it has to bear.

Working with hydroquinone and other fairly simple soluble substances, I have grown long needle crystals or whiskers (Chapter 4) which thicken by the growth of sleeve-like surface layers which are geometrically not unlike the growth layers in a tree. The initial whisker crystal or filament is often highly bent and the growth layers can be seen to exert a very strong straightening

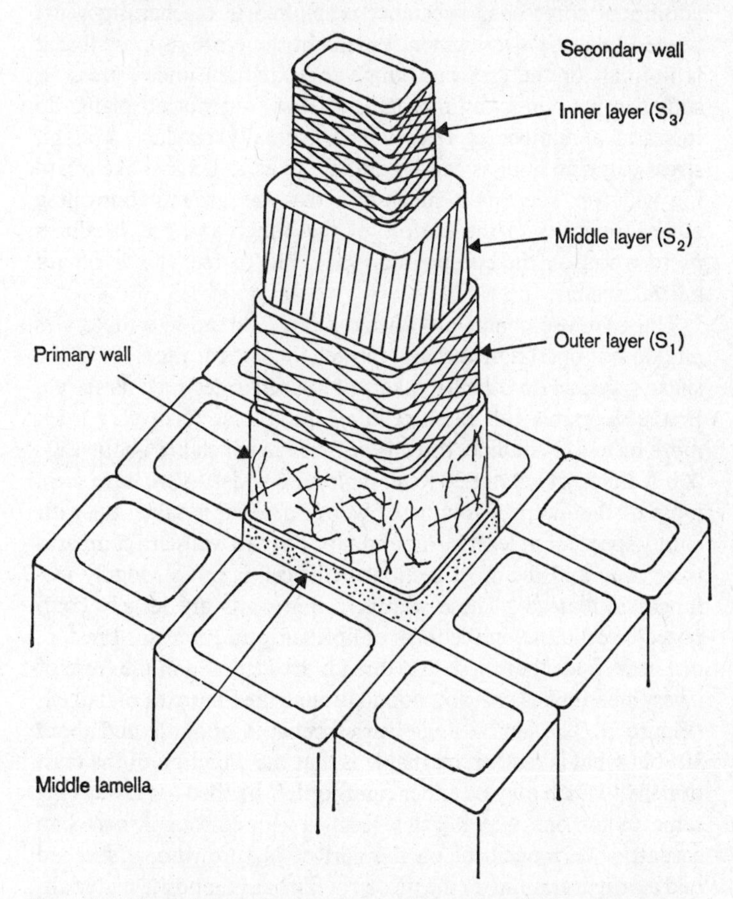

Figure 3. The cells in timber are very roughly rectangular in cross-section. The morphology of the cell walls is complicated but the disposition of the cellulose molecules and fibrillae is preponderantly helical, something like this diagram. (© Crown copyright.)

action on the bent filament, such that, by the time the sinuous initial thread has grown to a millimetre or so thick, it is invariably straight. From this it is clear that the growth layers of these crystals are formed under considerable mechanical stress if this is needed to straighten the crystal. This occurs quite frequently in simple, non-biological systems and there is no question of any additional controlling substance or biological mechanism being needed to cause it to happen. We might therefore suppose that it is normal for the growing bough to straighten under stress by some simple non-living mechanism. However, not all plants do this and a number of trees which normally produce straight, stress-carrying boughs can be grafted so as to behave like weeping willows. There is a suggestion that the growth-controlling auxin gravitates to the bottom of the bough and this produces more wood on the compression face, but to me, this is only a partial answer.

The cellulose chains are always simple thread-like molecules and do not branch by forming oxygen linkages at the sides of the sugar rings, as do other, weaker, polysaccharides such as starch. In the vegetable cell these cellulose molecules form very long, more or less crystalline, threads or fibrillae which are about 150–200 Å thick, say about 30 to 40 molecules wide. As we have seen, most of the internal volume of wood material is taken up with empty space, or at least by air and sap. The cell walls are comparatively thin and the cross-section of the cell is often roughly rectangular (Plate 8). These relatively thin walls are largely composed of cellulose, in the form of fibrillae, and Professor Preston, of Leeds, finds that these thin threads are disposed in the form of a very steep spiral or helix, wound around the long axes of the cells (Figure 3). The helical angle varies between about 6° and about 30° but what is really remarkable is that the direction of the twist or helix – which may be either right- or left-handed – is always the same in any one tree. All this seems a very curious – indeed an eccentric – arrangement on the part of Nature who, if she had had a proper training in the theory of fibrous composite materials, would surely have known better.

A little while ago Dr Giorgio Jeronimidis came to work with me on just this subject. The first thing that George found was that the work of fracture of wood was quite exceptionally high, although of course it has nothing resembling a dislocation mechanism to help it. In fact the work of fracture, *W*, turned out to be around 10^4 J/m^2, which, weight for weight, is at least as good as a ductile steel and a good deal better than 'tough' composites like fibreglass. In fact the figure is much better than one would predict from composite theory (Chapter 8), supposing wood to behave like an artificial composite. As Punch would have said many years ago, 'collapse of Stout Party'.

Since this high work of fracture – which makes trees able to stand up to the buffetings of life and which makes wood such a useful material – cannot be accounted for by any of the recognized work of fracture mechanisms which operate in man-made composites, George set out to find out what was really happening.

Now the various cells in wood are glued to each other (by means of the various non-cellulosic constituents which exist in timber) in a way which is reasonably effective, but not very effective. This is why the paper-maker is able to make a fibrous pulp for your morning paper from wood. If a crack begins to penetrate into the wood across the grain, the Cook–Gordon mechanism – which we discussed in the last chapter – comes into operation in the region around the crack tip and the various cells become separated so that each of them operates as an independent helix, something like a drinking straw. When this happens the thin walls of the tubes are able to buckle, the helical fibrillae can then straighten themselves out and so the cell is enabled to elongate under the tensile load by something like 20 per cent. Both by calculation and by experiments with model cells, George was able to show that the process of buckling and elongation absorbed a great deal of energy. This process shows great cunning on the part of Nature, also a good deal of cleverness on the part of George. It adds, very usefully, to our repertoire of work of fracture mechanisms and, as we shall see, it seems likely to turn out extremely useful in the design and manufacture of artificial composite materials.

In fact the arrangement of the cellulose molecules in wood is partially crystalline and partially amorphous. The crystalline regions are held together sideways by hydroxyls which have got rid of all their attached water molecules and once the system has locked solid into a regular crystal, the interstices of the crystal become inaccessible to water. We know that this is so because the X-ray diffraction pattern, which shows the crystal lattice spacing, does not change when cellulose swells in water. On the other hand, cellulose absorbs both liquid and atmospheric moisture very actively and this, from the engineer's point of view, is one of its worst vices.

The proportion of crystalline material in natural cellulose varies a good deal but may be about thirty or forty per cent of the whole. The non-crystalline, that is the amorphous cellulose, has no mechanism for protecting its hydroxyls from moisture, since most of them are not firmly attached to their neighbours, and so they pick up a shell, round each hydroxyl, of any water molecules which are available. This naturally reduces their attraction for each other and so the forces holding the cell wall together laterally are diminished and the cell swells. It is stopped from passing completely into solution, partly by the large size of the cellulose molecules and, more, by the fact that, in natural cellulose, the whole system is tied together mechanically by the presence of the crystals, which are water-proof and form a good proportion of the whole mass. So-called 'regenerated celluloses', such as Cellophane, are made by dissolving natural cellulose by chemical methods which break up the crystals. The resulting solution is then precipitated to form a transparent film which is largely a tangled-up felt of individual molecules, and is much less crystalline. When such films are wetted they become very flabby indeed and lose all their strength. The Cellophane which is made for wrapping and packaging is therefore protected by a very thin coating, on each face, of a water-resistant lacquer. This gives sufficient protection for its ephemeral purpose but, after prolonged wetting, such materials are hopelessly weak, whereas natural celluloses retain a good part of their strength.

The natural celluloses which we use include a very large number of timbers, bamboo, cane, flax, hemp, cotton, ramie, sisal, esparto and so on. However, as we might expect, their mechanical behaviour and especially their swelling in water and the relation between their temperature and moisture content and their strength, differ only in detail and present much the same general picture.

The properties of wood

Trees grow in all shapes and sizes and their timbers look very different. These variations are however more or less superficial and the main differences between timbers lie in their density. Seasoned balsa has density of five to ten pounds per cubic foot (s.g. 0·1), spruce around thirty (0·45), oak about fifty (0·7) and lignum vitae between seventy and eighty (1·1). With quite minor additions and subtractions the actual wood substance has in all cases about the same chemical constitution and about the same density of ninety pounds per cubic foot (that is, much the same as sugar – say 1·5).

As we have said, the main structure of wood consists of large numbers of tubular cells or fibres of squarish cross-section fitting very neatly together (Figure 3 and Plate 8). There are minor distinctions in the geometrical arrangement of the fibres in different species. For instance, some timbers, notably oak, have a certain number of fibres, medullary rays, running radially in the trunk and thus crossing the longitudinal fibres at right angles. From the engineering point of view, however, all woods may be considered as bundles of parallel tubes, rather like bundles of drinking straws. Since the tubes are made of substantially the same material the large range of density is caused by the various thicknesses of the cell walls. One consequence of this is that, to a first approximation, most of the mechanical properties of different timbers are proportionate to their densities; a timber twice as dense will be about twice as strong and so on. This is not quite true but it is roughly so.

Wood substance consists of about sixty per cent of cellulose, various other sugar compounds and lignin, a substance having affinities to a resin, which impregnates adult wood substance in some fairly intimate way. Unlignified cellulose is birefringent, that is to say, it rotates polarized light because of its highly directional nature and it also stains brightly with certain dyes. Normal wood substance containing lignin does not do either of these things.

However, immediately before mechanical failure, and before any weakness can be distinguished by mechanical methods, wood becomes both birefringent and easily stained by characteristic dyes. This is probably due to the early stages of George Jeronimidis' fracture mechanism of which we talked on page 135. These phenomena cannot be used as a warning of incipient fracture because, to observe the effects, it is necessary to cut thin sections of the stressed part and to look at it in an optical microscope. However, the method can be very useful when investigating accidents and it also serves to show how subtle is the nature of wood substance. Some tropical woods such as teak and greenheart contain small amounts of toxic chemicals and also of silica. These protect the timber from insects and rots but they also help to account for the high cost of working the best tropical woods because the silica blunts tools very quickly and the splinters of greenheart are poisonous.

As we have seen, wood depends for its defences against crack propagation partly upon Jeronimidis' work of fracture contrivance – which ensures that the critical Griffith crack length is a long one – and also, by way of a further safety device, upon the Cook–Gordon mechanism for stopping any crack which gets past George. The other mechanical properties of wood are very much what we should expect from a bundle of tubes or fibres. Laterally, that is across the grain, they separate or crush quite easily, so that the lateral tensile and compressive strengths are very low, only a few hundred pounds per square inch. The lighter woods, such as balsa, can be crushed with the finger. On the other hand, it is just because the fibre tubes can be crushed locally that wood can be nailed and screwed without splitting, provided we do not abuse the wood too much. Incidentally, nails and screws of reasonable size, put in with reasonable care, do not weaken the wood, as a whole, in any measurable way,* in other words wood is astonishingly resistant to stress concentrations.

The tensile strength of spruce, for instance, is around 17,000 p.s.i. or 120 MN/m^2 when carefully measured. This represents an elastic strain or interatomic separation of about 1·0 per cent, per-

* Dr Richard Chaplin finds that, if you take a screw *out*, the wood will be weakened in compression by the hole which is left – so leave them in.

haps between a tenth and a twentieth of the theoretical strength. These figures are much better than those for most other engineering materials, especially cheap ones. A commercial mild steel strains elastically about 0·15 per cent. Weight for weight, the tensile strength of wood is equivalent to that of a 300,000 p.s.i. steel, which is four or five times the strength of the steels in common use. In practice, as we shall see, it is not very easy to make effective use of the high tensile strength of timber.

The weakness of wood is in compression along the grain. In this respect it is the opposite of cast iron, which is strong in compression and weak in tension. Again, a bundle of drinking straws glued together provides a realistic model. Under a compressive load the thin wall of one of the tubes decides to buckle or corrugate and all the rest have to follow it (Figure 4). The com-

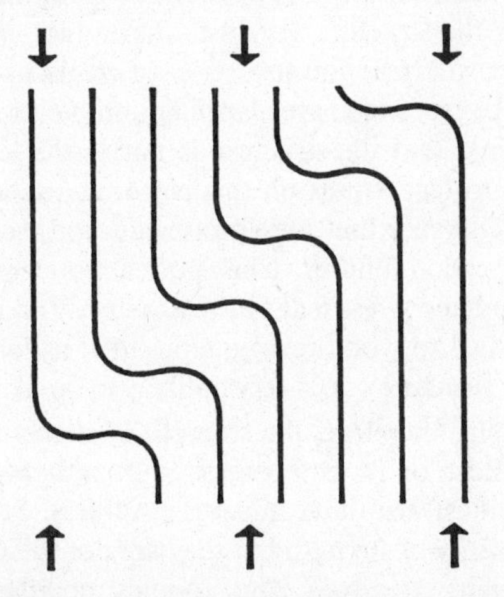

Figure 4. Compression failure in wood. On the clean, planed side-grain of the timber the failure can be seen with the naked eye as 'creases' running across the grain direction.

pressive strength of spruce generally lies between 4,000 and 5,000 p.s.i., say 30 MN/m^2. Weight for weight, this is still quite respectable, as compared with steel, but it is of course much less than the tensile strength.

When wood begins to fail in compression little lines of buckled fibres can just be seen running diagonally or across the grain but these are easily missed unless the surface is clean and you know what to look for. For some time after the initial failure nothing very sensational or catastrophic happens, the wood just yields gradually. In most cases wood is used in bending and the result of gradual crushing on the compression side of a beam is to transfer load to the tension side. In this way, the nominal stress in a wooden beam before actual collapse occurs may be up to twice the true compressive stress. It is this which makes a structure made out of timber such a safe one, generally one can very nearly get away with murder. Again, timber is noisy stuff and it will frighten the wits out of you before it is in any real danger of breaking. Sailplanes are often launched by means of half a mile or so of wire, reeled in by a winch. Having no engine, gliders are delightfully silent, except for a slight noise from the wind so that one can hear the structure very well. On a fast, gusty launch a wooden glider will treat you to a series of creaks and groans, and occasionally bangs, which are alarming until you realize that it is all pretence and that the structure is not in the least danger of breaking up. In fact it puts on this performance several times a day. I am pretty sure that these noises do not proceed from incipient compression failures. I have often wondered where they do come from but confess that I have absolutely no idea. They are however counted to wood for righteousness: as long as one can hear a timber structure one is very unlikely to break it.

For its weight, therefore, the strength of timber is as good or better than most of its competitors. Strength however is not enough: one must also have adequate stiffness. Substances like Nylon have plenty of strength but they are not sufficiently stiff to make engineering structures. The Young's modulus of spruce is about $1{\cdot}5$ to $2{\cdot}0 \times 10^6$ p.s.i. (12,000 MN/m^2) and the other timbers are, roughly, more or less stiff than this in proportion to their densities. Curiously, weight for weight, the Young's modulus of timbers is almost exactly the same as steel and aluminium and much better than synthetic resins. The good stiffness, combined with low density, means that wood is very efficient in beams and columns. Furniture, floors and bookshelves are usually best made in wood and so are things like flagstaffs and yachts' masts. The railways in America could be built very quickly and cheaply in the nineteenth century partly because of the efficiency of the timber trestle bridge.

As against these virtues, timber creeps. That is to say, if a stress is left on for a long time, wood will gradually run away from the load. This can be seen in the roof-tree of an old house or barn, which is generally concave. The creep of the wood is the reason why one must not leave a wooden bow or a violin tightly strung. The cause of the creep is most probably simply that, in the amorphous part of the cellulose, the rather badly stuck hydroxyls take advantage of changes in moisture and temperature to shuffle away from their responsibilities. It is unlikely that the crystalline part of cellulose creeps to any measurable extent.

Swellulose

No doubt it would not be beyond the wit of nature to join up the cellulose molecules sideways with primary chemical bonds so that it would be thoroughly tied together and would have much the same strength in every direction. However, as we said in the last chapter, it seems to be a condition for the strength and toughness of materials of this type that there should be planes of weakness parallel to the strongest direction. If not, wood would be something like a lump of sugar: homogeneous but weak and brittle. For its weight, there is really nothing wrong with the mechanical properties of wood and the weight of wooden structures is generally at least comparable to that of metal ones. We pay for this however in the vulnerability of wood to moisture.

Wood is affected by liquid water in the form of rain, rivers, seas and so on with which it may come into contact but, more importantly, it is affected by the moisture vapour which is always present in the air.

Air at any given temperature can hold so much moisture; any excess is precipitated as rain, fog, mist or dew. Such air is called saturated and thus the 'relative humidity' on a wet day is around 100 per cent. Indoors, or in drier weather, the relative humidity decreases, although it seldom falls much below 30 per cent even in hot dry climates.

All timbers tend to come to an equilibrium with the relative humidity of the surrounding air. Exposed for a long time to moist, saturated, air timber might settle down to a moisture content of 22 per cent or 23 per cent. In a very dry climate the moisture content might reach as low a figure as 5 per cent. Regarded as mere changes of weight these figures are of secondary importance. What is important is the effect of the moisture on the wood. The most important effect is that the wood shrinks or swells. The movement in the direction along the grain of the wood is negligible, as one would expect from the molecular structure. The cross-grain swelling and shrinkage is however very large. Every one per cent change of moisture content may cause about a half per cent shrinkage or swelling. Over the range of moisture contents likely to be reached in air the lateral dimensions of wood can thus change between five and ten per cent, that is up to an inch on a ten-inch-wide plank. Amateurs rather like to use wide planks if they get the chance, professionals are wiser and prefer narrow ones so that the movement at each individual joint is smaller. Of course one does not often get shrinkage and swelling as gross as ten per cent but as little as one or two per cent can be sufficiently troublesome. Paint and varnish slow down moisture changes in wood but they do not prevent them for no paint is impermeable to water vapour.

Even indoors, the relative humidity is changing all the time, especially between night and day. Floor boards and furniture tend to follow the humidity and this is the reason for the ghostly noises one hears in the house at night. If wood is physically restrained from shrinking when it wants to do so it will split, because it has almost no tensile strength across the grain. If it is physically restrained from swelling when it wants to swell, very considerable pressures are built up. The Egyptian method for quarrying large blocks of stone, such as Cleopatra's Needle, was to outline the shape by means of a stress concentration, in the form of a groove in the surface of the rock. Deep holes were made along this groove into which dry wooden pegs or posts were driven. These wedges were then supposed to have been soaked in water until the rock split along the required line.

The shrinkage of cordage and textiles is much the same in

principle as that of wood. Individual fibres change their thickness but not their length with moisture changes, and it is the helical geometry of ropes and textile yarns which causes rope and cloth to get shorter when it gets wet. Flax sails, especially, were very porous and sailing ships 'in chase' would wet their sails to swell the fibres and reduce the porosity.

As we see, the most important effect of moisture on wood is to cause it to swell. A rather less important effect, from the practical point of view, is to change the mechanical properties. Thoroughly wet wood has something like a third of the strength and stiffness of completely dry wood. Biological materials always operate in the saturated state: this gets rid of the problem of shrinkage and swelling at the expense of a reduction in strength. In engineering, cellulose is never used in the completely dry condition so that the range of strength and stiffness is not quite as bad as it sounds.

Wet wood is rather easier to bend than dry but the principal agent for bending wood is heat. Traditionally, wood which has to be bent for tennis racquets and boat ribs is steamed. It is often supposed that the steam does something because it is steam. In fact the steam is a convenient way of heating the wood without drying it out and the mechanism is exactly the same as that used by hairdressers for curling hair. Sometimes amateurs wrap wood in hot wet rags when they want to bend it. The wetness of the rags does not accomplish much but the wood gets heated and the rags may insulate the hot wood and prevent it from cooling too quickly. Wood will not come to much harm in moist heat below about 140° C. but, of course, in dry heat it will soon crack due to shrinkage.

Seasoning

A great deal of rubbish has been talked about the seasoning of timber by craftsmen and by romantic but ignorant amateurs. Wood, as we have said, consists of closed tubes which, in the living tree are partly full of water, or rather sap. In freshly felled wood the moisture content varies but may be over 100 per cent of the weight of the dry wood substance. About 25 per cent of this water is absorbed in the hydroxyls of the fibre wall, the remainder is liquid water inside the cell. Seasoning consists in removing most of the water in a controlled way: essentially it is a drying operation and nothing more. It is necessary to bring the wood to a moisture content which is nearly at equilibrium with the environment in which the timber is going to be used for if this is not done one must expect warping and shrinkage. For external use a moisture content of perhaps 20 per cent may be suitable, for an unheated building about 15 per cent, and for a steam-heated environment about 8 or 10 per cent.

Since the cells are closed, spindle-shaped tubes, the liquid water inside them is not very easy to get out. It can only be dried out by diffusing it slowly through the tube walls. This would present no great difficulty if one were dealing with a single cell but real lumber contains many thousands and it is necessary to diffuse the water from the inner cells through the walls of most of the other cells which lie between them and the outer world. To do this it is necessary to maintain a moisture gradient between the inside and the outside of the wood. The sharper this gradient is, the faster moisture will be lost from the inside. On the other hand if the moisture gradient is too steep the outside will be notably drier, in the intermediate stages of seasoning, than the inside and so it will shrink more and will thus split. This is why one cannot season too fast without ruining the timber. Traditionally, wood was seasoned 'naturally' in the open air or in open, unheated sheds. This might take a year or so for planks an inch or two thick and seven years for large oak ship's timbers. With primitive methods and knowledge this is about the best that one can do. One of the reasons why the better shipyards and coachbuilders were expensive was that they kept large stocks of valuable timber seasoned and seasoning.

A great deal of technological work has been done recently on the seasoning of wood, and safe accelerated drying schedules have been worked out for all kinds and dimensions of timber. By carefully controlling the drying rates in large kilns the time for seasoning can be reduced to a matter of days or weeks. Another factor which reduces seasoning time is the modern tendency, because of the existence of efficient glues, to use timber in much smaller sizes, which of course dry more quickly. Timber which has been properly kiln-seasoned (which needs expensive kilns and close supervision) is in no way worse than 'naturally' seasoned timber and indeed is rather less likely to have picked up the infections of rot during the seasoning process. However, original or commercial sin keeps breaking in and there is undoubtedly a great deal of badly seasoned wood on the market.

The moisture content of wood may be determined simply by weighing a small sample before and after oven drying. In industry it is usually done with portable meters which measure the electrical resistance between two needles pressed into the wood and thus give the answer much more quickly.

Up to about 25 per cent moisture content the whole of the water in wood is held in association with the hydroxyls in the cell walls. At about 25 per cent moisture content however these hydroxyls become saturated and the cell walls can absorb no more water; this is known as the 'fibre saturation point'. Up to the fibre saturation point the lumen or hollow part of the cell is empty of water, above the fibre saturation point virtually the whole of the additional moisture exists as loose liquid water within the lumen. All the dimensional and mechanical changes in wood which are due to moisture occur below the fibre saturation point, that is between 0 per cent and 25 per cent moisture content. After that no further swelling takes place and the additional water simply adds, very considerably, to the weight of the wood.

Wood substance has a specific gravity around 1·4 but freshly felled timber floats (unless it is a very dense species) because, even in the unseasoned wood, there is a good deal of air. Wood will, however, eventually become waterlogged and sink though, like seasoning, this takes a considerable time. The crew of the Kon-tiki raft were worried lest their balsa logs should sink under them on their long voyage although, in the event, the soakage was not very great. The American clipper ships of the 1850s, the famous 'soft-wood three skysail-yarders', became water-soaked within about ten years by which time they had no doubt paid for themselves very handsomely. The hardwoods from which English ships were usually built are more resistant to soakage and there are several instances of wooden ships afloat and in service for over a hundred years.

Rot

Rot is caused by fungi which live parasitically on cellulose since fungi have no chlorophyl and cannot photosynthesize sugars for themselves. The spores of various fungi are nearly always present in woodwork, just as the germs of many diseases are present in our bodies, but they do not become active unless the conditions are favourable. Rots cannot flourish if the moisture content of the wood is below 18 per cent although the spores can remain alive in quite dry timber, waiting for a rainy day. Even when the moisture content rises above 18 per cent the fungi may not grow if the ventilation is good. As the moisture content of the wood in an unheated structure may be around 15 per cent, it only requires a small amount of damp in an unventilated corner to get the rot going. One cannot always control moisture content but one can generally arrange for ventilation and this is usually a sufficient preventative.

Many chemical treatments are effective in killing active fungi in wood but, in an old and complicated structure, the practical difficulty may be to reach the diseased parts without pulling the whole structure expensively to bits. If the rot is accessible one can generally arrange for ventilation anyway.

In the cyclic natural scheme of things some kind of decay is essential, otherwise not only would the earth be cluttered with the stems of most of the plants which have ever lived, but most of the world's supply of carbon would be locked up in cellulose so that life could not be carried on. This is a general objection to the use of biological materials by man for nature's planned obsolescence may be in conflict with ours.

Wooden ships

'*But not long after there arose against it a tempestuous wind called Euroclydon. And when the ship was caught, and could not bear up into the wind, we let her drive. And running under a certain island which is called Clauda, we had much work to come by the boat: which when they had taken up, they used helps, undergirding the ship; and, fearing lest they should fall into the quicksands, struck sail, and so were driven.'*

Acts of the Apostles, Chapter 27.

The wooden sailing ship was *par excellence* the artifact which made the expansion of Western civilization possible and thus, more than any other device, was responsible for our present condition. Wooden sailing ships explored the world and later surveyed it. They carried passengers and troops, emigrants, convicts and slaves. They carried gold and coal, machinery and books, tea and wool, cotton goods and cheap tin trays, not only to the ends of the earth but also round the coasts and up the rivers. For hundreds of years the ship of the line was the ultimate argument of kings, frequently used. Ships like this are not things of a dim past, there were first-class passenger sailing ships on the Australian run within living memory* and there are Admirals alive who first went to sea in wooden sailing ships.

Although about the middle of the nineteenth century large improvements were made in both the hulls and the rigs of ships, for three or four hundred years before that the basic methods of construction remained nearly constant. The two controlling facts were that wood swelled and that metals were expensive.

Large ships were heavily framed from 'grown' timbers. That is to say the curved members, such as ribs, were built up of naturally curving wood, chosen to have the right shape. The watertight skin and deck were put on over this closely spaced framework of ribs and beams in the form of planks, nearly as thick as they were wide, which ran longitudinally at right-angles to the ribs. The

*The last major wooden (actually composite) *passenger* sailing ship seems to have been *Torrens* which ceased carrying passengers to Adelaide in 1903. Iron and steel sailing ships of various lines were carrying first-, second- and sometimes third-class passengers to Australia well into this century. Contrary to modern popular opinion these were splendid ships with excellent accommodation and many modern conveniences for both crew and passengers. Steamship competition was the cause of many hardships in cargo sailing ships but passenger sailing ships had to compete by offering more comfort. See for instance ***Painted Ports*** by A. G. Course (Hollis and Carter, 1961). The largest wooden, sailing, cargo ship – the six-masted schooner ***Wyoming***, of about 6,000 tons burden – was built in America in 1910.

planking and the underlying ribs thus formed a rectangular trellis with no diagonal bracing or shear members. The edges of adjacent planks were not fastened together mechanically but stood open so as to form a V-shaped groove.

Into this groove oakum, made by picking old rope to pieces in the prisons and workhouses, was driven by means of a mallet and a caulking iron which is a chisel-like tool with a groove along the edge. Outside the caulking there remained an open groove between the planks nearly half an inch wide. In the case of decks this had to be 'payed' which was done by running in hot pitch from a special ladle. When cold the surplus pitch was sufficiently brittle to be scraped off, leaving those pleasing black lines in the deck.* The bottom and topsides were payed or stopped with a putty-like composition. The point of all these arrangements was that the flexible caulking could accommodate shrinking and swelling of the planking, and to some extent movement of the hull, without leaking very much.

The whole structure was, and to some extent was intended to be, quite flexible, almost like a basket. Besides accommodating the shrinkage and swelling of the skin planks, it was supposed, perhaps correctly, that the flexibility of the hull contributed to its speed and sea-kindliness; certainly the Viking ships and the Polynesian canoes were even more flexible. When the much more rigid 'composite' constructions came in in Victorian times one or two of the racing clippers were built with hulls of deliberately controllable rigidity. Of one such ship her rivals would say, as she drew ahead, 'They've unscrewed the beams and we shan't see her again today.'

This was all very well and most wooden ships were watertight in harbour but, without exception, they all leaked when they got to sea. The rate of leakage varied from 'enough to keep the bilges sweet' to something very serious indeed. In spite of all the centuries which he had to learn about it the traditional shipwright seemed to be unable to understand about shear. Any shell structure subject to bending and torsion puts heavy shears into the skin and bending and torsion are just what a ship, especially a

*The Devil, incidentally, was a particular seam and the correct expression is 'the Devil to pay and only half a bucket of pitch'.

sailing ship, receives at sea. The orthodox ship construction was like a five-bar gate without the diagonal member.

Since there was no official way of taking the shear it was taken, unofficially, by the caulking which was squeezed and relaxed alternately, like a bath sponge. Occasionally, but surprisingly rarely, the labouring ship spat the caulking from some underwater seam, in which case she probably foundered. More often she just leaked and leaked and leaked. The danger was then, not that she would sink immediately, but that the crew would become exhausted from continual pumping and general misery, after which anything might happen.

When the situation became intolerable an attempt might be made to undergird or frap the ship by passing cables under the hull as St Paul describes in the Acts of the Apostles.* It has been done repeatedly since and very likely, in some corner of the ocean, an Arab dhow is being undergirded at this moment. The whole point of the undergirding cables was to provide some shear bracing and so unless the operation was done with a knowledge and accuracy which were rather unlikely in the circumstances, so as to get the cables roughly at forty-five degrees, the expedient probably had usually as little effect as it seems to have had upon Paul's ship.

As far as the Royal Navy were concerned the nuisance of excessive leakage was largely put a stop to when Sir Robert Seppings (1764–1840) introduced diagonal iron bracing into wooden hulls about 1830. Seppings, who used to say 'partial strength produces general weakness', seems to have been one of the first Naval Architects to have a clear mental picture of the stress systems in a ship's hull. In the merchant service wooden hulls were to a considerable extent replaced by composite and iron and steel construction after the middle of the century. A number of wooden ships continued to be built without adequate shear bracing, however, and such ships got more leaky as they got older, until, in an age when most of the pumping was done by hand, it became uneconomic to run them any longer. Up till 1914

*The word translated as 'undergirding' is 'υποζώννυμι in the Greek testament and it is quite clear that the operation was familiar both to the ancients and to the translators of the Authorized Version.

Norwegian shipowners were still making money by buying up British sailing ships and running them with windmill pumps.

In spite of their faults, wooden sailing warships were in use for between three and four hundred years and were abandoned by Admiralties with reluctance because they were, in their context, most effective and economical weapons. They had a range and endurance, an independence of overseas bases and an ability to vanish indefinitely into vast spaces which we have only lately regained with the atomic submarine.

Fleet actions were rare, and strategic pressure was generally exerted by blockade and by the threat of a 'fleet in being'. However, until the middle of the eighteenth century it was considered impracticable to keep fleets continually at sea throughout the winter because of the severe and rapid deterioration in the condition of the ships. However, these difficulties were overcome by the efforts of devoted officers. To anyone familiar with the coasts, with sailing ships and with the cellulose molecule, the maintenance of the blockades of Brest and Toulon, winter and summer and in all weathers, must appear as an almost incredible feat. 'Those far-distant, storm-beaten ships, upon which the Grand Army never looked, stood between it and the dominion of the World.'*

Rope and spars came mostly from the Baltic states and the convoys got through with difficulty. Although the blockading squadrons very rarely saw the French they had daily and hourly to struggle with rope and canvas and timber which stretched and broke and rotted. Nelson wrote 'I have applications from the different line of battle ships for surveys on most of their sails and running rigging which cannot be complied with as there is neither cordage nor sails to replace the unserviceable stores and therefore the evil must be combated in the best manner possible.' In spite of this, Mahan wrote 'For twenty-two months Nelson's fleet never went into port, at the end of that time, when the need arose to pursue an enemy for four thousand miles, it was found massed and in all respects perfectly prepared for so sudden and so distant a call.'

*Captain A. T. Mahan, *Influence of sea power upon the French Revolution and Empire*, 1892.

When a sailing ship has a fair wind, even though it be a gale, the loads in her rigging are moderate. However when she is heeling and lurching her way to windward the aggregate of the tensions in the shrouds and stays which support the masts is comparable to the ship's displacement and may thus amount to several thousand tons. Until the middle of the nineteenth century the whole of this load, equivalent to the weight of many railway trains, had to be carried by hemp ropes which were always shrinking and swelling, rotting and stretching so that it called for great skill to avoid the loss of some or all of the masts and spars. There was therefore an understandable reluctance to undertake regularly long voyages to windward in rough weather. A voyage round Cape Horn, for instance, was quite different in character to the routine voyages to the East coast of the Americas or even to India. Bligh's crew, for example, in the *Bounty* mutinied after one appalling attempt to beat round the Horn in which the ship could barely be held together structurally. Eventually Bligh had to turn round and run in the other direction, right round the earth, into the Pacific. Bligh, though unpopular, was a superb seaman and, if he could not succeed, probably nobody else could.

Wire standing rigging was introduced into the Royal Navy in 1838. Its adoption by the merchant service seems to have been fairly gradual (and was not complete until the 1860s) because about this time hemp rope was improved by being laid up, or twisted, mechanically, and thus much more tightly, so that the creep was considerably reduced. By chance the introduction of better rigging more or less coincided with the gold discoveries in California. About half of the emigrants and all of the heavy cargo went by sea and by then numerous clippers were prepared to beat regularly from New York to San Francisco in a hundred days. In the years 1849 and 1850, 760 sailing ships beat round Cape Horn carrying between them 27,000 passengers. It is difficult to determine what proportion of these ships had wire rigging and which used the improved hemp but in any case it is clear that the West was largely won with better rope.*

Another important development was in the matter of chain

*Incidentally wire mining-ropes were introduced in Germany in 1830 and did much to make deep mining safe and economic.

cable. Hemp anchor cables have certain advantages but their drawback lies in the space needed to stow them; the enormous ventilated cable tiers in H.M.S. Victory are impressive. Chain, which was introduced in 1811, could be stowed in a small damp locker and so it can almost be said that chain cleared the space needed below for engines and coal bunkers.

When ships were slow and there were no dockyards on the other side of the world, the fouling of ships' bottoms by weed and the attack on timber by boring animals was a serious matter. Both problems were solved to a large extent by the introduction of copper sheathing about 1770. This did more than any other eighteenth-century innovation to increase the speed and range of ships and it was so successful that shipowners were most reluctant to use iron hulls which could not be coppered directly on account of electro-chemical action between the iron and the copper in salt water. Some iron hulls were sheathed with wood and then coppered. This was popular for warships but it made for a heavy hull. Many of the best racing clippers were therefore composite built. *Cutty Sark* (launched 1869) is planked with teak and greenheart bolted to wrought-iron frames, with adequate shear bracing. The bottom was sheathed with a brass alloy called Muntz metal. There are people who consider this arrangement as being the most perfect construction yet devised for ships of medium size. This may well be true but it is unfortunately also a very expensive one.

The fall in the cost of iron and steel plates in the 1870s made composite shipbuilding uneconomic and, towards the end of the nineteenth century most of the world's deep sea cargo was carried by big sailing ships of almost standardized construction with steel hulls, steel decks, steel spars and steel rigging. Such ships were completely watertight and could be manned by small crews. The loss of speed from their rougher bottoms was compensated by the fact that they could be sailed harder than wooden ships in blowing weather. Over the centuries officers had had to nurse their wooden ships for structural reasons and this had provided a certain measure of protection against excessive sail-carrying. Hard driving clipper captains regarded their new ships as unbreakable and, when expostulated with, would reply 'Hell, she's iron isn't she?' Quite a number of iron and steel ships were driven under and lost by this attitude of mind.

Steamships were in a minority until about 1890 and in any case tended to take the shorter voyages. Of course plenty of wooden steamships were built but the tendency was to turn to iron and steel earlier than in the case of sailing ships. This may have been partly because iron hulls resisted the vibration of the early engines better than wooden ones and also because fouling was less of a problem with continuous speeds and shorter voyages. It is the becalmed sailing ship which fouls quickly.

Orthodox wooden construction is still being used today for fishing vessels, minesweepers and yachts of up to four or five hundred tons. For racing yachts it generally provides the lightest of all hulls and it is also the cheapest way of getting a 'one-off' design built. In its cheaper forms it still suffers from the classical trouble of intolerable leakage in bad weather, especially because of the much higher loads put into the hull by modern rigs. It is true that it is possible to get over this by good workmanship and sophisticated construction but then the cost is higher than that of building in steel or plastics.

Chapter 7 Glue and plywood

or mice in the gliders

*'When all else fails
Use bloody great nails.'*

Until recently the fact that the strength of engineering materials is usually only between one and five per cent of the strength of their chemical bonds was of little practical significance because the joints between the various component parts of structures were so inefficient that even the strength which the material had was scarcely used. Properly made knots and splices in rope are from forty to eighty per cent efficient; that is, the joint has that fraction of the strength of the continuous rope. Nailed, bolted, screwed, pegged or dovetailed joints in wood are far less efficient than this, at any rate as the joints are generally made. In pure strength, apart from their flexibility, the lashings, sewings and bindings used by primitive peoples, and by seamen down to recent times, are more efficient than metal fastenings, indeed sledges are still made in this way. About 1920, flying boat hulls were made by sewing them together with copper wire.

Wood-screws, beloved of amateur carpenters and boatbuilders are the least efficient of all joints. Between the wars the Germans did a good deal of research on nailed joints and also invented new and clever forms of mechanical connectors. This information is sometimes used today in building wooden houses but, on the whole, mechanical connexions of all kinds have been driven out by modern glues which have made the efficient use of wood possible but have introduced problems of their own.

Glue

Various pundits and committees have made a great mystery about gluing. In fact the elementary theory is simple enough, it is the practice of gluing which is difficult. As we said in Chapter 3, all surfaces have an energy, just because they are surfaces, and this applies both to solids and to liquids. If we consider a solid and a liquid separately, each being in contact with air, then of course each surface has its own surface energy. If now the liquid is brought into contact with the solid, so as to wet it, then the energy of the interface between the solid and the liquid will be less than the sum of surface energies of the two surfaces when they are in contact with air. Thus wetting involves a reduction of energy and will take place whenever the liquid is given the opportunity to meet the solid.

After it has wetted the solid surface, the liquid may be hardened, by freezing it or otherwise. If this is done, the energy of the interface will not be greatly changed and to remove the hardened liquid mechanically will now need strain energy and therefore a mechanical force. Thus, in principle, adhesion is very like cohesion and there is no great difference between the stick of a glue and the strength of a solid. The surface energies of glue-solid interfaces are generally rather less than the free surface energies of strong solids, but not very greatly so. In fact this difference is not usually of much consequence because in both cases the practical strengths are well below what they ought to be. The causes of weakness in adhesion are rather less understood at present than they are in cohesion but no doubt they are generally similar in character.

Any two solids can therefore be glued together if we can find a liquid which will wet them both and then harden. The difficulties which arise are practical ones. Wood can be glued very well by wetting it with water which is subsequently frozen. Such joints are said to pass most of the tests in the specifications for wood adhesives. Hide glue or carpenter's glue may be considered as a variant on ice in that the melting point is raised to a more practical temperature. Hide glue is the same as table jelly, except that less water is added to the gelatine, which may be made from hide, hooves, bones, fish and so on. A stiff solution of gelatine melts in a heated glue-pot at 70° or 80° C. After it is painted onto the wood it sets very quickly as it cools and the joint is soon firm. Unfortunately the process is easily reversed by heating the joint or by soaking it in water. Gelatine is also excellent food for fungi and bacteria. For these reasons hide glue or Scotch glue is only suitable for use indoors. Nevertheless it was used in the early aeroplanes and an attempt was made to protect it by binding the joints with varnished tape which was never very effectual. Until lately, fishing rods were glued with hide glue which was hardened and rendered partially waterproof by soaking the rods in formalin. This treatment was of no use for aeroplanes because it could only be used when the component was small enough for the formalin to penetrate.

Bad as they were, gelatine glues were better than the alternative, the gums or starch glues which were made by boiling some kind of flour in water. Rather strangely, a much better glue had been known but unregarded for centuries. Casein was used as a glue in ancient Egypt and as a vehicle for pigments by the medieval painters. In modern times it was used as a glue from about 1800 in Germany and Switzerland. Why it was not introduced into engineering earlier is not clear. Casein became a recognized adhesive in aircraft and yacht work some time around 1930. Its use made the modern wooden aeroplane, and the Bermuda rig in yachts, practicable.

Casein is the whey in milk and is therefore similar to cheese. Whey is soluble in alkaline water but not in acid. It is thus precipitated from milk by any weak acid, in the nursery notably by rhubarb juice, in industry usually by weak hydrochloric acid. The precipitated whey can then be redissolved in water containing, say, a little caustic soda. On the other hand, casein will react slowly with lime to form an insoluble chemical, calcium caseinate.

Casein glue, therefore, is sold as a white dry powder consisting of dried whey, caustic soda or something similar, and lime. When the powder is mixed with cold water it first of all dissolves to a creamy white paste and then slowly sets to a hard solid. As a glue it is easy to use and nearly foolproof. The only thing that upsets it is leaving the lid off the tin for long periods during storage when the reaction to calcium caseinate takes place prematurely because moisture gets in.

Casein joints set hard in a day or two and are more or less waterproof. However, although calcium caseinate is not soluble in water it does soften to some extent after soaking. Casein glues were very widely used during the war in aircraft and one day somebody discovered that the tensile strength of specimens of wet casein is one-fifth of that of dry casein. It was not unreasonably feared therefore that the strength of wet aeroplanes glued with casein might also be one-fifth of the strength of dry aeroplanes. Because of the resulting flap we got hold of a hundred similar wooden casein-glued tailplanes. Fifty we sunk in a pond for six weeks, the other fifty we kept dry. In the meantime a jig had been prepared such that the tailplanes could be broken under loads not dissimilar to those they would meet in the air. When all was ready we broke the lot. To our surprise and to many people's relief, they all broke at about the same load, the strength of the wet and the dry ones being very much the same.

The reason for this happy result is instructive. The stress distribution in a glued joint is very far from uniform and, in a typical joint, such as Figure 1, virtually the whole of the load is

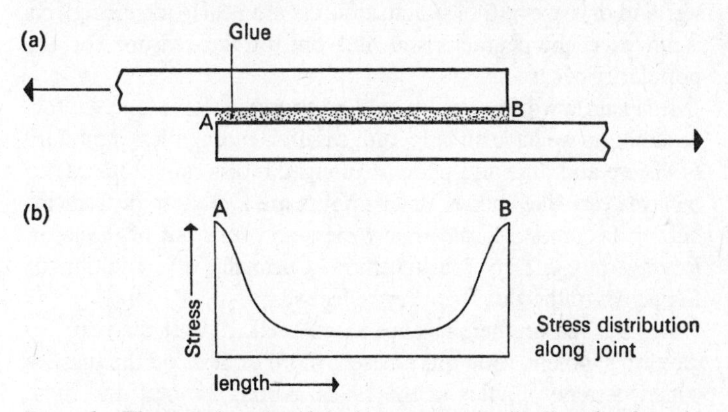

Figure 1. The stress in a glued joint is very unevenly distributed and nearly all the load is transferred through the ends of the joint.
(a) Glued lap joint.
(b) Distribution of stress along joint.
A and B show points of maximum stress.

carried in the extreme ends or edges of the joint. Very little load gets across through the middle. This is merely a variant of our friend the stress concentration which governs so much of engineering and materials science. As a consequence, incidentally, the strength of a glued joint does not depend upon the area of the joint, but mainly upon its width. This is just as true of a mechanical joint as it is of a glued joint and most of the load in such joints comes upon the first and last bolts or rivets. This is one of the reasons why a designer's life is a hard one.

Now dry casein is a hard, brittle substance which transmits loads in the best style of Mr Hooke. When the stress at the ends or edges of the joint reaches the strength of dry casein therefore, cracks appear at the edges of the joint which immediately produce their own private local concentrations of stress, and so the cracks run through the middle of the joint, much as they would in glass. Damp casein is very like damp cheese and its elastic behaviour is anything but Hookean. As a result, it just yields in a soggy sort of way to the concentrations of stress at the edges of the joint and the load is shared by the glue in the middle. With a glue like casein the various effects cancel out so that the wet and dry strength of practical joints are nearly identical. This is an excellent characteristic and one of the reasons for the popularity of casein.

In a sterile world casein would be nearly an ideal glue. Unfortunately, as we have already said, casein is more or less a mixture of cheese and lime and under prolonged moist conditions casein behaves very like cheese. Its last hours are like those of Camembert; it becomes a liquid smelly mess and runs out of the joint, leaving only a dirty mark behind. Curiously, the addition of fungicides to the glue is not very effective.

For this reason there has been a great effort, over the years, to develop synthetic resin glues based, more or less, on the plastics which became popular in the 1930s. About the best and most durable of these, in the early days, was phenol-formaldehyde or 'Bakelite'. This was available in the forms of either a treacly liquid or a dry powder. Under heat and pressure, the powder would melt and both it and the liquid would then set permanently to a hard, insoluble solid nearly immune to decay. Where hot-setting conditions could be used, phenol-formaldehyde became the basis of a series of really excellent glues. Since it is essential, not only that the glue should be heated to about 150° C. but also that there should be no appreciable gap or space in the joint, the gluing operation had, in practice, to be carried out in a heated hydraulic press. For this reason it was really only suited to the manufacture of plywood, for which it was immensely successful.

Although phenol-formaldehyde glues resulted in good waterproof plywood, they left the problem of the gluing of joints in the assembly of aircraft and boats unsolved, since it is generally impracticable to heat the joints of large structures in a controlled manner. It is true that phenol-formaldehyde resins can be set in the cold but this requires large additions of a chemical catalyst, or hardening agent. These catalysts were strong acids which damaged both the wood and the workmen.

The first synthetic assembly glues were therefore of the urea-formaldehyde type which could be set with much weaker catalysts. Although successful in their way, the earlier glues of this kind were structurally rather dangerous. When used in a properly fitting, thin joint they were reliable enough but, when the joint fitted badly so that the glue-line was thick, the shrinkages and internal stresses set up when the glue hardened often caused the glue to craze and to fall to bits in the joint. As it was impossible to inspect the inside of the joint after manufacture this was a potential cause of accidents.

Another trouble was that, once the catalyst or hardener had been added to the glue, setting began, so that the safe working life of the liquid glue was a matter of minutes. Moreover there was no infallible way of telling how long ago the hardener had been put in. With the usual frailty of human nature this led to all sorts of mistakes. This defect was ingeniously got over by developing a hardener which could be painted by itself on to one half of the joint while the glue was painted on the other half, nothing began to happen in the glue until the two halves were brought together. As a further guard against human frailty the hardener, and occasionally the glue, were dyed characteristic colours.

This is about as far as the development of glues had got by the end of the war. Excellent and highly waterproof plywood was universal. For assembly glues the arguments were about even between casein and urea-formaldehyde. Casein was nearly foolproof in application, of excellent strength both wet and dry, but rotted catastrophically when it got the chance. Urea was resistant to rot but in these early forms was tricky to apply and rather apt to fall to bits without warning in middle life. Since then, urea glues have been much improved and we have two new synthetics in particular, resorcinol formaldehyde and epoxy resins which, though they are rather expensive, have nearly all the technical virtues, bearing in mind however that epoxy resins frequently cause dermatitis.

Among the dozens of glues now available the arguments for and against are mostly on the grounds of ease of application, durability and cost. With all reputable glues the joint, when properly made, is stronger than the surrounding wood. Typical failures exhibit a thin layer of wood covering the glued surface. The strength of a well made glued joint in good condition is not increased by nailing or screwing the joint in addition to the glue. On the other hand, all glues need to be tightly clamped while they set and the simplest way to do this is generally to assemble the wet joint with nails or screws; having once done this, there is no particular benefit in taking the fastenings out afterwards.* Furthermore, a joint in poor condition may peel, like a banana skin, and the presence of mechanical fastenings is a great insurance against this. In the old days, with casein, it used to be said of some of the aircraft in the tropics that they were held together by the assembly brads. In most cases this was slander but I have seen instances where it was not far from the truth. Where glues are concerned, I, personally, would not scorn to wear both a belt and braces.

Laminated wood and plywood

One of the troubles with wood has always been getting it in the right sizes and making sure that it is free from hidden defects. Years ago one could buy great logs of Kauri pine from New Zealand, yellow pine from Quebec and so on which were virtually perfect but those days are long gone. Nowadays most of the wood which is used in engineering is laminated in one way or another. This means that it is cut up into comparatively small pieces which are then glued together again, usually in hydraulic presses with synthetic glues. In this way members of any size can be supplied and practically the whole volume of both large and small trees is made use of. Furthermore any serious defect is seen

* See *Structures*, Penguin Books, 1978, Ch. 13.

and rejected. Such members can quite easily be made in curved shapes and a not uncommon obstruction on the roads of England is a lorry carrying vast timber arches for some architectural project. The shortage of high-grade timbers for aircraft and boat-building would have been a serious matter during the War if all these woods had not been 'upgraded' by lamination with perfectly satisfactory results.

These laminated woods were simply ordinary timber cut up and glued together again. There existed, however, a distressing class of material known as 'improved woods' which had very much the properties and fate that one would expect from so hubristic a name. In these materials the wood was impregnated to a greater or less extent with a resin and then compressed to a considerably higher density. The intention was that the mechanical properties would be thereby improved; they were, but generally only in proportion to the increase in density, at the same time much of the toughness of wood was lost. Worst of all, they liked to swell back to their original dimensions in water and this swelling was generally unpredictable and irreversible. To be fair, these materials performed a useful function for a time in the propellers of Spitfires and similar aircraft.

Plywood is a different story and can almost claim to be a new material and a most successful one. It is made by gluing together three or more veneers, or thin sheets of wood, with the grain directions crossed. Veneers are made either by slicing or peeling. In the case of sliced veneers a baulk of timber is clamped and slices are peeled off it by a machine very like a large plane. With peeled veneer, a round log is heated in a steam pit for about twenty-four hours and then set up and rotated in a lathe in which a long knife peels the veneer circumferentially at a speed which is wonderful to watch. The veneer is cut up, dried, the defects are removed and finally stacks of plywood are glued in large presses.

The early plywoods were glued with vegetable or blood glues and, having virtually no moisture resistance, the word became almost a term of abuse. The introduction of phenolic glues changed all this and, incidentally, presents an interesting picture of the way in which the public image of a material can be changed. Modern phenolic glued plywood is quite impermeable to water, in the sense that the veneers will not come apart when it is soaked, and it has become an important material in modern boatbuilding.

As one would expect, the dimensional movement due to moisture changes is about halved. In other words the maximum movement, which now occurs in both directions, is around five per cent and in practice generally a good deal less. However, when the surface veneers dry, as in the hot sun, they are subjected to cross-grain tension and may thus 'check', that is produce a large number of small cracks. These, in themselves, do not do much harm, but in unpainted ply they form little traps for moisture and bacteria and so lead to trouble. Most of the original infections in plywood are killed in the hot pressing process, but if the material is subsequently exposed to bacteria or fungi and water it will rot quite quickly.

Wooden aeroplanes

It is generally a mistake to despise any form of construction and this certainly includes the 'stick and string' biplane. The main factor which governs the choice of materials and structural form is the ratio of the load on the structure to its dimensions. When the loads are comparatively small in relation to the size it is generally best to concentrate the compression loads into a few compact, rod-like members and to diffuse the tensions into fabric and cords. This is clearly the case in the rigs of sailing ships, in tents and in windmills and with certain variations it is true in balloons as well. Any other arrangement would be heavier, more expensive and inconvenient.

All the early aircraft had very low wing loadings for sufficient reasons. Their actual dimensions were, in many cases, not much smaller than those of equivalent modern aircraft, but their weights were less than a tenth of modern, hard-skinned machines. In the circumstances, a construction of fabric over a wire-braced framework of wood or bamboo was logical and efficient, and sometimes, nothing else would have got off the ground with the power available. The biplane form enabled efficient lattice girders, and also an efficient torsion box, to be achieved in a very robust form with little weight. The solid members needed only to take compression and since the principle danger in this condition was buckling, such components required to be as thick as possible for their weight and for this purpose bamboo or spruce was especially suitable. The numerous tension members could be simple piano wires. The problem of tension joints in bamboo, however, was always a serious one.

This philosophy produced strong and excellent aeroplanes so long as one was quite sure which members were in tension and which in compression, for, though a strut could at a pinch take tension, a wire could not take compression. In some of the more elaborate biplanes it was not always easy to tell which way the loads were going and it was a stock joke at one time that the way to check the rigging of a certain aircraft was to put a canary between the wings; if it got out something was wrong. S. F. Cody, of the 'Cathedral' biplane, was addicted to elaborate rigging and furthermore, not very technically minded. My grandfather, who was one of the aircraft pioneers, told me that he had a long argument with Cody about whether a certain member was in tension or in compression in flight. Cody maintained that it was in tension and had provided a wire. It turned out that my grandfather was right for Cody was killed a few minutes afterwards for just this reason. By some kind of irony this was exactly the reverse of the trouble with masonry cathedrals which fell down because they turned out to be in tension when the builders held that they were in compression.

It took some time, and many lives were lost, before the stressing conditions to which an aircraft is subject were sufficiently understood. In this country this achievement was largely due to the group of highly intelligent young men who were gathered together at Farnborough in the famous Chudleigh Mess in the first War. The principles of stressing and testing aircraft have remained much the same from the days of wooden biplanes down to supersonic fighters although there are many differences in practice.

When an aircraft has been designed and built a full-sized specimen must be tested for strength and stiffness. Stiffness testing is relatively simple but strength testing may involve engineering which is both heavy and difficult. In the 1914 period the custom was to turn the aircraft upside down and then to load the wings with bags of sand or lead shot distributed so as to represent the various aerodynamic loads which occur under the worst conditions, such as pulling out of a dive. Quite soon the loads on aircraft got too big for this method (though shot-bags are still used from time to time for certain simple tests) and nowadays the loads are applied by means of hydraulic jacks operating through very elaborate multiple lever or 'family tree' systems; each of the hundreds of branches ends in a mechanical attachment to the wing surface. There are so many of these attachments that the diffuse nature of the aerodynamic load is imitated (Figure 2).

In its better forms, such as the Avro 504 and the various Moths, the wooden biplane was almost everlasting* and the structure

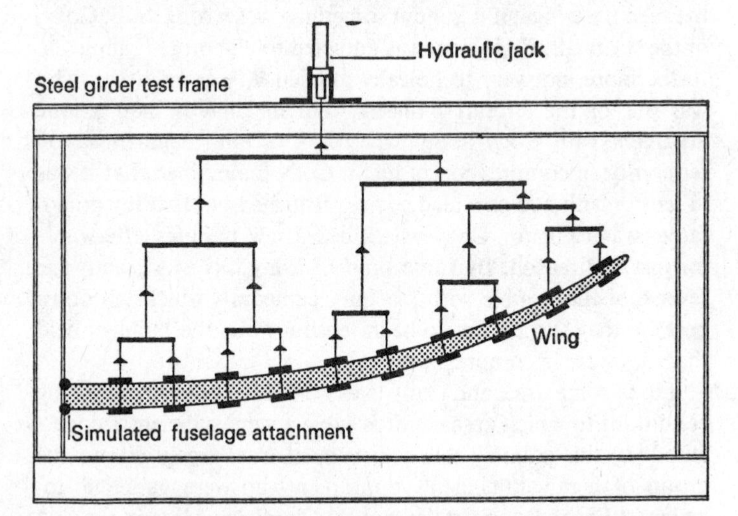

Figure 2. When an aircraft wing is to be tested, it is mounted by its root fitting in a large steel framework. Many hundreds of attachments, distributed over the wing surface in both dimensions, are used. In this way the effect of aerodynamic pressure is imitated.

*These wooden biplanes are much longer-lived than motor-cars. There are still plenty of Tiger-Moths about – presumably 30 or 40 years old – and only the other day (1975) I saw a de Havilland Rapide – a twin-engined cabin biplane – flying around very happily; it had probably passed its fortieth birthday.

could really only be broken by flying it into the ground. The feeling of structural security about flying in strutted and braced aircraft was very comforting but unfortunately did not always extend to the engines with which they were fitted. Cantilever monoplanes felt much more dangerous.

As loads increased the general trend of design was however undoubtedly towards monocoque, or hard-skinned, monoplanes in which the loads, as far as possible, were taken in the skin. There is no difficulty about taking tension in a thin membrane, the problem is how to take compression without causing the skin to buckle. In practice this was done by a compromise, the thin skin being stiffened by attaching to it spars and stringers, with which it shared the load, the whole rather elaborate surface forming a shell stiff in bending and therefore unlikely to buckle.

The outstanding early example of this was the D.C.3, later known as the Dakota, and this was followed by the Spitfire and by many of the famous aircraft of the last War. All these were metal aircraft, built of aluminium sheet to which were riveted L-shaped aluminium stringers. This system proved almost exactly equal in structural efficiency, that is in weight, to wood and fabric with the advantage of a smoother outside surface and the almost total elimination of airframe maintenance.

This construction proved very successful and, with minor modifications, is still the standard way of making aeroplanes. By 1939 it was widely believed that no more wooden aeroplanes would be built and this might have come true if the War had not created shortages of aluminium and of the machinery and skilled men for handling it. Furthermore there were furniture firms short of work and again the development time for a wooden aeroplane has always been much shorter than that for a metal one.

One expert achieved unwanted fame by stating, categorically, that it was no longer technically possible to build modern aircraft out of wood. The ink was scarcely dry upon this document when the Mosquito appeared. This wooden aeroplane was one of the most successful aircraft of all time, and 7,781 of them were built. It was probably more detested by the Germans than any other Allied plane.

Besides the Mosquito and a large number of trainers, the other big production of wooden aircraft was of gliders. Most of these were large machines with spans up to 110 feet (33 metres), frequently made to carry tanks and other heavy equipment. The original idea was that the gliders should be built to make one flight only. This turned out to be impracticable, partly because they were needed for training and also had to be moved between aerodromes because of changes in the strategic and tactical situation, but also, more importantly, just how do you build an aeroplane for one flight only? In practice the gliders became much like any other aeroplanes, except that they had no engines.

On the whole the wooden aircraft were extraordinarily successful and I suppose that we could hardly have won the War without them. Far too many of them, however, soon started to produce technical problems of one kind or another which almost immediately swamped the tiny number of experts in organic materials who were available at the Royal Aircraft Establishment. It was most fortunate that a young Cambridge biologist called Mark Pryor was extricated by the powers that be from a searchlight unit and sent to Farnborough to take over this work. The fact that the accident rate in wooden aircraft was kept to a reasonable figure and that enough gliders arrived in France in adequate structural condition was due in a considerable measure to Mark Pryor. Quite a number of soldiers and airmen owe their lives to his interminable wartime journeys between his microscope and the aircraft factories and airfields.

Given all the circumstances, it is difficult to see how most of the problems which arose could have been foreseen. The old fabric biplanes were entirely satisfactory but then they were made out of small pieces of wood, they were well ventilated and they were kept in good dry hangars. None of these conditions applied to wartime aircraft. First of all the new machines were of monocoque construction with comparatively heavy spar-booms and stringers rigidly glued to thick plywood webs and skin. We shall come to the further consequences of this construction shortly. Its immediate result was to divide the aeroplane up into a large number of badly ventilated and inaccessible compartments. As the aircraft were left out 'dispersed' most of the time in English or in tropical rain these compartments soon became little damp boxes, often with a puddle at the bottom. Rot, either in the glue or the wood or both, was only too likely within a few months. It is not very easy to arrange ventilation schemes when the designer has forgotten to do so and often the best that could be done was to arrange to leave the inspection doors open when on the ground.

Many aeroplanes, however, collected loose water inside, often in the most inaccessible places. The cure was to provide drain-holes, not just anywhere, but at the lowest point in each compartment. This was done with almost no result. It turned out that mechanically drilled small holes in plywood were fringed on the inside with a little coronet of splinters which could not be removed because it could usually neither be seen nor reached. These splinters soon collected enough dirt and fluff to block the drain holes and there we were with a puddle again. The cure for this turned out to be to burn the drain-holes with a red-hot skewer which, of course, gives a clean edge to the hole. Obvious, when you have thought of it. This solution was applied both to aircraft and to Motor Torpedo Boats, which had much the same troubles as wooden aircraft. The burnt drainage holes did a lot of good, but there seemed to be no cure for mud. Mud is apt to be thrown up by aircraft wheels in landing and taking off, muddy water enters the aircraft through drainage holes and all sorts of other orifices and then the water drains out, leaving a film of wet mud. This often contains the seeds of grass and other plants which before long sprout, like mustard and cress on a damp flannel. Internal gardens do no good, of course, to aeroplanes.

On the whole these troubles were less severe with powered aircraft than they were with gliders. Powered aircraft naturally flew more frequently and the consequent draughts were good for the aeroplane and bad for the fungi. More and more gliders were being produced all the time and it was quite impracticable to house them all in hangars, so they stood endlessly around the edges of airfields in the rain, waiting for an invasion which might come this year or might come next. As rather over 5,000 gliders were built in this country it was not possible for 'experts' to inspect them all continually so Mark Pryor issued instructions that he should be informed if they stank.

Now an unpleasant smell in a wooden structure is due to one of three things; drains, mice or rot and they all smell very similar. Drainage smells arose because there weren't any drains and could cause damage. Mice entered aircraft in pursuit of sandwich crumbs, usually under the floorboards. By the time they had eaten up the crumbs they had forgotten the way out and in their hunger ate the insulation from the wiring. Mark dealt with mice by obtaining an official issue of cats. Rot was more complicated and difficult. In all the circumstances some rot of some kind was almost inevitable in a good proportion of gliders. Perfectionism is out of place in war and the practical problem was to condemn and ground those gliders which were dangerously attacked and to detect and stop the rot in those in which the attack was trivial. This called for a great deal of judgement because there are about forty different species of rot, and the damage which they do varies and is not necessarily proportional to the visible effects.

Problems of rot were always with us but there were other problems as well which were just as serious. As I have said, the general structure of these aeroplanes was quite different from the old fabric biplanes. The main spar booms and other main structural members were sizable pieces of laminated wood, several inches square, and were generally boxed in on three sides by the plywood skin and shear webs. Now the spruce spar boom wanted to shrink and swell about twice as far as the plywood which was glued to it and this naturally gave rise to serious stresses near to where the two met along the glued joints (Figure 3).

Large pieces of timber take some considerable time to come to equilibrium with the surrounding humidity and, because the English weather changes so often, there was generally no time to build up dangerous differences in swelling strains so that we had comparatively little trouble from this cause, so long as the aircraft were in this country. When they were sent overseas the situation was different. In many climates there are long dry seasons followed by long wet seasons, each season giving ample chance for the wood to dry out thoroughly and then, in due time to soak up a great deal of water and swell. In such places there

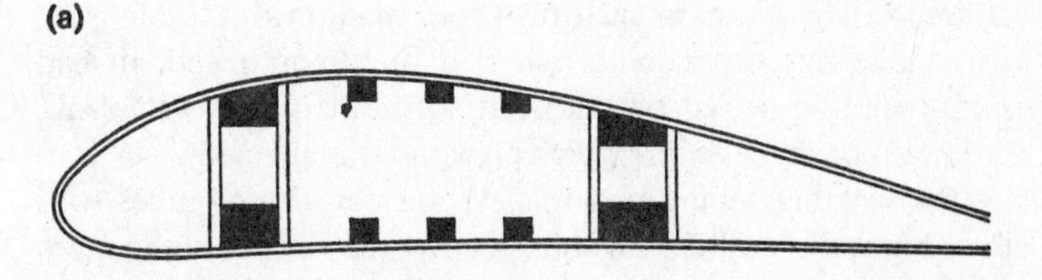

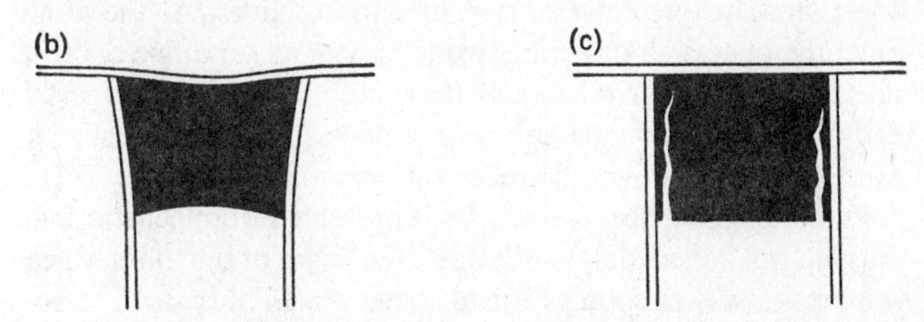

Figure 3. Effect of moisture changes upon the structure of a wooden aircraft wing.
(a) Diagrammatic cross-section of typical World War II wooden wing.
(b) What happens when the spruce spar booms shrink more than the plywood skins and webs.
(c) The final result – fracture of spruce spar boom or else glue failure.

was serious trouble. Big stresses were built up near the glue-lines; if the glue was in bad condition it broke; if not, the wood failed near the glue. There was really no cure for this except to bring the aircraft home.

Gluing troubles arose, not only from the glues themselves but from other causes. The worst of these was the so-called 'case-hardened' failure. It will be realized that there is no way of testing a glued joint which actually forms part of an aeroplane except by breaking the aeroplane, which is a self-defeating activity. One is therefore guided to a considerable extent by the appearance of the joint and also relies upon the inspection procedure during manufacture.

Soon after wooden aircraft went into large scale production it began to be realized that a proportion of aircraft plywood was ungluable. The joints in such plywood, made with all due care, looked like any other joints but had no strength and, in bad cases, could be peeled off with one's little finger. Worst of all, there was no way of telling which plywood was affected.

What was happening was this. Wood consists of tubes with quite thin walls and when wood is cut on the side grain the tubes are very seldom accurately parallel to the surface. Such a surface therefore consists of a large number of tubes emerging at a fine angle so as to present an array of slanting holes. At the same time, the operation of cutting wood is, viewed on a fine scale, a brutal one and the cut edges of the tubes are therefore damaged and mechanically quite weak. For a wood glue to be effective it has to penetrate down the tubes for some distance so as to get hold of the undamaged wood. If it is prevented from penetrating, the glue will adhere only to the damaged edges of the tubes which will break away as soon as a load comes on. In the case of 'case-hardened' plywood the edges of the tubes are bent over and turned inwards by the hot plattens of the press which makes the plywood, so that the glue is prevented from penetrating and the joint has no strength (Figure 4).

This is a very lethal condition and has been responsible for a great many accidents and much loss of life. The only reliable cure for it is to sandpaper off the damaged surface of the plywood. The sanding must be done thoroughly, merely scratching the wood is no good. Since one never knows what plywood is affected it is absolutely necessary to sand *all* plywood which may find its way into an aeroplane. This turned out to be a major administrative problem. It proved impossible to rely on hand sanding and a system of mechanical shot-blasting was instituted, after which the plywood was dyed or stamped to indicate that it was safe to use.

Wood is not a material which suffers fools gladly and a great deal of the trouble with wooden aeroplanes was due to wooden people. This could occur at all levels. Some designers felt that wood 'ought' to behave like a metal. If they made a mistake on this account then it was the wood's fault, not theirs. Engineer Officers, or at least the more recently joined ones, were brought up to consider metal the thing and sometimes had no patience

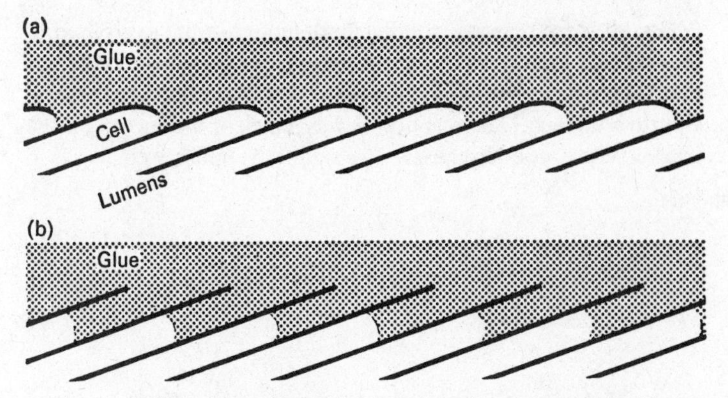

Figure 4. Many accidents could be traced to the use of so-called 'case-hardened' plywood in aircraft. Plywood can be rendered 'ungluable' as a result of heat and pressure during the manufacturing process. The cure is to sand the surface thoroughly before using the plywood.

(a) 'Case-hardened' plywood. Emergent edges of cell walls are burred over during hot-pressing preventing adequate entry of glue into the tubes of the wood.

(b) Properly sanded plywood. Glue is enabled to enter cell lumens in considerable depth and thus to provide a reliable joint.

with wood. There was the Engineer Officer, in civil life a garage proprietor, who lined up his wooden aeroplanes on the tarmac every morning and had them well hosed down.

In the factories, experienced inspectors were few and overworked. Some mistakes were due to genuine misunderstanding or fatigue; others I am afraid can only be accounted for by criminal stupidity or irresponsibility. There are always a few people for whom the most obvious sequences of technical cause and effect have no meaning. Gluing is not so much a skilled job as a responsible one and a large number of mistakes are available to a determined man, all of which can have dangerous results.

Herein, I think, lies the real difficulty about wooden aeroplanes. If they are wanted at all they are probably wanted in large numbers and to be made in a hurry by unskilled labour. Wood, which is really a craftsman's material, does not take kindly to the inevitable abuses of an emergency.

For all these reasons wooden aeroplanes are under a cloud at the moment. However it would take a brave man to prophecy that they will never come back. One never can tell where wood will turn up next. There is now a very efficient motor car on the market with a wooden chassis. It is said to be selling well.

Chapter 8 Composite materials

or how to make bricks with straw

'Then the officers of the children of Israel came and cried unto Pharaoh, saying, "Wherefore dealest thou thus with thy servants? There is no straw given unto thy servants, and they say to us 'Make brick': and, behold, thy servants are beaten; but the fault is in thine own people."

'But he said "Ye are idle, ye are idle: therefore ye say 'Let us go and do sacrifice to the Lord'. Go therefore now, and work; for there shall be no straw given to you, yet shall ye deliver the tale of bricks."'

Exodus, Chapter 5.

Ever since Pharaoh had labour troubles about putting straw into bricks there have been reinforced materials of one kind or another although they have only come into prominence as strong materials quite recently. It seems probable that the purpose of putting chopped straw into the Egyptian bricks was just the same as that of the Inca and Maya in putting plant fibres into their pottery, that is to prevent cracking when the wet clay was dried rapidly in the sun. Egyptian bricks were not fired in an oven but since it hardly ever rains in Egypt this did not matter very much. Clay, of course, makes a nice plastic paste when it is wet but the shrinkage on drying is considerable and the problem of drying clay is very much like the seasoning of timber. If it is not done slowly the clay will crack. The Egyptian sun is an excellent agent for drying clay but also a very rapid one and a little straw is effective in controlling and reducing the consequent cracks. It is most likely that the reinforcing effect of the fibres on the clay after it had hardened was incidental.

However, even quite small additions of fibre do have a considerable effect in improving the strength and toughness of weak, brittle materials and there are a great many instances of this. For instance it used to be the habit of English builders to add a little hair to household plaster. I remember being told, as a child, by a workman that bull's hair was much better than cow's for the purpose because, of course, bulls were stronger than cows. I have never made any actual experiments with either bull's or cow's hair and so I cannot pass any opinion on the subject but I have put paper pulp into plaster of Paris. The results, which are excellent, are shown in Figure 1. The trend of improvement in

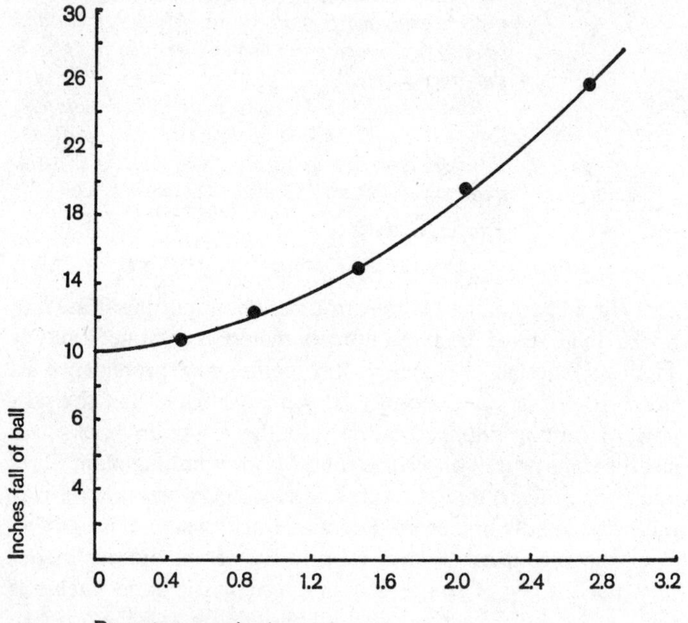

Figure 1. Brittle solids are often made much stronger and tougher by the addition of quite small amounts of fibre.
Effect of added paper fibres on the impact strength of plaster of Paris.

impact strength, that is to say in work of fracture, is steeply upwards and even very small additions of fibre make a big improvement. Unfortunately, adding fibres to wet plaster very rapidly thickens it and somewhere between two and three per cent of fibre results in a paste which is too stiff to mix. To some extent this difficulty can be got over by using a different type of cement and by consolidating it in a hydraulic press. Figure 2 shows the effect of asbestos fibres in a phosphate cement very like the cements dentists use in one's teeth; the results are much the same except that we can get more fibre in and thus more strength and toughness.

For a time during the Battle of the Atlantic the worst shipping losses were taking place in the central parts of the Atlantic where

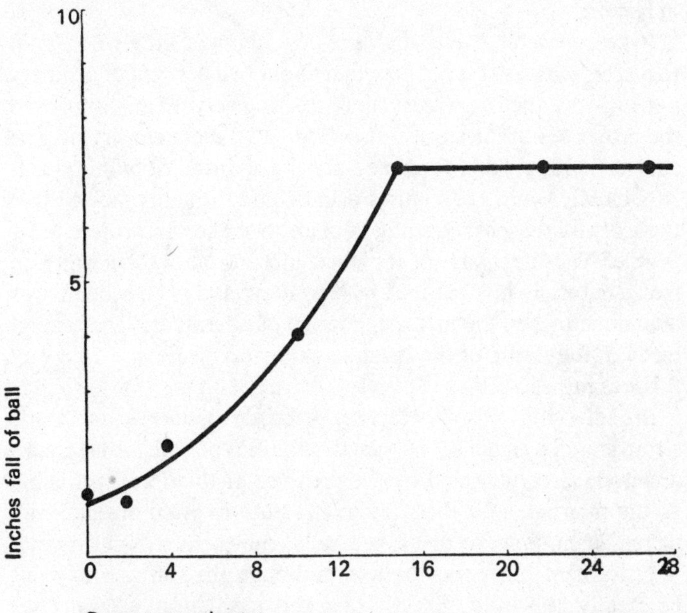

Figure 2. Asbestos fibres have an excellent effect upon the impact strength of a ceramic cement, in this case a phosphate compound. However, no further improvement occurs with fibre additions of more than 15%. I do not know why.

it was not then possible to provide air cover. It occurred to that very eccentric genius, the late Geoffrey Pyke, that one solution would be to tow an iceberg into the middle of the Atlantic and use it as an aircraft carrier. In some ways this was probably an excellent idea, but it was found on investigation that the mechanical properties of natural ice were unsuitable. Ordinary ice is quite weak in tension, it is brittle and cracks spread easily, which is why icebreakers can earn a living, and worst of all, the strength of ice was very variable. An iceberg would probably break up if it were bombed or torpedoed, but, even if it were not attacked, an iceberg large enough to operate aircraft would span at least a pair of Atlantic waves, which run about five or six to the mile in bad weather, and it was calculated that it would then fail as a beam in bending.

Pyke countered these objections by adding a little wood-pulp to his ice. He was able to show that about two per cent of ordinary paper pulp added to water before freezing very greatly improved the properties of the ice and also rendered it more consistent. The curve of strength and toughness for the addition of pulp to ice is very closely similar to Figures 1 and 2 and the sums showed that the ice would then be strong enough to make the project practicable. The idea was to add the pulp and allow the water to freeze naturally in a sea-loch in Newfoundland. The scheme was abandoned when the increasing range of aircraft and the general trend of the Battle of the Atlantic made it unnecessary. In a way this was rather a pity.

Broadly, the reason why weak, brittle materials are made stronger and tougher by very small additions of fibre is that cracks are stopped or deflected by the presence of the fibres, probably at the interface and the work of fracture is often dramatically increased; in practice this is generally equivalent to a substantial improvement in tensile strength, although the stiffness may not be greatly improved. Exactly how this mechanism works is not entirely clear and the subject would probably repay further research. In the form which we have discussed so far, that is to say quite small additions of random fibres to a brittle matrix, there is not much market for it at the moment, perhaps because nobody seems to want sun-dried bricks or mobile icebergs. However I would not be at all surprised if this approach came into fashion again in some different guise. At the moment the mode is for rather a different way of using fibres.

Those who work in the field of fibrous materials receive, in one way and another, a liberal supply of suggestions about schemes which we ought to try. Nearly all these schemes ignore the fact that, in order to compete with the quite efficient existing materials, it is necessary to get a large number of fibres into a given volume of the new substance and this is just where one begins to get into practical difficulties.

The simple systems which we have described contain about two per cent of short fibres, added to a matrix which, at one stage, is more or less liquid. Up to this point the fibres can be incorporated, if necessary, by stirring them in with a spoon. Beyond about two per cent however this becomes impracticable and the operation shows serious signs of getting out of hand. Suspensions of long thin fibres in liquids behave very like solutions of long thin molecules; both have a thickening effect which it is difficult to credit unless one has actually experienced it. The pulp (that is a suspension of wood fibres in water) for the paper from which this book is made had to be pumped and handled at a concentration of about one half of one per cent in order to be in any way manageable.

Papier-mâché

Beyond about two per cent, therefore, it is impossible to add fibres to a matrix and it becomes necessary to add the matrix to the fibres. This naturally changes the whole approach. Nearly always the fibres are packed tightly together in some form such as paper or cloth which is then soaked in a resin or some other binding agent. This form of the idea, too, turns out to be very old, again Egyptian. Elaborately shaped mummy cases were made from papier-mâché. This material is made by sticking pieces of paper together with paste or gum over a mould. When the glue is dry the shell is removed and painted. In Egypt papyrus was used, in the form of old manuscripts. When steamed apart by archaeologists most of the scraps of papyri turn out to be dull stuff, as one might expect, but the process does yield a small trickle of important Greek literature and is probably our only hope of recovering the works of Sappho.

After classical times papier-mâché fell out of use because papyrus fell out of use, but it was revived, almost unchanged, in the eighteenth century, especially in France, for making furniture using paper. It was used in England, until very recently, for advertising models and, during the last War, a great many fuel tanks and other aircraft parts were made in this way. The methods used, down to about 1945, were in no way different from those employed by the ancient Egyptians except that paper was used instead of papyrus.

Since it might be useful, it is worth mentioning how the process is done. A mould of some kind is needed which can be made from clay or Plasticine or plaster of Paris. This mould is then covered with soap or linseed oil (or possibly silicone car polish) to prevent the papier-mâché from sticking to it. Almost any paper will do but soft papers such as used to be used for sugar bags are most suitable. For glue a sloppy mixture of Scotch (hide) glue and office paste (starch) is best. It should be about as thick as pea soup. When all is ready, tear off pieces of paper about the size of the palm of one's hand and dabble them thoroughly in the glue until they are quite soft. Then press them on to the mould. Go on doing this until you have built up the necessary thickness, which may be more than you expect. When the moulding is thoroughly dry it may look rather like something the cat found (but do not despair, no doubt the Egyptians felt the same); however, it is much improved by sandpapering and painting. Many coats of oil paint are needed since the material depends entirely for protection against the weather on paint. The moisture resistance, of course, is bad, but not as bad as one would think. The mechanical strength is surprisingly good. Do not try to use synthetic glues or the result will be brittle, probably because the adhesion is too good.

If the resistance to moisture and fungi had not been even worse than that of natural timber, probably papier-mâché would have been more widely used because technology is always demanding a way of making light, strong, shell-like structures with elaborate curvature for coachbuilding, boats, armour, baths, furniture, luggage, fuel tanks and so on. For centuries, however, the process was stuck for lack of a strong waterproof adhesive and people were impelled to beat heavy, easily dented shells out of metal with great labour.

Moulding powders

However, in 1906 Dr Baekeland discovered that phenol and formaldehyde could be reacted together to make a resin which, though initially liquid or treacly, could be hardened by heat to an infusible, insoluble solid. Baekeland had a mind well open to commercial possibilities and he had already made a fortune by inventing and exploiting 'Velox' photographic printing paper, but even he does not seem originally to have been too optimistic about the applications of his resin, which was originally sold as a substitute for natural resins in lacquers and varnishes. I have been told that the great Bakelite Company started life in Edwardian times as the 'Dammard Laquer Company' and that it marketed three grades of varnish, 'Dammard', 'Dammarder' and 'Dammardest'.

Bakelite resin by itself is, when set, a hard, brittle substance of no great strength, much like natural rosin. It was of some use as an ingredient in lacquers, especially as an insulant in the electrical industry, and it was later to prove an excellent adhesive for plywood, but it was quite useless for mechanical purposes in solid lumps in the pure form. The turning point occurred when Baekeland noticed that the addition of fibres to the resin before it was hardened transformed its strength and toughness.

Most of the early applications were as a moulding powder. In this manifestation the partly set resin is mixed with short cellulose fibres, generally wood-flour. The resulting dry powder can be put into a heated steel mould in which the powder softens and, as the pressure of the hydraulic press is exerted, it flows to fill the interstices of the mould and then hardens irreversibly. The first commercial Bakelite moulding is supposed to have been made in 1916, the gear-lever knob for the Rolls Royce car.

Because of its light weight, low cost and the enormous saving of labour in making complicated shapes, Bakelite mouldings became extremely numerous between the wars and at one time there was even a major project to flood the undertaking market with Bakelite coffins. A well made Bakelite moulding can be a serviceable and reasonably attractive object but, naturally, such a process was a crying invitation to shoddy and ugly design. Moreover, in order to get the powder to flow easily and quickly in the mould, and thus keep down the cost of manufacture, the fibre added was very short in length and its power to reinforce the resin was quite modest so that the ordinary commercial powder moulding was both weak and brittle.

The immediate result of the introduction of moulding powders was to extinguish the Birmingham brass trade. A secondary and rather ineffectual result was a wave of indignation on the part of the consumer both on account of the ugliness and the brittleness. I have been taken aside often enough and told 'They say they put sawdust into the stuff to make it cheaper?' One then had to explain that without the sawdust it would have been even worse and that, anyway, what could you expect when the trade price of small mouldings such as switch covers was about three shillings a gross? Latterly the design has improved a good deal, partly as a result of the competition from the much tougher thermoplastics such as Polythene and Nylon.

Powder mouldings can be made, in effect, by throwing a (weighed) handful of moulding powder into the hot mould and pressing the button which causes the press to close. However complicated the shape of the mould the powder flows like a liquid to fill it. This process is very valuable when we want to make elaborate little gadgets and especially for electrical devices such as wall plugs where the plastic has to flow around numerous brass pins and inserts. However, to get this flow it is necessary to use quite short fibres and, as we have said, the result is a material which is comparatively weak and brittle. One reason for this is that, with very short fibres, a crack in the resin which encounters a fibre has only to make a shortish detour to get around the head of the fibre and then proceed on its way.

Cellulose fibre laminates

Material of the highest strength needs to be reinforced with long fibres carefully packed together and for such systems the flow in the mould is very limited. These materials are therefore different in character from moulding powders. In the laminates developed in the 1920s cellulose paper or fabric was impregnated with a solution of phenolic resin, usually in alcohol, dried, and then the impregnated sheets were laid between the carefully trued, parallel, heated plattens of a hydraulic press where they were hardened under a pressure of about a ton/in^2 (15 MN/m^2).

The resulting material was expensive but of good quality and in some grades the strength and toughness were quite high. Phenolic resins are either black or dirty brown and so these boards were not used for decorative purposes. Originally most of the paper-based material was used for electrical insulation; the fabric-reinforced laminates, being very tough, were sold for machining into cams and gears and bearings. After the last War, melamine resins, which were colourless, came in. This enabled the surface to be made from a coloured and patterned paper, the bulk of the thickness being still of phenolic impregnated brown paper which is cheaper and stronger. As might have been predicted, material of this type has been very successful for table tops and panelling and it has played a big part in the Kitchen Revolution.

The decorative plastic sheets which are generally sold are comparatively weak and brittle but, since they are nearly always glued to some kind of rigid substrate, such as a wooden bench, this does not matter very much. It is not very easy to realize that before these materials came on the market no really satisfactory surface existed for table tops and an unthinkable number of woman-hours were spent in scrubbing wooden surfaces which, because of their porous nature, merely absorbed the dirt.

Although the cellulose in cellulose-phenolic laminates retains most of its affinity for water the worst exuberances of the cellulose can be restrained by drying the fibre before the material is moulded and then moulding and hardening the material in as dry a state as possible. When this is done the fibre is, as it were, clamped and restrained by the matrix and by the other fibres which cross it, so that, although all resin matrices are permeable to water vapour, the swelling is much reduced. Since the paper or fabric must be coated with resin at an early stage in the manufacturing process and the drying must be done immediately before pressing, the resin naturally gets dried as well as the cellulose. Now the ease with which a phenolic resin flows in a hot mould before it sets depends very sharply upon the amount of water present, so the dry resin needs a high pressure to get it to distribute itself uniformly and bond the material together properly. For this reason it is usually not possible to manufacture such materials with reasonable water resistance at pressures much below a ton per square inch. The total load which has to be applied by the press to a standard four foot by eight foot panel is therefore about five thousand tons, which is one of the reasons why the process needs a certain amount of capital.

The moisture resistance is also affected by the chemical details of the impregnating process. It is possible to reduce the moisture pick-up considerably by the right choice of resin and this is often done with materials for electrical purposes. Unfortunately good moisture resistance means blocking the hydroxyls in the cellulose and this makes it brittle and so unsuitable for mechanical applications. Immediately after the War I saw an aeroplane which the Germans had built from a paper-based phenolic material. To ensure toughness they had reduced the water resistance of the material as far as they dared – too far as it turned out. When I saw it, it had been in the open for about three months and was falling to bits.

A lot of work was done during the War in this country to develop cellulose-reinforced sheet as a potential substitute for aluminium sheet for covering aircraft. Retaining reasonable toughness, we managed to get the total moisture movement in the plane of the sheet down to 0·8 per cent and then covered parts of the surfaces of twelve service aircraft with the material by way of experiment. The plastic material never caused an accident but it did give a lot of trouble. The sheet was, of course, riveted to an aluminium framework which did not shrink and swell with it. In consequence, in the desert the plastic became so taut that cracks appeared along the line of rivets while, in a wet climate, and especially after melting snow, the sheet buckled and waved in an alarming way. Eventually we pulled the material off. In practice the dimensional movement of cellulose-reinforced materials will be about 1·0 per cent or about one inch in eight feet. This matches neither metal nor wood nor plywood and generally condemns the material for large-scale applications.

Nowadays the use of strong cellulose laminates is almost

confined to flat sheets which can be pressed between accurately trued plattens. When shaped shell mouldings are wanted two shaped steel dies are needed. These are expensive anyway (and nearly impossible to alter) but what makes shaped moulding peculiarly difficult is that the material has almost no flow during pressing. For this reason the clearance between the two halves of the mould must be very accurately maintained. If this is not done, then all the press load will be carried at the tight spots and the rest of the material will not get pressed at all. The difficulty and expense of all this is generally enough to frighten people off, especially as there are nowadays several better ways of getting shaped mouldings. Around 1940, however, this was not so and a few serious large mouldings were made in spite of the heavy tool cost. The best remembered of these was the standard fighter pilot's seat which was used in the Spitfire and elsewhere. This was a fairly large and elaborate structure, made by bolting several shaped mouldings together. It had to withstand loads in the region of a ton and never gave serious trouble. On the other hand the saving in weight and cost over a riveted metal seat was not very great.

Glass fibre materials

Modern reinforced plastics really date from the introduction of inorganic fibres about the end of the War, mainly, in the first instance, for radomes; that is, for the dome-like structures which house radar scanners and therefore have to be transparent to radar and thus must be made from electrically non-conducting materials. The most successful of these fibres so far is glass. Except that the composition of the glass is sometimes changed in detail, these fibres are identical with those pulled by Griffith over fifty years ago. The drawing process has been mechanized in that the glass is generally melted in an electrically heated platinum cistern in the bottom of which are usually either two or four hundred small teat-like holes. From each of these teats a fibre is pulled, the glass being hard and cold by the time it reaches the revolving drum beneath the furnace on which it is wound. Commercial fibres are usually about a third to half a thousandth of an inch thick, from five to ten microns. The pristine tensile strength of the fibre is perhaps 400,000 to 500,000 p.s.i. (3,000 MN/m^2) though this gets reduced by subsequent handling. Because the new fibres tend to stick to each other and cause mutual weakening, the fibre is treated with an organic protective film applied between the drawing teat and the winding drum. This film enables the fibre to be handled during subsequent processes, such as weaving, with less damage than would otherwise occur. On impregnation the film combines with the bonding resin.

What happens after the fibre is drawn and reeled up on the winding drum depends upon the purpose for which the moulding is required. As we said earlier on it is necessary to get as much fibre as possible packed into the moulding, simply because the fibre is at least a hundred times stronger than the resin, so that, other things being equal, the strength of the finished material is proportional to the fibre content. The solids content of loosely packed individual fibre mats is very low indeed so that the fibre is seldom used in this form except for special purposes such as the so-called 'finishing sheet' which is often used to get a good surface on mouldings. Fibres pack best in parallel bundles, that is to say as threads or yarns. These yarns usually contain several hundred individual fibres. Because these fibres are continuous it is not necessary to put much twist into the yarn to hold it together.

Sometimes such glass yarn, after being impregnated with resin, is wound into cocoon-like structures intended for tanks and pipes and pressure vessels. For many high-grade applications however the yarn is woven into a cloth which looks not unlike an expensive white satin. During the days of clothes rationing and before glass cloth was widely familiar I had a large roll of such cloth stolen from the laboratory, no doubt to be made into underclothes. Since glass fibre is an irritant to the skin I watched the women employees, over a considerable period, to see if they scratched themselves. However, either they were all innocent, or else possessed of great self-restraint, for I never caught anybody.

Though the strength of laminates made from glass cloth is good, the cost is fairly high, not only because the woven cloth is expensive but also because cloth is not very suitable for automatic handling in making shaped mouldings. The greatest tonnage of glass fibre reinforcement is therefore handled as what is called 'chopped strand mat'. In this the yarns are chopped up into short lengths, usually of two or three inches. Most of this chopped strand goes into the manufacture of flat mats which are made by blowing the short lengths of yarn against a wire gauze with a little adhesive. This adhesive dries very quickly so that the mat can be removed from the gauze and handled like paper. For shaped mouldings suitable pieces of this mat are cut up and attached to the mould until the component is built up to the required size and shape.

When considerable numbers of shaped mouldings are to be made a blown preform technique may be used as this is almost a fully automatic process. The process is used for such things as helmets and typewriter cases. Instead of blowing the fibre on to a flat gauze it is blown and sucked by air on to a shaped gauze mould after which the lightly stuck together preform is automatically transferred to a heated steel die in which the main bonding resin is applied and cured under pressure.

Apart from its high strength, glass fibre has the great advantage of not swelling in water and for this reason, among others, it is not necessary to carry out the moulding operation under high pressure. This means that, if required, cheap moulds can be used, which can be altered about as the design is changed, and large hydraulic presses are unnecessary.

It is possible to bond glass fibre mouldings with phenolic resins but generally it is better to use the special resins, such as the polyesters and epoxies, which are developed and sold for the purpose. Many of these will set, not only with negligible pressure, but also at room temperature, after a catalyst has been added.

This has lead to what is rudely known in the trade as the 'bucket and brush technique'. These methods, which are popular with amateurs and with small firms, are almost identical with Egyptian papier mâché. Alternate layers of cold-setting resin and glass mat or fabric are laid up by hand over a simple plaster mould and left to set in their own good time. Given careful and conscientious methods there is not very much wrong with this construction, though it is expensive in labour if more than a few mouldings are needed. For very large mouldings, such as boats, it is the only practicable way of doing the job.

One of the objections is that no two mouldings are the same and that adequate inspection and supervision are almost impossible. Since it is difficult to predict the strength of any individual structure, the method has drawbacks for aircraft parts. For reliable mouldings the resins must be set in a dry, warm, controlled atmosphere and this may not be available in a back-street workshop. Many of the complaints about glass fibre in boats can be traced to the cold, damp shed of some local boat-builder. The larger firms are taking to using carefully heated (and expensive) building sheds and perhaps the most satisfactory role for the local builder or for the amateur is that of finishing off moulded hulls made by professionals with proper facilities.

For large mouldings like boats the cost of the mould is important because the number of orders is not usually very great. It is better to use a cheap mould and let the resin set slowly at room temperature. Furthermore one can put up with a lot of hand finishing on the moulded shell. When we come to such things as helmets and luggage the economic picture changes. In these cases it is usual to provide matched pairs of heated steel dies. A glass fibre 'preform' is dropped into the die and then a determined quantity of hot setting liquid resin is added at the last moment before the die closes. The setting rate is arranged so that the resin has just time to penetrate the fibres uniformly before it hardens and the moulding is ejected. Because of the smooth finish on the steel mould the moulding needs little hand labour in the final smoothing. The whole process of making the fibrous preform, laying it in the mould, impregnating it with resin and hardening the resin may be carried out in one large machine in a matter of seconds as against hours or days for the hand lay up process.

In the earlier reinforced materials small amounts of fibre were used to ameliorate the worst faults of a weak brittle matrix. Such materials could be correctly spoken of as 'reinforced'. In the newer materials the function of the matrix is simply to glue together a number of strong fibres and, as the weak constituent, we use as little of the matrix as we possibly can while still effectually bonding the fibres. Such systems would be more accurately called 'bonded fibre materials' – in fact, they are often called 'fibre composites' nowadays.

A serious study of the properties of these systems is a difficult and highly mathematical subject which has latterly become respectable and indeed fashionable in academic circles. Without going into any detail it may be said that the properties of a lot of fibres glued together are more or less what one would expect from engineering common sense.

It is usually difficult to get more than about fifty per cent by volume of fibres into any material. Glass fibres may be taken as having a tensile strength of about 300,000 p.s.i. (2,000 MN/m^2) by the time they have been processed and a Young's modulus of 10×10^6 p.s.i. (70,000 MN/m^2). A material, like a fishing rod, made from parallel glass fibres in resin will therefore have a tensile strength of about 150,000 p.s.i. (1,000 MN/m^2) and a Young's modulus of 5×10^6 p.s.i. (35,000 MN/m^2), since the resin contributes almost nothing to the stress situation, though of course it adds to the weight. Calculating from the simple law of mixtures, the specific gravity of the material will be 1·85, if all the air voids are filled as they should be. (The specific gravity of glass is usually 2·5 and that of resin 1·2.) We can therefore put down the following simple comparative table:

		Tensile Strength		Strength for weight		Young's modulus		$\frac{E}{\text{S.G.}}$	
Material	S.G.	(p.s.i.)	MN/m^2	(p.s.i.)	MN/m^2	(p.s.i. $\times 10^6$)	MN/m^2	(p.s.i. $\times 10^6$)	MN/m^2
Parallel fibre-glass	1·85	150,000	1,000	81,000	550	5·0	35,000	2·7	19,000
Crossed fibre-glass (woven fabric)	1·85	75,000	500	40,000	280	2·5	17,000	1·85	9,500
Mild steel	7·8	60,000	400	7,700	50	30·0	210,000	3·85	27,000
High tensile steel	7·8	300,000	2,000	38,500	260	30·0	210,000	3·85	27,000

From which it will be seen that direct comparisons between steel and fibre-glass are not very simple. However, very roughly, fibre-glass is stronger than steel, especially for its weight, but it is not nearly so stiff, even when we take account of its much lower density. In this respect it is also worse than wood.

Like wood, comparisons depend to a certain extent upon how many directions one wants to be strong in. Naturally such materials show up best when all the fibres and all the strength are put in one direction, though the engineering applications for unidirectional materials of this kind are fairly limited. When equal numbers of fibres are crossed at right angles we get a material like plywood, with half the strength of a unidirectional material at 0° and at 90° but rather less at 45°. This can be achieved with woven glass-fibre cloths.

Theory says that, if we want truly uniform properties in all the directions in a fibrous sheet material, then there are several arrangements of fibres which will give it and they will all achieve strengths and stiffnesses equal to one-third of that of a unidirectional system. Experiment shows the theory to be perfectly right here, provided of course that the resin contents are comparable. However, the case which generally occurs in practice with fibre-glass is that of chopped strand mat. With this reinforcement it is seldom possible to attain fibre contents as high as fifty per cent (because the fibres do not pack so well) and so we have generally to reckon on rather less than a third of the unidirectional strength in real life. However, chopped strand mat is usually used for comparatively cheap jobs where the utmost strength may not be needed. Even so, chopped strand mat will generally beat mild steel, strength for weight. It is in stiffness that reinforced plastics in general, and fibre-glass in particular, cannot compete with metals and wood. This is one of the main difficulties about using the material in largish structures such as boats and car bodies and it quite rules it out for the main structure of conventional aeroplanes at present. It is true that one can stiffen up car bodies, for instance, by putting in inserts of steel tubes, but then much of the attractiveness of the job has gone.

Metals, of course, are nearly isotropic, that is to say they have almost equal properties in all three dimensions. This is very useful if one wants to do the sort of things one can do particularly well with metal, such as making engine crankshafts, but it is not particularly useful for the shells and panels which one usually wants to make out of fibrous plastics. This is just as well because it is almost impossible to get isotropic properties in practice in a fibrous material because it is difficult to get fibres to pack tightly and to point in three directions at once. Even a haystack is apt to be a layered structure. Theory indicates that the strength of a three dimensionally random arrangement of fibres would be one-sixth of that of an all-parallel system, so it is really not worth trying anyway.

The work of fracture mechanism in fibre composites like fibre-glass is not without interest. As we have said, the work of fracture of glass fibre itself is no better than that of any other kind of glass, which is to say, abysmally bad. The resin is, perhaps, a little tougher, but not very much so. When the two are put together however the resulting composite is reasonably tough – tough enough, at any rate, for things like boats and crash-helmets.

The way in which this works is a little complicated. If we suppose a crack to be proceeding through the resin it will very soon encounter a fibre; if the material has been properly made – that is to say, if there is not too much and not too little adhesion between the fibre and the matrix – then the fibre will not be broken at that point but the material will crack at the interface between the glass and the resin for the reasons which we discussed in Chapter 5. This crack will spread along the fibre (this is called 'crack-back') so that the fibre becomes detached from the matrix, often for a considerable distance (on the left of Plate 11). Furthermore, for reasons which have been elucidated by Richard Chaplin, the crack in the resin is very apt to fork wherever it meets a fibre so that the number of cracks in the resin is greatly multiplied. We can generally see this process quite easily whenever a fibre-glass article has suffered from a blow because the material in that region, though not broken, usually turns white. This whiteness is due to the reflection of light from the surfaces of the many internal cracks. Material in this condition is not much weaker than it was before, although it has already absorbed a good deal of energy, simply in providing all those internal surfaces.

Before the composite can actually break, all the reinforcing fibres must, of course be broken. Since the strength of glass is very variable, the fibres do not break in any one plane in the composite but rather, fractures occur in a scattered or random manner throughout a considerable volume of material. The final phase of fracture therefore involves pulling all these fibres out of their holes or burrows. In order to do so a great deal of friction has to be overcome and this is where the bulk of the work of fracture of composites of this type comes from.

The whole process had been reduced to algebra by Kelly and others and it is found that the experimental works of fracture correspond pretty nearly to the theoretical maximum and so not much further improvement is to be looked for in composite materials of conventional design. This work of fracture is usually around 10^3 J/m^2 which is distinctly on the low side as compared with, say, mild steel. This consideration becomes important when we come to consider such matters as the safety of car bodies made from steel and from fibre-glass. Using his helical fibre work of fracture mechanism George Jeronimidis has recently been able to make glass-fibre composites with works of fracture in the region of 10^5 J/m^2 – roughly a hundredfold advance – and this may perhaps afford a break-through in this respect.

With all their drawbacks materials like fibre-glass are slowly spreading and becoming more widely used as they become more widely understood and appreciated. The cost per pound of the raw materials is something like fifty pence and this seems a great deal compared with steel at about 5p and aluminium at perhaps 30p. However the proof of the pudding is in the fabricating. The cost of making complicated shapes in plastics is usually so much less than it is in metal that the finished structure may well be cheaper. However, before this can happen it is usually necessary drastically to redesign the product and this may meet with resistance.

Very much depends upon the type of product. Nobody would try to make, say, a petrol engine out of plastics. But then metals are usually inefficient for light thin shells. There is quite a good argument for building the hulls of larger boats in steel, at least if one isn't in a hurry and doesn't mind the weight, but steel is hopelessly inefficient for the smaller hulls because the plates become so thin that, even if we can put up with the buckling, denting, oilcanning or whatever one likes to call it, a few months' corrosion will eat right through. In this field fibre-glass seems to have established itself very firmly and the costs are certainly competitive.

There have been many improvements in motor cars during the last generation, but in my opinion, the pressed steel body is not one of them. It is enormously heavy and its weight puts up the petrol consumption and reduces the performance, it requires a great deal of sound-proofing, and, worst of all, it starts to rust soon after one first gets the car home and body corrosion, rather than mechanical wear, is probably the reason why the majority of cars are eventually scrapped.

The use of fibre-glass in the bodies of mass produced cars is generally inhibited by three things. It is still marginally more expensive than steel in large-scale production and also it is difficult to get quite that showroom gloss on the surface finish which the motor trade seems to think that the public want. Furthermore – and more importantly – the crash protection afforded by a steel body is much better than that of a glass-fibre one – for the reasons we have just discussed. Yet nearly all the numerous non-mass production cars seem to have fibre-glass bodies. Indeed this is probably the factor which enables these cars to keep going economically because the sales are too small to justify die-pressed steel bodies while the old-fashioned 'coach-built' body would be too expensive anyway. By using a fibre-glass body the specialist car builder can turn out a car of roughly half the weight and thus get a flying start in performance at an extra cost which is often only about a hundred pounds. In spite of its disadvantages the world production of glass-fibre mouldings is said to have reached nearly a million tons per annum and to be increasing rapidly. This compares with a world production of about four and a half million tons for aluminium and its alloys. The expansion of the glass-fibre industry is likely to be limited, in the end, by the relatively low stiffness of the material.

High stiffness composites and carbon fibres

Over the last fifteen or twenty years various Governments have spent a great deal of money on the development of high-stiffness composite materials, some of which have received publicity out of all proportion to their actual usage. The main incentive for this work has been the requirement for weight-saving in critical structures and especially in aero-space, for it has been calculated that it would be practicable to treble the payload of long-range commerical aircraft by the use of improved structural materials and there are comparable advantages with space-travel and in military applications.

Before going into details it is worth reviewing the thinking which lies behind the development of advanced materials for applications of this sort. Presumably we can do very little to change the properties of natural wood but we might perhaps change the properties of a metal, such as aluminium, or else we might substitute a new and better metal. At first sight it would seem that all we have to do is to increase the strength of our metal – after all aircraft parts are designed as near to the bone as possible, that is as near to the breaking stress as seems safe. As we shall see it is not unduly difficult to strengthen a metal and, if the material were stronger then the part could presumably be made thinner and therefore lighter. To a limited extent this is clearly true – but only to a rather limited extent.

It will be remembered that, although we can now modify the strength and toughness of solids very considerably we have no real control over their stiffness. The Young's modulus depends solely upon the chemical nature of the solid and cannot, as a rule, be changed by tinkering with it. If we want a different modulus then we must change to a different substance. Thus, if we increase the strength of any solid, such as a metal, we do so by increasing its elastic breaking strain and, in order to make use of its higher strength we must operate it at higher strains. That is to say that the deflections of the structure as a whole will be higher; if we have put up the stress a lot, so as to save a useful amount of weight, then the deflections will be much higher. The consequences of this kind of action can be seen in the picture of the bent aeroplane in Chapter 2 and clearly such shapes are not acceptable.

Another reason why we need stiffness is that much of the structure of an aircraft, for instance, is in compression and moreover the compression parts are usually struts and plates which are thin in proportion to their length. Members of this sort fail under compression, not by direct crushing, but by elastic buckling and the cause of such failures is not lack of strength but lack of stiffness. This is called 'Euler collapse'.

Yet again, many parts of an aeroplane are liable to break, not by simple loading in one direction, but by what is known as flutter. That is by flapping violently in the airstream like a flag. This is guarded against by increasing the stiffness of the parts, not by increasing their strength.

For these reasons we find that if we simply increase the strength of a material we shall soon run out of Young's modulus and it is therefore as important to increase the Young's modulus as it is to increase the strength. Now when we are dealing with structures of minimum weight, as we are in things like aeroplanes, we are not so much interested in the actual or absolute properties of our materials as in their specific properties; that is, how much strength or stiffness we are getting for a given weight. Specific figures are obtained by dividing the actual values by the specific gravity or density of the material. It is salutary to look at the Young's moduli of the common engineering materials in this light. The figures are given in Table 1.

TABLE 1

Young's moduli of orthodox structural materials

Material	Specific gravity grams/c.c.	*E* p.s.i. × 10^6	*E* MN/m²	*E*/S.G. p.s.i. × 10^6	*E*/S.G. MN/m²
Molybdenum	10·5	40·0	270,000	3·9	25,000
Iron and steel	7·8	30·0	210,000	3·8	25,000
Titanium	4·5	17·0	120,000	3·9	25,000
Aluminium	2·7	10·5	73,000	3·9	25,000
Common glasses	2·5	10·0	70,000	4·0	26,000
Magnesium	1·7	6·0	42,000	3·7	24,000
Wood – spruce parallel to grain	0·5	1·9	13,000	3·8	25,000

It is remarkable that the specific Young's moduli of all these materials should be almost the same and, although this is more likely to be due to chance than to any deep philosophical reason it does make things a bit awkward for engineers and materials men. It also accounts for the fact that, for a great many years, steel and aluminium alloys and magnesium and wood (and latterly titanium) have competed with each other in the aircraft industry on roughly level terms. If you design airframes for the same aircraft in any or all of these materials they are apt to come out at much the same weight.

This is tantamount to saying that, if we want to make any large or dramatic advance in materials for this kind of purpose, then we shall have to reject all the common engineering solids about which we have accumulated experience. What can we do about it? What chemical entities are there which have higher moduli? The answer to this is – not an enormous number but quite a lot. Some of the better ones are listed in Table 2.

TABLE 2

Some high specific modulus materials

		E		*E*/S.G.		
Material	S.G.	p.s.i. × 10⁶	MN/m²	p.s.i. × 10⁶	MN/m²	Melting point °C
Aluminium nitride (AlN)	3·3	50	340,000	15	103,000	2,450
Alumina (Al_2O_3)	4·0	55	380,000	14	95,000	2,020
Boron (B)	2·3	60	410,000	26	180,000	2,300
Beryllia (BeO)	3·0	55	380,000	18	130,000	2,530
Beryllium (Be)	1·8	44	300,000	24	170,000	1,350
Carbon whiskers (C)	2·3	110	750,000	48	330,000	3,500
Magnesia (MgO)	3·6	41	280,000	11	78,000	2,800
Silicon (Si)	2·4	23	160,000	10	66,000	1,400
Silicon carbide (SiC)	3·2	75	510,000	23	160,000	2,600
Silicon nitride (Si_3N_4)	3·2	55	380,000	17	120,000	1,900
Titanium nitride (TiN)	5·4	50	340,000	9	63,000	2,950

In some ways Table 2 is a cheering document because it shows that there are in existence solids which have specific Young's moduli which are, very roughly, ten times as high as those of the traditional engineering materials and so they hold out the possibility of a rather spectacular 'break-through'. In other ways the list is a daunting one. All these materials are normally very weak and brittle, they can usually only be made at all at very high temperatures and some of them are toxic.

The only metal in the list is beryllium. Now beryllium can be dangerously poisonous (for instance it may be fatal to get it into a cut), but supposing for the moment that we discount the toxicity, can it be made tough and strong? The answer seems to be that in certain cases it can be made fairly strong but that it is very difficult to make it reliably tough. This is for the fundamental reason that, at normal temperatures, dislocations are only mobile in four planes in the beryllium crystal and, as we shall see in Chapter 9, we really need dislocation mobility in five planes if the crystal is to be immune from cracks attacking it from any angle. Although this characteristic of beryllium was predicted by the theoretical crystallographers quite a long time ago a great deal of money and effort has been wasted by the British and American Governments in trying to make ductile beryllium.

Though one cannot make beryllium reliably ductile one might perhaps be able to make it tough by making use of the composite approach. Working on these lines the Americans have experimented with matrices of magnesium or of magnesium-lithium alloys, reinforced by plates or particles of beryllium. So far, this has been only moderately successful, partly because magnesium – and to an even greater extent magnesium-lithium alloys – corrodes very rapidly. Another approach remains to be tried. One might be able to toughen beryllium by putting into it a small percentage of fibres, like wood-pulp in ice. However, I do not think that this last method has actually been tried or, if it has, I have not seen any results. If any of these experiments proved practicable I suppose that one might be able to arrange for some sort of protection from toxic hazards; yet a further objection lies in the fact that beryllium seems to be an unavoidably expensive metal, partly because of the precautions which have to be taken.

If we cannot civilize beryllium what else might one do? Clearly one might try to make a composite material based upon fibres which were much stiffer than ordinary glass fibres. Most conventional glasses have, very roughly, the same Young's modulus but again, a great deal of time and money has been spent by Governments in trying to develop high-modulus glasses suitable for fibre-drawing. It turns out that the only way to get a large increase in stiffness is to incorporate beryllium oxide, beryllia, in the glass. This is even more toxic than beryllium metal and the project has had to be abandoned for this reason.

One is therefore driven to try to make strong fibres from one of the other substances in Table 2. In the matter of dislocation mobility we require all or nothing. If dislocations are really mobile then we can make a reliably ductile material, like a metal, and do not need to bother with fibres. However, if we do make fibres, then the thing is to avoid any dislocation movement at all. Such movement does no good and it may do a lot of harm by weakening the fibre. For this reason beryllium and magnesia are not very suitable as fibre-forming materials.

Most of the other solids in Table 2 however are predominantly covalent bonded so that the dislocations remain immobile at normal temperatures – which is just what we want. In nearly every other respect however, most of these substances are what the materials man calls 'perfect stinkers'. Generally speaking they can only be formed with considerable difficulty and at high temperatures. If the substances themselves are not toxic then one or more of the ingredients needed to make them probably is. Moreover some compound needed in the process is almost certain to attack the walls of the apparatus.

It was pointed out in Chapter 4 that the problem about strength is not so much to explain why materials are strong as to explain why they are weak. In other words all solids are 'naturally' strong unless they are weakened by defects which are nearly all of a physical nature. It will be recalled that, in the case of brittle solids in which the dislocations are immobile, the weakening defects are small geometrical irregularities which set up stress concentrations. If the interior of the solid is reasonably homogeneous, then the dangerous defects are usually surface irregularities. Most of the covalent solids in Table 2 normally occur either as powders or else as irregular lumps. The task is to get these substances into the form of threads which are homogeneous within and smooth without.

This is what several laboratories, in England and abroad, have been working on for a number of years and there are now a variety of processes which will produce very stiff, strong fibres but none of these processes is easy or very cheap. For one thing the manufacturing temperatures needed are usually somewhere in the range between 1,000 °C and 3,500° C and at present the fibres have usually to be treated at high temperatures for hours or days. The engineering problems of getting furnaces to operate under corrosive conditions while maintaining reasonable chemical purity in the reaction chambers are severe. Moreover the amount of energy used per kilogram of fibre produced is very high.

These 'superfibres' usually fall into one of two broad categories, whiskers and continuous fibres.

Whiskers

These are not different in kind from the whiskers of water-soluble substances which we talked about in Chapter 3. It is however enormously more difficult in practice to grow whiskers from the covalent ceramic compounds than it is from, say, hydroquinone. There are a number of processes and all of them are scientifically very complicated. Processes intended to produce high quality whiskers are usually vapour-phase ones, that is to say the ingredients of the reaction are handled as vapours in high temperature furnaces. There is no difficulty in getting gases such as nitrogen or oxygen into the reaction zone but elements such as silicon, carbon or aluminium cannot be transported satisfactorily as elements and it is necessary to use what is known as a 'transport species'. These may be such compounds as SiO, $SiCl_2$, CH_2, AlO and so on. The object is to produce strong, smooth whiskers in quantity and as quickly and cheaply as possible. Unfortunately, when the reaction is speeded up the quality of the whiskers grown is liable to be reduced and the whole problem is very difficult. The extremely complicated chemical reactions which occur are analysed by computers.

So far practical whisker farming has been attended by only rather moderate success. Silicon carbide whiskers have been grown in kilogram quantities in England, in Switzerland and in Japan and can be bought commercially. It is also possible to buy alumina (sapphire) whiskers in smallish quantities from America.

At present the demand for whiskers is limited because the price is high and the price is high because the demand is limited – moreover the fashion has been for continuous filaments such as carbon fibres. There have been fairly persistent rumours that the Russians have been growing diamond whiskers; however, since I was nearly put in prison for asking questions on the subject behind the Iron Curtain, it seems safe to assume that no official information is available.

Continuous fibres

As reinforcing fibres, whiskers have several potential advantages. In the long run they seem to offer the possibility of cheap large-scale production (though this has not yet been achieved), as short fibres they are much better suited than long ones to cheap fabrication by modifications of paper-making methods and, moreover, they are generally very much stronger than continuous fibres since, because of the growth processes which are used, their surfaces are almost perfectly smooth. Most good quality 'commercial' whiskers reach a mean elastic breaking strain of about 2 per cent, which corresponds to a very high stress. The importance of this lies not so much in the possibility of making materials of very high tensile strength – as we have seen this is not generally the most important problem – but rather that, exploiting modern composite theory, this strength can be employed to increase the work of fracture of the composite. As we shall see, it is lack of work of fracture which is generally the fatal handicap in advanced continuous fibre composites of the carbon-fibre type.

Having burnt their fingers once over the brittleness of beryllium one might perhaps have supposed that Governments would have learnt to pay some attention to theoretical predictions about work of fracture but this does not appear to be the case and, of course, continuous fibres do have some substantial advantages. Thus most Governments have chosen to put their major effort into continuous fibre developments. The properties of the principal continuous fibres are given in Table 3.

The first of these fibres to be developed was boron – an entirely American achievement – dating from about 1960. In the preferred process a thin (0·013 mm) tungsten wire is drawn through a reaction chamber which is filled with either a mixture of boron trichloride (BCl_3) and hydrogen or else with a mixture of boron hydride (B_2H_6) and chlorine. The tungsten wire is heated electrically, like a lamp filament, to something over 1,000°C when a fairly thick (0·05 mm) layer of boron is deposited on its surface. What is wound up on a drum at the end of the process is therefore a thickish (0·1 mm) fibre consisting of a thin tungsten core surrounded by a thick skin of boron. Both boron trichloride and boron hydride are beastly substances but the process works quite reliably although it is both slow and expensive. This invention was greeted with great publicity and was described by a five-star general as 'the greatest technological break-through for three thousand years'. In fact composites based on boron fibres have been developed with both resin and aluminium alloy matrices and they have been used in service aircraft, in helicopters and in space-travel. The cases of very large rockets have also been made by winding tubes from boron fibre and resin and it is claimed by sober and responsible Americans that the development costs have been more than paid off by specialized uses of this sort. In any case the development cost of boron fibres – which might have been one or two hundred million dollars – would be a drop in the ocean compared with the American aero-space budget.

Although all this seems to be true and the material has many technical virtues, boron composites have not caught on for commercial purposes because the process of making the fibres is inherently expensive (about $700 per Kg.) and, moreover, boron

TABLE 3

Some modern high-stiffness reinforcing fibres

		Young's modulus		Tensile strength	
Fibre	S.G.	p.s.i. $\times 10^6$	MN/m²	p.s.i.	MN/m²
Boron	2·5	58	400,000	450,000	3,100
Carbon	2·2	60	410,000	300,000	2,000
Kevlar 49	1·45	19	130,000	400,000	2,700

fibres do not easily lend themselves to cheap fabrication processes.

Carbon fibres of a rather fragile kind date back to the end of the last century when Edison made electric lamp filaments by heating bamboo. However about 1964 Bill Watt at Farnborough was able to carburize polyacrylonitrile fibres – which are the basis of the dress-fabric 'Courtelle' – under rather special conditions so as to produce a fibre which combined a very high modulus with substantial tensile strength. Like boron, this fibre has suffered from a great deal of irresponsible Government publicity.

Although frequently described by the newspapers and on television as a wonderfibre of 'exceptional strength', carbon fibres are not, in fact, particularly strong; if anything they are a little weaker than glass fibres. They are however, for their weight, something like eight times as stiff as either glass or the normal engineering metals. As might be expected the resin-fibre composites made from carbon fibres are very stiff but not especially strong in tension. They are also, at present, rather inconveniently weak in compression. While it might be possible, in theory, to put up the compressive strength of carbon fibre composites by using a metal matrix, this does not usually work in practice because of the chemical reactions which occur between the carbon and the metal. In fact most attempts to manufacture carbon fibre-metal materials turn out merely to be very expensive ways of making acetylene gas (C_2H_2).

However, for many purposes where weight saving is important but where the strength requirements are not too critical – such as artificial limbs, golf club shafts or the stiffening of car bodies – carbon fibre composites have been very successful. When we turn to more exacting applications, like aircraft parts, the trouble is generally lack of sufficient toughness. When the composite is made in the conventional way the work of fracture which is actually achieved is not far short of the calculated theoretical limit – but unfortunately this limit is, in practice, not sufficiently high. This was at the root of the trouble with the carbon fibre fan blades in the RB211 engine which contributed to the Rolls Royce debacle a few years ago. These blades were unable to withstand the impact of the small birds which would have been sucked into them from time to time and, in the event, nothing could be done about this except to replace the plastic blades by titanium ones at the expense of the performance of the engine.

In the light of modern knowledge two ways of increasing the work of fracture of such materials suggest themselves. One way is to increase the strength of the fibre; if this can be done then the theory of the work of fracture of composites shows that the toughness can be increased. Although Bill Watt has been able to make considerably stronger carbon fibres on a small scale in the laboratory, it has not so far been practicable to put these fibres into production. The other way would be to use George Jeronimidis' timber mechanism, giving to the fibres a helical geometry. Working in the laboratory with carbon fibres and epoxy resins George has recently been able to make very dramatic improvements along these lines. It will be interesting to see what comes of this.

The last fibre on the list in Table 3 – Kevlar 49 – is something different, both because it is made from an organic polymer (with no nonsense about carburizing, which comes expensive) and also because it has been developed by private enterprise and not by Government defence laboratories. Messrs Du Pont, in America, have been quietly working away, to my knowledge, for at least twenty years on the development of high-stiffness fibres. They have explored the field very thoroughly and must be presumed to know what they are doing. Essentially, this material is made up from benzene rings joined together without folding, much as the sugar rings are joined in cellullose; in fact, both the density and the modulus are closely similar to those of a high-grade cellulose, such as flax. The strength however is about four times as high as that of the best flax and, of course, the material is virtually immune both to moisture and to rot. Weight for weight, the stiffness of Kevlar is not quite as good as that of boron or carbon but it is not so very much worse and the fibre may well prove to be both cheaper and more practical.

Reinforced concrete

Although the reinforced concrete people and the plastics people have been rather slow in communicating, the ideas involved are obviously parallel and it seems worth ending this chapter with a tailpiece on reinforced concrete. The origins of both materials seem to lie in the dim past and the differences are mostly in the matter of scale, the reinforcement being much coarser in concrete than in plastics. The Babylonians used reeds to reinforce structures of dried mud and various forms of 'wattle and daub' have been used all over the world. The Essex village in which I am writing this chapter is mostly built of mud or plaster over wattles, i.e. mud huts.

The use of iron as a reinforcement seems to be specifically Greek. As we said in Chapter 2, in normal masonry everything has to be kept in compression because masonry is not usually able to withstand any appreciable tensile stresses and so this condition leads normally to arches and domes which enable large openings to be bridged without the use of tensile stresses. However, although they were well aware of it, the Greeks seem to have rejected the arch, at least for formal architecture, very possibly on aesthetic grounds. In fact, in spite of John Keats, the Greeks were in some ways the least functional of people, especially in their architecture, which grew out of wooden architecture. The Parthenon and all other Doric temples are an exact copy in marble of wooden buildings, down to imitations in marble of the pegs which held the wooden beams together. As the result is dazzlingly successful and most of our own buildings are hideous we are in no position to jeer at the Greeks about this.

Wooden architecture is essentially an architecture of beams because wood is available in long pieces and has good tensile strength; Greek architecture was thus an affair of beams and columns. This is beautifully illustrated by American 'Colonial' architecture which, having timber in plenty, naturally reverted to classical styles with grace and success in wood. One cannot be 'Gothic' in wood because Gothic is a compression architecture originating in stone arches. Although marble is rather better than other stones in tensile strength it is really too weak and variable to make reliable beams of any length. In the early Doric stone temples this weakness was counteracted by keeping the spans of the beams short and by using very wide capitals at the heads of the columns. Even in the Parthenon (begun in 447 B.C.) the free span of most of the beams was kept down to about eight feet, though it looks more. However, when Mnesicles came to build the great gateway to the Acropolis, the Propylaea (begun 437 B.C.), both the architectural proportions and the need for ceremonial processions to enter called for much wider spans which in fact vary between thirteen and twenty feet. To deal with the tensile stresses Mnesicles caused iron rods about six feet long to be concealed and cemented within grooves in the marble. Thus we have iron reinforcing marble so as to make it behave like wood.

However, Mnesicles was not being particularly advanced because the Greek colonists at Akragas (Agrigentum) in Sicily were using iron reinforcing members fifteen feet long and of five- by twelve-inch cross-section as early as 470 B.C. How such large forgings were made is a mystery and it suggests that the Greeks would have had no technological difficulty in making steam engines and other heavy machinery if they had given their minds to it and if it had occurred to them to do so.*

As we have said, Gothic churches fell down if a tension load made its appearance, which it did quite frequently; the cure or palliative was to provide buttresses, pushing in the desired direction. Much the same thing applied to late classical and Romanesque architecture and although the outward thrust of the dome of St Sophia, in Constantinople (begun 532 A.D.) is countered by the inward thrust of the half domes on which it rests, the arches are tied across the base by iron tension rods.

The domes of St Peter's and St Paul's Cathedrals stand upon drums or cylindrical towers and there is no possibility of taking the outward thrust by means of subsidiary domes or buttresses which would have completely spoiled the effect of the designs with their isolated cupolas. As is well known the problem was solved in both cases by taking the thrust in a circular tension

*But of course the supply of fuel in the Ancient World would have been a difficulty.

chain which is embedded in the masonry around the bottom of the domes.

A more general approach was initiated by a Frenchman called Soufflot (1713–81) who tried to increase the tensile strength of masonry by burying a number of iron rods in the joints between the stonework. However, the wet got in along the mortar and rusted the iron, the expansion of the corrosion products then crumbled the masonry. The great I. K. Brunel (1806–59) later tried to do much the same thing, putting hoop-iron (that is the thin iron strip used for barrel hoops) between the joints of his brickwork with exactly similar expensive results.

Apparently it fell to three people to discover, almost simultaneously, that iron reinforcement in Portland cement did not rust sufficiently to cause damage. A French gardener, Joseph Monier (1823–1906), made flowerpots, or rather large tubs for orange-trees, by embedding a mesh of thin iron rods in concrete in 1849. These tubs were successful and attracted attention. An Englishman, W. B. Wilkinson, seeking a use for old mining ropes, of which a large quantity was available, made reinforced beams for use in building (much like the Greeks), putting the wires on the tension side of the beams. Finally, a French engineer, J. L. Lambot, exhibited in 1855 a rowing boat made of concrete reinforced with iron bars, presumably the first of a long line of not very successful concrete ships. Lambot patented, a little late in the day it would seem, the combined use of iron and cement in building.

Iron reinforcement does enable cement to carry tension loads quite successfully but the tensile breaking strain of concrete is low so that the concrete cracks long before the iron is seriously strained, and if any serious tensile load is put upon the combined system an elaborate pattern of cracks appears in the concrete. If these cracks are small they let the water in, if they are large the concrete may fall out piecemeal. To avoid this the best thing to do is to put the concrete permanently into compression by putting the steel reinforcement permanently into tension. In one form or another this arrangement, which is known as prestressed concrete, began to come in about 1890 but although it was quite successful it has been slow in catching on and it has only been applied seriously and on a large scale relatively recently. The use of pre-stressed concrete enables much more efficient and highly stressed structures to be built than were possible using concrete with ordinary reinforcement. One might say 'Why not make it all of steel?' In fact there is a considerable economy in the weight of steel used, mainly due to the fact that the steel has not to take the compression, and is, anyway, stabilized against buckling. Also, because the steel is protected from rust by the concrete, the maintenance of the structure may be nearly eliminated.

In the traditional 'reinforced concrete' the reinforcement – which usually takes the form of steel rods – is on quite a gross scale. However, during the last few years modern composite and fracture mechanics theory has been applied to the problem. This has resulted in the development of concretes with a fine-scale reinforcement. These materials are much more like the 'reinforced plastics' which we discussed earlier in this chapter. The reinforcement is generally thin steel wire but is sometimes a special sort of glass fibre. Though the potential for such materials in building construction and civil engineering seems to be large, there are still a number of difficulties to be overcome and at the time of writing, their actual usage is not very great.

Part Three

The metallic tradition

Chapter 9 Ductility in metals

or the intimate life of the dislocation

> *'We will now consider iron, the most precious and at the same time the worst metal for mankind. By its help we cleave the earth, establish tree-nurseries, fell trees, remove the useless parts from vines and force them to rejuvenate annually, build houses, hew stone and so forth. But this metal serves also for war, murder and robbery; and not only at close quarters, man to man but also by projection and flight; for it can be hurled either by ballistic machines, or by the strength of human arms or even in the form of arrows. And this I hold to be the most blameworthy product of the human mind. In order that death may reach men the more speedily, we attach wings to it; we deck iron with feathers and thus the fault is not nature's, but ours. A few examples prove that iron could in fact be an innocent metal. Thus in the alliances which Porsenna established with the Roman people after the expulsion of the kings, it was established that iron should be used for no purpose except agriculture.'*
>
> Pliny, *Natural History*.

As we said in Chapters 4 and 5, toughness, work of fracture and crack-stopping are very essential qualities in any useful strong material. To recap, 'toughness' implies, perhaps a little vaguely, a general resistance to the propagation of cracks; rather more precisely, 'work of fracture' is a measure of the energy which has to be consumed in propagating fracture through the material and thus of the length of a critical Griffith crack; 'crack-stopping' implies that the stress at a crack tip is reduced, usually by diminishing the stress concentration, to such an extent that the crack cannot proceed, even if the energy balance is in its favour. As we have seen, both natural and artificial non-metals rely upon a series of characteristic and highly ingenious mechanisms to provide these qualities. Metals achieve the same effects by a totally different method, basically by the dislocation mechanism – which scarcely occurs in nature. One effect of this mechanism is that many metals are 'ductile'.

If a metal possesses adequate ductility not only is the work of fracture high – which of course is a good thing – but the shape of its stress-strain curve is modified in such a way as to ensure large departures from Hooke's law. When this is the case one of the effects is that stress-concentrations are often very greatly and usefully diminished; in other words ductility tends to stop cracks. It will be realized that all calculations and assumptions about dangerous concentrations of stress assume that Hooke's law is obeyed. We speak of concentrations of stress but what the mathematical calculations really supply us with are concentrations of strain. Thus, if we calculate that the material immediately at the tip of a crack in a loaded structure is strained or stretched by 200 times more than the average for the structure as a whole then we assume that the local stress is also 200 times as high and we say that there is a stress concentration of 200.However, if Hooke's law is not obeyed by the local material at the tip of the crack then this is no longer true.

This is the classical metallurgist's way of crack-stopping but, since the local increase of strain at a crack tip is usually many hundredfold, it is of no use invoking minor departures from Hooke's law, such as might be caused by the shape of the inter-atomic force curve (Chapter 2). What is needed is a really whole-hearted lack of elasticity which is just what ductile metals provide. However, there is more than one way of departing from Hooke's law and it may be worth glancing at a mechanism which will *not* provide toughness.

Why viscous materials are no good

Viscous liquids will strain under a constant stress by any amount, if given sufficient time. In other words they flow. Like a quagmire, if you go on pressing, a viscous liquid will yield although it will resist a sudden load. All liquids are viscous but some are more viscous than others. The most viscous liquids are hard to tell from solids. In this class are pitch and tar, toffee and the baser sorts of plastics.

We have already remarked that a blow from a poker will shatter toffee which has resisted more adult and slower attacks and the same is true of pitch and the more deplorable plastics. These materials, given time, are very tough indeed because they can flow sufficiently at the crack tip to relieve the stress concentration. As structural materials, however, they combine the worst of both worlds. If they are subject to a sustained load they will flow in bulk and slowly run away from their responsibilities. Under a sudden load they are unable to yield in time and behave like solid glass. Once the crack is running it soon builds up to a speed to which the flow mechanism cannot possibly respond and so the material shatters.

Materials like wood and reinforced plastics creep a little, that is to say they behave in a slightly viscous way at high stresses and this, of course, is a bad thing. Quite apart from this creep however they are to a small extent non-Hookean so that the stress-strain curves generally look something like Figure 1. The departure from Hooke's law, though, is far too small to cause a useful

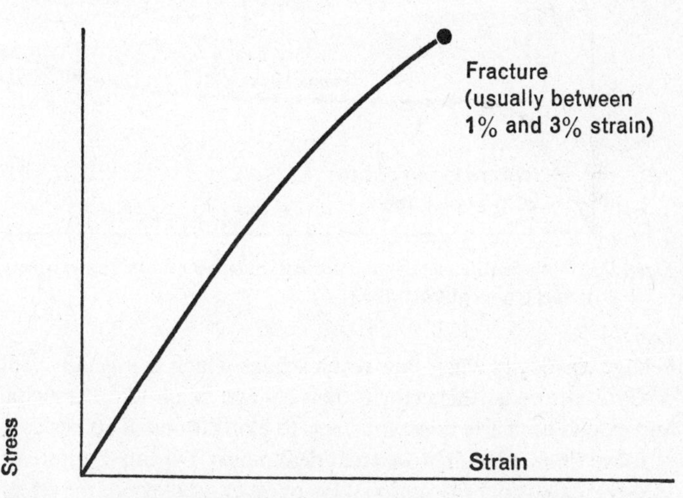

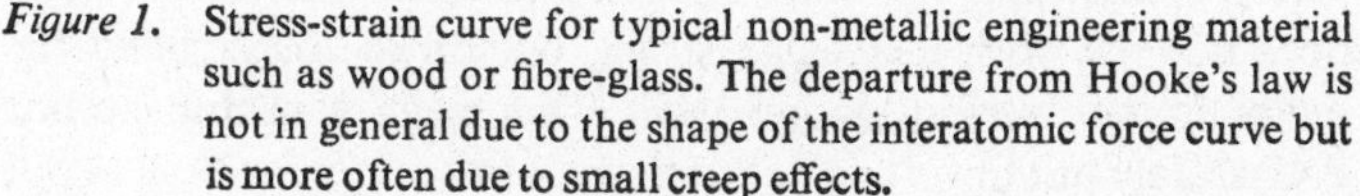

Figure 1. Stress-strain curve for typical non-metallic engineering material such as wood or fibre-glass. The departure from Hooke's law is not in general due to the shape of the interatomic force curve but is more often due to small creep effects.

reduction in stress-concentrations and these substances have to depend on weak interfaces to stop cracks.

Crack-stopping by dislocations – stress corrosion

At its best the dislocation mechanism provides a very desirable combination of elasticity at low strains with rapid and extensive yielding at high strains. A typical stress-strain curve for a ductile metal is shown diagrammatically in Figure 2. Such metals cease to

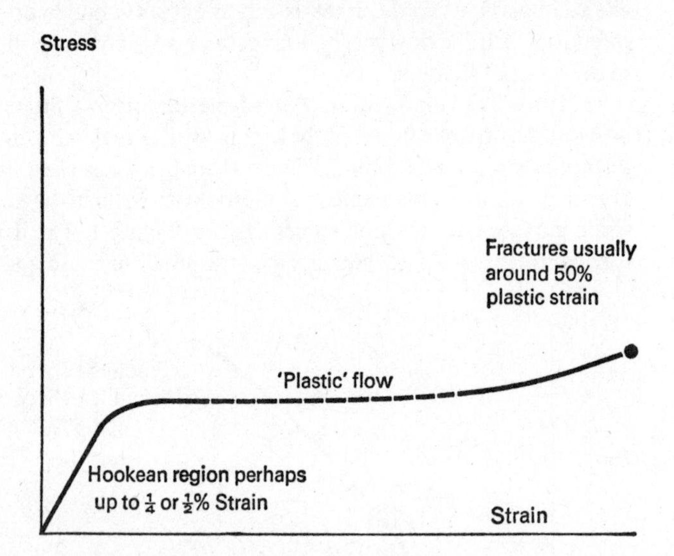

Figure 2. With ductile metals the stress-strain curve usually shows a very long region of plastic flow.

behave elastically when they reach strains which are usually well under 1 per cent; thenceforth they behave much like Plasticine and extend at nearly constant stress to elongations of 50 per cent or more (in fact locally to a great deal more). During the state of 'plastic' extension, the material is not much weakened, the stress does not rise with increasing strain, but on the other hand the metal is not seriously damaged. The mean working strains deliberately put upon engineering structures seldom exceed about

0·1 per cent and, as the metal may be able to yield locally by 100 per cent or more, local concentrations of strain at crack tips in the region of perhaps 1000 to 1 can be accommodated.

Figure 3 shows that on either side of the actual tip of a crack there are small local regions of very high shear – shear stress

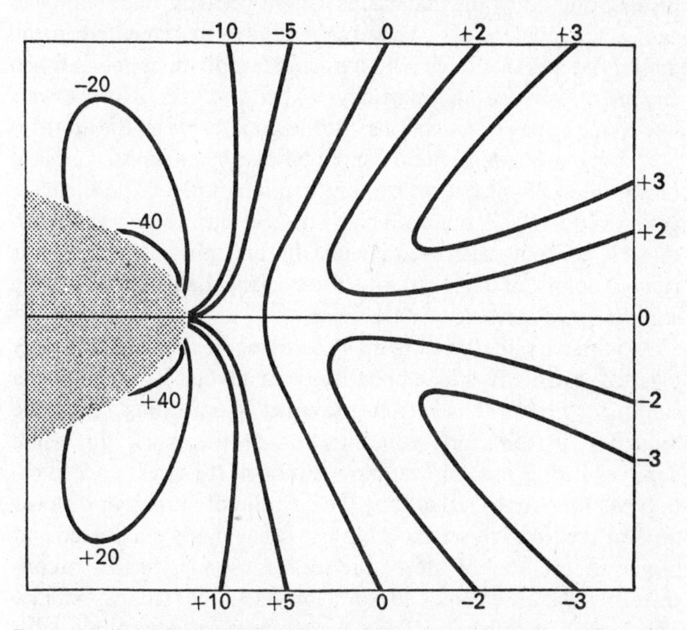

Figure 3. In addition to the concentration of tensile stress at the tip of a crack in a stressed material there are also concentrations of shearing stress which exist on either side of the crack tip. In a ductile metal these shear stress concentrations are able to nucleate hundreds of dislocations and thus help to relieve the stress concentration. This is a diagram of shear stress around a crack tip. Shear stress has a sign – positive or negative – either kind can nucleate dislocations.

concentrations. These are sufficient to initiate sources of dislocations in fairly soft metals and the new dislocations flow from these points in profusion. Slip occurs on two main planes, like ears, at forty-five degrees to the crack surfaces and so the worst of the stress concentration is relieved. This is roughly equivalent to rounding off the tip of the crack and thus, even if the Griffith energy balance (Chapter 5) is favourable to the propagation of the crack, the mechanism for implementing it may be frustrated for lack of a sufficient stress concentration.

The crack is thus not able to proceed under purely mechanical instigation and so the material is safe in perhaps ninety-nine per cent of practical cases. However, we have to remember in all materials work that there is no hard and fast dividing line between chemistry, physics and elasticity. Experts in their ivory towers like to make these distinctions but the bond between the atoms is not aware of them. A bond can be broken by chemical, physical or mechanical means or by any combination of these causes acting additively. A bond which is strained elastically is more susceptible to being dissolved chemically and physically. For this reason points of high stress are especially liable to attack by solvents or to corrosion by chemicals.

As we have said, there are many cases where the Griffith energy balance is usually still emphatically in favour of spreading a stationary crack. It is merely prevented from doing so by the reduction in the stress concentration at the crack tip which deprives it of a mechanism. Now although the stress concentration has been much reduced by the creation of numerous dislocations at the tip of the crack it has not been wholly eliminated and moreover the way of life of the local molecules has been considerably disturbed and all sorts of fine-scale strains remain. The bonds in this region are therefore more susceptible than elsewhere to attack by any aggressive solvent or chemical in which they happen to be immersed at the time. This is why metals which are tough in air or in other reasonably dry gases may crack when stressed for any length of time when wetted with sea-water or in chemical plants even though they may last for years submerged in the corrosive environment without a load. Some brasses are notorious traps for amateur constructors in this respect.

Ductility in crystals

The word ductility comes from the Latin *ducere* to lead, meaning, I suppose, that the material can be led by a stress to distort in a desired direction. In the engineering of metals it has two extremely useful consequences. It makes the metal tough so that cracks do not readily extend and, secondly, it may make the metal malleable (Latin *malleus*, a hammer), that is, able to be shaped, either hot or cold, by hammering, pressing or bending. Generally speaking, more capacity for flow is needed to obtain a useful degree of malleability than is needed to make the material reasonably tough. On the other hand a great deal of fabrication is carried out when the metal is hot when practically all crystals are much more ductile.

Ductility is exclusively a property of crystals for the reason that true dislocations can exist only as departures from the ordered crystalline state. Most solids are crystalline and dislocations exist in nearly all crystals. On the other hand, in the great majority of crystals, the dislocations are not sufficiently mobile at room temperature or are not mobile in the right way. Nearly all crystals contain quite large numbers of dislocations which arise from the nature of the mechanisms by which they grow but these dislocations are dispersed throughout the body of the materials in a very roughly uniform way. However, the stress concentration at the tip of a crack is a very intense and localized affair and there are generally not enough dislocations available naturally in the immediate vicinity to provide enough slip to relieve the situation, even if the dislocations are very mobile. It is therefore necessary that many new dislocations should be born on the spot, nucleated by the stress concentration itself. Furthermore, this must be able to happen very quickly if the material is not to be vulnerable to a sudden blow.

In real life, cracks are not two-dimensional diagrams on a sheet of paper but are flat, wedge-shaped holes trying to penetrate a solid three-dimensional material. To relieve the stress concentration adequately, there has to be slip on five planes in all.

The number of crystals which satisfy all these conditions at once is very few: out of all the thousands of crystalline substances which exist, perhaps only something like a dozen metals. With the rather dubious exception of silver chloride, no non-metallic crystal at present can be considered as truly and reliably ductile.

Although an enormous amount of research has been done on dislocations during the last thirty years and there now exists a really frightening volume of theory and information, it cannot be said that all the causes which determine the mobility of dislocations in different substances are fully understood. However, it may be worth looking at some of the more obvious reasons.

First of all, bonds vary a good deal in the ease with which they can be broken and reformed, and, of course, every time a dislocation jumps a step bonds have to be broken and remade. In this respect the most mobile bonds are those which exercise their attraction symmetrically in every direction, most notably the metallic bond and after this the ionic. The worst is presumably the covalent bond which is often highly directional and has an all-or-nothing character. Unfortunately the covalent bond is also the strongest and stiffest and the most generally desirable of the chemical bonds. Dislocations in covalent crystals are never usefully mobile at ordinary temperatures.

Again, the crystallographic structure of the crystal is important; that is, the geometrical pattern according to which the atoms or molecules in the crystal are stacked. If the unit cell or repeating pattern in the crystal is large, then a dislocation jump will generally be more difficult. Even if the unit cell is small but the packing is geometrically slightly more complicated, then the number of directions of easy slip may be unduly restricted. On the whole, crystals with cubic arrangements of atoms are more easily ductile than hexagonal ones. Furthermore the size of the crystals and the impurities they contain all have an important effect.

Although the vast majority of crystalline substances have no useful ductility at ordinary temperatures, those which do have tend to be altogether too ductile. Pure crystals of iron, silver, gold and so on, are too soft to be of much practical use and the art and science of metallurgy consists very largely in making such crystals harder and stronger without making them too brittle. This has to be done by controlling and restricting the movement of dislocations without stopping it too much.

Engineers are very apt to talk about and to specify 'elongation' as a measure of ductility. This is a rough practical test of the amount by which the metal can flow before total fracture occurs and has nothing at all to do with the elastic breaking strain of the material which is usually somewhere below 1 per cent. Elongation is measured, quite arbitrarily, by seeing how far two marks on the stem of a test-piece, initially two inches apart, have separated when the broken halves of the specimen are fitted together after fracture. If the total distance between the marks is then, say, three inches, the elongation is called 50 per cent, and so on. As with most popular engineer's tests it is very difficult to relate elongation in any consistent way either to the flow properties of the material or to the end usage. However, many engineers have an almost religious belief in the value of the test and if you tell them that wood and fibre-glass will give an elongation of nil but yet are very tough, they will merely reply that that is why they do not use wood and fibre-glass. As with most emotionally held beliefs this one presumably arises from fear, a very reasonable fear of brittle failure.

In practice, with most metal alloys, an elongation of about 5 per cent or 10 per cent is usually sufficient to ensure a tough material. The materials which are really popular, like mild steel, may have elongations in the region of 50 or 60 per cent even though the attainment of so much ductility implies the acceptance of quite low tensile strengths. This is partly due to an attitude of over-insurance against cracks but also to two other reasons. Many structures are fabricated from sheets and bars and tubes of metal and it is convenient and cheap to be able to bend these things to shape in the cold. One can also use rather brutal methods to make things fit. During the War I was told by one assembler of aircraft that the only way in which he could get the wings of his Spitfires to fit on to the fuselages was to bend the root fittings with a sledge hammer. I never saw this done with my own eyes so that I cannot guarantee that it is true but things of this sort certainly do happen on occasion though perhaps not in the aircraft industry in peacetime.

The second reason is that stresses can sometimes be relied upon to readjust themselves within the structure. In a complex structure it may be very difficult to calculate the loads in all the various members with any accuracy, or perhaps one is just too idle to do so. If the material yields and has a long 'plastic range', as it is called, then an overloaded member may stretch and be little the worse for it. Many engineers have a strong belief in the 'self-designing structure'.

These are very real benefits in an imperfect and commercial world and they go a long way towards explaining the immense success of mild steel, copper and soft aluminium. There are two drawbacks however. The ductility of even the softest metal is not inexhaustible and since there is generally no way of measuring how much of it has been used up in the manufacturing operations, one is left to guess how much of the initial ductility is left over to provide toughness in service. This is at the root of many complaints about failures in mass-produced goods. Annealing is a relatively expensive and troublesome operation, small components are costed and sold on tiny fractions of a penny and so the temptation to deform the metal in the cold as much and as often as possible may be irresistible. Perhaps it will not actually break until after the guarantee has expired.

The other drawback is that the requirement for maximum ductility necessarily implies a low tensile strength, because the metallurgist must arrange for dislocation movement to begin at a low stress. This has the consequence that structures are often much heavier than they need to be.

Dislocations, the edge and the screw

Dislocation theory is immensely complicated and, after all, perhaps mainly of interest to dislocation experts. We must however mention the two main varieties, the edge dislocation and the screw dislocation. The edge dislocation, which is that postulated by G. I. Taylor in 1934, is perhaps the easiest and simplest to think about. It has already been described in Chapter 4 (see Chapter 4, Figure 5). As we have said, it consists essentially of an extra sheet of atoms slipped into the crystal like a sheet of paper partially inserted between the pages of a book. Edge dislocations can be formed when the crystal grows, for instance at what are known as 'small angle boundaries'. That is, when two growing crystals meet at a fine angle so that they join up to form, effectively, one crystal, the join is marked by a line of edge dislocations, which may afterwards, of course, drift away.

Screw dislocations were postulated by Professor Frank, of Bristol, around 1948, not so much to explain the mechanical properties of crystals, as to explain their growth. For atoms or molecules to come out of solution or out of vapour and to settle down, more or less permanently, in a solid crystal, requires an energy change. Whether it happens or not depends upon what is called the supersaturation; roughly speaking, on how badly the molecules want to come out of solution or out of the vapour. One can cool solutions of sugar or salt, for instance, well below the temperature at which crystals should be deposited without any crystals appearing unless some surface is provided which is to their liking.

For an ordinary plane, flat surface the supersaturation which can be attained without actually depositing material can be calculated and is found to be quite high. What worried Frank was that, in practice, many crystals grew healthily at supersaturations very far below those calculated for deposition on a flat surface. In fact, if we had to depend upon deposition on a flat surface very many crystals could hardly be got to grow at all. It can be shown that if the surface possesses an irregularity such as a step, even if it is only one molecule high, deposition is much easier.

The re-entrant part of the step provides a welcoming and comparatively cosy home for wandering molecules which tend to settle down there, just as a bricklayer lays a brick in an existing re-entrant in a course of brickwork. As with a course of bricks, the result is not to abolish the re-entrant but to cause it to move along the top of the wall as more bricks are laid. This mechanism had been observed in operation by Bunn and Emmett around 1946. It will be remembered from Chapter 4 that this is the cause of the steps which mechanically weaken the surfaces of whiskers and other crystals (Chapter 4, Plate 10).

Frank's difficulty was that, admitting the existence of growth steps, what happened when a moving step came to the edge of the crystal? Presumably it would be extinguished, as the step in a course of masonry is extinguished when the bricklayer reaches the end of a wall. If so, then how could it be regenerated all over again for the next layer?

Frank's solution was brilliantly simple. Crystals are not built like a house out of level courses of bricks or molecules. The growth step was never extinguished at the edge because the crystal is built like a corkscrew staircase. Thus the crystal simply went on screwing itself into existence, using the same step indefinitely. Like G. I. Taylor's hypothesis of the edge dislocation, the screw dislocation is so intellectually satisfying that one feels it must be true and again, it turns out that it is. The screw dislocation was confirmed observationally by Forty and others not long after Frank conceived it (Figure 4).

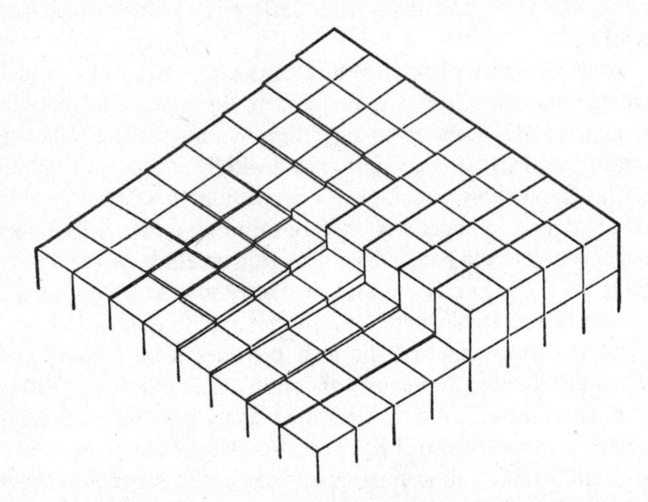

Figure 4. It is not very easy to visualize the arrangement of atoms in a screw dislocation. This diagram attempts to do so with rather moderate success.

The difficulty with corkscrew staircases is what happens in the middle. There is of course a hiatus or mismatch, in the form of a line of misfit up the middle of the screw and this is the actual dislocation. As with the edge dislocation the interatomic bonds are naturally highly distorted or strained at this point although in the normal way there is nothing one could call an actual hole. However it is not uncommon for whiskers to be hollow, like a tube. Possibly the reason is that these whiskers have grown with a screw dislocation of which the step is not one but several molecules high. If so, then the strain at the centre of the dislocation must be very large. The crystal may thus perhaps trade strain energy for surface energy, that is grow with a hole down the middle.

Like most successful hypotheses the screw dislocation has been rather overworked and almost every aspect of the growth of almost every kind of crystal has been attributed to it. It now seems that quite a number of crystals manage to grow without using the Frank mechanism but the fact remains that a very large number do use it and it is a very real and important phenomenon.

It is not necessary for dislocations to be wholly of the edge or wholly of the screw type. A single dislocation line can begin as an edge and end as a screw and vice versa. In between it partakes of the character of both and is spoken of as having a screw component and an edge component. However, the rules which govern the motion of the two types of dislocation are different and this is one of the reasons why the behaviour of real dislocations, which are usually lines curved in three dimensions, is very complicated.

The study of dislocations is now an elaborate and well-supported science in itself which has undoubtedly thrown a great deal of light upon the behaviour of solids in general and of metals in particular; to a considerable extent we now understand why metals behave as they do. On the other hand it cannot really be said that the knowledge of dislocations has led directly to any radical improvements in the mechanical properties of materials. As far as metals are concerned it does seem rather as if most of the possible important improvements have already been made by traditional and empirical methods and that the role of dislocation theory has been to explain the reasons for the improvements afterwards.

The energy of dislocations and the work of fracture of metals

Although it often requires only a small stress to move a dislocation through the body of a crystal – so that the strength of highly ductile metals is often very low – yet it will be realized that both the screw and the edge dislocation involve the existence of very high strains and distortions among the atoms in their immediate neighbourhood. Thus a considerable amount of strain energy is necessarily associated with every dislocation; this is known as 'the energy of the dislocation'. This energy, which does not differ very greatly between edge and screw dislocations, can be calculated quite easily and turns out to be about 10^{-9} Joules for each metre of dislocation length for most metals.

This amount of energy may not sound very much but it is to be remembered that, when a metal is extensively sheared, enormous numbers of new dislocations are created, in fact about 10^{16} per square metre. Thus the amount of energy stored in the dislocations in a cubic metre of highly strained metal is about 10^7 Joules. If we suppose the metal to be distorted to a depth of about one centimetre when it is fractured, which is roughly true, then this corresponds to a work of fracture of about 10^5 J/m^2,* which is in fact the case for metals like mild steel. So everything adds up very nicely and that is where the work of fracture of a metal goes. Thus the dislocation mechanism not only acts as a crack-stopper, it also provides a very high and useful work of fracture.

The observation of dislocations

However plausible and intellectually satisfying a scientific hypothesis may be it remains an abstraction without subjective reality to most people unless one can actually touch or see it. Indirect or mathematical proof is not enough. Heat is a case in point. Everybody knows, from elementary physics, that the temperature of a substance is due to the motion of its molecules which are in perpetual but highly irregular movement. However, since one is also told that molecules are far too small to see and since the

*This value of energy is roughly equivalent to the area under the stress-strain curve.

sensations of heat and cold do not in any way resemble that of moving particles the idea of heat as molecular motion is usually not very real to us.

The botanist Brown discovered in 1827 that fine particles of pollen in certain flowers appeared under the microscope to be in perpetual dancing motion. The Brownian movement is most easily seen by making a suspension of fine scraps of solid in water. This can be done with ordinary Indian ink or with the water-colour gamboge. A drop of this can be put on a microscope slide, preferably covered with a cover-glass, and observed with a fairly high magnification in an ordinary optical microscope. The finer particles can be seen to be spinning and dancing in a most erratic jig for as long as one cares to watch them. What is happening is this. The particles themselves, which are perhaps a micron across, are a few thousand times larger than the molecules of the the liquid which surrounds them. These molecules are rushing hither and thither in a thoroughly random way. The particles of ink or gamboge are therefore being jostled in a rough and irregular manner. For the smaller particles these jostlings do not necessarily cancel out, as they do for large particles, and so the little particles are pushed or kicked around in a fashion which is visible in a quite ordinary microscope.

Once one has watched the Brownian movement one's apprehension of the *nature* of heat will never be the same again. It is not that one can be said to have learnt anything in an objective scientific way but rather that one has come to terms with the kinetic theory of heat at a subjective level. It is the difference between having a sunset described and seeing one.

It is very much the same with dislocations. What began as an abstract hypothesis has become a very tangible phenomenon. What are the ways of observing a dislocation? Well, firstly one can etch it. As we have said mechanically strained bonds are more easily broken by chemical and physical means than unstrained ones. Thus one can prepare etches, usually acid brews, which will attack dislocations where they emerge on the surface of a crystal, in preference to the surrounding material. This produces a series of little pits which are usually easily seen in the optical microscope. This is a very common experimental technique and the expert can draw quite extensive conclusions from the series of pock-marks produced in this way on the surface of a crystal. One trick is to split a crystal in two. Any dislocations existing in the crystal before the experiment and which cross the cleavage surfaces will naturally be the same for both cleavage faces. One half of the crystal is selected as a control and etched immediately, thus showing up the pre-existent dislocations. The other half is distorted or otherwise experimented upon before it is etched. By comparing the etch-pits on the two surfaces one can see which dislocations were generated under the experimental conditions and also which have moved.

Etching is useful but it cannot be called a direct observation of the dislocation itself and so is perhaps not subjectively very satisfying. The next step in this direction was taken by Dr Hirsch in the Cavendish Laboratory, Cambridge. Very thin metal films are practically transparent in the electron microscope, but any distortion of the crystal lattice may show dark. The line of a dislocation thus shows as a dark line on a white background. So far so good, but one wants to see them move and it takes a stress to do this. It is not easy to apply a direct mechanical stress to films thin enough to be transparent to an electron beam. Hirsch however used the heat of the electron beam itself to expand the film and thus to stress it. This worked very well and he was able to film dislocations in motion. The impact of this film is considerable. The dislocations give an uncanny impression of scurrying mice.

In Hirsch's pictures, however, there was no question of seeing individual molecules or the three dimensional chequer-board of the crystal lattice. Hirsch's dislocations were simply moving black lines of strain on a white or grey ground. What we really want to see, I suppose, is a layer of molecules coming to an end in the crystal lattice. After all, if one saw a course of bricks doing this in a brick wall one would be highly surprised. However, in order to see a dislocation in a crystal lattice one must first see the crystal lattice.

Now in metals and in the majority of ordinary crystals the lattice spacing is about two Ångströms. At the time I am talking about, around 1955, the very best resolution of an electron microscope was about ten Ångströms so, in the ordinary way, there was no hope of resolving the layers in normal crystals.

Jim Menter at Hinxton Hall, near Cambridge, got over this difficulty by making and using thin crystals of a substance called platinum phthalocyanine. This is a flat, roughly square, organic molecule about twelve Ångströms across. In the middle of the square is a hole, and in the hole, in the case of platinum phthalocyanine, is an atom of platinum. (Copper phthalocyanine is a first cousin, the synthetic pigment Monastral Fast Blue, familiar in the blue paint on innumerable front doors.) In the crystal the flat molecules stack so that the lattice spacing is about twelve Ångströms and in the middle of each row of molecules is a line of heavy platinum atoms, standing out from the light atoms of the surrounding organic molecule. There are thus lines of platinum atoms in regular crystalline array, but spaced twelve Ångströms apart instead of the normal two. The organic part of the molecule may be regarded as a transparent padding or spacer keeping the dense, opaque, platinum atoms separated.

By adjusting the microscope to give the best resolution it proved possible to resolve the lattice of the phthalocyanine crystal. The result looked like rather woolly charcoal stripes on a lighter grey background very like the lines on a television screen. The first impression was that of the incredible regularity of this tiny scrap of crystal. On big enlargements the innumerable fuzzy black stripes extended perfectly straight apparently for ever and there were an enormous number of layers, millions upon millions of molecules, each one perfectly in its place.

Many pictures were needed before, after diligent searching, an edge dislocation was found. It looked exactly like the diagrams people had been drawing for twenty years. One dark fuzzy stripe came to an end and the others came together to close the gap (Plate 14). Jim Menter was able to send this photograph to Sir Geoffrey Taylor in time for his seventieth birthday.

To those of us working at Hinxton at the time, these pictures, coming wet from the darkroom, had a numinous quality not far short of a religious experience. A visiting Russian scientist looked at them for a long time and then he said 'You are looking up zee trousers of God.'

Jim Menter's visual revelation of the crystal layers and their dislocations by means of the electron microscope is satisfying and has become famous. There is however another approach with a strong subjective effect. As we said in Chapter 4, David Marsh devised a most sensitive tensile testing machine for whiskers and other fine fibres. This machine can detect extensions of as little as four or five Ångströms, which is about the resolution of a modern electron microscope. The shear slip movement caused by a single dislocation is about one Ångström and therefore cannot be measured by the machine. A dislocation source however releases sufficient dislocations to provide from one hundred to about five hundred Ångströms movement and thus can easily be detected by the Marsh machine.

Now if we take any ductile material, such as a soft metal, and pull an engineering-sized test-piece we shall get a load-extension diagram such as Figure 5, a smooth curve of a type very familiar to engineers and metallurgists.

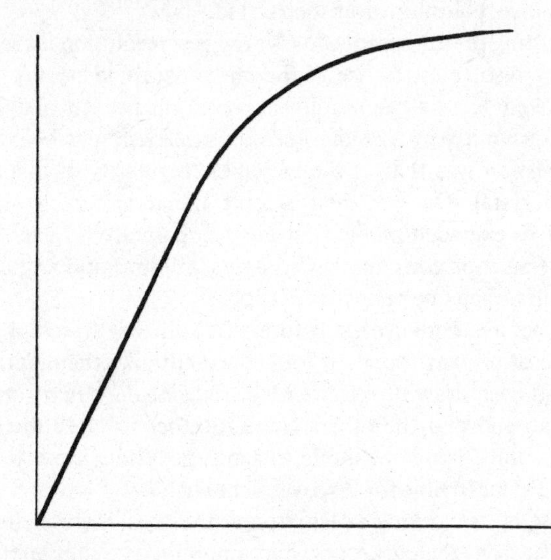

Figure 5. Normal macroscopic load-extension curve for a ductile substance.

If we now take a really thin but ductile test piece, such as a large whisker, and test it in the Marsh machine, we get a load extension diagram which is something quite different. A typical example is that in Figure 6. Here we have an elastic extension

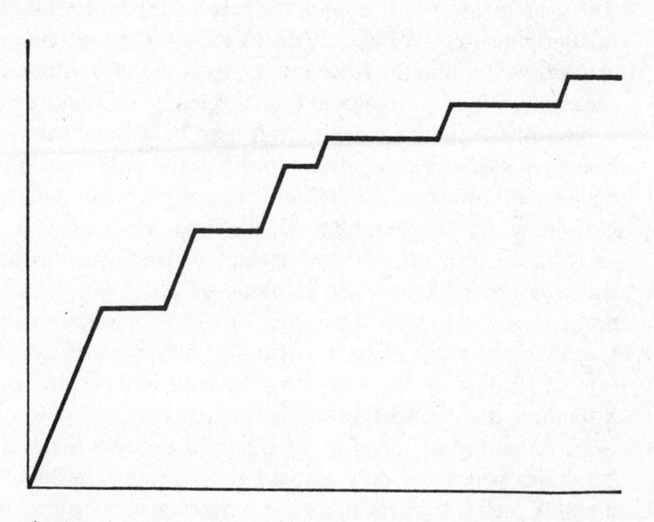

Figure 6. Similar material tested on a fine scale in the Marsh machine. Plastic extension is broken down into steps, each of which corresponds to the operation of a dislocation source.

interrupted by the sudden operation of sources. These sources operate quite erratically and the slip they produce is virtually instantaneous. The load extension diagram therefore has the form of a series of steps. What is happening is that, at each level of stress there are dislocation sources almost ready to give birth. What triggers them into doing so is a random thermal shove, just like the shove or jostle which pushes the particles around in Brownian movement. In a laige specimen the same thing is happening but in so many places and so frequently that the gross effect is that of a smooth curve.

With a small specimen in the Marsh machine the complete randomness and suddenness of the movements yet again impresses upon one the reality of dislocations.

Creep and temperature resistance

The consequences of this upon the behaviour of metals in service are fairly obvious. Well below the elastic limit or yield point, that is to say well within the Hookean region of the stress-strain curve, the elongation of the material is unaffected by time and we might subject it to a stress for centuries if need be without causing any change in strain or any deterioration. Near to the limit of elastic behaviour however the material becomes markedly affected by both time and temperature. As we have seen, even at room temperature random thermal pushes will activate dislocation sources so that plastic strain accumulates with time: the material gets longer and in some cases may break. Thus we cannot really specifiy the strength of such a material unless we also specify the rate of loading or say how long the load is to be left on for. Structures like suspension bridges which are loaded for many years on end must therefore be designed to lower stresses than structures which are only stressed rapidly and occasionally. In practical metals there is often *some* creep even at quite low stresses and this has to be watched where dimensional accuracy is important.

As we might imagine, the stress at which creep becomes serious is very dependent upon temperature and this is a factor which frequently governs the design of machinery and especially of heat engines such as gas turbines. On the whole the hotter the hot parts of an engine can be run the more efficient the engine is likely to be, especially in the matter of fuel economy. Since iron melts at over 1,500° C. and other metals at even higher temperatures it might be thought that there would be no great difficulty in running engines at temperatures of, say, 1,200° C. which are well below the melting point. This is very far from being the case.

It is true that iron does not melt below 1,500° C. but then the concept of melting implies that the metal flows under its own weight which is usually a negligible stress. As soon as we introduce a mechanical stress, however, even a small one, flow and eventually fracture occur at far lower temperatures. Even for comparatively rapid loading, that is to say loading as rapid as can conveniently be applied in a testing machine, the strength is drastically reduced. Furthermore, when components are subjected to prolonged stress in one direction, such as the centrifugal stress in turbine blades, we have to be very careful indeed about the creep.

For 'short-term' loading the strength of a metal varies with temperature much like Figure 7, in other words the material dies

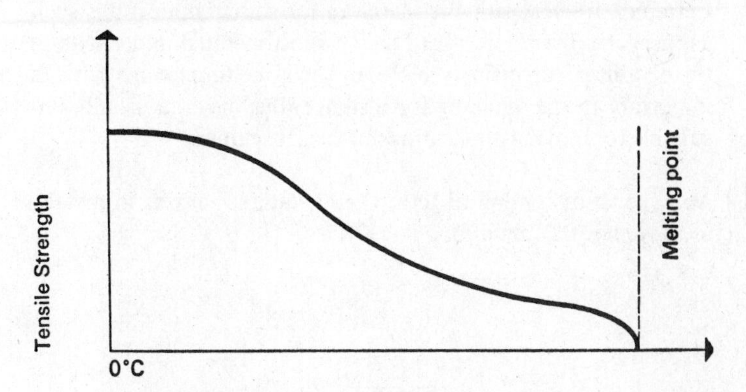

Figure 7. Most metals get weaker when they are heated and the weakening effect begins to operate surprisingly early. Thus although the melting point of iron is 1535°C. many steels cannot be used above about 300°C.

with a whimper not a bang. As a very rough working rule, which is true for most metals, one cannot work a metal at a temperature which is higher than half its melting point in degrees Kelvin. (Degrees Kelvin = degrees Centigrade+273. See Appendix.)

The way to get the operating temperature of an alloy up is, of course, to impede dislocation movement by one means or another. The difficulty is that most of the additions which one might use for this purpose tend themselves to become mobile. (Naturally one must avoid oxidation of the surface of a high temperature alloy but the additives introduced for this purpose may conflict with those intended to prevent creep). The subject is an extraordinarily difficult one and metallurgists have probably done well to achieve working temperatures as high as 950–1,050° C., which can just about be done with the recent very special turbine blade alloys. The normal run of engineering steels have to be operated far below this temperature.

It is true that dislocations are largely immobile in many ceramics at temperatures up to about 1,500° C. but then these materials are usually dangerously brittle at lower temperatures. Ceramics are very suitable therefore for static applications such as furnace refractories where they can be operated under load at temperatures surprisingly close to their melting points (this is important in steel-making for instance) but they are usually unsuitable for moving applications such as machinery.

Note: for a discussion of 'creep' and 'fatigue' effects in metals, see *Structures*, Penguin Books, 1978.

Chapter 10 Iron and steel

Hephaistos among the Satanic Mills

'I will send them the locomotive to be the Great Missionary among them.'

George Stephenson (1781–1848).

Simply because wood and masonry have always been the commonest materials of construction and metals are relatively recent intruders in technology and engineering we are peculiarly conscious of the role of metals as innovators although, as we have seen, they are still in a minority on a tonnage basis. However, metals, especially iron, were remarkably well suited for making the sort of machines which were both the curse and the glory of the Industrial Revolution. It was the development of means of making and working iron cheaply and in quantity which made the spread of mechanization possible. Steel, as we know it, only came in as a cheap material in the second half of the nineteenth century when the main impetus of the revolution was over.

Important as iron was, it was only used to the smallest practicable extent in most of the early machines, even in steam engines. In Fulton's first steamship on the Hudson River even the boiler, incredibly, was of wood; the actual heating of the water took place in a separate arrangement of iron pipes. Even the Americans thought that this was going rather far, although the river steamers which carried the bulk of the American inland traffic until after the period of the Civil War used wood in their machinery, as well as in their hulls, to a degree which a modern engineer finds hard to credit.

Broadly speaking there are two problems with all metals – extraction metallurgy, the separation of the metal from its ores; and physical metallurgy, which is how to get the metal into the most useful condition of hardness, strength and toughness. As we have seen, a pure metal is usually very soft so that physical metallurgy consists, notionally, of impeding the dislocations to just such an extent that the metal is strengthened without being embrittled. Technologically however the processes of extraction metallurgy frequently do not yield the virgin metal in a pure condition so that both extraction and the subsequent processing have to be considered together.

In their chemical and technical details the treatment of the different engineering metals varies widely but in every case the physical objective remains the same – the control of dislocation movement by adjusting the size and structure of the metal crystals (dislocations can cross grain boundaries but they do so with some reluctance) and by adding other substances and 'impurities'. Complex alloy systems may ensue in which it is hoped that the diversity of crystal structures will impede the dislocations by just the desired amount. Very small particles, even single impurity atoms, will 'pin' the forward movement of a dislocation line wherever it meets them. The stress required to bow out and eventually to detach the dislocation line between the pinning points is calculable and depends upon the separation of the points and therefore this is a useful and powerful means of control. Almost anything which is added to a metal will affect its mechanical properties for good or for bad – sometimes for both since one has to be careful that an additive which is beneficial when dispersed does not end up concentrated around the grain boundaries where it may have a serious weakening effect as we saw in Chapter 4.

When we consider the number of ductile metals and also the number of hardening mechanisms which are available the permutations and combinations of physical metallurgy are very numerous and the subject is a most complex one. To the non-specialist, however, who is chiefly interested in principles and in the end results, the consequences of these processes are very much to a pattern.

Many of the engineering metals are listed in Table 1 of Chapter 8 where it will be seen that – although there is a very considerable range of specific gravities, from about 10·5 for molybdenum down to 1·7 for magnesium – for all the metals in that table the Young's modulus divided by the density of the metal comes out to an almost constant figure, namely $3{\cdot}9 \times 10^6$ p.s.i. (25,000 MN/m^2); there are a few common metals not in the table, such as copper and brass, which have specific moduli which are a little lower than this. There is no ductile metal with a higher stiffness for its weight and thus nearly all the useful metals give one in stiffness exactly what one pays for in terms of weight, neither more nor less.

As has been said, all these metals are very soft and weak when in the pure state and it is the business of metallurgy to raise the strength and hardness without rendering them unduly brittle. Seen as *strain* the achievements of metallurgy are remarkably constant. Usually the maximum *elastic* strain which can be imparted without unduly embrittling the metal is around 1·0 per cent, give or take a little. However engineers generally regard metals in this state as having too little ductility for most purposes and for the majority of uses they are satisfied with a maximum elastic strain between 0·25 per cent and 0·5 per cent, when the elongation is likely to be around 50 per cent to 60 per cent.

Very, very roughly therefore all the metals may be taken as constituting a family with similar specific stiffness, specific strengths and elongations. This generalization is only approximately true and it is not quite fair to metallurgists who do, as a result of their labours, continue to attain rather better combinations of specific strength and toughness (specific stiffness they can do nothing about) although the limits are fairly narrow. What metallurgists have been more successful at is making metals retain their room-temperature properties up to elevated temperatures. For many uses of course this is more important than getting more strength at room temperature.

It is not necessary to describe here the special metallurgies of all the various engineering metals. There are innumerable books on the subject including an excellent general review of technical metallurgical processes in *Metals in the Service of Man* in the Pelican series. However, the great social and technical importance of iron and steel renders some account of these materials necessary. In attempting it I am only too well aware of the size and difficulty of the subject. Perhaps before doing so I should have sacrificed to Hephaistos, smith and purveyor of weapons to the Olympians, the only technologist to have reached the rank of a major God.

Iron

The elementary facts about iron and steel tend to be obscured by the jargon of the trade. First of all there is a confusion about what is meant by 'iron' and 'steel'. Naturally in both cases the predominant chemical element is iron. 'Iron' by itself usually means iron in the relatively pure chemical form. 'Cast iron' on the other hand means iron containing nearly as much carbon as it will hold, perhaps about four per cent. 'Wrought iron' is different again and is usually a special sort of fairly pure iron containing glassy inclusions. 'Steel' usually means iron with a little carbon in it, generally less than 1·0 per cent. The implication is that in steel the content of carbon or other alloying element is under fairly close control. Since the mechanical behaviour of iron is profoundly influenced by very small amounts of carbon and other additives the control which is exercised over steel is important. 'Alloy steel' is usually a generic term for steels which are alloyed with elements other than carbon. Alloy steels, incidentally, are generally a good deal more expensive than carbon steels.

The strength of iron and steel is governed by the extraordinary sensitivity of dislocation movement within the iron crystal to quite small traces of carbon. Of course, dislocation movement was not understood until recently and even the comparatively simple chemistry of the extraction metallurgy of iron was not appreciated until fairly late in the Industrial Revolution. However, the practical metallurgy of iron was worked out without benefit of these ideas and it remains today largely a traditional process. Just as, in the textile trade, spinning and weaving go back to prehistoric times and all that the most advanced factories have done is to mechanize and rationalize the simple hand process, so the steel trade operates techniques which are sophisticated versions of immemorial practices. On the whole therefore the iron and steel making processes are best understood in their historical contexts.

Apart from his scientific ignorance, the biggest difficulty that the primitive metallurgist had to encounter was that of getting a high enough furnace temperature. In a modern steelworks the availability of high and controlled temperatures enables short cuts to be taken which by-pass a number of ancient procedures. Naturally everything is on a much bigger scale and a modern furnace may produce a thousand tons a day where the medieval smith would have been content with a hundredweight.

Unlike bronze which can be melted at about 900° to 1,000° C. – which is just within the reach of an ordinary wood fire – pure iron melts at 1,535° C. which for long centuries was out of the range of human technology. However, the addition of quite small proportions of carbon lower the melting point of iron considerably and, of course, carbon is readily available when a carbon fuel, such as charcoal, is used to heat iron ore. The lowest melting temperature attainable in this way is about 1,150° C. which occurs when 4 per cent to 4½ per cent of carbon has diffused or seeped into the metal.* If a mixture of iron with excess carbon is heated to 1,150° C. therefore, it will melt. Such a temperature was not very easy for primitive people but it could just about be attained by a blown charcoal fire.

Iron ores are usually oxides of iron, typically haematite, Fe_2O_3, which is so called from its blood-red colour. The iron oxides, incidentally, are used as pigments in painting; Venetian red is largely Fe_2O_3. The first thing to do is clearly to get rid of the oxygen. When the ore is heated with charcoal or coke this occurs almost automatically:

$$3Fe_2O_3 + 11C \rightarrow 2Fe_3C + 9CO$$

The oxygen goes off with some of the carbon as carbon monoxide gas, leaving iron carbide or cementite, a compound containing 6·7 per cent of carbon. However in practice we also get the reaction:

$$Fe_2O_3 + 3C \rightarrow 2Fe + 3CO$$

So some pure iron is produced as well as cementite and we

*The amounts of carbon present in iron and steel appear surprisingly small considering the effect which they have upon the material. It is to be remembered however that the proportion of carbon in iron is always quoted as a percentage by *weight* and that the carbon atom is much lighter than the iron atom – roughly a fifth of the weight. The percentage of carbon by volume, or by numbers of atoms, is thus considerably larger and may reach about twenty per cent.

usually end up with a mixture of iron and iron carbide containing, as a whole, 4 per cent or so of carbon. Iron and iron carbide are mutually soluble and it is this solution which forms the liquid whose low melting temperature was the key to the extraction of iron in primitive furnaces – it is also what the modern blast-furnace produces.*

Iron ores do not consist solely of iron oxide but contain various mineral impurities, mostly oxides of other metals. These have usually, by themselves, also a high melting temperature and if the ore were heated solely in contact with a carbon fuel there would be a danger that it would not melt properly. To ensure that it does so a 'flux' is added, usually lime or limestone. This lime performs exactly the same function as it would in glass-making, that is to say it reduces the melting temperature of the non-ferrous oxides by forming with them a glass with a lowish melting point. This is called slag. In commercial practice it is a dirty brown or grey substance which is nowadays sometimes made into fibres and sold for insulating houses.

What we are apt to get at the bottom of the furnace is therefore a mixture of iron, iron carbide and slag. In the most primitive processes this mixture could hardly be melted and was extracted as a cake or 'bloom' containing bits of charcoal and other impurities. Apart from the question of these impurities, iron carbide is a brittle substance unsuitable for making tools and weapons. This is because, while crystals of nearly pure iron are held together by metallic bonds which favour the passage of dislocations, crystals of iron carbide are held together by bonds which are partly covalent in character so that dislocations do not

*This description applies to normal extraction processes operated at or above 1150°C. The earliest iron-making seems to have been carried on at considerably lower temperatures, perhaps as low as 700°C. Under these conditions no melting takes place but the *second* of the two reduction reactions takes place, rather slowly, in the solid state. The initial product of this process is a bloom consisting of iron which, chemically speaking, is fairly pure but which is of course full of bits of charcoal and other forms of dirt. This bloom is also beaten or wrought with hammers, in this case partly to get rid of the larger impurities but also to disperse carbon through the metal. This leads eventually to some sort of mixture of iron and iron carbide which can be hardened by quenching.

become appreciably mobile until a temperature of 250° C. or so is reached. The metal in the fresh bloom is thus malleable when hot but brittle when cold.

The early smiths therefore took the crude iron from the extraction furnace and, after reheating to some temperature perhaps about 800° or 900° C., they hammered it. Originally the iron was 'wrought' or hammered by hand, with immense labour, but latterly this was done by water power, supplied by 'hammer ponds'. The hammering had two effects. It squeezed out mechanically most of the impurities and some of the slag and it also reduced the carbon content of the iron. This occurred in the following way. Iron heated in air to a moderate temperature forms an oxide scale, the commonest form of which is FeO. Iron which is heated and beaten out flat thus becomes covered with oxide and, when, after it has been beaten into an elongated form, the smith doubles it over like pastry and beats it out again, the film of oxide is included between the layers of hot metal with which it is hammered into intimate contact, so that the simple reaction occurs:

$$Fe_3C + FeO \rightarrow 4Fe + CO$$

In high-grade work the beating out and folding over were repeated, sometimes for thousands of times. This is why swords show a delicate wavy pattern, each line corresponding to a thin layer of metal and to a beating operation. If the job was properly done almost the whole of the carbon was removed, leaving iron which was nearly pure except for a little silicon which was on the whole beneficial. This 'wrought iron' contained however streaks and strings of slag which again were to some extent beneficial. This was because the purified iron was now generally too soft and the glassy filaments limited flow to some extent. Furthermore, the rust resistance of wrought iron is generally excellent. This is partly due to the purity of the iron itself but many people hold that the initial film of rust is anchored to the surface of wrought iron by means of the slag inclusions so that it remains to form a protective skin instead of dropping off to make way for fresh corrosion as it generally does with steel.

Wrought iron direct from the anvil was too soft for weapons

and cutting tools and therefore for these purposes it had to be hardened by putting back a certain amount of carbon, at any rate into the surface. This was done by a process almost identical with that which is still widely used, that is to say 'case hardening'. The sword or other weapon was packed inside a mass which consisted essentially of carbon but which often also contained a number of secret ingredients of dubious efficiency. It was heated in this environment for a period so that carbon diffused into the surface to a depth of perhaps half a millimetre to a millimetre.

This surface carbon hardened the metal considerably but, to get the best effect, the 'steel' might be quenched by cooling it suddenly in a liquid. The exact mechanism of this quenching is complicated. Briefly, the hot steel consists of 'austenite' which is a solution of cementite in iron which is unstable at room temperature. The way in which the austenite parts with the excess carbon when it is cooled depends on the details of the cooling process.

If cooling is comparatively slow the result will generally be 'pearlite', so called from its iridescent appearance in the microscope caused by its banded structure. Pearlite consists of alternate layers or laminae of pure iron (ferrite) and iron carbide (cementite). In this form and because of its regular structure, the steel is tough and fairly strong but not particularly hard. However, if the austenite is cooled very quickly the result will be mainly 'martensite'. Martensite is yet another variant of the iron-carbon crystal which has the carbon atoms squeezed in in such a way that dislocation movement is impossible and so the crystal is extremely hard. On cooling, austenite transforms to martensite at a very high speed indeed, about three thousand miles an hour, and so to get as much martensite as possible, it is necessary to quench as quickly as one can.

Quenching can be done in water and it usually is but, historically, there seems to have been a preference for using urine and other biological liquids.* It turns out that this practice really was

*'Another sort of tempering of iron is also made in this manner, by which glass is cut and also the softer stones. Take a three year old black goat, and tie him up for three days within doors without food; on the fourth day give him fern to eat and nothing else. When he shall have eaten this

beneficial for two reasons. The first reason is that the cooling was rather quicker. When water is poured on hot metal a film of steam is formed so that the liquid water does not actually touch the metal and the heat transfer is consequently bad. This is easily demonstrated by dropping water on the hot plate of an electric cooker. With urine, however, crystals are formed on the surface of the metal as the water evaporates and these tend to bridge the steam gap and improve the heat flow. Furthermore, urine contains urea and ammonia both of which are nitrogen compounds. There was therefore some degree of nitriding of the surface, that is nitrogen diffused into the iron. This formed hard needle crystals of iron nitride, Fe_2N, and, also, individual nitrogen atoms insinuated themselves into the iron lattice as what are known as interstitials. Interstitial atoms pin dislocations. As a matter of fact the degree of nitriding effected during quenching is very small. In modern commercial practice periods of two or three days in urea or ammonia are needed, for this reason it is a rather expensive treatment, used where only the best will do.*

It will be noticed that the preparation of iron and steel consists of a series of approximations, each process going too far and being in turn corrected. Thus we first make cast-iron or pig iron which is too hard and contains too much carbon, then we generally remove all the carbon and find that the iron is too soft so that we have to put some carbon back again. This iron or steel, as has been explained, is generally 'quenched' by cooling suddenly in a liquid when we want a hard tool or weapon.

---

for two days, on the night following enclose him in a cask perforated at the bottom, under which holes place another sound vessel in which thou wilt collect his urine. Having in this manner for two or three nights sufficiently collected this, turn out the buck, and temper thine instruments in this urine. Iron instruments are also tempered in the urine of a young red-headed boy harder than in simple water.'

Theophilus Presbyter (eleventh century), *Scheme of various arts*, translated by Hendrich, 1847.

Note that 'tempering' is often popularly used when 'quenching' is really meant. Quenching is a hardening process, tempering tempers or softens extreme hardness.

*Of course the iron has to be hot for the nitrogen to enter the metal. Dogs do not harden lamp-posts.

Quenched carbon steel (or carburized iron) is often too brittle and so yet another and this time final process is often needed, that is tempering.

For tempering, the quenched metal is reheated to some temperature between about 220° C. and 450° C. and allowed to cool naturally. This softens the steel to some extent by transforming some of the martensite into a softer, more ductile structure. The higher the tempering temperature the greater the effect. Traditionally the temperature for tempering was judged by the colour of the oxide film found on the surface of the metal which varies from yellow through brown to purple and blue. It will be obvious that simple carbon steels of this kind cannot be operated at high temperatures without spoiling their properties.

Cast iron and pig-iron

As we have said, the earlier extraction furnaces could barely melt the iron which they made and this iron was usually removed from the bottom of the furnace as a rather messy cake or bloom. By the middle of the fifth century B.C., that is about the time of Pericles, Greek furnaces were able to melt the iron properly and so run it out into moulds as 'cast-iron'. Although cast iron was available through the classical period, the uses for such a brittle material were limited and it does not seem to have become economically important. Most classical iron is wrought iron.

With the dark ages the temperature of furnaces fell and cast iron does not seem to have been made again in Western Europe at least until the thirteenth century. It really found its métier however after the invention of gunpowder. The earliest cannon (the word comes from *κάννα*, a reed or bamboo, and is connected with the ecclesiastical sort) were made from wrought iron staves bound with iron hoops, like a barrel. However, as the capacity of furnaces and the skill of ironfounders increased cannon began to be cast. The early cast guns burst nearly as often as the built-up wrought iron ones but they must have been much cheaper.* In

*As a matter of fact cast-iron guns never did become very reliable. *Victory's* opponent at Tragalgar, the *Redoubtable*, burst two guns before she surrendered. The guns were little better in the Crimean War. See page 249.

its traditional form cast iron is not only very brittle but it also contains little layers or veins of carbon in the form of graphite which act as built-in cracks. As a result, cast iron was both weak and unreliable in tension. It was therefore really a very unsuitable material for a pressure vessel like a gun barrel. However until about 1860 it was the only economic one available, brass or bronze being usually too expensive. In consequence, guns were extremely heavy; one throwing a thirty-two pound shot, such as the main armament in H.M.S. *Victory*, weighed between three and four tons. The weight of the guns therefore formed about ten per cent of the displacement of a warship. Because of her age, *Victory* can no longer bear the weight of her own guns and they have been replaced with wooden replicas.

At one time it was usual to cast iron directly from the blast furnace but this is not very often done today. This is partly because blast furnaces have become much bigger and it would not be economic to cast iron from them in penny packets, and partly because iron cast straight from the blast furnace is hard, brittle and weak. Nowadays, it is usual to cast the whole of the production of the blast furnaces as pig-iron. Part of this goes on to be turned into steel and part is remelted and its composition modified so as to produce cast iron with more acceptable properties. By taking thought, it is now possible to produce cast irons which are reasonably tough and have quite good tensile strengths. As it is generally cheaper to make a complicated shape by casting it in iron than by forging it in steel there is still a considerable incentive to improve cast iron which is nearly always used for the cylinder blocks of car engines, for instance, because of their elaborate shape.

In England iron was originally extracted with charcoal in the forests of the Weald and later in Shropshire, but during the first half of the eighteenth century the problems of using coke in place of the increasingly scarce charcoal were gradually solved. The change to coke was fairly complete in England by about 1780 although it did not take place on the Continent until much later. This not only enabled more iron to be extracted more cheaply but it was one of the reasons why the iron trade gradually migrated to what we now call the 'Industrial North'.

Thus, by the late eighteenth century large castings, up to about 70 feet long, were available in England quite readily and cheaply and they could generally be transported by water. These castings however were very weak in tension by modern standards and so they had to be used in applications where the stresses were predominantly compressive. An obvious use was bridge-building. Here the iron could be used in compression to make arches, much like stone arches. A stone arch is built up from wedge-shaped stones called 'voussoirs' each of which has to be cut laboriously by hand. The early iron bridges were made from cast voussoirs in the form of open or lattice frameworks which fitted together like a stone bridge.

The famous Iron Bridge, erected over the Severn at Coalbrookdale in 1779, was the first large iron structure and is more or less of this type. It has a span of just over 100 feet, a total length of 196 feet and rises 50 feet. It contains 378½ tons of iron and was built in three months. It cost £6,000 to build and, even at the values of 1779, this was much cheaper than such a bridge could be built in any other material.

Although the Iron Bridge was successful, it gave trouble from its very virtue. An arch bridge, like an arch in a cathedral, thrusts outwards at the base, and whereas in a church this thrust may be opposed by buttresses, in a bridge the outward forces are balanced by the opposite push of the masonry and earthwork approaches. We are not apt to think of cast iron as a light-weight material, but compared with traditional building materials it is so. As a result, the arch at Coalbrookdale showed, perhaps for the first time in history, the opposite fault to that of stone arches and domes. It was too light to oppose the inward thrust of the approaches whose weight, tending all the time to slide into the river, forced the iron arch inwards and upwards. For this reason the conventional approaches had to be replaced by cast-iron subsidiary arches. This must have been an early case of that difficulty of putting new wine into old bottles which constantly troubles materials engineers.

Puddled wrought iron

After coke began to be used in mechanically blown blast furnaces crude cast iron became relatively cheap and plentiful though its uses in this form were limited by its brittleness and low tensile strength. For most purposes the stronger and tougher wrought iron was needed and as long as this had to be hammered out laboriously, wrought iron remained, even with water-driven hammers, a scarce and expensive substance. If one had to pick upon any one material as being the key to the Industrial Revolution, then that material must surely be puddled wrought iron. Steel in its various forms did not appear in quantity until much later and its social and economic implications were less important.

Puddling, at least in any practical form, seems to be due to Henry Cort (1740–1800) who patented the process in 1784. Cort invented a coke-fired furnace in which the chimney ran for a short distance horizontally before turning upwards in the usual way. On the bottom surface of this horizontal section was a basin shaped hollow in which could be melted a pool or puddle of pig-iron. This puddle of molten iron could be stirred through ports in the side of the furnace by long iron tools called 'rabbles', shaped rather like a hoe.

When the pig-iron was molten the puddler stirred iron oxide into it with his rabble. This oxide, often the scale from the rolling mills, when well stirred reacted with the carbon in the pig-iron in much the same way as it did in the hammering process, removing most of the carbon as carbon monoxide. The evolution of gas agitated the bath into a 'boil' which drove most of the slag out of the furnace. As the carbon was removed, so the melting point of the iron increased, and, as the furnace temperature was around 1,400° C., the iron began to 'come to nature' or to grow pasty. It was then rolled up into a ball weighing about a hundredweight and removed from the furnace. Although puddling was very hard work a puddler could puddle about a ton of iron a day which was perhaps a ten- or twenty-fold increase on the hammering process. Puddling was a very skilled trade and for many years after the Napoleonic wars English puddlers earned good money by travelling around on the Continent giving instruction in puddling.

When puddled, the hot pasty iron was usually passed through rollers which, after many passes, squeezed it into plates or rods. In the process the hot surface oxidized and the resulting scale fell off as the iron cooled and was fed back into the puddling furnace. As will be seen, the whole process was chemically equivalent to beating out the iron in the old way but was considerably more productive. Nowadays puddling is almost extinct because, even with mechanization, the output of a puddling furnace can only be raised to about a hundred tons a day whereas, by blowing air through the iron in a Bessemer converter, such as is used for making steel, an output of about 800 tons per day is possible. In any case the market for wrought iron nowadays is limited since steel is both cheaper and stronger.

Many of the problems of engineering are really concerned with how much strength and how much toughness one can get for how much money. The whole of the Industrial Revolution has to be seen and judged against a background of the gradually falling price of wrought iron and mild steel. This is very clearly illustrated in the history of the railways.

Railways began as colliery tramways in which wooden rails were laid to ease the passage of horse-drawn waggons. Towards the end of the eighteenth century many of these wooden rails were replaced by cast iron ones which lasted longer and showed less rolling friction than wood, so that a horse could pull four or five loaded waggons on the level. For the transport of minerals this was considered quite satisfactory and probably no further modifications would have been made had it not been for the sharp rise in the cost of horse fodder at the time of the Naploeonic wars. This turned the minds of colliery owners to the possibility of using the coal which they produced themselves at 3/9d. per ton as a source of tractive power. The pit owners, of course, already used steam engines extensively for both pumping and winding but these stationary low-pressure (3 p.s.i.) engines were far too large and heavy in relation to their power output ever to become mobile.

The inventor of the high-pressure locomotive, and therefore

the true father of railways, was Richard Trevithick (1771–1833), a genius who died in poverty, unlike the Stephensons who both lived and died in the odour of great prosperity. Trevithick produced a high-pressure (50 p.s.i.) locomotive in 1804 and another in 1805 (Plate 15). Both were successful as locomotives. It was the track which let them down.

In spite of the relative costs of hay and coal, locomotives were expensive both to build and to run. The annual running costs of an engine, including capital charges and so on, were estimated at a little under £400, which of course was far more than that of a single horse, even if the cost per horse power was less for the engine. To be economic the locomotive must therefore either draw a greater load than the horse or else draw the same load faster. Since horses were already working along the line it was impracticable to increase the speeds very much and hence the engine must be made to pull more trucks.

As we know there is no particular difficulty about getting enough adhesion between smooth metal wheels and rails to draw any desired load, always provided that the weight on the driving wheels is sufficient to prevent them from slipping and this was where the real impediment lay. The existing cast-iron rails were just sufficiently strong to support reliably the three-ton trucks in use but an engine weighing only three tons itself could not be made to draw thirty or so trucks of the same weight without slipping. If the engine were made heavier then it broke the cast-iron rails so frequently as to be uneconomic. The failing of Trevithick's engines was that they broke rails in a wholesale manner and so they had to be converted to stationary uses.

After this the story of the development of the early locomotive is that of a struggle for adhesion without breaking the rails. Part of the trouble was that the early engines were not sprung because no strong enough steel springs could be made. In consequence the load on the rails was multiplied at every jolt. Engines were built with eight driving wheels in order to spread the load (Plate 16), but one of the most popular solutions was to cast the rails with teeth which meshed with cogs on the engine like a modern mountain railway (Plate 17). These devices were troublesome and never worked really well.

George Stephenson met the spring difficulty by providing his engines with 'steam springs', that is by supporting the axles on pistons floating in cylinders filled with live steam, a suspension exactly similar in principle to that recently introduced for motor cars. However, because of the problem of sealing the pistons properly Stephenson abandoned steam suspension as soon as steel springs became available.*

In 1821 John Birkinshaw of Bedlington near Morpeth patented a method of rolling puddled wrought-iron rails of I section and one of his early customers was George Stephenson who was thoroughly worried about the track for the Stockton and Darlington line at the time. Birkinshaw quoted £15 per ton for his wrought-iron rails and, although this was more than twice the cost (£6–15) of cast iron, the effective cost per mile turned out to be the same because, the wrought-iron rail being stronger, a lighter rail could be used. The length of Birkinshaw's rails was 15 feet which, it will be remembered, was the length of the forged bars made at Akragas in 470 B.C.

The American approach to the same problem a few years later was different. In many cases they seemed to have reverted to a system which was used in Scottish colliery lines about 1785. This involved laying a flat strip of wrought iron on top of a substantial wooden rail. This was used in America for some years and worked fairly well. The iron strip was however merely nailed or spiked to the wood beneath and from time to time the butt joints worked loose. When this happened the end of the strip might curl upwards under the weight of a train wheel and when this happened it could penetrate the floor of a carriage above it, sometimes with fatal results to the passengers.

Such tracks were replaced by the usual wrought-iron rails but for a great many years the American practice was to use rails of much lighter section than in Europe, supporting them by very closely spaced wooden sleepers. This habit of course reflected the cheapness of timber and the high cost of iron in America.

Although cheap steel became available about 1860 it took nearly thirty years to oust puddled wrought iron. In 1883 some

*One of the revolutionary features of the Rocket (1829) was the introduction of piston rings in the driving cylinders to replace oakum packing.

seventy per cent of the pig-iron produced in Great Britain was puddled, and it is doubtful if more than ten per cent was turned into steel. By the 1890s these proportions were roughly reversed. The real reason why puddled wrought iron hung on for so long was that, although weaker, and sometimes more expensive than steel, it was considered, with some justice, to be more reliable.

The first sensational success for the new Bessemer steel occurred when fast paddle steamers, such as the famous *Banshee*, were built in the early 1860s to run the Northern blockade into Southern ports during the American civil war. This they did with almost contemptuous ease, having a speed of twenty to twenty-two knots compared with the fifteen or so of the fastest ships of the Northern navy. Some of these vessels ended their days, comparatively recently, as passenger steamers on the Clyde. Although the saving of weight, by the use of steel, was very great, accidents occurred quite frequently and the British Admiralty would not build hulls in steel until about 1880. The use of steel for really large and important structures could not be said to have become established until the Forth railway bridge was built of open-hearth steel in 1889.

Steelmaking

The making of steel, especially under modern conditions, is an extraordinarily complicated business and only quite a brief outline can be given here. What we now call mild steels and carbon steels consist of iron having between 0·1 per cent and 0·8 per cent carbon content, little or no slag inclusions and with or without controlled small amounts of other elements such as silicon and manganese. What the traditional producer of wrought iron made however was iron almost free from carbon but containing extensive slag inclusions and also small but uncontrolled amounts of other elements. As we have said the biggest difficulties faced by the early ironmasters arose from the fact that, as they removed the excess carbon from the pig-iron, they also raised the melting point from about 1,150° C. to around 1,500° C., a temperature beyond the capacity of their furnaces. Thus slag could not be removed by melting and carbon could only be put back, to give the necessary strength and hardness, by carburizing the hot but still solid surface of the iron by blacksmith's methods.

However, throughout the eighteenth century the temperature of furnaces was slowly rising and about 1740 Benjamin Hunt found that he could melt wrought iron with a little added carbon in small batches of up to about 90 lb. in covered clay crucibles in a furnace. When this was done, the slag also melted and separated and rose to the top (because it was lighter), leaving molten iron containing a little carbon, but still with its original quantities of impurities, underneath. The carbon content could be adjusted to give the desired strength and hardness and the resulting steel could be poured off, free from slag, into moulds.

Crucible steel was expensive, partly because it was made from the already expensive wrought iron, and moreover, since no purification or control of impurities – other than slag – took place, its quality was variable. Even so, it was generally cheaper and better than most of the smith-made 'steel' used in swords and it was used extensively in small quantities for tools of high quality.

Crucible steel had the advantage that, instead of making a tool or a weapon dead hard outside and soft inside, any required strength and hardness could be achieved right through. For some purposes however the steel was still carburized or 'case-hardened' to give a more durable cutting edge, as indeed is still sometimes done. Nowadays nobody would try to make plain carbon steel in this way, except experimentally, but small batches of expensive alloy steels are usually made in crucibles.

Bessemer or Mushet steel

Until the middle of the nineteenth century crucible steel remained the only steel available and the metals of large scale construction were still cast iron and puddled wrought iron. The production of cheap steel in large quantities was originally due to Henry Bessemer (1813–98) and Robert Mushet (1811–91). Bessemer was a prolific inventor with a strongly developed business sense. After doing well with a number of inventions such as the manufacture of 'gold' paint and the consolidation of graphite for 'lead' pencils, Bessemer was drawn to steelmaking by the publicity given to the weaknesses of cast iron guns during the Crimean war.

After various experiments Bessemer had the revolutionary idea of blowing air through liquid pig-iron to remove the excess carbon and other impurities. He took out his master patents in 1855 but, in its original form, Bessemer steel was of poor quality because it contained excessive oxides and sulphur. However, in 1856 Mushet took out his own series of patents for a very similar process which differed from Bessemer's mainly in that the impurities which had not been burnt out by the air blast were controlled by the addition of something called 'spiegeleisen', a special cast iron from Germany containing manganese. It was the addition of manganese at the end of the blowing operation which ensured the success of the Bessemer process.

Bessemer steel is made in a contrivance called a Bessemer converter which consists of a pear-shaped crucible or container mounted on trunnions so that it can be tipped. It has no external means of heating. At the bottom of the converter are a series of holes or tuyeres through which air can be blown.

To operate the converter, the vessel is tilted so that its spout is under the outlet from a blast furnace and a charge of from five to thirty tons of molten pig-iron (that is iron at perhaps 1,200° C. containing about 4½ per cent of carbon and small amounts of silicon and manganese) is poured in. Since the converter is on its side the charge lies in the belly of the vessel and does not block the tuyere holes. Air is now blown through these holes and the converter is allowed to swing upright so that the air is forced to bubble through the molten iron. Under the conditions in the converter the air first oxidizes the manganese and silicon in the iron to form a slag which floats on top of the charge. The process is traditionally controlled by watching the colour and character of the flames produced in the mouth of the converter. At this stage they are short and reddish brown.

After a few minutes the manganese and silicon are fully oxidized and the air begins to remove the carbon; at this stage the flame changes to whitish yellow and becomes longer and more alarming. Finally, when all the carbon is eliminated, the flame drops and the blast is turned off. During the blowing period the burning of the carbon, manganese and silicon, which together amount to about six per cent of the charge, produces a great deal of heat; enough not merely to raise the temperature of the charge to keep pace with the increase of melting point due to loss of carbon, but so much that it would be overheated were not a little scrap steel added to cool it – otherwise the furnace refractories would be damaged.

By the end of the blow we have what is called 'blown metal' or approximately pure iron in the converter and it is usually desired to put back some carbon and manganese and also perhaps silicon. This is done by adding solid carbon and the special form of cast iron – spiegeleisen – which contains a high proportion of these elements. Manganese is wanted in steel both for its own sake as an alloying element and also because it controls the sulphur which is not removed from the iron during the Bessemer process.

Sulphur is a great nuisance in steelmaking because it does not oxidize to SO_2, as one might expect, but forms iron sulphide, FeS, and this has the peculiarity that it is soluble in molten iron but not in solidified iron. As a result, on cooling, the iron sulphide separates out at the crystal boundaries and weakens the steel (Chapter 4). The addition of manganese changes FeS to MnS, which is insoluble in liquid steel and so passes into the slag. Manganese also reduces the solubility of oxygen in steel which again is beneficial because oxide particles also tend to end up at the crystal boundaries.

Bessemer described his process to a meeting of steelmakers in 1856 in a paper called 'On the manufacture of malleable iron and steel without fuel'. Such was the enthusiasm of the audience and such was Bessemer's reputation that £27,000 was immediately subscribed in advance patent royalties, after which the steelmakers went home to build themselves Bessemer converters.

As it turned out none of them could make satisfactory steel, for the original Bessemer process was sensitive to the kind of pig-iron which is used and moreover it requires some skill. Not unnaturally, Bessemer became exceedingly unpopular. He then built a complete working model of his converter in his laboratory in St Pancras and used it to demonstrate steelmaking to his licensees. As these demonstrations did more to show up the incompetence of the licensees than to improve Bessemer's popularity, the agitation against Bessemer continued and no steelmaker would operate his process. In consequence, in 1859 Bessemer set up his own steelworks in Sheffield and made steel which sold extremely well, notably to the French and Prussian governments for the manufacture of guns.

The palpable success of Bessemer steel led steelmakers all over the world to seek licences and Bessemer received about one million pounds in patent royalties over and above the profits of his own steelworks. Those of Mushet's patents which were connected with blowing air through iron were probably anticipated by a few months by Bessemer but Mushet's patent on 'spiegeleisen' should have been valid and immensely valuable. Unfortunately Mushet forgot to pay the stamp duty when renewing the patent and thus extinguished his legal rights. In consequence Bessemer always refused to pay any royalties to Mushet and a long quarrel ensured. Towards the end of his life Bessemer paid Mushet an annuity of £300 a year.

It is difficult to quote representative figures to illustrate the economic effects of Bessemer steel. However, while in the 1850s steel fetched from £50 up to £100 per ton, by 1900 steel rails were being sold for less than £5 per ton. Although shipbuilders' tons are different from anybody else's it was possible to build steamships in the 1890s for around £10 per ton. (Nowadays, in spite of technical improvements, the price of steel is around £50 a ton and ships cost upwards of £200 a ton.)

Part of Sir Henry Bessemer's fortune went into building a cross-channel steamer, the *Bessemer*, in which the first-class saloon – which was large and luxurious – was hung, like a Bessemer converter, on trunnions and was intended to remain level at sea. Seasickness was further discouraged by blowing fresh air vigorously among the passengers by means of an ingenious arrangement of pipes in the floor.

In practice, the swinging cabin never worked properly and after a few voyages the ship was scrapped. The original saloon of the *Bessemer*, firmly fixed, is still in existence, as a conservatory, in a garden somewhere near Dover.

Nowadays, although straight Bessemer steels probably only account for a few per cent of the gross steel production, modernized and more sophisticated versions of the Bessemer system are making headway. In the Kaldo process, for instance, the converter is blown with oxygen instead of air and the extra heat which is produced is used to melt a flux for removing the sulphur directly and also to consume more scrap. What is gained in extra efficiency in such processes can however be lost by damage to furnace refractories and by the cost of the oxygen.

Open-hearth or Siemens-Martin steel

In a sense the Bessemer process was a cause of its own obsolescence because, as steel became cheaper and commoner, so did steel scrap and the availability of scrap began to exert an important influence on the economics of steelmaking. Nowadays about fifty per cent of the steel manufactured finds its way back to the steelworks as scrap The Bessemer process, however, in its traditional form is essentially a process for converting pig-iron from the blast furnace into steel and it only makes use of scrap in trivial quantities so as to get rid of a small excess of heat.

In the open-hearth process much of the charge consists of scrap steel which has the advantage, not only of being cheap in itself, but of already having most of the excess carbon and other impurities removed. Moreover it is rusty. As we have said, the Bessemer converter cannot use very much scrap because to melt it would need more heat than is produced by blowing the charge.

In 1856 the German-born Frederick Siemens (1826–1904) and his brother Charles William Siemens (1823–83), both of whom, like Bessemer, were prolific inventors with a strong business sense, developed the regenerative furnace. This is a furnace whose outlet and inlet are reversible and are both furnished with extensive labyrinths or honeycombs of firebrick through which the gases have to pass. Much of the heat in the outgoing gases is therefore stored in the outlet honeycomb. The furnace, however, is arranged so that the gas flow is repeatedly reversed and thus the incoming air is always being drawn over heated bricks and so picks up some of the heat which was in the exhaust gases. These furnaces are usually gas-fired and, as a consequence of their design, the temperature could be raised as high as the refractories would stand, in practice to something over 1,500° C. which was sufficient to melt pure iron.

In steelmaking the Siemens furnace was originally used simply as a convenient and economical way of melting crucible steel. Later, the Siemens brothers applied the regenerative principle to the traditional puddling furnace and made steel by melting pig-iron with iron ore. The addition of large quantities of scrap is due to a Frenchman, Pierre Martin, and dates from 1864.

In operation, the open-hearth furnace is charged with a flux – usually limestone – about equal quantities of scrap steel and pig-iron and some iron ore, perhaps Fe_2O_3. On heating, the whole charge is melted and the iron ore removes the carbon present in the pig-iron. The flux converts not only the non-ferrous oxides present in the iron ore to slag but also the sulphur present in the steel. For this reason it may not be necessary to add manganese. One of the advantages of the open hearth process as compared with the Bessemer converter is that much closer control is possible over the composition of the steel and until recently about eighty-five per cent of plain carbon steels were made in this way. However the open hearth furnace is slow and rather expensive to operate and it has therefore been losing ground to the oxygen blown converter processes such as the Kaldo which are quicker, rather cheaper and can take liquid iron directly from the blast furnaces. In consequence only about half the steel in the country is now made by the open-hearth process which seems to be declining rather rapidly.

For still closer control over cleanliness and composition it is usual to employ electric furnaces and a comparatively small, but significant, tonnage of high grade steel is made in this way.

Chapter 11 The materials of the future

or how to have second thoughts

'In fact we have to give up taking things for granted, even the apparently simple things. We have to learn to understand nature and not merely to observe it and endure what it imposes on us. Stupidity, from being an amiable individual defect, has become a social vice.'

J. D. Bernal, *New Scientist,* 5 January 1967.

Before the first edition of this book was published in 1968 I was persuaded, rather against my judgement, to add a final chapter called 'The materials of the future' with the defensive sub-title 'or how to guess wrongly'. Much to my relief there do not seem to be any real technical clangers in the original chapter and, in the present edition, it has been possible to transfer most of these prophecies, as accomplished factual information, to their appropriate places within the body of the book.

The weakness lay, I think, not in the facts but in the emphasis. Much of the discussion was about what it is now fashionable to call 'High Technology' and we are less inclined to be impressed by this kind of thing than we were a few years ago. Getting to the Moon has turned out to be, perhaps, just a little boring and that enterprise was, in any case, a very expensive way of developing non-stick frying pans. Students tell me that space-fiction keeps its popularity but surely its appeal is no longer chiefly technical, it is simply the fairy-story or the fable in modern dress.

More and more one comes to see that it is the everyday things which are interesting, important and intellectually difficult. Furthermore the materials which we use for everyday purposes influence our whole culture, economy and politics far more deeply than we are inclined to admit; this is, indeed, recognized by the archaeologists when they talk about the 'stone age', the 'bronze age' and the 'iron age'. It is significant that, from very soon after the introduction of bronze for tools and weapons, there was a sort of polarization between the metallic and the non-metallic technologies.

Although the ductile metals have their limitations and they are by no means infallibly tough or even particularly strong yet, for a number of purposes in peace and war, they were so much superior to the other solids which were available that a whole range of popular beliefs and superstitions and emotions have become associated with them and especially with iron and steel. In one shape or another these emotional situations have continued down to the present day and, because they still influence many people's thinking, it seems to me that it may be worth spending a little time on the historical and psychological background of the subject.

Because of their interest in tools and weapons the early civilizations were inclined to have smith-gods. The Norsemen had Thor and the Greeks had Hephaistos, who is also the Roman Vulcan after whom volcanoes are called. The stories about Hephaistos are many and not always edifying. Hephaistos, be it noted, was an Olympian god and the Olympians were not indigenous to Greece but came, as it is sometimes said, with the Dorian invaders from the North, who may have conquered the Greek world with iron weapons – possibly at the fall of the Minoan kingdoms around 1400 B.C. At any rate Hephaistos looked after the supply of iron and of weapons and was regarded by gods and men with rather mixed feelings. Hephaistos was rather a big-wig as gods went and he has a magnificent temple in Athens which stands to this day. It is interesting that there was no god of any consequence specifically connected with any of the non-metallic materials; one or two scruffy little low-class demons were associated with pottery works – where they sometimes caused the pots to crack in the kilns – but these hobgoblins were of no real importance in the world.

In the middle ages Wayland Smith, who is Wieland, who is Voland and who lived in Heligoland, or possibly near the White Horse in Berkshire, was continually turning up in improbable circumstances. There were magic swords almost innumerable, Miming, Flamberge, Excaliber and so on; some of these were quenched in Dragon's Blood. If he was not too busy with a magic sword Wayland Smith would shoe your horse for you for a very modest sum. Again, I do not think that there was any real non-metallic equivalent to Wayland.

Although this sort of thing died out – or was suppressed by the Church – the strength of the feeling about the special nature of iron and steel continued and was reinforced rather than diminished by the Industrial Revolution. The Victorians could not really be said to have had smith-gods but they did everything they could with iron – short of affording it actual formal worship – and iron and steel became synonomous with industrialism and technical progress. Everything done with metal was important and to be taken seriously; it followed that anything done with non-metals was old-fashioned and quaint and unimportant.

About 1912 an ex-theological student called Joseph Djugashvili (1878–1953) changed his name to Stalin* since 'Iron out of Calvary is master of men all'. He proceeded to live up to his name and, incidentally, spent much time later on in building up the steel industry throughout the Soviet Empire. Actually it looks as if he may have rather overdone it since most Communist countries now seem to be suffering from a surplus of steel.

Of course, from Boulton and Watt down to Henry Ford, iron and steel have been, above all other materials, the agents of development, industrialization, enrichment and 'progress' and, historically, we could not have done without them; the question is whether we ought now to be growing out of that kind of thing. Everything has its bad side and the bad side of metal technology did not come to an end with the Factory Acts. What really made the industries which were based on iron and steel so successful in modern times was that they lent themselves best to disciplined mass-production and to the dilution or elimination of skill and individual judgement at the bench level. All the worthwhile decisions were taken at the top and imposed from the top. Such manufacturing systems placed enormous power in the hands of managers and accountants and, eventually, in the hands of governments and trades unions. Governments and trades unions are no more enthusiastic about giving up this power than the managers and accountants and they are even more apt to talk about the economies of scale and the benefits of 'rationalization' and centralized control.

*Both the English and the Russian words are supposed to derive from the Old Teutonic 'stah' or 'stag', to be firm or rigid.

What is left out of account is that most ordinary people don't like this kind of thing and nowadays they find ways of not standing for it and of being bloody-minded which more than nullify the economies of scale. A factory may be an accountant's paradise but if it is on strike it is not producing anything at all and surely it would be better to have a less 'efficient' system which did produce something?

These large and highly interdependent organizations presuppose a willing and disciplined labour force of a kind which is most unlikely to exist for long under any political system. In my opinion nationalization and high wages or even 'workers' control' do not really improve the situation because they do not deal with the roots of the trouble which are to a large extent inherent in the size and in the inhuman nature of so many manufacturing processes.

The difficulty has been that, until recently, no economically practicable alternative to bigness has existed and, on the whole, the economists from Marx to Keynes seem to have taken the economies of scale for granted; indeed most of them have rather welcomed bigness, partly because it appeals to tidy minds, but also because bigness puts more power into the hands of the Children of Light. But the Children of Light are few in this world and people furiously disagree as to who they are; also all power corrupts and ought to be diminished.

But then what shall we do to be saved? There is nothing like Leather, says the cobbler; nothing like Sound Management, says the business man; nothing like Taxation, says the politician; nothing like Equality, says the trades unionist; but I think that the problem might very well be a technical one. Although about twice as much timber is used as steel, it is interesting that the woodworking industries in the Western world are seldom in the news, whether for good or for bad and they do not seem to be especially plagued with troubles or dissention. Somehow steel and its dependent industries is never out of the headlines and nobody associated with it ever seems to be really happy. Whether we are concerned with making swords or making motor-cars steel somehow remains the material of power and politics. It has been the fashion, especially on the Left, to regard steel as being in some way a 'People's material', a key to all sorts of enlightenment and progress. Of course steel is extraordinarily useful stuff, we cannot get on without it and it is wrong to take too simple a view, yet there is a strong case that steel is the agent of a sort of faceless industrial oppression, the life-blood of the Dark Satanic Mills. Indeed steelworks are gloomy places.

The differences between the social records of the industries based on wood and those based on metals is unlikely to be due to pure chance and can probably be traced, however indirectly, to the physical characteristics and properties of the materials themselves. For one thing, speaking comparatively and in a very general kind of way, people seem to *like* working with timber; for another, the very manufacturing limitations of wood impose constraints upon the sociology of the industry which may well be salutary. If this is true, then it might be a good idea to study the whole question of how materials affect the happiness of the people who work with them in much more depth. Now that we can design new industrial materials to suit ourselves we ought surely to bear this psychological element in mind much more than we do. At present nobody seems to care.

Designing materials to suit ourselves

All this brings us to the question of designing new materials and we might begin by harking back just a little. Materials science – the study of materials as a whole rather than in their special chemical, physical and engineering aspects – is a fairly recent development. Indeed it has only lately become respectable. However, in spite of its youth, the new discipline has been rather successful and I think it is fair to say that we now understand a great deal more about the reasons for the mechanical behaviour of solids than we did only a very few years ago. This may be because many of the raw materials of understanding were lying to hand already. There was a great body of orthodox physical and chemical knowledge and there was also, although in different hands, an accumulated mass of engineering experience and tradition. To fit them together and to make one explain and confirm the other required only a moderate amount of original experiment and fresh thinking – once a sufficient number of workers had considered it worthy of their serious attention. As so often, the real difficulty about the solution of a problem is to recognize that the problem exists.

Naturally enough, the first task was one of understanding the observed phenomena – why solids in general, and especially the familiar materials, behave in the way they do. Although there are still a good many loose ends, this stage can broadly be said to be accomplished. The problem now facing materials scientists is what use to make of their knowledge. The possibilities are not unlimited – one of the things which has been learnt is that there are a considerable number of things which cannot be done even if we wanted to do them. A cognate aspect of our knowledge is that many lines of improvement had already been exploited, almost to the full, before the scientists got there. Some of our knowledge is useful simply in telling the engineer what to avoid – what sort of stress-concentrations are dangerous, for instance.

However, when all due reservations are made, the ambitious will want to apply materials science in radical ways, either by making substantial changes in the older materials or else by inventing new and perhaps better ones. However, the more intelligently we examine traditional materials like wood and steel the more we ought to be impressed by how cunningly they are made. What is wanted is not one property in isolation but rather a balanced combination of properties and this is provided in such materials by means of exceedingly subtle and complex mechanisms such as dislocations and hollow helical tubes. Modifications to the older materials of construction are more likely to spoil them than to improve them.

If we are going to set out to invent entirely new materials then we had better watch our step because the requirements for any really successful material are likely to be very complex indeed. Nevertheless, it is probably worth trying and the eventual rewards, both economically and socially, may be very great. As Academician Rabotnov remarked in his introduction to the Russian translation of this book 'this is a noble task to which young people might well devote their lives'. Although I might not have expressed the sentiment in quite those words, I cannot but agree with Professor Rabotnov.

Before we can discuss the subject of new materials intelligently we have to begin by asking ourselves the question – 'What do we really mean by a *better* material – better for what?' The answer to this is anything but obvious and the question is really the central one in materials science at the moment. As we have already said, the whole problem is made more difficult by the extraordinarily complicated way in which the technical, social and economic aspects are interwoven.

Many business men however seem to have no serious doubts about what they want – theirs is a simple Faith and they want the stuff to be cheaper. For this reason a high proportion of materials research is directed towards getting the cost of production down. There are, of course, some materials which are unduly expensive and which could and ought to be made more cheaply. However, I do not think that this is true to any important extent of the engineering materials of construction in general, such as steel. The cost of steel was reduced very greatly during the nineteenth century and it is now fairly cheap; on technical grounds it seems unlikely that such marginal economies as are likely to be made in future can really justify the investment of any large scientific effort.

Even if it were practicable to achieve large reductions in the cost of constructional materials it is worth asking who would benefit. In many finished products the cost of the materials, as such, is only a few per cent of the cost of the finished article and so, even if the material were to be supplied free, the benefit to the consumer would be small compared with other changes which might be introduced.

Secondly, the very cheapness of materials may actually have a bad effect upon design and performance. When materials are unduly cheap the designer has too little incentive to economize in using them and the result may not only be heavy, clumsy design (involving waste of fuel and damage to roads) but it may also, in the long run, lower the professional standards of engineers. The reason for much bad, heavy, ugly design is partly to save fabricating costs but as often, I am afraid to save the designer from the trouble of thinking. Economists tell us that, in a given context, there is generally an optimum price for both land and labour which results in efficient social development and I fancy that the same reasoning might apply to the price of materials.*

There is another aspect of the price of materials which is also important. The cost of the various fabricating processes is frequently very many times higher than the cost of the bare material. For instance it is cheaper to buy a plastic at 20p a pound which can be moulded into its final shape for a further 5p than to buy steel at 5p per pound which needs to have 50–100p spent on it in pressing, machining and finishing operations.

Cheap fabrication is, at root, the reason for the commercial success of plastics which are always expensive raw materials compared to most metals. It is not only that, from the economic point of view, such materials can offer large savings in processing, manufacturing and finishing but also many of these processes can be carried on competitively upon a very small scale. I have seen the extrusion of plastic tubing carried on as a village industry in Hungary and indeed, all that is needed is two or three extrusion machines and a shed to house them. It is difficult to see how the process could benefit, economically or otherwise from being done in a big factory. When I was on the Board of a large plastics company I was able to watch our extrusion business being run off the market by little back-street firms whose overheads were lower and whose thought-processes were quicker than ours.

Very much the same sort of thing applies to the injection-moulding of thermoplastics; an industry which makes millions upon millions of toys and kitchen gadgets and useful what-nots at an incredibly low price. Given a suitable (and rather expensive) mould, injection moulding can be carried out in almost any barn

* During the nineteenth century Edward Gibbon Wakefield (1796–1862) pointed out that an important obstacle to the colonization of Australia and New Zealand was the very low price of land. This, he showed, led to so wasteful a use of land that no colony could flourish. When, at his instigation, the price of unoccupied land was controlled and raised colonization was successful. There are many books on Wakefield.

or garage. It may suit the convenience or the vanity of administrators or business men to group these activities in large factories but there does not seem to be any compelling reason for doing so. Though I find it difficult to go all the way, politically, with either William Morris or Dr Schumacher, there can surely be no doubt at all that Small is Beautiful?

Extrusion and injection-moulding are very well as far as they go and they enable jobs which are inherently dull and repetitive to be carried on by smaller groups of people in pleasanter surroundings – which is all to the good and, after all, some people like repetitive jobs – but, of course, it does not give much scope for initiative and variety in the design of the product.

This is achieved, to a considerable extent, in the wood-working industries, making products like furniture in comparatively small numbers and to comparatively individual designs. By using modern machinery and adhesives and finishes the cost can be kept competitive with the big factories. The same thing applies to a still greater extent in the fibre-glass industry where all sorts of shell-like products, from swimming-pools to boats to car bodies to flower-pots, can be produced in little factories with very low capital costs.

Naturally, there are plenty of small industries which are based on metals but these people generally find it more difficult to compete with the big boys and it is the non-metallic small industries which are going ahead much the faster. This is probably an area where a moderate amount of materials research could do a great deal of good.

Energy conservation

Latterly it has become very fashionable to talk about energy conservation and, quite apart from political questions about oil-wells, it is probably high time that we gave this aspect of technology more consideration and respect. When power had to be provided, in very small quantities, by men or horses, vehicles were generally made from wood and other light materials. It is most instructive to look at sedan chairs and horse carriages in museums and to see how light and robust some of these things were.

Traditionally, railway trains were drawn along smooth and level rails by engines burning lots of cheap coal and a railway carriage is an interesting example of just how heavy and clumsy one can make a moving structure. To some extent the prodigal use of material in railway rolling-stock arises from the nature of trains themselves; that is to say trucks and carriages have to be constructed to resist what are called 'buffing loads' which occur because of the mutual impact of strings of vehicles during shunting and manoeuvring. Light, modern rolling-stock has usually to be worked in conjunction with older, heavy vehicles which are liable to smash anything near them and, in my experience, it is difficult to save very much weight or fuel in trains by advanced structural design. In any case, I doubt if the real problems of the railways are the technical ones.

Nevertheless, the whole tone of traditional engineering was set for many years by railway and by marine engineering and by bridges and stationary engines and all these things were generally constructed as if weight were no object. 'The English think that weight means strength.' The requirement for weight saving arose with the invention of the motor-car and the aeroplane but even here engineers were generally more interested in increasing the power of the engine than in saving weight in the structure. It used to be said that 'a tea-tray will fly if only you put enough power into it'.

By running internal combustion engines at very high speeds on high-octane fuel it was possible to increase their power output very dramatically indeed. Much of this power output has been needed to cope with the large increase which has taken place in the tare weight of cars during the last fifty years, mainly due to the introduction of the pressed steel body. As long as oil was comparatively cheap and plentiful I suppose that this did not matter very much. In fact the fuel consumption of a car is roughly proportional to its weight and so nearly half the petrol which is imported into this country is used or wasted in propelling heavy rusty steel shells along the roads.

The only real argument in favour of pressed steel bodies for cars is the safety one. These steel shells are in fact very good at absorbing impact energy during an accident – due to the high work of fracture of mild steel – and so each of us drives about inside his own private tank. However, according to my sum, the extra fuel needed to move all this armour around costs about £1,000, at present prices, taken over the life of each average car. One would think that there would be cheaper forms of protection than that. The total cost to the country in imported oil is enormous and, of course, the extra weight does no good to the tyres or the roads.

Fibre-glass car bodies save a great deal of weight and, in fact, they are already quite widely used. The trouble is that such bodies have barely enough energy absorption and they are probably distinctly less safe than steel bodies. What is needed is a large increase in the work of fracture of the material and also, perhaps, some increase in stiffness. As we saw in Chapter 8, tougher, stiffer composites seem to be only just around the corner and, if so, we may see a large swing to plastic car bodies together with a saving in fuel which might well be as high as 30 per cent. Since such bodies do not rust cars would probably last longer.

Light-weight car bodies are one good way of saving energy; improved building methods and house insulation are probably another. Unfortunately development in building materials is a good deal handicapped in this country by conservative building regulations and by the Building Societies. It does, however, very much look as if a new approach to the whole question of building materials and insulation is overdue.

The new materials might perhaps be sophisticated ones based on polymers or other 'advanced' substances but they might equally, and perhaps preferably, be based on traditional local materials, modified where necessary in the light of modern knowledge. Professor Biggs tells me that if one looks at housing from the total energy point of view – that is to say, if one considers the energy needed to make and to transport the materials, as well as the energy consumed during the life of the building in heating it – then the traditional English thatched and half-timbered cottage is probably better than anything else. Rather predictably, this is just what one is not allowed to build under the present regulations.

A variant of the same problem exists in connection with overseas developments. In many tropical regions, such as parts of Africa, it is difficult to improve upon the traditional construction of mud and reeds which can be put up cheaply and quickly and which is cool to live in. Most of the drawbacks of these buildings can be got over by making use of various forms of modern technology. I am told however that the inhabitants reject this construction with scorn and insist on building with concrete and corrugated iron which are both hot and expensive. As long as such attitudes prevail it is difficult to see what science can be expected to do.

So far we have talked about saving energy; however, if we are going to go out and actually collect energy from primary sources, such as the sun and the wind, then we shall probably need to invent and to make use of a whole new range of materials. For something like 200 years engineering 'progress' has consisted of making machinery and other engineering devices more and more compact, of working at higher and higher stresses and of 'processing' more energy in less space. A modern ten horsepower engine is at least a hundredfold smaller and lighter than it would have been in the eighteenth century. This has been possible because of the concentrated nature of fossil fuels. Primary energy sources such as the sun and the wind are not concentrated and have to be collected in driblets, as it were, from over a wide area. Plants are superbly good at collecting the energy of sunshine but the structures and materials which they use are different from those which are popular with the modern engineer.

If we want to revive the sailing ship and the windmill, under modern conditions, as I am fairly sure that we should, then we shall have to devise ways of reaching out and collecting small amounts of kinetic energy from quite long distances very cheaply and simply. One has only to sit down and study the problem from the economic and structural point of view to see that this probably cannot be done with existing materials and we shall probably have to go about the job in some more intelligent way and, again, this will undoubtedly call for new kinds of materials and structures.

The disposable technologies

There is no doubt at all that the introduction of 'disposable' materials, such as cheap paper and plastics, has been, on the whole, decidedly beneficial. It has reduced the incidence of infectious disease and dramatically diminished the less attractive kinds of domestic chores. The question is, how far ought we to go in this direction? What do we really mean by 'disposable' anyway?

It is all very well to throw away things like towelling and packaging and it is probably an excellent thing to throw away your morning paper, but what about refrigerators and motor-cars? It is perhaps possible – just possible – to exaggerate the cynicism of manufacturers and shopkeepers about 'planned obsolescence'. Of course, Nature arranges for all her creatures to die and there is no good reason why the works of man should last for ever. A paper towel is very cheap – much cheaper than one made from cotton or linen – and furthermore the cost of washing a durable towel is probably greater than that of throwing away many paper ones. But all this is not true of motor-cars or refrigerators. In such things a small addition to the first cost would result in a much longer life and in reduced maintenance costs.

One of the biggest contributions to the total economy would be to make 'consumer durables' durable. After all, if such things last twice as long, that is roughly equivalent to doubling the production of the article; in other words one need only make half as many. This does not necessarily cause unemployment because one can use the money which is saved to buy something else – or else perhaps just save it.

Many products wear out – or rather go out of service – for silly, shoddy reasons (Oh no, sir, we don't stock spares for out-of-date models). However, the biggest single reason for throwing things away is probably rust. As we have seen the introduction of plastics in place of pressed steel shells is one way of getting over this and very often these plastic shells can be manufactured on a 'Small is Beautiful' basis.

I suppose that industries which deliberately live by 'planned obsolescence' ought not to be surprised if they become obsolete themselves; perhaps we need some form of euthanasia for declining industries. At present the policy is to pension them off so that they can continue to exist comfortably at the taxpayer's expense. One does see that there are political and social problems about lame ducks and disposable industries but it is seldom pointed out that it is precisely those industries who, in their hey-day, were most ruthless in superseding the stage-coachmen, the canal boatmen, the coastal seamen, the sailmakers, the millwrights and such other excellent people who now call most loudly for subsidies on social grounds. Times have changed since the nineteenth century but are they changing fast enough today?

If 'consumer durables' wear out too quickly, do houses and other buildings last too long? Very possibly more houses have been built during the last thirty years than were put up in the whole span of previous history; most of them are ugly, or at any rate commonplace, and our grandchildren may well want to get rid of them. Also it would perhaps be better if our houses could be altered quickly and cheaply to suit our changing requirements and better still if we could take them with us when we wanted to move to another part of the country.

Unfortunately the local authorities have joined with the Building Societies to ensure that houses shall be as expensive and as immoveable as it is possible to make them and also very difficult to modify. It is quite true that both caravans and also most temporary buildings, in their present forms, are nearly always ugly and shoddy and to be discouraged. But is this necessarily so? We have got it firmly into our heads that anything temporary or disposable has to be ugly but, after all, one could hardly have anything more temporary or more disposable than a crocus or a daffodil and it might be worth giving some thought to the way in which Nature does these things.

We have, I suppose, the biggest aesthetic opportunity in the whole of history and what are we doing with it? Nothing, or rather we are producing miles and miles and miles of the dull and the commonplace. Does everything really have to be Fabian grey? By making use of modern ideas and modern materials I suppose that we could all of us be pavilioned in splendour – quite comfortably and cheaply – if we really gave our minds to it.

Because the influence of materials and structures upon almost every aspect of our lives is so great, the fact that we now at last understand, pretty well, how materials work and have some idea of how to invent new ones, is very important indeed. So far the implications of this new knowledge have not been sufficiently widely appreciated. Our modern understanding of materials has been brought about by getting engineers and physicists and chemists to talk to each other, which they were rather reluctant to do. What is wanted now, I think, is to bring materials science together with economics and aesthetics. If this can be done in a really imaginative way then the opportunities are enormous and surely the challenge is great enough to satisfy the most able and the most ambitious?

Appendix 1 On the various kinds of solids

and what about treacle?

Atoms and molecules

There are roughly a hundred different kinds of atoms, not counting isotopes (that is atoms with the same chemical properties but slightly different nuclei.) About ten of these are ephemeral things which have been made by atomic scientists by artificially transmuting other atoms. The rest have existed naturally, almost since the beginning of time, and usually in a more or less immutable state. Of these only about twenty or thirty are sufficiently common to concern us in this book. Each kind of atom is called an element. All the atoms of any one element are virtually identical but the atoms of the different common elements differ greatly in their properties. This is basically why matter displays the enormous variety which it does.

The atoms of an element can exist in a pure, homogeneous state as elements, e.g. iron (Fe) or carbon (C); they may exist as any kind of mixture or solution (whose properties are as a rule simply a mixture of those of the constituents) or as definite chemical compounds, e.g. iron carbide, Fe_3C. In this last case the atoms usually combine in quite definite fixed proportions to yield a chemical compound which is an entirely new substance with its own characteristic properties. For instance chlorine (Cl) is normally a green poisonous gas; sodium (Na) is a soft shiny metal. Equal numbers of atoms of each combine to form sodium chloride, NaCl, a white harmless powder, ordinary table salt.

The twenty or thirty common elements can and do combine to form a huge variety of substances, solid, liquid and gaseous and this, of course, is what chemistry is about. The four common elements, carbon, hydrogen, oxygen and nitrogen can combine in virtually infinite variety to form nearly all the substances which are found in living matter besides a great number of non-living and artificial compounds such as plastics, petrol and oils, drugs, paints and so on. Compounds of this type are called 'organic'. Other compounds are lumped together under the label 'inorganic'.

This includes most compounds of metals such as minerals (other than oil), ceramics and so forth.

In the game of atomic Meccano which is called chemistry the basic unit is the molecule, that is the smallest particle of a compound possessing the properties of that compound. For instance a molecule of sodium chloride is NaCl, that is, one atom each of sodium and chlorine. A molecule of benzene is C_6H_6, that is a construction containing six atoms of carbon and six of hydrogen. Again, a good many elements exist in the form of molecules, combined so to speak with themselves. Iodine, for example, exists as I_2. It will be realized that the word 'molecule' is used rather loosely to describe a small grouping of atoms according to chemical principles. This does not mean however that the chemical bonds which hold some molecules together are not sometimes very strong indeed. Molecules vary in size from little things made from a couple of atoms up to elaborate structures made by joining together hundreds and sometimes thousands of atoms.

The biggest organic molecules can be relatively quite large, perhaps several hundred Ångströms long. Inorganic molecules are generally, though not always, smaller, typically perhaps about ten Ångströms. However there do exist long inorganic chain molecules, such as asbestos, which are quite as long as anything organic.

Chemical bonds

Matter, that is atoms and molecules, is held together by chemical bonds. These are of several types which vary a good deal in their properties.

(*a*) BONDS WHICH USUALLY HOLD ATOMS TOGETHER WITHIN THE MOLECULE

Covalent bonds These occur when two atoms share a pair of electrons. It is usually the hardest bond to make but, when made, it is often very strong and rigid. This is the type of bond that occurs within organic molecules and sometimes in ceramics.

Ionic bonds The individual atoms of elements are, as a whole, electrically neutral since the charges of their constituent particles balance out. When sodium reacts with chlorine the metal gives one outer electron to the gas so that the sodium is now positively charged and the chlorine negatively charged. As a result the two atoms now attract each other. In solids, ionic bonding is particularly common with metallic compounds. It is quite common for the bonds in some compounds to have a composite ionic and covalent character. Whereas covalent bonds are strongly directional, ionic bonds operate more uniformly in space around the charged atoms.

Metallic bonds These are the bonds which, in general, hold together metals and their alloys when these elements are not in the form of a definite chemical compound. In this case, some of the outer electrons are not held permanently in orbits related to particular atoms but can rove freely through the material being, as it were, the communal property of all the atoms in that piece of metal. They form what is sometimes known as an 'electron sea'. Metallic bonds are comparatively easy to form, to break and to reform. Because of the free movement of electrons within the material, metals are good conductors of electricity.

(*b*) BONDS WHICH USUALLY ATTACH MOLECULES TO EACH OTHER

Hydrogen bonds Although the water molecule, H_2O, for instance, is, as a whole, electrically neutral, the distribution of the charges within it is such that there is a strong local charge imbalance which can be highly attractive. Many organic compounds, in particular, have along their molecules numerous $-OH$ groups each of which is capable of attracting other $-OH$ groups, water and so on. It is these forces which, in general, keep the molecules of plants and animals attached to each other. These $-OH$ groups are often called 'Hydroxyls'.

van der Waal forces These are much weaker forces which arise from small local variations of charge which tend to occur all over the surfaces of any molecule and are not generally associated with any particular chemical groups. Cohesion depending upon van der Waal forces is not particularly common in nature but is quite frequent in plastics and between other artificial organic molecules. Because of van der Waal forces, almost anything will stick to almost anything else in rather a feeble sort of way provided that the surfaces are sufficiently clean and in good contact.

Heat and melting

Although temperature can rise as high as you like, it cannot fall below absolute zero which, as Kelvin calculated, occurs at −273° Centigrade (which is not all that cold, considering that one can get temperatures of +4,000° C. or more without much difficulty). At absolute zero all atoms and molecules of whatever substance are at rest and everything is a hard solid.

As soon as the temperature starts to rise, all the atoms and molecules begin to vibrate. The higher the temperature the more vigorous the movement, heat being, of course, simply the random vibrations of the atoms and molecules in a substance. Up to 0° C. water, for instance, remains in the form of a hard solid, ice, although its internal cohesion is subject to more and more battering from the thermal agitations of the molecules as the temperature rises. Finally, at 0° C., the internal cohesion of solid ice gives up the struggle and the molecules acquire the sort of shuffling freedom which characterizes a liquid. The ice has melted to form water. If the temperature rises further, the water molecules shuffle more and more energetically until at 100° C. the water boils to form a gas or vapour, steam, in which the molecules, released from any kind of mutual cohesion, fly about quite freely, like a swarm of bees. If the temperature is then lowered, the same sequence occurs in reverse so that the steam will condense and eventually freeze. These changes of state are usually considered as physical ones since the only bonds which have been broken and reformed are the hydrogen bonds between the water molecules which are, within themselves, unaffected.

Although the melting and boiling temperatures of various substances vary enormously, the general principles are very much the same for everything. A few substances (such as Iodine and smelling salts, ammonium chloride NH_4Cl) pass straight from solid to gas without the intervening state of liquidity. Quite a number of complicated solid compounds decompose chemically when heated before they get a chance actually to melt or vaporize.

Crystallization

As we have said, all molecules attract each other to a greater or less extent and, if they are not torn apart by thermal agitations, they will cohere into some kind of clotted solid. Since the molecules attract each other, they naturally try to get as close together as possible and this is to be achieved, not by huddling together in some hugger-mugger way, but by systematic packing. A loose heap of bricks occupies more volume than bricks properly stacked. In so far as the molecules have a more or less free choice of sites, therefore, they tend to take up regular positions, like bricks in a wall, when they solidify. This can occur when a liquid remains quite fluid up to the moment of freezing, as happens with water and metals for instance. In these conditions a molecule, looking for a desirable residence, will shuffle around for a long time till it finds a 'closely packed' position to sit down in.

Mechanisms of this kind lead to the formation of crystals which are essentially highly regular arrangements of molecules in a solid. In a good crystal the number of molecules and the regularity of their arrangement is breathtaking.

All solids have a tendency to be crystalline but not all achieve it. However, all metals and many simple inorganic substances are invariably crystalline. Other substances may be so to a greater or less extent. Good crystals are often quite large, up to several inches across, and may show characteristic simple geometrical shapes.

Glasses and ceramics

If a liquid is very viscous before it freezes, or if it is cooled very quickly, most of the molecules will not be able to select the most closely packed sites and the material will solidify in the form of a hard irregular mass of molecules. The most usual cause of high viscosity, when a liquid approaches its freezing point, is that the molecules, instead of remaining independent until they crystallize, associate while still in the liquid, to form sluggishly mobile chains or networks. This is particularly the case with some metallic oxides such as silica, SiO_2, that is to say sand, which melts to a viscous liquid and when subsequently cooled very readily forms a glass. The melting point of pure silica is inconveniently high (1,600° C.) and so most practical glasses consist of mixtures of sand, lime and soda which can be melted in ordinary furnaces.

Sugar, as bought at the grocer, is normally crystalline (and there is, of course, a special trade in large, well shaped crystals for coffee). However, if sugar is melted and cooled fairly quickly, it will form a glass, toffee. Treacle, of course, is a viscous liquid on the way to becoming a glass.

'Fudge' is devitrified toffee. That is toffee which has wholly or partly abandoned the glassy state and has crystallized. Because of the consequent shrinkages fudge is full of cracks and thus weaker than toffee (Chapter 4).

Metals and substances like sugar and salt are crystalline and so are the majority of rocks, which had plenty of time to cool. Glass, obsidian and toffee are glassy. Some materials are a mixture of the two. Most common ceramics, such as domestic pottery, consist of small crystals of metallic oxides and silicates which, when they are 'fired', become stuck together with a thin layer of glassy material. If the pottery is glazed this is done by melting on to the surface a layer of a low melting point glass.

Polymers

Most living matter, both animal and vegetable, and all plastics are in the form of polymers. Polymers are in many ways very convenient solids to make, both for Nature and for the plastics technologist. The basic idea is that convenient small unit molecules are built up, on the site as it were, into large chains or networks.

Elastomers

This includes things like natural and artificial rubbers. These are rather like ordinary polymers, in that their molecules consist of long chains, but these chains are not closely tied together laterally, so that the chains can fold and coil up. The enormous mechanical extension of rubber is due to the unfolding and uncoiling of these chains.

NOTE ON CONVERSION OF UNITS

Length	1 metre	= 32·8 feet
	1 foot	= 30·48 centimetres (exactly)
	1 micron (μm)	= 10^{-4} centimetre = $3{\cdot}937 \times 10^{-5}$ in.
	1 nanometre	= 10 Ångströms = 10^{-9} metre
Area	1 square inch	= 6·4516 square centimetres exactly
Force	1 kg force	= 2·205 lb. force
		= 9·81 Newtons
		= $0{\cdot}98 \times 10^{6}$ dynes
Stress or pressure		
	1 p.s.i.	= 6895 Newtons per square metre
		= 0·0705 kg per square centimetre
		= $6{\cdot}9 \times 10^{4}$ dynes per square centimetre
	1 atmosphere	= 14·696 p.s.i. 1 MN/m^2 = $10^6 N/m^2$ = 146 p.s.i.
		= 1·033 kg per square centimetre
Energy	1 Joule	= 10^{7} ergs
		= 0·239 calories
		= 0·734 ft. lb.

Appendix 2 Simple beam formulae

or do your own stressing

The basic formula for the state of affairs at any given point along a beam is:

$$\frac{M}{I} = \frac{s}{y} = \frac{E}{R}$$

Where $M =$ the *bending moment* to which the beam is subjected at this point. Bending moment is load multiplied by distance, e.g. in inch pounds. If M is not, for a given case, obvious from first principles it may be obtained from the data given below.

$I =$ the *moment of inertia* of the section of the beam at this point, e.g. in inches^4. Moments of inertia are treated in text-books of elementary mechanics. The moment of inertia in question here is that about the neutral axis which, in most beam problems, will be a line through the centre of gravity of the section. If the I of the section is not already known it is usually easily calculated by applying one of the following formulae.

For a rectangle:

$$I = \frac{bd^3}{12}$$

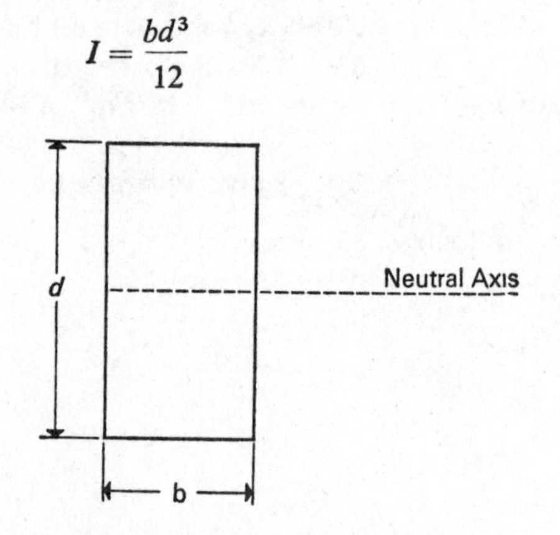

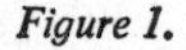
Figure 1.

Hence sections made up of rectangles, such as rectangular tubes, *H* beams and channels can often be calculated by subtracting the *I* of the empty areas.

For a circle:

$$I = \frac{\pi r^4}{4}$$

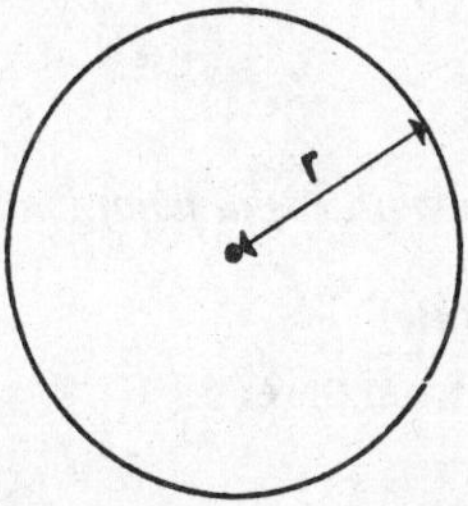

Figure 2.

Again hollow tubes can be calculated by subtraction.

s = stress in material.

y = distance from the neutral axis. In a symmetrical section this is the distance from the mid-point or centre of gravity of the section.

E = Young's modulus.

R = radius of curvature of beam when it bends under load.

Of these various properties we most often want to calculate the stress in the beam and so:

$$s = \frac{My}{I}$$

For a simple rectangular beam:

$$I = \frac{bd^3}{12} \quad \text{and} \quad y = \frac{d}{2}$$

at the surface where the stress is greatest. So:

$$s_{max} = 6\frac{M}{bd^2}$$

Which is why a beam twice as thick is four times as strong and so on.

For specific beams the following information is useful. Information covering virtually every imaginable form of beam is given in *Formulas for Stress and Strain* by R. J. Roark (McGraw-Hill, 1954) which should be referred to for more complicated cases.

Point loads

(*a*) *Simple cantilever length l with point load W at end.*

FOR BENDING MOMENT

at any point distant x from the end:

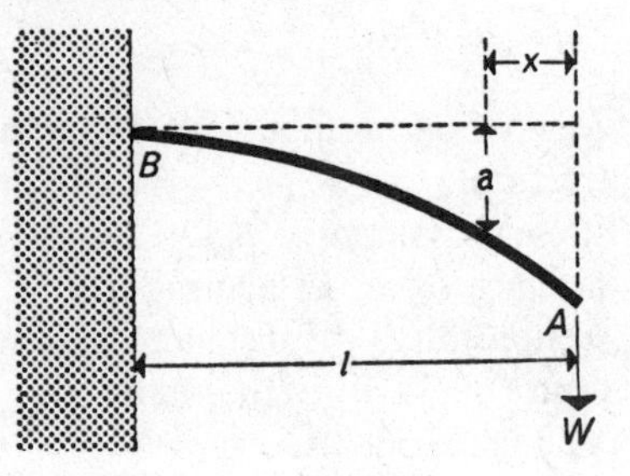

Figure 3.

$$M = Wx$$

$$\text{Max } M = Wl \text{ at } B$$

FOR DEFLECTION

at any point:

$$a = \frac{1}{6}\frac{W}{EI}(x^3 - 3l^2x + 2l^3)$$

$$\text{Max } a = \frac{1}{3}\frac{Wl^3}{EI} \text{ at } A$$

$$\text{Slope at } A = \frac{1}{2}\frac{Wl^2}{EI} \text{ radians}$$

(b) *Simply supported beam length l with point load W in middle.*

FOR BENDING MOMENT

at any point:

$$M = \frac{1}{2} Wx$$

$$\text{Max } M = \frac{Wl}{4}$$

FOR DEFLECTION

at any point:

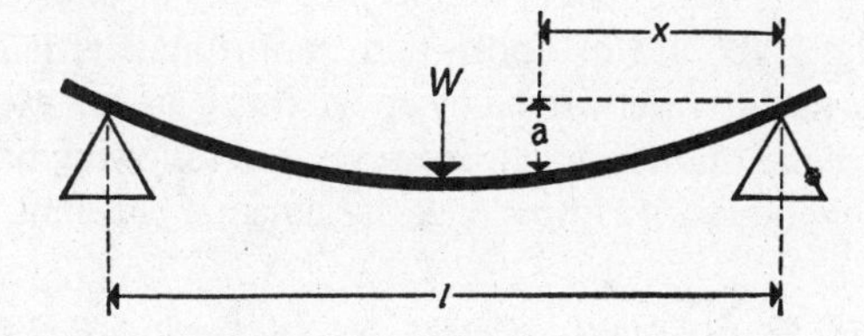

Figure 4.

$$a = \frac{1}{48}\frac{W}{EI}(3l^2x - 4x^3)$$

$$\text{Max } a = \frac{1}{48}\frac{Wl^3}{EI} \text{ at centre}$$

$$\text{Slope at ends} = \frac{1}{16}\frac{Wl^2}{EI} \text{ radians}$$

(So, *inter alia*, a beam twice as long deflects eight times as much.)

Suggestions for further study

It is not possible to acquire a catholic knowledge of materials entirely by reading books; one must also use direct observation and experience. Just as the real knub of learning photography or drawing or painting lies in learning to see, so one has to cultivate the habit of noticing and observing the structures and materials around one – even the commonest of them – with a seeing eye.

Equally, it is not possible to interpret many of one's observations without the aid of books and, unfortunately, it is not a subject particularly well served by books which are not excessively specialized and mathematical. However, the following books are open to anybody with a knowledge of elementary algebra.

Introduction to Materials Science, by B. R. Schlenker. John Wiley, 1974.

Materials Science (2nd edition), by J. C. Anderson, K. D. Leaver, J. M. Alexander and R. D. Rawlings. Nelson, 1974.

Materials in Industry, by W. J. Patton. Prentice-Hall, 1968.

Structure and Metals, by Michael Hudson. Hutchinson Educational, 1973.

Fibre-Reinforced Materials Technology, by N. J. Parratt. Van Nostrand, 1972.

The Structure and Properties of Materials, Vol. 3, 'Mechanical Behavior', by H. W. Hayden, W. G. Moffatt and J. Wulff. John Wiley, 1965.

Strength of Materials, by Peter Black. Pergamon Press. 1966.

History of the Strength of Materials, by S. P. Timoshenko. McGraw-Hill, 1953.

Strong Solids, by A. Kelly. Oxford University Press, 1966.

The Mechanical Properties of Matter, by A. H. Cottrell. John Wiley, current edition.

Mechanical Behaviour of Engineering Materials, by W. D. Biggs. Pergamon Press, new edition, 1977.

Formulas for Stress and Strain, by R. J. Roark. McGraw-Hill, current edition. (This is the Bible of do-it-yourself stressing.)

LESS TECHNICAL BOOKS

Philosophy of Structures, by E. Torroja (translated from the Spanish). University of California Press, Berkeley, 1962.

Metals in the Service of Man, by W. Alexander and A. Street. Penguin Books - current edition.

On Growth and Form, by D'Arcy Thompson (abridged edition). Cambridge University Press, 1961. (This is the classic account of the shape and structure of animals, originally published in 1917 but still readable and important.)

Biomechanics, by R. McNeil Alexander. Chapman and Hall, 1975.

Mechanical Design of Organisms, by S. A. Wainwright, W. D. Biggs, J. D. Currey and J. M. Gosline. Edward Arnold, 1976.

The Southseaman, by J. Weston Martyr. Blackwood, 1928. (An excellent account of classical wooden shipbuilding in the 1920s.)

Engineering Metals and their Alloys, by C. H. Samans. Macmillan, New York, 1953. (This is a good general account of practical metallurgy, rather more advanced than *Metals in the Service of Man*, but very comprehensible and readable.)

Ceramic and Graphite Fibers and Whiskers, by McCreight, Rauch and Sutton. Academic Press, New York, 1965.

Structures or Why Things Don't Fall Down, by J. E. Gordon. Penguin Books, 1978.

Much information about timber can be obtained from the various publications of the Forest Products Research Laboratory which are published by H.M.S.O.

Finally, the *History of Technology* (Oxford University Press, 1954) is a mine of information on all matters connected with the history of materials and structures. This is a forty-guinea five-volume book which is available in many public libraries.

Index

Library of Congress Cataloging in Publication Data

Gordon, J. E. (James Edward), 1913-
The new science of strong materials, or, Why you don't fall through the floor.

Reprint. Originally published: 2nd ed. Harmondsworth: Penguin, c1976. (Pelican books: A920)
Bibliography: p.
Includes index.
1. Materials—Popular works. 2. Strength of materials—Popular works. I. Title.
[TA403.2.G66 1984] 620.1′1 83-43103
ISBN 0-691-02380-8 (pbk.)